THE TALK OF THE TOWN

Even in the propriety of Stuyvesant Square, the gossip spread . . .

The gossip turned on the fact that in two days "that woman," the notorious Mrs. Restell, owner of that brooding Fifth Avenue mansion uptown, keeper of unmentionable secrets, would go to trial, perhaps for her life. The question that titillated those it did not frighten was how much the lady would reveal. Her clients included not only the poor, the desperate, but the rich, the powerful, the respected.

The city waited in fascination . . .

Stuyvesant Square

MARGARET LEWERTH

AVON BOOKS NEW YORK

AVON BOOKS
A division of
The Hearst Corporation
105 Madison Avenue
New York, New York 10016

Published by arrangement with E. P. Dutton, a division of NAL Penguin Inc.
Library of Congress Catalog Card Number: 87-512
ISBN: 0-380-70596-6

First Avon Books Printing: April 1989

K-R 10 9 8 7 6 5 4 3 2 1

To my father,
Daniel Lewerth,
who knew
Stuyvesant Square.

The characters involved in *Stuyvesant Square* are fictional except for:

Mrs. Caroline Restell
Mr. Anthony Comstock

The details of Mrs. Restell's death in New York City on March 31, 1878, were drawn from the newspapers of the time. The case was closed as a suicide.
I have taken a different view.

Margaret Lewerth

1

When the great Comet hurtles past the Earth to embrace the Sun, so the ancient wisdom goes, birds change their migrations, animals their paths, and men their dreams. The very Stones, those chalices of secret energies, renew their powers.

In the spring dusk of the late, glorious century, a year and a half before the young Princess Victoria was summoned to the throne, a man could be seen running on the Plain of Salisbury in the south of England. He was not young, and his breath came hard. His face, despite a cooling mist, was covered with sweat. His goal loomed ahead, more menacing than the dusk itself. He must reach it before dark.

Faith goaded him on, faith and the figures he had poured over night after night at the kitchen table. Will Lyman had once dreamed of being a schoolmaster. He had become, instead, a dirt farmer, with no hand for the plow and a head in the clouds. But this night would change all that.

For this was the night the Great Comet would come. His figures had proven it. And wasn't it so that a man had only one chance in his life to see the Comet? If he dared take that chance within the circle of the great ruined Stones on Salisbury Plain, he would be touched by its fiery currents. He would prosper.

So confident was Will that he had already boasted in the Swan and Thistle that before summer passed he, with his young daughter, would sail for America, that land of riches. Now as he stumbled across the sloping barrows of the plain he was sure of this. His plow mare Mollie, which he had ridden out from the village, had balked, laid back her ears, and refused to put a hoof on the path to the Stones, leaving him to go on alone on foot.

Suddenly out of the dimness, the Stones arose, so ancient, so huge, so awesome that no man knew whether sorcery or idolatry had placed them there. The mist rising from the ground made of them enormous pendants. The villagers called them the Hanging Stones. To believers in magic, they were Merlin's mighty crown. To the larger world, of which Will had no part, they were known as Stonehenge.

To stand alone after nightfall within that monstrous broken circle would test any man to the bottom of his courage. Will hesitated, his foot struck a shard of rock, bringing him to his knees. He rose, gasped for breath.

"God give me strength! I'm a poor man. My wife is dead. My land is worn barren. My Nora, my little girl, must have a husband someday. God, send the Comet!"

There was no one to see him fling out his arms and run through the black opening into the circle of the Stones.

In the white fog of morning, the young girl faced the villagers.

"That's all I know. The mare came home without him."

"We'll find him, little Norrie, don't ye worry. Now we all know yer Dad was a little daft. . . ."

"He wasn't daft!" Her eyes blazed. "He liked to go out of a night and look at the sky. And he said the Comet was coming. . . ."

"Maybe if he'd tended to his land more and his sky gazing less. . . ." That brought a chuckle.

She turned on them. "He did tend his land. Anyhow he didn't need his old land. He said we'd be going to . . ." She stopped.

"Go on, Norrie. Goin'? Where?"

"Leave the girl alone!" A thick-set, muscular man stepped by her side. Ben Fitch, who raised pigs, had long eyed Will's expanse of acres and, at closer range, his pretty, blossoming daughter. He laid a thick protective hand on the girl's shoulder, a thumb under the blond curls at her neck.

"Don't you worry, Norrie. We'll find him, and I'll give a hand with yer Dad's plantin'."

Nora fled.

By mid-afternoon they had discovered Will. He was lying within the circle of the Stones, against a fallen fragment. From a gash in his forehead the blood had flowed and blackened. He was breathing. His eyes stared at them with a childlike brilliance. He was without speech.

Ben Fitch saw to the planting and harvesting. Little Nora tended the house and her father and avoided the red-bearded man who came to the kitchen door, sometimes for water, but more often, it seemed, to look at her.

At last speech returned. Will could move about, answer questions.

"I saw the Comet. It came out of the sky. . . ."

"Did you duck, Will?" His neighbors winked at each other.

He was patient. "It lit up the Circle so you could see it like day. It turned the Stones red. It had a tail of fire like a broom. . . ."

"A tail, eh? Like Mollie the mare? Or Fat Mary's, when she's carrying her wash?"

Amid bawdy laughter, Will grew silent. He did what work he could in the fields, and afterwards drew into himself.

The Comet had put no money in his pocket. It had blocked forever the way to America. Worse, talk of his daftness hung like cobwebs around him and his pretty daughter. Her eyes distant, young hands overworked, he ached to see the girl given to fits of brooding for a world she was never to see. White linen on the bed, silver on the table, ladies with jet-black curls and small feet, silk dresses, carriages with lemon-coated footmen, all spun from his own talk and Nora's fairytale images of a faraway land of sunlight and splendor that was America.

As he slumped in his chair more often, Will found himself increasingly grateful to Ben Fitch, who could do the work of two men in a day.

"He's an honest man, Norrie. Show him your pretty ways. Something good might come of it."

"What good?"

Time and poverty are the twin enemies of all dreamers. As the seasons turned, Will saw spring rains flood the seed from his fields, winter storms tear the thatch off his roof, and Nora grow thin, her brief blossoming already withering.

"Marry him, Norrie. Have done with it!"

On a day bittersweet with fading summer, the villagers saw Nora walk primly into church beside Ben Fitch and pledge her dreams away. She emerged a married woman with sober step, her fingers barely touching her husband's arm. When his hamlike hands helped her into the waiting wagon, no one saw her flinch.

In the tenth year of her marriage, Nora conceived her first, and, as it turned out, her only child. When she held the boy in her arms, peace at last filled her. Peace and a long-buried pride that she had once harbored for a new life and a new country. This child was hers, flesh of her flesh, soul of her soul. His fuzz of dark hair, the intelligence of his large dark eyes, the fineness of his hand as it curled around hers had come from nowhere but the depths of her own longing.

Secretly she searched for a name appropriate to her beautiful son. In a yellow entry in the church registry, she found it. JULIEN EDMOND, MARQUIS OF ABBINGDON, B. 1682, D. 1687. Five years of life, was that all? Such a little Marquis would not have used the name long. He would not even miss it. She pronounced it over and over, delighted with its nicety. Julien Edmond Abbingdon . . . someday when he was far away and rich, in America . . .

"Not my son, you won't! What kind of name is that? Julien Edmond! If you've nothing better in your head, my girl, I'll tag him myself. Ned, plain, no nonsense Ned."

Sunday morning at the baptismal font, Nora in her best brown woolsey dress glanced down at the infant held tightly in her arms and marveled again at the fine shaping of the head, the long lashes fringing transparent eyelids, the delicacy yet strength of his small, straight bones.

He was different, this child of hers, and she would raise him so. She would teach him to read and write. In time he would go to Salisbury, to the Vicar's school. He might become a page in the Duke's estate near Bath. Or go up to London and catch the Queen's eye for the Household Guards. But in the depths of her mind she saw something else . . . her son, a gentleman in America.

"In the name of the Father, the Son . . ."

An episcopal hand, white lawn at the wrist, lifted.

"I baptize thee . . ."

Julien Edmond, Nora breathed. Julien Edmond Abbingdon.

The white lawn wrist descended. Icy, if holy, water touched the tiny forehead. The infant yelled. The Parson pushed on.

"Ned Fitch."

Ned Fitch it was. He would know nothing of all this. When he grew old enough, he would wonder at first why his mother called him Julien when they were alone. Why when she took him to the village on market days, heads would turn, glances follow, women whisper. As he was taken less and less to the village, he forgot.

He knew his father as a huge red-faced authority whose thick arm collared him one day to watch his first slaughtering. Ned had been fond of the old sow now past her use. He had liked to scratch her snout, hear her grunt. He imagined her smiling at him through the fence. Pigs were like that. Now as he watched her blood spout in searing bright mockery of life, he cried out and wretched.

The second time his father forced him to hold the knife.

"You're a pig farmer's son, Ned. You're going to learn your trade, for all your mother's fancy notions."

The work-hardened hand clamped over the small unscarred one, guiding the knife to the squealing animal's throat. This time Ned neither cried nor retched. When it was over he walked across the fields, out to the edge of the heath, and sat down. In the darkness, long past supper, his mother found him.

"I saw it all! You are meant for better things, Julien. Oh yes, you are! Someday you'll wear fine clothes and carry a fine cane and ride in a carriage of your own . . . oh yes, you will. I promise, my little Julien!"

He moved from her closeness and faced her.

"My name is Ned. He said I was not to forget it. If I'm to be a pig farmer I'll be as good a one as *he* is!"

But what young Ned Fitch would remember all his life was the figure bent and dozing beside the kitchen hearth. His grandfather, who the villagers said was "away," which meant daft. But when the old man lifted him to his lap and began one of his stories, Ned knew better. Stories of places too strange to pronounce, stories of heroes with names like Alexander and Achilles, Caesar and King Arthur. Names that leapt from the flames and loomed larger than his father's shadow on the wall.

The day came when old Will found strength to hitch up the wagon and drive Ned across the Plain to stand within the circle of the Hanging Stones.

"Feel that, Boy? Feel the power of 'em? I was right there on that broken block you're standing on when the Comet came. With a roar and a flame brighter than hellfire it passed right through as if the Stones were there to catch it. It knocked me down." It was then that Ned saw the daftness, but he did not interrupt. He heard a tremor in the cracked voice.

"You'll see it in your turn, Boy. Every seventy-five years it comes. The Stones tell you. Come over here. See that ridge there? There's another just beyond it. They run right around the Circle. There are holes along 'em. Like post holes. Thirty-seven on the inside, thirty-eight on the outside. What's that make?"

"Seventy-five!" Ned would remember his delight.

"Seventy-five. That says something, doesn't it? What the Stones know. Seventy-five years. When the Comet comes back, you'll be a grown man. Settled. But now you're young and strong. And the Comet's a long way off. It can't help you or harm you. It can't stop you as it stopped me. The land drains a man. Takes all he's got. In the end the land's there and the man's done for. Go to America. The door will open. When it does, go, go! It's when a man stops, when he no longer listens to what's inside him, that he fails."

When the winter settled in, Ned escaped when he could to the shed off the kitchen. There, wrapped in shawls, old Will claimed rheumatism. But when the door closed he managed to hop quite nimbly out of bed to a dusty sea chest that stood in the corner. Taking a key from a shriveled leather thong around his neck, he would lift the lid. It was a moment of intense anticipation for Ned. Secreted inside were the old man's treasures. A brown-paper-wrapped parcel. "Clothes to lay me out in, Boy. So I'll do you proud."

Tucked in one corner was "the Box," as Ned thought of it, four inches by four. It was carved on all sides. On top was a ram's head. Between two curved horns a grinning imp's face.

"Came from Egypt, by way of Spain. See what's in it."

But turn it over as he might, Ned could not open it.

The old man chuckled.

"Not yet, Boy. Not yet."

The remaining space in the chest was crammed with books. Small books, fat books, six- or eight-inch volumes bound in faded buckram, stained and tattered from long use and long storage. With a gnarled and shaking hand, old Will lifted one out.

"Gift from the Comet, Boy. When you've read this one through you'll have another. No nonsense here, not the airy-fairy poems your mother likes. Just good hard words that'll tell you what men have done and what they've thought long before you came. And maybe you'll learn what you can do when your time comes. Words, Boy. And ideas. And your own ambition. What else is there?"

For a while Ben Fitch took little notice of his household. Better to have the boy with an addled old man than in the shadow of a foolish woman. But too often he had come upon a book beneath the blanket of Ned's loft bed. Outside where he was stacking cord wood, Ned heard the thunder in the kitchen.

"Books, Nora! Books! That's what he's giving the boy. As

if your teaching him how to bow and hold his spoon and knife like a city fop ain't bad enough. What are you and the old man making of the boy? A waxwork? I need a son to muck out the stall, swill the pigs, truss up a sow. That's what a man's sons are for. Bad enough, isn't it, you only gave me one!"

Ned saw him clutch his mother's arms, his mother wince.

"I'm hearin' things, Norrie. Talk at the pub. Hints, like. One day I'm going to ask you a question and you'd better have the answer. Straight to me."

Ned's schooling was almost over, as much as he would get. He was not sorry. The sullen silences of the house, his mother's helpless pretenses, his father's increasing harshness, set him apart. His closest companion was the Plain, the emptiness of springy turf, undulating over flat meadow lands and the ancient burial mounds of the barrows. In summer the grass was sweet. In autumn driving rains shrouded it. In winter fierce winds rebuked the intruder.

The long summer twilights Ned liked best. Then he would walk until he could see the Hanging Stones, black, mysterious, against the melon sky. They became for him a mystic city, magic beckoning, where lights would glow, people pass, and where, when he reached it, he would belong.

Then one cold, autumn night it all changed. Lying in his loft bunk, a candle glimmering on another forbidden book, Ned heard the kitchen door below slam violently. Then the heavy tread of boots and a crash as of an overturned chair, a grunt, a muffled curse.

His father had taken to spending his evenings at the village pub. Tonight he must have stayed till closing time. Ned heard an unsteady creaking on the ladder to his loft. He blew out his candle. But his father was already silhouetted in the light of a half moon.

"I'll take that!" Ben's voice was thick and ominously low. "Get your clothes on!"

By the time Ned was dressed and in the kitchen, Ben stood confronting Nora, shaking the book in his hand.

"It's the last time, you hear me! I'll not have any more of it!" With a powerful thrust, he hurled the little volume directly into the kitchen fire. "Now I'll have yer answer!"

"You've been drinking, Ben." Nora was calm, almost remote.

"Aye. I've been drinking. Four nights and you've not taken notice. Rolling away from me in the bed as you've tried to do since the day he was born! Not that I let you or . . ." Ben caught himself. It was always easy for her to take him off the thread of his thinking with her quick tongue. "I want my answer, plain and proper between us!"

"If you want a proper answer then ask a proper question."

The devil take her neatness with words.

"I'll ask a proper question, my girl!" He seized her wrists and caught his breath as if it burned. "What the whole village is asking!"

"What is that?"

"Is the boy mine?"

The slight smile at the corners of her mouth set his temples pounding with rage.

"You know the answer to that, Ben."

"What do I know? That I married you when no one else would? That your father was daft and you were like him? That you were barren, or that maybe I was? And you put the horns on me?"

"Is that what they're saying?" Her mouth thinned. "Because my son is beautiful? Because I want him to be better than all this, because someday he . . ."

"No! That's not what they're saying! They're looking at me and the boy and seeing the strangeness between us. My son, with none of me in his face! They're lookin' at you and saying a woman, taking long walks by herself . . . for God's sake, answer me!"

She looked at him without pity. "You should have known better than to listen. They're jealous and spiteful. That's all they know! But I'll answer you. And it's God's truth. Julien—oh yes, I'll call him that I will! Julien isn't your son. Or mine. Not rightfully. He is different. He's meant for something better than you or me. And I mean him to have it. If there are lies about me, I'll face them. But Julien will have his chance. I swear on the Holy Book!"

It was not the answer Ben sought. It was no answer at all. It was Nora's way of twisting him when the drink had tossed all his thoughts askew. He wanted no more.

He turned and saw Ned staring at him, with those eyes that belonged to no one. He lifted a fist, then dropped it.

"You're my son! You heard that! Mine! If I catch you sneakin' books again or puttin' on airs to me, I'll strip every inch of hide off your body!" Then he stomped out the door, and the night swallowed him.

Old Will peered into the kitchen.

"Come in here, Boy."

Ned obeyed dully.

"It's no great matter, Boy. He'll get over it. Maybe you will, too, when you're a little older. What book was it?"

Ned shrugged. *"Tales from Homer."*

Old Will sat down. "Troy burned again, eh? Old Homer won't mind. He never even wrote the words down. But they stand higher, bigger than the Stones out there. And almost as old. No one can burn a book, Boy. The words will still be there, somewhere. You'll find 'em again." He sensed he was talking to fill an emptiness, to return to normalcy, to cool the stark anger, the furious outrage in Ned's face. He could not even guess whether Ned was listening.

So the time had come. Will went to his sea chest, opened it, and took from its corner the little carved box.

"Here, Boy. Maybe you ought to see what's inside. Just press that imp's face between the horns."

Ned had not expected it this way. Not when he was filled with a seething rebellion, not when he had seen his mother hurt, his father turn from bully to brute. Not now. . . .

Mechanically he touched the spring. The lid flew open. Within, on a piece of shoddy green baize, lay a single coin, gold, shining.

"Minted in America, Boy. Philadelphia 1816. Five dollars, it says. That's near a guinea. It was to take me and Norrie to America. But the Comet—the Comet . . ." A dim emotion choked him. Then he gave Ned a watery smile. "Your turn now, Boy. Take it. Take it! And go. Go now. Tonight. Before he—before—before the Comet gets in your way. Go, Ned, for God's sake! Don't you understand? I'll be going with you!"

Frightened, giddy with the vision, Ned felt the bindings on his life slipping as the aged and bony hands urged him on. He threw his arms around his grandfather, sharing for an instant his young strength with the spent old man.

In the kitchen he stopped only to snatch his coat from the nail on the wall. Not the fine new one his mother had fashioned for him. He wanted nothing that would draw him back. Only his old work coat with the ragged sleeves. He forgot the torn pocket.

Slipping the gold coin into it, he opened the door. Then he began to run, down the road into the beckoning night.

The night was half gone when Ben Fitch stumbled into the house.

"Supper ready?"

Nora's face was as white as her small clenched fists.

"He's gone, Ben. You drove him away! Where is he? Where's my son?"

"My son, Norrie. Bad cess to him and what you done with him. And good riddance!" He smiled at her, craftily, as his red-rimmed eyes fastened on her.

"On second thought, I've not a mind to eat. I'm that cold with the night. I've a mind for a wife. Come to bed, Norrie. Yer husband's home!"

As he pushed her toward the bedroom, he fingered something the ray of his lantern had caught outside the doorstep. A gold coin, the astonishing turn of a blind, uncaring fate.

2

The sign hung on the gates of Buckingham Palace, PREMISES TO RENT. Ned stared at it, then at the awesome building. No shining Household Guards, no marching band, no royal standard against the mottled sky. A group of idlers cheered and jeered, backing away as a guardsman stiffly tore it down. When Ned gazed at the Palace again, the sign had been restored.

It was not what he had expected, this first sharp disappointment in London. It would be some time before he understood.

The sign was the citizens' angry resentment at their widowed Queen. Victoria had chosen to withdraw into her grief in solitude at Windsor. She had remained there too long.

No, it was not what Ned expected. But then he had not expected London at all. Chance had brought him here. Chance, the loss of his gold coin, and the cold, hungry days on the Bristol waterfront.

"America? No ship leavin' now for America. You look strong. If you can load coal, I'll take you aboard to London."

Somewhere along the Thames' docks the captain found him an apprenticeship with one Mr. Loftus, tanner. It was food and shelter, dirty imprisoning work, and the company of youths who taught Ned to be quick with a curse, quicker with his fists, and that survival meant striking first and the devil take the loser. In his rare hours of freedom he would prowl the streets, to find what must be a different London. He discovered Russell Square with its lofty porticoed houses, Hyde Park with its parade of carriages and holiday strollers, and St. James's Park where men in silk hats and polished boots descended from hansom cabs to enter the forbidding doors of what he learned were gentlemen's clubs. Meanwhile, the years of his youth were blowing away in the boiling bubbles and the stench of steaming vats.

One day he made a more disturbing discovery. When he smiled at a girl, she invariably smiled back. Sometimes she smiled first. But when he approached, she'd look at him in some bewilderment and lose herself in the crowd. The apprentices set him straight. "You stink, Neddie. We all do. Takes a hardy street wench to put up with any of us."

On his next hour off, he walked out of Mr. Loftus's employ and did not return.

But London's squalid sub-life had already enveloped him. He hired out for whatever work he could find. On the rear step of a carter's wagon, he was carried into the world of grey, faceless streets, into Cheapside, Holborn, Smithfield, and the back doors of a city that ignored him. Here people worked in shops, offices. But even for that a man needed skills.

The carter looked at him thoughtfully one day, coughed and wheezed a bit.

"You'll make a good carter, Ned. I'll not be fit much longer to do the load. I've a daughter. Plain, maybe, but a hard worker. I seen her watching you. You can have the daughter and the wagon and the route. It's a solid chance in life for you, lad. More than most get."

The daughter, a muscular determined wench, had already come to his bed. The wagon had a cracked axle and the old dray horse was aging. Ned thanked the carter, made the bow his mother had taught him. That night, he mucked out the stall, fed and watered the horse, and took to his heels.

He was no nearer to his mother's promise of Better Things than to his grandfather's urgency. He had long made up his mind, in the harsh grip of London's rigid society, that if he could not go to America as a gentleman, he would go at least as a young man of parts and purpose.

One evening that flirty doxie, Chance, who can lead a man to heaven or hell at her whim, took him into The Nailhead, a smokey beer hall in Leicester Square. With a shilling and two ten-penny pieces in his pocket, he found a seat, pulled his jacket sleeves over his wrists, and looked around. The girl was seated alone in a corner. She had strawlike hair, a hat with a single red artificial rose, and round, expressionless eyes. They were fixed on him.

Uneasy under her gaze, Ned studied his pint of bitter. She was not what he had ever imagined for himself. Yet she had a curious magnetism. Perhaps it was her very aloneness, which he so well understood. He sensed, as a man can, that such intensity could lead to involvement. He finished his glass and left.

But Chance was not done with him, as it never is with any man or woman. Debating whether he should again repair to The Nailhead, Ned found himself walking the tangle of streets beyond Leicester Square. In the lingering London sunlight his eye caught a square white card in a dusty window. He stepped idly from the stream of jostlers to read it.

YOUNG MAN WANTED. MUST BE ABLE TO READ, WRITE, MOVE HEAVY WARES. The sign on the grimy bricks above the door informed Ned that this was BELLOWES FINE BOOKBINDING, EST. 1835. It was a wry prod of memory, his grandfather at the hearth. "1835, Boy. Never forget it. The year the Comet came. Changed everything. . . ."

Ned pushed the door open, heard a bell jangle, and looked around. Clutter spilled everywhere. Off a table onto the floor sheets of heavy paper, discarded bits of fabric and leather, spindles of twine. A seedy desk with the top unrolled, accounting books thrust into it at random. On a shelf above stood a row of immaculate volumes bound in dark blue leather and lettered in gold. Mr. Bellowes did good work.

A wizened little man behind the table lifted his eyeshade. "Come for the job, have you?"

Ned met the shrewd eyes, appraising him. Had he? "Maybe."

"Read this." Mr. Bellowes thrust a dog-eared volume at him, the cover fingermarked. It had obviously been opened many times.

"Plutarch's Lives," Ned read.

"Don't bother with the title. Any fool can read that. Start on page ten."

Word by deliberate word, Ned read. With each completed sentence he was aware of how far he had slipped from his youthful vision.

"You could do better. Write your name." Ned took the quill. "Ned Fitch. Your full name? When I hire a man I want to know who he is."

Ned picked up the quill again. In letters dark and full and ending in a flourish that cracked the nib, he wrote "Julien Edmond Abbingdon-Fitch."

Mr. Bellowes glanced at it sharply. "Where you from?"

"Wiltshire."

"Wiltshire's a good-sized county."

"Avebury. North of Salisbury, three miles east of . . ."

"I know. I know. That's where the Hanging Stones are. People make a lot of fuss trying to understand 'em. But they're there for any man to read who has the wit. And the imagination. Imagination. They's the real mystery. Use that and you're a free man. Come with me."

Without waiting for an answer, Mr. Bellowes led Ned through a rear door, down a flight of dark steps into the perennial dusk of an extensive cellar. A narrow window near the ceiling was the only skylight to the street.

Ned made out a ghostly stacking of bales, rows of barrels, and when his eyes adjusted, piles of tanned hides in uneven shapes on the floor. The air was choking and he recognized the smell.

"You'll get used to it." Mr. Bellowes tapped a barrel. "Like the glue. Best you can buy. Dutch. Mostly cattle and horse bones and fish. Many a worn-out horse might feel better going to the knacker's, knowing that someday he'd hold Shakespeare's *Sonnets* together. This is where you'll work. Check deliveries against invoices. Keep a record of what's needed. Sweep, clean, see that the stock's neat and dry. Seven to seven, midday meal provided. If you haven't lodgings, there's a cot right off the storage. Table, stick, and candles provided. You didn't come with a character or you'd have offered it before now. Which means you haven't stayed in one place long enough to get one. So I'll ask you to sign a year's bond. Not worth teaching you if you're running off again. Well, Mr. Abbingdon?"

Ned started to correct him, thought better of it. He had never heard the name spoken. He liked the sound.

"Let's see, had it backwards, didn't I? Well, Mr. Fitch?"

"I'd like to think about it, sir."

"How long?"

"Tonight."

"You'll have to take your chances."

In the front office, Mr. Bellowes resettled his eyeshade.

"You need improving, young man. A great deal of improving. But I think you're capable of it. Take this. Don't bother to return it. Good day."

It was the dog-eared volume from which he had read. In the street Ned had an impulse to pitch it into the first trash bin. The work offered at Bellowes Bindery was no better than other imprisonments he had escaped.

The day was gone. A lamplighter touched the street with tawdry illusion. Ned was aware of his own hopelessness, the futility of his days, of an unseeing world that, try as he might, walled him out. And he was hungry.

His last two shillings and a sixpence reminded him that Mr. Bellowes had made no mention of wages. Perhaps there were none in that dank employment. He jingled the coins together. He would spend them grandly.

The Nailhead was beginning to fill up with coarse faces and coarser voices. Ned took a seat beside the window. A bowl of hot soup would lift his spirits. A meat pie would do the rest. He looked at his face reflected in the darkened glass. *Mr. Abbingdon.*

Mr. Abbingdon, well-tailored, silk-hatted, hailing a cab with a walking stick.

The image faded. He saw that his cuffs needed mending. Gravy had spotted his coat. He'd have to tend to all that before presenting himself to Mr. Bellowes in the morning.

He thought of the girl. The corner table had been empty when he came in. He glanced at it again, her straw-colored hair, her round eyes as vivid in his mind as the first time he had seen her.

A stranger sat there.

3

Respectability, as the denizens of The Nailhead would tell you, was for those who could afford it. Departure from it was labeled sin, a splendid umbrella of a word that could be thundered from the pulpit or whispered at tea tables, with delicious titillation and no offense to good manners.

Nevertheless the primal urge flourished copiously and enjoyably in the Queen's London. The smothering monotony of the marital double bed could be relieved as often as a gentleman met a dewy adventuresome eye. A lady bent on mischief could find it any time she entered her opera box and lifted her opera glasses. The servant girl could, and often did, expect a tumbling by the heir and/or master of the household. The layers of clothing, the corseting, the thick woolens and the thicker modesties merely added to the delights of anticipation.

It was noted that the Queen herself bore a child as often as nature permitted, totaling nine in little more than sixteen years.

Sex, a banished word, was the gaudy underskirt of proper society. Sometimes it held a surprise.

The girl with the round, china-blue eyes stayed in Ned's mind through the first long grueling weeks in Mr. Bellowes' basement. Twice he returned after the day's work to The Nailhead, to find the tables crowded with noisy beer drinkers and no sign of her strawlike hair and the little round hat with its artificial rose. Ned told himself he had only to walk around Leicester Square to find another like her. Yet her aloofness, the aloneness that seemed to enwrap her, the expressionless gaze piqued him. He was used to more warmth in female eyes.

But if the frowsy beer hall did not yield the girl, it offered something else. Human company, thick bodies pressed close in conviviality, rowdy voices, the thumping of beer mugs to raucous songs as the smoke grew denser, the air hotter.

Late one evening, after a long day that alternated between stacking glue barrels and outmaneuvering the basement rats, Ned walked again into The Nailhead. There, in the corner, as he had long imagined her, sat the girl, the red rose brave on her hat. Her eyes widened to meet his, solemn, unblinking, unseeking.

He walked to her table.

"May I sit down?"

As she said nothing he sat down beside her. Preliminaries seemed futile.

"Like a beer?"

"No, thanks."

"Waiting for somebody?"

"What girl isn't?" She sat back. "But I don't expect him. Not for a while."

"This evening?"

"No."

She was thin-bosomed. He could see a thin ankle in a white cotton stocking above a black boot thrust beyond the table's edge. The boot began to tap as the next song began. When it was over she clapped her small rough hands. Her mouth was too narrow, her teeth too small, her features drawn. But her skin was the texture of new cream.

He wondered if this was all she came for.

"What's your name?"

"Millie." She did not ask his.

In the overheated air, her face began to lose its strain. She was prettier than he had first thought. They sat in silence, until the next rowdy song began. This time she joined in, with a giggle for no one in particular.

She loved not the savor of tar nor of pitch,
But a sailor might scratch her where 'ere she did itch,
Then to the sea, boys. . . .

The smell of spilled beer, the leering laughter, faces red and sweaty above the mugs, made the girl brighten in response. While Ned's presence seemed to content her, her indifference made him uncomfortable.

"Where do you live?"

"Gower Street."

"Do you work?"

"I'm a respectable girl. I sew feathers and fur on ladies' bonnets. All the time I think of the poor little dead birds and the poor little dead animals that would be prettier to look at than them ladies."

It was more than she had said in an hour.

"Let's go somewhere."

"Where?" The girl's round eyes were full on him again.

"A walk. To get some air."

"Oh." She made no move. He suspected that she no more wanted to leave the warmth than he did.

"Do you live alone?"

She was silent for a long moment. Then her voice was sharp. "If you want to come to my room, why don't you say so? I've got no mind for talkin' when the singin's going on."

She rose, he followed. They had passed the last table when a man called out.

"Goodnight, Millie darlin'. If anyone comes asking fer you we'll tell 'im where to find you."

The laughter that followed her was not without affection.

The night was wet with fog. Millie took Ned's arm as if she'd been doing it all her life. He sensed, out of her silence, her air of indifference, and the reality of her arm close against his, a possible involvement that could not further or aid the future he saw for himself.

The room she took him to had its own surprises, like Millie's rare outbursts of talk. It was at the top of four flights of rickety stairs, under the roof, so the ceiling slanted. It contained a narrow bed, a commode with a chipped white pitcher and basin, two straight-backed chairs and a little table. Whatever else Millie possessed was hidden behind a curtain drawn across a corner. A single window opened to a roof-filled landscape of London's chimney pots.

There must have been hundreds of lonely little top-floor rooms exactly like this one, except for one thing. Millie had hung every available inch in bright red. Red glazed cambric covered the window. A torn fragment of turkey red carpet concealed most of the floor. The bed was covered in a crimson-and-yellow India print. The corner was shut off by a piece of ancient scarlet damask. Grey dawn would mellow it to rose. Only the brief slant of noon sun could strip it to its tawdry truth, a bit of cruelty that soon passed.

Into this carmined and diminutive Venusberg, Millie led Ned. As the kerosene lamp spread its glow, she glanced anxiously at him.

"Nice," he said.

She urged him to one of the stiff chairs, disappeared behind the scarlet damask and returned with two cups of tea, two tin spoons, and a flowered saucer of sugar. She sat opposite, her eyes full on his, stirring the sugar into her tea as he drank his. When he was nearly finished, she lifted her own cup, holding her little finger up, straight as a kitten's tail. Perhaps it was the flushed closeness of the room, perhaps the warmth of the tea that made speech unnecessary. When she had cleared the table and smoothed the red calico cloth, she stood motionless before him.

"I'm ready," she said.

In the night that followed Ned discovered that Millie was as generous with her thin body as she was with her silence.

As the weeks passed he could only guess that she was as content with his presence, his lovemaking, as he with her.

He had never known such unquestioning calm. She no longer visited The Nailhead. He would come directly to her room after work. The door would open before his knock. She would take his cap and his coat with little brushes of her hand and hang them neatly. If he chose to sweep her at once onto the crimson India print of the bed, she would yield without protest.

In the long spring twilights they would walk up the Strand to Piccadilly, like settled folks. On Sundays he would take her to Hyde Park, where he would buy her an ice or a sweet-cake. They would sit on the grass and she would make her hand into a little cup of crumbs for the sparrows.

"I'd like to buy you a present, Millie. What would you like?"

"Oh, and are you that rich?"

"I'm not rich at all."

She surveyed him thoughtfully. "But you're gentry, Neddie. I knew that from the first." He let that pass. He found it pleasant to accept the fantasies she spun about him, when she had a mind to talk.

But he could grow impatient with her chatter. What he relished was her quiet.

"I work for a living, Millie, like everyone else."

Her round eyes were wary.

"What do you, Neddie? Is it honest?"

"Yes, it's honest. I work in a bindery."

"What's that?"

"It's where books are bound together. Pages and covers."

"Books!"

He would never again, he was sure, hear the word spat out with such disdain. It unleashed a small fury.

"Books! Tell me what they can do for you, Neddie! Except to make you think you're better than you are. At home the Vicar was always plaguing me to read books. 'You've the sense to raise yourself, Millie,' he'd say. 'I can help you if you'll come read with me.' But Tim, the coachman's son from the manor, said if I took to reading books he wouldn't marry me someday. 'Come up to the manor and work in scullery, Millie my love,' he'd say. 'We'll have a future, the two of us. Vicar will give you a character.' Oh, I was that torn. One day Tim caught me behind the hedgerow and just as I was down the Vicar comes riding by on his big nobbledy-kneed old horse and peers over the hedgerow. Tim runs off and the Vicar says to me, 'Whatever are you doing down there, Millie, my dear? Shall I come help you?' I said, 'No thank you, Vicar, I'm looking for star flowers but there's none here,' and I got up and ran away. So I lost my character and didn't get to scullery and instead came down to London. I had a quick needle so I found steady work. Oh, I do hate books. They can twist a body's life all out of shape and cause misery. Just misery!" She dabbed at her eyes. When she lifted her head Ned saw they were round and expressionless again and quite dry.

On the way back to her room he bought her what she most coveted. A parasol of lavender silk with white stripes and a pink ruffle, the whole no bigger than a soup tureen.

The quarrel, if it was a quarrel, sank like a stone into the marshy comfort of life with Millie. Yet it seemed to Ned to lie there invisible but solid, leaving him with an unease he preferred not to think about.

He was doing well at the bindery. Mr. Bellowes was now inviting him to the front office to show him accounts gained, debits lost, credits made, and other mysteries of business for profit. But it was stifling boredom. His one reward was the full tea Mrs. Bellowes served up with admiring chirps and encouragement.

And there were the books. Millie's outburst notwithstanding, Ned was by now opening book after book with a sense of time lost, amid the cramped horizons of his unproven life.

On Saturday afternoons, Millie invariably went to visit a cousin in Cheapside. "Duty bound," she said. "A promise is a promise, isn't it?"

On Saturday afternoons, Ned found himself making his way to the Thames' docks, where the great Atlantic packet ships were berthed. Powerful ships, half steam against the battering of the Westerlies, half sail when the coal might be running low. Wonder-ships, he saw them. It was said the grand salons held gilt chairs, rosewood pianos. The ladies' bedrooms were hung in silk with private baths. Below, in the dark bowels of the ship, a man for four guineas could book steerage passage, provided he brought his own blanket, a sack of dried oats, and a supply of tea. Water would be supplied, within limits.

It would take a long time to save four guineas on Mr. Bellowes' wages.

But the talk on the docks, whenever Ned would wander there, was heady. At this midpoint of the Queen's reign, America fever gripped the English imagination. Enormous wealth buoyed upward on the black smoke of England's factories, but too little of it seeped through the sooty haze below. America might be a land of savages and bad manners. It was also a mirage of quick wealth and classlessness. A man would never become a Duke in such a country, but he could, with a little hard work, move his children into quality.

Ned perched on a capstan, watched the gulls dip and cry above an off-loading ship.

"What's in the bales?"

The seaman at a hawser grinned. "Buffalo hides from America. Keep the draughts off backsides in them old Scottish castles."

"What's America like?"

"It's big. Big. They got a thousand miles of nothing but grass high as your waist. And gold? They got spikes of gold in the railroad tracks."

"Have you seen all that?"

"All I seen is Mother Bell's on South Street, New York." The seaman winked. "But that's enough for me. Maybe if I was younger I'd try my chances. But it's England for me, and the Widder, God bless 'er."

On a day of driving rain, Ned pushed his way into the beery refuge of The Anchor and Sail and up to the bar.

"Here's a likely fellow! We're short a swabber, man. What d'ye say?"

A heavy hand dropped on his shoulder. Ned whirled and knocked it off. Among his other presentiments of gentry he disliked a coarse hand laid on him.

"Come now, we're techy, ain't we?" The mate stood off, swaying slightly. "I'm offering you the chance of a lifetime. New York, sir. Houses of solid marble. Even the whores ride in carriages. Who'd stay in London, I ask you? The Queen sittin' on an ivory throne now—Empress of India. What's right about that? To be an Empress of the heathen? Are they better, I ask you, than the free and honest men of England?''

The mate and his followers swung out the door. In the silence that followed, the old barman leaned across the counter.

''Don't listen, young sir. When I was young they sent me to America. For poachin'. Three woodcock and a brace of rabbits from the Earl's park. Afeared I'd bring more disgrace on the village, they took up a collection in church. The schoolmaster wrote to his cousin in America up in a village called Harlem that I had a bit of a green thumb. Me mither said you'll make the flowers grow like England, son. So I went.'' The barman glanced around. He poured a drink for Ned and one for himself.

''Well, sir. I got as far as New York. They told me the village of Harlem was ten miles north. I wanted none of that. Maybe get scalped with a tommyhawk that far into the wilds.'' He drained his glass and looked through it to his youth. ''New York was a fair little town there on the rim of the water. Or might have been. But for the mud in the streets and the pigs. Not even a park. Just rocks and stubbles and hills where the goats graze and a few shanties to keep the cold from a poor man's belly. But any man with a trade could get work. I hired as a gardener to Mr. Rutherford. He was gentry. Had a nice house on the edge of town. His lady wanted an English garden. Garden! What man could grow a garden in that climate? It was so hot in summer that the horses dropped dead in the streets. So did workin' men. In winter, what with the ice and the snow and the piercin' wind, the ground froze six inches deep and every root in it. I stayed three years; then I come home. If you're goin', go when you're young, sir. An old man would perish in that city. No, no. I'll not take yer money. It's my wish for luck to ye.''

One day, as summer was ending, Ned lounged beside Millie on the faded grass of Hyde Park, watching the elegance of horses and riders on that wide strip of soft earth, known to fashionable London as Rotten Row. Occasionally he glanced at her face, pretty in the play of shadow and light through the absurd lavender parasol. She was absorbed in the antics of a small boy trying to fly a kite. He did not try to understand the hold she had on him. He began to suspect it was his need to keep what little had come his way that made him want her.

He owed only two months more of his written bond to Mr. Bellowes.

"Would you like to go to America, Millie?"

She looked so startled he had to amend his statement. "It's only an idle question, Millie. I've got my bond."

"But you're thinking of it?"

"I think of a lot of things."

She sat for a while pulling the petals off a limp daisy she had found lying on the grass. Then she lifted her eyes.

"When?"

"When what?"

"When are you going to America?"

"Oh, for heaven's sake, Millie. I don't know. I have no plans. It takes a bit of doing. It was only a little joke."

"Oh." She tossed the torn daisy away and sat quite straight under her parasol.

"Oh! Look! There!" She pointed with a stiff forefinger. "The little boy lost his kite!" The loose kite, buffeted by an erratic wind, swept over the Sunday strollers.

Ned saw something else. He was on his feet and running when the chestnut horse with a lone rider cantered by. A toss of wind carried the kite straight into the horse's face. The horse reared with a squeal, whirled, and plunged off the bridle path. Ned barely heard Millie's scream as he lunged for the animal's bridle. With a quick spring he caught the reins. Another tug and the horse came to a trembling stop, sweat foaming on its copper-chestnut neck.

"You are very strong, young man."

The lady's face behind her veil was as white as her stock. Her silk riding hat was pitched forward and her breath was coming rapidly. Otherwise she was so lovely on her sidesaddle that Ned could only stare.

She gathered up the reins, adjusted her hat unsteadily. "It's all right, now. Sun Knight never shies like that. Really. But he had such a fright." She stroked the horse's neck. "Didn't you, darling?"

"Any horse will, ma'am, when something comes at him from above his head."

"You understand horses." She was looking at him so directly that the statement seemed irrelevant.

"I like them."

"That's all it takes." She smoothed her riding skirt. "Oh, my stirrup! Could you?"

He fitted the small polished boot into the stirrup. She smiled, her eyes warm.

"I can only say thank you. From my heart."

"You're welcome, ma'am."

It was an instant caught in crystal. Ned groped for something to say to keep her there, but he was too late.

To a thudding of hoofs, a heavy man in a grey top hat rode breathlessly up to them.

"Helene, whatever did you have in mind? I thought for a moment the brute would throw you!"

"Horses rarely throw people, George. People fall off. I might have gone off, too, but for this young man."

"Very good of him, I'm sure." The man thrust into his pocket for a coin. "For you, my man. Come along, Helene. The Royal Carriage is due in minutes."

"Bother the Royal Carriage," said the girl, her eyes still on Ned. "I do thank you," she said softly. Then she permitted her escort to lead her away.

Millie had seen it all. They walked home in silence, which was not unusual, but this was a silence filled with unsaid words. Millie looked straight ahead, ignoring shop windows and passersby. The sunlight had gone, the sky turned grey. At the first drops of rain, Millie furled her parasol. Ned's thoughts were taken up by the incident, the perfection he had glimpsed, the girl's air of belonging and the coin dropped into his hand to remind him he never would.

He realized guiltily that he had quite forgotten Millie.

He took her arm. "A bit of tea now?"

"I don't really feel the need, Ned."

He showed her the coin still in his hand. "My reward for the day. Where else would I spend it?"

The closeness of the tea table restored warmth to her cheeks, and her hurt began to evaporate.

"You were very brave, Neddie. I thought that horse would trample you."

"The last thing in the world a horse wants to do is to trample anybody. He hates to put his foot on anything soft as a human body if he can help it."

She shuddered delicately and accepted a second cup of tea, stirring it mechanically. Ned was grateful that she had apparently forgotten the unfinished talk of America. It was not a subject he should bring up until he had faced the question honestly. Did he want to take Millie with him?

"She was beautiful, wasn't she?" Millie spoke suddenly.

"Who?" He indulged her. He knew the answer.

"The lady on the horse. Like the princess in that old picture book they sent us down from the manor once. Only she rode a white horse and wore a tall, pointy hat and . . ."

A giggle broke the chatter.

"You've put lemon and milk in your tea, Neddie! You can't drink that!" She poured the brew into a saucer and peered into the cup. "Oh, my." There was a pause. "Did you know I can tell fortunes, Neddie?"

"In the tea leaves?"

"Yes. And in your palm, too. It's better in your palm. Then you can see it for yourself. I'll show you."

Her oddly ineffectual little hands clasped his so caressingly that he felt a throb of titillation, as he did whenever she touched him.

"Oh, my," she repeated.

"Well, what is it? Am I going to conquer the world?"

"That's your left hand. See, that line there, rather raggedy, uneven. That's what you were born to. Now, here's your right hand. See?"

She peered intently at his right palm, her forefinger tracing a highly visible line around the base of his thumb.

"That's what you're going to be. It's very strong. See. It gets deeper right there. And there's change and then . . ." She pushed his hand away. "I can't tell you any more." Her voice held a flutter.

"You mean you can't or you won't?"

He did not like the turn the afternoon had taken.

"Well, what does it all mean, Millie? Am I or am I not going to be rich?"

"I don't know about that. Maybe you'll be a real swell someday but . . ." The words drifted. Then came one of Millie's rare moments of earthy shrewdness that never failed to unsettle Ned. "You'll always be easier with people like me than—than people like her."

The scattering raindrops had turned into a steady drizzle. Millie furled her parasol and protected it as best she could, under her arm. When they reached her room, she took out the cold remnants of a meat pie, sliced two spotted pears, set the inevitable kettle to a boil.

After eating, Ned threw himself on the bed and watched her.

When she had returned the room to neatness, she unbuttoned her plain boots, took off the summer dress, hung it neatly behind the scarlet damask curtain and went to the six inches of mottled mirror on the opposite wall. She brushed her straw-colored hair exactly twenty times. Then she came and stood stiffly before Ned, slowly unhooking her camisole. He had told her he liked that. She blew out the wick and lay down beside him, waiting silently, as if nothing had happened yesterday and nothing would happen tomorrow.

In mid-November the early darkness of London's winter began to settle in. Ned noticed a change in Millie. Her silences were longer. On occasion she showed flashes of irritability he had never suspected. He had let her parasol fall to the floor. He had left uneaten his half of the salt haddock. He had arrived half an hour late on the evening he had promised to take her to the penny show. And the day she had saved enough stale bread to make a hot pudding, he had failed to come. There was never a quarrel. Ned discovered that even a single word less than loving could silence Millie.

Down at the docks, his barkeeping friend at The Anchor and Sail added fuel. "There's money aplenty in America," he would admit. "Gentry, too, I suspect, if you know where to look. But it's no more for the likes of you and me than here in London. If you've found your place, stay with it, I say."

On Christmas day, Millie refused to see Ned, saying she would have to spend the time in Cheapside with her cousin, who was feeling poorly. The following two Sundays he waited until mid-afternoon in the little red room. She arrived breathless and penitent in her heavy shawl. He found himself crushing her in his arms, his anger dissolved in the relief that all was as it had been.

"I had to be gone, Neddie. You understand, don't you? Look what I've brought. A half loaf of Dundee cake from the second-day man. We'll have it for tea."

He did not want tea. He wanted Millie. Even as he took her he acknowledged the humbling hold this inscrutable girl had on him. Millie knew who she was. He needed that confidence himself.

Toward the end of January, Mr. Bellowes came down to the bindery's storage basement at the unusual hour of ten in the morning.

"You've done very well, Ned. You're clever. You're learned. And you've taken to heart Mrs. Bellowes' advice on reading. Your bond is up in another five weeks. I've been thinking about it. Expect you'll be settling down soon if you've found the girl. Mrs. Bellowes thinks maybe you have."

Ned waited, suppressing a ripple of something like panic at Mrs. Bellowes' perspicacity.

"I never question Mrs. Bellowes. She has woman's instinct. Mighty powerful. Like a high wind. Best to bend before it. You'll find that out for yourself one day. I'd like to say I'm pleased with your work. You've caught hold of things here, right and proper. I'd like to offer you a future, steady, dependable. In the front office of Bellowes' Book Bindery."

Ned was startled and alarmed by his good luck. He was not prepared for such finality. On the other hand, never in his life had he been rewarded with more than a day's wages for a day's work. Here suddenly was a place for him in the established order of things. Little as he knew of domesticity, he sensed Millie would make a good wife—steady, dependable as Mr. Bellowes' front office. What else did a man want? A new suit for holidays, a mutton joint on Sundays. Respectability. Millie would like that. So would his mother. Julien Edmond Abbingdon-Fitch, Bookbinder. A long way up from a pig farm.

For three days he kept the good news from Millie, thrashing it out on long solitary walks.

On the fourth day, wearing a clean shirt and carrying a bouquet of snowdrops only slightly brown at the edges, he climbed the stairs to Millie.

The door was locked. That might mean she had not yet come home. He felt for the key on the lintel. It was not there. That might mean she was inside sweeping and tidying and did not like to be discovered. The image irritated him. The snowdrops looked foolish. He knocked. There was no sound. He knocked again, impatiently, and heard a step. The door was opened cautiously.

The man standing there was neither young nor old. He was slight, his head was large and his face leaden grey.

He stared, blinking, at Ned.

Ned felt his fists tighten. "Where's Millie?"

"She'll be back." The door was opened wider. "Better come in."

Ned flung the snowdrops down the stairs behind him and pushed into the room. The man he confronted had a shock of sandy hair, a thin mouth framed in deep lines, and in his eyes the bloodshot weariness of an underfed street dog.

"I'm Artie," the man said.

A basin of dirty water stood on the dresser. Across the bed lay a black overcoat, green with age. Otherwise the room was as neat as always. Millie's parasol hung on its nail.

"Where is she?"

"Gone to get me a kipper. It's a long time since I've had a kipper." The man picked up the basin of water and carried it behind the scarlet damask curtain. "Best to rid up. She doesn't like things out of place, Millie doesn't. But I guess you know all about that, Mr. Fitch."

"Who the devil are you?"

"Like I told you. I'm Artie. Artie Riggs. Didn't she tell you about me? She told me all about you. Oh, come now. No cause for hard feelings. If I don't have 'em, why should you?" A shiver ran through him. He coughed. "I guess it comes as a surprise to you, maybe, seeing me here like this. But Millie's a sensible girl, and if she figured it was the right way to do things, I guess it was. You might not have stayed around if you'd known about me. And then things would have gone bad for Millie. All I can say is I thank you for takin' care of my girl the way you done. Saved me a lot of worrying after they took me in."

With easy familiarity, the man turned up the lamp. It was the room Ned knew so well, but the rosy comfort of it was gone. In its place Ned saw the tawdry shabbiness, not alone in the red curtains, the rag of a carpet, the forlorn damask, but in the soul of the place, the threadbare illusion Millie had tried to create. He wanted to slam the door on it. Yet he wanted to see Millie once more. A hope that she would deny it, she would explain it away. Reason told Ned that this man, fragile as smoke, and beyond Ned's anger, spoke the truth.

"You might think I had some shame, Mr. Fitch. Some pride. Millie, too. But people like us can't afford what the rich have. We've got to make do. I'm good at my trade. I could have had that wallet out of your coat pocket before you passed the door sill if I'd pleased. I'm as good as they come and I've got a few pounds stashed away for Millie and me to begin all over. I've no cause for shame either. Show me a rich man who hasn't picked somebody's pocket on the way up! I'll go at it a little longer until Millie and me can open the little pub we want down in Eastbourne near the sea. Millie would like that. She's a respectable girl, Mr. Fitch. I guess you know that, too. That's why I'm grateful to you. Being her protector, like. Though looking at you now, I kind of wished Millie had told you how it was. She's a brave girl, Millie is. But you can't expect everything, now can you? I guess it was easier for her to tell you she had a cousin in Cheapside when she came to visit me. A cousin in Cheapside! Gor! If she hadn't she'd not have kept this room till I got out.

"You see, Mr. Fitch, I understand Millie. It's what you got to do with a woman, now isn't it? Try to understand her even when she's different. Millie's not afraid of being cold, or hungry, or of hard work. She's known all those things with nary a word of complaining. She's only afraid of one thing and it's best you understand it, being she's my girl. She's mortal afraid of being alone in the dark."

They both heard the light steps ascending the stairs.

Artie leaned toward Ned, making him feel unpleasantly like a conspirator, as he whispered, "You see, Mr. Fitch, that's why I owe you my thanks. If it hadn't been you, it might have been . . . others."

The door opened. Millie wore her brown shawl over her head. The dampness had curled the straw-colored hair showing around her face. Her cheeks were pink from exercise. Ned had never seen her prettier. In one hand she carried a brown-paper package, in the other a few bruised snowdrops. She stood for an instant, her round eyes staring at the two men.

"Oh," she said at last. She closed the door, laid the package and the snowdrops on the table, shook out her shawl and hung it neatly on the nail beside the parasol. She smoothed her hair before the green-tinged piece of mirror and, at last, turned to break the silence.

"It's best you're here, Neddie. I got two kippers, Artie, they're small. End of day, the fishman said, so they were cheap. I'll fix them with a bit of lard." She scooped up the bedraggled snowdrops. "Whoever do you think could have dropped these flowers on the stairs? Poor, darling little things. I thought only rich people could have snowdrops. And the Queen . . . they'd do with a bit of water. . . ."

"I'll get you better than those, luv," said Artie, "the day we're married."

The last word seemed to pierce an inner wall.

"Neddie. . . ." She gave him her hands.

They were cold. His were surprisingly warm, his voice calm. He had already left her.

"I understand, Millie. Don't talk. Artie's told me. I'm glad for you. Glad you won't be alone. Because I came to tell you I'm leaving for America."

She stared at him.

"In a few weeks, as soon as my bond is up. You remember. You read it in my hand."

She pulled from him, ran past Artie, and returned with the parasol. "You'll want this back, Neddie." Tears stood in her eyes.

"It's yours, Millie. Carry it at your wedding." He turned

his back to Artie. Gently he took her face in his hands, kissed her forehead. Then he turned and left, quickly and forever, the rosy entrapment of his youth. He would never know whether Millie's last tears were for love or for a lavender-striped parasol.

The next day Ned did not go to work. Instead he went down to the docks. The new coal-and-steam packet, the H.M.S. *Boedicia,* was signing on crew to depart in four days for the port of New York. Ned signed, third-class able seaman, divesting the captain, the ship, and the owners of all responsibility for his person and property during the voyage.

Then he went to the front office of Bellowes Fine Bookbinding.

Mr. Bellowes pushed back his eyeshade. "America, eh? Why? Never mind. I don't need an answer. You want to be rich and you think that by some manner of sea change you'll get rich there when you won't in London. Well, maybe you will. Then again, maybe you won't. But it's not my experience that a young man who breaks one agreement is going to do better anywhere else. You owe me five weeks."

That night, beneath a well-worn feather quilt, Mrs. Bellowes moved closer to the long-familiar spine of her husband.

"Let him go, Mr. Bellowes. He's a good lad. Can't you see?"

Mr. Bellowes reluctantly shed his armor of sleep.

"See what? I can see he's broken his word."

"He's broken his heart, that's what he has. The girl refused him, she did. A woman knows these things by instinct. I don't blame you for not seeing it outright, being a man. He's going away so as not to pine to death." She pushed her billowing softness closer. "Why, Mr. Bellowes, don't you remember when we were courting and your uncle said he'd set you up in the East Indies trade if you'd sign on with him and go? But you said there was nothing prettier in all East Indies than my blue eyes and you'd marry me instead. But what would have happened to you if I'd said no? Why, it would be a crime against nature to make Neddie stay here and suffer. I'd suffer with him."

Mr. Bellowes was not at all sure about the crime against human nature, but he was very sure about the crime against his peace of mind, which Mrs. Bellowes regularly committed.

He waited until mid-afternoon to summon Ned. He methodically finished a full page of his account book while Ned stood at his desk. Finally, he looked up.

"Here's your agreement. Do with it what you want. And here's a character. You've done good work so I won't begrudge you that. I don't hold with this way of doing things. Not at all. But it's a new day. Maybe honor's old-fashioned when a man wants first thing to serve himself. Not that I begrudge that either."

He rose and lifted from the table a square package wrapped in brown paper and tied with a heavy cord. "Mr. Crowne of Crowne Booksellers would be obliged if you'd take this with you and deliver it safe and in person to the address in New York. It missed the last sailing. There's a guinea for your trouble."

"You can depend on me," said Ned.

"I hope so," said Mr. Bellowes dryly.

Ned was free at last, albeit uneasily. They had been kind to him. The echo came from the past, his mother. *A gentleman's word is his honor*. It occurred to him that perhaps honor, like soap, had to be afforded.

He pocketed the guinea and read the address on the package. "Dr. Hugo Lendler, 72 Stuyvesant Square, New York."

Stuyvesant Square. It had a foreign ring to it. But that was what he wanted, wasn't it? A new life.

He repeated the address as H.M.S. *Boedicia* lifted her bows into the North Atlantic's winter gales.

Stuyvesant Square. A place where no one need know where he had been or what he had done.

4

Having done its mischief, the Great Comet streamed from the Earth toward its apogee, its most distant point beyond the Sun. It would not return to trouble human fate for another near-century.

It would seem an auspicious time for Ned to break with all he knew, for all he imagined. Lying on the damp boards of a bunk in the black bowels of the *Boedicia,* he wondered what trick Chance had played on him. Because he hadn't much else to do, he thought about those faint, long-ago promises.

"You'll be a gentleman someday, Ned. You'll see." His mother's foolish doting words. He had learned soon enough in the sunless alleys, the sooted backstreets of London, that in the bare-knuckled struggle for a day's bread no man became a gentleman. He was born to it or he wasn't. He was of "gentle" birth, or not.

He thought, too, of the old man, a dim silhouette against his mother's hearth, but a kindly friend who had taken him out to see the stars, and the Hanging Stones, and best of all, the world's horizon.

"You'll go to America, Boy, because you can't help it. The Comet promised it. You'll go in my place."

"When, Grandfather?"

"You'll go when you're a young man or there won't be much point to it."

"Where will the Comet be?"

The old man had made a calculation. He was never as daft as they made him out to be. "The Comet will be as far from us as it can get. Maybe just coming around the bend of the Sun on its way back. That is to say, it won't do you any harm, but it won't do anything for you either. Not way out there. Whatever you're after, you'll have to do it on your own."

Lying in the dark, an angry sea not an arm's length away

pounding the hull, Ned considered what he had made of himself.

The voyage so far was a disaster. The swabbing, the scrubbing, the holystoning of the deck, the fetid odors below, the long rain-soaked hours on watch, the hardtack, thin tea, and strips of leathered beef had been bad enough. Ned had expected hard work. When had he ever been without it? But he had counted on brief moments of freedom for glimpses of the future. A girl at the rail of the first-class deck, her scarf blowing in the wind, her gloved hand clinging to her hat, all grace and poised motion. A sedate couple arm in arm, balancing their steps against the deck's slant.

Three times he had managed to steal up to the top deck to peer furtively at the gilded comings and goings of the Grand Salon. Women in silks, jewels gleaming on bare arms and throats; men in formal evening dress, as much at home at sea as in any London club. The music he could barely, teasingly hear but felt came from an orchestra of black-coated musicians, with instruments brighter than the brass he polished daily.

The third time he made one of these furtive journeys he had been collared. The First Mate had pushed him roughly down three decks into a dank hole.

"I've seen you, Fitch. Ye may think yer too good for yer mates, m'lad, but you'll stay in the brig until ye learn yer proper place. And yer dooty."

The turn of a key had locked him into darkness.

At first it had been a relief to be left alone with his own images. But as time lost its measurement, bitterness, like the film of bilge water at his feet, began to seep into Ned's soul. He had brought it on himself, of course. But had he not as much right as the next man to a glimpse of brightness and beauty and warmth? Could he not, given a chance, fill the polished boots of any man on the upper deck with as much flair and good manners?

His first youth was gone. It had left him with two rock-hard convictions. Trust no man. A man could lay a whip on your back, order you to work you hated. A man could hold the power of death over your body if you were not strong enough to defend yourself.

But he had made a more subtle discovery. With a second glance, a slow smile, he could turn a girl his way. But having done that, she would claim possession with an uncanny instinct for where his weaknesses lay. Ned had come to the conclusion that beneath the bonnets and airy shawls, the fragile finger mitts and ruffles, lurked an awesome and invisible power to be approached warily, invoked knowingly. Women, he discovered, were drawn to him. The trick lay in knowing when to move out of their reach.

So inevitably his thoughts returned to Millie. He remembered her silences and, oddly, the two rows of tiny, perfect teeth in her young, soft face. As a woman she would fade, a bisque doll soon to be lost among former playthings. Yet he found himself shifting uncomfortably away from the words she had left festering in his mind.

Go as high as you will, Neddie, you'll always be more comfortable with my kind. . . .

As he had before, he turned face down against the roll of the ship, buried his head in his arms, aware that neither vindictiveness nor denial could obliterate some recollections.

It was easier to think about the distant Comet while he lay in this dark, awaiting rebirth.

Providence proved a harsh and sudden midwife. Out of the north, within a single watch, winds of hurricane force struck the *Boedicia,* a giant fist that could wipe a wooden splinter of a ship from the thundering mountains of the sea. Every man was needed. Ned was sprung from his prison to pit his body with the others against the fury of the waves. He saw, helplessly, two men swept from the deck, their cries thin and final as the ghosts of long-departed gulls.

As the storm screamed around him, he found himself bargaining with fate, with the deity, with himself. What a man was or did made little matter. Survival was the essence of life. Let him only live through this green and black hell and he would ask no more.

The storm would pass; the evil times of his life always did. He had not come this far to be drowned like a blind kitten by a blind fate. But the sea in its fury had spared nothing. Water had seeped into his sea chest, coating his few possessions with a salt slime, nearly obliterating the address on the package of books he had promised to deliver. Could he recall it? Fatigue paralyzed his mind. He would remember, perhaps . . . sometime. . . .

The *Boedicia,* slowed by her battering, steamed at last into a vastness of calmer water. Ned, at the taffrail beside Combs, his bunkmate, saw a scattering of islands in the distance and, to starboard, some low-lying hills with a rim of buildings at the shoreline. The glittering sea was cluttered with sails of all kinds, but of a city there was no sight.

"The Lower Bay." Combs enjoyed a sense of superiority.

"New York harbor's shaped like an hourglass. We'll go from here through the Narrows into the Upper Bay and you'll see the city soon enough. Sew your money into your pants, lad, but if you've got any to spend you'll see more than you ever saw in London. There's Jolly Dolly's down along the old docks on South Street. Every woman in it weights nearly twenty stone. For a sixpence she'll show you anything you want. There's Madame Maude's Hall of Venus on Pearl Street. After midnight, not a stitch on any girl in the place. Then, if you fancy real style"—Combs's thick red face creased into something between a smile and a taunt—"yer kind of style, Ned, you can go uptown to the Gemini . . . the Gemmy . . . two houses with an upstairs door between. You can gamble in the first but you got to start with a hundred dollar bill. If you lose they say you get free champagne and the loan of another five hundred. If you win . . . if you win, lad, you can take your money and go through the door to the other house. You sit in your own booth behind curtains, there's a stage below. What you see there they say you see no place else in the world . . . even Singapore. I never been there. It's what I heard tell, for the swells."

Ned looked into the faint mist that still concealed the city. "Do you know where I can find lodging?"

"Lodging?" Combs's laugh was cynical. "What would you need lodging for? At most, you get only three nights ashore. When you've seen all you can see, there's a sailor's flophouse where you can get a few winks. Don't waste your time ashore sleepin', lad. We're nearly a week overdue now. They'll be pretty smart about casting off for home. If we get three full days this time we'll be lucky. Come to think of it, you've been in the brig. It'll stand black on your record, and just maybe the First Mate'll not take too kindly to giving you shore leave. He's not got much likin' for you as it is. You've only one chance, as I see it. He's got a little doxie up on Beach Street and he mayn't have the time to notice you. So when he's gone ashore . . ."

Combs stopped. Ned was staring at him.

"Nobody can hold me on this ship. I've done my passage."

"Ye've done half your passage. You signed on for the round trip."

"Oh, no I didn't. I said I'd work my way to New York."

"That you did. Not too well I'd say, until the storm came up. But if you read the small printin' on what you signed, you'd see it was for the round trip. You'll get your money when you get back to London. And I wouldn't try to jump ship if I was in your shoes. The Line's sharp about that. They got men watching. They find you, they bring you back. And with the record against you. . . . Ned, believe me, I see what you're thinking. But you got it wrong . . . if they let men go in New York they'd be havin' the devil's own time filling out a crew to sail the ship back. It's not worth trying, boy. They keep after you until they find you. If you give 'em too much trouble you'll go back home in irons. You signed round trip and that's the end of it."

The grainy voice dropped into silence.

Ned was looking past him, across the expanse of sunlit water to where a city was emerging like his own future from the bright sea mist.

"No man ever kept me where I don't want to be, Combs. And no man ever will. Thank you for your advice. I take it kindly."

In the lee of the protective islands, the *Boedicia* slowed to a stop.

"Taking on the pilot," said Combs. "Rules. You don't get through this harbor on yer own. No sir. They got their own Yanks here to do it."

Ned watched the harbor yawl come alongside, the pilot grip the rope ladder, and the small boat tack away. Slowly the *Boedicia* nosed past the islands, through the Narrows of the double harbor, and into the thicket of masts, sails, packets, paddle-wheelers, and barges that was New York's Upper Bay. As the southern tip of Manhattan Island came into view, Ned felt a sting of disappointment. He saw a clutter of wooden houses, with sagging roofs, deteriorating wooden piers, and ancient pilings tilting crazily in the water. All old, all abandoned, all bespeaking what Ned had vowed to escape forever. Poverty.

"All hands stand by!" It was the First Mate. "Think you can dawdle here like a bloody first-class passenger, Fitch?"

Ned risked another couple of minutes on deck. The *Boedicia* held a slow course north northwest. Disdainfully, she passed the rotting piers of South Street, leaving them to the ghosts of those early Dutchmen who, two centuries before, had built them and piled them high with beaver pelts, a now-forgotten trade disappearing like them into history.

It would be Ned's first lesson, although he had no way of knowing it, that this muscling young city on which he pinned his uncertain hopes waited for no man, scorned failure, and took only one measure, success.

The *Boedicia* pushed on into the North River, up past brick houses and crowded wharfs, to dock neatly at a modern pier. Ned returned to the deck to hang over the fore-rail as the passengers disembarked. A clatter of voices, seamen's shouts, a rattle and banging of trunks, added to the brawling traffic on the cobblestoned street below. He watched small boys darting like silverfish along the pier to carry bags, hold horses—anything for a penny. He watched barrels being noisily loaded onto a dray. He saw two sailors in a fistfight outside a pub across the street. He had known the London docks. But he had never seen such confusion, such a tide and flow of humans, horses, and freight at home.

"It's a wild town, Ned." Combs was at his elbow. "Come along with us and we'll get you back safe."

Ned shook his head. "Not me."

"Didn't get yer shore leave?"

"No."

He watched Combs and a boisterous gang of hands descend the gangplank and lose themselves in the melee of the dock.

Then he saw what he was waiting for. The squat figure of the First Mate emerged on deck, glanced around, and went quickly down the gangplank, to disappear in the street.

Ned's sigh was not so much of relief as of revival. He detoured around the deck and went quietly up to the deserted Grand Salon. He lingered for a moment to savor its luxuries, seeing himself at ease among the velvet chairs and gilt tables. Then he went quickly, quietly down to his silent bunk, took the water-stained package of books from his soggy sea chest, found his way to the gangplank, and was free at last in this city that held his fortune.

Later Ned would not remember the labyrinth of narrow streets through which he walked that day. There seemed no design or order, as if the city had tumbled over itself in its push to grow. Warehouses jostled sail-making lofts, fish markets squeezed between public houses and shabby boarding houses. Vegetable vendors, pants makers, printing shops, and harness repairers elbowed each other for space.

By mid-afternoon, Ned was hungry. He was also lost. It gave him a measure of security when he turned into a street labeled Park Row. He had two guineas tied into his pocket. It was time to look for lodging.

The green-painted door, no different from the others in the row of small brick houses, opened slowly, as if Caution stood behind it. Which indeed it did, in the tightly corseted, high-bosomed person of Mrs. Greta Luskin, owner, proprietor, and landlady of 34 PARK ROW, LODGERS ACCEPTED. From behind her cotton-lace parlor curtains she had watched the stranger come down the street. She knew the type. Seaman's jacket, rough cap, and trousers. No baggage. Peering up at each house he passed. Either wanting a bed after a drunken night or jumping ship. In either case he would bring her trouble. More than once she had earned a welcome half dollar by going around to the shipping office and reporting on a delinquent sailor. But all in all, she preferred quiet lodgers with a degree of permanence about them.

She had had no time to remove the "Vacancy" sign before the doorbell jangled. The stranger removed his cap.

"I saw your sign, ma'am. I'm looking for a room."

He was not what she had expected. He was not Greek or Polish or Portuguese or, save the mark, Irish. To Mrs. Luskin's limited ear, he spoke a gentleman's English. Furthermore, he was not without luggage. Under his arm he carried a brown-paper-wrapped parcel tied with good stout twine. And he was—the black bombazined bosom smothered a sigh—undoubtedly good-looking, in a romantic sort of way. Like the penny novels to which she devoted her nights. Still, she was a business woman. Widowhood had seen to that.

"A room for how long?"

Ned stepped easily into the tiny hallway.

"Two weeks. Three. Maybe longer. I've come in on the *Boedicia* from London. Rough trip. My personal things were pretty badly damaged. I need a place to stay—get my bearings. I liked the look of your house. . . ."

This was no jump-ship, she thought. Not free with his information like that. She knew the *Boedicia* had come through a violent storm. She kept an efficient tally on ship arrivals. She began to suspect he wasn't a common seaman. A passenger, more likely, in borrowed seaman's clothes. He might even be—the penny novels fluttered within her—a young English lord in disguise.

Ned smiled. "I realize I don't look like a very good risk but if you'll tell me how much the room costs, I'll pay—" he made a lightning calculation of his total fortune of two guineas and took the plunge—"three weeks in advance." Mrs. Luskin returned his smile.

As if the matter were settled, he set the package on a table where the light fell on it. Part of the address, blurred by salt water, had returned as the paper had dried. In wispy clarity a name emerged and beneath it the angled letters of "Stuyvesant Square."

"I am entrusted by friends to deliver this. But naturally . . ." He made a deprecating gesture toward his jacket. Mrs. Luskin nodded, black jet earrings bobbing—"when I've straightened my affairs a bit, I will rely on you, Madam, to tell me how to find Stuyvesant Square."

Mrs. Luskin had been to Stuyvesant Square only once, and that after a spell of faintness on the dizzying new Third Avenue elevated railroad. She had sat for a stolen half hour on a wrought-iron bench beneath lofty shade trees. She had never forgotten the unhurried grace of that little uptown world.

"I'll be glad to, sir. It's truly elegant." Something close to eagerness replaced the business in her voice. "I have a very nice room, my best. New painted and my mother's rosewood bedstead. Second-floor front. . . ."

Ned saw that he had overreached himself. Much as he liked the best of anything, he had never been able to afford it. Nor could he now. He relied on the new warmth in Mrs. Luskin's voice.

"Second-floor front? Without a view I would guess. I'm a man who likes heights. A glimpse of the world. As a boy I used to climb the tallest tree on my father's property. . . ."

Mrs. Luskin looked at him thoughtfully. She had one other room. Fourth floor. She did not add, cold in winter, hot in summer, a slit of an attic window and no fit room for a gentleman. She merely said two dollars a week.

"Done." He flashed her a grin. "Up where a chap can live like a bird. Free to the sky."

Mrs. Luskin went to her desk and opened her ledger. "Name, please."

"Edmond . . ." He hesitated. Abbingdon would free him forever from the ship's master roll. Yet it was the one card up his sleeve he would need when the stakes were higher. "Fitch," he said quickly.

He glanced around the tight little parlor. Striped brown wallpaper, heavy brown hangings, a round table with a red felt cover reaching, bell-fringed and dusty, to the worn red carpet. And everywhere a clutter of china shepherdesses, lute players, and perched birds crowding the surfaces. The room stifled him.

"I'm going to be very happy here," he lied. To prove it he stooped to stroke a yellow brindle cat curled in sleep on a bamboo settee. And withdrew his hand abruptly. The cat was an exemplary instance of the taxidermist's art. Mrs. Luskin touched a finger to her eyelid.

"Bluebell died four years ago next September. I keep her with me always."

Ned had one more request.

"I've always found that the best way for a stranger to learn his way around a city is to read the daily newspapers. I wonder if I might take a journal or two off that table."

A white card propped against the table lamp stated that it was forbidden for any lodger to remove reading matter from the parlor.

Mrs. Luskin felt the young man's arm brush hers as he placed his deposit on the desk. She gave a sudden little high-pitched laugh.

"Oh, don't mind that sign. That's for boarders who take the journals out to wrap things in. There's today's *Sun*. And last night's *Police Gazette*. A little livelier for a young man, I'd say."

His landlady could be arch, Ned realized. He bowed slightly and allowed himself to breathe easier. "You're very kind."

He followed her dutifully up three dark flights of stairs, through a prevailing odor of fried onions.

The room was even less than he had expected. An iron bedstead with a single thin blanket, a black-painted basin and pitcher stand, a single straight-backed chair, a plain oil lamp on a rickety bedside table, and a row of nails for clothes he did not possess. A second's inexplicable nostalgia caught him. Millie had lived in such a room, triumphantly concealing it in red. Ned had no intent of either concealing or triumphing over its shabbiness. He would be out of it as fast as opportunity allowed. Even sooner. He would force opportunity to come to him. He hated every board and nail of Mrs. Luskin's lodgings.

Mrs. Luskin set a box of sulphur matches beside the lamp and the door key next to it.

"I'll send up the girl with water." Her glance lingered. "I hope you will be happy here, Mr. Fitch."

He waited for the door to close and the measured steps to descend. Then he pushed open the shallow window and, kneeling, leaned out to the coming night. Below, a pinched alley had begun to fill with shadows. Opposite, a wave of roofs darkened against the sky. Behind it another wave, and another, until he imagined the great city cresting and surging against the March sky. Names like golden lights pricked the March night. Fifth Avenue, somewhere in the deepening dusk, with palaces of marble. And Stuyvesant Square. Elegant, the woman had said.

Reluctantly, he turned his back on the night, touched a match to the oil wick, and spread his newspapers on the bed.

As if by magic, the city sprang to life. He read, slowly and with care, living each item on the front page of the *New York Sun*. "The Haymarket, for the prettiest girls, the liveliest music in town." "To J.D. Missing you, Heartbroken. Come home." "New invention on display, Telephone Concert, Thursday next. Tickets much be purchased before six. Mr. Embry's piano concert in Philadelphia will be carried by telephone wire to New York audience in Aeolian Hall, Seven prompt." "Will the young lady wearing mauve gloves at Billings' Penny Arcade Tuesday last communicate with admiring gentleman who wishes to pursue respectful acquaintance. C.V. Box 107." "Employment for extra waiters, Wednesday 20th, for Mr. Perry's Horseshoe Dinner. Apply rear door Delmonico's restaurant."

At the bottom of the second column, he reread a two-line notice. "Gents Clothes for Hire. Day, Evening, All Occasions. Elias Monk, 23 Bowery." He took out the small penknife he kept with him, then decided against defacing Mrs. Luskin's morning paper. He committed the unfamiliar address to memory: 23 Bowery.

He turned the pages slowly, loathe to miss a word. On the social page he learned that Mrs. Mortimer Wilberforce would give the last of her Winter Receptions at her Fifth Avenue mansion Friday next. She would open the Summer Season in June at her palatial Newport "cottage" with her usual Lawn Tennis and Croquet Sociale.

On the editorial page he read that prominent members of the distinguished Citizens Committee applauded the dismantling of the brilliant new arc lights in Madison Square. The ladies had declared that the lights gave their faces a deathly pallor and refused to walk beneath them. ". . . the dismantling will undoubtedly bring cheer to pickpockets and other rowdies stalking the periphery of decent society, but our ladies must be served."

Ned saw himself offering his arm to a timid patrician lady in the dimmed park. He saw himself entering a magnificent drawing room for Mrs. Wilberforce's last Winter Reception. He saw himself in a box of The Haymarket, handsomely tailored and confident, catching the eye of the prettiest girl in the chorus. And he heard himself addressing, to outbreaks of applause, the prominent members of the Citizens Committee, whatever that might be.

Two hours of this heady, imagined New York success and splendor passed before Ned reached for the second journal, the *Police Gazette.* Its blaring headlines made more enticing reading, but he had not forgotten Millie's odd little warning that he would always be more comfortable with her kind. It had stuck like a burr in a corner of his mind.

With disdain he read the first page. MADAM RESTELL TRIAL SET APRIL FIRST. BRIBE OF $40,000 FAILED. NOTORIOUS MIDWIFE AND ABORTIONIST RELEASED TO AWAIT TRIAL.

Woman matters. He remembered only one midwife in his life, an aging creature with a wen on her nose and forearms beefy enough to birth a calf. Mattie, they called her at The Crown and Anchor, where she'd drop in for a glass of gin after her day's . . . or night's . . . work. Her eyes were small and deep with ancient mysteries. The bar customers withdrew from her as if she carried a plague.

He turned the page quickly and there he stopped. A pen-and-ink drawing pictured a dark-haired woman in a wide-brimmed hat, flaunting the ostrich plumes of a duchess. A fur cloak reached to her knees, beneath it billowed ruffles of silk and lace. She was shown stepping, with the aid of a footman, into a fine closed carriage.

Her face was sketched in harsh lines, the nose bent as if the artist hated her. But the evidences of wealth were unmistakable.

"The True story of Madam Restell, once Caroline Lohman, nee Anna Trow. Her rise from Gloucestershire servant girl to Fifth Avenue millionairess. . . ."

Ned turned up the lamp wick and drew the *Gazette* closer.

In her parlor below, Mrs. Luskin sat at her desk, her fingers tapping impatiently to her thoughts. She had been upstairs twice in the last hour to see the knife edge of light beneath her new boarder's door. As if lamp oil flowed like water. Heedless of cost. Perhaps of other things.

She opened the ledger. In the space above Ned Fitch's name she wrote in cramped letters: Reference, Dr. Hugo Lendler, Stuyvesant Square.

Mrs. Greta Luskin was, after all, a careful woman.

5

"Read all about it! Read all about it!"

Mr. Walter C. Tremont, his tailoring faultless over his solid girth, his silk hat brushed to a subdued shine, nodded pleasantly and pursued his way up Broadway. It was his custom to buy his evening paper from a feisty little urchin who had staked his claim to the northeast corner of Fifteenth Street and Third Avenue. Walter Tremont was a man of fixed habits. Like his father before him, he walked to the offices of Tremont & Sons in the morning and back in the evening to his home, now on Stuyvesant Square. "Stimulates the brain for the day's work, airs it out at day's end," was the old gentleman's advice.

Waiting to cross Broadway, Walter wondered as he often did, what his father would have thought of this noisy, seething modern New York. In less than four decades, the rustic town of quiet roads, pleasant meadows, and tree-lined streets had vanished. Macadam and Belgian blocks encrusted its thoroughfares. Its neat brick houses, spaced by front yards and white fencing, had surrendered to relentless rows of houses of brownstone, what one visitor called "New York's chocolate coating." No man's sleep was safe from the clatter of iron-rimmed wheels and iron-shod hoofs, and the roar of the new elevated railway.

As for Broadway, his father had known it as a wide stagecoach route and carriage way to be followed northwest through rolling hills for a day's outing in the countryside. It was now engulfed in a ceaseless flow of horse cars, drays, delivery wagons, stylish broughams, and common hacks, sometimes wheel to wheel. It was as much as a man's life was worth to cross Broadway, Walter thought irritably. He had willingly joined other prosperous business men and the fashionable merchants of what was called "Ladies' Mile" to petition for a footbridge over the traffic.

Safely across, Walter turned east on Fifteenth Street.

"Read all about it! Getcha evenin' payper!" A skinny boy flashed an Irish grin. "Here y'are, Mr. Tremont!"

"Thank you, Jimmie. How is your mother?"

"Foine, Mr. Tremont. Foine. Come out of the fever real good. Och! I gave you two paypers."

"I'll take them." Walter found a second coin.

"Thanks, Mr. Tremont. You won't be sorry, sir. Plenty of good readin' in 'em tonight. That rich lady up on Fifth Avenue they say murders babies is goin' on trial. Do you think she'll go to prison?"

"That's what trials are for, Jimmie. To decide."

"Maybe they'll hang her." The boy's eyes danced. "Me mither says she'll go to the gallows sure in all her foine furs and plooms, you'll see. . . . Getcha evenin' payper!"

Walter thrust the papers under his arm with distaste. He found it less than dignified to have acquired two copies of such sordid matters. But he would not hurt the boy's feelings.

More had changed in his beloved city than its streets and buildings. The culprit was money. In the decade following the War Between the States, great new industries, the iron works, the cotton mills, the coast-to-coast railroads, the seemingly depthless coal and copper mines, the vast empty West, fallow for exploitation, all were pouring into the city a flood of wealth never seen before. With it had come a slackening of everything Walter Tremont believed in, standards, self-discipline, and high morals, public as well as private.

Not a month ago, a prominent clergyman had preached from his pulpit against the spread of vice. There were more prostitutes, he had announced, than there were Methodists in New York City. Two ladies had fainted dead away, requiring spirits of arnica. The gasp from the congregation had joined a windstorm of outrage through the city.

As a responsible member of society, Walter Tremont had done his part. He had joined the Citizens League for Decency. Only today he had learned that he had been elected to its presidency.

The thought of it mellowed him. His step quickened. It was not only an honor, it was another in the chain of pleasurable events that had followed his marriage to Adrienne. The house they had settled into on Stuyvesant Square, the charm with which she had decorated it, the grace with which she filled it. Adrienne, blonde, lovely, too young in some eyes for a middle-aged widower. But did other eyes matter?

He entered the Square, warming as always to the small park with its black iron railing, fine trees, well-kept walks, wrought-iron benches, the stately gates opening into it.

The mild March dusk filtered like smoke through the leafless branches. Here and there a front window glowed. Through the Brussels lace curtains a shadow of a maid could be seen setting a dinner table. Mist rising from the damp ground would soon blend the facades of pressed brick, newer brownstone, granite, and the marble of the older houses into a single enclave of well-being and order that was home to Walter Tremont.

At a corner he stopped and lifted the top of a trash bin. With a quick motion he dropped his two newspapers into it and closed the lid.

"Throwing the world away so early in the evening, Walter?"

It was his old friend, Professor Lendler, whose modest brownstone house on the east side of the Square had long brought Walter a sense of neighborliness and the Square a taste of scholarly, if remote, distinction. Not that the professor cultivated social contacts. He taught languages at Columbia College, collected learned books, and gave lectures. On a spring evening when the windows were open, he could be heard playing his violin.

In Stuyvesant Square he was regarded as the most courteous if also the most private of gentlemen.

Walter had known and respected Dr. Hugo Lendler since the years of his own first marriage.

"Good evening, Hugo. I can't say I found the world in tonight's newspaper, at least not the part of which I wish to be informed."

"Ah, the weaknesses of the flesh. . . ."

"I'm well aware of them," said Walter dryly. "But I hardly think the trial of that infamous woman is a subject for family reading."

"Quite," murmured Dr. Lendler. "Quite. So you've made a proper disposal of the business. And how is your dear wife?"

"Adrienne is splendid, thank you."

"And Miss Noel? Over her indisposition?"

To the best of Walter's knowledge his only daughter was not only in sound health, but thriving and as independent as ever.

Noel had her own ways of handling her affairs, much of them remote to Walter.

"My daughter's well, thank you, Hugo."

A bow to his old friend, and Walter turned up Rutherford Place, the west side of the Square, passing the red brick Meeting House of the Society of Friends. A gentle reminder in the midst of the new prosperity that humility and service were among life's riches.

Beyond the Meeting House rose the venerable bulk of St. George's Church, thrusting twin spires into the sky, the double-sworded guardian of the Square's respectability.

There were few cabbies in New York who did not know St. George's as "Mr. Morgan's church." Mr. Pierpont Morgan, whose enormous power in high finance loomed larger on the city's horizon than any house of God or man, was a dedicated worshipper, senior member of St. George's vestry and mentor of its destiny. Mr. Morgan especially enjoyed hymns and gave them full voice. Any member of the congregation daring tardiness risked the beatling severity of that heavy brow. Somewhat to his own surprise, Walter Tremont now possessed a pew in Mr. Morgan's church. Adrienne had asked so prettily for it. The solidity, the timelessness of the old church had more than once given Walter comfort. Now as he passed in the fading light, another old friend hailed him.

"The top of the evenin' to ye, Mr. Tremont." Old Dougherty, wizened and bent beneath the burden of his ladder, emerged from the shadows. Like most of those who served prosperous New York, Dougherty had been hurled without mercy by the potato famines of his native Ireland to the new shores. Few knew where he laid his head at night. But on the city blocks he served, every child and household could tell the hour by the arrival of Dougherty leaning his ladder against a cast-iron lamp post and climbing, agile as a monkey, to light its flame.

Since the years of Walter's first marriage to Maria in the brownstone house on Sixteenth Street, he had known old Dougherty. In bitter twilights, Maria, who had given him three children, would throw a shawl around her small shoulders and rush out with a jug of hot tea for the lamplighter. Maria was never aware that what the old Irishman really wanted was a belly-warming taste of whiskey. Nonetheless his face would pucker in gratitude, which sent Maria back into the house with snowflakes netted on her brown hair and a pink glow of kindliness in her cheeks. Maria, who had shared twenty years of Walter's life. Dougherty was a link, an echo of loyalty that Walter would not, perhaps could not, relinquish.

Walter crossed to the north side of the Square. His own handsome house of whitened brick was aglow. Maria would have gasped at such extravagance. He must stop making comparisons.

He glanced upward. The third-floor windows were still in darkness. Noel's room. She had chosen it for herself. She had claimed it gave her greater privacy despite Adrienne's plea that she use the spacious second-floor rear that had been arranged for her. She was one of the family, too, her father had reminded her. Noel had given them both a quick smile and, as quickly, a no-thank-you. It was one of the many small differences he had seen growing in this only daughter he loved so dearly, an estranging too subtle to be named.

Any hint, even in his own mind, that his remarriage might be the cause, he dismissed angrily. Noel had seemingly welcomed the event with joy that his loneliness had ended. She had lent her special brightness to the wedding plans, to the move to the Stuyvesant Square house, to Adrienne herself. She had no fault to find, no suggestion to add. It seemed as if she had insulated herself within a determined pleasantness to make matters go well. From the first she had gotten on with Adrienne. They had become in the course of time almost like sisters. He was a lucky man, his friends told Walter, to have two such attractive young women to escort, a comment he did not particularly enjoy.

He did not want Noel as a "sister" to his young wife. Any more than he approved of the, to his mind, dreary trivia with which Noel filled her days. Attending lectures at Cooper Union, the free, liberal college on East Ninth Street, she could learn such forward subjects as Women's Suffrage, Freedom of the Mind (whatever that was), and, he had heard it rumored, Free Love.

"It isn't quite that bad, Father," Noel had said lightly at the dinner table, despite the presence of the serving maid. "It's simply for some people a different way of living and therefore . . ."

"Therefore we won't discuss it," Walter said, catching a slight frown on Adrienne's lovely face at the other end of the table.

Adrienne delicately changed the subject. "How are your duets coming with Dr. Lendler, Noel? Your Mozart sounds excellent."

"I really haven't had time"—Noel swept the table with her

enigmatic little smile—"for either. Besides, Father, I do serve three afternoons a week at the Angel of Hope Mission. That should make up for some of my defects," Noel added, not quite meekly.

Walter was aware of sounding elderly when he admonished Noel.

One night, with Adrienne warm and silken beside him, the scent of her breath on his cheek, the suppleness of her body curled against his, Walter had tried to put his daughter from his mind. A whisper reached his ear.

"Don't worry too much about Noel, Walter. Don't you understand? She should be married by now. She knows that time is passing. In another few years . . ." Adrienne, snug in her young widowhood and second marriage, spoke with confidence. "It's really up to us to see that she meets a suitable man."

That had been some weeks ago. Walter came back to the immediate present. This should have been one of Noel's afternoons of music with Dr. Hugo Lendler, a youthful kindness she had carried over from the Sixteenth Street years. Not a lively occupation for a girl of her age, Walter admitted. Still, a genteel one. He glanced up again to the darkened third-floor window. She should be home by this hour. He must give more thought to Noel's days.

He pushed open the solid oak door with its fanlight of fine-cut opaque glass.

"Good evening, sir."

Mrs. Jessup, overseer of the household, was Scottish and inclined to dourness in which he sometimes fancied a note of disapproval. A sparse wren of a woman, she would always look older than her age. He had promised Adrienne a butler someday.

"Good evening, Mrs. Jessup. Has Mrs. Tremont come in?"

"I've just sent Madam's tea up, sir."

"Send a second cup up for me, will you?"

He had grown to like Adrienne's custom of the tea hour, brought back from her English schooling. He had fallen into the habit of leaving the office early to share it with her. Adrienne, lying on her chaise lounge in a sweep of mauve ruffles, her blonde hair fanning over her shoulders, the silver service at her elbow, her softness coming to him through the steamy warmth of the tea. She had the gift of attentive listening, and he found himself shedding, like a schoolboy, the barnacles of the day.

This evening he had news that would please her, the presidency of the Citizens League for Decency.

He handed his hat and cane to Mrs. Jessup.

"You've a caller waiting, sir."

"A caller? At this hour?"

"Mr. Weldt, sir."

Walter had forgotten Josiah Weldt, retiring president of the Citizens League, whose place he was taking. He must keep a tighter rein on his affairs in his new euphoria.

His visitor was seated on a straight-backed chair, an old-fashioned mutton pie hat squarely on his knees. Walter did not like the man. Whether is was his parsimony, his ill-gained wealth, or his habit of sniffing as he talked, Walter would not say. But he could not remember a time when the wagons of Josiah Weldt, Dealer in Clean Coal, were not lumbering through New York's streets, the drays overloaded, the horses overburdened, the drivers sharp with the whip.

Josiah Weldt's money had brought him an invisible wife, a dark Italianate mansion on lower Madison Avenue, and the presidency of the Citizens League, which was his single joy. Society ignored him.

Now, thin-mouthed, and looking oddly misplaced in the cream and blue velvet of Adrienne's drawing room, Mr. Weldt came to the point.

"I congratulate you, Mr. Tremont, on your achievement of the presidency of our league. You were my choice, you had my full endorsement, and it is a source of satisfaction to me that the election committee saw wisdom in my recommendation. It is my belief that the city of New York offers no higher civilian honor than to direct its vigilance against those who would abuse and despoil the decency, the character, and the nobility of this great city."

Mr. Weldt resettled his hat on his knees. Walter waited, conscious of a wariness threading his patience.

"The honor has come to you. I am sure you will fulfill its goals to the satisfaction of us all. To be brief, the next meeting is thc last I shall attend after eight years of deeply gratifying service. I shall have certain proposals to make as my valedictory. I thought it best that you should be acquainted with them so that we may strive together in mutual purpose."

Walter shifted a cramped knee. Mr. Weldt folded his hands on his mutton pie hat.

"I believe the time has come for the Citizens League for Decency to take a more active part in the battle against vice, and in the protection of the purity of our women, and the innocence of our youth."

Mr. Weldt was sitting bolt upright now, his fingers working on the rim of the hat.

"The fine-spirited Society for the Suppression of Vice has made some progress. Its distinguished member, Mr. Anthony Comstock, has proved his mettle with his aggressive attacks and his commendable victories in the relentless prosecution of vice. Today's paper carries his latest triumph. When no one else could do it, Anthony Comstock has at last brought that infamous woman, Caroline Restell, that abortionist and murderess—"

"That has not yet been proven. . . ." Walter heard himself murmur.

". . . single-handed to trial. I remind you, sir, that it was Anthony Comstock who had the moral courage to go to her very door, to enter that mansion of depravity and death, to demean himself by passing as a poor man with an ailing wife unable to bear children, and asking for the infamous devices that Mrs. Restell possessed." Josiah Weldt drew a sharp breath that whistled through his teeth. A dew of perspiration shone on his bald head. "And obtaining them! Obtaining the hard irrefutable evidence on which stands the woman's guilt! I believe, Mr. Tremont, sir, that it is time for the citizens of New York to express their appreciation. In short, I intend to propose at our next meeting that the Citizens League make a public declaration of support of Mr. Comstock, for his untiring vigor and the sacrifices he has made. . . ."

Walter turned his head sharply. The front door had opened. He heard voices. Noel was home. He waited a moment for her to go upstairs before turning back to his caller. Privately Walter damned the retiring president of the Citizens League for imposing his presence on his home.

Mr. Weldt rose stiffly. "I count on you, sir, to see that support for Mr. Comstock is voted." The eyes narrowed. In a mind's instant, Walter saw the coal-driver's whip on the tired horse.

Walter allowed Mrs. Jessup to show Josiah Weldt to the door. After it had closed he stood alone in the emptiness of the paneled hall. Opposite the curve of the stairs hung one of Adrienne's treasures, one of the few objects in the house he actively disliked. A bull's-eye mirror, a circular walnut-framed glass erupting into thirty-six bulbous little mirrors, reflecting at this moment thirty-six tiny Walter Tremonts. One would have been too many, he thought wryly.

He had been elated with his election to the presidency of the Citizens League. He had come home tonight, eager as a champion from the lists, to tell Adrienne. He had vowed to do his honorable best. Perhaps eventually move on, into politics, even diplomacy. Adrienne would like that. She belonged on a larger stage.

As for Mr. Anthony Comstock, a declaration of support was no more than any group of grateful law-abiding citizens normally voted. Certainly, Comstock had flung himself unsparingly against the city's purveyors of vice, gathering in his net a shabby collection of dealers in pornography, operators of nude art classes, midwives and their underhanded trade in "ladies devices." His latest, greatest achievement, bringing the Restell woman to trial, would be acclaimed by Christian congregations throughout the city.

Walter could endorse, even applaud, the results of such diligence. But the man's methods disturbed him. The hypocrisy of Comstock's friendly approach, the deceit of his pretended "need," until his victim had trapped herself. Are the means always justified by the end? It was a question Walter had not faced before, any more than he had understood the ephemeral burden of obligation he had been made to realize toward Josiah Weldt.

"Good evening, Father."

Noel was coming lightly, quickly down the hall toward him.

"Noel! I thought you had gone upstairs."

"You hoped I had, Father dear." Her instant smile took the sharpness from her words. It did not quite reach her eyes. "You needn't have worried. I had no wish to meet Mr. Weldt. What are you going to do?"

"I'm going to dress for the evening. As I hope you are."

"You know that isn't my question. What are you going to do about supporting Mr. Comstock? Oh, don't frown. I wasn't eavesdropping. I was in the den—I must remember to call it the library, Adrienne says—Mr. Weldt's voice does twang, doesn't it? Especially when he's sniffing out some particularly juicy scandal."

"Whatever you're talking about, Noel, I have neither the time nor the inclination to continue now."

"Of course you haven't. You wouldn't be my dear honorable father if you did." She touched her lips to his cheek and brushed past him to the stairs. "Tell Adrienne not to worry. I'll be ready before she is!"

He watched her go, unreachable as the wind, and sometimes as invisible. All he had ever wished for her was happiness. Now in the midst of his own, the wish had become an ache.

The day had lost its buoyancy. He would not tell Adrienne about the presidency yet. She would sense a shadow across it. Instead he would confirm that Noel was going out with them tonight. That would please her.

Perhaps Adrienne had the key. Noel should be married by this time. There was no reason why not. She was as attractive as any young woman he had seen at the balls and receptions he now found himself attending. She was intelligent. Perhaps too intelligent. He sometimes regretted his liberality in her schooling. Did any girl need all that study? But Adrienne could coax her out of that. Adrienne knew the art of charming a man. Not the least of it was the generous dowry he would settle on Noel when she did marry.

Her happiness would round out his own life. Yet where did it lie? A nagging self-blame accompanied him up the stairs. Before his new marriage, Walter had settled part of his patrimony on his two grown sons, each receiving a third share in his business.

Noel had made only one request. It was as startling as it was unthinkable. She had asked for her dowry, then and there, in full.

He had refused.

6

Gossip served only one purpose, Noel Tremont told herself grimly. To make dull people sound interesting and dull parties appear lively. This week it was darting like grass fire all over the city from backstairs to boudoirs, from corner salons to gentlemen's clubs, from raucous street vulgarity to delicious whisperings behind evening fans.

Even in the propriety of Stuyvesant Square, where such talk was considered unfit for the dinner table, the gossip spread. Late at night many a husband was discovering that his wife's release from the day's restraints could be as curious, as ribald, as human as his own.

The gossip turned on the fact that in two days "that woman," the notorious Mrs. Restell, owner of that brooding Fifth Avenue mansion uptown, keeper of unmentionable secrets, would go on trial, perhaps for her life. The question that titillated those it did not frighten was how much the lady would reveal. Her clients included not only the poor, the desperate, but the rich, the powerful, the respected. The city waited in fascination.

A light tapping brought Noel back to the immediate present. She was seated in Dr. Hugo Lendler's parlor at his aging walnut piano. He had removed the violin from his chin, rapped lightly on the music rack and was looking down at her with an expression so compassionate, so intense that she turned from it. Her hands dropped from the keyboard to her lap.

"I'm sorry, Dr. Lendler. I lost count, didn't I?"

"Merely misplaced it. Mozart put it there to stay. It will be there when you need it again."

After several weeks' absence, she had come, out of kindness, for an hour of music with the little professor. And out of something deeper, something she could share with no one.

A sense of finality. She was no longer a little girl, he the old family friend. Sometimes when he looked at her with those deeply brilliant, compelling eyes, she felt uneasy, almost fearful. Other times she thought he understood her better than anyone else ever had.

Neither was a comfortable thought.

She had been foolish to come. Even kindness could not coat over the incident of last winter. They had been playing Schubert when his violin rose to the passion of "Du Bist die Ruh," far outsoaring her piano. It had ended with a shimmer, a hush, meant only for her. He had put down his violin, seized her hands, held her seated at the piano to search her face.

Thou art my rest, my perfect peace. . . .

"Noel, Noel! If I could only do all I wanted to for you!"

She had slipped away, too embarrassed, too touched to answer.

Now sitting, hands motionless, the music broken by her inattentiveness, she saw the incident lying ephemeral but real between them.

Dr. Lendler laid his violin gently on the faded green velvet of its polished case and closed the lid. The gesture had a finality.

She rose. "I'm afraid I'll never be a dedicated musician, will I?"

"You are more than that, Noel. You are a woman of courage. That is the essence of living. To do what you must, with grace." She gave him a startled glance that within the instant turned coquettish.

"My goodness, that doesn't sound attractive at all."

His tone became fatherly. "You make it attractive, my dear. Thank you for coming today. You will never know how kind you are, humoring an old professor's love of music."

Noel walked slowly through the lingering light of the little park. This must be her last visit. What did he mean by doing what she must do, with grace? What did he know of her at all, this friend of her father's who had seen her grow from young heedless girlhood to—to this careful constraint? The next thing she knew he might ask her to marry him. It was not the first time the idea had occurred to her. Marriage to Dr. Lendler would solve so many things. He would make a gentle, honorable husband. He had a searching mind that would keep her interested. She could discipline herself to his misshapen body. If she told him that love was impossible he would offer her the haven of his devotion. Like her own father.

No. When she needed shelter she would find it for herself. Marriage to Dr. Lendler, or any man, for that purpose was out of the question. She knew that deep within her was a capacity for love, for passion, that could be stirred were the right note struck—the touch of a hand, a glance, a shared image in a dancing flame or simple nearness. But the cost was betrayal. She told herself she must remain who she was, what she was, in the tight little whale-boned world she occupied. Miss Noel Tremont, daughter of Mr. Walter Tremont of Stuyvesant Square and its fences of do's and don'ts, its numbing duties and proprieties at once her protection and her fate. Why had Dr. Lendler said "with grace"? He should have said "with a locked heart." But then he did not know her, nor did anyone. She found herself walking faster, as if to escape her own thoughts.

"Well, now, fancy this!"

Her unseeing steps had carried her squarely into the path of a figure who seemed to have come from nowhere. With some annoyance, she glanced up and noticed several things at once. He was dark-haired, young, and his smile was clearly presuming. He had neither stepped off the path nor bowed. In spite of all that, Noel did something she clearly should not have done. She giggled.

His grin widened.

"My fault, I'm sure, Miss. But I was looking for an address. . . ."

"You should have looked first where you were going," she said, unreasonably.

"I was doing just that. Minding my own business, in a quiet way, like any stranger. Or aren't strangers allowed here?"

Noel managed severity. "Manners are preferred."

"Indeed they are, Miss. Nice to have, like change in your pocket, what?"

His accent was English, his clothes barely respectable. His jacket too short, his shoes . . . "You can tell a great deal about a man," her mother used to caution, "from his shoes and his linen." Noel saw blunt, scuffed black boots and below his coat sleeves not a vestige of a shirt cuff.

"Inspection finished?"

She flushed. "If I may pass. . . ."

"Why not? As you like to say here in the States, it's a free country. And a free walk. I've heard that American girls are too independent to be polite."

He stood looking down at her. She knew that she had been rude. She had not even offered him a direction to whatever address he was looking for. But the moment for apology had passed. The instant of indecision had made her too conscious of him, his overconfident good looks, the boldness of his manners, the sheer physical presence of him, which she could not, would not, put into words, but which prompted her to speak when she intended to pass him in silence.

"You have a great deal to learn about American girls and American manners.'

"I'm looking forward to it. When I find a proper teacher." He doffed his cap again, bowed, and stepped aside.

She walked past him, turned the corner to the north side of the Square and to the slender railings, the granite steps and carved oaken security of her own front door. She might have walked longer this mild March afternoon but for the encounter. Yet her spirits had lifted. A healthy dose of irritation was probably just what she needed. By the time she reached her room, she had thought of a dozen withering things she might have said to him, might say if they met again. She banished that absurdity immediately. But not the echo of it that sounded a tiny warning, not once, but twice, and then again before she managed to dispel it. Yet not quite. The presentiment lingered. If they did meet, what would she say?

From the bay window fronting the Square, Dr. Lendler turned back into his parlor. The small room had never seemed so drained of life. He had witnessed Noel's encounter in its entirety. If he could not hear, he could watch the lingering moment. How long would she stand there, her face tilted upward to the tall young man? As he mounted the stairs to the cloister of his study, Dr. Lendler felt every one of his forty-four years. But as he told himself severely, he had made one mistake with Noel, he must not make another.

Of the trio, Ned Fitch left the Square with the lightest heart. He had no idea who the girl was or how he would meet her again. She was not beautiful as he had imagined beauty. Yet he would not forget the fine modeling of her face, her light slenderness, the proud lift of her head, brown hair, smooth in its net, shining beneath an absurd little hat. He had no word for it all. Quality, elegance, or something else—a fire banked beneath that indignant self-control, an awareness that met his? He would find her again, he promised himself. He glanced down wryly at his scuffed shoes. He might bring her down a peg or two for that inspection. He remembered the flashing brown eyes. She might even enjoy it.

The long shadows of early spring were beginning to slide through the park, touching strollers with a sudden coolness, softening the shapes of waiting trees, hinting at a stirring of senses and sap.

Noel had let the day go too easily. Sitting at her dressing table, she told herself the useful things she might have done. Shopped for the lace ruching Adrienne wanted, or walked to Cooper Institute to browse among its bookshelves and dip into the censured *Leaves of Grass* by the bearded Walt Whitman, or find back issues of the outspoken *Weekly,* published by the irrepressible Victoria Woodhull, who had once dared to and succeeded in running as a candidate for the Presidency of the United States. It was not, Noel told herself, that she sought out only defiers of public approval, but they enlivened her mind, thus her days. She envied them. They seemed to have been born with a flair for self-freedom and an immunity to hurting those who cared for them.

She was not. Enough of herself. She had let half an afternoon waste away for a trivial reason. She simply had not been willing to recross the Square and risk another encounter with the overbearing young man who had no manners and obviously wanted none.

If her purpose was to fill her days, her nights held a different kind of emptiness.

She picked up the ivory-backed, time-mottled hand mirror that had belonged to her mother. She grimaced into it, with the usual satisfying results. Her mouth went awry, her nose parted at the center, her eyes slid out of alignment, and the left side of her face took on a greenish malevolence. The image never failed to restore her armor of good humor.

The day had gone. She lit the oil lamp.

In a few minutes Annie-Mae, the new maid, would knock on the door with a pitcher of hot water, a reminder that it was time to dress for the evening.

Had Noel not so obstinately refused the second-floor room arranged for her, she would only have had to turn a swan-handled tap and warm water would have come gushing from the pipe. But the plumbing newly installed in the Tremont house did not go as high as the third floor, hence the reliable old pitcher and basin for Noel, like the servants above. She did not mind. The pipes rattled alarmingly when Adrienne drew her bath. The water, lumbering heavily up through the larger kitchen pipe, had been known to spew tadpoles into the kitchen sink.

The ironies of society, Noel thought, the new extravagances of this new-rich city. New York's finest houses were now equipped with running water. "Croton" water it was named, piped through an enormous tunnel from distant Westchester farmland into the massive reservoir at Forty-second Street. It takes two whiskies, the saying went, for a man to drink Croton. One before, one after.

All of it, as Noel knew, provided the empty chaff of social chatter. How delicious it was to know that Mrs. Mortimer Wilberforce had abruptly ended her winter season a year ago, not because of the death of a dear aunt as stated, but because the Rodent Inspector had discovered thirty thriving specimens big as cats in the Wilberforce sub-basement plumbing.

Or was it three hundred? The number had become as merry a guessing game as the worth of the pearls cascading over the full Wilberforce bosom.

Society, where a head would roll for a moment's amusement. Idle chatter because there was so little of substance to say. Men bored until they could return to their full-time pursuit of making money. Women parading gowns so lavish over corsets so tight that they could not draw a breath deeper than the curve of their breasts. It was accepted that after making one's entrance at a party a lady could escape to a boudoir above to loosen her stays before the three-hour, nine-course dinner anticipated below.

This was the world into which Adrienne was leading her father. Noel would not let herself despise it, but she could not, would not, follow.

She had only to decide on her little lie for this evening.

Adrienne had been delicately firm. "No excuses this time, Noel dear. It is Cousin Kitty's last *soiree* of the season. She has a young man dying to meet you. So eligible. His father has millions. Montana copper, I think. Or is it silver? Wear your rose *peau de soie,* I'll lend you my amethysts."

It was once Adrienne's rose *peau de soie*. And amethysts had never suited Noel, but she could not fault her stepmother. Adrienne lived as though she had been born to please. Her eagerness to include Noel not only gratified Walter but seemed to imbue Adrienne herself with an added sunniness. If at times Noel heard a kind of nervous insistence in Adrienne's generosity, she understood. It was a reflection of the unanswered question that lived phantomlike in the house, a small bell ringing in Noel's ear at every social gathering.

When is Noel Tremont going to marry? Or put differently, Noel really must get married before . . .

Before it is too late? Before Noel Tremont, spinster, settles permanently into the third floor of her father's house, her days filled with needless tasks, her presence like her very soul, gathering dust in the proscribed fate of the unloved woman.

How little they knew her.

The knock came. A pretty little Irish girl, stiff as the apron over her striped dress, entered. So young to be in service. Too young, thought Noel.

"Yer hot water, Miss Noel. Mrs. Tremont says to tell you the carriage is called for eight." The Tremonts were still renting their carriages. Tardiness was not excused.

Noel took the pitcher, swathed in a towel, and set it on the basin stand. She smiled at the girl.

"Are you happy here, Annie-Mae?"

"It's very nice, Miss Noel. Thank you."

"Have you had your evening off yet?"

"Oh, no, Miss Noel. Not until I've done me first month."

The girl was as simple as water, a relief from the complexities of Noel's thoughts.

"I pressed your rose silk, Miss Noel. It's hanging in the wardrobe."

"I saw it, Annie-Mae. It's beautifully done. Someday, if you like it, I'll give it to you."

Disbelief, confusion flooded Annie-Mae's face.

"Oh, no, Miss. It's not for the likes of me." She bobbed, turned, and fled.

It was, Noel reflected, so easy to give people pleasure when one could be oneself. Oneself. How did one know? This afternoon, running headlong into the stranger in the Square, she had behaved like a schoolgirl. She had been caught off guard. He must have seen that or he would never have talked so familiarly, so boldly. She had had no proper answer. That was not the posture she had set for herself. Her life was accounted for, settled. She had only to maintain it.

She idled for another moment at the dressing table. Beside the hand mirror lay her mother's ivory-backed hairbrush, another inheritance. Centered on the white runner was an unlikely companion piece, a conch shell, no more than seven inches long, its outer convolutions coarsened by the ocean's churning sands, its interior a glistening pink, visceral in its delicacy.

She touched it, then, unable to resist, she held it to her ear. From its depth, for it was not a very large conch shell, came only the faintest whisper of the sea. But fainter than that, came inevitably that other voice, distant, intense, for her ears alone.

"You're mine, Noel. For all time. No man or woman can part us."

He had said it one shimmering, treacherous hour at the sea's silken edge. In God's name, would his memory never fade?

She put the shell back on its white runner. Why had she kept it? Why had she not hurled it from her and stilled forever the words it contained? Because it was a thing of beauty? Because even the pain it held was dear to her? Perhaps because of a deeper truth, that no woman can entirely relinquish all remnants of her own passion.

Tonight, emotion betrayed her. The stranger in the park, his laugh that compelled her to share it, his glance that compelled hers to meet it. How long had it been since any man had looked at her that way? Never, she told herself. The man who had come into her life in all her youthful innocence had the look of—she could use the word now in all its harshness—lust. This afternoon she had seen an inexplicable compassion in Dr. Lendler's face. But the stranger in the park, with his inexcusable manners and easy smile, had looked at her as if they shared an immediate, unspoken secret. She found herself at once irritated and bemused by the thought. A spark, like the new electricity she had seen demonstrated once, a spark that jumped the space from wire tip to wire tip.

Where on earth was her mind wandering?

She turned to her dressing table, picked up her hairbrush, and mechanically, even savagely, began the end-of-day disciplines.

Twenty minutes later she entered the drawing room in a plain plaid-twill street dress. Adrienne was not yet downstairs. Her father, in the full splendor of evening dress, stood before the grate fire. A little overweight, a little too florid, perhaps, but beaming his contentment.

She kissed his cheek and put a forefinger to his lips.

"Not a word, Father. No. I am not dressed for the evening. I am not going to Cousin Kitty's. I am needed at the Mission. I received a message. There is a special hymn meeting tonight and Miss Prior is ill. They need me to play the piano."

Somewhat elaborate, but plausible enough to escape the evening ahead. She could make it a half-truth by actually going around to the Mission, although it was not her night.

Her father looked at her thoughtfully.

"Quite proper, Noel. Of course. It will disappoint us all but you are always free to make your own decisions."

Free. She might have smiled wryly, but he so obviously believed what he said. It was one of the reasons she could not bring herself to hurt him.

"Thank you, Father."

Had he even heard? His head was already half turned toward the hall to listen with a keener ear for the rustle of Adrienne's French taffeta on the stairs.

Then he surprised her. With a clumsy gesture, he reached for her hand.

"Noel, my little girl. Never forget this is your home. It will be as long as it is mine. It's what your mother would have wanted. So do I."

He hesitated as if to curb the next words. They came in spite of him.

"I need you."

Kitty Merriman surveyed her crowded salon with mild exasperation. It was all she would permit of the anger within her. This, her last "Thursday" was to have been the brilliant climax of a season of triumphant maneuvering. Brilliant was a word Kitty used frequently, wrapping herself and her image in its patina. Far from brilliant, the evening was progressing heavily.

Her first disappointment had been the "Regrets" of Mrs. Mortimer Wilberforce. No reason given, but then Mrs. Wilberforce never gave reasons. Her absence was sufficient to alert the world that Kitty Merriman had not quite arrived as quality. It meant, too, that Kitty would not receive the long-sought invitation to Mrs. Wilberforce's April reception, the last of the season. It banished the last hope of an invitation to Mrs. Wilberforce's tennis weekend at Newport. Unless of course one of Kitty's gentlemen admirers . . .

But that was not the worst of the evening's blows.

Noel Tremont had sent her excuses, once again slipping beyond Kitty's reach. For distant as Noel had become she was the unmentioned, unwitting key to Kitty Merriman's grand design.

Grand indeed it was.

It had to be. Kitty, petite, well-rounded, with black curls glistening and decolletage devastating, had not always had her pretty foot on the unsteady ladder of New York's new society. She had been born into shabby mediocrity as the youngest member of the Dancing Nealeys, a theatrical family troupe that had criss-crossed America's small towns and bare board stages, always a few natty steps ahead of the bill collectors. Kitty had learned early that stage troupers were admitted, if at all, through the back entrances of nice houses, and then only as entertainers, never as guests.

Her mother, stricken with consumption and dying at twenty-eight, had put it bluntly.

"You're pretty, you dance well. Men look at you. But it's not enough. You'll never be a first-class dancer, Kitty child. Go to New York, into a chorus. Meet a man who'll take care of you. Not a millionaire who'll give you diamonds, a carriage, furs, and forget you for the next pretty girl. A man of substance, Kitty, who'll marry you. Give you position that will last the rest of your life. Respectability, Kitty. You can build on that. You're clever enough . . . to . . . go . . . far. . . ." Her last words had trailed off.

But Kitty had never forgotten them.

They returned now as they so often did at moment of disappointment, of near failure. For hadn't she accomplished exactly what they had promised? Her pretty face had brought her to New York, her pretty legs had brought her onstage as a dancing "extra" in the most extravagant spectacle the city offered, *The Black Crook*. For an instant Kitty saw not the melding colors of her own drawing room, but the excitement, the glorious silk and satin pageantry of that incredible production, the longest-running theatrical show in New York's history.

She had worn tights, shyly at first, then as casually as the others. One wag claimed that tights made ladies look shorter but gentlemen look longer. To it all she had responded with the fullness of her small, dream-filled soul, each night abandoning herself to the enchantments of Herzog the evil sorcerer, who, with his magic black crook, opened grottoes, caves, heights heavenly and dens hellish, each a setting for more and more lavish spectacles of flimsily clad dancers and bosomy show girls, each spiced with the provocative indecency of those flesh-colored tights.

The performance ran four hours and forty-five minutes, no encores permitted. It had also run for a decade and was soon, Kitty had heard, to return to New York.

The Black Crook had been her youth. On its airiness, she had succeeded in dancing her way across the flickering candles of the footlights into the stolid, bemused heart of Henry Merriman, partner in the successful tailoring establishment of Tremont & Sons.

If marriage to Henry had proved dull, it had also provided the substance wherewith to begin her rise in society. She had made the most of it. She had succeeded in introducing an impoverished, orphaned but bewitching cousin (third cousin, to be truthful, named Ada but successfully blossoming to Adrienne) to the widowed Walter Tremont, thereby doubling her assets. With her bright black eyes on the future, and her social contacts expanding, Kitty had persuaded Henry to leave the plodding security of Tremont & Sons for the wildly beguiling world of investments, stocks, bonds, and markets cornered, fortunes won overnight. (Also lost, but Kitty never admitted that word in her pert repartee.)

When Henry proved less than adaptable to his new state, Kitty discovered that fortunes could be made by other means than the uncertainties of high finance, particularly if there was an eligible daughter in the family. For Kitty now saw herself as part of the Tremont family. What was good for them was good for her. There were young, eminently marriageable heirs to the vast new monies. They were bored, often vapid, but available to a clever hostess. Part of Kitty's expected triumph for this evening had been inveigling young Jasper Quinley (Quinley Iron Ore) to come to meet Noel.

"I'm not sure Noel's going to find that young pinhead interesting, for all his money," Henry had observed mildly as he lay on the chaise lounge watching his wife powder her soft shoulders, and sipping his first whiskey of the evening.

Kitty had risen to snatch the glass from him.

"Henry. You promised. You have to keep your wits about you tonight. Of course Noel won't find him interesting. That's not the point. It's whether he finds her interesting, buried in books all day. But she has to marry someone or she'll be an old maid before she knows it. Twenty million in Quinley iron ore would put us all where we should be."

"If the old man would ever let the boy have a nickel."

"Don't spoil my evening, Henry. It's costing us too much!"

Kitty's efforts had all been in vain. Young Quinley was already showing signs of boredom with her party. Noel had slipped through her fingers again. The girl was unknowable. She had a way of seeming to accept whatever one advised, then doing precisely the opposite, as if words were raindrops, to disappear as soon as they fell.

Kitty rearranged her features in a bright smile. Irritation put lines in the face, anger deepened them. She could afford neither. Her glance swept the groupings in her green damask salon, the rainbows of silks and laces of women sitting with women, of men clustered together, sombre as crows.

A white-gloved footman, one of four hired for the evening, made a noiseless appearance.

"Excuse me, Madam. Madame Rossari and her accompanist have arrived. She said to inform you that she will be ready to sing in thirty minutes."

Kitty's eyes were still hard. "She is already twenty minutes late. Advise her that she is to sing at nine as agreed. Show her to the back sitting room and serve her supper there afterwards."

"Your opera singer, Kitty?" Despite his depression, Henry's spirits always rose watching Kitty in command.

"Not the one I wanted. Unfortunately Madame Rausch sailed for Europe last week." She did not add that the celebrated contralto had not deigned to answer her note.

"Aren't we to meet the lady?"

"In the best houses, Henry, the entertainers do not sit with the guests. Well, what is it?"

The footman lingered. "If you please, Madam, Madame Rossari has asked for a little gin to, uh, clear the vocal cords before she sings."

"Tell the butler. But no more than a cordial glass."

She heard her own sharpness. For an instant she saw again that special place of make-believe—the singers, dancers, musicians, and players with the magic to touch a drab workworld with a moment's enchantment. Madame Rossari, aging and for hire, was one of those, an artist, a giver. . . . Kitty closed her eyes against her betrayal. But where on the tightrope she now walked could she hang the weight of a heart?

"Henry, you will talk to Walter tonight?" Kitty said, putting her past behind her once again.

Henry heard the command through the question. He always did. He watched her drift away, a small golden flame, her head held high like a premier dancer, her body taut in yellow satin, her black curls Greek fashion, the tendrils in subtle abandon at the nape of her neck. Under her spell, her arch little laugh, the evening would begin to stir.

Left to his own devices, Henry skirted the edge of the long salon. Snatches of female voices reached him.

"Would you go to the trial if you could?"

"If my husband wouldn't find out. . . ."

"Do you think the Restell woman will name names?"

"It's her revenge. . . ."

"If she does, I wouldn't be in her shoes next week for anything!"

There was a ripple of suppressed laughter, shrill with sensation. This was the favorite new subject of gossip—the coming trial of the woman Restell. Henry moved on. As he passed, a hush descended.

He caught a glimpse of Walter Tremont among a group of men that included a Washington senator and two well-known bankers. He recognized again his wife's extraordinary talent for assembling people.

But he would not go begging to Walter tonight. He would not humble himself again to admit his failures. He had been treated like a brother as well as a partner in the Tremont firm. He had left with a sense of guilt. Walter had been more than generous. Now he could only envy his old friend's comfortable ease among successful men while he . . . he needed a drink.

"Oh, Mr. Merriman, do come sit with me!"

Fluttery Millicent Price laid her hand on his arm. Mouse-blonde, doll-like, Millicent would inherit eleven million dollars made by her father in one extraordinary cornering of the silver market. Amid pink tulle, rosebuds, and genuine pearls, Millicent still wore around her throat a wide black velvet band of mourning, the banner of her loss.

It must be three, or was it four years ago . . . Henry remembered the story vaguely. The young man, blond as a Viking, not a dollar to his name, had come courting her. They had been engaged only three weeks when the accident happened . . . a drowning, he recalled.

He would hear it all again now in Millicent's endless litany—her true love lost at sea, her hero sacrificing himself for others.

He would indeed like a drink. He would also in kindness bring Millicent a sherbet. He suspected few young men would linger in attendance to hear her relentless eulogy.

It was not to be. Kitty was coming toward them, her hand firmly, persuasively, through Walter Tremont's arm, her voice lilting.

"Millicent dear, I have a young man dying to meet you. Do let's leave these dull businessmen to their own affairs!"

She released Walter and swept up the pink tulle and rosebuds. Walter bowed to his hostess. Then he turned a keen glance on Henry.

"Well, my old friend, suppose we have a taste of your excellent brandy first. Then you can tell me how much money you need."

7

Ned Fitch leaned against the counter of Elias Monk's store, Second Hand Clothing, and waited for the tooth-rattling roar to end. Light and shadow alternated at the dusty window, a shower of soot and sparks glanced off the glass, somewhere a terrified horse squealed. Ned no longer ran into the street to see the spectacle. In three weeks he had become familiar with a great deal that was new and amazing in his adopted city, including the four cradlelike, brown-and-yellow coaches and the stubby, smoking engine roaring one hundred feet above the street it darkened. It was New York's latest achievement, the Third Avenue Elevated Railroad.

Mr. Monk, stooped, weary-eyed, and beyond surprise, sighed as quiet returned.

"Two dollars and seventy-five cents past due, Mr. Fitch. And you want to rent a suit again?"

Ned managed a tone both lofty and confiding. "I'm starting a new position tomorrow. You shall have every cent, my good chap, within a fortnight or two."

Half of the statement was true. Ned had no wish to cheat the man, any more than to default on past rent due his shrewd, watchful landlady. By certain well-aimed compliments, a warmth in his voice, a slight pressure of hand on hand, a lingering brush of that solid, black bombazined shoulder, he had managed to stave off a crisis. Obviously Ned needed different tactics with Mr. Monk. He could think of nothing better than a much-worn "exaggeration," he preferred to call it, which at least held hope. He disliked the harsh finality of "lie."

Once again Ned found himself wondering why it was so difficult for people who could pay their bills, eat at their own table, sleep soundly in their own beds at night, and buy what they needed to understand what it meant to have nothing. Yet he was not quite destitute. His pocket contained three quarters, a ten-cent piece, and six pennies that he would need for carfare tonight. And one last British tuppence, which nobody here would accept.

Mr. Monk blew air through his pursed lips. He had no quarrel with the good-looking young man. Actually he had taken a liking to him. No other customer filled the Elias Monk merchandise with such flair. A regular walking advertisement you might say, had anyone guessed the clothes were rented. But Mr. Monk saw easily through the "new position tomorrow." Most of his customers claimed they were starting work, when the truth of the matter was that they needed his clothes to find work.

"The same suit, Mr. Fitch? Young gentleman's daytime wear?"

Ned hesitated. He had rented the suit three times, thereby plunging himself into debt. Each time for the purpose of making a presentable appearance at the door of Dr. Hugo Lendler of Stuyvesant Square with the package of Mr. Crowne's books. Each time he had lingered in the Square hoping to catch a glimpse of the girl again, dark-haired, coal-eyed, who had both bewitched and irritated him and would not leave his thoughts. He had alternated between wanting to meet her in proper tailoring and telling himself he'd meet her as he was, and she could take it or lump it, in all her bloody pride. He had retracted that instantly. No more London street talk. He had learned that much.

Beneath all this wavering, this uncertainty, Ned recognized the force of an attraction, unlike anything he had known in the quick, easy camaraderie of girls available to him. In London he would have considered it hopeless. In the free air of this surprising city, who knew? The girl on the path had not brushed past him, head high. She had stopped, answered his impertinence. Despite her loftiness, he had caught a half laugh, or so he thought. He could not forget her.

He had not seen her since. Nor had he delivered Mr. Crowne's books. He told himself that they might not yet be properly dried out. Might need the touch of a flatiron to their pages. Moreover, wasn't it foolhardy to risk presenting himself to Dr. Lendler (whoever *he* was) until the H.M.S. *Boedicia* was safely on the high seas bound back to London, when he would no longer be sought as a jump-ship?

So he had procrastinated, while aware deep in his conscience of a sterner truth. Once the books were delivered he would have no further excuse to loiter in Stuyvesant Square, asking directions, while actually searching the paths, the passersby, for a quick, slender figure. . . .

"Well, Mr. Fitch, I'm not one to stand in a young man's way. If it's the grey worsted you want once more . . ."

But Ned, jolted back to the present, was struck by a daring notion.

"Oh, no, Mr. Monk. What I need today is an evening suit. Full dress, as they say. Silk hat." His eyes darted around the racks and pegs of Mr. Monk's overstuffed shop. "And I'll need a cane, too. That black one with the carved top."

"Whoa, now! That takes money. That cane's ebony with a genuine ivory head and silver banding. I take a deposit for that."

"How much?"

"Two dollars."

"Add it to the bill."

Mr. Monk could not resist a little sarcasm. "Goin' to a fancy ball?"

Ned had not wasted his first weeks in New York. He had not explored day after day the dazzling immensity of the city, nor pored over the daily journals, studying the doings of the rich and privileged, for nothing. The plan forming in his mind had taken the shape of reality.

"A reception at Mrs. Stephenson's." The tone was not patronizing, merely informative.

Mr. Monk sighed once more. Human nature could be as unguessable as the cast-off clothes he collected, patched, and pressed to further service. No doubt he would be gulled again. On the other hand, the young man had style, even quality. Maybe somewhere an inheritance . . . he'd heard of them British dooks, sometimes flat broke waitin' for the money. Elias Monk hadn't built his business without taking a chance or two.

"Oh, one thing more. I'll need a pair of shoes."

"Don't have many. Maybe not your fit."

"If I can get into them I'll take them."

Tonight for a little while he would be a free man. Tonight he would put a daring dream into effect.

Mr. Monk shoved the package across the counter to him. "Careful with the champagne, young feller. No dribblings on those clothes." He gave a dry chuckle. Ned took no offense.

In the street he found a knot of people gathered around the latest disaster left in the wake of the perilous overhead train. A crippled fish wagon, one wheel gone, tilted crazily against the elevator's iron girder-support. Spilled baskets of gittery fish were already attracting dozens of the city's thousands of stray cats. Street urchins picking the slithery bodies from the mud were slapping them at each other or any unfortunate passerby. The cause of it all, a terrified horse, free of its traces, stood trembling, white-eyed, as the fishman held the broken reins, cursing.

Ned passed the wreckage, eyed the horse.

"Young, isn't he? Do they get used to it?"

The man shook a thick fist upward. "No more than any of us."

"He's cut a hock back there."

But his troubles made the man surly. "Mind your own business, limey."

The street children were delighted. "Limey! Limey! Mind yer own business, limey!"

Something soft struck between the shoulder blades and slid down the back of his jacket.

He tightened his hold on his bundle, strode rapidly away from the dust, the dimness, the stench, and the small cruelties of poverty.

Beyond him lay the city, brilliant, waiting. His step quickened.

It was well known and duly reported that for her receptions Mrs. Potter Stephenson insisted on candlelight. A thousand candles would be used in one evening to replace the glare of common gaslight. As for the new electricity installed in a few of the great houses, Mrs. Stephenson would have none of it. It blanched the ladies to deathlike paleness. Electricity required a thunderous generator in one's own basement to reinforce the current, and a hired private engineer to keep the thing running. Even then it was anything but reliable. Society still merrily recalled one lamentable party in a most correct New York mansion. Dinner had run later than the four hours planned. The engineer in the basement, uninformed of the delay, had gone home on schedule, turning off the generator and plunging the entire house into darkness. The guests. . . . An entire season had been diverted by speculation as to fallen reputations at that affair.

So on this night, from the tall windows of Mrs. Stephenson's French Renaissance castle, the assured and lovely glow of candlelight poured into the mist of Fifth Avenue. A line of carriages two blocks long inched toward the handsome mahogany doors.

Ned, in his rented evening clothes, his hired cab, sat nervously fingering the dwindling change in his pocket. He had walked as far uptown as high tight shoes permitted. He had boarded a Madison Avenue horse train to within a block of the Stephenson mansion. He had flagged a hansom cab to take him around the corner. The irate driver had snapped, "Waiting time extra."

At last the cab edged to the lordly Stephenson doors. Ned thrust the fare into the driver's hand and walked so briskly up the granite steps he did not notice the man spit after him. He moved with the line of guests through the marble entrance and found himself in a large circular hall. It was illuminated by four gilded candelabra suspended from a ceiling painted in rosy-fleshed cupids. Or were they angels? To the left, three life-size, discreetly draped marble nymphs balanced a fountain of flowing water. In niches around the paneled walls, tall Chinese vases held bursts of white roses. Through an archway ahead he caught a glimpse of gold damask walls, heard distant music, bursts of laughter, the buzz of voices. But it was the curved stairway to the right that held his eyes. Down it came a stream of jeweled, white-bosomed women more dazzling, more splendidly gowned than he had ever imagined. He caught himself staring. And he caught something else; their quick, curious glances in his direction.

"Good evening, sir. May I . . . ?" The footman in silk knee britches bearing down on him had a stiff back, a cold eye, and, to Ned, a voice oiled in suspicion.

Ned had rehearsed the moment. He handed the man his rented opera hat, his ebony cane, glancing through the crowd as if searching for someone. He must see all, hear all, a sponge to soak in all he could of high society and somehow postpone as long as possible the inevitable.

"Haven't we met?" A voice tinkled beside him. A woman, in white satin and black lace, a collar of diamonds above a nearly bared breast, looked directly at him.

Ned bowed. But he could take no chance. "I never forget a beautiful face, Madam, but as I've just arrived . . . from London. . . ."

"Oh, then perhaps not. We must make it up." Another bright glance before she turned to the gaunt, greying man beside her and disappeared with him through the archway. Her boldness startled Ned. Was conquest so easy in this brash, indulgent city? Or had she seen through him?

The butler loomed before him.

Ned had hoped with better luck to slip unnoticed into that splendid room ahead, to mingle, perhaps to turn the escapade into a joke to amuse the ladies whose glances he so freely caught.

"May I announce you, sir?"

He should have expected this. If he was to make his way up this slippery ladder he must be better schooled. He must take more care. No lapses like this, in details. Unbidden, although in reality not very far away at any time, the image of the girl in the Square returned to his mind. Her disdain, her proud little head. She would think differently of him to-night. He was even struck with the unlikely coincidence that she might be here now, within these elegant walls. If she were, any chance would be worth it.

"May I have your name, sir?"

He detected iciness. What was there about him to deserve suspicion? He stood as tall, his evening dress as good as any man in sight. He was unaware that he had been stretching, on uncomfortable tiptoes, to scan the staircase, the room be-yond. If she were here—common sense came to the rescue. If she were here, and she did not give him away, he might carry it off as a jest. But he would have met her under pre-tense. He rejected it all. Proud as she appeared, distant as she sought to be, he would have her know him for the man he was—no more, no less. He could not have explained even to himself the depth of that feeling. But with it, the evening had turned suddenly to a sorry charade.

"Your name, sir?"

He must play it out. He was angered with himself for the betrayal of his own resolve, and angered that the image of a girl could by mere recall turn him from the evening's glitter-ing promise.

The butler's mouth thinned, his eyes hardened.

Ned waved an imperial hand.

"Yes. Yes, of course, my good man. My compliments to Lady Bramwell and be good enough to announce Mr. Julien Edmond. . . ."

"Bramwell?"

Uncertainty alternated with suspicion, a state of mind not expected of Mrs. Potter Stephenson's second butler.

"I'm afraid you've made a mistake, sir. This is the resi-dence of Mrs. Potter Stephenson."

"Oh. Oh, bless me. Indeed I have made a mistake. A quite dreadful mistake. Please present my apologies to Lady, uh, Mrs. Stephenson. I must have been given the wrong address in London."

Out on Fifth Avenue, the cold mist threatened a drizzle.

Ned did not look back to the streaming lights of the great house. The comedy was over. He had had his glimpse of splendor. It was all that he had imagined. All that he had dreamed. The shadow that had crossed it was of his own making. As he started downtown an odd memory slid through his mind. A red-and-yellow kite he had made as a boy. He was trying to fly its brightness up into a clouded sky when the harsh-faced man who was his father found him. The man had snatched the string from his hand, snapped it, and pushed him homeward. Ned had only time to look back to see his splendid kite snagged, tattered, and broken on a bare tree limb. Tonight the butler wore the face of his father.

Ned turned up his collar. Using his cane, because in the dampness his shoes pinched, he began the long walk, ten, twenty, thirty blocks, and more. At Forty-ninth Street and Fifth Avenue he paused. The block was occupied by a somber, darkened mansion of Gothic style. Ned had seen it before in his explorations. But now at this eerie, mist-filled hour it took on a more sinister shape. He knew whose it was. He studied it with interest, to rest his feet and to ponder its mystery.

Police Officer Malley, coming around the corner, looked at the young man leaning against the lamppost as if there was no such thing as a DO NOT LOITER sign. A gentleman he looked to be, a real swell in evening clothes and doing no harm. Except maybe a drop too much of the evening. Still, Officer Malley had his orders.

"Beggin' yer pardon, sir, but there's no loiterin' on this block tonight. Police rules, sir."

Ned shifted his weight. "I seemed to have mislaid an address. I've just arrived in the city. I'm looking for Bramwell, the Bramwell residence."

"Never heard that name, sir . . . not on this part of the avenoo. This here"—he thumbed at the mansion he was patrolling—"is Mrs. Restell's house. You've maybe read of her. She's done crimes in there, they say, to make a judge blush. She's going up for trial tomorrow. We're keeping the rowdies off the block. Beggin' yer pardon, sir."

"I quite understand." Ned glanced up at the darkened house. "Is she there now?"

"Of course she's there now. No matter what they're saying. She's not escaping with the New York Police watching her. You can be sure of that. If you ask me she's on her knees now to God Almighty—or ought to be. It's like to go hard with her tomorrow."

"Indeed. Well, thank you, Officer."

Ned moved down the side street, into shadow, from where he could hear the patrolman's heavy plodding into the mist and from where he could clearly see a side door of Mrs. Restell's notorious mansion. He knew well enough the crisis in that disreputable career. He had followed the story day by day in the *Police Gazettes* from the boarding house parlor table. He had listened to the leering talk at mealtime. The young men at Mrs. Luskin's, all come to make their fortunes in the new Babylon, relished the story of the former English servant girl who, without a penny to her name, had reached the pinnacle of a Fifth Avenue mansion. Easier for a woman, they allowed, who was no better than she should be. But there was the stony fact that Caroline Trow Restell had made two respectable if unlucrative marriages before widowhood left her nearly destitute on these shores. From then on she had slid into darker ways, with a knowledge of medicine gained no one knew where, and that no woman should possess. "Skills," they called it, for murder, skills that even the rich came to buy. The young men around Mrs. Luskin's supper table winked at each other for solace. Oh, yes, it was easier for a woman to get ahead on those terms, but she had had her comeuppance now. They'd like to see the sport of a good hanging, even if her skirts were tied around her ankles.

Ned, standing on a street corner at this late hour, remembered it all as he gazed at the home of the woman who now called herself Madam Restell. He had been rebuffed this night, but a whole city lay around him, still there for the taking. A curious idea was taking shape. He longed to see the interior of the great mansion looming ahead of him, with its closely draped blind windows, its elaborate cornices, its four, full-square and solid stories. He would even like a glimpse of the ill-famed woman who occupied it.

His thoughts skipped like stones across deep waters. She was worth millions. Suppose he befriended her, suppose he offered her the solace of a fellow countryman, suppose . . . He already knew enough of this excitement-craving city to be aware that notoriety of any kind was better than oblivion. By tomorrow she would be on public trial. It would be too late.

These and a dozen thoughts like them tumbled through his mind as he scrutinized the house. He had already discovered a sliver of light at a second-story window. He searched the facade. Suddenly, he caught a movement of some kind at the side door, a deepening of shadow, an opening? At that moment Officer Malley plodded into sight. The side door closed abruptly.

Behind him, the avenue traffic was thinning. Ahead the side street lay deserted. Ned moved cautiously through the dim circle of gaslight and into the shadow, until he was nearly opposite the side door. He saw it open again. He backed quickly into the darkness.

The veiled woman who stepped through hesitated as if the house held more shelter than the hostile street. Then quickly, lightly, she crossed the areaway to the gate set into the iron grilling that fenced the house. There she half turned and with a lift of her head glanced backward. There was nothing furtive in her movements, nothing desperate. A kind of pride, Ned thought, or defiance. As she swung the gate open, her skirt seemed to catch on the granite corner of the gatepost base. She was held, in silhouette, a skiff straining at its mooring. She tugged sharply at her skirt. Then, set free, she ran eastward into the empty night. Ned peered down the street for sign of a waiting carriage. There was none. The darkness engulfed her.

It was not Caroline Restell. He had seen too many newspaper sketches of the thickened woman of sixty. This woman was lithe, graceful, slight. And the lift of her head . . . his mind searched for something, lost it. But she was young. No doubt of that.

There was no sign of the patrolman. Ned went to the gate and saw, in the faint pallor of the night, a dark blotch on the granite corner. He bent over and picked up a patch of dark cloth, ruffled, as far as he could make out the texture, heavy, and silklike. On an impulse he could not name, he thrust it into his pocket.

The gate, at his touch, had swung open. Disbelieving, he saw that the young woman had left the side door ajar in her flight.

If Ned Fitch believed in anything, he believed in Chance. Not your lucky card, throw-of-the-dice chance, but an inexplicable turn in the deep flow of a man's fate. It was all that he had ever been able to count on in the twists of fortune his youth had taken. Now here was Chance again. The most talked about house in the city, a side door left ajar. . . .

When a door opens, Boy, go through it. . . .

Not exactly what his grandfather had meant. Yet here was a house of great wealth, of mystery. The portals of respectability had already closed on him this night. Great as the risk might be, it was better than the nothingness of his tomorrow.

His agile mind already began to invent the excuses he would give for intruding.

He looked up and down the street. In another few moments, the patrolman might again appear. Ned slipped through the gate, crossed the twenty feet of areaway, pushed the side door open wider, and stepped into what at first seemed total darkness.

As his eyes adjusted, he saw that he was in a long, narrow hall. To the right he made out a flight of bare wooden stairs. Backstairs, he guessed, to the servants' quarters. To his left, at the far end of the corridor, a faint glow emanated from a single globe, the gas jet turned so low as to be almost extinguished.

The silence was complete, so dense he could feel it in his throat. Was the house deserted? Had the black-plumaged bird flown? Was that wraith of a figure in the street the last to leave? Ned found himself hoping so. In his two-and-a-half decades of less than elevating experience, he had arrived at the wisdom that the law was the scourge of the poor, the shackles of the timid, but for the rich a mere inconvenience, a mote in the eye. Madam Restell was very rich. She could well have flouted it once more.

Driven now by a compulsion beyond curiosity, Ned moved along the corridor toward the faint light. A white reflecting object ahead proved to be a doorknob. It turned easily in his hand. The door pulled open. All that barred him now from what must be the front part of the house was a curtain of heavy brown velvet. He listened, heard nothing, parted the curtains, and stepped through.

He found himself in a large main hall, softly lit as if the owner had gone out for the evening and would return. Whatever else the heavily draped mansion held, it was not mediocrity. Diamond-shaped black and white marble tiles paved the hall. A wide gilt-bannistered staircase flared onto it. He listened and heard no sound, except the pulsing against his own eardrums.

A few cautious steps carried him to where he could see into a grand salon where the very air was hung with the flamboyance of wealth. Like the hall, it was softly illuminated. He saw lush scarlet carpeting, ruby satin drapes closely drawn, a careful clutter of bronzes, jardinieres, heavy gold-framed paintings, deep sofas, tables, and carved chairs intimately grouped. He could not identify all the objects crowding the room, but even to his untrained eye it added up to uninhibited luxury.

He could well believe the penny journal stories that through these rooms flowed the full tide of the city's most powerful men—the politicians, the merchants, the gamblers, the financiers, and the brilliant demimondes they escorted.

He dared go no further. The grandeur, the emptiness, the total silence began to play tricks. His imagination peopled the upstairs rooms. He saw himself trapped, exposed, a jump-ship on the run. His explanations, that he had heard a cry, seen an intruder, come to offer a gentleman's help, seemed tissue-thin and irrelevant.

Slowly, cautiously, he moved past the imposing front door through which a gentleman might be expected to enter, aware of the squeak of his left shoe on the polished marble. All he had to do was to reach the safety of the velvet curtain and the darkness beyond it. He passed an elaborately carved wooden stand that held a large open book. A Bible. A reassurance to the fearful among Madam Restell's unfortunate clients? Or a false beacon to the trusting?

He came to a door, half opened. A cautious look through it showed him a small, officelike room with a desk, a couple of straight chairs, and walls lined with glass-fronted cabinets containing unguessable shining metal objects.

Looking down he saw something else and heard the quick intake of his own breath.

On the floor, half hidden by the desk, lay a woman. Face upward, her black hair tumbled in a satanic halo around her, the ruffles of a cream dressing gown spilling foamlike over her entire inert body. Ned knew the sight of death—the open mouth, the surprised eyes, the mottled, drained face. Nor was there any doubt of her identity. The penny journal artists had filled the newspapers with the strong features, the determined chin. Caroline Restell, alias Caroline Lohman nee Annie Trow, a former scullery maid, feared as a murderess, despised as an abortionist, or, depending on one's place in life, a cruelly persecuted benefactor of the unfortunate, laid beyond vulnerability. By whatever unknown means, she had escaped a society whose very private needs she had served, whose confidences she held. She would tell no secrets tomorrow. Death, he guessed, had struck without warning.

It was this last thought that brought Ned to his senses. His eye took in an open ledger on the desk. Near the awkward twist of her neck lay a torn page.

Then he heard it. A sound that might have been a footfall, or a sigh, or merely the ghostly awareness of a presence created by his own overwrought nerves. He listened. The silence beat in waves. He heard it again.

With that, Ned abandoned all daring, all images of Chance and Fame that had feathered his mind. Across the marbled hall, through the brown velvet and into the dim back corridor he fled, pursued by the squeakings of his own shoes. Once in the corridor, he saw the side door mercifully still showing a slant of night mist. Another five seconds and he was outside, across the areaway, and through the side gate into the street. Streamers of fog curled around the distant street lamp. Ahead lay Fifth Avenue, where the clatter of hoofs, the rumble of wheels promised normality.

He did not look back. He did not note that the sliver of light he had seen in the second-story window of that monstrous, silent house had gone out.

He walked on, unseeing, as unaware of the steady drizzle as of his own soggy, pinching shoes. Two facts lay rooted in his mind—the dead woman's face and the torn piece of heavy silk his hand could feel in his pocket, a testament of the night.

A mile and a half downtown he reached the quiet of Washington Square. He dropped onto a bench, no longer trying to remember what his mind sought, found himself nodding with fatigue on the wet wood. But as so often happens to a numbed consciousness, his eyes suddenly opened as his mind fumbled with an image. The straight-backed young woman he had seen veiled and leaving Mrs. Restell's darkened mansion, the lift of her head, the backward glance, the slight, erect figure, disappearing down the street. He had seen her before. Or had he? It was impossible, of course. The mischief of a tired memory? He knew if one lived too acutely in need or in hope, impressions gained or lost their significance. Only a settled mind was a balanced mind.

The young woman in the night. Try as he would to erase the idea, he found the image returning with it, a probing suggestion of similarity. He would deny it to himself again and again, but superimposed on that fleeting figure in the dark, he saw a slim, proud girl walking swiftly from him in Stuyvesant Square.

8

Walter Tremont folded the newspaper hastily, dropped it into his lap, and watched the new maid pour his breakfast coffee. She was untrained, unsure, and as yet neither Adrienne nor Noel had mentioned her name. Nor had he asked. Household matters had been and would always be, in Walter's world, the province of women.

He saw that the girl's hand was unsteady. He also noted that she filled the starched bosom of her striped uniform becomingly. She had the pert prettiness of many of the Irish immigrant girls who, if they were lucky, went from the horrors of the ship's steerage into service in respectable and proper homes. They would lose their youth early in long hours of work, short hours of rest, their hands reddened from ash soap, their lungs imperiled from sleeping in cold attics. Walter knew little of that, but he did believe in all his honesty that the young girls who found employment and refuge in homes like his were at least protected from the immoralities of an increasingly immoral city.

This girl had lost neither pertness nor prettiness. Not more than seventeen, he guessed. Much too young to see even the headlines of the early "Extra" edition hawked by newsboys around the Square. He had gone outdoors himself to purchase it before it found its way, uncensored, into his home.

"Agh!" The young maid's face flushed. The starched bosom rose in a gasp. The coffee had overflowed into the saucer.

"I'm that sorry, sir."

Walter waved a hand. "It's nothing. A little *fussbad.*"

"A what, sir?"

It was Maria's word when a cup overflowed. The German for footbath. "Don't worry. It's quite all right. You're new here, aren't you?"

The maid bobbed. "Three weeks, sir. I'm a tweenie"—she saw the perplexity in his face—"that's a startin' girl, sir, who works between scullery and best floors. Yesterday Mrs. Jessup promoted me to upstairs and breakfasts but now . . ." The soft round chin trembled.

It was beyond Walter, but he certainly didn't want the pretty little thing to cry. "I'm sure you'll do very well. Just bring another cup." He leaned toward her confidentially. "A little larger this time. A kitchen cup, perhaps? Just between you and me, I like a stout cup of coffee in the morning."

She stifled a giggle of conspiracy and ran from the room. He drew the newspaper from his lap but was not ready to open it. He thought of Adrienne upstairs, faintly scented, delicious in sleep, the curve of her lovely breast half revealed. They had been out late the night before, at the Academy of Music to hear *La Traviata*. To the melting music, she had sat close, warm beside him. The image treacherously dissolved. Opera had been no part of his life with Maria. But how she loved to hum the Italian tunes of the hurdy-gurdy in the street.

A thick white cup stood at his elbow, the little tweenie's eyes bright on him.

"Thank you. That will do nicely."

"Yes, sir. Will that be all, sir?"

"Quite. Uh, you do have a name, don't you?"

"Annie-Mae, sir." She bobbed. "Would you be likin' the same cup every morning, sir?"

"Yes. But don't set it out. It will be our little secret."

For all her youth, her smile was knowing. Walter regretted his unbending. She was the kind who could get herself into trouble. A mere youngster. Needed strictness—Mrs. Jessup's strictness.

Still reluctant to open the newspaper, Walter turned his mind to the morning ahead. The usual first-of-the-month meeting on accounts before the store opened. Tremont & Sons had finished last year with its usual comfortable margin of profit. This year looked to be about the same. Past fifty, Walter was more and more inclined to leave responsibility to his elder son, Orrin, with his terrier nose for laxness and his instinct for opportunity. His younger son, David, had already demonstrated a pronounced lack of interest.

There was, though, an immediate personal matter. His old friend and former partner, Henry Merriman, up to his ears in debt because of his foolish wife. Walter had never deserted a friend in his life. Henry was as close to him as a brother.

Walter took a swallow of strong coffee and turned with

distaste to his duty of reading the morning's special edition, as any man must who values the sanctity of his home, the protection of his family. The headlines stood black and bold:

> RESTELL TRIAL OFF. NOTORIOUS MIDWIFE-ABORTIONIST COMMITS SUICIDE.
>
> On the eve of her trial, the infamous Madam Restell made her restitution to society last night. At dawn this morning her domestics, alerted by an overflow from her bathroom, had found Mrs. Restell lying nude in her bathtub, her throat slit from ear to ear. Her white ruffled dressing gown lay on the floor beside the tub. A kitchen knife at her side gave evidence of what had happened. Running water from the tub's open faucet had drained away all the blood from the body. Police estimate that the unfortunate woman had slashed her throat between ten o'clock in the evening and two in the morning, during the time the servants had been dismissed for the evening.
>
> When notified, Mr. Anthony Comstock of New York's Society for the Suppression of Vice, the man responsible for bringing Mrs. Restell to justice, said that he could only give thanks that the sinner had found God. . . .

"Good morning, Father."

Walter half rose, crushing the newspaper behind him.

Noel stood in the doorway. She was dressed in a light tan traveling suit. A small hat, defiantly free of bird's wing, tilted above her chignon. She held a pair of traveling gloves in one hand.

"You're up early, Noel."

"I'm always up early, Father. Don't get up. I've had coffee." She crossed the room and dropped a light kiss on his cheek. She had her mother's small tipped nose, but the large dark eyes, filled with a veiled, sometimes mocking intelligence, came from heaven knows where. "It's a lovely day. I'm going up to Riveredge."

Riveredge was a small hamlet on the Hudson River beyond Irvington, an hour's train ride from New York. Noel had old friends there, a girl she had known since school days, she had explained. Walter had not pressed. Noel had good judgment and common sense. She was free to make her own friends, visit where she would. There had been a time, during Walter's engagement to Adrienne, when Noel had stayed several weeks at Riveredge. The visits did her good. After country air and country food, she always came home seeming rested and happier. This morning she looked particularly tired. He saw dark shadows beneath her eyes, her face, too pale, showed strain. Maria would have ordered a spring tonic.

"How long are you staying?"

"Just for the day. I expect to be home tonight."

"Why not take a few days in the country?"

"Perhaps I will, Father. I'm not sure."

With a light step, she was gone. He heard the front door close. He knew so little about her these days. Perhaps he should be firmer. He liked order, good planning. He liked to know each week ahead where he and the members of his family would be. This impetuous dashing off was part of the restlessness of the new era. He felt somehow that his role as pater familias was dimming, control seemed to be slipping from him.

He rang the silver table bell.

"Annie-Mae, I do not want any newspaper brought into the house today."

"Yes, sir. Lord, ain't it a horror, sir."

"You've seen it?"

"Yes . . . sir." She looked frightened. "I fetch the morning paper for Miss Noel, sir. She likes it with her early coffee."

Walter dabbed at his mustache and rose, leaving the coffee cup half full. A shadow of uncertainty, he could not call it by another name, had intruded on his morning.

From behind the small-paned windows of Tremont & Sons, Gentlemen's Tailoring, Est. 1847, Orrin Tremont watched the street. He was a spindly, undersized young man, his forehead too high, his hair too sparse, his mouth too narrow. He wore a pince-nez and the grey complexion of a man who spent all his hours indoors. He looked twenty years older than his age and would presumably look that way the rest of his life.

He was aware that he was not the likeliest member of the family. Four years ago he had made up for it by marrying into the impeccable but penniless Van Broot family. Tall, gaunt Charlotte traced her ancestry to the city's earliest Dutch days when New York was still Nieuw Amsterdam. She had two solid silver Dutch tankards, heavy as mallet heads, on her mantel to attest it. The rest of her dowry consisted of entry into New York's most exclusive inner society of old families and dwindling fortunes. It was a marriage of silent endurance, but it had carried Orrin into society.

Its side rewards were the gifts from his father—promotion

to partnership in Tremont & Sons and, on his father's remarriage, the old Sixteenth Street house. Such generosity implied loyalty. Not loyalty in return (his father would have abhorred such a suggestion), but the natural loyalty of a loving son to a close-knit family.

Loyalty. Virtue. His father had a way of reducing the most complex matters to such simplistic formulas. As unworkable in today's world as they were unanswerable.

The ponderous Dutch clock (Orrin's contribution to the front office) began to strike. His father was never late. He would not be late this morning. Orrin returned to his father's office in the rear to wait. The confrontation ahead would not be comfortable.

Walter Tremont paused long enough outside his place of business to note that the window panes sparkled, the gilt lettering was without blemish, the brass knocker and doorknob shone, and that the dark green door bore silent testimony to old-fashioned good taste.

As always, the walk from Stuyvesant Square to Bleecker Street had done him good. In the pleasant April sunshine, his disappointment in Noel's behavior had faded. He had thought instead of Adrienne's words, her light voice, faintly amused. "But Walter, my darling, you are not an old man. You must not think like one. You are still young. Your new life is just beginning. Of course we must get Noel married. And we will. Orrin manages very well downtown. You and I are what matter now. . . ." Her young body had pressed against his. Walter had believed her. The morning recaptured its spring brightness. He felt disposed to kindliness as he pushed open the front door.

"Good morning, Mr. Tremont." Miss Brickley did not permit herself the familiarity of a smile.

Upstairs in the lofts, thirty sewing machines would be humming, flatirons steaming. Fitters, their black aprons strung with pins and chalk, would be shaping and cutting with the expertise for which Walter assured himself he paid well. Many had worked for his father and grown old in service. The apprentices, fresh-faced and neat, were well taken care of. Sixty-three souls and their families for whom he, Walter Tremont, was accountable.

Feeling more like a father than he allowed himself to feel at home, Walter crossed into his private domain.

"They're all ready and waiting for you, Mr. Tremont," said Miss Brickley.

They?

Orrin was at the door to greet him. Behind him, to Walter's surprise, sat the spare figure of Adam Billings, family lawyer and adviser to the Tremont affairs, his spectacles hanging on a black ribbon against his black vest. Bland, bland, Walter thought for the hundredth time. Adam was always bland until he was losing.

Then to his surprise Walter saw a third figure perched on the corner of the library table that centered the room. Blond hair tousled, coat half buttoned, tie awry, David, his youngest, threw his father a twisted impersonal smile.

The meeting began matter of factly. An accounting for the first three months was profit three percent, down a half from the high of last year.

"To be expected," said Walter drily. "The price of Leeds worsteds has risen three pence. The British Empire is enjoying considerable prosperity. British woolens move with it. We shall continue to buy Leeds worsteds because they and we have always stood for quality before cost."

He saw Orrin and Adam Billings exchange a glance.

Other matters related to warehouse inventories and a surplus of Indian summer pongee.

Walter cleared his throat. "I daresay any first-class tailoring house in New York would be happy to have such a surplus. Our stock is made entirely from tussah, genuine wild silk which is becoming harder to get. If President Hayes lets import duties go much higher, it will be impossible. Oh, I remember, Orrin, you thought my purchase two years ago was a bit foolhardy. But pongee isn't going out of style. It's the lightest, coolest stuff a man can wear in our summers. In Washington, where summer is insufferable, Senator Walsh has ordered four suits from us. We stock the best because our clients depend on us for the best. I promise you, we'll use every yard of that surplus and wish we had more. Anything else?"

It seemed that six of the thirty-eight sewing machines needed new flywheels, four more would have to be replaced. "That," added Orrin, on a note of near satisfaction, "will bring profits for the next quarter down to two and a half percent. Or lower if we're unlucky."

"Luck has nothing to do with it," snapped his father. "These are investment expenditures in a sound business. We'll get it all back in increased efficiency before the year is out. Get the repairs made and buy the new machines." He was enjoying himself. He liked to make quick, confident decisions. It revived his sense of command.

"Well, is there anything else?"

He was aware of an uneasy lull. Adam Billings was stacking his papers, squaring the corners neatly. David shifted his position on the library table. Orrin rose slowly.

"Father, are you really satisfied with a three percent return on your business?"

"Your grandfather was satisfied with one percent. If it represented the best he could do."

"Times are different, Father."

"Times are always different. They change every day with the sun's rise. But that doesn't change a man's character. He's a fool if he lets it change his purpose. Oh, I understand profit, my boy. On a steady three percent I have provided for my family and my home. I've educated my three children. I've kept my men at work through good times and bad. When I die my wife will be provided—"

Walter hesitated. Time enough later to bring Adrienne into this. He hurried on irritably. "Tremont & Sons had its chance at big profits. Every merchant in this country with a government contract during the War Between the States had the same. You're too young to remember Artemus Briggs. Next door to Tremont & Sons before we moved up here. Tailoring business like ours, though he liked to cut close on the seams. Artemus had a government contract, too, to supply uniforms for the Union troops. President Lincoln ordered good wool for the men. What Artemus supplied was sleazy linsey-woolsey. He made forty-eight percent profit the first six months. Profit on the backs of men going out to die! Profit on rotting young corpses!"

Orrin opened his mouth, closed it, slowly swung one foot. David looked down at his knuckles. The old man's intensity was sometimes embarrassing. The war was a decade behind them. So were its causes. But they knew that once embarked, Walter would live out his vision.

". . . by the time the war was over Artemus had made a fortune. He invested it in railroad stock. The hope of the country, everybody said. What he didn't know was that among the big sharks he was a very small fish. He had no chance. Grant was in the White House and he was repaying the men who'd put him there. He permitted corruption such as this country had never seen. Stock was being sold on railroads that had gone bankrupt or had never been finished or that didn't exist. Stock was being watered as thin as the sleazy stuff Artemus had sold to the Union army six years ago. Then the market crashed. That was in '73. Banks failed. Artemus lost everything. Two years later he killed himself and followed his wife to a pauper's grave. His children—God knows. . . ."

Walter pulled out his handkerchief and found nothing better to do with it than wipe his hands. He had not meant to say so much. There had been no argument, no debate. He had dueled with empty air, with things unsaid.

Still he was not finished. He had not made his point—a fading point, but he would make it. "You boys are young, you think the city was always like this. Overcrowded, noisy, greedy. But when my father brought me here I was only a little shaver . . . why, I remember seeing the Great Comet, Halley's Comet. . . . The point is, we came from an old and tired European city. Strasbourg. My father saw this new country as a new heaven. Untouched. Full of opportunity. He believed that if every man who came here did his best this would become the greatest nation on earth. Tremont & Sons was my father's best. It will remain the best as long as I have breath to say it."

In the silence that followed, Walter pulled the heavy gold watch from his vest pocket as if to feel its substance.

"Have we covered the business of the morning? Then I would like to bring up a matter that's very close to me." He smiled benignly. "And, Adam, I welcome your presence, too. We'll need your help to expedite it. You know how much I value the friendship—the long friendship—between Henry Merriman and myself. He was my partner. He stood me in good stead during the years when we first knew of your dear mother's illness. He carried on this business almost single-handed." Walter paused. There was still nothing in the faces around him to encourage him. Nothing to tell him what they were thinking.

"I feel that both my sons should know. Henry is in trouble. Oh, I agree that his wife has been extravagant. But Kitty is, after all, my, uh, well, Adrienne's cousin. So I shall not look kindly on any criticism. But the fact is, Henry has come to me for a loan of $25,000. An awkward, but I do not think impossible, figure."

"Did you tell him that, Father?" Orrin's nasal voice thinned.

"No. Indeed not. I told him that I would consult my sons, now partners in my business, but that in all probability . . ."

"Well, I told him it was out of the question."

Walter stiffened. "You told Henry that we would not help him? You spoke for me? When, may I ask?"

"The same night he talked to you. At Kitty's party. Charlotte went home early. She's always tired with our fourth on the way. I stayed late. Kitty's parties get better, you know, nearer to midnight."

"I am not asking for a report of your personal life, Orrin. I want to know just when Henry Merriman talked to you about his debts."

"A little past midnight, to be exact. In his own library. He was quite drunk. He had been a little, shall we say, playful with poor, rich little Millicent. If he wants money, why doesn't he go to her father? One of her strings of pearls would take care of everything Henry owes. But of course Kitty wouldn't hear of that. In fact, Kitty may not even know how deep Henry's in for." Orrin's mouth bent into a knowing smile.

Walter told himself he would not interrupt. He would quietly pray for forgiveness for the distaste he felt this moment for his elder son.

"Henry spotted me in the library. Came in, poured himself another whiskey, which you will be pleased to know I had the character to refuse. Told me his troubles. He needed $20,000. He must have lowered the ante to me, Father. It was $20,000, or he'd go under, we'd all go under, whatever that means. But I guess he thinks we're all one happy family now."

Orrin met his father's eyes. Walter sensed something like arrogance in the direct stare, then it was gone.

"I told him we didn't have that much to throw around. The answer was no."

His son could be cruel, too, Walter realized, but that was not the point now.

"You didn't know he had already talked to me?"

"Oh, he told me, but as I said, he was drunk. Wanted to talk. He said you'd told him you'd think about it. But he thought you wouldn't understand his situation, 'couldn't,' I believe was his word. Wasn't sure you were close enough to the business these days to, well, make the decision. You've left a lot to me, Father. I think this is one of the things you might also leave to me."

Walter rose. Although he was given to slouching as his girth widened, when straight he seemed to tower. At this moment he felt not the weight of years, only his anger and the solemnity of his moral duty.

"We have, I believe, about $20,000 in the reserve account in New York Trust. As we have no immediate emergency, I shall put that money at Henry's disposal. That will solve the matter."

Orrin's head thrust forward, reminding Walter of a small angry turtle. Yet his tone attempted to match the ease of his father's.

"We *had,* Father. It was you who ordered the work lofts remodeled last year for better air and the workers' rest areas heated with coal stoves. And now you want four new machines ordered. If I may remind you, we lost one hundred bolts of Lyons lining silk when the packet *Arcturus* went down. . . ."

The front doorbell jangled. It was nine o'clock. Tremont & Sons was open for business.

Orrin stood up, straightened his coat, ran a hand over his thinning hair.

"Father, I think you must realize that even if we all agreed to make Henry his loan, which we decidedly have not, this business does not permit it. A three percent profit is totally inadequate for today's style of living, much less such unguaranteed generosity. I am sorry, sir."

Adam had completed the squaring of his papers. He thrust them into his case.

Walter watched him.

"You agree with that, Adam?"

Adam was careful.

"We are approaching a decade, sir, when money will be made in such enormity in this city that no man will be satisfied with a small business. Last week Western & Platte bonds went on the market. Eight percent interest guaranteed for five years by the house of Morgan. The entire issue is already bought out."

"I'm not a gambler. Neither, I trust, are my sons. Nor do I wish to become one of those men who use money to make money, instead of using the hands and skills God gave them."

Adam Billings thrust out a cold, skinny hand. "Nor should you, my old friend, if you like the world better as it is than what it is becoming. Always nice to see you, sir. Good day, gentlemen."

The lawyer departed soundlessly. As if he hadn't been in the room, thought Walter. But he had. Oh, he had.

A sense of defeat dimmed the morning, a feeling of something hinted at, not yet spoken. Something Walter could not name stuck like a stone in his throat. Yet he must be fair. Orrin was the most reliable, the most disciplined of his children. From the moment he had entered the business, Orrin had set himself to mastering every detail of it, working longer hours than were ever asked of him. Walter could not recall a day when, on arriving at his office at nine, Orrin was not already there, the workrooms humming, the day's fitting schedule completed. He had shown more than loyalty. He had become the linchpin in the comfortable happiness of Walter's present life. Orrin was certainly entitled to the strength of his own opinions. He must be fair, Walter told himself again.

Fair. Not emotional.

His second son, David, slid from the edge of the table. David . . . the golden child, whose headless lead soldiers, whose lost ball, whose tailless hobby horse had concerned him most. At this moment, with a lock of tawny hair fallen across his forehead, youthful impatience stamped on his face, David was for an instant the beloved small boy, his and Maria's youngest. The instant passed. This muscled young man, already distancing himself, was no longer a boy. He had moved out of their old home a month before Walter's remarriage. He had not yet visited the new house on Stuyvesant Square.

The father surveyed him, managing an easy smile.

"It seems I'm lacking in relevancy, David."

"We all are, Father, when we're not understood." David had indeed grown beyond the old perimeter. Walter decided he would not ask David why he had joined the meeting this morning. He had already begun to see the shadowy outlines of its purpose. He would not lend it any further weight.

"Sit down, David. It's a while since we've had a chance to talk. Adrienne is complaining that you never come to dinner with us."

"Her stepson? I'd be an albatross around her neck. And yours, Father."

The words carried something Walter did not understand. The alert young eyes were clouded. But he would not let these few moments with his son dissolve into distance between them.

"Where are you living now, David?"

"I've two rooms in Perry Street. One to sleep in, the other to work in. A Mrs. Skally does for me. Five feet tall, five feet wide, wife of the corner saloon keeper, keeps one ear or the other to the ground. Invaluable, I assure you."

David's style. Chatty, courteous, revealing nothing. Walter felt awkward. "And you're busy?"

"More work than I can handle. I have the *Gazette*, the *Express*, the *Sun*, and I may get a chance at the *World*. . . ."

"Those are newspapers. I thought you were becoming a painter."

"A sketcher, Father. I get fifty cents a sketch if I'm quick on the scene. More if it's a big story."

"I don't think I understand. . . ."

"Here. I'll show you." From the floor beside him, David lifted a bulky canvas roll. "My wares in my pocket, Father. Work done fast, accurate, cheap."

With the flip gesture of a card dealer, David spread the contents of the roll on the table—pen and ink sketches, clipped from newspapers.

"What'll you have? Street fight at the Brooklyn ferry wharf? The woman there with the bucket of slops stopped 'em. Slum fire at Five Points? That's the mother of one of the victims. A five-year-old child. Sulky collision at Jerome Raceway? They had to shoot Walcott's $10,000 mare. That's the Carterwell wedding. Bride isn't too happy, but look at her father. He was the son of a grocer. The groom is a French marquis. Little old spindleshanks. Doesn't look as if he'd make the altar, much less—"

"Do you sign these things?"

"Right there. Goodfellow. My pen name. I'm that merry wander'r of the night. Courtesy doddering old Doude, at Latin school. Remember? He thought a chap was educated if he knew the subjunctive, the ablative, and twelve plays of Shakespeare."

The sketches were more than good. They were powerful. In harsh, spare lines, David had caught the violence, the grief, the greed, the cruelty, the very anguish of the city seething below the ordered surface of Walter's own world.

But why? Why would David, so carefully, thoughtfully raised, throw away his youth on the vulgar, the mean, the sordid in life? Walter picked up the last two sketches. One, a tall, somber mansion and a black carriage disappearing down a side street. The other, a woman's head in a large plumed hat, the heavy face, the thickened chin framed in smooth black fur.

"The Restell house and carriage. That's the lady herself the night she was arraigned in court. The *Gazette* was going to pay me a dollar and a quarter for every day of the trial. That's been taken out of their hands. For the better, I'd say. They've promised me five dollars to do her funeral tomorrow. Up at Tarrytown."

David gathered up the clippings. But not before his father had looked again at the face of Caroline Restell. Haughty.

Sensual. Evil, as he saw it. What he was not prepared for was the compassion David had drawn into the deep-set eyes.

"You've met that woman?"

"How else could I sketch her?"

"Have you been in her house?"

"Anyone could enter her house. There's one side door without a lock. Only an attendant, a woman, on duty. In case some helpless unfortunate girl was too nervous or too frightened to go up to the front entrance and ring the bell."

Walter made a gesture of distaste. "I'm not interested in those details, David."

"You should be, Father. So should every right-thinking man and woman in this city."

Walter's sense of outrage returned. Yet anger would do nothing. This young, impudent stranger was his son, his beloved David. He must remember that. He rose to end the unpleasantness of the scene. Yet he could not turn his back on it.

"Am I to believe that you have given up all serious work, David, for this?"

"This is my serious work. The most serious work I've ever attempted. To get at the truth of things. To show it as best I can underneath all the piety, the hypocrisy of this city. Come with me someday, Father, and I'll show you things. . . ."

Miss Brickley was standing in the doorway.

"A messenger from Colonel Gordon, sir. The Colonel wishes to know if you were able to obtain the grey twill for his coaching coat in time for the Hedley Meet?"

Walter felt in his pocket for a coin as if he were reaching for order. "Mr. Orrin knows the schedules. Give this to the messenger boy."

David had left. Walter took his hat from the rack. He needed to breathe. The office stifled him, the air was heavy, his nostrils clogged with a scent like dead ashes.

He would walk. He would breathe the decent air of this city that had been so good to him. He would remind himself of the old-fashioned ideals that, as his own father had promised, had brought him to this position of substance.

A man's true profit is pride in his work. A man's integrity is his first business. A man's loyalty is the measure of his heart.

The April sun warmed his back. He would walk up Broadway to the Hoffman House and its double-length bar, the most popular meeting place of the day for men of affairs. He'd take a quick brandy to restore his sense of well-being and pick up the latest foreign textile prices. Then he'd take a cab uptown to the Union Club at Twenty-sixth Street to which, among his new honors, he had recently been elected. Adrienne would be returning soon from her social rounds. She had promised him an evening at home.

He was the head of his house and his firm. He was still in command. He would make the loan to Henry Merriman because Henry was a trusted friend. The money was there, lying unused in the Exchange Bank. A private account of $20,000, available only to himself. Henry, his old partner, would return it long before it would be needed.

The sense of betrayal that had shadowed the unpleasant little office meeting lifted. He had the wisdom of his years. It was up to him to take care of those he loved.

If he chose to make a loan of Noel's dowry, why not? It would seemingly be a long time, if ever, before his cherished and inscrutable daughter could claim it.

9

The crack in the ceiling widened, undulated, and narrowed. Sometimes it looked like a long wound, sometimes like a mirage of escape through which a man might push himself if he knew how and vanish.

Ned lay on the iron bedstead in his attic room staring up at it. He had slept little if at all after his night's adventure. He had come home in pouring rain, shivered under the thin blanket his landlady considered adequate for April, and had lain listening for the sounds of the coming day: the rattle of cart wheels, the smell of refuse newly dumped in the rear alley, and finally the defiant clatter of pans and stove lids as the girl-of-all-work started the dawn's drudgery.

He had waited for full daylight, or whatever remnant of it his narrow skylight would admit. Finally morning had come. He had dressed, gone down to the street for a cup of coffee a lady fruit vendor usually had waiting for him.

A newsboy thrust an early morning "Special Edition" into his hands. He glanced at the headline, took a second, more careful look, and returned abruptly to Mrs. Luskin's rooming house, tiptoeing up the creaking stairs to his attic room. There he had remained, except for periodic sorties into the street for newer editions.

Now it was past noon. Fully dressed in his old seaman's pullover and trousers, a stubble of beard on his face, Ned lay again on his iron bed, staring at the ceiling. It was the only privacy he knew in the vast hubbub of the city in which to be alone. And to think.

It would soon end. On his last trip downstairs, two hours ago, he had caught a glimpse of Mrs. Luskin watching from her sentry post at the desk inside the parlor door. He had slipped past her. Last night's business was his own. Meanwhile, on the opposite wall of his room hung Mr. Monk's evening-suit-for-hire, which would have to be returned. At present, suspended from a nail, it drooped shapeless from the night's rain, filling the room with a dank smell. It would cost a pretty penny to clean and press. Mr. Monk would have to wait for his suit. As for cash, Ned's last handful lay on the table. No pretty penny, all told.

Nor was there any use in reading again the newspapers scattered around him on the bed. He knew every appalling word. The woman he had discovered last night lying dead in her first-floor consulting room was reported this morning to be "a grisly suicide, found by a servant in an upstairs bathroom with her throat cut. . . ." The newspapers, depending on their editorial quality, differed only in details: "Mrs. Restell's powerful hand still clenched the handle of the kitchen knife . . ." or "The kitchen knife lay beside her in the tub . . ." or "The faucet she had turned on to carry the blood away had gone dry . . . so much water had drained through the tub that the roof tank was empty . . . no blood was left in the body . . . the back of the skull showed a bruise where her head had struck the tub's edge . . . no bruise was found anywhere on the body . . . Mrs. Restell's ruffled peignoir lay unstained across the bathroom chair, white as the stark nude body in the tub . . . Mrs. Restell's suicide was as gore-stained as . . ."

None of it true. Not one bloody word. The old woman had been dead as a haddock in her own office at ten o'clock last night. He had seen her with his own eyes. Yet to come forward, to admit that he had been in the Restell house last night, he a foreigner, a jump-ship, maybe still wanted by the shipping line—that would be putting his head in a noose for certain.

No. What he knew he had to keep to himself. At least until he could find a way to use it to his own advantage, not to his peril. Yet his mind would not let go of it. Someone must have come into the office, carried the dead woman up the wide staircase to that bathroom. Someone of cold gut, of considerable strength had set up that gruesome scene. Why? If the woman was already dead, wasn't that enough? How had she met death in that office? If it had been by natural causes, why make a suicide out of it? But if there had been foul play. . . . Ned recalled again the sound he had heard that had driven him from the house—not quite a footstep, a sound of movement, of stirring. A line of sweat broke out beneath his dark hairline. Someone had been in the house, perhaps watching him. Someone who could identify him.

Then there was the younger woman; this was the nail on which Ned tossed. Young, slender, graceful . . . he had seen her leave by the side door of the Restell mansion only minutes before he had come on the body. Had she known?

In his pocket, carefully transferred from the wet evening clothes, lay the only reality of the night, a jagged piece of brown silk—heavy, lustrous, the kind of silk worn by a woman of quality. The memory of that disappearing figure had flitted mothlike in and out of his mind all night.

It was past noon when a double knock broke the pinwheeling of his thoughts. The door was pushed open.

"Neddie! Are you all right?"

In a cloud of violet scent, the full-bosomed bulk of his landlady bore down on him. The flaxen pompadour, jet earrings bobbing, bent over him.

"What's wrong, Neddie? Taken sick, running around the city all night? Where you've no business being?"

There was no scolding in her voice, rather something knowing, satisfied. It didn't make sense, nor did anything else this April morning.

"If I'd known you were still up here, Neddie, I'd have come up sooner. You had a visitor."

Ned pushed newspapers away from him and got to his feet.

"I don't know anybody in this city who'd call on me, ma'am. Or even know where I live."

But her eye had fallen on the scattered sheets of the journals.

"So that's it! You're not sick, Neddie. You've been lying on your back wasting the whole day with that trashy story in the papers!" With a powerful stroke, Mrs. Luskin swept the offending newspapers from the bed.

"I'm ashamed of you, Neddie. No better than the others. There isn't a *Gazette* left whole on the parlor table. Well, all I can say is that woman came to her just desserts. Maybe now the papers will be fit for decent people to read!"

Ned focused innocent eyes above Mrs. Luskin's pompadour.

"That . . . woman?"

"Don't play shy boy with me, Neddie. I know my lodgers. I'd have to or I'd be out of business. The Captain, my late husband, rest his soul, used to say to me, ship with a good crew or don't leave port. I knew you, Neddie, from the day you walked in. A jump-ship? I could guess. . . ."

Ned slid from the bed. He had not expected this.

". . . but something about you was different. I thought

you'd go far. I had high hopes for you, Neddie, and here I find you lyin' abed knee deep in that Restell trash as if your soul . . ."

What else did she know? The woman had the tongue of a magpie, the eyes of a hawk.

"You're not fancying I know the woman?"

Mrs. Luskin looked at him uncertainly.

"Know Mrs. Restell? Of course you wouldn't know that woman. Nor would any respectable person. You can't guess her wickedness, Neddie. Calling herself a midwife, taking into her house every hussy, with an illegitimate brat coming, while decent women have to work to the bone to keep body and soul together!"

The black-bombazined bosom rose and fell. Ned began to understand the thrust of her outburst.

"Oh, Neddie, Neddie! Where's the justice? That witch woman with her coach and pair, driving up Fifth Avenue with the best of high society while I . . . while honest women work and—" Mrs. Luskin had dammed her indignation too long—"slave she's making millions out of sinning. Well, she's past that now and good riddance. It must have come to her in the dead of night, like the fist of God, to make her cut her own throat. Thank the Lord I'm a woman with peace in my soul. Trying only to do my best to comfort the lost and help the friendless to find their way."

She gave an explosive sigh. But she had not yet met Ned's eyes, nor could she relinquish the pleasurable details.

"They're going to bury her with a marble angel on her grave as if God was waiting with a bunch of pink roses. And her three grandchildren there to make her look respectable. I'd say a hanging and a pauper's grave would have done her better. But I don't envy her. Not me. She must have lived with a terrible conscience for all her money. Oh, Neddie, it's a hard and ugly world"—she leaned toward him—"when you're a woman alone. It's not everyone I can bare my heart to."

"I'm sure, Mrs. Luskin." Ned stopped to pick up some of the fallen newspapers. "You said I had a caller?"

Mrs. Luskin stiffened and touched her pompadour. She had lost a skirmish but not yet the field. She gave Ned a bland smile.

"A Mr. Elias Monk. You know him?"

Ned had already decided on candor.

"Yes, I know him. I've rented clothes from him once in a

while. I had to. I couldn't go around the city in these now, do you think? I rented that evening suit from him yesterday."

"I know. He said it was due back before noon. It's now past two, Neddie."

"How could I return them? I've no way of getting them cleaned up from the rain."

"Oh, Neddie, Neddie. How could you waste your money on fancy clothes and going out to see fancy sights when you haven't even a job?"

"I've asked myself that, lying here this morning. I know now it was reckless of me. And wrong, Mrs. Luskin. Wrong. I'm paying for my bad judgment. I was carried away by the city, the lights, the people. And"—this time he looked directly at her—"by the kindness I've found here." He paused, then continued. "I might as well be honest about it, for it's what kept me lying here idle today. I am in debt to Mr. Monk as I am in debt to you. I shall honor those debts as soon as I can. I've made up my mind that tomorrow I'll take work as a hostler. There's always a public livery that needs one and I've a hand with horses. I'll be able to bed over the stable, I should think."

"Ned, you must not do that!"

He waited.

"You must find something better. You will find something better. Something you're fitted for." With a surprisingly quick movement for a heavy woman, she scooped the damp evening clothes from the nail and hugged them within her arms. "You must not think of leaving here, Neddie. I'll just carry you along until you've found proper work. As for Mr. Monk"—she gave Ned an inscrutable smile—"I told him I'd see that these things got back to him before the day was out, fresh pressed and clean. And—" her triumph was unmistakable—"I paid your bill."

He stared at her. "You paid Elias Monk for me?"

"The whole bill, Neddie. You have nothing to worry about. I've just added it to your account in my books. Why, it's so much better this way. That man might have put you in debtor's prison. Then how would you find a job? What are friends for? I was happy to do it. You can pay me when you're able. Well, aren't you pleased?"

He'd heard what he wanted, but he was not pleased. The old sense of entrapment returned. His own affairs had been taken out of his hands, and by a woman. But it served him right, he told himself grimly. He had wanted so much, so quickly. His revulsion to poverty, his knowledge of its debasement had sent him skipping across very thin ice.

"I'm grateful, Mrs. Luskin. Very grateful."

It was not the effusion she had expected, but neither was the expression in his face, as if she had already gone from the room.

"There's one thing more, Neddie." Her voice was cooler. "Mr. Monk said with the clothes, he rented you an evening cane. . . . " She glanced into the corners. "If you'll give it to me I'll return it with the other things."

"I don't have it."

Her eyes sharpened. "Where is it?"

"I must have left it on one of my, uh, calls last night."

"Where was that?"

This was possession, bought and paid for. But he would take the matter lightly until he could rid himself of the woman's presence.

"Dear Mrs. Luskin, would a gentleman reveal to a lady where he went on a night of pleasure? I'll get it back. Don't worry about that."

For a florid woman she went quite red. "Mr. Monk said the cane was worth twenty dollars at least."

Twenty dollars. An impossible sum for him now or at any foreseeable time. But it was not the value of the cane that disturbed him. It was the brink he saw himself approaching.

He laid a light hand on Mrs. Luskin's tight black sleeve. "The responsibility of the cane is mine. You are to forget it. I shall find it and return it. And . . . I can only say again how grateful I am for your generosity."

With a shake of her head that might have been despair or forgiveness, Mrs. Luskin turned and to Ned's boundless relief closed the door behind her.

He stood frozen in the center of the room.

The cane. Where had he left it? He tried to retrace the events of the night. He could remember with precision the frosty gesture with which Mrs. Stephenson's footman had returned his rented evening hat and the chilling angle at which the ivory-headed cane had been thrust at him.

He remembered grasping the cane on his uncomfortable walk downtown on the wet sidewalks of Fifth Avenue. He had leaned on it while looking at the Restell mansion. Yet he had no recollection of it after his ill-fated intrusion into the house. At some point it must have slid from under his arm. There was only one place where that could have happened noiselessly. On the thick brown carpeting of Madam Restell's consulting office, where he had stopped at the sight of the prone figure.

For an instant Ned heard his own heart thud. He could almost see the cane lying there. Yet he had read every word the newspapers carried. No mention was made of a gentleman's cane found in the consulting office.

Yet someone must have found it. The person or persons who had carried Mrs. Restell's body upstairs? in that event, whoever he was would have as little liking to come forward with the wretched cane as Ned was to retrieve it. And as there was no identification on it . . . or was there?

Ned took himself in hand. The animal cunning that had enabled him to survive the snares and quicksand of London's waterfront came to his rescue. He was on the verge of making a fatal mistake, surrendering to his own imagination. No one could associate him as yet with the violent death of Madam Restell.

Besides, he held a card or two himself—a fragment of fine silk and, in his memory, the quick toss of a girl's head.

He swung his sea cap from the wall and slid his remaining coins from the table into his purse. He had not eaten in twenty-four hours. Experience had taught him that a man never thinks his best on an empty stomach.

He would spend what he had to for a decent meal. Then he would plan a careful next move, the delivery of a sea-stained package of books to one Dr. Hugo Lendler of Stuyvesant Square.

10

With a gasp of relief, respectable New York welcomed the suicide of Mrs. Caroline Restell. Do-gooders saw in it a fitting solution to a long-endured scandal. "Justice done," "Peace with God," "Cleansed her soul of guilt," and other such sentiments filled the press and the pulpits. Society could drive comfortably at last past the shameless Gothic mansion on uptown Fifth Avenue. More than one judge, politician, and high-living millionaire could settle himself at his family dinner table with new ease.

In the days immediately following, the voice of conscience occasionally spoke. The *New York Sun* roundly berated Commissioner of Vice Anthony Comstock, for his method of obtaining the evidence that had at long last run Mrs. Restell to earth. The *Eagle* took pains to point out that she was the fifteenth of Mr. Comstock's victims to take her own life. As far west as Rochester, the press rumbled that "Comstock is as unimportant to New York as last year's flies," and that "no group of people in this country carry more stupidity and cowardice than the humbugs of vice, the Comstocks."

The penny journals served the prurient with stories of searches of Mrs. Restell's cellar for the bodies of murdered infants and young women. None were found. The ladies' journals tried to keep the story alive, and circulation up, by debating the suitability of the gravestone. Neither an angel nor a child seemed appropriate. Civic authorities could take comfort that Mrs. Restell would be buried in the distant village of Tarrytown, thus avoiding a city spectacle. In the whole great wash of print, no question was asked, no doubt surfaced about the assumption that she had died by her own hand. Mrs. Restell's suicide had the satisfying ring of divine justice.

In the end, Mr. Anthony Comstock, her relentless persecutor, had the triumphant last word. Raising his eyes heavenward, he answered his maligners, "I serve one Master. I bear patiently my burdens. I do something each day for Jesus. I labor only to protect the innocence of youth and shield the purity and beauty of womanhood."

"Treacle!"

In the small private sitting room of her old-fashioned house on the south side of Stuyvesant Square, Miss Phoebe Bliss threw down her newspaper. After five decades of spinsterhood, she was quite used to talking to herself. One must, she would say also to herself, if one expects an honest answer.

"Treacle *and* nettles!" This time she addressed a large, iron-grey striped cat whose pale green eyes were fixed on her from the ottoman. "If there is one thing on this earth I despise, Wellington, it is a hypocrite!" She snatched up the cat and held its warmth against the mauve pleating of her bodice, the fingertips of her right hand moving gently into the thick fur. "That is why I adore you, my little love. You are what you are. With the evil in you as plain as your paws. It is my opinion that Mr. Anthony Comstock should ask a lady first if she wants—what is it—her purity and beauty of womanhood protected. When I was a girl, a lady did that for herself. Or she didn't. But it was a much better time, Wellington. Soft dresses and dancing. I blame the Queen for all this stiffness today. I really do. As for Mrs. Restell, why shouldn't they put a pretty little marble angel on her grave? Who knows . . . ?"

The rest was lost in the tinkle of the Dresden clock on the mantelpiece. She pressed the cat against her an instant longer, then dropped him unceremoniously onto the ottoman.

"Time for my walk, Wellington. And it is a lovely day. You have the night, remember, but the daylight is mine. I think the cashmere shawl will be quite enough."

Suitably wrapped, Miss Phoebe, as the Square knew her, returned to the ottoman, lifted the cat, and deposited him on the window seat where with a throaty purr and an acknowledging flick of his black-tipped tail he settled himself on the bottle-green velvet.

"There. Now you can watch me in the park. And when our Mr. Christopher comes downstairs to his activities he'll know where I am. We must never, never worry Mr. Christopher, Wellington. We've agreed on that."

After a last small stroke of love on the fur between the cat's ears, Miss Phoebe departed, stepping into the mild sunlight of the April afternoon with a sigh of pleasure. Clouds, drizzle, even cold rarely deterred Miss Phoebe from her walk.

Good weather would regularly find her on a wrought-iron bench within view of the comforting bulk of St. George's. She was as familiar and reassuring a sight to the inhabitants of the Square as the twin spires themselves. A tiny, bonneted figure with the trace of a limp, she carried an unstylish black satin reticule and was the last woman in New York to wear black lace fingertip mitts. It was also said that no sparrow molted in the Square but Miss Phoebe knew the feather's drift.

Today as she walked, she was Deploring. Miss Phoebe's intensities came in capital letters. Now her quick eye noted clumps of Weeds where grass should grow, bushes in need of Trimming, black paint Flaking from the benches. There was no doubt the park needed a Spring Uplift. There was also no doubt that dear Mr. Morgan, for all his fierceness, would see to it.

Still she was thankful that dear Pa*pa* was not here to see it. That is, half thankful. Her emotions concerning Pa*pa* had mercifully faded, although that dimly awesome figure, dead twenty years now, could still reach across time to remind her of principles. She had never married. She had cared for him dutifully, in return for which she had inherited the huge unwieldy house, one of the first built on the Square, a self-assumed responsibility for the little park and, her most telling inheritance, advancing age, about which she could do nothing. Yet, she reflected, as she seated herself on her favorite bench, she had done a few things. Quite a few, considering.

She sat back and let the sun warm her face. The first spring softness always put her in what she called her pink mood, taking her back merrily to that long lost day of her youth when her waist had measured seventeen inches and she had sat primly in her apple-green-and-white striped muslin on the parlor divan. Mr. Horace Witterly, round as a frog in the middle, but a man of great property to the North, had come to propose. There he had been, down on one knee before her, clasping her hand. "My dear Miss Bliss, Miss Phoebe, my dear Phoebe . . . your father has given me permission to offer my suit." At that moment a most curious thing had happened. The room had filled with pink light. Out on the street she had heard voices, shouts. Without an instant thought, she had jumped up and run out into the street where a crowd was gathering, and the street and the sky and the whole world were turning pink.

When she had returned to the house, Mr. Witterly was standing, his hat firmly on his head, his left hand solidly gloved. "My dear Miss Bliss, you will condone my departure and frankness. I perceive I have failed to judge accurately certain aspects of your estimable character. Since triviality, I might say, uh, flightiness, are no part of my own way of life, I do not see that an understanding between us. . . . To be brief, my dear Miss Bliss, I am not a man who could consider an abberation in the heavens sufficient motive for interrupting one of life's most significant decisions."

He had marched down the street, a round black cutout in the pinkness of the light. In later years Miss Phoebe could never quite remember whether it was the arrival of Halley's Comet or the departure of Mr. Horace Witterly that had made her day so luminous.

Forty years or more, was it? It did not matter. It was spring and the pink mood was upon her again. There would be strollers out this afternoon, although it was early for Dr. Lendler. For an instant the errant imps of her thoughts put Dr. Lendler on his knee in place of Mr. Witterly in that long-forgotten parlor. In such an event, Miss Phoebe admitted privately, she would never have run out for all the comets in the sky.

But what the Square needed now was Young Blood. Like Noel Tremont. Miss Phoebe always enjoyed a few minutes' chat in the park with Noel. The girl was lively and gracious and had a style of her own. Yet there was something about her, a reserve that Miss Phoebe, for all her sharp observance, could not put a finger on. A reserve, a distance. Miss Phoebe found herself in the unusual situation of groping for words. It was as if Noel were somewhere else, as if her pleasantries were merely a shell while she inhabited a place known only to herself. It's what comes, Miss Phoebe thought, of having too young a stepmother, or of being urged too blatantly into marriage. Possession may be nine-tenths of the law, Miss Phoebe told herself, but when people try to possess each other, "That's a sin," she added aloud.

"I beg your pardon, Madam."

The man addressing her was tall. Miss Phoebe had to shade her eyes against the bright April sky to look up at him. He was also young. And she noted, with an inward ripple of pleasure, quite good-looking. In fact, she would say, handsome. She disliked mustaches and beards with which men today cluttered their faces. This young man's cheek was as smooth as polished pine. Which was quite a lot to notice before the young man spoke again.

"If I may beg your courtesy. I am looking for . . ."

"Oh, sit down, young man. I can never think with the sun in my eyes."

Ned sat, and congratulated himself on his luck. He had walked the Square to find someone who might be useful. This little old absurdity could be just the party.

"My thoughtlessness, Madam. I beg your forgiveness."

Miss Phoebe's laugh bubbled. "That's three begs, young man. Don't you know that when you're young you don't need to beg from anybody? What is it you're looking for?"

Ned was in no hurry. "Information, Madam."

Miss Phoebe measured him. His manner was at curious odds with his seaman's cap and jacket.

"You're from England?" Her eyes were shrewd.

"Yes."

"Recently?"

"Quite recently."

It was Miss Phoebe's habit to sit with her left foot curled under her skirt, the Unlucky One she called it since the accident had left it twisted. Her right foot was thrust forward, the hem of her skirt delicately clearing it. In her youth Miss Phoebe was known to have a well-turned ankle. Now the little black boot swung, gently conspicuous.

"May I ask from what part of England?"

"Near Salisbury, ma'am."

"Ah, Salisbury."

Ned was not prepared for coincidence. He waited.

"Salisbury," Miss Phoebe sighed. "Thirteenth century. Splendid nave. A bit dark. Not like Ely. Ely is pure white and built right in the middle of a marsh. Or York, with the Seven Sisters and the Rose window. And Lincoln, with the haunted crypt, or is it the other way around? I was brought up on the cathedrals. Grandfather hung them all over his house. He was such a Tory. When everybody here was talking about Independence from England, Grandfather went right out and signed the Declaration of Dependence on the Crown. He left a copy among his papers to remind us. When the British Fleet arrived to put down the rebellion, Grandfather had his coachman row him out to the flagship. He stood up in the boat and sang 'God Save the King' and then fell overboard. Well, there's nothing like the British navy for pulling people out of the water. Grandfather caught the grippe and had to live on chamomile tea and cabbage soup for a week. When the Rebellion was over and the Yankees came and stole all the silver, Grandfather took the first ship he could for England, which was a mistake. Because Pa*pa* said when

Grandfather got to London he was neither fish, fowl, nor very good herring. He was a sort of tainted Tory. A Loyalist who had lived right on here through the Rebellion. Pa*pa* said we had settled in America and would stay here and be Americans. But England is so very dear to me. I hope to see it someday. Who was your father?''

Ned fixed his dark intense eyes on Miss Phoebe.

''I'm the second son of a second son, ma'am.''

Miss Phoebe took an instant to reflect. ''Oh, I do see. They're the ones who never inherit. And you've come to America to make your fortune. Yes, of course. Well''—she gave him a weighing look—''I'm sure you won't have any trouble.''

But Ned's attention had shifted. Miss Phoebe followed his glance.

Down the street on the walk outside the iron railing came a straight-backed young woman in a tan suit, with black passementerie outlining a neat waist.

''Why, there's Miss Tremont. Noel Tremont, a charming girl. Do you know her?''

''No. No.'' Ned returned to Miss Phoebe, keeping a partial view of the girl. ''For a second she reminded me of someone.''

''That does happen, doesn't it? You must meet her. The Tremonts are rather newcomers to the Square but such nice people. So well mannered and substantial. They do fit. Their house is on the north side, white pressed brick, one of the older ones . . . oh, dear!''

The girl had come to the open iron gates, in full view of Miss Phoebe's bench, then abruptly seemed to change her mind. She darted across the street and, in another moment, was lost behind the great oak doors of the church.

''Oh, dear, I thought she was coming this way. Noel, that is, Miss Tremont, does a great deal of good work for our church but I can't imagine why she's gone there now. The Mission Society met at eleven and the Ladies Guild doesn't meet until tomorrow. Well, to be young is to be vigorous.''

April clouds had begun their drift across the sun. Miss Phoebe pulled her shawl closer. ''It's been a pleasure to hear about England, Mr. . . .''

Ned was looking past her toward the church. Luck had brought him to this moment. Instinct told him that the moment had come. The girl he had just seen enter the church was indeed the girl who had collided with him that first day he had visited the Square. She could not be the same young woman he had seen leaving the darkened Restell house. Yet there was the light walk, the head carried high—the figure haunted him like a shadow on the retina when the eyes are closed. Miss Noel Tremont. He at least knew her name now.

". . . Mr. . . . uh?"

He was aware of the tiny woman beside him.

He bent his head deferentially. "Edmond Abbingdon-Fitch." He dropped a gentle emphasis on the middle name.

"Mr. *Abbingdon*-Fitch. How very English! My name was hyphenated, too. Once. Handon-Bliss. Miss Phoebe Hortense Handon-Bliss. But Pa*pa* said there was no better way to salute our new country than to drop the hyphen. So we saluted." She rose abruptly. "Oh, dear, I am forgetful. You wanted information."

Ned rose with her, edging away for a fuller view of the church doors.

"I can't impose on your time any longer, Madam."

"Nonsense. What do you want to know?"

What had he wanted to know? It had been an idle question, to learn something about the Square, or about Dr. Lendler, or perhaps merely to talk out of loneliness and forget the disturbing uncertainties of the past week. What he wanted now was to escape, to follow the girl. If he delayed he might lose even this small chance.

"I have plenty of time, Mr. Abbingdon-Fitch."

There was no help for it.

"I was merely wondering about that fine old church, but it's of no matter."

"Ahh. Our dear St. George's." Miss Phoebe launched into this pleasurable subject. "In 1752 it was known as St. George's Chapel of Ease. Isn't that sweet? On Beekman Street. Church of England then, of course. In 1846 it moved as a full-grown church to Stuyvesant Square." She waved a small possessive hand. "This was the last of Governor Peter Stuyvesant's farm, you know. The family deeded it to the city in 18 . . ."

Ned stole a glance at the closed doors of the church. It was not missed by Miss Phoebe.

". . . Protestant Episcopal now. Everything changes. They are even talking about abandoning private pews. Well, we are a republic. We must never forget that. Pro publica dear Pa*pa* used to say. Pro publica. Dear St. George's burned down twice. It's Romanesque now. Visitors are always welcome. Sunday service is at ten. When you're settled, Mr. Abbingdon-Fitch, you must come and tell me how you're getting along. I live on the south side of the Square, number 15. Good day, Mr. Abbingdon-Fitch."

Miss Phoebe's slight limp became a half skip as she hurried down the path. Beyond the security of two stalwart elm trees, she turned and looked back. She was not surprised to see the young man already crossing the street toward the church. But she had not expected quite the agility with which he bounded up the five steps and pulled at the heavy doors. It was, Miss Phoebe concluded homeward bound, a most unusual encounter.

In the basement choir room of the old church, rehearsal was going badly. The young tight-lipped choirmaster, Mr. Charlesworth, rapped impatiently, looked up, and saw with pleasure Miss Noel Tremont standing in the entranceway. His sallow cheeks pinked. Miss Tremont, as he so often told himself, was fresh air. At more secret hours he would sometimes add "and temptation." Not that she had ever given him so much as what he would call a real look. But the thought of Noel Tremont more than once slid between his concentration and the pages of the liturgy. There was something about her, a not-quite-Christian lack of humility. It would never do in a cleric's wife. But when he sometimes turned at service to catch a glimpse of her sitting twelfth row center left, her head held a little higher it always seemed than the others—oh, she had spirit. Indeed, one could say Miss Tremont had spirit.

"Do come in, Miss Tremont."

Heads turned. Noel smiled beneficently on the group. "I just wanted to tell you how splendid you all sound."

The young cleric felt his spectacles steam. "We try our best, Miss Tremont. We do indeed. Won't you stay and listen?"

There was a shuffling but Noel saw no extra chair.

"Another time I'd love to, Mr. Charlesworth. But I'm on my way to the Mission. Could I go out through the robing room?"

"I should think so. They're washing the floors, but I'll go with you."

"No, no. Please don't bother. I'll take another way out." She gave him a lovely smile. "But you're needed here, Mr. Charlesworth. Do go on with your rehearsal."

The young cleric blushed again, fumbled for words and lost.

To the uncertain strains of "Look ye Saints, the sight is glorious," Noel reclimbed the stairs into the body of the church, annoyed at herself and her playacting. She had let the mere sight of a stranger on a park bench, a man she had seen once and would not see again, send her running into the church like a schoolgirl. It was not only the sight of him that irritated her, but her own quick recognition of him, the unsettling recall, the quickening of her pulse, the flush of her face, which had cooled but could not be denied. She had believed that she had put the man out of her mind. Suddenly there he was again, with, of all people, Miss Phoebe Bliss. There was apparently no limit to his forwardness. She would not permit even Miss Phoebe to manipulate her into another confrontation with him.

She moved down a side aisle of the empty church, passing a center pew with a new brass nameplate, TREMONT. This outward evidence of social acceptance always made her uncomfortable. She slid instead into the dimmed quiet of a public side pew. She needed to clear her mind, to make sure of her own strength. And not on her knees. She had gone to church dutifully since she was old enough to be buttoned into a Sunday pinafore. She had been led then. Later she had gone, walking quietly beside her parents on pain of missing the Sunday roast beef dinner and the outing that followed up Fifth Avenue to the great reservoir. In her teens she had gone in silent rebellion, to see her mother, so kind, so devoted to them all, on her knees declaring herself a miserable sinner.

At her mother's coffin Noel had bowed her young head in compliance, but refused to beg God to take her mother among the angels. What other place could there be for such selflessness?

As time passed, the same demand for selflessness had begun its tug on Noel. In the now motherless family, someone must put order into the household. Someone must see that brothers had their chance. Someone must provide comfort for a lonely father. Noel found faith a weakening reed. She developed a stubborn self-reliance. Her inner life would be her own. There would lie the strength she needed. Or so she had thought until . . .

For an instant she covered her face with her hands, as if to shelter herself from the rush of emotion. Slowly it ebbed away. She had thought she was beyond such weakness. Why should she be vulnerable at this moment? Had she faith, she told herself, she might have seen this sudden yielding as a release, a gift of peace. But even in this place she barred self-indulgence as she barred intruders. There could be no release for her. She alone was responsible for the course her life had taken. It must be forever secret and alone.

Refreshed in spite of herself, she made her way down the aisle looking neither right nor left, her footsteps echoing like dropped pebbles of identity.

In a dark corner at the rear of the church near the tall doors, Ned waited. He had dismissed any twinge of propriety. The moment, the opportunity, that had flitted through every waking hour and broken his sleep had come. He would meet her, speak to her, convince himself that she was as he remembered her. She could not possibly have been that veiled figure he had seen through the darkness, hurrying from the scandalous house of Mrs. Restell. Yet the image, the similarity, haunted him. What if she were? Nothing could come of it. She might have gone there in charity, in kindness to that desperate woman, or to one of her patients. Found the house empty, silent, taken fright and fled, knowing nothing about the death that lay in the consulting room. Death that only he had seen, that not even the newspapers reported. He had gone over and over the sordid event, returning always to the same wishful conclusion. He could in no way relate this proud, proper, lovely girl to any of it.

He took a step forward. She had suddenly appeared from the side of the church. He watched her enter a pew. He saw her abruptly drop her face in her hands. Piety? He wondered about that. Hidden grief? The sudden gesture moved him. He felt awkward, prying, an outsider on the verge of a discovery he had no business to make.

She was at last coming down the center aisle toward him. In another instant, she would be out through the heavy doors.

"Good afternoon."

She blinked in the spring light and turned. He was nearly faceless, a darker silhouette among the shadows of the church to her light-struck glance. But she knew him. She would know him anywhere, she realized. And that was not to be tolerated. "Oh, it's you again."

"Nice of you to remember."

He moved nearer, shielding some of the light of the afternoon. "Now, don't run off as you did the last time. I simply wanted to say that our meeting in the park was entirely my fault. I was looking for an address and I thought you were the most likely person to give it to me. You see—oh well, a little honesty never hurts a man, does it?"

"Well, really. . . ."

"I could guess that a lot of men look at you."

"That is impertinent."

"Isn't it? But I have to make an impression in some way,

now, don't I? You see''—Ned's mind was working on two levels, the nearness of this girl and a searching to imagine those delicate features through a veil in a night mist—''I have some books to deliver here in Stuyvesant Square and the house number has been rain-washed off the package.''

Was that a flicker of a smile at the corners of her lips?

''A bad crossing. Terrible storm, everything soaking wet. The books dried out but''—he paused and looked down at her—''my name is Ned Fitch.''

''I'm sure the Curate can help you.'' Her voice was not as cool as she would have wished. ''It's his livelihood to know. You'll do him a favor.''

''The books are for a Dr. Hugo Lendler.'' He had to keep her there another few minutes. He felt like a drowning man, trying to stay afloat. Any life line would do.

''Well''—she had not quite turned away—''why didn't you say that? Although I still think it would be a kindness to ask the Curate. He tries so hard.''

''You know Dr. Lendler?'' Not that Ned cared. The devil with Dr. Lendler and his wet books. All that mattered at this moment of shadow and light was the nearness of this girl.

Noel in her own mind had committed a blunder. She had permitted herself to establish a connection with this total stranger. By lingering here, she was compounding it. Let him find his own way. She would, she must, leave at once. Then she made a second blunder. She met his eyes. The mischief of spring slipped between them.

''Dr. Lendler lives at number 72, directly across the Square.''

''Thank you,'' said Ned gravely.

''Good day, uh, Mr. Fitch.''

Miss Noel Tremont departed, down the granite steps, taking the afternoon light with her.

Ned stood for a moment longer, yielding to emotions unlike any he had known. All he knew of this girl was her name and where she lived. And the look she had not quite managed to conceal in her eyes. The mystery surrounding her had only deepened her fascination for him.

''Anything I can do for you, my good man?''

A young cleric in a long black gown, his nose twitching like a rabbit, was bearing down.

''No, thank you.''

''You're welcome to meditate. The side and rear pews are public.''

"Well now, fancy that!" Ned found himself unreasonably irritated.

The young cleric sighed. Why were the unfortunate of this world so difficult to help when Christian hands were so readily outstretched?

"If you're in need of food, there's a charity mission two blocks north, one block west. The Angel of Hope."

"Much obliged—your Worship."

Ned briskly left the church. He was indeed hungry, but he had no wish to return to the staleness of Mrs. Luskin's boarding house. Not yet. Charity soup it would be.

The sky had faded to a luminous melon-green as Ned reached Third Avenue and turned north. Along the side streets he could see the endless lines of roofs, pitch black against the dying afternoon. Overhead New York's forest of telegraph poles swung delicate scallops of wire into the light. Everywhere there were people, as if the throbbing city were pouring its entire population into the April twilight. Those not sitting on doorsteps were crowding the sidewalks. Newsboys, their fingers inked, bawled the evening editions. Fruit vendors briskly pushed their emptied carts through the traffic. Shawled women hawked yesterday's violets at passersby. Nursemaids hurried their infant charges home in basketlike prams. Young matrons, skirts ruffling to the sidewalk, carried spoils of the day's shopping—hatboxes, parcels of lace and ruchings, the delicious refubishings of spring.

From the river to the east came the hooted calls of ferry boats. Ned had heard that there were men rich and eccentric enough to live across the river on the wooded heights of Brooklyn and make the journey each morning and evening to and from their city offices by ferry.

In another two hours the horse-trams would be jammed with clerks and shop workers. Already traffic had slowed to a sluggish crawl. It was said to take a man two hours to travel by cab from his business in Wall Street to his home on Thirtieth. In another decade, wags predicted, congestion would bring all traffic to the ultimate, impenetrable halt; a man might leave for work a bridegroom and return a grandfather.

Ned crossed the street, skidding in the melted drippings of an ice wagon.

"Look where yer goin', y'fool!" A whip cracked past him.

The Angel of Hope Mission turned out to be a former store, its windows reasonably clean, the name in plain black letters on a dull green door. Ned found himself in a long narrow room, with mustard-colored walls, half filled with rows of unpainted wooden chairs. Against the right-hand wall stood a square piano, its varnish long gone, its lid supporting a stack of worn cloth-bound books. Hymn books, Ned saw. Across the rear of the room stretched a counter, its white oilcloth cover gleaming in the half light. Although there was no evidence of food and the oil lamps had not yet been turned up, a few men had already taken chairs.

Ned could not guess their ages. Their clothes were a comic-tragic assortment of misfits, worn with the grey dust of defeat. From whatever lost hopes they had come, they shared one thing in common. They were hungry.

Ned chose a chair beside a squat little man with bowed legs. The man's knitted cap showed a gaping tear. Through it Ned could see a skull bald as an egg. The man's eyes held the blunted weariness of a worn-out horse. He pulled constantly at his lower lip, revealing two blackened teeth—one upper, one lower. They did not meet.

When he spoke at last his breath was fetid.

"Best to be early, son. Then wait a bit. Soup's thicker near the bottom of the pot."

The room was filling rapidly. The little man leaned confidentially again toward Ned.

"I've been to all of them, son. Angel's the best. Shall I show you something?" He gave a grating chuckle and opened the flap of his outsized coat. In a cavernous inner pocket Ned saw the outline of a bottle. "Meet my friend, Johnnie B. Best friend a man could have. I shoveled coal three days for him. I couldn't leave him behind, now could I?" Under the shield of his coat, the little man ducked his head. Ned heard a long, gurgling sound. The head emerged and the little man opened his coat to Ned.

"Go on, son. You've a good face. Meet my friend. He'll see you to the end of a bad day. Go on there, go on!"

Ned took the bottle. To avoid an argument, he told himself, but the truth was that he was beginning to enjoy himself. No pretense here. No false manners. No trying to please or fear of making mistakes. He was among comrades he understood. All of them like himself. Hungry.

The raw liquor burned his throat. But the heat reaching his empty stomach brought unexpected solace. He took another draught, long, deep, and satisfying. The little man snatched at the bottle and thrust it back into hiding.

A woman enveloped in a long white apron, a Mother Hubbard as it was known, began to turn up the oil lamps. From her bearing, the correct upsweep of her fine brown hair, the severity of her glance, Ned would have called her a lady.

"That's the old turkey hen herself," the little man whispered. "She sees everything. After the soup, she passes out the hymn books. You gotta sing by way of paying for the food." He patted his overcoat. "I tell you, my friend comes in handy then."

Another white-aproned lady carried in a large carton containing stacks of saucerlike tin bowls. A third followed with a shallow box of tin spoons. Piles of bread on tin plates appeared on the counter. The men began to shuffle into line. Two steaming cauldrons were set in place, eyed eagerly.

The little man beside Ned opened his overcoat and in a new bright beneficence held out the bottle. It was a mistake.

The "turkey hen" bore down on him like a bird of prey. "It's you again, Mr. Lafferty!"

The little man, a stricken field mouse, cowered and released the bottle to the talon fingers.

"You've been warned, Mr. Lafferty! Time and time again! It's against the rules. I'm ashamed of you. You're a disgrace to this Mission and a sinner in the eyes of God whose kindness has brought you here!"

Straight-backed, she marched to the door, opened it, and hurled the offending bottle into the areaway of the building. The shattering glass seemed to thrust a splinter into the breast of every man watching. A silence followed.

The little man rose. He pulled once on his mouth, a watery brightness filled his eyes and threatened at any moment to furrow down his dirty grey cheeks. In dignity he walked to the door, turned, and lifted his head to his tormentor.

"That was my friend. You—you killed him."

The door closed quietly behind him.

A communal sigh swept the room. The gaunt woman regained command. "Move along now. We can't let the soup get cold."

But in Ned, the fire of bad whiskey coupled with the anger of injustice climaxed a long day. He jumped up on a chair, gathering stolid looks from the men.

"They call this charity? If God's kindness has brought you here what in hell has He been doing with you the rest of the time?"

There was a spattering of grunts and a half laugh or two.

"I haven't tasted their soup, but I'll wager it's boiled from one old mare's shank without marrow and last week's vegetables rotting on the grocer's floor. What do these fine ladies know about the hunger in a man's gut? That little chap needed his drink, like any one of us when the kindness of God has us down on our backs and struggling. Maybe he'll find another. I hope he does. But while he's holed up somewhere, cold and friendless tonight, these fine ladies will be home at their grate fires with their warm clothes and clean tables. Another day's charity soup served up, and be damned to the man who wants anything else!"

If he heard feminine gasps he ignored them. He turned his back on the fluttering white aprons.

"You're supposed to sing for your supper. All right, I'll give you something to sing. Something to entertain these ladies! If they had men at home half as good as you chaps, they wouldn't be here now, would they, mates?"

A few uneasy cheers answered him.

With a voice as robust as it was off pitch, Ned roared out the old song. In his blurred mind he was back in The Nailhead pub, Millie beside him, and the river mist rolling yellow in the night. . . . "She loved not the savor of tar nor of pitch; yet a sailor might scratch her where'er she did itch! Then to sea, boys, and let her go hang!"

Worn faces broke into grins. Through hoarse laughter the men picked up the bawdy words. Ned shouted the last two lines again, swung his cap with a wild flourish. It fell from his hand. He jumped from the chair, made a low, unsteady bow and lifted his head to look directly into the face of Miss Noel Tremont.

Without expression, she picked up the fallen cap.

"You've given us quite a novelty," she said icily. "But misguided as we may be, we must have order." Her glance swept the group of silenced men. "If any of the rest of you believe that our performance here is inadequate to our intention, please feel free to leave. Otherwise you are all welcome. But I must ask for your usual courtesy and patience just a little longer. We pride ourselves on beef soup that is hot!"

Her face was dead white and oddly young beneath its authority. As she thrust the dusty cap out to Ned, a faint flush stained her cheekbones. She turned abruptly away.

A round bundle of white apron descended on him.

"There's not much to be said for you, young man, but we don't turn anyone away." She pushed a broom into his hand and an empty flour sack. "Sweep up that broken glass in the areaway and put the bag in the trash bin. That'll be for penance. Then you may have your soup."

Mechanically he took the broom and sack and walked out

into the night. He had no desire to return. His sudden confrontation with Miss Tremont had sobered him to icy reality. "A fine wrinkle of things you've made now, Fitch, my lord. A Cheapside bloke you are and no better. And all it took was the worst drink a man ever poured into his gut."

He descended to the areaway and began to sweep, because it was better than doing nothing. Miss Noel Tremont was a lady. She was also, in a rare, old print way, very lovely. Worst of all, she was intelligent, the kind who knew too much to forget or forgive.

He swept the broken glass into the sack and dropped it into the bin. He would stand out here all night if necessary for the chance to see her again. He wondered what he, or any other man in his worn boots, could offer as an apology.

The first spring warmth had fled. A cold night wind blew from the river. What a climate this city had! A man could freeze solid even while he was looking at the first crocus. People were the same way—take a man at his best or his worst, no halfway about it. Ned pulled his jacket closer and waited.

From above came the thin strains of payment due for a bowl of soup. To the accompaniment of a tinny piano, a forthright female voice, and a few quavery male mutterings, Ned could hear the words of salvation. "Throw out a lifeline, throw out a lifeline, someone is drifting . . . drifting to shoore. . . ."

Suddenly in the semidark outside the Mission door, there she was, Miss Noel Tremont, on her way home. Ned moved faster than he could ever remember and forgot any prepared speech.

"Miss Tremont. . . ."

"Oh, it's you." She seemed to come back from a distant place.

"Miss Tremont, I'd like to apologize, or to try to apologize—"

"I'm sure you would. But there's no need. A man says what he thinks. I admire that ability. You were quite accurate. Charity is a cold business. Miss Pendleton should not have thrown away Mr. Lafferty's whiskey. She should simply have put it away. But she's lived for forty-five years with a very irritable mother and one does have one's limits. Good night."

"Miss Tremont, isn't there something I can do or say. . . ."

She turned abruptly, her face a cold cameo in the ring of gaslight.

"Yes, there is, Mr., what is it? Fitch? You can stop following me."

"Follow . . . ?" He was losing ground. It was not going at all as he had planned. "Follow . . . ?"

"I am not stupid." For the first time she looked at him fully, directly. "I am not unaware of when or how a man looks at me. I have seen you. Once, twice . . . and now tonight. Without being either coy or brazen, I must tell you the simple truth. Nothing can come of your following me. Or trying to know me. Nothing. Please do not intrude in my life again. Now or—ever!"

It seemed to Ned that a tremor belied the severity of that final word. But it was too late to protest or to make amends if any could be made. She had turned and was gone, a vanishing yet somehow familiar figure down a dimming street.

It was not the way Ned had planned or even imagined their next meeting. It was to have been courteous yet knowing, mannered yet aware. Instead she had seen him at his worst, as vulgar, as loud, as the lowest street bummer in a London pub.

Yet out of the black despair of his mood, an odd thing happened, a sensation bordering near-relief. There was no need for pretense now, there could be none between Miss Noel Tremont and himself. He could almost smile. So much contained fury beneath such a small hat. So much indignation in that careful, precise voice. He was conscious only of her nearness. And he believed—no, it was more than belief, it was as deep as a man's instinct could tell—that she had been as conscious of him.

Common sense returned and with it reality as chill as the newly risen wind from the river. A fool he was, standing on a dark street corner in need of decent clothes, a living to be made, a food in his belly. Mooning instead over his instincts, his dreams, and a girl who in all likelihood would never speak to him again.

But if she did, Ned told himself vengefully, Miss Noel Tremont might indeed consider offering him her own apology.

He picked up his neglected broom and went into the Mission. There might still be dregs in the charity pot. Hadn't his recent friend told him it was better near the bottom?

11

The young Mrs. Walter C. Tremont was giving one of her much admired *dîners intimes,* small parties of twelve to fourteen guests at which her youthful beauty shone unrivaled.

They were, Adrienne admitted to Cousin Kitty, a good deal more tiring than a single large *soiree* that, if the musicians and champagne were above average and the supper of adequate sophistication, would usually run by itself.

"Of course small parties always take more effort." Kitty was airy and knowing. "But a young hostess entering society should be known for a speciality. Your little dinners are already being talked about. And it's a master stroke to serve five courses instead of eight. People are noticing. Besides, Ada . . . Adrienne . . . I'm here to help you."

Very easily Kitty Merriman had slipped from the role of doyenne and marriage maker to social mentor, planner, and inevitable guest in the Tremont household.

"Why shouldn't I?" Kitty asked defiantly of her husband as she sat at her dressing table powdering the deep decolletage above her camisole. "I don't propose to see Ada stuck down in Stuyvesant Square while Walter dozes the evening away behind his newspaper. And Noel will do nothing. Absolutely nothing. Oh, she'll be at dinner. She'll sit there looking as if she were a hundred miles away. I sometimes wonder what the girl thinks about." Kitty whirled from the mirror. "Now, lace me up!"

Watching his wife dress was one of Henry's few remaining marital privileges. It would not last, he knew, after Kitty obtained the French maid she coveted. That hardly seemed likely yet, but he would not bring the ugly question of their finances into the anticipation of the evening.

She stood clinging to the bedpost. He tugged at the corset lacings until the seventeen-and-a-half-inch waist was achieved, her breasts thrusting youthfully upward and her flesh warming. Henry sank back onto the chaise lounge, florid and perspiring above his stiff dinner collar.

"Are we going to be late as usual?" He asked more out of irritation than concern.

Kitty's hands moved among her jars.

"Of course we're going to be late as usual. Considering most of the guest list is mine, it would hardly do to upstage the hostess. Now, Henry, don't get that look. Cousin Ada owes me a great deal for that comfortable marriage of hers. And her social success. She wouldn't have the faintest idea of how to begin to enter society without my help. Besides . . ."

She studied her face and touched her lips. Beet juice, she had told Henry; all the ladies used it. But he knew better. Among her salves and pomades was French rouge, the stuff to him of questionable reputation. But she was clever about it, as she was about so many things. Clever and daring. Henry turned his blunt, honest mind to the contemplation of his wife's shoulders.

"Besides," she continued, "Walter can well afford Adrienne's little dinner parties that are so convenient for us."

He did not remind her that Walter had recently been very generous. His loan of $20,000 could well have taken them out of all their financial difficulties. But Kitty had had a better idea. She had heard that shares in the proposed West Shore Railroad, on the west side of the Hudson River, were on the market. She had been assured on the very best authority that they would triple. Walter's loan—Henry would not bring that up now. Kitty looked so pretty, so pert, she was obviously anticipating the evening.

She rose from her mirror.

"Henry, I wish that just once you would understand all that I try to do. Not only for Adrienne, but there's Noel. I'm mortally tired of going to Adrienne's dinner parties with Noel sitting there, so obviously single and the only available man there that dreary little professor with all the books. Oh, for heaven's sake, Henry, don't make me explain everything! All a man has to do is go out and make money. A woman's duty is to manage everything else, make it sensible, civilized. Henry, you will be nice tonight?"

"She's a damn good-looking girl."

"Who?"

"Noel."

Kitty shot him a curious glance.

* * *

Adrienne's *dîners* were always innovative. The dining room, like the entire house, defied the smothering plush of New York fashion. Cream walls, spills of floor-length draperies, delicate French carved mahogany and pearwood invited pleasure. The long Chippendale table bore the airiness of cut crystal and vermeil, and two bowls of yellow primroses and hothouse daisies low enough to permit guests not only to see but to talk across the narrow table. Over it all, Adrienne reigned, in the palest of apricot silk, as if wrapped in candlelight.

Dinner was limited to nine. Senator and Mrs. Franklin Walsh, at Kitty's suggestion, and a large lady wrapped in purple tulle, also Kitty's addition. The novelty was a three-inch square of gold-edge Limoges china at each place announcing, in Adrienne's fine penmanship, the menu for the evening. "Consommé tortu, truite amandine. . . ."

Everyone pronounced the idea charming and so French. Adrienne smiled. Kitty's laugh tinkled, light and brittle, her dark eyes flashing at the Senator. Down the table at Walter's left, Mrs. Walsh watched silently. Kitty Merriman, lively as she was, was no more than a common climber, the kind of woman dear Franklin could never abide. Which was in fact the effect Kitty wished to achieve. She could charm the Senator any time she needed him. Someday she might need the Senator's wife.

For Noel, seated next to Henry, the scene was as transparent as it was distant. To her relief, no young man had been produced for her benefit. She could watch Kitty flirt. She could speculate whether Senator Walsh's absurdly high collar was celluloid or stiff linen. Or she could fix her gaze on a corner of the room, grateful that Dr. Hugo Lendler had for once not been placed conspicuously beside her. His attention was dutifully turned to the lady in purple, with the long face of a mournful horse.

Noel glanced at her father. Couldn't he see what these dinners were? His benign expression warned her to channel her thoughts.

Channel them she must, as she must ignore a letter that lay thrust beneath the taupe silk bodice of her dinner dress. It was not a letter she might secretly like to receive. It had come joltingly in the afternoon mail, on coarse white paper, postmarked Riveredge. It lay like a blade against her breast, and, as it seemed to her, visible to anyone.

The purple-tulled lady was trumpeting through her prominent nose.

"Ah yes, dear friends. Water! Heaven's mystical gift. We come from water. Ninety-seven percent of our body is Water. Water holds the secret of all healing. Discover its power. On the mind. The flesh. And for men who have reached the age . . ."

At that, Henry rose unsteadily to his feet.

"Water, my dear lady, is to wash streets. Wine is to waken love. A toast to our lovely hostess, our Venus of the night, and to my old friend Walter, who has found perfection!"

A gasp from the Senator's wife, a sharp look from Kitty, as Walter nodded gallantly.

"Thank you, Henry. Doesn't every lady carry her own perfection?"

What would they say, Noel thought, if she suddenly pushed from the table, ran from the room, the house, the faces, forever? Or better still, stood up and defied the trivialities, stripping away the layers of whalebone and pretense, or propriety and boredom and malice, revealing the truth about themselves and about herself? She closed her eyes.

"Are you feeling quite well, my dear?"

She returned to the present. "I'm feeling splendidly, thank you, Uncle Henry. I was remembering something. Remember, Father? The time the minister from St. George's came to dinner? I imagined there was a mouse in the soup tureen and surely enough when Mrs. Jessup lifted the lid . . ."

Noel was conscious of startled faces turned toward her. What did it matter what she said or what they thought? Tomorrow or the next day might blow them all away from her life, like smoke.

Dinner was nearly over. It would be followed by another of Adrienne's innovations. No port and cigars at the table for the gentlemen, no retirement for the ladies to the boudoir for titillating gossip. Adrienne would conduct her guests to the drawing room for coffee, after which she would move gracefully to the piano.

Noel was aware of her father's concerned glance. Had she spoiled Adrienne's—no, Kitty's—little party? It had not been her intention. In a way she cared for them deeply. They were the fabric of her days. Yet when they cornered her . . .

To her relief the lady in purple suddenly drew a long breath and boomed.

"I feel a mystic influence in this house. A kindred presence. Does anyone here know a man named Goodfellow?"

"Goodfellow!" Kitty echoed the name, eager to restore the evening. "Adrienne, didn't you tell me that was the name

David . . . ?" Adrienne's eyes were fixed on her plate. "No, of course you didn't, dear. I was thinking of someone else."

The lady in purple held to her course. "I share a psychic message with Mr. Goodfellow. We have been touched by the same spirits beyond the grave."

There was an awkward pause. Walter felt his spine stiffen. While spiritualism might be fashionable among susceptible ladies of leisure, it had no place in the home of a sensible man.

The Senator's wife leaned a heavy bosom against the table, eyes bright as a chipmunk's. "Pray do go on, Mrs. Palstead."

The lady in purple beamed. "It was the picture, dear, the drawing Mr. Goodfellow did in the newspaper. A coffin being lowered into an open grave. He had sketched a woman's picture above it. No mistake. That noble brow, those plumes on her hat. Mrs. Restell! Over it he had printed a caption. 'Willing or Unwilling?' That was all. 'Willing or Unwilling?' But it told me that Mr. Goodfellow had received a message from beyond. That poor woman's spirit is seeking to tell us something!"

A glass tipped, its stem shattering against a plate. It was the wine goblet at Noel's place.

"Oh, I'm sorry, Adrienne. Your lovely glasses!"

Senator Walsh dropped a fist on the table. "Mrs. Walsh, ma'am, has a morbid curiosity about the hereafter. I should be happy not to have it gratified. The Restell matter has been thoroughly and satisfactorily disposed of by the police. I doubt if that woman has any wish to return from wherever she took herself."

Walter scowled. This is what came of eliminating the sound masculine custom of after-dinner port and cigars. Subjects like this brought up in mixed company. He cleared his throat.

"My young son, David, has a rather misguided sense of whimsy. He adopted the name Goodfellow, Shakespeare's Puck, you recall, for his newspaper articles. He is a young man of more than average talent. He has elected to waste it on the sordid aspects of city life. He no longer lives at home. Adrienne, my dear, what is the address of David's rooming house?"

Adrienne's brow displayed a small furrow, her smile was bland. "Why, I don't know, dear. I don't believe you ever mentioned it."

Dinner had ended. Adrienne gathered her guests with that

serenity that seemed to erase all undercurrents and cross purposes beneath the evening's surface.

At Adrienne's signal, Noel dutifully seated herself on the tasseled piano stool. Adrienne extended an exquisite arm on the piano's polished rosewood. Her light, silvery voice rose chastely. "I hear the wee bird sing. . . ." It was followed by the favorite ballad, the season's most popular extravaganza, "Evangele." With melting directness Adrienne sang to her husband, managing both naïveté and passion. "Come to me quickly, my darling," the youthful voice coaxed. The applause was instant.

Walter stirred in his chair. He already regretted his quite unnecessary question to her about David's address. He knew the deep-buried dark area in his mind that had prompted it, the shadow never quite banished. An incident that had occurred the evening he had presented David to Adrienne, his stepmother-to-be. Yet it was hardly an incident. It was more like an instant's second sight, a double image when he had seen them standing together. The sudden girlish flush in Adrienne's cheeks, David's lingering glance. How well-matched they were, how young, how golden, and he himself a middle-aged—no, aging—man between them. He had banished the idea as unworthy, yet he could still feel his guilty relief when David announced he would no longer live at home.

The evening ended. Noel took her place dutifully beside her father and Adrienne as the guests departed to their carriages. Dr. Lendler was the last to leave. He took her extended hand, concern in his voice.

"My dear—your playing . . ."

"Dreadful, wasn't it? I hate gushy ballads."

"Mozart will take care of that."

She gave him a lovely smile. "I'll practice, Dr. Lendler, I really will."

At last she stood in the empty hall, the door still open to the spring night. The letter beneath the silk of her bodice told her that the time for frivolity was over. Yet she did not close the door. So little time was left to her, to be herself, to look into that innermost core of feelings, to remember what could not be hers to remember.

Ned Fitch was his name, his manners as plain as his behavior had been outrageous. She saw him at the Mission, had it been as long as a week ago? His dark hair tousled, fury in his face, his song shockingly bawdy. And the Mission ladies! Noel smothered a giggle, her imagination darting like a firefly in the dark. She saw Ned as he might have been in evening clothes at her father's table tonight, handsome, bantering, holding them all with his talk. Kitty would bat her eyes, Adrienne would practice her languorous seduction, her father would be courteous, but careful, measuring. Ned would be seated next to her and none of it would matter except their awareness.

So does the spellbound mind work. A lifetime of imagined events lived in seconds, leaving a drop of radiance distilled in the dragging monotony of the days.

Abruptly Noel returned to reality and stared into the night. Across the street, against the railing of the park leaned a man—tall, motionless, disturbingly recognizable. Had her own thoughts conjured him?

She heard steps behind her in the hall.

"Noel? Still downstairs?"

In the bull's-eye mirror, thirty-six diminished fathers were coming toward her to emerge in a single bulky figure, weighted with weariness.

"You'll catch your death of cold, my dear, at that open door!"

Mechanically she pushed it closed.

"It was a lovely party, Father."

But Walter's good humor had gone. "I regret the turn it took. Give Frank Walsh a little rope and he'll talk about anything. I don't want the Restell woman discussed in my house again. I'm afraid Adrienne sets too much store by these little parties." As if to end what was nearing criticism he tested the doorknob. It was firmly latched. "Noel, you're looking too pale these days. Your mother would have ordered spring tonic."

"I'm past the age for sulphur and molasses, Father."

"A girl needs pink cheeks to be pretty. Maybe a little salt air. You'll open the Far Rockaway house again for us this summer, Noel?"

Their sprawling old-fashioned summer home on the ocean's edge was the place her father loved most. Adrienne had tacitly but unmistakably rejected it. It had become Noel's duty.

She left the question unanswered. "I—I'm going up to Riveredge before that, Father."

"Splendid. A visit up there always does you good I've noticed. Good country living. When are you leaving?"

He had made it easy. "Probably tomorrow."

"Splendid. You'll need a little money. Cab fare, a ticket, a present for your friends." He enjoyed head-of-the-family generosity. From his wallet, he counted out a five-dollar bill and three singles. "There you are, my dear, don't stay too long. I don't think I can spare you."

Eight dollars when she might need eighty, or eight hundred? The solid wealth her father had made of his business was all around her, yet unreachable as the understanding on which he prided himself, as the love that had no other expression than this bearlike protection.

"It's late, Noel. Time for you to be in bed."

"Yes, Father."

She watched his slow tread on the stairs, heard the bedroom door close. The figure in the darkness of the park? Was he still there? If he was, would she dare? A giddiness seized her, impulse with a magnet's force.

She tiptoed to the closet and took out a shawl. She would not be long, she told herself, not long at all. In another instant she was down the steps and into the safe shadows of the trees.

"What kept you?"

He had stepped to meet her as if for a carefully planned tryst. She had made it that. What could she say? She was never very good at fluttering.

"Oh! Mr. Fitch! I hardly expected. . . . I—I came out for some air."

"Miss Tremont, you stood at the door. You saw me. And high time. If the truth were known I've been walking up and down outside your elegant house for hours. I saw you through the curtains at the piano. Charming—"

"You watched me!"

"And the lady standing beside you with her mouth open. Singing, I take it. It seemed forever. I had about decided if I were to see you at all I'd have to ring your doorbell. Oh, don't look so startled. I'm prepared. I've a proper suit, obtained on my last, positively last, credit from my friend, Mr. Monk, dealer in secondhand clothes. But would you understand that? To make matters plain, I had to see you again."

The cold air did little against the heady flow of his words. She tried in deepening waters, to clutch at the raft of reality.

"Really, Mr. Fitch! You have the most astonishing way. . . ."

If she expected an answer, she found herself listening to silence, what seemed a river of it. He was looking down into her face.

"You knew that I wanted to see you. I had an idea that you might not be unwilling."

Her shawl felt suddenly too close, the night seemed to have

warmed. She searched for words, proper words, and did not find them.

"Too soon to talk, isn't it?" His smile was knowing, confident. "So we'll walk. Do they lock up your park at night?" He touched her arm, then firmly took her elbow. He shortened his steps to match hers, the whole unlikely incident slipping into the semblance of a dream.

The Square was deserted. The promise of spring enclosed them, as palpable as a curtain against the passing of time, against the world beyond. In a pool of dim lamplight she found herself looking up at him, surprised at a gentleness in his face.

He caught her look. "You're smiling."

"I sometimes do."

"It's becoming."

The last gate into the park had been closed. But by now the night's sweetness bound them, an unspoken awareness, a subtle tension, as exquisite as the mingling of desire and denial those locked gates imposed. They walked more slowly, as though even a word would shatter the hushed spell of the night.

Timeless, close, they walked the four sides of the Square, Noel's arm now tucked unbelievably beneath his. At the steps of her father's house, she stopped, drew a short breath, and drew her arm away. Ned tightened it to his side.

"Not yet, Noel."

Her first name! It lit the sky. By every social rule, a gentleman waited weeks, months, before he dared use it. Ned had turned it into immediate intimacy, confident, accepted.

"I must go in. I—I must."

"Very well." But he was not ready to release her. "But one question. Just one. And an honest answer." In the vibrancy of his voice, the night's magic lingered. "Be honest, Noel."

"I usually try."

He hesitated. "Is there any possible way? For us?"

What could she say? What right had she to allow a man into her life now? What dared she tell him that she could tell no one else? Spring's giddiness dissolved. The letter lay sharp against her breast.

"I—I can't talk. Not now."

"I understand." The gentleness had gone from his face. The familiar mockery edged his words. "No answer, is that it? Better no answer than the wrong one. But I should warn you. I'm a stubborn man, not to be managed by a slip of a girl after a pretty walk in the night air. You'll see me again. I'll walk past your door by day, your windows at night and between times. Unless you choose to call the patrol."

Banter. But at least it was safe ground.

"I do my own defending, Mr. Fitch."

"Then we shall manage very well, Miss Tremont."

Then he did an extraordinary thing. He bent his head and touched her hair with his lips.

In her room, Noel held cold hands to her face. She had been as vulnerable as a schoolgirl. She had invited, no, sought the encounter. She had willfully gone out to meet this man, no more than a stranger, a man who challenged her at every turn, matched wits with her every time she spoke and promised to see her as often as he wished, not as she wished. Even in the folly of the night she should have cut him short. But she had done just that on two other occasions. It had not worked. Had she wanted it to work?

She began to pack mechanically for her journey. She opened the wardrobe that contained her suits and dresses. And gasped. The brown moire silk street dress she had discarded weeks ago hung before her, cleaned and mended. Annie-Mae had done her best. But Noel could see, at the bottom of the skirt, the damage that could not be repaired. A piece of the fabric had been torn from it.

The dress had become a symbol, a persecutor of her buried fears. She snatched it from the wardrobe, rolled it up, and flung it into the wastebasket. Annie-Mae could keep it or do with it as she wished in the morning.

Shaken, Noel finished her packing. She took from the bodice of her dinner gown the letter she had concealed since afternoon. She had no need to read it. She knew its contents by heart. Without heading or signature, three words lay as if shaken from a desperate hand. "Come at once."

Her journey had taken on the semblance of flight.

12

A crash shattered the early morning silence of the quiet little house. Dr. Hugo Lendler retrieved the exercise dumbbell from where it had rolled and stored it in a felt-lined box. The noise, he knew, would reach his formidable housekeeper, Frau Gruen, in her kitchen. Faint, but sure enough to cause her to roll her eyes upward and mutter. Should he drop the other one, she would come into the hall. A third untoward noise from his attic gymnasium would bring her halfway up the stairs.

"Herr Professor! Ist etwas los?"

Of course nothing was wrong. He disliked the question. He wondered peevishly at what age the women in a man's household began asking about his welfare. Like twenty years of a dull marriage, when a wife masks her irritation with overconcern. He was, after all, not yet forty-five.

He placed the second dumbbell beside the first and set the box on its shelf. He covered the parallel bars in the center of the room with a dust sheet and aligned the pulley rings hanging against the wall. His exercises had gone clumsily and he knew the reason. To obtain the best for his body, his mind must be emptied, freed of distraction. It was anything but that, this morning. It was cluttered with disturbing impressions from Adrienne Tremont's lamentable dinner party. He foresaw the time when he could settle into the eccentricities of accumulated years and decline all social invitations. But that hour had not yet arrived. Not while Noel Tremont could sit at her father's dinner table, smile steadily, say nothing, her face white as chalk, her eyes as distant as if none of them were present.

As if, he thought to himself, there was anything he, in truth, could do for Noel. The present was forbidden him, as was the future. He reached for a towel and stepped into the tin-lined shower closet adjoining his apparatus room.

All this Dr. Lendler had designed for himself. It was, as he often admitted, at considerable distance from its inspiration, a sketch he had once seen in a Vienna quarterly. It had portrayed the stark efficiency of a gymnasium that Empress Elizabeth of Austria had ordered for herself within the very grandeur of the Hofburg. Recognized as the most beautiful woman in Europe, the lissom Empress had no intention of thickening into the accepted shape of royalty.

Dr. Lendler had applauded. If more women exercised, smelling salts and corset strings might become as vestigial as the human tail. As for himself, long hardened to discipline, exercise was a fourth dimension. In the privacy of his narrow brownstone house, he had converted a dusty pitched attic space into four walls just large enough to contain his equipment. The room was without windows and without a mirror. A narrow skylight let in barely sufficient illumination, but as it was morning light it satisfied Dr. Lendler. For here, within these close walls, the little professor started each day, deriving from this lonely half hour an inner knowledge of himself, of his own strength, of the man the world did not see.

Stripped as he was now, Hugo Lendler was a powerful man. His legs were built to support a tall frame. The muscles of his thighs and forearms moved with well-developed ease. Only an accident in infancy at the hands of a perverse fate had pushed a vertebra so sharply out of place that his shoulder had been thrust forward and his spine shortened. Hugo Lendler stood shorter than most men. His mother, her eyes heavy with guilt, would look at his young body in silence. But his father was harsher. It did not matter how tall a man stood, but how tall a man thought. The mind was the essence of a man. What he did with his mind would govern his life.

Hugo Lendler had long ago rid himself of self-pity, or the self-indulgence of wondering to what heights a straight back would have taken him. He did what he could for his body each morning and finished the discipline by stepping into his shower. It was an ingenious contraption, a wooden washtub suspended by chains from the ceiling. A valve in its base released water into a perforated bucket attached below. A simple tug on a rope and Dr. Lendler stood for precisely two minutes in the icy spill. In winter the water was nearly freezing. In summer he hoisted a cake of ice up into the overhead washtub.

Another three minutes and Dr. Lendler, wrapped in a plaid

woolen robe, reentered his second-floor bedroom. Promptly at quarter to eight he sat down to his breakfast, a sense of restored well-being warming his Viennese *Gruss Gott* to Frau Gruen.

She returned an unsmiling nod. She regarded the apparatus in the attic as no less sinister than the cabinet of a stage magician. It was *her* ministrations that kept Herr Professor in health, not that monstrous *teuflische Falle* that threatened to drown them all. Who all was, she could not have said, for Frau Gruen would have no other woman in service to the house. She relied for whatever help she needed on a scrawny youth named Billy Gribbs who in winter cleaned the coal grates and in spring rolled up the carpets and carried them into the backyard. There for a week he could be seen performing the seasonal rite of beating them clean, a thin dancing figure in a cloud of dust.

Frau Gruen would have been outraged to know that young Billy's wages went directly to a shiftless father whose response was likely to be a cuff on the cheek and a berating for taking the dirty money of a Jew.

Dr. Lendler would have been less surprised. He had met bigotry early, as early as childhood. Even in this brash new city of a thousand hopes, he had found it, funguslike, in the dark places of men's minds, in ignorance, in distrust, in deprivation. He lived with it because he must, as with winter dust. Someday in the spring sunlight, in a warmer, kindlier world, there might come a time. . . . At that point Dr. Lendler would bring himself up short. Fancies were for the idle, the undisciplined. Better to be a good teacher than a bad poet. He had a day's work ahead. And there, in Dr. Lendler's philosophy, lay a man's salvation.

Now, finishing a hearty breakfast of Frau Gruen's excellent potato pancakes with lingonberries, Dr. Lendler walked to the bow window in his parlor that looked out on Stuyvesant Square. He was an observer of people. He cherished these few minutes when, hands clasped behind his back, he watched the little park come to life. Schoolchildren, the girls walking primly together in their thick white stockings and their top-heavy hats, the boys in black stockings and knickers, coats open to the spring day, peaked caps awry. They would swing their schoolbooks by long canvas straps at each other or, more daringly, at the girls who would squeak and scatter like small birds until it was safe to group again.

It was early enough to see an occasional laborer with a lunch pail take a shortcut through the park's paths or a new-style office girl, her hat sensibly straight, her serge suit unadorned, her black buttoned shoes sturdy enough for the puddles she must walk through.

But Hugo Lendler did not deceive himself. In this early morning interlude at his bow window he could sometimes catch a glimpse of that slight, erect figure with the small, tilted hat, the brisk step, the skirt that swung with such elegance. He did not try to guess all the errands that took Noel Tremont from the comfort of her father's house. He knew deeper than instinct her need of freedom.

But he had made one never-to-be-repeated mistake. Caught in the closeness of the music they shared, he had revealed his feeling. She was too intelligent not to have understood, too kind to rebuff him openly. He would never put her to such a test again. It was in his nature to protect what he held dear. His role was and would be forever as her silent, secret guardian. An acute memory returned. It was at this same window he had seen her walk swiftly, unseeingly into the arms of a tall stranger. In Dr. Lendler's imagination, she had seemed to linger there. He had turned abruptly from the window. Yet it was not the incident that had imprinted itself so lastingly on his mind. It was the intensity of his own emotions.

From the mantel the porcelain Bidermeier clock with its bright brass pendulum struck a warning. Frau Gruen was in the hall holding his loose overcoat and soft wide-brimmed hat.

"I have an appointment this morning and a lecture this afternoon. I shall not be home for lunch." Dr. Lendler knew she took pleasure in following his routine.

But he did not tell her the purpose of his appointment. She would not understand that in this new country one could be summoned to the police station for a purpose other than being arrested and jailed.

"Guten tag, Herr Professor."

Captain Joseph Schwartz of the Eighth Precinct glanced up at the white-faced wall clock in his cluttered little office and walked to the door. His visitor would be prompt. At the desk outside a young lieutenant commanded a bleak waiting room. A single barred window threw a shaft of dusty grey light across the floor. A long bench was fully occupied with an assortment of human beings, some angry, some restless, a few numb and expressionless, all chips of flotsam on the swift currents of an indifferent city, robbed of a sense of time and place.

Captain Schwartz lowered his voice. "I'm expecting Dr. Hugo Lendler. Show him in as soon as he arrives."

"Yes, sir." The young subordinate looked toward the bench. " 'Madam' Rosanna said her appointment was for nine."

"Appointment, is it? Tell Rosie she's late and she'll have to take her turn. She can wait or go."

"She won't like it, Chief. She says your bully boys have been coming around bothering her."

A large woman in puce sateen rose from the bench, the ostrich plumes on her hat waving furiously. Captain Schwartz bowed and turned a hefty back. The woman sat down.

"Sure they did, on my orders. She's used to paying well for her protection. I had to put new men on her beat. I can't blame the boys. Her business is good and she's generous. And she has friends higher up. That's what she's here to tell me."

"Yes, sir." If the young lieutenant had any envy of the more lucrative jobs in the police force, he kept it to himself. Someday he hoped to replace this self-righteous plodder and get rich like his brother who had worked for old Boss Tweed. That was the way to run a city. Money for everybody and no questions asked.

The captain took a second look at the bench.

"Who's the sport in the grey bowler? Hasn't he been here before?"

"That's O'Finney. Owns a beer parlor with just a few darlin' waitresses to sing. . . ."

"Sure. All of them out of a convent and in bed by nine. Somebody's bed. We've had three complaints of customers losing their wallets. He'll wait."

The captain returned to his office.

Stockily built, Joseph Schwartz had the bright blue eyes of an Irish mother, the strong face bones of a Polish-born Jewish father. He held the private opinion that if his name had been O'Schwartz he might be police commissioner by now. Not that he took time to consider justice in his life. He hadn't found much yet, but his father had bequeathed him a lively inquisitiveness. "Learn, my boy. Learn everything you can. Knowledge is power. Learn something the other man wants to know. That's the way to success." From his mother had come a feisty if sentimental humor and a vague promise of the blessings of heaven. "Be good, my son. Go on your knees to God and He'll reward you."

Neither piece of advice had proved practical. In the summer pestilence that spilled annually from the city's festering slums, both parents had died, and his own young, pregnant wife had followed. Thereupon young Joseph Schwartz had abandoned faith and personal ambition for a bare-knuckled attack on the city's depravities. And a fight with anyone who asked for it. He joined the police force. His work became his life.

Along the way he developed an uncomfortable reputation for thinking beyond the call of duty. And for an honesty that could only be considered a handicap. In a word, Captain Joseph Schwartz was too bright, too blunt, too "different" to climb any higher in the Irish hierarchy of city politics.

But what he had to do, he'd do thoroughly. He did not look forward to this morning's meeting with Hugo Lendler.

The door opened. Captain Schwartz rose and extended a powerful hand.

"Good of you to come so promptly, Dr. Lendler."

"I rather expected your message, Captain."

An odd friendship had existed between the two for some years. It was born of mutual respect and mutual interests. New York considered itself an intellectual capital, second to none—not even that Athens of America, Boston. For respectable and informed middle-class citizens, the lecture hall or "Lyceum" was a favorite place of entertainment. One might on any evening attend "The Glories of Rome with Lantern Slides," or "The French Revolution Exhibiting 'Madame' la Guillotine," or "The Poetry of Sappho with Harp," the harp innocently veiling that Lesbos enchantress's true intent. For livelier curiosities, there was "Animal Magnetism" and "Free Thought." For controversy, "Women's Rights," or "Suffrage and the Home," or, more enticingly, "The New Woman."

So popular were the lectures that Dr. Hugo Lendler, the Vienna-born scholar, was persuaded to give a series on a subject of growing fascination—"Mind Control," popularly known as hypnotism. His scientific dedication, his impressive demonstrations, inevitably filled the hall.

It was after one such lecture that a stocky man in a plain dark suit approached him.

"I found your talk very interesting, sir," said Police Captain Schwartz, "but I have a question. In your opinion could hypnotism be used in proving guilt in a criminal case?"

Dr. Lendler liked the question and the man who asked it. The discussion continued late into evening at a nearby coffeehouse. In the course of time, a kind of professional friendship developed between the two men. Occasionally Captain Schwartz would call on the professor for a glass of schnapps laced with a little talk on the quirks and vagaries of human nature. But he had never before asked Dr. Lendler to come to the police station.

"Bad time to bother you, Dr. Lendler, this hour of the morning."

"As I assured you in my message, Captain, I am at your disposal." Dr. Lendler sat stiffly in the straight-backed chair beside the captain's desk.

The captain grinned. "I don't intend to dispose of you. Just a few questions. Your answers will be a great help." He cleared his throat as if to delay the inevitable.

"It's the Restell case. A nasty business."

Dr. Lendler nodded. It was what he had expected. The preliminaries were over.

"You knew Carrie Restell?"

"Yes, indeed."

"How well?"

Dr. Lendler could have admonished his friend that this was an imprecise question that could only receive an imprecise answer and was therefore of little value. Instead, he chose to be direct.

"I would like to think that she considered me a friend."

"That would have been fortunate for her. She didn't have many."

"On the contrary, Captain, it's my belief that she had a great many friends. Not, of course, among the so-called respectable, but among those of a scientific rather than superstitious turn of mind. And, of course, those she helped were devoted to her."

"How long did you know her?"

Dr. Lendler shifted in the uncomfortable chair. He was not surprised at the thrust of the questions. He suspected this would come. He had never disguised his acquaintance with the notorious woman. He had never had to. It was simply a facet of his life not suitable for social discourse.

"I met Caroline Restell when she came to my lectures on Mind Control. If I remember the first occasion—"

Captain Schwartz made a brusque gesture. "I'm not taking testimony, Doctor."

"Then I'll shorten my answer. I've known her perhaps seven or eight years."

"You liked her?"

"I admired her. She was an intense young woman, plainly

dressed. She always sat in the back row. After the lectures, she would come up to me, much as you did, Captain"—Dr. Lendler's eyes showed a momentary twinkle—"with all kinds of questions. Eventually she asked me if I would be willing to come to her home. She would pay the necessary fee. I assured her there was no fee. . . ."

"And you went to her home."

"Many times. She was humane and intelligent. She wanted to find every means possible for relieving pain. If hypnotism would help, then she wanted to know how to practice it. If she had the ability."

"Did you think she had?"

"Most assuredly I believed she could have made an excellent practitioner. She had a powerful empathy with people. Her black eyes were almost magnetic. And she was kind. When I studied Mind Control in Vienna, hypnotism was considered a valuable aid to the practice of medicine. I told her so. But whether she ever attempted it, I don't know. Hypnotism has become today a vaudeville stunt of charlatans, a trick used by spiritualists at their seances. Some sectors of the public see it as witchcraft. Mrs. Restell could not afford that. Her work was too serious."

"Do you still believe in the power of Mind Control, Dr. Lendler?"

"Oh, yes. In some distant day I believe it will take its rightful place among the sciences as a method of discovering ourselves. Of relieving our internal guilts, even healing our physical disorders." The little professor was becoming animated. "But I'm taking too much of your time, Captain. Is that all you wanted to know?"

"Not quite. When you met Carrie Restell, did you know her profession?"

"She had told me that she was a midwife. When I visited her home, I realized there was a greater pain than childbirth with which she dealt. Spiritual pain, mental torture that could not be done away with by a whiff of opium. Suffering that is beyond the skill of medicine or the compassion of faith. In her work she had nothing to sustain her but her own lonely courage."

Captain Schwartz lifted a paper from his desk.

"One question more, if you're willing, sir. Knowing Mrs. Restell as you did, do you believe she was a woman who would take her own life?"

Dr. Lendler looked beyond the police captain. When he spoke, the words came slowly.

"The human impulse for self-destruction is sometimes—"

The captain's hand slammed on the desk. "Damn it, I'm not asking for scientific analysis. I'm asking what your reason tells you. What my mother used to call the living heart of you. Carrie Restell had courage. You and I know that. She practiced abortion when no one else would. She flouted the law. She bribed anyone who tried to stand in her way. She charged the rich enormous fees so that she could take care of the poor. And when she was taken to court the first time, ten years ago, she declared she would hang before she would reveal the name of any client. Is this a woman who would put a kitchen knife to her throat and drain her blood down a bathtub pipe to escape public trial?"

Dr. Lendler looked directly at the police captain. Then he spoke softly. "I never thought so."

The captain released a sigh. He did not usually let emotion drive him to such oratory.

"I wanted to hear you say that."

He thrust out the sheet of paper he had been holding.

Dr. Lendler took time to settle a pince-nez on his nose, a convenience to deliberation; his eyesight was excellent. He began to read:

> FROM THE OFFICE OF THE COMMISSIONER OF POLICE:
> To all Precinct Captains
> THE SUBJECT: Mrs. Caroline Restell, alias Lohman, nee Annie Trow.
> The Coroner's Office reports no evidence, bodily or circumstantial, of foul play in the death of the above subject. Therefore the verdict of self-inflicted death is formally accepted. The case is hereby and in finality closed. . . .

Dr. Lendler returned the paper. "The machinery of the law moves quickly."

"Too damned quickly."

"An affront to your authority, Captain?"

"No. To my conscience. They began stripping the house the day after the funeral. They ordered me to call my three men off special patrol. I went to see the commissioner as soon as this letter came. He said there was not one shred of evidence that anybody had even been in the house to see Mrs. Restell that night. If there were, it would prove nothing. The truth is they don't want to prove anything. God knows how many politicians and private citizens want this case closed. The anti-vice committee wants more funding from the city, so it doesn't dare stand up against the politicians. And Mr. Anthony Comstock wants to gratify his peculiar pleasure in running sinners to ground. So there it is."

He crumpled the paper in his fist.

Dr. Lendler removed his pince-nez.

"I appreciate your feelings, Captain. In fact I share them."

"They are not feelings. This is something my mind tells me. Carrie Restell did not take her own life. I believe that as sure as I'm sitting in this chair. Somewhere in this city whoever killed her walks free. And will walk free unless . . ."

"Unless?"

Captain Schwartz shook his head. His anger had drained, leaving his face stolid. He knew the futility of personal involvement in police work. It served nothing, nor was it encouraged by his superiors. An officer's private morality had nothing to do with carrying out the law, which, as any politician worth his bribery knew, was not enforcement but compromise.

The captain went to the wooden filing cabinet and reached for an object lying on top of it.

"One of my men picked this up. He found it lying beside the door in Mrs. Restell's office and brought it back. I showed it to the coroner but he dismissed it as evidence. There was no wound or bruise of any kind on the body except for that knife cut. Mrs. Restell was known to cultivate rich clients. Anyone might have left it. Someone who might be important to the political machine. Wouldn't that be embarrassing, now? What do you think of it?"

It was an ebony evening cane with a carved ivory head and a band of silver joining ivory and ebony.

"Very fine, I should say. And of considerable value." Dr. Lendler's fingers encircled the shaft. "You see, slightly elliptical in shape. Designed to carry a rapier. That would date it as eighteenth century, possibly earlier. The ivory head I should think more recent. The lotus carving is typical of early nineteenth century when Chinese motifs became so popular. . . ."

The captain was impatient. One thing he could count on from the little professor was a full and learned answer, which he certainly had no need for now.

"Well, it's a cinch nobody's going to claim it. Or even admit to owning it. If the investigation were to continue, it might lead somewhere. As it is, what to do with it? I certainly don't want it around here." Affability returned to his shrewd, blue eyes. "You appreciate fancy gimcracks, Dr. Lendler. Why don't you take it along?"

"It takes a taller man than I to carry it, Captain."

"Keep it as a favor. I'll know where it is—if I should ever want to see it again."

The captain was searching through his wastebasket. "Ah, yesterday's paper. Useful, sometimes." He took the cane from Dr. Lendler, rolled it tightly in the newspaper, and handed it back.

Dr. Lendler accepted it without comment.

The captain's mood had become increasingly genial.

"We were talking about hypnotism. Do you still practice it, Dr. Lendler?"

"I have never practiced it professionally. I did scientific experiments in Mind Control for my lectures."

"I believe you once said that a person might confess to a crime under hypnosis."

The little doctor smiled. "I believe I also said, my friend, that such speculation is dangerous. No court of law would accept a confession obtained by Mind Control."

"Not today, but someday?"

"I see no way. For a subject to admit to anything he wishes hidden he must be under the deepest kind of hypnotism. It has not yet been proved that even under such hypnotism a man can be made to deny his every instinct, his entire will-power. In the event he did confess to a crime, how could it be proved that the crime was in the mind of the subject and not put there by the controller? No, no. That was my belief when we first talked about this, Captain. I've found nothing new in my studies to change it."

They parted with friendly ease, Dr. Lendler carrying the wrapped cane stiffly before him. He used it to hail a cab.

The wind was rising when Dr. Lendler reached home. April was blowing a gust of rain across the deserted Square. In the vestibule of his own snug house, a light glowed. Frau Gruen looked at him searchingly as he came in. The day must have been troubling. She took his hat and coat.

"Thank you, I'll not have coffee this afternoon, Frau Gruen. A little nap, I think. A touch of spring fever, perhaps. A little late in life, wouldn't you say?" He turned toward the stairs.

"*Herr Professor,* please. I am sorry but must tell you—there is a young man sitting in the parlor."

"Eh? A young man. One of my students?" He was dismayed. He had assured his students he was always available to them. But it was late in the day, the pain in his shoulder was pronounced, always a warning to rest.

"A student? No, *Herr Professor.* No, no. I'd say certainly not. He had a package to deliver. I told him to go around the alley to the rear door where deliveries are made. He said he wanted to hand it to you. I told him you were not at home but he came in anyway."

Ordinarily Hugo Lendler would have been quite willing to see so zealous a messenger for he had an ever-questing curiosity about his fellow men.

"Give the young man this for his pains. Thank him. If he looks hungry send him off with a few of your fresh crullers."

Frau Gruen thinned her lips at the coin in her hand. A quarter. To that impertinent young man who had towered over her and had the shamelessness to wink at her as he had seated himself without being asked in *Herr Professor*'s best mustard-velvet armchair. She would give him the money, of course, but not one crumb from her kitchen. Yet as she hurried to the parlor, a sigh, a wisp of long-forgotten girlhood escaped her. The young man was indeed *sehr nett.* . . .

Hugo Lendler climbed the stairs slowly, his mind returning to the day behind him. For all the pleasantries of his meeting with Captain Schwartz something was missing, something remained unanswered. The single, simple question—why? Why had his friendship with that tragic woman, Carrie Restell, been so overtly probed? Why had this curious and probably valuable cane been given to him?

He lay the cane in its wrapping on the desk. He would examine it at his leisure. But the daily newspaper around it had loosened and Dr. Lendler disliked untidiness, or more exactly, he smiled to himself, loose ends. He unrolled the cane and looked down its ebony length. He saw scratches and chips that no varnish could conceal, tarnish on the silver banding, and a dismal yellowing in the carved ivory petals of the lotus blossom head.

The old cane had known better days. In fact, Dr. Lendler discovered, even the joinings were weakened. The ivory and banding could be twisted. And removed. Beneath the silver top he found a thin strip of paper glued to the wood. Property of Elias Monk, 23 Bowery.

So that was it. Secondhand, rented, or purchased, perhaps from a dealer in old clothes. That would explain how it had been left in Carrie Restell's office. No man accustomed to carrying a cane would leave it behind him, any more than he would leave the hand that carried it.

Captain Schwartz had undoubtedly made the same inspection and arrived at the same conclusion. Yet rather than pursue it he had wanted to rid himself of the evidence. The case was closed. Even as honest a man as Joe Schwartz was helpless before the political machine of the city. And Carrie Restell, for all her courageous work, had depended on that machine for her survival.

Dr. Lendler rolled up the cane in fresh newspaper and thrust it on the shelf of his closet. Then he sat down and pulled off his boots. Time solved all things. He dismissed this absurdity at once. Time solved nothing unless a man could think for himself.

He stretched out on the tufted black leather couch and pulled up the latest afghan Frau Gruen had knitted for him in her relentless blacks and browns. But his mind was still churning. It occurred to him what that parcel downstairs, delivered by the strong-minded young man, contained. At last, the long-awaited books from London. His bookseller, Mr. Crowne, had written they would be sent on the packet-ship *Boedicia,* in care of one Ned Fitch, whom Mr. Crowne considered sufficiently trustworthy for the mission. The *Boedicia* and Mr. Crowne's letter had long since arrived. Only this week Dr. Lendler had noted in the shipping news that the *Boedicia* had departed. He had given up on the books and the trustworthy young Mr. Fitch and had planned to write Mr. Crowne a reorder.

Now it seemed the young man had been sitting in his parlor this very afternoon.

Dr. Lendler recalled Frau Gruen's indignation with a smile. Within the bosom of that worthy woman duty and propriety lay as solid and sustaining as her own dumplings. He wondered what she would have to say when Mr. Fitch returned.

Dr. Lendler pulled the afghan to his chin and turned on his side. Oh yes, young Mr. Fitch would return. His manner had said it for him. Only the motive remained obscure.

Dr. Lendler closed his eyes. For a little while he would surrender to his privacy, to a memory of lost duets, and to a secret image, intense and lovely, that could warm a lonely man as night fell.

13

The fat-bellied steam locomotive grunted to a halt, its black-grated cowcatcher protruding like the thrust of a defiant chin, its funneled stack venting clouds of dingy smoke. The string of coaches it pulled jolted and rocked to a stop.

The aging stationmaster crossed the platform to catch the mail pouch. Say what you like, he thought, about Mr. Vanderbilt and his railroad—and upcountry people said plenty—but his trains kept to their schedules. And the coaches were clean except for the soot that came through opened windows.

The morning was cool, so for the time being the windows had remained shut. The stationmaster watched a lone passenger descend from Coach Two—a young woman, slim and neat in a grey suit and violet hat. She was no stranger. Usually she passed with a small smile and a nod, and the bleak platform seemed friendlier. If he were not busy he would go out to the street and signal one of the hacks at the stand for her.

This morning, despite the early hour, she must have been in a hurry for she crossed directly to where the hack horses were tied, tails toward the smoke-belching monster to which they never would become numbed.

The stationmaster did not know the girl's name but he knew where she always went. During long winter nights, the hackies consoled themselves for thin pay and long hours with the warmth of the stationhouse wood stove and the lustiness of their gossip. Yet, as often as he had heard the talk, the stationmaster found it hard to accept the fact that a young lady of such refinement could be visiting the farmer, Gustav Hansen, and his hardworked wife, Sophie. To be fair, Gus Hansen had not always come into town, surly and alone, to buy his provisions, take a single beer from the red-haired barmaid at the Traveler's Hotel, and depart offering his hand to no man in greeting.

Time was, and not too long ago, people remembered, when Gustav Hansen kept the tidiest farm along this part of the Hudson River. An apple orchard, Macintosh and Northern Spies, big as a man's fist. Pigs as fat as they were clean. A half dozen Guernsey cows with milk the color of spring dandelions. At planting and harvest he employed a farmhand and, in good seasons, a handyman to mend fences and replace shingles.

Every Sunday, rain or shine, snow or storm, Gustav would load his three children and his pretty, bonneted wife into a neatly painted carryall and drive ten miles to the three-hour service of his faith. There, head bowed in long periods of humility, he would give thanks, ask God's help, and walk out with a word of kindness for everyone and the look of a refreshed and strengthened man.

The children, it was noticed, two boys and a tiny girl with flaxen hair hanging straight under an oversized bonnet, bore no resemblance to each other. Or to Gustav and Sophie. It was speculated that they were adopted.

Then, of a sudden things changed. The Hansen family ceased coming to church. A neighbor riding past the farm reported the front shutters half drawn, a broken fence rail left dangling. Others noticed paint on the barn beginning to peel. The apple trees showed long whips left unpruned. And the Guernsey herd was down to two. Gustav could be seen working his fields, but he never turned his head for a passerby. To cap it all, one blustery autumn night, Gustav's farmhand arrived at Grady's saloon to tell all who would listen that he had been discharged, thrown out, with a dollar and a shove from a madman.

After that, Gustav Hansen was seen in town only when he bought supplies. And always alone. He never stinted on his farm purchases, though Miss Hankle at the Ladies Drygoods reported that he no longer stopped for a measure of fine muslin or a pair of ladies' Sunday gloves. On occasion he took time for a stop at the Traveler's Hotel. There, at the far end of the bar, he would sit silent and grim, while Ruby, the full-bosomed barmaid, filled glasses and wiped up beer suds. It was commented by the faithful that Gustav never attempted the usual sorry jokes and coarse play Ruby was known to enjoy. Yet she treated him with gentle courtesy and would lean over the bar to chat with him, deepening the crevice of her large breasts. He would down his drink quickly, lay his money on the counter, and leave, looking neither left nor right.

Through all the gossip and the guessing, the young lady who had just descended from the train continued her visits. A friend of Sophie Hansen's? The stationmaster hoped so for the sake of the poor isolated woman. Yet why was this young lady admitted when the neighbors were shut out?

The stationmaster watched her cross the street to the hack stand. Too thin by far for his taste. But when she smiled, she was someone you'd like to talk to, which in itself made her different. In the stationmaster's greying experience, women had many uses. But the Lord forbid that a man should have to spend time talking to them.

He waited only to watch her mount the carriage step with the prettiest turn of ankle a man could hope to see. The hack pulled away from the stand. The stationmaster sat down at his telegraph ticker. He wished her well. But the wish was uneasy.

Noel, stiffly upright on the dusty hack seat, was aware of a deepening dread. So deep that she had overlooked the simplest courtesy of nodding to the stationmaster. Every turn of the hack wheels sharpened the uncertainty of what lay ahead.

She tried to think of the country through which she was being driven. A mile north the hack would turn west onto a tree-lined road and the moment would come that Noel usually awaited, the moment that severed her past from her present. The road curved, the sky opened, and the quiet grandeur of the Hudson River burst into view, reaching nearly a mile across to the cradling cliffs opposite.

At this moment Noel would yield to the river's serenity. She would imagine the teeming, shining shapes of river life beneath the silver surface. She would imagine the saline ocean tides that at the moon's pull rolled and swelled up the vast river bed, against the current's flow. Up from New York City's distant sea harbor, up past the awesome Palisades, the lower-lying hills of farm and pasture lands, the blue-grey mountains of unmolested oak and spruce, pine, elm, and ash. And on, on, two hundred miles it was said, to the still-provincial state capital of Albany. There, at the moon's release, the salt tide would ebb back to its distant sea womb, leaving on certain days a new crispness in the air, and on Noel's lips the salt-sweetness of the distant sea. The sea had betrayed her, but it had for a brief hour brought her ecstasy.

Her mood would change as the hack approached the red farmhouse. From the yard, children's voices would float like bells. Noel would open her arms, snatching the tiny girl to her. With the child she would joyously climb the porch steps to where Sophie Hansen stood, wiping her hands on a long striped apron, smelling of fresh-baked bread, and smiling warmly.

But today?

The hack made its turn into the farmhouse lane and stopped. She jumped out unaided and held out the fare.

"Real pity in there, ain't it?" The hackman swung from his seat. "Will you be needing a ride back to the station today, Miss?"

"I don't know. I mean I don't know when. I'll send word, thank you."

The man touched his cap and slapped the reins on his horse's rump.

Noel walked quickly up the unkempt path. Sophie was not on the porch to greet her. A toy wagon lay overturned at its edge. A child's white stocking gathered dust. A cat leaped from the porch step and fled. Only stillness met her. As if no voice were there to speak, no wind to stir, as if morning had passed the house by.

She pushed open the front door. It squeaked on its hinges. In the grey half-light she saw him, Gustav Hansen slumped in his chair, his head drooped. His big frame seemed to have gone boneless.

She had seen little of Sophie's husband on her visits over the last years. His heavy back had retreated when she arrived. He had not shared meals while she was there. But if he had grown sullen with the years, she had given him little thought. She had come for a different purpose, and it filled her being.

Now she stood staring at him. The man in the chair lifted his head.

"Where's Sophie?" Her voice was cold with apprehension, colder than she intended. "Where are the children? What's happened?"

He did not look up. After a pause that seemed to Noel an eternity, he nodded toward the closed door of the downstairs bedroom.

She waited for a word, a tentacle of communication. Nothing came. She crossed quickly into the bedroom.

The coarse linen curtains were full-drawn, letting in only a hint of morning. In the rocking chair beside the window sat a strange woman. A purplish twill best dress was at odds with her red hair. Noel could see that in a full-fleshed way she was young and good-looking. She was buffing her nails.

But the room had been tidied. On the wide sleigh bed, deep in shadow, lay Sophie. Noel stifled a gasp.

Sophie's apple-round cheeks were grey and sunken. Two slashes of bright, unnatural color stained the cheekbones. The skin on her forehead had the look of putty and gleamed with a film of moisture. The brown hair lay moist, pushed back from her brow. Only her hands, lying above the quilt were familiar, blunt, work-worn. Noel covered one of them with her own.

Sophie's eyes opened.

"Noel . . . you're here!" Her eyes, overbright, moved to the woman in the rocker.

Noel nodded and smiled at the woman.

"I'm an old friend of Mrs. Hansen's. I've come to help. Perhaps you'd like to take a rest or get a little fresh air before the rain starts."

"Sure. That's all right, Miss." The woman was younger than Noel had guessed. "I got to be gettin' back to work. When Mr. Hansen came into the Traveler's yesterday, looking so scared like, I told him I'd come out until he got somebody. Guess it's all right if he drives me back now." Her voice dropped. "The doctor came. Water in the lungs."

Her eyes sharpened as if something stirred in her mind that she was unable to say. "I sent the boys up to the barn." She gave Noel a curious stare. "The little girl didn't want to go. She's out in the shed with her doll. I gave her a piece of cornbread with jam."

At the door her voice rose with brisk artificiality. "I hope you'll be better real soon, Mrs. Hansen. You got a real worried husband. The medicine's in that brown bottle on the table, Miss."

The pungent scent of carnation trailed her from the room.

Noel felt the faint tug of Sophie's dry fingers.

"Noel, I must talk to you. . . ."

Noel felt again the chill that had come with Sophie's letter. "Later, Sophie. You must rest. I'll be here. . . ."

"No. No. Listen, Noel! Now . . . !" A rasping cough shook her. The red cheek stains deepened. "It's . . . it's . . ."

"It's what, Sophie?"

"It's Posie. Gustav knows."

Time seemed to stop between the two women. Noel was the first to break the silence, her voice far way in her own ears.

"You told him?"

"Oh, no. No. He guessed. Oh, Noel, haven't you realized? Look at yourself! Look at your child! All these months haven't you seen? Posie's face . . . her little nose . . . her smile. Yours, Noel! She walks like you . . . even the way she holds her head! Oh, I've prayed on my knees to God that she'd grow up different . . . with her blond hair . . . but Gustav saw it all, he guessed. . . ."

Sophie was half upright now. Noel, stifling a threat of panic, gently pressed the dying woman back.

"How long has he known?"

"I—I can't think. Yes . . . maybe more than a year now."

A year. For four years Noel had been making these trips believing herself safe, letting a small seed of security begin to grow. Four years, with her innocent bags of taffy, her fairy tales, the little games she stored in her mind for each visit, behind the careful discipline of her days.

A year. Wasn't that about the time Gustav had begun to avoid her, to turn his back on the house itself while she was in it?

"Why didn't you tell me before, Sophie?"

"I meant to. Each time. But I couldn't make the words come. I'd say to myself, next time. Next . . . oh, Noel, once he guessed it was terrible. He—he made me tell him everything. Right here in this room, standin' right there, forcin' me to my knees. How did I come to know a—a woman like you? What brought you here? To our house? I had to tell him. I couldn't help it! He kept on drivin' the questions into me like nails. I told him about Mrs. Restell—"

"Oh, Sophie!"

"I had to. Don't you see? Once I started I couldn't stop! No matter what I'd done, or he'd do, he's my husband. Oh, I was scared. I had told so many lies. It was a powerful release to tell him I had worked in Mrs. Restell's house . . . how kind she was . . . how she had found me the position with the Reverend Blake's family. That's where I met Gustav."

Sophie's eyes brightened, her thoughts skittered.

"I'll never forget that fair, Gus driving his team of oxen, shiny as satin, going like lambs . . . and never a meanness in Gus. I loved him, Noel, from the first when he came courting me at the parsonage, I thought heaven had opened. . . ."

The flush in the drawn cheeks faded. Sophie's head rolled fitfully.

"But nothing changes the past, does it, Noel? Nothing can. Gustav knew I—I wasn't a virgin on our wedding night. When children didn't come to us, Gustav said there were plenty of children who needed a home. We drove to the orphanage and found the two boys. Then the letter came from Mrs. Restell. There was a baby girl. . . ."

"*I know.* Sophie. . . ."

The thin hand tightened on hers.

"No, no, Noel. Let me talk. . . . Make you understand. Mrs. Restell knew you couldn't keep the baby, being who you were. I wanted a little girl. She would be like my own. I agreed to your visiting. But after you left, she was mine. It was easy to pretend when I had to pretend so much. Until that night when Gustav stood here in this room asking about you and . . . Posie. I couldn't lie anymore. I told him I—I had . . . fallen . . . I had wanted to kill myself. Mrs. Restell took me in. She did the—the operation. She saved me. I begged Gustav to forgive me. But he didn't say a word. He didn't ask another question. He just went out. He put a cot in the shed and not another night did he sleep in this bed. Nor look straight at me again."

Noel sat rigid. She had seen the changes and deliberately blinded herself to them. All she had cared about was her child's safety.

"If Gustav felt that way why did he let Posie stay here? Why did he let me come?"

Sophie looked past her with blank eyes. "I don't know. . . . Sometimes I think he liked to—to look at you."

A light rain fingered the window. Sophie closed her eyes, her breath faint but even. Pain had drained from her face, leaving it almost pretty.

Noel might have envied that peace she saw there. There was no more time to think of Sophie or herself. She must find Posie, take her away as soon as she could.

To her relief, Gustav's armchair in the parlor was empty. She hurried out to the rear of the house.

The shed was separated from the house by a half dozen yards. The low door hung half open on rusted hinges. There was no window. The place had been used for years as a catch-all for stacked wood, an assortment of ropes, chains, a spade or two, and a few garden tools handy for Sophie.

Noel, pushing her way through the narrow door, saw a low-slung cot of woven hemp and across it a torn square of flowered carpet.

It was on this the child lay, pale as the light that filtered in. A battered-faced wooden doll had slid to the floor, as had a half-eaten square of cornbread, sticky with jam. Jam smudged, too, the sleeping child's face—unevenly, as if tears had run through it. A tiny girl, skin of ivory (like her own), eyes dark brown (hers), nose with that tilt she had found so unclassic in her own. Cheekbones high. *Why had she failed to see?* The likeness was as sweet as it was damning.

Only the hair, fine and light as spun flax, was not of her. It was a reminder forever of the young summer of her life, when first love (or its counterfeit) and the sound of the sea had wrapped her in oblivion and left her with this child, the core and meaning of her life.

She lifted the child to her and held her close.

"Mistaffy!" There was a warmth of recognition, then a wiggle, a squirm, and Posie slid to the floor. "Is Mama better?"

"She's sleeping, Posie. Let's go into the kitchen. It's cold out here."

Mistaffy had come about in the directness of children, in ripples of delight for the three red-and-white striped paper bags of taffy that always accompanied Noel's arrival. For Noel the name had become an easy disguise, a clown's face she had gladly adopted. *Mama* would have to be dealt with later, as would so much that was new now.

Posie snatched up her doll, ran from the shed and across to the kitchen. Noel gathered the broken pieces of cornbread and followed. In the kitchen she found Sophie's faded blue coverall apron hanging on its nail. She tied it over her city clothes like armor. There was work to do. That in itself held a kind of relief.

"You look like Mama now." Posie settled herself on a stool and watched with solemn eyes. "The stove's gone out."

Noel thrust wood into the cast iron under-box, blew into it, and saw a glow. The iron pot on the top held cornmeal mush and bacon. When it was heated Posie ate obediently if not with relish. She was an amenable child.

A slant of sunlight touched the child's bent head, turning it to near silver. Noel caught her breath against the sudden reminder. *She must not think back,* now or ever. The rain had stopped, the overcast was lifting. In the changeable moods of the Hudson Valley, sunlight was breaking through the great river's mist.

"Perhaps later we can take a little walk, Posie."

The child slipped from the stool.

"We can't, Mistaffy. Mama is sick. Are you going to stay?"

"Yes."

"Can I go out and play with the wagon?"

"On the porch, Posie. The grass is wet."

She watched Posie retrieve the little wagon from the path,

seat herself on the bottom step, and push the broken toy back and forth in the unfettered absorption of childhood.

The aloneness of the small figure, the stalwart movement of delicate head and hands. . . . Noel felt a pain so stabbing that the artifices of her life seemed to crumble. This child was her own flesh. Against all scandal, all propriety, she would never again deny her, never again let go of her.

She filled a wooden pail at the outside pump and found a half-used piece of darkened yellow soap. It was not thinking and feeling that pushed a woman through a day, nor was it dressing and sitting. Whatever lay secret and bruised within her could be blanketed at least for the time being by the numbing routine of brush and broom.

When kitchen and parlor were cleaned, and the three pinched little rooms on the second floor tidied, Noel took off her apron and went downstairs. Against the afternoon light that was beginning to fade, she saw him. His arms hung straight at his sides. His look, hard, direct, was empty of even the kindness of recognition. Standing there, silent and heavy, Gustav Hansen filled the room.

When he had come in, Noel had no idea. Had he been in the house while she worked, moving from room to room, watching from a distance? Or had he been outside, listening, peering.

"Why aren't you in there?" He gestured to the closed bedroom door.

"She's sleeping. I've put the house in order. And the children will need supper." Noel tried to match his coldness. She would show no servility to this man. Or to any other, she added to herself. She was as alone as the woman lying in there, alone because their betrayers had left them no choice. But she would not bow. Nor would she, she promised herself, show fear.

"I'll manage my house. You stay with her." Contempt roughened his voice, but some of the menace had gone.

In the bedroom, Sophie still lay in sleep, the flush faded, leaving her face sunken and grey. Her breath came slowly and unevenly. When darkness came, Noel drew the curtains and lit the kerosene lamp, turning the wick low. Once she opened the doors to hear movement in the kitchen, but no voices. The nearness of death leveled all things—the cruelties, the kindnesses, the enigmas, the pretense, all the threadbare hopes and artifacts of human delusion. There was no place on that grey plain for past or future.

Near midnight Sophie stirred as if gathering the last of her strength.

"Noel . . . ?"

"I'm right here, Sophie."

"It's about Posie"—for an instant the tired eyes were lucid with demand—"she can't stay here . . . she must not."

"I'm going to take her. She'll be safe with me."

"No . . . listen to me!" Sophie seemed to grope for a thought too elusive, too distant for her efforts. "You must go straight to Mrs. Restell. Do you understand? Straight there." Sophie raised a hand against interruptions. "When I took sick . . . when I guessed how it might be . . . I wrote a letter. The woman up the road took it. Didn't Mrs. Restell tell you? Didn't you see her?" The voice became a single high-pitched string, plucked with anxiety. "Noel . . . didn't you?"

"Sophie! Sophie dear! You mustn't fret. Posie will be safe."

But beneath the soothing words, Noel stared at a hard fact. Sophie did not know of Carrie Restell's death. Isolated, without neighbors or confidants, Sophie had been spared the ugliness, the sordid brutality of it. For an instant, the black-haired woman seemed to stand beside them in this small room of death, a presence as reassuring as it was secret. Sophie's brow was wet with effort.

"Noel, listen. There's a place for Posie. She will never have to go to an orphanage or be unhappy, ever. Mrs. Restell knows. Promise you'll see her! Promise me. . . ."

"Posie will never go to an orphanage." Noel had already made the vow to herself.

"Noel, promise me you will see Mrs. Restell!"

Answer the dying, release them in peace, the old minister at her mother's bedside had said so long ago. But where was peace for Sophie in the truth? There had been so many lies. What harm in one more, if it would ease her torment?

"I will."

Noel saw anxiety give way to a little-girl smile that flickered on Sophie's lips as if a friend, as if anticipation itself, had entered the room. But she was not yet done with her burden.

"Oh"—a sigh so faint Noel bent to hear—"Gustav . . . dear God . . . help him . . . help . . . Gustav. . . ."

As the first bird chirped in the false dawn, Sophie died. Noel turned out the lamp, folded the hands and kissed the dry cheek. Her own sense of loss would come later. Noel was used to the postponement of her emotions.

Gustav, in his chair, was not asleep. At his blunt glance, she merely nodded and went up the stairs. She heard the chair springs squeak, steps, the opening and shutting of the bedroom door where Sophie lay.

Had whatever harsh God he served endowed the man at last with compassion?

Sophie would not know.

As the first light whitened the east, Noel, sleepless in her narrow bed, heard him leave the house. Then the creak of wagon wheels and the plod of a horse's hoofs. For a little while perhaps she would sleep.

14

At noon the next day, a murmur of sounds, rough unidentifiable reached Noel in the quiet of the farmhouse. Looking out she saw an appalling sight. Down the lane at a wary distance from the front gate a crowd had gathered. Lanky youths, grown men, their farm hats pushed back, and women, a few in the decency of black skirts and black shawls, were waiting. What had drawn them was not the house that still contained the dead, but the preposterous spectacle at Gustav Hansen's gate.

Full in the sun stood a glossy black hearse, drawn by a pair of equally glossy black horses, black pompoms nodding between their ears. The glass sides of the hearse sparkled. From each corner hung a luxuriant black silk tassel. The center of the roof was crowned with a cluster of black-painted wooden feathers, encircling the black-painted figure of a triumphant angel. On the driver's cushioned seat sat a long-faced man in a black suit, black gloves. From his stovepipe hat hung several yards of black "weeper crepe."

The splendor, the incongruity, held the crowd. Death, like marriage and disaster, provided what drama their hardworking lives possessed. But this dazzling display surpassed anything ever seen in Riveredge. Had Gustav Hansen provided all this for his poor wife to whom, it was said, he had denied even a kindly word? Talk in whispers ran back and forth, threads of gossip to be woven together on cold winter nights.

Noel turned from the window in choked revulsion. The tawdry splendor, the farce, how Sophie would have hated it. Then she caught herself. Or would she? In Sophie's bleak life, it might have been what Gustav intended, a plea, a need to remember, the inarticulate grief for a love that had not quite vanished.

Gustav had told Noel nothing. But she had washed and

readied the children, polished their buttoned shoes, and found what would pass for Sunday clothes. For herself, she had taken Sophie's black funeral shawl and mourning veil, staples in life when the unexpected came with such frequency.

She herded the children out onto the porch, trying not to stare as they did at what stood at the gate. Behind the hearse, Gustav's grey plow horse, Ben, shifted uneasily on the shafts of the farm wagon.

There were sounds of heavy movement in the house.

The front door opened. The crowd in the road hushed. Noel took the children's hands.

Two hired pallbearers and two official mourners, their crepe floating behind them, carried a varnished pine coffin down the steps. It was lined, as Noel had seen, in fluted lavender silk, finer than anything Sophie had ever worn in her troubled life. Gustav followed, his face granite.

Noel shepherded the children quietly after him.

Halfway down the path, he looked back. He wheeled, flinging out an arm like a cudgel.

"Away! All of you go away! You hear me!" His voice rose to take in the crowd. "None of you belong here! She was mine! I'll see her buried!"

There was a moment of confused and stricken silence. The crowd backed off. The two boys at Noel's side froze in terror, then fled in relief. Noel caught Posie's cold little hand but the child would not be drawn away. Her feet planted firmly, she watched solemnly as the gleaming box was pushed into the lustrous coach. Blinding sunlight was reflected from the glass siding.

Noel snatched her up, a fullness in her own throat.

"It's all right, Posie. Mama"—she stumbled on the word, using it for the child's sake—"Mama's with God now." She found herself resorting helplessly to that worn, too facile explanation of the unexplainable.

The child pushed down from her arms. "Why did those men put Mama in a box?"

Posie stuck her fists into her eyes but that did not stop the two tears that rolled large and free down into the sparse grass below.

Noel dropped to her knees.

"Cry, Posie. Cry all you want. Sometimes it's good to cry."

"You're not crying."

"I never learned how."

The child's arms went hungrily around her neck.

The crowd in the lane drifted off, voices returning to normal as the paraphernalia of death disappeared. Only a few remained, a hard core, emboldened by raw curiosity, the pleasantness of the day, and the lure of the game, whatever it might be.

Later in the day, through the front window, Noel could see them, overgrown, heavy-faced youths, still lounging beyond the gate. As soon as Gustav returned she and Posie must leave. Noel's mind was not fully focused on the future. She would take the late afternoon train back to the city. She would find a quiet, respectable hotel. She had money enough for that. Tomorrow she would buy Posie some proper clothes. Then she would face her dilemma squarely.

Meanwhile she would pack her bag, with a change of underthings for Posie. She would spend the rest of the time in the few rites she might still do for Sophie.

How quickly a room was made barren by death. The empty bed, the bared mattress covered only by a quilt. On the bureau top a few pathetic possessions. A heart-shaped brooch stuck into a chintz pin-cushion; a colored picture postcard, "Lovers Leap, Mohawk Falls" wedged to the side of the mirror; a round celluloid box with a small hole to hold the combings of Sophie's thinning hair. In the top bureau drawer lay a mock tortoise-shell comb and brush and four white handkerchiefs edged in Sophie's crocheting. Neat, immaculate, the sum of Sophie Hansen's small prides. Noel touched them gently, as if the time for tenderness had not passed.

It was then that she saw the piece of writing paper folded beneath them. It was well creased, the corners limp, as if it had been read and thrust away time and again. There were no secrets now between Sophie and herself, no differences in what the world considered their shame. If there was anything still to be revealed or hidden, Noel must see to it. She unfolded the sheet of paper. It bore a name in the unmistakable handwriting of Carrie Restell. A name she did not know.

"Mistaffy!" Posie was standing in the doorway, her eyes round. "Why are you in Mama's room?"

"I'm straightening her things. I have a picture card to bring you."

"There's somebody coming up to the porch. I don't know who."

Through the parlor window, Noel could see a black-topped buggy in the lane, a scrawny grey horse tethered to the hitching post.

The knock on the door was loud and rapid. Noel opened

it to a tall, spare woman with winter on her face. Her nondescript bonnet and shawl scorned both mourning and fashion. She stepped briskly across the threshold, looked past Noel into what recesses she could see of the parlor, then slid her gaze on Posie, who was clinging in awe to Noel's hand.

"Good day, Miss. I am from the Christian Endeavor Society."

Noel had long learned the value of a patient smile. "Good day."

"We are, of course, very sorry about poor Mrs. Hansen. We heard what happened here this noon." If she hoped for an assent from Noel she got none. "That is, well, shall we say, uh, Mr. Hansen's instability. . . ."

Noel's smile remained fixed, waiting.

"Well . . . is Mr. Hansen on the premises now?"

"Not at the moment."

"I see. We thought that might be the case. There are three minors in this house, I believe?"

"Yes, indeed. Two fine boys and this little girl." This time Noel did not smile.

"And you"—the woman's glance traveled over Noel's city suit—"you are a visitor?"

"What is it that you have in mind, Miss . . . Mrs. . . . ?"

"Miss Quill, if you please. I have come, it seems, at the right time. We have a shelter for children such as these. We are prepared to take them as soon as they can be got ready and keep them until they can be sent to Haverstraw."

"Haverstraw? What is that?"

"It is a suitable place for abandoned and neglected children to be cared for, taught regular Christian Doctrine and prepared for the toil and hardship of life."

"I see." Noel's voice tightened. "But there must be some misunderstanding. The children in this house are not abandoned. When Mr. Hansen returns . . ."

The woman might have some reason for her assumptions, Noel thought. Posie's hair was in tangles, her best dress crumpled, her pinafore milk-stained, her thick white stockings dirtied and wrinkled. One black boot was unbuttoned.

She lifted her chin. "I could not possibly release the children unless Mr. Hansen . . ."

But Miss Quill was no longer surveying the child or the premises. She was staring at Noel, then at Posie, then back to Noel as if measuring inches, shapes, heaven knew what. What she saw brought a splash of dull red to her cheeks.

"Well . . . well, I declare . . . the child . . . you say you're a visitor? She's the very image of you, Miss . . . Mrs. . . ."

Noel's hand held tightly to Posie's, who was returning the woman's stare.

". . . I didn't realize. I wasn't told. I'll report of course. The Society will be in touch with—with Mr. Hansen. I do declare. Good day."

"Good day."

The door closed. For an instant Noel leaned against it. Then with a smothered laugh, she swung the child high.

"Oh, Posie, Posie! We'll beat them all yet, you and I!"

A red sun slanted low through the curtains. It was too late to think of the afternoon train. If there was an evening train, Gustav would have to drive her.

For the first time it occurred to her that he might not intend to return. He would be right in guessing that she would not take Posie away and abandon the boys. Yet he was a farmer. She had witnessed his hard labor filling the needs of his land, his animals. He must come back.

As the light faded, Noel found herself unable to shift her thoughts from the harsh, gaunt man. She had taken him for granted as she had taken so much for granted, here in this place. A backdrop that allowed her to see her child and, for a few illumined hours, to be herself.

Yet now, alone in Sophie's house, the presence of Gustav Hansen was everywhere.

She put the children to bed early and went outside.

A sickle moon hung in the west. Below it, the evening star, Venus, glowed with the unnatural brilliance of its spring cycle. The violet sky was draining of light, filling the twilight mist with the sounds of April—of the peepers, those tiny frog heralds of renewal, and the raucous farewell of wild geese as they lifted from lush meadow grass to the refuge of a distant pond for the night. The air pulsed with the myriad scents of spring, of damp earth, of the mysteries of hidden growing and budding. Never, it seemed to Noel, had she been so aware of all that was living, all that was around and beyond her. The coming night dwarfed her, yet in a curious way held a mystic reassurance. The hushed immensity, the soaring beauty, the completeness, each element in its place, as eternal as the planet's turn. Surely she and Posie were part of it. Surely there would be a place for them, as surely as for the first white moths winging out of the darkness.

Yet she was not solitary in this crystal universe. Fragments of memory, some painful, some heartening, fluttered around her. Of Mrs. Restell, when Noel had first entered her office in the huge, formidable house.

"I ask no questions, Miss Tremont. I make no judgments. I believe in life above death, in peace above pain. I believe that happiness, not misery, nourishes the human spirit and error lives in every heart. You are a strong young woman. There is no reason why you should not have a lovely child. But you have a choice. . . ."

Noel had already faced that ugly fork in the road.

"I am here, Mrs. Restell, to have my baby with the best care and privacy."

The severe features softened. "I am here to give it, Miss Tremont." Then the penetrating glance. "You loved this man?"

And her response.

"Doesn't every woman believe that, Mrs. Restell?"

So, like others before, she had regularly slipped, cloaked and veiled, through that always open side door until the time had come when she told her father, preoccupied with his new wife, that she would be away for a while. An old school friend now in Boston . . . there were no questions. She had moved into a neat white bedroom on the third floor of the great mansion and Carrie Restell had girdled her world.

Now Carrie Restell, her benefactor, was dead. As was Sophie—dear, warm Sophie who had betrayed her at the end, overwhelmed by the double burden of guilt and love.

So, Noel had come to this now, her child at last her own. It would never again be otherwise.

For a moment longer she yielded to the twilight, the radiance of the rising planet, the pulse beat of birth and renewal. Sharp and unheralded her heart suddenly skipped within her. Was it only two nights ago, in the same spring softness, she had walked with him, truancy in every step, her girlhood returned, the enchantments of life newly ahead? Ned, a man she barely knew, yet now would know forever.

She turned and fled into the house.

It was nearly daybreak when she awoke in the parlor rocking chair, stiff and chilled, to hear wagon wheels. They were followed by the whinny of a homecoming horse, the splash of pump water at the rear of the house.

Gustav Hansen stood in the doorway. His hands were muddied, his boots scuffed. Clinging to his black Sunday suit were blades of grass, dead leaves, fragments of soil. As if he had thrown himself across the earth. Across a new grave. In the black brooding of his face lay something a woman might fear.

Noel pulled her shawl, Sophie's black shawl, closer. She had found it easy to ignore Gus Hansen, his thick features, his coarse, curt manner. He had never seemed a part of her days with Posie. But now in the emptiness of the hour, the isolation of this room, she found she could not ignore him. He filled it with his presence, with his misery. What lay in her mind lay deeper than fear. The knowledge that she had hurt this man and no power on earth could change that. She wanted only to escape his house now, with her child. But wasn't there a little time left for pity, a little kindness out of her own guilt?

She rose from the chair.

"Are you hungry? I can get you something to eat, Gus."

"No."

"Then I'll go up, get my things ready."

"Stay where you are." His eyes were fixed on her. "I've let you come here. Even when I knew what you were. You'll stay until I've said my mind. Things I . . . couldn't say . . . to her." His head jerked toward the closed bedroom. "I'll say 'em so you know. You and every other whore who'd trap an honest man into marrying her! You stare at me. You didn't know a man can suffer, did you? You didn't know that to a man there are only two kinds of women in the world. The wife he wants . . . and the woman he can have with a little sweet talk or a half dollar!"

He tugged at his collar, as if it were choking him, yet he couldn't stop. "A man must have three things to be a man, to live as a man. Did you know that? Then I'll tell you. Or some other man will. Pure water to drink. Pure faith to give God. And a pure woman to give his name to, to sleep in his bed, to bear him children! I know now I had no wife. But I loved her. God forgive me. I—I still do. If I know the truth, the last truth she would not tell me, I could drive that love out of me with the devil's curse. But you know it—and you'll tell me! Or I'll shake it from you!"

For the first time Noel sensed fear. But you don't run, she told herself. Not from a dog. Or a horse. Or a man, his eyes red with fury.

She spoke gently.

"I'll tell you anything I know, Gus. I have no reason not to."

It seemed to steady him. The wildness drained from his face, the anguish remained.

''Tell me—tell me the truth. Did Sophie kill her child?''

''Oh, no. No! Oh, she couldn't do that—not Sophie! There was an operation. . . .''

''Say it for what it is. Abortion . . . murder!''

''No. To save her life! Can't you understand that!''

''I understand it as God understands it! The devil has her soul!''

She could feel even pity now. He stood a broken man before her. She had started from the room when he spoke again, his voice lifeless.

''Get your things and the child's. I'll take you to the station. The milk train comes through at five.''

Twenty minutes later, Noel mounted, tight-lipped, into the wagon beside Gustav Hansen. Within the circle of her arms, Posie drowsed in sleep.

Clouds had settled on the river and beyond the road ahead. She wondered when, and where, they would lift.

15

"Move along there, boy. Old Josh is on the next shift."

"You can't send that horse out today, Mr. Malley."

"I can't, can't I? And who'd be after telling me that, at all?"

The squat, heavily muscled foreman of the Sixth Avenue Omnibus horse barn moved down the long dim corridor to where Ned Fitch was standing.

"He's lame, Mr. Malley. You can see how he holds up that hoof."

The foreman peered into stall 16, a rectangle no wider than needed to contain a standing horse and let a man slide by him. A big roan stood tethered to a ring in the wall.

"Untie him."

Ned slipped into the stall, untied the halter, and gave the old horse a gentle push. The horse backed dutifully. Ned heard the sting of a whip on the rump.

"No need for that, Mr. Malley. He's moving." He tried to keep the raising anger out of his voice.

"Can't I see that for myself, now?" The whip struck again. "Sure, and if he can move he can pull. And if he can pull, he can work. And if he don't, then it's to the knackers with 'im." He spat on the corridor floor, already soggy with slime and manure. "Hey, you there, Joe, harness up number sixteen with Sal. She'll do more than her share. I'll have a word with this young gentleman later."

But the noon whistle blew and Ned's shift was over. He had worked since midnight with one fifteen-minute recess at six for bread and coffee. But even that was hardly enough time for five stable hands to feed, brush and curry, muck out, and ready the forty workhorses. There were not always five men on duty. Under Malley's rule the turnover was frequent. Hungarians, Poles, Greeks, and the ubiquitous Irish—

muscled, unschooled youths, nursing their ignorance like their ambitions in sullen silence—came and went.

To Ned, the wide stable doors at each end of the half-block-long barn had looked like the Gates of Hope. Steady employment at fifteen cents an hour, six days a week, seven if he volunteered Sunday. Money at last in his pocket to buy the secondhand suit of clothes he so desperately needed. He had gone deeper into debt to his overindulgent landlady for the extravagance of visiting Stuyvesant Square that one night to see Noel Tremont. His success had been more than he dared hope and as empty as the next day. Those few moments of closeness, of the pure magic of her, had served only to widen his distance from her. He had skirted the Square once or twice after that but had caught no glimpse of her. He had avoided the house of Dr. Hugo Lendler. Never again would he be told to go to the rear door of any house in Stuyvesant Square. In the back of his mind lay a half-framed plan to call on Dr. Lendler, if only to return the quarter tip. When he did, he would be properly dressed. He might even ask for an introduction to a reputable position. But that was in the future. The stubborn pride that had brought him this far would not bend to anyone in that elegant and remote enclave that had become the hidden core of his life.

So Ned had found work. Lowly as it was, it had put his first earned dollars into his pocket. Then he began to see those open stable doors for what they were. Barriers. For all his understanding, for all his willingness to take on the dirtiest stable work and the spent horses, he could not please the foreman. He dared not leave without a character. And it was beginning to be plain that he had made of Mr. Timothy Malley an enemy.

"You don't go about it the right way, Ned."

A greying man with a veined nose, carrying two heavily padded and worn horse collars, spoke to him from the yard outside. Ned finished washing his stained hands in a bucket of water, wiped them on a blackened rag, and stepped out into the bright noon light.

"I hate to see horses mistreated."

"Ah. Mistreatment." The stoop-shouldered man set down his burden. His thin mouth slanted in a wry smile. He used English carefully and he might have been fifty to sixty years, Ned guessed. Mr. Keefe was the one friend he had made.

"Mistreatment can be a matter of inheritance as well as stupidity, Ned. I hold no brief for Malley but he likely had the daylights whipped out of him by his father. And his father by his father. In the hands of barbarians, the whip means no more than a sharp tongue."

"What don't I go about right?"

"You talk to Malley with your head too high, Ned. Oh, I know it's put on that way, but he's got the idea you're his better. You're not, are you, for all your good looks?" The man cocked his head to one side and squinted at Ned. "A farmer's son? Pigs and corn in Sussex?"

"Wiltshire."

"I can always tell with an Englishman. I'm one myself. What you've really gone the wrong way about, is coming to work here in the first place."

"A man needs to eat. And he needs to start somewhere."

"Ah. Start. Something depends on where he's thinking of going. Now if you happen to have in your pocket the price of a smallish glass, for a man with a largish thirst . . ."

Ned knew exactly what he had in his pocket—four small coins and a single, carefully folded dollar bill. Secreted in another pocket, not for spending, was the solitary quarter. Ned could still remember how that pudding-shaped dragon woman guarding Dr. Lendler's household had dismissed him with it. He had taken it curtly. Only in the street had his resentment asserted itself.

You were meant for better things, Julien. Was he already taking his mother's dim, fatuous prophecy for the fact? He did not have to. He had discovered it for himself in every turn of this brash, gilded city. A man could have anything he wanted if he put his mind and muscle to it.

There'll be a place for you, Boy, you'll find it. His grandfather's wishful promise. Hadn't he already been inside one of the most lavish houses in New York? More profound than that was the look he had seen in the eyes of Noel Tremont. Fleeting as a mirage, yet it lived with him. For an instant Ned let his mind dally.

The vision faded. It took money, hard-earned, tightly saved. Money not only for proper clothes, but for the proper attitude of independence.

Mr. Keefe stood eyeing him, forlorn hope masking hidden desperation. Ned swung the heavy horse collars up and grinned.

"Come along, Mr. Keefe."

The Harp of Tara was beginning to fill. Ned elbowed his guest through the swinging doors into near-stygian darkness. With the ease of familiarity, Mr. Keefe found a rear table and bench, waved Ned to be seated.

"Best left to me, friend. I know the ways of the place."

Mr. Keefe went to the bar, spoke a few words to the bartender, who looked across the room at Ned. Ned nodded and Mr. Keefe gave his order. Then he moved along the counter. With a gesture that only practice could have made so swift, he swept onto a saucer from the waiting platters four thick pieces of bread, two slabs of white cheese, four hardboiled eggs, and what looked in the dimness to be two large green pickles but turned out to be two small pigs feet. Free lunch at the Harp was generous. It was also, on Mr. Keefe's visits, unprofitable.

He deposited the victuals on the table and returned to the bar for the two glasses, one short, one tall. He set the larger glass, with its collar of froth, in front of Ned. The smaller glass he set at his own place. Then he sat down, took a gulp of the whiskey, and rubbed the tip of his tongue lovingly around his lips. He followed that with an expansive sigh.

"Yes, Ned. You're the wrong way about it. The wrong way indeed."

Ned decided against an answer. His companion, with his dusty grey face, houndlike red-rimmed eyes, his skinny frame, and his ill-fitting, cast-off clothes, was a figure of human dilapidation. Only Mr. Keefe's speech indicated a mind at work and Ned saw no purpose in interrupting that.

"You see, lad, it's not the first mistake a man makes that's bad. Nor the next. Nor even the third. Maybe. But after that it's deeper in the quagmire until you've no way to pull out one foot for the other. How did you come to this country?"

"Worked my way, third-class seaman. . . ."

"Ahh, mistake number one. You should have paid your way steerage, then you'd have arrived fresh for opportunity, owing no man anything. Where do you stay?"

"A rooming house on Park Row." Ned might have resented the brisk questions, but Mr. Keefe, despite his shabbiness, managed to endow himself with an aura of authority as well as concern.

"Park Row, eh? Where all the jump-ships go? Second mistake. Put a label on yourself. Your third mistake was coming to work in the horse-car barn at all. No future. Nobody there to give you a leg up."

Which could not be contested. Mr. Keefe's oratory was rising.

"Your last mistake, lad, was working for a man like Malley. Maybe it's news to you, young friend, but there's only one thing on earth an Irishman likes better than a fight. That's the spectacle of a down-and-out Englishman. You're down on your luck, lad, anyone can see that. But you don't act it. That's a mistake, or maybe not, depending. But Malley saw that. He couldn't lord it over you. So he did what he could. Every time you came in sight he'd lay a whip on a horse, just to see your face. Someday he knows he'll get your dander up and there'll be a fight. Malley was a fistfighter once. He figures he can give you a good drubbing, and if he's lucky, finish you off."

"I'm not so sure."

"Neither am I, Ned. But it's Malley's thinking. And you're getting short of patience."

It was true. Ned had already promised himself a swing at the foreman's jaw the next time he saw an animal abused.

"So there you are. But now, lad, there's a fifth wheel on the wagon. Being as maybe you're a jump-ship?" The skinny little man's eyes were sharp as pins. Ned sat silent. He had given enough of himself away. "If Malley finds that out and he will, somehow . . . he'll take it within his rights to drop a shoeing iron on your skull and see you sent back to old England in chains."

"He'd have a damned hard job. . . ."

Mr. Keefe stroked his empty glass. "We're talking about your future, lad. Not your muscles. So we come to your last mistake. . . . Wouldn't mind a second now, would you?"

Ned went to the bar and returned with a whiskey, and the ale he didn't want.

"My thanks, lad. Keeps my mind clear and to the point when I'm trying to be the father to you that you haven't got. Your last mistake which could not rightly be called your mistake at all. That's being English."

"I'm not ashamed of it!"

"Of course you're not! God save Her Majesty the Queen!" He tilted his glass to his mouth, spilled a few drops on the wooden table top, wiped them up with the curve of his thumb, and licked that member clean. "I'd have stood up but for the unfortunate company we're in. The sun'll never set on us, lad. But for all the Widow of Windsor, the fleet, and the crown jewels, the Dukes, the Earls, the gentry right on down to the footmen, the fishermen, the pitmen working the bottom of the mines, they all have the same trouble as you and me."

Ned looked around. Malley had just entered the saloon and had taken a seat on the far end of the bar from which he had a full view of Ned and his guest. Ned debated an exit. He wanted no further scene with the foreman. But Mr. Keefe's philosophies had winged into full flight.

". . . the same trouble. Being English we all have a terrible, terrible sense of place. It besets us like original sin. We can no more get rid of it than we can take the bones from our skulls or peel the hide off our backs. A man's proper place in life. What he was born to, where he'll stay, and where he'll die. An Englishman believes that like the Roman Pope believes in his own holiness."

Time was passing but not for Mr. Keefe. Ned saw Malley had fixed his eyes on them.

". . . and who can say they're wrong, lad, when it's history? Take this New York where we are now. The Dutch owned it. And there they were sitting comfortable with their muskets and their gin holding the redskins off. In sails, the British. Three ships, lad, just three. Well, the Dutchmen look through their spy glass and see those three ships, every manjack aboard in his proper place. In the bows, the rigging maybe, astride the gunwales. Every man where he ought to be. What happened? The British took the whole island without firing a shot. Changed the name to New York and here we are."

The fiery dark liquor was returning color to Mr. Keefe's sunken cheeks. That and the warmth of unexpected kindness. Ned saw that Malley was sipping his beer slowly, watchfully.

". . . but of course, lad, it didn't always work so well. Take that nasty bit of unpleasantness they call the American Revolution over here. The British troops had to come and teach the upstart Yankees *their* proper places. But how did they come I ask you? Breeches and neck cloths, white and proper. Boots and bullets polished. Every man in his proper place in the line and down the square. Now, there's no man under the sun beats an Englishman when he's fighting. But the Yankee Doodles in their ignorance didn't know anything about a man's proper place. They shot from anywhere they could, behind a rock or a tree, or a hole in a field. Like the savages. And what could a proper British line do? Fall back, that's what, fall back, each man in his proper place."

Mr. Keefe sighed as much for the dwindling in his glass as for the lost causes of history.

"Well, the English don't give up that easy. So now they're coming back. Five hundred thousand, they say, in the past few years leaving the old country and more than half of them coming to America. It'd be easier if they'd all go to Canada or Australia where a man's proper place might likelier be understood. But here they come with all the trouble again of being English."

Mr. Keefe nibbled on the last fragment of pigs' foot.

"Now comes the moral of my story. My dad . . ."

"I think we'd better be going, Mr. Keefe."

"Going, lad? And not finish the free lunch? And a little to wet it down?"

It would, Ned reflected, be wiser to let Mr. Keefe's exuberance deflate quietly in this dim corner than to risk it at large in the saloon. Malley might be spoiling for a fight.

Ned signaled a gangling youth in a soiled apron who had materialized as a waiter.

Mr. Keefe gallantly lifted his refilled glass to his host.

"You'll make a proper gentleman someday, Ned. With your open hand and the advice I'm giving you. Now, my dad. Coachman to his Lordship back home. No man in all England could tool a coach and four, six if you like, like my dad. Then one day her Ladyship ran off with a painter fella to some heathen place like Burma, leaving a nude picture of herself in his Lordship's gun room. His Lordship in revenge gave up his horses and hounds and carriage and moved up to London. Nearer the tarts, he said. My dad, knowing his place, announced he'd go to America, finding it more settled, you might say, for a man of his character. But my mother, being lady's maid, said she'd stay in England. She didn't think there'd be any call for her work in a land of savages. So my dad brought me. Well, lad. . . ."

Mr. Keefe leaned forward as confidential as he was comfortable in his deepening aura of raw whiskey.

". . . to go on. My dad and me arrived here September the year '60, having to go through the immigration to prove we'd make decent citizens. Decent! And my father speaking the King's English. But that year of '60 was a bit of luck for us. The papers were full of Mr. Lincoln likely being the next president, only some of them called him Ape instead of Abe, which my dad didn't like. 'Not their proper place,' he'd say. And there was talk of war maybe coming to split the country north and south. I couldn't see that it would matter, with all the empty space I'd heard about. But the Prince of Wales was comin' to make a visit to New York the next month, October, and the gentry and the mayor were giving him the grandest ball ever seen. That is, in America. Well, there wasn't a fine house in the whole city that wasn't looking for an English coachman or an English butler for the proper way of doing things. My dad took employment right away. Rich people.

Rich? They had a fine mansion with gardens running right down to the East River''—Mr. Keefe gestured eastward—''and a carriage house for four vehicles, and stables. And three marble bathrooms. More than the Queen herself, I dare say. And you know where all the riches came from? Here's the point of my story, lad. When the old man who hired my father came to this country, a Greek he was, he went out on the roads peddling brooms. Good brooms, I don't doubt. Two kinds. One short-handled for shelves and closets. The other long-handled for sweeping the floors. He painted the handles all different colors—green and pink and purple and blue and yellow. Well, ladies being usually uncertain to make up their minds, they didn't buy one sensible broom. They'd buy long and short and maybe another one or two for color. And pretty soon he was rich, that Greek. And my dad, there he was, driving a coach and dusting out lap robes for him just as if he'd never left England. Well, it wasn't my cup of tea and I told my dad so. 'Dad,' I said, 'this is a bigger country than you ever saw. Nobody owns it all yet. There's so much land out beyond they're begging people to take it free. Why you can own land and be gentry if you'll just get up and start. You don't have to be anybody's coachman!' My dad looks at me as though I'd spit in church. And he says, 'Son, I have the finest gift the world can give a man. A respectable place in life. If you have the sense of your betters, you'll fit yourself to take my place when I'm gone.' That was all he'd ever say on the subject.''

Mr. Keefe drained his glass and set it down with finality. To Ned it seemed the pale, rheumy eyes had filmed but now he wanted to hear the rest of the story. It had more bearing than he had supposed.

''So did you go west on your own, Mr. Keefe?''

Mr. Keefe shook his head. ''That was nearly twenty years ago, lad. And I'm still here. My dad's gone, so he's spared the shame of seeing me tack cleaner and night watchman in a horse stable. There's always a root cause to things.'' He studied the wall behind Ned. ''She was a minx. Daughter of the house where me and my dad found employment. A fairy of a little thing. A waist you could span with two hands. A foot that would fit in your palm''—it occurred to Ned that Mr. Keefe had made measurements—''light and heedless as a dandelion seed. I was footman on the coach the night she went to the Prince of Wales ball. It was said her father had paid two thousand dollars for the dress she wore because she was one of the young ladies chosen to dance with the Prince.

But the next day, the very next, she was down at the river wall at the end of the garden pretending she didn't know I was working on the border bed of tulip bulbs. And I couldn't tell her to go away, now could I? In her own garden. The next day and next and on I'd look up from my work and see her, kicking the toe of her slipper into the soil, or twisting off ivy leaves as if they were in her way. She asked me why hadn't I the spunk to move on, go west? That's what she'd do, go west and raise sheep . . . sheep! I doubt she'd ever faced one of the dumb creatures in her life. I said it was in my mind and she said she'd help me . . . she was stifling here in the dull city, being presented by her aunts to Society and . . . well, that's the way the talk went, until one afternoon on the far side of the summer house, my dad caught us. Me with my hand where it oughtn'a to be . . . that was the end of it. My dad gave me a belt or two to teach me my place and said I was to leave, with no character. Her dad, I guess he knew her, said she was in need of marrying." Mr. Keefe's eyes brightened at a private vision.

"So you never went west for the land, Mr. Keefe?"

"Somehow I lost the taste. The city held me . . . it can, lad. It can."

Ned looked around. The noontime crowd was thinning. The bartender had fixed an eye on their empty glasses.

Ned rose, tapped his guest's shoulder.

"Time to go, Mr. Keefe."

The man lifted a face from which all life had drained. Slate grey, deep-lined. His arm shot out and he clutched Ned's sleeve.

"You're young, Ned. You've got no proper place yet. Don't look for one. Get out of that stable. Put on a suit, like a gentleman. Those hands'll need a little pumice and a pair of gloves. Go out and find what you want from life. It's the way you see yourself. What you can be. If I were your age again . . ." He rose unsteadily, found his footing, and walked to the bar. With a lordly gesture he dropped a small coin on it, then turned to Ned and made a bow of stiff courtesy.

"Thank you for your hospitality, friend." He turned to no one in particular. "Good day, gentlemen."

It occurred to Ned that Mr. Keefe was not as old as he looked. He was like a tree, swept and stunted by prevailing winds. He could be fifty, even less. An odd thought struck Ned. Something he had read at Mr. Bellowes' bindery? Or was it a moment of second sight, an instant's extrasensory image, a fleeting chill on a warm day? But there it hung in his mind. For every man, there is always another who has followed in the same shoes to the same fate. He would not take Mr. Keefe's path. But he would take, whatever the cost of debt or borrowing, that blurred and bitter advice.

They reached the swinging half-doors of the Harp of Tara together.

"Keefe!"

Mr. Malley had emerged from his place at the bar. He was a short, broad man, hunched with muscle, his face beefy, his eyes small, and at this moment dangerous.

"Keefe!"

"Yes, sir?" Mr. Keefe swayed.

"You're drunk, Keefe!"

"Not very, sir. Just a nip. My friend here . . ."

"I saw it. You listen to me. I've given you warning before. I'll tend to your 'friend' later. You're drunk all right, but not too drunk to get back to the stable yard. There's a dead horse lying there. I've sent for the knacker. Go back and see that they get it out of there."

"I'll do that, Mr. Malley." Ned's voice was as cold as his eyes.

"Oh you will, 'Mister' Fitch? Get on with it, Keefe, and you'd better still be standin' on your two feet when I get back."

The little man pushed his way unsteadily through the swinging half-doors and out into the spring light, strands of sparse grey hair standing upright, an aureole in the light breeze.

Ned waited, a tightening in his gut telling him that the moment was here.

"You're fired, Fitch." Malley's face was bloated with hatred. "One, for getting my man drunk on duty. Two, for interruptin' my orders. Three, I don't like you."

"Understandable, Mr. Malley. I'll finish out my time today and. . . ."

"You'll finish nothing. You'll pick up your pay at the office and get out. Now. If you're on the premises when I get back it'll go bad for you. Get me?"

"I do, indeed."

"You goddamned limey. Yer a jump-ship and . . ."

But Ned had gone.

In the stable yard it was as Ned suspected. The tired old roan, Josh, lay dead in the mire, mouth open, knobbled legs stiff, an open slash on his rump already filling with flies. But it was to the heavy head that Ned walked. As he moved, he was aware of the stable workers gathered near the horse, eyeing him in silence, as if waiting, testing. Mr. Keefe was nowhere in sight.

Ned stooped. The old horse might have known better times. The neatly turned ears, the long straight slope of the withers showed bloodline. And something else. Ned found what he was looking for. Between the ears there was an ugly bruise, as if made by a piece of metal. There was another on the side of the forehead. Old Josh's great heart had not given up in the traces. He had been beaten to his knees first.

Ned looked around the half-circle of men and saw neither emotion nor hostility, only watchful curiosity. They were waiting. It did not take long. Malley, his powerful short-legged stride, deliberate, was crossing the yard toward them. His hand grasped a two-foot length of pipe, easily, familiarly, as if he knew its uses well.

"I told you to get out, Fitch!"

"You killed this horse, Malley."

"I run this stable. I do it my way!"

Malley was close now. If he swung the pipe he could easily have knocked Ned to the ground. But as with all bullies, Malley needed to be sure. There was always an instant of uncertainty, of someone at his back, of treachery like his own. He glanced around. In that split second Ned sprang. He pushed Malley's arm back, twisting the pipe in Malley's thick grip, and at the same moment forcing his foot between Malley's shins, the old London street trick for unbalancing a man.

But Malley was a fighter. He did not go down, nor did he loosen his grip on the pipe. He swung a heavy left fist at Ned's jaw as he regained the use of his weapon. A man shouted a warning. Even as Ned ducked, he felt the pipe graze the side of his head and a dizzying warmth of blood on his temple. Blindly, with all the considerable strength he possessed, he punched the beefy stomach.

Both men fell. Ned lay for an instant, winded and silent. Then slowly he pushed himself to his feet. Malley lay sprawled, the pipe gone from his hand, his eyes shut. But he was breathing. Ned controlled a raw, red urge to sink his fingers into the man's short neck and finish the job. He looked around. The stable hands had melted away. Mr. Keefe was coming toward him.

"Better go, Ned. He'll come around all right. But he's a killin' man. He'll never forgive you."

"I'd be ashamed if he did. All I ask is that he doesn't forget me. Or that animal lying there."

No man could end the tragedy of man's cruelty to man and beast, but as he left the stable yard Ned felt unaccountably good. The blood had dried on his face, his dizziness had disappeared. He was dirty, disreputable, and his left trouser leg was torn across the knee. But once again the city loomed open and challenging around him. He was free.

What was it Napoleon had said? "Circumstances *make* circumstances." What one man could do, he, too, could do. As he turned south, a faint smile twisted his face. What would Miss Tremont of Stuyvesant Square say if she saw him now?

The answer came, not from his mind, not from reason, not even from knowledge, but from somewhere in a region of his heart that he had held so long at bay. In his mind's eye he could see her coming toward him with her proud little head held high, surveying him with that cool, measuring look up and down. He could almost hear the cool, measured words she might say.

"Why, Mr. Fitch, what a perfectly splendid thing to do!"

Stuyvesant Square, mottled by spring sunlight, lay in its usual mid-afternoon languor. Three o'clock, to be precise, the nadir of New York's social day. At eleven in the morning, calling cards might be left, one corner correctly bent. At noon, luncheons summoned. At four, tea wherever that British custom remained rooted. But at three, Society's tireless arbiters had decreed a vacuum for quietude, detachment, and unlacing of corsets.

It was therefore startling when at this unlikely hour the front doorbell of number 269, residence of Mr. Walter Tremont, jangled. Annie-Mae, now a parlor maid, dozing in a chair in the rear hall sprang to duty, straightening her apron, tucking tendrils of curls under her flounced cap. Any sound or diversion was welcome. For Annie-Mae, although she would die before admitting it, was lonely. Belowstairs, Cook wielded a broad-based tyranny. Abovestairs, housekeeper Mrs. Jessup practiced the unrelenting severity of a Scottish Presbyterian. A far cry for Annie-Mae from the whitewashed cottage of her childhood, overflowing with brothers and sisters, her mother with a laugh quicker than a slap, her father returning at nightfall with a barrow of peat.

Annie-Mae hurried to the front hall. Never let the bell ring twice, Mrs. Jessup had warned. Breathless, becomingly flushed, she opened the door. The gentleman standing there was as tall as anyone she had ever seen, his hair black against the sharp light. He carried a square white box tied with a pink ribbon—flowers, if she had learned anything in the new country. He removed a grey bowler. He was all in grey, not unusual on a spring afternoon, she guessed. Blinking at the splendor, Annie-Mae was unaware that the caller had moved deftly past her into the wide hall before identifying himself.

"Miss Noel Tremont." He smiled down at her as if he were a familiar and regular caller of the family.

"Miss Noel isn't home, sir." Annie-Mae bobbed, not at all sure she should do it.

"Really? I had understood. . . ." He looked down at her.

"She's gone to visit friends, sir. Up the Hudson River. She's gone now two weeks near, but I expect she'll be back soon—" Annie-Mae stopped abruptly. Should she talk so much?

"How very nice. A little holiday at this time of year. Very pleasant. But my bad luck." His eyes held hers. "Perhaps, if you will be so kind, and I'm sure you will be . . ."

"Oh yes, sir." Annie-Mae felt a little giddy with the kindness.

By this time Ned had maneuvered himself to a marble-topped table and a mirror above it with what looked like a hundred eyes. From there he caught a glimpse of the drawing room, all gilt and blue velvet, as elegant as he had dared to imagine. Whatever his secret gratification, it was momentarily dimmed by the presence of a lady in the entranceway. She was as slim as Noel, of about the same height and age, he guessed, blonde and cool, in an ice-blue dress that matched almost exactly the blue of her eyes. Ned sensed that beneath that disdain could lie danger.

"A gentleman, ma'am, to see Miss Noel. I told him . . ."

"That will do, Annie-Mae."

Annie-Mae vanished. The lady moved forward to confront the three o'clock intruder.

"I am Mrs. Tremont, Noel's stepmother. You are . . . ?"

"Edmond Abbingdon-Fitch. At your service." Ned bowed and smiled. The lady did not return the smile. She was not looking at him as much as directly through him.

"And you are an acquaintance of my stepdaughter, Mr. Abbingdon-Fitch?"

"Yes, of course. Or I wouldn't presume . . ." Ned knew the type. High-mannered as the ladies he had seen at a distance in London. But that was long ago and this was America. Although the situation surprised him, he congratulated himself on arriving at it. ''I had the privilege of making Miss Tremont's acquaintance on an occasion and I wanted to express my appreciation of her graciousness.'' He held out the box.

''I quite understand.'' Adrienne Tremont was openly measuring him. ''I had not heard her mention your name. It is unfortunate, as my maid told you . . . and I'm afraid she isn't quite trained yet . . . that Noel is away visiting. We really don't know when she's returning. But I shall of course accept these for her with your card.''

She had him there. Ned had tried to think of everything in the two days he had planned this assault. His look held a touch of boldness.

''I do not carry calling cards yet, Mrs. Tremont. I've come only recently to this city.''

''I see. You're English, are you not? I was schooled in London. It is my second, I might say almost my first, home. We must talk about it someday.''

But she did not mean it. She was dismissing him as surely as she had the little parlor maid. Ned glanced past her into the drawing room. A young man with his back to the entrance stood seemingly lost in study of an oil painting in a heavy gilt frame. His left hand was smoothing his tawny hair.

''Oh, David''—the cool voice lilted—''do come here before you go. Mr. Abbingdon-Fitch, you must meet my stepson, Noel's brother. David, this is Mr. Abbingdon-Fitch from England who came to call on Noel and . . .''

The young man stepped forward, smiled, held out his hand. Ned liked him. He was open-faced, friendly.

''Welcome to the land of the dollar. Hope you like it here. I don't, but if you don't like something you stay and change it, right? You don't back off. Thank you for early tea, Adrienne.'' He glanced sideways at Ned with what seemed a half grin, though it might have been closer to scrutiny. ''My stepmother's a bit of a problem. Can't call her Mother. I've tried but she won't hear of it. Good luck to you, Mr. . . .''

''If you'd only stop talking, David, you'd have heard. Mr. Edmond Abbingdon-Fitch.''

It surprised Ned that she had picked up the syllables so precisely.

Mrs. Tremont's laugh was as impersonal as her speech.

''You must forgive David. He's our youngest and something of a bohemian. He's an artist and his father wants to send him abroad to study. But David prefers a more, shall we say, commonplace career in journalism. Oh well, this is a day of change. One can't advise the young in ways they don't wish to go, can one?'' The words came oddly to Ned from a woman as obviously young as the man waiting for her in the drawing room. ''I shall tell Noel when she returns that you called, Mr. Abbingdon-Fitch. Though I am never sure when. My stepdaughter doesn't always take me into her confidence. Good day, Mr. Abbingdon-Fitch.''

The dismissal was final. Had Ned turned back as he left the house, he might or might not have been surprised to see the composed young woman in ice blue give a little gasp as she faced her stepson.

''David! How could you?''

''Could I what, my sweet?''

''I asked you to stay out of sight.''

''With the fellow halfway down the hall peering at me, like a squirrel in a cage? What's wrong with being seen at tea with one's very own stepmother?'' Adrienne's face flushed. ''Anyhow, everybody can rest now. In peace. Noel has a beau, and a presentable one at that. I trust I made him welcome. Let the family rally.''

Adrienne's mouth tightened. For an instant an observer might have glimpsed in that lovely, youthful face the aging woman that would someday come, features pinched and sharp.

''Presentable! With no calling card. His cuffs frayed. A bowler looking as if it had come out of some theatrical shop. And at three in the afternoon when no gentleman calls on a lady.''

It struck David that Adrienne had been rather zealous in her scrutiny, but he merely grinned.

''I thought you and Kitty wanted nothing more than to marry Noel off to somebody, anybody. And relieve the family of the stigma of spinsterhood. Father will give her a handsome dowry. So what does it matter if Mr. Edmond Abbingdon-Fitch is a fortune hunter?''

''It matters a great deal. I am not so sure I favor Noel's marriage to anyone. In the last two weeks since she's been away, I've begun to realize how much company, even contentment, she provides for her father. Walter quite adores her, you know. Without her the burden rests entirely on me. That''—she looked squarely at him—''I find at times awkward.''

She took a step toward him, reached out her hand to touch his face, her forefinger lightly brushing his mouth.

''You are naughty, David, not to understand.''

"And you are Circe, luring me to my ruin." He caught the hand to his lips.

She stepped closer, her fragrance enveloping him. His arms dropped stiffly to his sides.

"Not here, Adrienne. For God's sake. Not in my father's house."

Ned walked slowly, thoughtfully, into the Square beneath the new shade of its fine trees. He was angry at himself, at fate, at his own clumsiness in the turn of events. It had not occurred to him that Noel could be away. He had fixed her so completely in this place, coming and going from the house he had just visited. He had only, in a manner of speaking, to charge through the front door. His meeting with her would be as inevitable as the next day's sunrise.

It had gone quite differently. The young stepmother who had managed to be both lofty and enticing. The young man, David, Noel's brother. There had been no welcome, no talk of Noel's return, no curiosity about Ned himself. He had been subtly made to feel the outsider, the intruder.

But he had made no mistake about Noel. He had thought of her in terms too intimate to deny a future. The meeting in the park, the stroll together, the shared vibrancy. Later she had chosen to wrap herself in mystery. What woman didn't?

Ned brought himself up short. He would see her again. He would find her wherever she was. If one door closed, as his not-so-daft grandfather had dinned into his ears, another would open.

Meanwhile, like it or not, he must set himself to the rigors of survival. He glanced down at his secondhand suit, his too closely fitting vest. Perhaps he had overdone it a bit. He would do better. Then he would call on Dr. Hugo Lendler. And damn the dragons.

16

The woman opened a second-story window, and set a pot containing a single geranium, blighted of leaf and limp of bud, in the fragile May sunlight. Then she leaned her heavy breasts and heavy arms on the windowsill to watch the day's course.

The lane below was so narrow that two wagons could pass only by mounting the sidewalks and sending pedestrians scurrying into the flaking doorways of small shops. Overhead, the tangle of telegraph wires, New York's ubiquitous signature of progress, left their knife-edge shadows crisscrossing the little street. The skimming urgency of the messages they carried from prosperous waterfront offices of commerce to prosperous uptown bastions of finance were, to the inhabitants of Barrow Lane, as remote as the migrations of birds, as unknown as the past.

For a peculiarity of this thrusting young city of a million inhabitants was its almost total indifference to its own history. Few sailed into its harbor with a taste for retrospect. Whatever energy had brought a new arrival this far was directed to the future, a vague, gilt-edged goal seen through the glow of ambition. No one came to New York to look back.

So, too, with the woman seated at the second-story window of a moldering mustard-brick building fronting on the cramped little street. A century and a half ago it had been the manor house of a successful Dutch-born merchant. Visions of those long-lost reaches of green lawn, shadows of elm and oak, scarlets and yellows of tulip beds might have provided her with some lift of spirit. But all that, like her own days, lay quieted forever beneath cobblestones and mortar and the sullen thunder of the city. How could she know that before another decade passed, the faded mustard-brick building would play gutted host to other masses of people, with swarthy faces, tongues as strange as their customs. Poles, Russians, Serbs, Estonians bringing each of their own idiom and their inflexible God to a bright tomorrow. Brightness would soon dim in the rooms of the old mustard house. In the decades to come, each room might hold an entire family, even two or three families of the desperate yet hopeful humanity surging through it.

But for the woman at the window it was still a self-respecting place. Slum was always a word for another part of the city. Nor had she any knowledge of the glib uptown dismissal of that ugly word. Slum, from slump, for those who had allowed themselves to slump into the hole of poverty. Hard work, sobriety, and righteous respect for one's betters would solve everything.

The woman leaned forward, her attention caught.

"Binnie!" she called. "Binnie, come here and see!"

A gaunt, younger woman arose from where she had been kneeling at a dressmaker's frame. She still had pins in her mouth as she came to the window. She removed the pins.

"Where?"

"Out there." The heavy woman pointed. "A cab left them at the corner. A cab, fancy that."

The gaunt woman watched with interest. "Well, you can tell where she's going. Young, I'd say, from the way she carries herself. But that black dress don't fit her at all. More cotton than silk, I'd say. Not much shine. And a veil that thick is out of fashion. The young ones today when they've lost one man don't want to hide their faces from the next. Not them." Binnie spoke with the bitter authority of the unmarried. She peered again at the two figures now directly opposite. "But look at the child. Pongee, I'll wager, that dress is. And a flounced hat. With a whole wreath of daisies on it. Not just front and side, but all around. A pretty penny for that!"

"There. I told you so!" The heavy woman crushed her breast against the windowsill. "Going toward Nater's. She's not carrying anything, so it must be joolry she's got. Binnie, later when you've finished on that skirt, take some coffee over to Mr. Nater and find out. My ankles are killing me or I'd go."

The gaunt woman rolled the pins between her fingers, preparatory to returning them to her mouth. "If she's that young, old man Nater isn't going to give her much on anything. Unless she throws in a little something on the side. If you know what I mean."

"How you talk, Binnie."

Down in the street the young woman in black stood, hesitating outside a dark red door. The child lifted her face beneath the flounced bonnet and stared at the three glittering golden balls directly above her. The young woman seemed to have come to a decision. Taking the child's hand, she pushed open the door.

The woman at the window turned her head. "She's gone in, Binnie. She must be recent widowed to wear that heavy black. Seems rightly the child should be wearing black, too."

"Rightly, yes," came the superior wisdom. "But who do you think would notice the widow twice without the child dressed up bright as a dollar like that? I know her kind."

The heavy woman returned to her vigil. She could not hear the jangle of the pawnbroker's bell. But in her mind, she could see, plain as a pike, Mr. Nater, proprietor, skeleton-thin, emerge from the dark green curtains at the rear of the shop. She settled herself, wondering with the morbid curiosity of a loveless woman how long the young widow's transaction would take.

In the circle of light thrown on the counter by an overhanging lamp, the pawnbroker loomed as tall as a prehistoric bird, his head bald, his nose beaked. When he fitted the black jeweler's loupe into his left eye and bent forward, Noel felt Posie start back from her grip.

"It's all right, Posie. The gentleman is just examining the brooch for me. Now why don't you look here, into the case? See all those pretty rings and chains."

But Posie's face, momentarily brightened by the sight of the three golden balls, had turned pale. Her hand within Noel's tightened. The premonition of defeat that had run through Noel's broken sleep last night confronted her again. For an instant she thought of snatching up her brooch and, with her child, running from the place, from the dust, the stifling odors of camphor, wood oil, resin, and unaired wool. Then common sense returned. Any weakness of her resolve would take Posie from her—to the care of an orphanage, of strangers, of enemies.

She felt a small tug.

"When can we go, Mistaffy?"

The man behind the counter glanced up with his one clear eye. Whether it was at the oddity of the nickname or for some other reason, Noel could not guess. The eye was shrewd.

"If the child is impatient, Madam, I have a rocking horse in the storage room. . . ."

"That's very kind but she'll stay with me."

All of this, Noel reminded herself, was her own fault. On that despair-ridden dawn three weeks ago, or was it three years, when she and Posie had taken the first train down from Riveredge to the city, she had discovered the safety of her widow's veil. It had brought deference, even kindness. It had permitted the cabdriver at Grand Central Station to suggest a small, respectable hotel . . . "West Twenty-second Street, ma'am. Very refined. With a ladies' entrance, like the best. You'll be comfortable there."

She had indeed been comfortable, too comfortable. A delphinium-papered room, clean white washstand, a brass bed wide and deep enough to hold herself and Posie, and meals included, two dollars a day. As expensive as one of the great luxury hotels along Broadway, but here she had also been safe. A round-faced chamber woman, her head nodding with sympathy, brought their trays and a kind of rationale.

"You've had your loss, ma'am. But you'll find yourself. And that pretty young 'un will be your solace and your strength. The very image of you, ma'am, if I do say so. God heals all who ask His help, in His own time."

Time. A gift for those with hope. For those in flight, a tyrant. She who had once had too much time, found herself counting her days against her dollars. The secret cache of saved money she had taken to Riveredge, she thought, would last her, with prudence, until she could solve her dilemma.

The trouble was that she had *not* been prudent. The two dollars she had spent a day might have kept them a week at a plain boarding house. But she could not bring herself to risk her privacy. And then with Posie's solemn, questioning eyes on her, she had quite lost her head. As well as buying herself a disguising black dress and a heavy veil, she had bought Posie a ribbon-sashed pale silk dress, a lawn petticoat, shiny black buttoned shoes, and the ultimate extravagance of a daisy-trimmed hat that turned the little face into a portrait.

Then she had set out gaily to show Posie the delights of the city, the goat-drawn carts in Central Park, the waxworks on Broadway, the horse-tram rides. At a deeper level, she had craved the mother-and-child closeness she had for so long denied herself. Sometimes in the self-searching moments of long nights, she had wondered if it could be achieved at all. This distant child, flesh of her flesh, seemed as politely unconscious of any tie save the sharing of a splendid new holiday.

The pawnbroker was taking his time. Posie drooped in silence beside her. Noel's heavy black veil added to the airlessness of the place. The clutter of objects seemed to crowd in on her. On a shelf along one wall stood clocks of brass, carved wood, enamel, some with pendulums, some without, in various states of dilapidated silence, the hands marking the long-ago hours that had at last stilled them. On the wall above hung a row of stringless violins, the veneer chipped, the patina gone, among them one polished mandolin, its string board inlaid with ivory, its strings in place, as if only yesterday the player had laid it on this counter of banished hopes. But what caught Noel's eye was a woman's cape hanging in one corner. Woven of gold thread now fraying, the borders of white fox long yellowed, it might once have graced a box at the opera, or a ball, like a beautiful woman's pleasures ended.

The pawnbroker lifted his head and removed the loupe from his eye. Intuition told Noel not to show impatience. It would encourage the man to give her a cheaper price. Then she was aware that he had turned his full scrutiny on her, his eyes moving from her face through its sheltering veil to her black-gloved hands, over her small black-clothed breast to her narrow waist.

"We don't give much on opals, Madam."

"It's a fire opal." Noel watched the man purse full, moist lips. It was no ordinary opal, as he must know. Hyacinth red, large as a sparrow's egg, in a filigreed setting of seed pearls and tiny diamonds, it had been her father's gift to her mother on their tenth wedding anniversary, a symbol of his growing prosperity. Noel remembered her mother's worried acceptance. "It's very rare, Papa says. And it doesn't bring bad luck like those milky opals. But my goodness, Noel, how can your father be so extravagant!" Noel could remember seeing her mother wear it only once, on an annual Ladies Night of the Lieder Society. It had come to her on her mother's death. She had prized it. In the early morning of her departure for Riveredge, she had snatched it on impulse from her jewel box, a fragment of innocence from a distant girlhood. Now, in her need, she had done what had to be done, without permitting herself the luxury of anguish.

"Twenty dollars." The man's long fingers fondled the brooch.

"Twenty! Why it must be worth . . ."

"How much would you like to have for it?" He lay the brooch on the counter and looked directly at her. "I could arrange more, perhaps." She saw his power, she sensed his brutality. He traded in human desperation. No one entered his shop without that burden. She was, as she was beginning to learn, step by step, no different from other flotsam of troubled humanity milling through the city's meaner streets.

"Twenty," she said icily, "will be satisfactory."

He did not notice her again. In a series of movements, so rapid as to be almost one, he pushed a long grey ledger and a pen at her, and slid a receipt and two dirty ten-dollar bills across the counter with his right hand as his left engulfed the fire-opal brooch.

"Redeem in three months. Two percent per month. Five percent after that. Forfeiture six months from current date. Mind the step."

She was out on the sidewalk, clutching Posie's hand as if it were no longer small round flesh but a life ring. A dray, topheavy with bloody beef and sheep carcasses, rumbled close, its iron-rimmed wheels scattering the street's filth. She was unaware of it.

Twenty. She had anticipated a hundred. No, she had dreamed a hundred. At this level to which she had brought herself, dreams were as unaffordable as indulgence.

She began to walk, numbly, rapidly, Posie's small steps drumming at her side. Exercise, the deep intake of fresh air, began to clear her mind. She must plan now, as she had always planned, sensibly and devoid of emotion.

She would begin by taking the Broadway stage uptown. No more cab rides. With care she could afford one more week in the delphinium-papered room. By that time she must find employment, suitable lodgings, and solve head-on the one dilemma that she had pushed from her day after sunny, spellbound day. Posie. Her child was no longer a pain-wracked secret. She was reality, filling to overflowing the inner emptiness of Noel's days, opening forgotten channels of warmth, spontaneity, of love, if Noel dared use the word she had so long denied herself.

In a practical, workable way, she would find a pattern of life in which to keep and care for this small, unspeakably dear human being whom she was barely beginning to know.

The streets, instead of widening toward Broadway, had grown drabber and more mazelike, one running into another, like small mud flows toward a river. She had never been in this part of the city before. Her brother, David, had once told her, because David knew everything, that if she were lost she had only to find the sun—east in the morning, west in the afternoon—and she would know which way to go. The brilliant May sun was directly overhead.

She walked on. Narrow houses of flaking brick or brownstone crowded each other as if here all life melded—a patchwork of lodging houses, dwellings, and printed white cardboard signs stuck into windows, ragged pennants of defeat. LODGING 30 CENTS A NIGHT, NO CHILDREN. FRENCH LESSONS, MLLE. LEPEY, 25 CENTS AN HOUR. MILLINER'S ASS'T WANTED. TO STEAM FRAMES. FEMALE PIANIST TO ASSIST IN CABARET ACTS.

Here was not so much the bedrock of poverty, but what would be referred to her at her father's dinner table as "working classes." Here was where people who served the comfortable, the wealthy, lived their private, cramped lives. The cabman who had driven her to the refined little hotel. The faded saleswomen who sold fashionable ladies their laces and threads. Perhaps even the bookkeeper at her father's business. All in their places during the day. Few uptown cared where, their hours of service over, these servants laid their heads.

It now occurred to Noel that here she, too, might work out her fragmented destiny. She spoke French, she played the piano, and her mother had adamantly trained her in practical sewing. Those talents, she was discovering, were salable.

Suddenly as birds fly from a tree, three children burst out of a side alley into the street. Two girls in ragged skirts, dirty and of undeterminable color. A boy in torn breeches and mismatched shoes, an oversized cap pushed to the back of his head. The younger girl carried a woebegone yellow-striped cat lashing its tail. Like imps of a dark fantasy, they danced toward Posie, the boy mimicking and squeaking.

"Give her the cat!" he shouted.

The smaller girl thrust the cat into Posie's arms, while the larger girl snatched the daisy hat from Posie's head. They fled, out of reach. But this time their street skills failed. They ran straight into the bulk of an approaching policeman.

"Hey, you ragamuffins!"

The boy yelped, the girl dropped the hat. The three vanished into an alley. The cat jumped from Posie's arms. Looking down, Noel saw a long, red scratch across the small wrist.

"Here's yer hat, little lady." The policeman bent toward the staring Posie.

"Very kind of you, Officer." But Posie had drawn away.

"Those brats. They spill out of the slums like mice. Can't keep 'em where they belong."

"I'm sure they meant no harm."

"Harm! They grow a little older, the boy'll be carrying a knife or a sandbag. And the girls . . ." He covered the end of the sentence with a cough. "Nobody lookin' after them, that's the trouble. Father drunk, mother going out washin'. Or maybe the mother drunk, father takin' French leave, if there was a father. No help for it. Except to keep them away from decent people. Beggin' your pardon, ma'am, but are you and the little lady getting yourselves into a bad section?"

"I'm trying to reach Broadway."

"You're walking away from it fast as you can, ma'am. Now, you got two choices. Walk west and you'll come to the elevated railway stop on Sixth Avenue, though some ladies are afeard of riding three stories up in the air. Or you can go north to Sullivan Street where you'll find a cab. Best that way, I'm thinking. For you and the little miss."

Posie still clutched the spattered daisy hat, holding it over her injured arm.

Noel stooped. "Don't worry, Posie, we can brush off the mud. And we'll bandage up that scratch."

Posie moved from her, toward the police officer, and held out the hat.

"She can have it. That girl. Give it to her."

"Oh no, little miss. You spoil 'em that way. What call would the likes of her have for it?" Posie stared at him.

In the soft spring twilight that turned the delphinium wallpaper to faint lavender, Noel watched her sleeping child. The nightmare of the day was over. The city had shown its savagery in a pawnbroker's lust, in the tragedy of poverty's children. She had glimpsed the horrors that lay behind crumbling facades of brick and stone where the destitute sought survival. She who had been taught that comfort was the natural reward for hard work, honesty, and determination was no longer certain. How often had she heard her father say of his father, when they had arrived long ago from their native Alsace and the Old-World limits of Strasbourg, "Here is a new country, a new city. Here a man can become anything he will work to be."

Could he? And what of woman? But Noel was not given to despair. She had twenty dollars now and a reprieve of time.

The light faded as she watched Posie sleep.

It was dusk when the chambermaid arrived. Not the motherly chamber woman Noel knew but a big rawboned girl with a country-hardened face and small inquisitive eyes.

"Good evening. Is Mrs. Muller away tonight?"

"Mattie? She's gone. Husband in an accident at the new bridge where he's working. Under the water. Real bad, they say." The girl was savoring the grim importance of her news.

"How terrible." Noel meant it. She could hardly remember when the monstrous new bridge being built to span the East River from New York to Brooklyn did not have its attendant list of accidents and casualties. New Yorkers had already declared it a million-dollar folly that would never be completed. "I'm so sorry for Mrs. Muller." A tragedy for a kindly, hardworking woman who had been a source of goodness in this now hostile city. Mattie Muller deserved better.

"They'll kill all those men yet, takin' 'em down in them great wooden boxes under that river." The girl looked at the child sleeping in the bed. "No need to turn the bed down, I guess. Anything else?" She glanced around the room, quick hard probings, from the stark black dress hanging like an exclamation mark against the closet door to the ivory-white cashmere of Noel's dressing gown, as if picking up chips of Noel's privacy.

"Yes, please." Anxious as she was to get rid of the girl, Noel had no choice but to use what service was offered.

"A bowl of warm bread and milk for my little girl." She tried to smile. "And she likes plenty of floating butter."

But the girl missed the smile. Her eyes were fixed on Noel's hands.

"Yes, ma'am."

"And tea for me, please, with milk. And some toast."

The girl nodded. Her eyes met Noel's for an instant. She turned on her heel and went out.

The look, hard and sullen, held something Noel could not quite define. But it remained with her after the door closed, as she unfolded a newspaper to the front-page columns of "Help Wanted" notices and picked up a pencil.

"Wanted. Young lady capable and sensible. . . ."

She was capable and sensible.

"Wanted. A teacher of pianoforte. . . ."

She made another checkmark.

From the bed came a stirring. Posie slid from the covers and came to Noel's knee.

"Mistaffy. . . ."

How did one teach a child?

"Mistaffy, tomorrow can we go to see the lady's arm?" Posie had her own way of coupling reality and fantasy.

"If you like?"

"And stay?"

"Yes. For a while." She took the child up. The newspaper slid to the floor. Despite the warmth of the small body against her own, Noel felt a chill. She remembered the servant girl's hard look. Noel thought she understood it.

The brilliance of the warm May morning had already brought strollers to the wide parklike area of Madison Square. Women in flowered hats and light graceful dresses carried parasols, trailing their skirts on the walks, knowing they could afford to. Nannies in summer uniforms pushed open wicker prams, their charges snugly muffled against sunlight and fresh air. Elderly men were finding their usual benches. And, as inevitable as a wine sack at a Dionysian festival, came that prime talisman of a New York spring, the organ grinder. Swarthy, muscled, splendid with menacing black mustache and a bright red Neapolitan hat, he pushed a hand organ, bulky as a steamer trunk, while a melancholy monkey hopped to a grinding Anvil Chorus. Verdi was the new opera rage in this city of new sensations. Children followed the mechanical music maker like butterflies.

Noel found an empty bench. She had no need to point out the organ grinder. Noel sat back, feeling safe behind the thickness of her mourning veil.

Madison Square had been created when Broadway on its diagonal thrust through the city crossed elegant Madison Avenue. On one side rose the dowagerlike eight-story Brunswick Hotel, its luxurious rooms already shaded against May warmth by green-and-white awnings. On its other borders, Madison Square boasted rows of handsome brownstone houses, four or even five storeys in height, with tall windows, carved lintels, and neat blocks of granite flanking the front steps that New Yorkers still called by the centuries-old Dutch name, stoops.

In this particular spring season, Madison Square contained a curiosity that at first brought hordes of spectators, then a growing indifference, finally a sense of mild irritation. It was nothing less than an enormous sculptured female arm, the hand holding upward a huge sculptured torch. A framed notice informed the curious. "Right arm of the great statue to liberty which on completion will be the gift of France to the United States, in lasting recognition of French-American friendship and the mutual ideal of Freedom."

But fate could be perverse even in man's most noble moments. The great statue was not ready. Worse, the French, with their natural logic, had assumed that a grateful United States would want to provide the 89-foot granite pedestal necessary to support the statue. The Americans, with eyes only on their own quickening future, were slow to grasp the opportunity.

In brief, the mighty gift, instead of lifting the hearts of men, was proving a dilemma. French practicality solved it. If the towering lady herself was not ready, a token would be sent to the Centennial. Specifically, the right arm, 42 feet long, with a hand 16 feet, five inches in length that grasped the torch. After this awesome member had boggled the minds of Philadelphia, it would go on tour. The mere sight of it would loosen pennies from schoolchildren and checks from America's well-known and increasingly numerous millionaires. The embarrassing lack of a pedestal would be resolved.

In due course the arm arrived in New York's Madison Square, where it rested in the open within a low railing. Some were repelled by it size, others thought it a hoax. "There's no statue in the world you could attach that arm to!" "If you ask me, it gives a person a queasy feeling, like we're all too little, sort of make-believe." "Money for a pedestal? Not me. Let them that has money give it if they want the thing here!"

On this morning of May sunshine, such comments floated above Posie like cloud puffs. Once again she was allowed to stand gazing in wonder at a fingernail, eleven inches long at the thumb, into which a child her size could walk. Nothing in all the city had so captured her attention. The carved lady to which it would someday belong overflowed her imagination.

Noel, seated near her, knew that Posie would remain motionless, self-contained, gazing at the arm until she was summoned. Then she would come quietly, obediently, giving no hint of what flights of fancy she had traveled.

Someday, Noel told herself, she would know this child of hers. Now she was grateful merely for her nearness. Whatever change Noel's life must take, Posie would be at the heart of it. The sun was growing hotter. Noel's black dress was too heavy for the day, stifled her. She felt a dizziness, her forehead was damp. She would like to have lifted her thick black veil, but that was too dangerous. Someone might pass, someone who knew her. Stuyvesant Square lay only six blocks to the south. Six blocks—six thousand blocks now. The city around her blurred, then came into view.

On a bench across the walk sat a portly man in a black

suit. His bulk, his mustache, the gold chain catching the sunlight across his vest brought to mind her father. She dismissed the notion. The man had an unsavory quality.

But the sight served to bring back the restlessness of her nights, the recurring dream that broke her sleep like a missing piece of her own life. In her dream she had returned to her father's house, as if from a long journey. Her father opened the door, kissed her, and bending over, had taken Posie into his arms. In the heady relief she had entered into the familiar hall, its sweet polished quiet, marble-top table, bull's-eye mirror with its thirty-six tiny reflections. Oddly, those mirrors were empty, like sightless eyes. With Posie's hand in hers she had walked through the hall, on and on, until it had become an endless tunnel. She had turned once to look back. There was no one behind her. And no one ahead.

Her cry had awakened Posie.

"Mistaffy! Mistaffy! Are you crying?"

"Oh no, Posie. I was dreaming."

"Was it a good dream?"

"It must have been. I was laughing because you were happy."

She must not give way again. She must channel her thoughts to her purpose, discipline every emotion, waking *and* sleeping. She must not let the warmth of the day, the drowsiness that seemed to beset her on this hard bench distract her. It was time to return to the hotel.

The manager had sent up a note with her breakfast tray that he would, if she would permit, ask the honor of waiting on her at three o'clock. She understood. Her rent was due. But now she had the money. She could engage the room for another week. She had checked at least five positions for which she might apply. It was quite likely that the manager himself could recommend someone in the hotel to mind Posie while she went out for interviews. The worst was over.

She drew her veil close and rose. Her mind spun. Posie was not at the railing. Where she had stood, looking at the arm, was emptiness, as if a cutout had been made in the sunlight. Noel looked around wildly. The opposite bench was vacant. The man in the seedy black suit was gone.

She pushed her veil against her mouth to stifle a cry and ran out on the broad path through the square. Strollers were filling it. She brushed past them. There ahead, walking rapidly northward, she saw them, the heavy man in the seedy suit, Posie's hand in his. The child was talking animatedly.

"Posie!" Noel's choked scream thinned in the air.

Posie turned, slipped her hand from the man's, waved to him, and came dutifully to her. The man looked back and, with what to Noel seemed sudden alacrity, crossed Broadway to disappear into a side street.

"Mistaffy, he was going to buy me peanuts to give the monkey."

"Posie, the organ grinder is playing on the other side of the park."

"But the peanut man is over there." Posie pointed to a red-and-green umbrella.

"Posie, you must never talk to strangers. And you must never, never go with them."

"Why?"

"Because"—the inevitable introduction of evil to innocence—"you don't know who they are."

"Everybody's a stranger. You're a stranger, Mistaffy, aren't you?"

"I'm your friend. I take care of you."

"But I don't know who you are. You're not Mama."

Noel caught her breath. It was neither the hour nor the place to tell Posie the truth. She knelt to straighten the daisy hat.

"Posie, listen to me. Please. You must come straight to me if a stranger speaks to you, do you understand?"

Posie said nothing.

In the afternoon, while Posie lay on the bed napping, Noel sat bracing herself for the manager's visit. Her unaccountable dizziness returned fitfully. The heat, she told herself. Her thoughts were riveted on this sleeping child, her own, who could so unconsciously bring her pain even as she filled Noel's life. What little control she had of her affairs seemed to be slipping into confusion. At the perimeter of it all, evil played like dark lightning. She must protect Posie, not from the daily world alone, but from her vulnerable innocence.

The knock came.

Money in her hand, Noel opened the door. The manager was a small man. The polish of his black hair matched the polish of his pointed shoes. His smile was fixed, his teeth large and white. He took only one step across the threshold, discreetly leaving the door wide.

"Very good of you to see me, Madam."

"I should have stopped at the desk, but my little girl . . ."

"Of course." He did not intend to waste time.

"I would like to engage the room for another ten days. I

understand it is available and we have been most comfortable.'' She held out the two ten-dollar bills, glad to rid herself of the pawnbroker's touch.

The manager kept his hands stiffly at his sides.

''I regret there has been a change, Mrs. Taylor.'' The name still startled her. She had chosen it hurriedly to sign the register. Mrs. Norton E. Taylor. At least it carried her own initials.

''What change?''

The little man cleared his throat.

''We have—shall I say—a personage arriving next week. I cannot say more than—a title. All front rooms on this floor have been reserved.''

''I see. I understand. We'll be quite as comfortable in another part of the hotel. Whatever you have.''

''We have nothing else.''

He glanced at her hands, a quick, furtive glance, but she caught it. He saw what the chambermaid had seen. She wore no wedding ring. In the world of respectability, no widow would divest herself of that sacred emblem at any price. Her mother had worn the wide gold band until it had tightened physically, spiritually, into her flesh. When disease had begun its final ravaging, she had wound thread around the thinning finger and covered it with glue to keep the ring in place. ''Never take it from me, Noel. Bury it with me.''

Noel remembered wryly that there had been rows of rings to be had, cheap in the musty trays of the pawnbroker, mute symbols of other women's faded sacrifices. It was too late for that now. The sharp-eyed chambermaid had probed her disguise, perhaps even to the fine-embroidered underthings in the dresser drawer, the neat walking suit in the wardrobe, the violet hat worn to Riveredge. For whatever compensation there might be, twenty-five cents added to wretched wages, the outright splendor of a dollar, or merely the approval of a harsh employer, the girl had reported the ''widow'' and child.

The manager waited, his official smile gone. Noel saw it now as a duel.

''I have paid for this room through Friday. If I do not find suitable lodgings for myself and my child before then I shall expect this hotel to accommodate me.''

As the door closed, Noel caught a glimpse of the chambermaid idling in the hall. The girl had been warped by deprivation, lured by temptation. Was she herself any better, who had succumbed to temptation and resorted to hypocrisy?

The room was hot. She saw Posie as through a mist, playing with an improvised handkerchief doll on the bed. She drew a chair to the open window and drew a deep breath.

Her victory over the manager was as passing as smoke. Long before Friday she must have a plan and shelter. She would find it. She would not lose this child she had not yet won.

Her forehead was burning. She rose to bathe it. Posie was now singing a rambling little tune to her handkerchief doll in the comfort of the wide bed. Shelter was the first thing Noel must provide. A clean, decent lodging house. There must be advertisements for such places. She returned to the chair with her newspaper. For a brief moment, she yielded to the half dreams, half nightmares of her nights. Her father's house. What would her father do, if she returned? What would Adrienne do? Her brothers? Before the small, lovely reality of Posie? How could a child be a sin? Had she herself not paid in silence for her shame, if that was truly what it was?

She opened the newspaper. On page three, as if coiled and waiting, a headline sprang at her.

WALTER C. TREMONT
PRESIDENT OF THE CITIZENS LEAGUE,
NAMED WITH COMSTOCK
TO MAYOR'S MORALITY COMMITTEE
Anti-Vice Committee to Lunch at White House

The letters seemed to dance in waves, but Noel read on.

> Mr. Tremont, vowing a return to decency and solid, family morality, has promised support to all sectors of the Mayor's crusade. He will urge the destruction of the infamous Restell mansion of Fifth Avenue, which has long been an affront to decent men and women and is now a cynosure for the prurient. Mr. Tremont's appointment to the Mayor's Committee is seen as another indication of this capable and respected citizen's emerging importance in city affairs. . . .

The newspaper slid from Noel's hands to the floor. There was her nightmare, her answer to a buried wish. The question was not what her father would do in the presence of Posie. But what she and Posie would do to the serenity, the rising prominence of that house in Stuyvesant Square.

She could not go home, nor could she hope for help. She was more alone than on that anguished day nearly five years ago when she had first suspected she would bear a child. She had gone to a stranger. And in that stranger she had found the strength, the trust, the secrecy with which to have her child.

But all Carrie Restell had done was reviled. In alternating shifts of anger and heat, Noel sat motionless. Staring into the future, Carrie Restell drifted into the past.

Yet something of her reassuring presence lingered. Noel recalled the piece of plain notepaper she had found among Sophie's handkerchiefs. The name, in Carrie Restell's handwriting, that had seemed meaningless. Noel had thrust it into her handbag then to avoid prying eyes.

Now she recovered it and lit the oil lamp to read it again. In her firm hand, Carrie had written, "Ducharde. 17 Pear Street." That was all. A name, a place, and the unknown. But it was a name. And a place.

At eleven o'clock the following morning, passersby, had there been any, might have seen a cab turn into a narrow, cobbled alley in lower Manhattan. A former mews, the alley boasted half a dozen sagging, low-roofed houses of a style abandoned a century ago. At the end stood the solid bulk of a grey-washed brick house, presenting shuttered windows, and a painted paneled door to the street. In place of a knocker, a wrought-iron grill indicated that this building kept to itself. Number 17 Pear Street.

Noel had barely touched the bell when the door opened. A young, red-cheeked maid in uniform nodded, opened the door wider, but said nothing. Noel, with Posie's hand in hers, followed the girl into an interior room, a parlor she might have guessed, but so dim she could make nothing of it, nor of the face of the tall figure standing there.

"You may remove your veil. We have been expecting you, Miss Tremont."

But something was wrong. The room was without walls, the veil oddly heavy. A chair began to revolve. I don't faint, Noel told herself. I have never fainted. Not now. Please God not . . .

"Salts, Terese!"

But it was too late. The room spun. Posie's hand slipped from hers. Noel felt an arm, assertive, commanding, around her. Then nothing.

17

WILL LEMONADE LUCY COME TO LUNCH? As all New York including Dr. Lendler knew, Lemonade Lucy was the name given to the wife of President Rutherford B. Hayes by a ribald and irreverent press. Mrs. Hayes had banned all drinking of spirits, beer, wines, whiskies at the White House so the name had clung.

But the doggerel following that headline was not directed at that virtuous and strong-minded lady. Dr. Lendler settled his gold-rimmed spectacles and read on.

Will Lemonade Lucy come to lunch
With Comstock and Tremont and all of that bunch
Who ferret out Evil, do battle with Sin
Deploring the Flesh with all of the din
Of knights in tin armor, tin heroes, that ilk?
Oh, snooping out lust puts a man in the silk.

It was yesterday's newspaper. Dr. Lendler did not usually pursue the daily sensations of the press, but that morning at Columbia College he had heard a group of his students chuckling, then an open guffaw. They had thrust the paper at him. He had glanced at it quickly. Pleading time, he brought it home. If only for his old friend Walter's sake he must read to the scurrilous end.

Now one word of caution before you go,
You warriors, sniffers of human woe,
Who root out the fallen, like hogs at truffles,
Finding the garter beneath the ruffles.
Your piety gladdens in naming Vice.
It's a four-letter word Lucy does not think Nice.

At the White House praise Purity, name no Evil,
Time enough later to sup with the Devil.
Dwell on Chastity, Virtue, Morals,
Dull to be sure but you'll win Lucy's laurels.
So into the fray, boys, with cymbals and trumpets.
Save for the night time your doxies and strumpets.
Oh, no one denies fighting Evil sure pays.
When it gets a man lunch with President Hayes!

"Trash," muttered Dr. Lendler. But he had to finish.

But there's more to you gents than meets the eye.
You Tremonts who Peep, you Comstocks who Lie.
If as you say, the truth you would tell,
Uncover the hand that burked Carrie Restell.
(signed) Pure Yorick

It was worse than trash, it was libelous. But the New York press was known for its savagery and the tawdrier journals, to the delight of their readers, had long turned their vaunted freedom from use to abuse. Libel suits were as rare as they were unwinnable.

Dr. Lendler tossed the newspaper into his wastebasket. He could only hope that Walter had not seen it. But that was begging the issue. By this time the whole city would have read it and quoted it. Besides, Walter in his new-found enthusiasm for public good read newspapers he would once not have permitted in his house. Having seen it, what was he likely to do? Take issue? Abandon his innocent tilt with immorality? Or, courteous and decent to the last, step deeper into unknown waters?

It was, Dr. Lendler reflected, a question of motive. He sat back in his parlor armchair, removed his spectacles, and let his thoughts roam on his favorite subject. Motive. The human mind does nothing from the single motive. Any more than a single wave breaks on the shore. Behind the outer act, behind the surface motive, stirs another motive, more personal, more secretive. Behind that lies hidden need, a buried longing, sprung from some long-forgotten scar or failure that set the waves in motion. What in the smooth unrolling of Walter Tremont's life could give rise to this thorny new direction?

The *why* of human behavior . . .

That was the crux, seeded in him those long-ago student nights in Vienna when lamp wicks burned low, excited young voices rose high, and eager beginners first saw the awesome vistas of a newly discovered universe, the human mind. How far had they all come? Young Freud would be heard from someday, and the others who had stayed in Vienna.

For a moment Dr. Lendler yielded to nostalgia. Vienna, that splendid dowager, encrusted in elegance, gilt, and ancient bias. But for him a Vienna whose very stones sang to the human soul. His childhood home had been in Leopoldsville, a cluttered section outside the old city walls between the Danube Canal and the great river. Here his own people had lived in close, mutual need. To the aging, the invisible presence of long-gone ghetto barriers still stood. To the young, there were no admitted barriers. They were such daring intellects, so sure of a welcoming world, at once and forever. The poignancy of those dreams stirred in Hugo Lendler like the scent of Vienna's lilacs on a spring night.

But this was a different time and place, this was where he had made his life. His immediate subject was motive. Motive and his good friend, Walter Tremont. He was to dine with Walter on the eve of the anti-vice committee's departure for Washington. He must be quite clear what his own thinking would be.

The little mantel clock chimed four. Almost on the instant, the doorbell jangled. Dr. Lendler found himself startled. This was the hour Noel had come to play duets, the hour when she had brought him youth, warmth, and sometimes merriment. It had now become the loneliest hour of his day. He had not seen her since Adrienne Tremont's dinner party, even to bid her good day in the park.

Frau Gruen was standing in the doorway.

"He's come back, *Herr Doktor.*"

"Who's come back?"

"The young man who brought the books."

"Indeed. Did he give his name?"

"Mr. Abbingdon-Fitch, sir. Would Dr. Lendler see Mr. Abbingdon-Fitch?" She pronounced each syllable with care.

Her usually severe mouth relaxed to a near smile. It was apparent that she had revised her opinion of the caller.

"Mr. Abbingdon-Fitch, eh? Yes, I'll see him."

"You would like coffee? I have made a fresh sponge cake, *Herr Professor.*"

The little man eyed her with amusement. Even this stalwart tyrant of his home and kitchen had her frailties. But his voice was benign, even kindly. "No, thank you, *Frau Gruen.* I shouldn't think it necessary."

She turned a disappointed back. Motive, thought Dr. Lendler. Even in trivia. Frau Gruen classed most men as women's undeserved burden. He sensed that he had, for the moment, joined that majority.

"Dr. Lendler . . . ?"

He saw a tall young man in a plain black suit a clerk might wear, a neat bowler in hand. It occurred to Dr. Lendler that he had seen the dark-haired young man before. The height, the straight, strong build, the thick unruly hair. Dr. Lendler was conscious of such details. Then it came to him. Through the trees in the park, it was the young man he had seen talking to Noel. Dr. Lendler took pride in logic and objectivity. Chance, guesswork were not the functions of an orderly mind, yet he was aware of a momentary tightening of throat muscles.

"Come in, come in. My housekeeper tells me that I am indebted to you for a package of books you were kind enough to transport from London. This is my opportunity to thank you, Mr. Abbingdon-Fitch."

Ned had been doing some thinking. His pomposity with the guardian dragon had been shortsighted. The stunted little man, Dr. Hugo Lendler, was not at all what he had expected. The courtesy, the slightly accented geniality were cover to the sharp intelligence now probing him. Anything less than honesty might make of this man an enemy. What Ned needed now was a friend.

"I go by the name of Fitch, sir. Ned Fitch."

"Very sensible. I'm sure you'll find Americans take to informality. The shorter, the quicker, the better. Sit down, young man."

Ned sat precariously on a chair that seemed too small for him. Now that he was here again, the house seemed smaller than he remembered, and browner. Only one detail remained clear in his mind, the mantel clock, whose round golden pendulum swung back and forth catching the sunlight.

"You are English, Mr. Fitch?"

"London, sir. Uh, before that Wiltshire."

"You have come to America to stay?"

"Oh yes. I'm looking for employment, a good respectable position in which I can rise in the world. I have found work, Dr. Lendler. Body and soul kind of work. To keep them together so to speak. I'm not the man to idle. Not to my taste."

"Ah . . . and where is this body and soul employment?"

"In a horse-car stable. I left."

"Indeed."

"Cruelty, Dr. Lendler. I saw one horse being worked to death."

It was difficult not to like the young man even while one suspected a sleight-of-hand with facts. Dr. Lendler walked to the bow window. For an instant he studied again the lean, wind-bronzed features, high forehead, dark unruly hair, eyes observant and perhaps too quick, the strong chin but a mouth that would twist easily into sensuality. A face to tempt a woman.

He picked up four small books from his coffee table and handed them to his visitor.

Ned had risen.

"No. Sit where you are, Mr. Fitch. I like to stand. I sit too much. Besides"—the little professor permitted himself a glint of humor—"there are times when I not only like the advantage. I take it. Those are the books you brought me from London. Have you read them?"

"No, sir. I didn't open the package. A bit water-stained, I see."

"Water. Fire. Even the ultimate cataclysm cannot stop the passage of human thought. Take them with you. Read them. All except this one, which is in German. Unless, of course, you understand that language."

"I speak only English, sir. And I may not be very good at that. I can read, if that's what you're asking me."

His young visitor had a quick pride. Good enough, thought Dr. Lendler. He must know the extent and variety of this young visitor's mood if a plan that was taking shape in his mind were to succeed.

"All I've asked, Mr. Fitch, is *that* you read. Not *whether* you read. Come back day after tomorrow at this hour. We'll talk then. I have need of a clerk. Too many books up there in my study, too many papers, too few hours to organize them myself. If you qualify, and I think you might, you may be quite useful to me. The salary to begin is twelve dollars a week. Good day, Mr. Fitch."

The salary was generous, as Dr. Lendler knew. He saw the young man's eyes brighten. He watched him down the street, the confident, almost arrogant stride. He watched him pass the iron grilling of the park fence, the spot where Noel had run into him that day.

Noel's private feelings were not his affair. Her welfare was. He had taken the step, Dr. Lendler told himself, which was the right one, the only one.

In the gathering afternoon silence, Dr. Lendler went up to his study. From the shelf of the closet, he drew down a long newspaper tube. He unwound it carefully. As a lover of all fine, dedicated hand work, he admired again the slender shaft of polished ebony, the exquisite lotus carving of ivory, the perfection of the cane Captain Schwartz of the Eighth Precinct had presented him.

Deftly, he pulled at the ivory top. It came off more easily than the first time. He might have to glue it back at some later date. But he needed to be quite sure about it again.

Beneath the silver banding was the address of E. Monk, 23 Bowery. He had taken the trouble to pay E. Monk a visit. For a price of thirty dollars Mr. Monk had been quite willing to relinquish to Dr. Lendler all title to the cane and offer the information that he had rented it on March 31, of current year 1878, to one Ned Fitch, Mrs. Luskin's rooming house, 34 Park Row.

Dr. Lendler rewrapped the can in its newspaper, replaced it on the closet shelf and lay down on the black leather couch, curved by this time to his form. Devious as Ned Fitch seemed to be, there was nothing about him that suggested the petty thief, the housebreaker or worse. Yet, he had been, on *prima facie* evidence, in Caroline Restell's house the night of her death.

Motive. Dr. Lendler stared at nothing. Motive, each one wave upon wave, each one deeper than the next, each one spurring the next. Motive, the why of human behavior when it contrasts so strongly with the externals of human appearance.

In a steamy upstairs room of the Anti-Vice Commission's office at City Hall, Walter Tremont sat stiffly with the six other members of the mayor's special committee. They were waiting for the arrival of the chairman.

It was not like Mr. Anthony Comstock to be late. But Walter did not mind. As soon as the meeting started, the only window in the room would have to be closed, what breeze there was shut out, so that a man could hear another above the pounding of iron-shod hoofs, the rattling of iron-rimmed wheels in the street below. He wondered irritably what benighted planners still ordered the city paved in cobblestones.

Yet he knew his irritation was not bedded in the unseasonable heat, the noise, or even the sordidness that seemed to be engulfing him since he had accepted the honor of the Mayor's appointment.

He was troubled. He could trace the malaise back to boyhood, back to the sailing ship that had carried him with his father to the New World, back to a twilight when he had stood at the ship's rail with his father's arm around his shoulders. Below, the white foam of the bow-parted waves surged past. Beyond, the emptiness of the ocean stretched vast, darkening. Suddenly at the rim of the world it had appeared, a fiery ball of light. Rigid with awe, his father's arm around him, he had watched it flare across the sky, the streaming fire of its tail burning the ocean itself.

He could hear voices, shouts in the background. He could see the masts, the spars, the great sails black against the glow in the skies. Then his father's voice.

"The Great Comet! You are lucky, my son." His father spoke his determined English with the half-French, half-German accent of his native Strasbourg. "It is not the end of the world. It is the broom of God to sweep the world clean for a new day. It means you will see great changes which I cannot imagine." The older man paused, his face carved in the unearthly light. "It means, God willing, we will find what we have come for." His arm tightened. "It is not easy for an eleven-year-old to understand, but you must try. We have come for justice. Where every man has a fair and equal chance before the law. Justice, my son. . . ."

Justice. That was what troubled Walter now, standing, waiting at the open window of the Anti-Vice Committee's meeting room.

The door was suddenly flung wide.

The man who entered was short of six feet, but must have weighed over two hundred pounds, his torso broad and powerful. At this moment, his ginger hair was awry, his close-set eyes sharp and angry, the narrow pursed mouth grim. Mr. Anthony Comstock's black alpaca frock coat was torn at the shoulder, his black trousers showed the dust of a street scuffle.

"I caught him! Collared him as he was escaping out the back of his shop. Held him down until the police arrived. They've got him now. That's one art dealer who won't sell filthy pictures and obscene books to smut lovers. Thirteenth Street, too. Just a block away from where good, decent women, their innocent children in hand, walk and shop."

Walter was not ready to admit his distaste for this business. The city's open evils were said to outstrip Paris, even San

Francisco, the Babylon of the West Coast. Anthony Comstock's self-ordained vice crusade had the support of the foremost churchmen of New York and many of its most distinguished citizens. Hadn't Comstock been responsible for the founding of that much-needed hostel for strangers to the city, the Young Men's Christian Association, where a gawky young country fellow might find a decent bed, clean surroundings, the guidance and proper literature to keep him from temptation and start him on a worthy career?

Nor could anyone doubt the man's physical courage. His right cheek still bore the knife scar of an infuriated bookseller in Ann Street who, on Mr. Comstock's third tour of inspection, had attacked him and thrown him bodily out. It had done no good. Mr. Comstock had returned with the police, seen the contents of the store confiscated and the owner arraigned. A week later, the unlucky bookseller was found hanged by his own hand from a beam in the rear of his shop.

"Think of the innocent, gentlemen. We must protect the innocent."

Mr. Comstock brushed at his coat and the knees of his trousers, swept back his sparse hair, and, beckoning to the waiting commission members, took place at the head of the long table.

"Mr. Tremont, would you please? The window?"

Mr. Comstock settled his eyeglasses on his narrow nose, one glass cracked and the frame bent.

"To the work at hand, gentlemen. But first I want to assure you that I did not walk aimlessly this afternoon into the art dealer's store. I was intent at arriving at our meeting on time when I passed it. I stopped appalled, as any decent person would. There in the window stood six pen-and-ink drawings, at least eighteen inches high. Every one of them a nude woman. Nude, gentlemen. Stark nude. In a variety of poses which we would deplore to be seen by the women we protect and cherish. I inspected each one carefully. I do nothing on impulse. I was driven by the hand of God into that store, regardless of time consumed. As you can witness, there was hostility. But righteousness has prevailed. Ladies may walk again from Fourteenth Street to Thirteenth Street in all the beauty of their purity. Justice has been done."

If Walter Tremont drew a slow breath, no one heard it.

"Vigilance, gentlemen. Vigilance is the key. I do God's work. No attack, no matter how vicious, how scurrilous, can touch me. I bear all in the name of the Lord."

The room was predictably warming. Several members were stirring uncomfortably in their woolen coats. Mr. Comstock wiped his brow and resettled his broken spectacles.

"I am happy to report, gentlemen, that despite the depravity of a sordid section of our press, resulting in the ribald doggerel written for the lowlife of this city, I have good news. Our luncheon at the White House has been reaffirmed this morning by telegram from the President's press secretary to our Mayor. The lofty integrity of our great President, Mr. Hayes, and that most noble of women, Mrs. Hayes, enables them to remain untouched by the evils of our sinful city. Two days hence, we shall take the ferry to Newark and there board the Washington train, leaving at ten in the morning. Accommodations have been arranged by the Mayor at the splendid new Willard Hotel. I assure you, gentlemen, you will enjoy every comfort. Running water in each room. The fixtures are all of solid brass, as are the cuspidors. The lobby is said to be a marvel of white marble and growing ferns. I have promised to bring Mrs. Comstock a picture.

"We shall attend at the White House promptly at noon the following day. President Hayes will receive us at twelve-fifteen. I believe several congressmen and an aide or two of the President will be at table. We shall finish lunch promptly at one forty-five and depart the White House at two. Carriages will be waiting. We shall return on the four o'clock train to Newark.

"That is all, gentlemen. Except"—Mr. Comstock lifted his eyes with a smile surprisingly boyish—"I pray that the good Lord whom we serve so diligently will permit us fair weather. The streets of Washington are rivers of mud in the rain. Are there any questions?"

The members were straightening their backs, reaching for their silk hats.

"Just one, Mr. Comstock."

"Ah, Mr. Tremont. May I repeat how pleased I am that you are with us? The Citizens League is indeed a valuable addition of support to our crusade for decency. And the question?"

Walter had surprised himself. But now that he had seized the moment there was no turning away. He leaned back and ordered his thoughts.

"Like you, Mr. Comstock, I am above the riffraff commentary of some of our newspapers. As for the verses, Mrs. Hayes is owed an apology and the writer a sound thrashing.

Also a lesson in scansion. . . ." One or two members smiled. Mr. Comstock did not.

"But one matter continues to disturb me. Not because of the verses themselves but because of a reference that seems to persist in the undercurrents of our city. Underground, you might say, but there it is. It is a matter of justice. Justice that may have miscarried."

"Yes, Mr. Tremont, yes?" Mr. Comstock's impatience suddenly flared, not only with Walter's sudden monopoly of attention, but also at the irrelevance.

"I am speaking, much as I deplore it, of the case of Mrs. Caroline Restell."

If he had materialized old Beelzebub himself, Walter could not have better shaken the airless torpor of the room. The members leaned forward. Mr. Comstock sat wooden, while his face assumed a blandly beatific expression.

"I am afraid I do not understand, Mr. Tremont, the relevance. . . ."

Damn the relevance, Walter said to himself. But outwardly he reflected a calm and kindly tolerance.

"There seems to be in the public at large a persistent, if not growing body of doubt regarding Mrs. Restell's death by her own hand."

Mr. Comstock's mouth thinned.

"Prurience, Mr. Tremont. Nothing but prurience for the titillation of the lower classes. Mrs. Restell was an immoral, depraved woman indulging for profit in the most abominable of practices. No one knows how many young women met their deaths within her walls, how many unwanted babies. I, myself, went into that house of crime. Asking God's forgiveness. I sat in the woman's obscene office. She herself gave me bottles, the nostrums, the God-knew-what instruments. I had the evidence. I myself rode beside her in her carriage at her arrest. It was on that ride she offered me forty thousand dollars to let her escape. Forty thousand dollars! I am not a rich man, Tremont, I live modestly. The guidance of God is my wealth. The night before the Restell woman was to go on trial my dear wife and I went on our knees in our simple bedroom, praying for her, beseeching God to show her the evil of her ways. Our prayers were answered. That very night the woman took the knife to her own throat." Mr. Comstock was perspiring, his eyes overbright with the pleasurable fires of self-salvation.

In the uncomfortable silence that followed, Walter felt his own repugnance of the scene. How had he stepped so blindly into this man's obsessed piety? How had he linked himself to these indecent probings, all in the name of God? Was it Anthony Comstock's province to deceive and then betray the unlucky of this world? Was it Walter Tremont's duty to abet it?

When the meeting was concluded, Walter walked slowly eastward. He needed the fresh air as he needed the normalcy of the city around him. Feeling the warmth of the afternoon sun on his back, he remembered it was almost time for his summer suits, his lightweight bowler. Maria had fixed that date firmly in mid-June. How habit gripped a man. If he could settle his mind on these pleasantries, he would enjoy this walk home. But his way lay through a thicket of troubled thoughts. He had a decision to make.

He loved this city in which four decades of his life had passed. He had grown with it. He still thrilled to the glittering currents of the two great rivers that cradled it. As a boy he had often walked the country roads, from the great placid expanse of the North or Hudson River to the racing currents of the East River. In his youth there had been little more to watch than the occasional stagecoach carrying travelers out of the city northward, past the awesome sight bordering the wilderness of Jones Wood.

A gigantic hole was being dug at Forty-second Street, between Fifth and Sixth avenues. A full square block, it would one day hold twenty million gallons of water. The young Walter would stand in endless fascination watching sweating Irishmen dig and blast at the solid granite underlying the city. The land itself had been for nearly two centuries a paupers' burial ground. The whitened bones of 100,000 bodies, a lost city in itself, were shoveled into waiting carts.

For nearly four decades now, the great Reservoir had stood, a fixture in Walter's own life. Its Egyptian-temple walls rose fifteen feet above street level to provide citizens with a splendid walk. Walter had taken his young bride, Maria, there, and his children, as they came along. Sunday afternoon walks on the reservoir were as fixed as Sunday itself in New York.

A city of rock and water. His own life had marched with it. Now in his prosperous late years, Walter held the belief that New York, having been so good to him, deserved the best from him.

Yet could he give his best through the meddlesome officiousness of Anthony Comstock? Or was he being too harsh on the man because of his own distaste for public calumny and for all matters sordid? Comstock was said to carry toys in his pocket for children and to enjoy a practical joke like a boy out of school. It was known that Comstock and his tiny black-garbed wife, ten years his senior, had lost their only child, a little girl of three.

Compassion came easily to Walter Tremont. Justice was a sterner matter. He could smile but still be warmed by his father's imagery of the Comet, the flaming broom of God come to burn away the old world's injustices. He wondered idly if on its return in another forty years the Comet would burn away the new injustices of this present world.

All of which had carried him eastward on Twentieth Street, along fashionable Gramercy Square, an enclave of tall, handsome houses. Fine as it was, the tidy little park they bordered did not suit Walter's taste at all. It was kept locked within its iron grillwork, the keys held by the homeowners. A park, Walter believed, should be open. Yet he would not judge. He was simply more comfortable with Stuyvesant Square's little park, freely accessible.

He lifted the thick gold watch from his vest pocket and flipped open the lid. He had time yet to walk all the way to the East River. He liked it best of all the city's waterways. Perhaps because he knew it best. The wild turbulence known as Hell Gate where East and Harlem rivers met, the salt inlets above the village of Yorkville where his father had taken him fishing, where the tide rushed in to depths of twenty feet. And the country road that bordered the great river estates. How often he had ridden it on horseback north to Yorkville to court little Maria Shuler on her father's truck farm? She had been young and pretty, awed by the young city man, and tremulous at the thought of the city itself.

He had won her.

He smiled at the memory. The afternoon rainstorm. He had gone into her father's barn, to rub his horse down and give him hay. She had followed, watching shyly from the loft. After he finished he had climbed the ladder to her as rain beat on the barn roof. In the lustiness of young manhood, he had swept away her shyness. She had come to him in a rapture he had not guessed beneath her quietness, the modest calico of her dress. The wedding had been as sweet as it was proper, except for a sudden summer shower pattering against the church windows. Maria, in white muslin with downcast eyes, had barely been able to repress a giggle as he had slipped the wedding band on her capable little hand.

"Mr. Tremont!"

He came back from his reverie.

At the crossing of Twentieth Street and Third Avenue, a frowsy little man in a cloth cap detached himself from the elevated railroad's iron pillar and came toward him.

"Sam!" Walter extended his hand. Sam Lipperson had been for twenty-two years the best cutter in the house of Tremont & Sons.

"A good day to you, Mr. Tremont, sir."

"Whatever are you doing here, Sam?"

"A day's work, Mr. Tremont. Not bad. Not bad."

Walter felt an awkward surprise. Had he allowed himself to drift so far from his business, his father's business?

"Aren't you with the company?"

"Not for a while, sir. No, sir. Times change, sir. I couldn't see you walk past without wishing you the good of the day, sir." The little man looked up and down the elevated tracks.

"Why not? What happened, Sam? I want to know."

The little man sighed. He seemed already to have said more than he intended.

"What went wrong, Sam?"

"I'm not saying things went wrong, Mr. Tremont. There's no man in New York can cut a sleeve shoulder better than I can, sir. If I do say so."

"Indeed you should say so."

"But like I said, times change. Always have. Always will. I can cut a shoulder. But Mr. Orrin wants four cut at one time. Says we have to turn work out faster these days. Guess it's true. Everything speeding up. But I couldn't do it that way. Couldn't make them come out fitting proper."

Walter looked thoughtfully at nothing in particular.

"What work are you doing now, Sam?"

"I been lucky. They need a flagman at this corner. Remember, sir, a few weeks ago? That young Mrs. Devere, driving her trap across Twentieth Street here. Had a young horse, too young for it. But you know the ladies these days. They do what they please and no man can tell them different. Train came along up there on the elevated tracks just as she was driving under. The horse bolted, flipped the trap over, and threw her out, her head against the iron column there. Dead, sir. Terrible dead. Well, you know, sir. When the rich have troubles they can do something. Mr. Devere went to the Mayor and said they'd have to keep a flagman at this corner as long as he lived in this city. That was my lucky day. I know the Deveres' coachman. Play pool with him once in a while and he spoke up for me. Not bad, sir. Not at all. Being flagman I see a lot of things I never saw at the cutting table." The thin cackle Walter guessed was Sam's laugh at fate.

"I think we can do something about this, Sam."

"Oh, no, sir. Please don't. I wouldn't want anyone to think I had a grudge or I was telling tales. I don't need so much now. My Bessie died two years ago. I'm living with my son. He's seventeen and got a good job. Works at the printing press for the *Tribune*. Fills ink drums and cleans the rollers. I go where I like when I'm through here. Sometimes I bring him back a news item. Something I seen happen . . . like a robbery or a stabbing or somebody going out the back door of one of them mansions during a party with a bag of silver. Oh, I can tell. The lad passes it on to the editors, helps him get along. . . ." Sam cocked his head, listening.

Walter heard it, too. The low rumble, the shrill whistle. Sam jumped to the iron pillar, picked up a tall pole with a yard square red cloth attached to the end of it, and began waving it furiously first on one side of the "El," then the other. Eastward, halfway down the block, Walter saw a cabriolet come to a stop, the horses skittish, arching their necks, sidestepping. A lone horseman turned his mount abruptly back toward the river.

It was not futile work Sam was doing, perhaps less futile than cutting four sleeves at once.

The rattle and roar overhead passed. The train slowed for the Twenty-third Street station. Sam leaned his flagpole against the pillar and returned to Walter.

"Excuse me, sir!" He snatched Walter's black silk hat, blew a live spark from it, brushed it carefully with his cuff and returned it with dignity.

"Begging your pardon, sir. Best not to stand too near under the elevated tracks when the train's going by. I saw a man's coat burned through, hole the size of a saucer, from a hot cinder." He paused and shifted his feet. It would seem that Sam Lipperson had something on his mind. "It's good seeing you, Mr. Tremont. And—if you don't mind me saying it, I got pretty mad at those terrible things I read in the paper. Those nasty verses, and your name in 'em, sir. It's wicked. Wicked, I said to my son. And, begging your pardon, sir, I hope you'll pay them no heed. When a man's doing the right and good thing . . .

It was more than Sam Lipperson had ever said to the head of Tremont & Sons. His tongue failed him.

Walter held out his hand.

"Thank you, Sam. I count on friends like you."

Walter did not walk all the way east to the river. Instead he turned south down Second Avenue, a quieter thoroughfare that cut directly through Stuyvesant Square.

He had guests coming to dinner. He hoped that they would be as generous as Sam.

18

"Your good health, sir." Hugo Lendler lifted a glass of excellent claret to his host.

Walter, at the table's head, bowed.

"Hear, hear!" Henry Merriman, flushed of face, leaned forward tipped his glass clumsily. "Oh, I am sorry. Awkward. Very awkward. Kitty would have my head for that. Good thing she isn't here. No ladies tonight. King of supper we used to enjoy, eh, Walter? Spiced pot roast on the sideboard, Maria's strudel for dessert. She could make strudel, that little woman. Had the sense to retire and let men enjoy themselves, didn't she?"

Mrs. Jessup's arrival with a napkin to cover the wine stain brought a temporary pause. Walter smiled tolerantly. Dinner was near an end. Yet not one word had been said, not one reference made to what lay uppermost in everyone's mind. By which Dr. Lender concluded that they had all read the contemptible verses in the newspaper and were determined to avoid the subject. Then what was the purpose of the dinner, with both sons present, David and Orrin, as well as Walter's former partner, Henry Merriman?

Henry's glass had been refilled and so, apparently, had his lungs.

"I tell you, and I have this from infallible sources, that the railroad will be built on the west shore of the Hudson River. It has to be if they're going to break Vanderbilt's monopoly of freight with his New York Central. Why, right now, he's setting any rates he pleases, robbing the public right and left. Making so much money that I've heard, though this isn't public yet, that Pierpont Morgan himself is buying up New York Central stock. But when the West Shore Railroad goes in, there'll be a different story, you can quote me on this, any man who buys West Shore shares will be a millionaire before the next decade's over. If I had your money, Walter . . ." Henry drew a breath, drank deep of his glass.

Orrin picked up the slack. "It isn't the railroads that worry me, Henry. We must have more of them and we will. The progress of this nation depends on its railroads. What worries me is the way this city is wasting its money."

"You mean the politicians, don't you? Money going into their pockets to make old Boss Tweed proud. He robbed the city of only thirty million." Humor lit David's boyish face. "Tweed's in jail, but there are plenty coming along who have learned his style. You can't clean up corruption, Orrin, if the voters don't want to."

Dr. Lender glanced at his host. Perhaps there was no more purpose to this pleasant male dinner than an evening among friends. Walter sat with an amiable smile.

Orrin seemed determined to keep the argument going.

"I am not interested in cleaning up anything, but I might remind you, David, I have a wife and three children to support, and another child on the way. We have paid officials to investigate dishonesty. What concerns me is the question of clearing Central Park three miles to the north. All the way up to One-hundred-tenth Street. What for? Who's going to use it? Nobody lives that far uptown. Clear it at the city's expense for more Irish squatters with their filthy shanties, their open garbage, their pigs and goats? It's nothing more than an encouragement to laziness and drunkenness!" Orrin's thin nose pinched at the unreasonable intrusion of poverty.

"Not everyone looks at it that way, Orrin." Walter's tone was mild.

"Sorry, Father. I forgot your Citizens League supports the park. . . ."

"It is not a question of supporting one side or another. It is a simple belief in fresh air. We must all breathe it. Therefore we must all have it to breathe. This city is now overcrowded. A million human beings. The more cleared parkland for people . . ."

Mrs. Jessup removed the remnants of poached salmon and grilled woodcock. She returned with a wide cut glass bowl containing a purplish mixture which she held out for Walter's inspection.

"Plum trifle, sir. Mrs. Tremont told me to plan only light desserts. Shall I dish it, sir?"

"If you will, Mrs. Jessup." For an instant images of strudel, baked molasses pudding, pies of Maria's splendidly solid mince floated before Walter. Yet he would not fault Adrienne.

She was taking care of him in her youthful way. He never told her that the only reason he could find for eating her ubiquitous trifle was the aptness of its name.

He looked past his guests to the rear window, opened between floor-length golden-hued drapes to the warm night. A breeze stole in, mellow with garden scents. The time had almost come, yet he wanted to delay the moment of truth a little longer. He had the unreasoning sensation that after it the course of life in this comfortable household might never be quite the same.

"Father." It was Orrin again. Walter found himself almost capable of distaste for the intolerance of this son who was no longer a boy. "Father, are you planning to open the Far Rockaway house this summer?"

"Of course."

"When?"

"When Adrienne returns."

"I wouldn't count on that, Walter." Henry leaned forward with a grunt. "From the rate Kitty bought hats and dresses for this trip to Bar Harbor with Adrienne, I think they're planning a summer siege. I've already had one wire from Kitty saying they're extending their stay another two weeks. She'll stay until she runs out of money, or I do."

"Well, let them. They're well out of this summer heat." Walter turned to his elder son. "In that case, Orrin, we'll open the house as soon as Noel gets back."

"Where is she?"

"Visiting those friends of hers up on the Hudson. She always returns refreshed and happy. I can't begrudge her the time." Actually Walter had hoped each day for Noel's return. He needed her special understanding, her unquestioning presence.

"How long will that be?"

"She hasn't written. Enjoying herself too much for letter writing, I presume. I didn't know you were interested in the old summer house anymore."

"Of course I'm interested. It can be worth a lot of money if it's kept up."

Walter smiled. "It's kept up, Orrin, I assure you. But it's not for sale."

Orrin sensed a rebuff. "Of course it isn't, Father. Nobody wants that. Lord, David, remember how Mother would move us all down on the nineteenth of June—trunks, hampers, boxes, and barrels—and turn us out free as Irish goats. I'd like my children to know that."

"No reason they can't, Orrin."

The port was passed. The cigars. Hugo Lendler's sense of waiting became more acute. Walter seemed to have drifted into a reverie of his own.

Yet he had not gone far. Only as far as the sprawling, weather-beaten, shingled house at the edge of the sea that he had built for them all so long ago. He was touched that Orrin should remember their summers there. By the time Walter would arrive on the first of July, the wide verandas, swept by ocean winds, would be readied and inviting with wicker lounges, chairs, and striped awnings against the summer sun. Maria's beloved roses would be in full bloom, his favorite hydrangeas already as blue as the sea. . . .

He was aware that David was on his feet, holding up his wineglass.

"Father, it is a pleasure to be at your table tonight." The young voice had lost its irony. "I would like to propose a toast. To the first Tremont to be invited to the White House. May you not be the last."

"Hear, hear!" came from Henry. Hugo Lendler followed suit. He found the moment a touching glimpse of family. Father and sons. Hidden bonds. Hidden pride. Twisted by time, unraveled by newer passions and purposes, yet the ghosts were there, more real at this instant than any pretty luxury in this still traditionless new home.

Walter rose, his voice husky. "Thank you. My sons, David, Orrin, my loyal business partner, Henry, my close friend, Hugo. I wish that my dear wife and daughter were here to join me in thanking you all for coming. But we can be grateful that the ladies have escaped the city heat. I appreciate the honor that has been done me. I have never aimed that high, any more than I anticipated the honor of the presidency of the Citizens League. I came humbly to these shores, a poor boy, son of a poor tailor. But there was opportunity here for honest, hard work, and reward, too. If any man owes a debt to this country, I am that man. . . ."

Dr. Lendler heard a shifting of feet. Walter's flights of oratory could be as dull as they were sound.

". . . I intend to pay that debt in full value with whatever abilities I possess."

"Hear, hear!"

But Walter was not finished. "When I enter the White House Thursday noon and shake the hand of the President of the United States, I shall not forget that I am there by God's grace and the help and support of those I love."

An instant of silence passed. Walter looked from one face to another. Orrin bit his lip.

"So you intend to go, Father?" he blurted out.

"Of course I intend to go. I was asked. I accepted." He drew a folded newspaper clipping from his pocket. To Dr. Lendler it seemed his hand trembled, his face appeared less genial.

"There seems to be a question prevalent in the city these days that as yet no one has answered. I don't like unfinished business so I shall attempt to answer it tonight. I do not know whether Mrs. Rutherford B. Hayes will lunch with us on Thursday. . . ." Walter looked around the table. There was no sound. "I assure you that that gracious, estimable lady will be most welcome, most honored. As will we all."

So the matter was out. There were a few murmurs, a stifled cough from Orrin, a half laugh from Henry and a sense of both relief and embarrassment like a mist above the table.

Walter unfolded the newspaper clipping.

"I need not say that I am enormously relieved that the ladies of my family are beyond reach of such contemptible journalism. However, among men, there need be no hesitation in discussing these, uh, verses which I am sure you have all read to the end. They don't scan. The writer reveals a deplorably limited vocabulary, an unfortunate tendency to repetition, and a sorry misrepresentation of facts. I admit the pun of Pure Yorick will have its admirers. Otherwise it is merely a vile attack on the fine woman in the White House and on respectable citizens of this city. So it's worth exactly . . . that." Walter tore the clipping in half, then in half again.

"However, the last line of this shoddy doggerel contains a lie which I will not allow to pass. It pertains to a matter so sordid that I would not permit newspaper reports of it in my house. The case of the Restell woman. I am aware of the rumors. We have discussed the case at the Citizens League. But I have come to the irrefutable conclusion with Mr. Anthony Comstock—"

"Oh, my God." It was a mere murmur from David.

". . . and the police, that the wretched woman took her own life and that the case is closed. It must be closed. The city must be healed of this scar. I do not agree with Mr. Comstock's methods. I despise them. But it is contemptible to keep the case open for public titillation. I am not without pity for the fallen women who ignorantly sought aid at her hands. The Citizens League supports orphanages for the unfortunate children resulting from their sins. But the case has been thoroughly investigated and closed, and I shall join my associates in assuring the President that this city does not tolerate immorality.''

Every man at the table heard it, the opening of the front door. Then the light, musical voice floated from the hall.

''Bring my dressing case, Annie-Mae. Tell the coachman to carry the trunks up the back stairs.''

Adrienne stood in the entranceway. For an instant she waited, poised, as if measuring the effect. Her tiny feathered hat still held a traveling veil. The folds of her coffee-colored summer suit revealed her fine figure.

''Walter . . . my darling.''

With a rush she was beside him, her lips full on his. Quickly she circled the table, trailing a scent of jasmine as the men jumped hastily to their feet.

''David, I knew you'd be with your father.'' Her gloved hand touched his shoulder. ''And Orrin. . . . Dr. Lendler, how kind . . . Henry . . . Kitty was coming back with me but Senator and Mrs. Walsh arrived yesterday at the hotel and Kitty is entertaining them Friday. Walter, dear, I just heard last night . . . we all heard. I was so humiliated, so . . .'' Her voice held a tremor. She completed the round of the dinner table and now stood slightly apart, a picture of pathos and bravery.

''We were at Mrs. Clark-Jones' reception for Sir George and Lady Buckwell—Kitty does know so many people—when Dollie Galeswood, you know, she's Mrs. Wilberforce's grandniece. She's going on to Newport for the season and I suppose she was so bored with the evening she wanted to liven it up. She's a spoiled little thing. Anyhow in the middle of the reception she flipped out that dreadful newspaper piece. Where she got it, I don't know . . . about you, Walter, and began reading it. About Lemonade Lucy—and—your name in it. Ours. Everybody laughed! Oh, Walter, I nearly died. But I didn't faint . . . I don't faint, Walter. You know that. Kitty said I was quite splendid. I simply hid my mortification and said that under the circumstances my place was beside my husband. And I took the train down this morning. Oh, Walter!''

She took a small step toward him but before his arm could reach her, she stiffened. ''It isn't hopeless, Walter, if we keep our heads. With David and Orrin and our close friends here, I think I should tell you. Senator Walsh has been a tower of strength. He called on me this morning while I was having my breakfast tea. He is not running for the Senate this fall.

He has decided to retire to private law practice and he said he will be more than happy to represent us in the suit. I assured him that we would consider it an honor. Oh, it was such a relief. He will be back in New York on Sunday and he will call on us. He will start the suit at once against the newspaper, the publishers, the writer. They'll have to pay us a lot of money, and he thinks we should go away until it's over. Oh, Walter"—she crumpled against him—"I've tried to be so brave—for your sake."

Dr. Lendler, leaving quickly with the others, found the scene stamped in his mind. Adrienne, so graceful, so sure, crumpling like a child, protesting with her small courage. Oddly enough, he believed her. Whatever her ambitions, her pretenses, Adrienne had revealed herself tonight a woman mortally afraid of being hurt, of losing what she had.

Orrin and David followed him down the steps.

"Good night, young gentlemen."

"Good night, sir."

He watched them turn west and part in the darkness. He could not remember, since Walter's remarriage, seeing the brothers together in that house.

"The night's young, Professor. Time for a nightcap?"

Henry Merriman was carefully descending the four steps, his hand on the curved iron railing.

"Thank you no, sir. It's bedtime for me."

Henry grasped the balustrade, feet planted. A corner street lamp threw his bulk into gross relief against the blanched brick of the house.

"She's right, you know, Hugo. Adrienne is. Walter could make himself a nice little pile of money from a suit like that. Frank Walsh could squeeze that newspaper dry. Walter doesn't belong in politics. He sees everything good or bad, right or wrong, God or the devil. No compromise. Take the Restell case. Half the people in New York suspect the woman was murdered. The other half are sure of it. Why? For what she knew. Show me a list of important men in this city and I can pick out a dozen or more who sent their mistresses to her. As for the ladies, I can name you more than one whose doors you and I couldn't get through, who have paid a visit to the Restell house."

Henry didn't elaborate on the source of his knowledge. He shifted his feet unsteadily.

"Think anybody wants all that coming from the witness box? That's why the case is closed. Truth is, a man can do anything he wants in this city, as long as it looks proper in the parlor. And a woman, too. Oh, especially a woman. Ask one of those fine ladies what she does while her husband's at his club for the evening, or downtown making the millions she wants. But no one will ask. That's why it all works, don't you see? That's how we hold things together. Don't embarrass anybody. Don't make anything obvious. Keep up appearances. That's all that's required. Poor old Walter thinks he's going to change all that—for the sake of decency. Public morals. Know anybody who wants 'em?"

Dr. Lendler escaped, crossing the Square beneath leafy trees. Henry walked heavily, alone, toward the lights of Third Avenue. The drawing room lamps of the Tremont house went out. Walter locked the front door for the night as he always did and climbed the stairs, weighted with a sense of foreboding.

Adrienne had not yet removed her traveling clothes. Only her hat and veil lay flung on the dressing table. Her face bore a faint tracing of the train's soot, left by the pattern of her veil.

She looked helpless, fragile, and distraught. He wished she had at least changed to a dressing gown, to the femininity he liked, the young wifeliness of her.

"Walter, why didn't you answer me in the dining room?"

"Answer what, my darling?"

"When I told you about Senator Walsh's help. You just looked at me and didn't say anything."

"I might have said I loved you, I was glad you had come home. But we had guests."

She was standing and distant, her hands twisting.

"But you will agree to it, won't you? You will give up this stupid Washington trip and leave everything to him? The *Excelsior* is sailing Monday for Le Havre. I looked it up in the newspaper coming down on the train. I can be ready. We can go to Paris. Paris, Walter—just the two of us and forget everything else. By the time we get back it will have blown over and Senator Walsh will have gotten quite a lot of money for us for the libel. Don't you *see?*"

She flung herself against him, clinging to him, her lips against his ear, her body pressed to him.

"Please, Walter. *Please. . . .*"

His arms went around her. But his mind betrayed him. It showed him a rift, opening at his feet. It showed him how deeply imbedded in him was his principle of Duty. And like a shadow across it, something he did not want to see in this marriage.

He held her closer.

"You're shivering, my darling. Come to bed."

"Will you, Walter? Will you?"

"We'll talk about it in the morning."

"No, I want to talk about it now. I want it settled."

He released her gently, as gentle as his words.

"Adrienne, I do not want Senator Walsh or anyone else interfering in my affairs. I do not take cheap and salacious doggerel seriously. I shall treat it as it deserves to be treated. I shall ignore it. I believe that should settle the matter, except for one thing." His eyes like his voice softened. "You are very dear to me. I have sworn to love, honor, and protect you and I shall do that to the best of my ability to the end of my life. I only ask that you put the whole sordid business out of your lovely head. You are my wife. I shall never let anyone or anything harm you. Now, I know you must be tired. . . ."

She had backed from him and taken refuge behind a chair, her hands white-knuckled on the back of it.

"You intend to go to Washington?"

"I have given my word."

"So that's all it means! All that fancy talk to me. You don't care about me or how I feel. I'm something pretty you like to have in the house. You don't respect me! Any more than your children do! You have no idea how I feel about anything, always being with old people, entertaining old people, living like old people—"

"Adrienne!"

"No, I might as well say it all. If you want somebody here, why don't you get your precious daughter home! She's the one you really want!"

"Adrienne, you don't know what you're saying! Listen to me!"

But she had moved beyond control. She flung out the reckless words as if they were weapons.

"What do you know about your Noel? Where she goes, whom she sees. You trust her! Anything Noel does is right. You don't even know that a man came here last week, to call on her. At three in the afternoon. With flowers! As if he were accepted. Overdressed, arrogant . . . tacky, if you looked twice! David called him a fortune hunter. . . ." Her voice suddenly trailed.

"David?" Walter was looking at her oddly. "Was David here last week?"

Adrienne's hands dropped limply from the chair. "Maybe it was two weeks ago. I—I don't remember."

"Of course not. I hadn't heard."

"He came to pick up books or something he had left here. I—I forget. What does it matter? What does anything matter?" She looked full at him, dropped her eyes, and turned quickly.

Walter watched the dressing room door close behind her. She had said nothing of significance, he told himself. Nothing. Merely the hysteria of a frightened, overtired woman. He was old enough to forgive that in so young a wife.

Yet something had shifted. It was as if he were suddenly seeing himself, his home, his contentment, in one of those distorting mirrors in a black magic gallery. He tried to dispel the image. But it was not imagery. It was a shift—invisible, unspoken.

For him, it was a return to loneliness.

19

Number 17 Pear Street lay shuttered to the early sun. Whatever movement stirred within the aged Georgian house, none reached a private chamber in the heart of it. Not much larger than an expanded closet, the tiny room was walled in dark polished wood, warmed by the reddish glow of a single votive lamp. Above a makeshift altar covered in gilt cloth and illuminated by the faint radiance of the lamp, hung a life-size lithograph of the face of a young Christ.

The lamp cast no shadow. In the windowless chamber no sliver of worldly light intruded.

Madame Ducharde, owner and proprietress of what her untutored neighbors called "the French woman's place," was at her devotions. Her beads moved soundlessly through long fingers. Her head was not bowed but uplifted. The ancient prie-dieu, the tasseled cushion beneath her knees, held her in rigid embrace. Freed from Madame's flowing skirts, the worn petit point would reveal a faded biblical scene of the Wedding at Cana, the figures long blurred, Wine and Water no more than threads, only the bridal whiteness of a gown and the brown robe of the Guest sharply discernible, as if renewed.

Around the base of the prie-dieu ran a carved legend in ancient French script, *La Coeur a Ses Raisons, que ce Raison ne Connait pas. Sauf que Dieu.* The Heart has Its Reasons that Reason Knows not. Only God.

The little *cabinet de prière* might be said to contain all that still lived of the faded passions of Madame Ducharde.

At last the beads hung still. Madame's lips had not moved. Rather, they were set thin and tight against speech. Her eyes were fixed on the lithographed face above her. It was not a suffering face crowned in thorns. Nor yet a face within a halo of forgiving pity. Rather it was the face of a young man of striking beauty, dark beard, rich dark hair to the shoulders, full lips, and deep, promising eyes bedeviled by an artist's trick. The eyes followed the observer from whatever angle one might look at them.

They followed Madame Ducharde through the disciplines of her days and the sleeplessness of her nights.

This morning, Madame lingered a little longer at her altar. Her pieties were threaded with a worldliness for which she had no remorse, a practical gratitude, an earthly triumph for what had finally, rightly, taken place. Madame had yet to discover what had delayed the young woman, upstairs in her *petit hôpital.* Perhaps she would never know. All that mattered was that Miss Noel Tremont had at last arrived with the child at her door.

A great weight had been lifted. Madame gazed upward at the lithograph, a flicker of girlishness in her smile.

"Tu a la puissance!" she whispered. *"Tu a le droit!* I shall manage now—against my enemies. *Remerciements, mon bien-adoré!"*

The whiteness around Noel shaped itself into walls. The pin scratch of light became the sun-struck rim of a wash bowl. The dark blur opposite her bed condensed into a plain wooden crucifix. And the fluttering bird sounds from outside her window turned into the voices of children.

She was awake, weak but free at last from the disorientation that had held her in its grip for days she could not yet count. Ducharde. 17 Pear Street. That was the address she had given the cabman. That was where they had taken her in. That was where—but it seemed better for the moment to lie still and take bearings. An open armoire revealed her grey traveling suit. On the shelf above she could see her violet-trimmed hat. Across the single straight chair her ivory dressing gown lay neatly folded.

Missing were her black dress, Sophie's black shawl, the thick black veil she had bought and, she realized with a start, any evidence of Posie. What had they done with her? Had the invisible forces of respectability, of society's harsh ruling that had pursued her since the day Posie was born, come to separate her from her child? So far she had beaten them. She had escaped with Posie, if she could only remember, if she had not been taken ill.

"Good morning, Miss Tremont."

Noel had not heard the door open.

"Well, you are better. A fine day, the weather's turned."

It was the pleasant-faced young woman who had flickered in and out of Noel's consciousness the past few days. Or was it weeks? A capable girl in a striped uniform, as impersonal as the narrow little room itself.

She set a tray of tea, toast, and porridge on the bed.

"You are to eat it all. You need your strength back. Madame Ducharde wishes to see you this morning. I will come for you at five minutes to eleven." At the door she added, "Your underthings are clean and ready in the drawer under the washstand. There is also a towel."

The door closed. Weakness surged again through Noel. Then she remembered what she had wanted to do. Cry out to the girl, to anyone. Where is Posie? The moment was gone.

She sipped the tea. The children's voices floated up, light as bubbles. Strengthened, she rose unsteadily and went to the window. Below her lay a wide enclosure, walled in rose-colored brick veined with new ivy. Within the walls spread a lushness of close-cropped grass, a scattering of low, trimmed bushes, and a winding graveled path. There were no flowers. But in one corner rose a willow tree to splendid height, criss-crossing the garden with shade and filling it with music as the morning breeze played like a bow across its drooping branches. Noel also saw two double-seated sliding swings with yellow awnings, a few white iron chairs, and a small white table.

The garden had a serenity, an aura of peace and shelter that seemed to remove it from any world that Noel had ever known.

Playing on the grass were five little girls of assorted ages in light summer dresses, starched white pinafores. Their feet encased not in sensible high-buttoned boots but light black slippers, as if they had learned to skip before they walked, dance before they trudged. Each child's hair was tied with a different colored ribbon. Pink, blue, yellow, violet . . . butterflies, thought Noel. They're butterflies.

Posie was not among them.

It was nearly eleven. Without knocking, the pleasant-faced girl opened the door.

Noel had managed to dress to her petticoats, brush and pin up her straight brown hair.

"I think I need help with my suit." She despised her weakness.

"No time for that, Miss Tremont. You've done very well so far." The girl shook out Noel's ivory dressing gown and held it up. "Madame Ducharde's not to be kept waiting."

Noel felt strong fingers clasp her elbow. She was propelled

down a long corridor, a right turn and into what appeared to be an upstairs sitting room, large, light, and richly furnished. A rose-tinted carpet covered the floor. Graceful, open-armed French chairs stood at intervals, their light brocade repeated in a divan stretching along one wall. Everywhere was a profusion of pillows, soft, inviting. For an instant Noel was not sure whether she should flee in the awkwardness of her negligee, or sink into that pillowed comfort.

"Good morning, Miss Tremont. Do come in. Thank you, Bessie. Close the door, if you please. Do sit down. We must make you comfortable. No, not that one, my dear girl. Take the deeper chair. There by the jonquils. A little late for them, but we are quite blessed this season. The morning sun has passed our willow tree so I trust the light won't bother you. Our willow is not only a protector of the garden, but a watchman of our comfort. And a dear friend. How are you feeling?"

The woman from whom these kindly, precisely enunciated words flowed was seated in a high-backed ornately carved chair, the window behind her. Undefined folds of grey material falling from her throat to her feet revealed only that she was above average in height and bone thin. Her face—Noel had seen it before. Narrow, elongated, prominent aquiline nose, high, sculptured cheekbones, the forehead lofty and wide. Steel-grey hair rigidly drawn back as if nothing must conceal or shadow the depths of those heavy-lidded eyes.

A face not out of life, not out of memory. Noel, weak as she was, knew where she had seen it. In effigy, carved in granite with headband and chin cloth, lying on a long forgotten dusty tomb. She had seen it pictured in lantern slide travelogues of medieval French castles and the crypts of French cathedrals. The face of the Renaissance queen, forever rigid in the enforced grace of power; or a twelfth-century prioress, unyielding even to death; or a crusader's wife, her iron chastity girdles, faithful and forbidding through eternity.

Noel felt her head spin with images, with the newness of it all.

"Have we asked too much of you too soon, my dear?"

"No . . . no." Noel groped for a form of address.

"Then let us at least make our acquaintance. Enough for one day, I should think. I am Adelaide Christine Isabelle Francoise Ducharde. This is my home. You are Noel Elizabeth Tremont, daughter of Walter Christian Tremont and the late Maria Shuler Tremont. So we already know something of each other."

More, Noel thought, than she could have guessed. But questions tangled in her mind, knots of faintness.

"You have had a fever, my dear. I have gone on my knees to pray for your recovery. And you have needed help. Oh, I know. And now you are here where you shall have it." Madame Ducharde sighed gently. "If only you had come to me when you were told."

"But I—wasn't—I mean . . ." Noel searched through the mists in her mind. No one had told her. There was the card. Or was it a letter? Sophie's dresser . . .

"Yet you had my address, my dear." The deep-set eyes studied her. "No matter. You are still very weak. We must build you back to health. The fever—oh, it's a miracle that you are here! There is plenty of time ahead for us to know each other. I am a rather formal person, but I should like to think that you have come to me as a daughter."

Madame's kindness was disarming even as her air of authority barred argument. Noel felt a return of dizzying helplessness. But she must cling to what was hers, to all that mattered.

"Where is Posie?"

"Posie? Ah, of course. Little Elizabeth. Quite natural. Forgive me. I should have thought of it." Madame reached for the bell pull.

The door opened at once. Noel recognized the pretty little maid who had admitted her at the front door—when? How long ago?

"La petite, elle est prête?" Madame's question was sharp.

It seemed to Noel the maid had barely left the room when she returned, to Noel's choking relief, with Posie. Posie in yellow dress and white pinafore, her feet in tiny black slippers, her hair caught back by a yellow ribbon that lay like gold against the silvery fairness. Released by the maid, Posie walked primly, directly, to Madame Ducharde.

"Bon matin, ma petite."

"Bon matin, Madame." Posie held her small skirt wide and made a curtsy, one tiny foot balanced precariously behind her.

"Trés bon, Elizabeth. A friend is here to see you."

Posie turned. Then she walked, slowly, sedately to Noel.

"Mistaffy. *Bonjour."*

She did not throw herself into Noel's arms. She did not entwine her arms around Noel's neck, crying out her lonliness, her fears. She made a second curtsy and stood waiting, regarding Noel with solemn eyes.

Noel caught the child to her.

"Posie! Posie! My darling! You are all right! Safe! Let me look at you! You're well? A little pale. But how pretty you look! Madame Ducharde has been good to you. You have not been unhappy? Or too lonely? I am better now, and soon we'll . . ."

Madame Ducharde, with a swift movement, was beside them. Gently she slid the child from Noel and stood her on her own small feet. Posie smoothed her pinafore.

"Elizabeth, Mistaffy has been quite ill. When she is stronger she will come and see you again. Now it is time for your *petit déjeuner.* And then it will be your turn with Emily and Pauline to play in the garden. *Dépêch-toi!"*

Posie curtsied to the tall woman, a smile lighting her face. Without looking back to Noel, she ran from the room.

"A charming child, Miss Tremont. As you see, quite happy. But, my dear girl, you look unwell. I'm afraid we have overtaxed you."

Madame Ducharde seemed to fade.

Noel was aware of talon fingers again piloting her down endless corridors. Dizzily, gratefully, she allowed herself to be put to bed.

She was not summoned the next day or the next. She found it was enough to lie cradled between reality and fantasy, to drift on the faint assurance that Posie was near, although even that sometimes eluded her. At times she awoke to a sense of uneasiness. At others, she gave herself to nothingness, or to a kaleidoscope of images that formed and re-formed against the blank wall of the room.

She was a child. She was free. She was running with David across a summer field. Lying in the scented warmth of a meadow, David searching the horizon beyond.

"David, what are you going to do when you grow up?"

"I'm going away."

"Where?"

"Anywhere."

"So am I!"

"You can't."

"Why not?"

"Because you're only a girl, Noel. And a silly girl at that. You have to get married and have babies. Like all girls."

She was grown, sitting stiffly in her father's brown parlor, her hair too straight, her skin too sallow—Kitty—Kitty Merriman, sharp-voiced, stylish, moleskin muff, moleskin tocque. "It's time, Walter. Noel must meet a suitable young man. I'll give a reception. Only a woman can arrange these things." And Kitty again. "You don't do well in pink, Noel. And without your mother, white is not appropriate." Kitty had bought Noel blue tulle, the color of kitchen rinse water.

The reception. Noel drifting among her images saw it again, in all its dry-mouthed misery. The sugaring of Thanksgiving snow, a room weighted with statuary, crowded with strangers. Noel standing beside Kitty, numbly nodding. Her father across the room with a young woman, a dazzling creature, golden hair in a coronet, shoulders glistening above a deep-cut gown of unadorned black. Her father moving toward the supper room, on his arm the young woman in black.

Noel, in her grotesque blue tulle, escaping to the upstairs dressing room, flinging herself into a high-backed chair where she would be neither seen nor spoken to. The silence. Voices somewhere behind her, Kitty's high and thin. "Yes, he's older. But settled, substantial." If there was an answer Noel didn't catch it. Kitty's voice again, a tone sharper. "Addie, I've gone to a great deal of trouble and expense to arrange all this for you. You don't think I gave this affair for that hopeless girl, do you? For you. You, Addie. This is your chance. Don't you see? As a widow, you can do nothing. As a married woman . . . with his money . . ."

Noel, holding her hands to her ears. But the words never went away. Living on as if waiting to spring to betray the kindly, unseeing man who was her father.

She, too, had betrayed him. The images came and went against the wall of her mind. The bright-haired stranger at the tiller of his skiff, docking at the lighthouse, urging her, coaxing her, daring her. The long empty curve of the beach. Wooing her. The intensity—the sudden pain . . . the magic that lifted her into make-believe. The first dawn on her body. She could no longer see his face—only a taut figure walking away, always away . . . leaving her, leaving her—Posie.

She must have cried out.

She was given something hot and bitter to drink. She slept and awakened and slept, this time to nightmares. She was in her father's house—it was empty, abandoned, and her father gone. She was walking down a long corridor, ending at a door. She went through. Gus Hansen. With Posie. But at last the limbo of images began to fade. A light edged her mind. She was conscious of searching, searching through trees, around corners, among shadows, searching for someone . . . someone. Laughing. She called out. . . .

Bessie stood at the foot of her bed.

"It's a lovely day, Miss Tremont. I've moved a chair to the window. It's time to sit up now."

Her private world vanished.

She swung her legs unsteadily to the floor. It had rained in the night. She filled her lungs with the freshness, her senses with the greenness below. She would dress, she would find Posie. She would thank—she sat down rather quickly on the hard chair, glad of the pillow at her back.

"You must take your time, Miss Tremont. You had a relapse. Doesn't do to try too much your first day up. You can sit in the chair and look out to the garden, until you're stronger."

Noel discovered that she had lost all sense of day or of month or of the real world. She must wait again, wait with her tray beside her, until the future took shape and time could be counted.

The full foliage told her it was summer. From the window, she could see the children—butterflies—playing in and out of the willow's weeping branches. She thought she saw Posie with the others. She wanted to call out. She was not ready.

When the garden was empty Noel felt its potency. There was no rioting of flowers, only the cool greens of shrub and grass, boxwood and ivy flowing together like sea currents, blending, parting, pooled in shadow or shining in the sun. She had no idea there could be so many shades of green. She liked to think of the wisdom that had decreed green the color of earth's fertility.

Sometimes she could see Madame, trailing the cobweb-grey folds of her gown on the graveled walk. Nun, priestess, or an eccentric woman of undiscernible power? Once she had seen her walking with a slight, young woman in summer dress, summer veil. The young woman had held a handkerchief, briefly touching her eyes.

Once Noel saw a man, his tall spare frame slumped in a garden chair, his head dropped motionless in his hands.

And once she had seen Madame with a heavy-shouldered man, his hair thick silver, his black coat relieved by the white collar of a clergyman. Madame was talking with unusual animation.

At eleven one morning, the summons came. Madame Ducharde requested her presence downstairs at four.

"Bessie, what will I do until then?"

"You will eat your lunch. You will dress." Noel had a sense that the girl was dismissing her.

She had nearly five hours to put her thoughts in order.

Though her mind was sharpening, her strength nearly returned, Noel realized her resources of will were thin.

Madame Ducharde had elected the garden. Seated in a fan-backed chair, the heavy grey silk falling about her, the woman looked more graceful, more at ease than at Noel's first meeting with her. Yet the ease that diminished her severity added to an aura of the unknown. Her deep-set eyes searched Noel's face.

"Well, you are improved, Miss Tremont. Almost well, I should say."

Noel caught the faintest of accents, not much more than an inflection, that she had missed before.

"I am quite well, Madame, thank you. And very grateful."

Madame lifted a hand as if to stop the words.

"Now we must talk about you."

Noel could have waited. She chose not to.

"First I would like to see my child, Madame."

"Naturally. This is the time for the little one's *chocolat*. After that, the music hour which Elizabeth so much enjoys. But if you insist. . . ."

A return of that shadowy sense of entanglement.

"I want to see that she is well . . ."

"She is as you saw her, Miss Tremont. Perhaps even happier. When she came she knew nothing. But she responds so quickly to teaching. She enjoys her little lessons."

A rebuke was not implied, yet Noel felt it. The present was rushing in on her. And the future.

Madame's gaze was on the willow tree beyond her.

"You do not quite trust me, Miss Tremont?"

"Madame, I assure you, I am deeply grateful. For myself and Posie."

"Of course, you're grateful. You are a civilized woman. So am I. But gratitude is hardly the point between us today. There is no reason, of course, why you should trust me. 'Should' is a word, incidentally, I dislike. It implies a surrender of will. And your will, Miss Tremont, is strong. As is your courage. And your silence. Qualities, I might say, that Carrie Restell admired in you. It does not surprise you, I am sure, that I speak of Carrie Restell. We are—were—old friends. I held her confidence for many years. It might have been easier for you if you had taken her advice and come to me directly. . . ."

"She didn't—" Noel bit her lip. Silence. She must keep her silence, until she understood more.

The heavy-lidded eyes held hers, probing, searching.

"As you well know, the young women who entered Carrie Restell's house came in desperate terror. They sought only one thing. To be saved from disgrace, from social ruin, from devastation of their families. If the child was to be born, then an orphanage must be found and total anonymity, total disappearance. But if Mrs. Restell's skills could free them? Carrie carried the weight of those tears, those pleadings, those tragedies every hour of her life. You were different, Miss Tremont. You wanted your child, heedless of past or future. Carrie admired that. Yet you surrendered her to a farmer's wife, telling yourself that your child would not only be safe, but she would be forever yours. You would see her whenever you wanted to, you would watch her grow, you were willing to live your life in a half world, as your child would.

"But, Miss Tremont, the most unpredictable gift God ever made to the world is the human heart." Madame Ducharde looked beyond the brick wall of the garden to where clouds billowed above the stubby steeple of the nearby church, snaring its cross in light and shade.

"So"—the low, throaty voice continued—"you were betrayed."

The long, lean hand lifted again as if anticipating Noel's answer. None came.

"The farmer's wife wanted your child as desperately as you did. From the moment she took the baby in her arms, she relived her own frustrated motherhood. You, Miss Tremont, were a visitor, a stranger who might or might not return, an elegant lady your child hardly knew."

"Why are you saying these things to me?"

"So you will not be surprised if Elizabeth should say them to you later. She is a perceptive child. Completely silent the first few days she was here. One day she asked me if I knew her mama. I asked her where her mother was. Oh yes, she said. She pointed to the sky. The gesture seemed to unlock her tongue. She began to talk. She said that Mama sits in a big chair. She wears a blue shawl. She has flowers in her lap and she holds out her hand. And if Elizabeth is good she will give her a flower. . . ."

Noel broke in, her voice shaking. "Madame, do you know what she's telling you?" She caught her breath. No emotion. She could gain nothing in a quarrel. "Have you ever seen the waxworks at the Eden Musée? I took Posie there in our first days in the city. It was a mistake. I learned that soon enough. I did not yet understand the literal mind of a child. The figure of the woman with the flowers in her lap was outside the entrance, a figure in wax, a make-believe flower seller. Posie slipped from my grasp and ran to the figure and touched the wax hand. She screamed and ran back to me. 'She's dead! Like Mama!'

"I took her away. I bought her an ice. We went to the park where I bought her a ride in the goat cart. By the time we went home, I thought she had forgotten. But here among strangers, without me, she's remembering!" Noel stopped. She dared not show anger. "Madame, I am grateful. But I would like to see Posie as soon as I can."

"And why not?"

But the tall woman in folds of grey remained motionless. So long that Noel shifted in her chair. Time seemed to flow in a thick, palpable current through this walled garden, at a rhythm unknown outside it. Noel reminded herself that impatience had always defeated her. She must wait. She must match this woman's impenetrable calm with her own.

Unexpectedly, Madame Ducharde smiled. The dark eyes warmed. Noel saw a moment of youth in the lean, disciplined face.

"Miss Tremont, do you know what makes a willow tree grow?"

In the pause, Noel heard the light afternoon breeze stir the trailing branches of the great tree as if it, too, knew secrets. The sound was lost in a sudden burst of children's voices and laughter through an open window on the second floor.

Madame Ducharde glanced upward, her face still warm. Then she fixed her eyes on Noel.

"A willow tree must have moisture. Its roots must have water. The rocks on which this great city is built once contained thousands of brooks and springs. They were bricked over, paved over. Houses and streets were built and smothered them. Do you not think it a miracle that a single willow seed carried by a bird or the passing wind dropped in a corner of this small garden, where it would thrust down its tiny roots and find sustenance? A hidden spring, an undiscovered river, unseen, unknown, but on which the willow tree would flourish? To me that tree is a daily affirmation of the force of life, the indestructible potential of a seedling if some kindly wind will carry it to where it can be nourished. So it is with a child, Miss Tremont. So it is with the children who come to this place."

The afternoon breeze had died down. The trailing willow

hung silent. In the setting sun its shadow lengthened to the chairs where Noel and the woman in grey sat.

"It is not too cool for you, Miss Tremont? No. A relief, is it not?" A smile briefly touched the skeletal features again. The tone lightened. "But our willow has found more than nourishment and love in our garden. It has earned our respect. Like the holly tree, like our own too human selves, the willow is either male or female. The seed must be fertilized to continue its kind. This tree, I am told, is female. Much"—amusement rippled the low voice—"preferred. The wood of the female willow is more flexible. More durable. So you see our lovely willow provides us not only with shade and shelter. But with a creed. That cross you see, over there on the steeple of St. Giles of the Innocents, reminds us we are Christian mortals. Here under our willow tree we might turn Druid." A hint of merriment spun out and was gone.

"Now, Miss Tremont, we shall talk about you. You are impatient. Only your good manners prevent you from interrupting me and demanding to see your child. Perhaps to take her away with you this very day. You are beset with a modern sense of time. As if time could be measured by a watch. Time, I assure you, Miss Tremont, is measured by what we do with it, not by what it does with us. And lastly, you have found as yet no reason to trust me. And yet you must. Because you will find ultimately that there is no other person you *can* trust. So we must be entirely honest with each other. As a token, I return this."

Madame Ducharde reached into the grey layers of her skirt and drew out a small tissue-wrapped package.

"Open it, Miss Tremont."

Within the thin white paper, glowing like an ember, lay the fire opal, her mother's brooch, that Noel had released to the grimy grasp of Mr. Nater, pawnbroker.

"We found the receipt in your handbag. Such a paltry sum for such a jewel, Miss Tremont. But desperation makes beggars and fools of us all."

"I will repay you."

"Please. . . ." The thin hand lifted. "There are more important matters. I ask your pardon for the necessity of looking into your purse but, you see, I had to know. You have been a source of grave worry since you refused Carrie's advice the last night of her life."

Noel felt her throat dry. She stared at Madame Ducharde.

"If you had come directly to me as she told you, you would have saved yourself a great deal of difficulty. Carrie Restell knew your child could no longer remain where she was. God's ways are mysterious. It happens sometimes that these innocents born of love, not wedlock, bear the very face of the mother. Or father. And so must be doubly protected from what society chooses to label 'disgrace.'

"Carrie dedicated her life to protecting unfortunate women and their blameless children from that stigma. In return she asked only their silence and their loyalty. So, if I am to help you, Miss Tremont, I must know why you failed to obey her that last night of her life."

The willow's shadow had enveloped them. The slow twilight had turned somber the garden's green motley and made faceless the long pale brick wall of the house. Through the open window on the second floor, the children's voices were stilled. Noel shivered. The place had an air of conspiracy.

"Surely, Miss Tremont, you trusted Carrie."

"I did not see Carrie Restell the last night of her life," Noel said quietly.

A long hand slapped the arm of the chair.

"Miss Tremont, we must understand each other. Nothing must jeopardize my work or all that Carrie Restell did. Whatever the world thinks it knows, only trust must lie between us. You were in Carrie's house the night before she was to go to trial."

Madame Ducharde paused, gazing over the wall at the streamers of tenuous clouds streaking the gilded sky. She gave a small sigh, as if releasing a burden of her own.

"You see, I know, Miss Tremont, because I, too, was in the house that night."

Noel sat motionless, straining to hear the reality of the children, of Posie, upstairs. Be silent, she told herself. Wait.

Madame Ducharde continued, her tone almost conversational.

"I was there because Carrie had asked me to come to help her the night before her trial. There was a great deal to be done. Nothing the servants could do, so she let them go out for the evening. But she had records that must be destroyed, or removed to safety. Provision made for the shelters she maintained for women after their ordeal. And for the children. Mostly for the children, until they could be placed. Carrie was obsessed with the children. The innocents. She had often said that someday she would want her grave marked with a marble cradle and sleeping child.

"Perhaps, Miss Tremont, you should know about the woman who befriended you. For Carrie Restell life had never been easy. She had come to this country, an ignorant young immigrant from England. She had married briefly and was widowed two years later. She married a man named Lohman, a printer who worked as a—what do you say—compositor at the *Tribune* newspaper.

"But there was never enough money. She was widowed again. To support herself and her own little girl whom she adored, Carrie opened a boarding house. It was a shabby part of the city. She came to know all kinds of people. Her closest friend was a gaudy young woman who practiced prostitution when she couldn't find work dancing. Dancing in entertainment saloons, or at bachelor parties. Stripped when she was asked. Prostitution, the girl told Carrie, was almost easier to endure. But she clung to her small dream of dancing because there was nothing else. Carrie saw the degradation, the helplessness, of such girls who put their bodies on sale.

"Carrie was mature and strong. And she was friendly. She discovered that women would talk to her, confide in her. She had something for them more important than sympathy. She had—what shall I say—understanding, a kind of simplicity. She was of the earth.

"She came to know an old woman living in a dilapidated house on Chatham Street. The woman was small and bent and very dark. She claimed to be half gypsy, half African. Carrie used to say she was the wisest woman she had ever met. She showed Carrie little instruments she had made of wood and metal that could cause less pain. She kept a garden of herbs and plants for medicines. She taught Carrie that the leaves of the foxglove plant would help a failing heart. That the seeds of a certain poppy when chewed would lighten pain. That cobwebs, common cobwebs from the attic, would drive infection from a wound. And that willow bark—" She broke off, then continued, as if reciting a litany.

"Carrie Restell became a midwife. To women who could not afford a physician's fee. To women whose modesty forbade their going to a male doctor. And the others . . ."

Madame Ducharde's grey folds were merging with the shadow.

"The others, Miss Tremont . . . women who came in terror of disgrace, married women who until one rash hour had lived respectable lives, rich women, famous women, who offered any amount to save their reputations. And most pathetic of all, young, unmarried girls who had succumbed to their own pent-up passions, or to the persuasions of men. They read the three little lines advertising her skills in the personal columns of newspapers. A specialist in female diseases. And her address. They knew what those lines meant. As you did. Did you not, Miss Tremont?"

Madame Ducharde seemed to be awaiting an answer.

"Did you not, Miss Tremont?"

"Are you asking me how I came to Mrs. Restell?"

"Yes."

"I heard of her at a lecture I attended. At Cooper Union. A lecture on the new woman."

"Ahh. You are even more independent than I suspected. Very capable I would say. But in the end the new woman is not so very different from the old one, yes?"

Madame Ducharde's long, fine fingers smoothed the folds of her gown. "Carrie Restell denied no one. She became notorious as an abortionist. Twice she was brought to court. Once she was declared guilty of manslaughter in the death of a young girl who came to her too late to save mother or child. Carrie served a year in prison on Blackwell's Island. But not in luxury as they said. That was a malicious lie! Out of it all Carrie Restell learned what men have always known. Money is power. With enough money she could buy protection, safety."

The dusk was deepening. Noel felt a chill, whether from the coming night, or the relentless voice. Madame glanced upward as if listening. A softness touched her face. From the open window floated again the sound of children's voices. They were singing.

". . . safety, Miss Tremont. For herself and *les petits innocents*. The children she brought into the world. *Les pauvres bâtards*. The children the world called shame children. These were Carrie's real concern.

"The night before she was to go on trial Carrie talked about them. And about her enemies. She had only contempt for the self-righteous. They could not hurt her. But her real enemies—and this was the tragedy of her life—her real enemies were those she had helped. Carrie knew they surrounded her, fearful that in the extremes of the witness stand she would be driven to revealing their secrets . . . she had a right to fear."

The husky voice fell silent. Noel glanced up at the window, now lighted, for reassurance and found none. This woman whom she barely knew, yet to whom she was so indebted, this priestess figure, draped in softness, hawklike in profile . . . who was she? What was she spinning out of the twilight and the past? She had shown only kindness, yet a warning stirred in Noel that this web of words and shadows was somehow entrapping her.

The sun had dropped into a bank of purplish clouds, staining them a brief crimson. A whitened curve of young moon hung timid, ghostly, in the drained sky. The willow gathered to itself the blackness of the coming night. But the garden still held a luminous glow.

Madame Ducharde's eyes were fixed on the distance.

"When you saw Carrie Restell the last night before her trial, Miss Tremont . . ."

"I did not see her, Madame."

Madame Ducharde sighed.

"Miss Tremont, there must be nothing but the truth between us. There is no other way."

The words lingered for an instant in the quiet air. Then Madame Ducharde continued as if there had been no interruption.

"Carrie expected you at nine o'clock. She had plans for the security of your child. She wanted you to know them before her prosecution began. She would see no one else that evening. As I said, she was fond of you, Miss Tremont. At five minutes to nine she went downstairs in her dressing gown—"

"Madame"—Noel heard her own voice, thin as a plucked string—"I tell you I did not see Mrs. Restell!"

There was a slight movement of the grey folds. Madame Ducharde leaned forward.

"Am I to believe that you failed to keep the appointment? Even for the sake of your child?"

Noel again sensed the faint warning within her. But there was no way to reverse the tide or words.

"I went to the house," she said dully.

"Ah . . . and you entered?"

"Through the side door. Mrs. Restell said it would be left unlocked."

"And . . . ?"

"I went directly down to the nursery as Mrs. Restell had written me. She said she would meet me there. I waited. When she didn't come—"

"You went upstairs."

"No. No, I did not. I waited so long that I became frightened."

"Frightened? You, Miss Tremont? When you knew the house so well?"

"I thought something might have happened. . . ."

"What might have happened?" Madame Ducharde leaned forward as if piercing every word for its truth.

"I thought perhaps Carrie had had to leave. Or might have decided to escape. I thought I might be discovered there by strangers. I thought . . . oh, why must we talk about all this? I ran up the stairs to the back hall and out into the street. What does it matter now?"

"It matters, Miss Tremont, because I, too, was waiting in that house. Carrie's carriage was to come for me at ten o'clock. Hannah, my trusted helper, and I were to take Carrie's private records and papers out of the house to where they would be safe. When I knew it was time to go I went out into the upstairs hall. I heard steps, Miss Tremont, steps across the marble floor of the front hall. . . ."

"I didn't go into the front hall!"

"Carrie gave you my address that night, or you would not be here, in this garden, now."

It was a thrust of steel but the effect was to cool Noel's overheated mind. Something was beginning to take shape in her mind, something beyond the walls of this place.

"Madame Ducharde, I found your address among Sophie Hansen's things, in Carrie Restell's handwriting. I—I finally knew I needed help."

"Is that all you have to tell me, Miss Tremont?"

"It is the truth."

There was no need to say more. Noel was at last beginning to understand. They were not adversaries, she and this strange, dominating woman. They were confederates, conspirators, each in her own way part of the sad underworld in which Carrie Restell had lived, that shadowy half life of fear and secrecy. Madame Ducharde was as afraid of discovery as Noel herself.

Emboldened now, Noel felt she had passed an invisible test.

"I assure you, Madame, no one knows where I am."

"You misunderstand. The tragedy of that last night of Carrie's life must be apparent to you. You and I were the last to enter that house. If either of us had waited a little longer, spoken a word, lifted a hand of compassion, Carrie Restell might never have yielded to that mad, lonely impulse to destroy herself. That is what I can never forgive, to myself or anyone else."

Noel hesitated, but timidity no longer served her.

"I have never been able to believe that Carrie Restell could, or indeed, did take her own life."

Madame Ducharde rose, revealing an unexpected agility within the grey serenity. Her eyes flashed.

"Then you defy God!" The shadows added to her height. The words came as if from a distant, musty pulpit. "The burdens of the human soul are understood only by our Heavenly Father. When the moment comes that the will breaks, God finds a way for us, with mercy for His stumbling creature."

Madame Ducharde stood, hands lifted, palms together, a figure as ancient as faith, as careful, as precise as art.

Then an extraordinary thing happened.

A light went on in the open second-floor window. It threw a square of illumination into the garden, across the stern, motionless figure. Madame Ducharde turned like a girl, lifting a face suddenly alight, expectant, toward the open window. Noel glimpsed the echo of a last beauty, of youth, like the laughter, the silks this woman might once have known.

"Listen!"

From the window came the children's singing.

"The old villanelle. Four centuries have sung that melody, Miss Tremont. I learned it in my childhood.

J'ai perdu ma tourterelle,
Est-ce point elle que joi?
Je veux aller après elle . . .

The children's voices rose gaily, confidently. In the dusk, Noel heard, to her surprise, a rusted contralto beside her.

Si ton amour est fidèle
Aussi est ferme ma foi
Je veux aller après elle.

Madame clapped her hands. "Charming, is it not? Do you know it, Miss Tremont?' 'If your love is faithful, as my faith is firm. . . .' "

For an instant Noel shut her eyes. The garden, the twilight vanished. She was in Stuyvesant Square. Ned was coming toward her. . . .

Reality returned. Madam was talking. ". . . but you must excuse now. The children like me to join them." Madame became crisp. "Tomorrow morning at eleven, if you please. In my downstairs office. We will discuss what arrangements are to be made."

There was no mistaking the finality. Noel was not to see

Posie now. She was to return to her cell-like room, another tray would be brought. She would wait through another night. She seemed to have passed a lifetime in this walled place. Yet in the curious new balance that had come about between Madame Ducharde and herself, she found a certain strength. She was neither beggar nor victim. She had learned more than she had revealed. Whatever the "arrangements" Madame had in mind, she need not bow to them.

Tomorrow. From her childhood, her father's good-night came back to her, gruff, tender, following her childish prayer.

"Tomorrow is a brand-new coin, little Noel. Spend it being happy and good."

If only she could. If only she had one of those lost new coins to spend again.

Madame Duchard was late.

It was nearly eleven-fifteen. Noel sat primly on a little chair of carved pear wood to which the parlor maid had led her. A French chair. Louis XV? Her idle speculations kept her thoughts from running in darker channels. This gaunt woman to whom she owed so much. A woman of quality, of manners, of a certain stark elegance, yet beneath it all Noel sensed hostility, an area as yet unknown.

She would insist on seeing Posie today.

Eleven-twenty. Noel rose and walked to the window of the small office. It had been left open and unshuttered. It fronted on the street. In the dusty white sunlight, she had a diagonal view of a frame house. The red paint had peeled away, the porch roof sagged, part of its railing was gone. Over the door hung a lantern.

As she watched, a man came walking heavily out onto the porch. He wore only an undershirt and dark baggy trousers suspended below a protruding stomach. He seated himself on the porch step and began to fan his bald head with a folded newspaper. Two girls also emerged from the house. Even at a distance, Noel could see that they were young, one a small blonde with hair frizzed into a tangle of dandelion fluff, the other taller, dark hair tumbling to her shoulders. Both wore what were popularly called kimonos, in wild floral patterns. As the blonde girl leaned forward to speak to the man, her wrapper fell open to reveal small white breasts. The man's hand reached upward, fingers idling over the soft flesh.

Noel turned from the window. The degradation of the scene swept through her like nausea—with it a sense of frustrated anger. They were little more than schoolgirls. She could only wonder what forlorn or vicious twist of fate had flung them into this dead end, frail discards of the city's indifferent lusts. Girls like these had come, too, to Carrie Restell. Noel found herself wondering how Madame Ducharde had chosen this street for her residence.

"I beg your forgiveness, Miss Tremont." Madame Ducharde entered briskly. She was dressed not in the trailing garments of a prioress, but in businesslike street dress of charcoal linen. Her hat bore a dove's wing.

"I have kept you waiting and I offer my apology. But if you saw the happiness I have seen this morning in the face of one of my *petites* I am sure you would pardon me."

She walked to the window and drew the shutters closed. The room faded to a soft twilight. She seated herself behind the desk and gestured to Noel.

"We use the rear of the house, Miss Tremont. There is a little hedged path from the garden to the rectory of St. Giles of the Innocents. You no doubt noticed the steeple beyond the garden wall. That is where I took my *petite,* Elaine, this morning. She is twelve. She has reached her *puberté*. She goes now to France, to the Convent of La Sacre Vierge where she will complete her schooling. At seventeen she will be presented. *Alors"*—Madame's eloquent hands opened—"a suitable marriage. Little Elaine's face was alight this morning with her expectations. I understand you are not of the church, Miss Tremont, but I assure you that within its fold, these *innocentes* are safe. I went to confession last evening, as I always do before one of my *enfants* leaves. So this morning I could go to Mass with confession. It leaves the soul washed, the heart cleansed. Not like your cold American puritans, Miss Tremont, who condemn all sinners to eternal fire and hold out neither the hand nor the heart of forgiveness. *Le Dieu est bon.* That is the first lesson my *petites* learn. Sit down, Miss Tremont. We meet this morning to talk about your affairs."

Madame had mastered the art of sitting motionless, of letting time pass until it became meaningless, a gulf that at this moment seemed to separate Noel from all that she knew, all that was dear and familiar. Her father, her brothers, the kindness of Dr. Lendler, Stuyvesant Square, and—no, she would not think of Ned Fitch now. He, too, was across the moat with which Madame Ducharde seemed to surround herself and Noel.

"The street outside, Miss Tremont, was not always as you see it. It was once a charming *allée* of locust trees running between a carriage house and stables on one side and kitchen gardens and orchards on the other, all part of a fine estate. This house was the home of an Englishman, a Mr. Dunne, who came to New York after the defeat of that madman, Napoleon. I believe he found the air fresher. Mr. Dunne and his American wife had three lovely daughters. The young ladies' pictures still hang in the drawing room on the other side of the hall. Sometimes I permit my little *innocentes* to go in and look at them. I tell them what grace and charm and elegance a young girl must have. It is always a treat for them."

It was a section of the house Noel had not seen. Nor did she sense the direction of Madame's leisurely discourse. Yet intuition told her that there was a purpose behind it.

"Then, Miss Tremont, something quite dreadful happened to the Dunne family. They were very fond of the theatre. One spring evening, they went to the Astor Place Opera House, I believe it was, to see a famous English actor, Mr. Macready, in *Macbeth.* But it seemed the American people had not yet forgiven the English. They wanted American actors. That evening an enormous crowd of, what do you call them, rowdies, the commonest sort, gathered outside the theatre. When the curtain went up, they started a riot. Paris, I am sure, had seen nothing worse. Mr. Dunne managed to lead his sweet little family to safety. But the youngest girl was struck in the head by a stone. She survived, but her brain was permanently damaged. Mr. Dunne packed up his family and sailed for England. They abandoned everything, the house, its furnishings, anything that would remind them of America. When I found the place, it was in a state of total neglect. The outer buildings were in ruin, stables and gardens gone. The surrounding land sold off. But the house still stood. And the fine brick garden wall. It suited my purpose. I closed off the front side, facing the street. Only the front door, the address, would be used by those who had need of it. The house itself I restored to its rightful elegance. As you would restore a broken life to its rightful place in the world. So I have made, for my little ones, a home, a place to grow, *un jardin, tendre, jolie.*"

The walls of the old house must indeed have been thick. Noel heard no sound.

"*Alors,* Miss Tremont," Madame clapped her hands. "Now we talk about you. You look almost well this morning. I should say quite able to make the departure you wish.

"I should like to see Posie, Madame."

"Of course. I have told her your plans."

"I have made no plans yet. I shall have to work them out."

There was a pause. Madame seemed to be expecting more.

"I shall make my life around my child."

"Of course. You will find work, I am sure, Miss Tremont. You are very intelligent and capable. You will find a little room somewhere, I presume. You will leave Elizabeth with a neighbor or a day orphanage while you work. You will come home from your work and make her little suppers. As she grows older, find her friends on the streets. Or, Miss Tremont, do you think you will go up to your father with her, beg his forgiveness, beg to be taken in? He will take you in. I have no doubt of that. But will he accept your *bâtarde?* The very image of you. Will he turn his back on his position? I read that as head of the Citizens League he went to lunch at the White House, with the President of this great country. Will you dishonor—"

"Madame!"

Noel was on her feet, her face white.

"Don't you think I've thought of all that? Every word of it is burned into my mind. Since that first day I walked into Mrs. Restell's house, carrying my unborn baby. I love my father. I would do nothing, nothing, to hurt him or dishonor him. But I want my child! I will do anything to keep her safe, to make her happy. . . ."

"Exactly. You want her. You will keep her safe. The contradiction seems to have escaped you. Worst of all, you are proud, Miss Tremont. You do not ask help. Or advice. Since you have come here you have behaved as if there were a conspiracy in this house to separate Elizabeth from you. Would you have had her see you in high fever, delirious, weakened until we feared for you? Yet when you did see her, you saw a happy little girl, fresh, pretty. What more can you ask? I am beginning to think we have both wasted our time."

But Madame did not rise. There was something, Noel sensed, still to be played out. Was it to be a humbling, an admission of Noel's dependence? It was as if in a span of moments, Noel must decide the course of a whole lifetime.

"I would like to see Posie, Madame."

"Very well."

Posie must have been once again readied and waiting. Madame went to the hall door and returned almost immediately, Posie's small hand touching the folds of her charcoal linen suit.

"Mistaffy is here, Elizabeth. *Fais-toi révérence.*"

With a gentle push, she urged Posie forward.

The child was dressed in the clothes in which Noel had

brought her. But the sashed dress looked fussy, the daisy hat dowdy, and the black high-buttoned boots worn and heavy. She walked slowly toward Noel.

"Darling!" Noel dropped from the chair and stretched out her arms.

Posie stopped just beyond their reach. For a long instant she stared at Noel with dry empty eyes, then she made a stiff little curtsy.

"Posie, dear! You've learned so much now. We're going to . . ."

The sound was so tiny Noel barely heard it. It was not a sob, nor a gasp. It was merely a very tiny sound as Posie took a half step backward. Then suddenly she spun around, ran past Madame, and out of the room, gone like a stray beam of light, the door pulled shut behind her.

Noel rose to her feet. Was this child so like her that she could not even cry? The pantomime was over. The future she had built of bright pretense lay collapsed like worn-out props.

Madame watched in silence.

Noel caught her breath, but the question came in spite of herself.

"What can I do?"

It was no doubt the submission the tall woman awaited.

"Sit down, Miss Tremont. It is time we talked before you expose Elizabeth to any further pain." Madame seated herself in a straight-backed chair beside her desk. "You are an intelligent, strong-willed young woman, but you are the victim, like so many others, of certain false concepts of society. You have borne a child. Your child must love you because you are her mother. You are not married but because of your love for her she must share your disgrace. Oh, do not misunderstand me. I do not think of you as disgraced. I think rather. . . ."

The heavy-lidded eyes focused beyond the room, the severe face turned as if listening, not to any sound in the house or the street but to an inner rhythm.

"I think of you as fortunate. You have known what is not given to all women, passion. And you have a child."

Noel sat rigid. The talk had taken an uncomfortable turn.

"So you are fortunate. I envy that fortune. I was deprived of it. My father put me into a convent at sixteen. I would not marry an ugly old man he had chosen. It was nothing new. The convents of France have been filled with women whose young living hearts have been torn out of them. When my father died and I reentered the world it was too late for me.

But God left in my heart a love of all children, *les pauvres innocents.* It is for them I live now.

"I can take into my home here, just twelve. I see them not as just sweet children, but as twelve little girls who, I believe, with proper schooling can become accomplished, lovely young women, properly prepared for suitable marriages and social position. I wish I could take a hundred, but I can only do so much. It is my way of making up for all the heart-starved misery to which society condemns women who break its laws. These little ones are *bâtardes.* Who knows that when they make their bows in Paris or London or Vienna?"

Madame gave one of her rare laughs, her face revealing again the ghost of long-fled beauty.

"It is my pleasure. My life. So I have created this"—the long thin arm swept the air—"my little *lycée,* my . . . my *revanche!*"

The sudden bitterness of revenge burst like a spark. Then went out.

"Carrie Restell was to tell you all this that last night, Miss Tremont. But you say you did not see her. I must accept that for the time being. There are many, Miss Tremont, who seek entry here. My terms are not easy, but they are just. The child who comes here will have her board, clothing, religious instruction. She will learn French and Italian. She will become proficient in pianoforte and the harp. She will learn deportment, dancing, painting, history, and the arts. At twelve she will go abroad for the *complétement.* . . ."

"And then what?" But Noel already knew. She had seen the figures in the garden, the woman in tears, the man, head bowed in his hands.

"The child's natural mother is permitted to come here twice a year. She may not visit, but she may see her child. On her name day and on Christmas Eve mass at the little church at the rear of us, St. Giles."

"That's all?"

"For the child's sake, that must be all. I have one empty place in the school now. Only one. My little Elaine has made her *progrès.* For Carrie Restell's sake, I can offer it to you."

So there it was. As if each step of her distraught way had led Noel to this decision. This logical, threatening moment of truth.

"There are terms, of course. Perhaps that sacrifice, too, would be too great."

"What terms?" Noel was hardly listening. She was trying

and failing to guess what the days ahead would be, bereft of feeling and purpose.

"They are very simple. Five thousand dollars to be paid when the child enters. That covers all costs here in my house for board and education until she is ready to depart for the convent in Paris. At that time another five thousand dollars is to be paid for her finishing, her preparation, her debut. Then her *dot* is to be provided. Two thousand dollars. Without a dowry"—Madame shrugged—"a proper marriage would be impossible. In all, a total sum of twelve thousand dollars. Not excessive, is it? To assure a young girl a fitting place in the world?"

Madame folded her long hands. Noel was reminded of her first impression. The aristocratic features carved in stone, the grey serenity obliterating forever the heated blood that must once have raced through those veins, the heart that must once have known passion, the fantasies, the expectations, that might have played in light and shadow across that proud face.

"Madame, I have no such sum of money."

Madame glanced at her sharply. "Then perhaps Carrie was wrong. She understood your father . . ."

"My father is generous and kind. He loves me. He believes it is enough to give me a home and his protection. But he would not entrust money to me. When my brothers came of age he made them generous gifts. If I had married I would have had my share—"

"As a dowry?"

"The dowry would be given to my husband. Not to me. Oh, Madame. I blame myself for what happened. I believed—I imagined—I was in love . . . I trusted. . . ."

Madame's hand lifted impatiently.

"The story is always the same, Miss Tremont."

"No, it is not! My child is my life. I knew I was wrong all those years I had to leave her with others. I suffered for it. When I took her away at last, I vowed that nothing on earth would make me give her up again. Don't you think I see what it has been for her here? Pretty clothes, fine manners, children to play with. I see the glow in her face, the happiness I haven't yet been able to give her. But she's mine. I haven't stopped telling myself that since the hour Carrie Restell laid her in my arms!"

The handkerchief Noel had been twisting tore. Yet in some way the shuttered little room had grown in size. For Noel the air had freshened.

"I—I hadn't meant to say all that, Madame. I . . ."

The tall woman sat sybil-like, expressionless.

"It had to be said. I believe we are finding each other human at last. Women do not trust each other easily. Yet we must learn to. The world of men is a distant place. Their so-called protection, their encirclement of us, their laws defining what they wish to see as our weakness, our innocence. We have little recourse against all that. Except our cleverness"—Madame paused, her eyes hard—"and our bodies. You need money, Miss Tremont. With a little skill, a little willingness it can be yours. If you marry—"

"Marry?"

"You are young. You are, you could be, attractive."

But it was not a lover Noel saw in her mind. It was the heavy face of Gus Hansen . . . the searing words, that she was the kind "who'd trap a man into marriage." No man would ever say that to her again.

"I will never marry, Madame."

"How little you know! How many women, Miss Tremont, do you think go to their wedding beds for love? You had your little dream. It did not pay the bills or assure position for yourself or your child. Since time began women have given their bodies because they must, while heart and mind fled to some kinder star. But our submission is outside of ourselves. What is inside no man can ever touch or possess. That, in the end, is our victory."

The mask of effigy had gone, a living woman spoke. She walked to the window, pushed open the shutter. The shabby wooden house across the street came into view, the porch now empty.

"For the desperate, that house over there is one way. For the more fortunate, marriage is another. But do not think the difference so vast." She swung the shutter shut. When she turned, all emotion, all intensity, had drained from her face. The effigy was restored.

"Elizabeth is a rare and sensitive child, Miss Tremont. It has been a pleasure to have her here. I shall make my *adieu* to her. Then she will be ready to go with you."

Madame Ducharde had reached the door before Noel found words.

"Madame!"

The gaunt woman turned slowly.

"Madame, would you give me time?"

"For what?"

"I need time . . . to think. If you could keep Posie here a little longer, until I have thought about it. . . ."

Madame Ducharde studied Noel's face. Her own was without expression.

"I am not a harsh woman, Miss Tremont. Nor an ungenerous one. I have seen too much of wrong, of evil, in the world. If I can make a little gift of time. . . . But I advise you, do not delay too long. It is your child who suffers."

She was gone. And with her, a part of Noel's life, the only part, she told herself, that would ever matter.

20

The man at the top of the ladder was in trouble. He clung like a monkey to the black bunting the wind was tossing around him. It was to be the final loop of mourning nailed across the red and gold sign of Engine House 66, leaving only the painted tiger's head, mascot of the fire crew, to be seen above it.

Ned, idling along the cobbled street, had joined the watching crowd. What he saw made him push his way roughly through it.

"And will ye not come down, ye old goat! And leave a man who's able to do the work proper!"

The shawled woman, shapeless as a bundle at the foot of the ladder, shook a thick fist. The gathering crowd cheered. "Dinna fash yerself, Grannie!" A toothless man, tobacco spittle on his chin, jigged with delight. "Yer Patrick's taken enough of the bottle to float him down like a fither!"

Then it happened. The black stuff whipped around the old man's head, the hammer slipped from his hand, the nail from his mouth. He clutched at the ladder and fell. The woman screamed.

Ned was the first to reach him. The old man lay flat on his back, mouth open, wrinkles crisscrossing the soiled face. But he was breathing.

"Glory be to God and to God's Mother! Sure and it's his head he's broken and me own heart with it," the woman keened.

The little man opened a baleful eye on her and shut it. Then he opened both eyes and saw Ned. "If you'll do me the favor, young man . . ."

"I wouldn't try to talk, sir. You've had quite a fall."

"If you'll just help me to my feet. That'll shut the old woman up and I'll get on with me work. It's the hot blast of her coming up at me that blew me off." His face went white and he grimaced.

Ned pushed him gently back on the cobblestones.

"You'd better stay where you are, Mr.—"

"Flaugherty's the name, young sir," the woman offered, crouching beside him. "And the divil curse the day me two young eyes, blue as the waters they were, sir, first laid on the old bog-trottin' calf!" She laid a tender hand on the stricken man's forehead. "Be ye hurtin', Paddy?"

Ned knelt, his hands gentle on the fragile frame. "Send someone for an ambulance. It's his leg."

"Agh, and sure it's the bone starin' at me. There through the leg of his pants!" The woman shrilled. "Birdie, go run for Dr. Jenny. She'll have the morphine."

Paddy's eyes flew open. "I'll have no female woman doctorin' on me! A slip of a thing like that. What does she know of a man's shank?"

"Plenty of 'em know yours, Paddy! A banty rooster in yer day!" A ripple of uneasy laughter betrayed relief.

"Get on with you all! Tom, be after telling Father Gillano we'll need the wagon. He's Eyetalian but maybe today the good God will hear him anyway." The woman rose heavily but surely for her weight and shape. "I'm grateful to you, young sir."

Ned had removed his own jacket, folded it and was easing it between a puddle and the little man's head.

"Now don't be doin' that, young gentleman." The woman snatched at the jacket. "It's a fine jacket and ye'll be ruinin' it on the like of an ol' fool who's known the pavin' often enough."

What was needed, Ned saw, was authority. He took the jacket firmly and replaced it. "What your husband must have, Mrs. Flaugherty, is quiet. He must lie very quiet."

"You're a doctor yerself, sir?"

"No, but I've tended a fallen horse or two."

"Ye hear that, Paddy, me love. The young man says yer to be quiet. All of you"—she roared—"stand back! Don't be pushin' as if you'd never seen a living corpse before! Paddy, Paddy . . . me dove. Open yer eyes! Look at me!" Paddy's eyes tightened shut.

"Agh, he's hurtin' bad! It's a jumpin' flea of a man he is, young gentleman. Or he wouldn't have been up that ladder. Only wantin' to pay his respects puttin' up the black crepe to the great man who's dead this very day with the church bells tollin' the noon hour. Right there in his prison cell."

She crossed herself and lifted her eyes to a heaven that bestowed such an abundance of grievances. "Dead. Of a sore and burdened heart, if you ask me. All them houndin' him and he doin' good like the arm of God. Ask Minnie there. Great and mighty as he was, didn't Mr. Tweed send the darlin' white coffin when her youngest was taken up to the angels? And when Agnes came with her five straight off the boat from the county Mayo, God help us, didn't Mr. Tweed send around a sack of coal and a bag of praties to settle her in? And Paddy"—Mrs. Flaugherty wiped a slow tear—"are ye hearing'? Yer own sister's son . . . didn't he have the grand job from Mr. Tweed? Paintin' the lampposts in the spring, on the days that it rained. And the paint drippin' off as fast as he put it on. So sure enough, he could start paintin' them all over and over again. Some said it was makin' the city pay three times and Mr. Tweed gettin' the profit, but I say it was steady work for the lad, and a good thing, too."

"Aye"—the toothless man took up the litany—"and didn't the great man invite us all to his social club, the Tammany, for a pint or two and a round of jiggin'? And all ye had to do was sign . . ."

What, Ned would never know. Down the street, skirts flying, spindle legs working like spokes, came the young girl Birdie, dispatched for Dr. Jenny. She threw her arms around the shawled woman, whispered something and burst into tears.

"Agh, the day of our sorrows. Who told you, Birdie? The policeman? And the door's locked?"

The girl, apron to her face, nodded.

Mrs. Flaugherty looked frightened. "It's Dr. Jenny." She lowered her voice to the nearest of the crowd. "She's been arrested. Last night, was it?"

The girl nodded.

"Arrested?" The toothless man danced up and down. "Arrested! Praise be to God. What Jenny was doin', she'd been better selling herself bare in the street!"

A howl went up. It would be difficult to say what part of the crowd was cheering, what protesting. Fists were raised.

To Ned's relief, two briskly trotting horses turned the corner. A grim, dark blue wagon came into sight. The crowd hushed, backed, and stared, immediate drama being more satisfying than argument. Two blue-uniformed attendants unrolled a canvas slung between two carrying poles.

"Out of the way, young gentleman."

"It's his leg there. A bad break. I'll help you move him."

They worked competently and confidently. The little man groaned, cried out, then fainted. The stretcher with its burden was tilted and shoved through the open doors at the rear of the wagon. With a crack of the whip it rattled off. Patrick Flaugherty had changed from a man to a cipher.

As quickly, the street emptied. Not even the shawled woman with the weeping girl remained. A younger man had climbed the ladder and was nailing the last black loop into place. Ned picked up his stained coat and slung it over one shoulder. Something was missing. Something had happened that he had not anticipated. Used to loneliness, he was surprised at this odd feeling. He could not have named what he wanted. Not thanks, God knew. Rather a share, perhaps, in the bitter emotions of the street, a forgetting in a glass of beer, some friendly banter at a pub, or a cup of tea lifting the spirits of a burdened family.

But he was alien to them even as he had joined them. Well as he knew this harsh world, he no longer belonged to it. He had taken himself from it. He was now a "young sir." Yet he was as faceless here as he was to the inhabitants of Stuyvesant Square. He had seen employment with Dr. Lendler as the door to a new life. Yet no door had opened to him. He lived with only the phantom of a girl he had found. She had disappeared as totally as the figures in the sad little street scene in which he had just taken part.

You'll always be happier with our kind than theirs. Millie's remembered words over the tea leaves—teasing or prophetic?

"Extry! Extry! Read all about it. Boss Tweed dead. Swindled thirty million! Extry, sir?"

With nearly a dozen newspapers in the city, every hour saw an "Extra" on the streets. Ned reached into his pocket. Not that he wanted the paper, not because it was a gentleman's gesture, but because of the pinched need in the boy's face. He could now afford to see it.

"You'll get yer money's worth this day, sir. Boss Tweed, dead as a haddock. And old Tony Comstock strikes again!"

It was later at night when Ned opened the thin, sleazy Extra. But what he found near the back page among the police items brought him bolt upright. He lay a long time, thinking. So long, in fact, that his landlady rapped on the door to inquire of his health. It was Mrs. Luskin's way of reminding him of his extravagant use of lamp oil.

The afternoon stillness suited Noel. In her own room, in her father's house, standing idly at her own window, she felt safe.

Because of her noticeable pallor and her quietness she was left alone. She had asked Madame Ducharde for time to make a decision. Actually, there was no decision to be made. She was being carried on an invisible river growing swifter, stronger each passing day until in her mind she could hear the menacing thunder of the falls ahead. She would be swept over, like the condemned Indian maiden in the penny arcade's lantern slides. She could never recall what the doomed Indian maiden had done. But she would always remember the Indian maiden's lover, a distant figure running along the bank, forever out of her reach, forever unable to help her.

She stood often at the window these days, looking out into the park, watching passersby in what seemed to her their unburdened freedom. Searching, searching—fearing yet longing to see a too-familiar dark head. Once she thought Ned was there, sitting on a bench, motionless, his gaze fixed on nothing. So vivid was the image, she had to stifle an impulse to run down the stairs and across the street to him. When she looked again the bench was empty. What could she expect from him now? The simplest need in the world—love, sharing, a completeness to the loneliness she had embarked on—she had turned away. She was a woman whose need was even simpler. A wedding ring, from a man suitable enough in her father's eyes to obtain her dowry. No questions asked, no emotions involved.

Noel turned from the window. She was thinking too much. If, as Madame had advised, she would accept her destiny as a woman in her circumstances must, she would find the way not only easier but straight. Straighter, Noel thought wryly, than it had ever been.

A light knock and the bedroom door opened. It was Annie-Mae, half buried beneath an enormous basket of white ruffles.

"Let me take it, Annie-Mae. It's much too big—"

But Annie-Mae had already set her burden gingerly on the floor. "There ye are, Miss Noel. All done, ironed and fresh. Fer your stay at the shore."

"Annie-Mae . . . my best summer dresses, my best petticoats! Who put you up to all that?"

"Mrs. Jessup said I was to have everything ready. I thought if I did it all right, you might be wishin' to take me as lady's maid with you like Mrs. Tremont does."

"Oh, my dear girl! My dear, dear little friend! I'm going to keep my father company. And, well, just be quiet."

"You'll be out to balls and parties, Miss Noel."

"It isn't like that. It's a big old house where we just enjoy summer. I'll be walking on the beach. And in the evening . . . watching the stars. Or . . . reading."

The disappointment in Annie-Mae's round face was as clear as her longing.

"But, Annie-Mae, if you think Mrs. Jessup will let you go, I'd be delighted to take you with me."

"No, Miss, not—not that way, she won't. Nor would I."

"Then I'll make you a promise." Noel knew what was prompting her. The closeness, the dear familiarity of all she knew, all she belonged to, and this girl, half-child that she was, trusting a future that could not exist. "Annie-Mae"—she took the girl's hands in hers—"I promise you that if ever in this world I should need a lady's maid, you will be the one, the only one." Color suffused Annie-Mae's face. "And if, when I leave this house—"

"Oh, no, Miss Noel. Or maybe you're meanin' the day yer a bride . . . ?"

"When I leave this house, I will find you a position of lady's maid to the most proper lady I know. And I know some very proper ones."

"Oh . . . I do thank you." It was all Annie-Mae could manage. She shut the door with a bang that Noel prayed Mrs. Jessup would not hear.

Slowly, Noel began taking out the sheer white linens and lawns, ruffles and eyelet embroideries. All she would not need. Now or ever. Her plans were more spartan. She heaped the clothes on the bed. The bottom of the basket was lined with white tissue. Beneath that, as protection against the dust, lay newspaper pages. Yesterday's, the day before, it didn't matter. Except that off center, at the bottom of the basket, lay five inches of print, like a thumbprint of fate, meant for Noel's eyes alone.

ANTHONY COMSTOCK STRIKES AGAIN.
WOMAN ARRESTED.

Genevieve Crater, aged 32, known as a practitioner of female medicine on New York's downtown west side, was taken into custody last night for the illegal practice of abortion. In the company of two police officers, Mr. Comstock entered Miss Crater's basement office to find not only instruments, morphine, and other incriminating equipment of her nefarious work, but plain covered pamphlets Miss Crater admitted to both giving out and mailing to women. As Mr. Comstock is now a federal postal supervisor, he has stated that Miss Crater will be prosecuted not only for her nefarious practice but for sending pornographic matter through the United States mails.

Miss Crater is known to have been a former associate and protegée of the late, notorious Mrs. Caroline Restell. Trial has been set for the first week in June.

Noel tore the article from the paper. She pinned on her summer hat, picked up her mesh gloves and went quietly down the stairs, leaving 269 Stuyvesant Square to its virtuous peace. At the iron grilling of the park fence, she paused, almost involuntarily, to peer into leafy shadows of the trees. Among the strollers, along the well-filled benches she saw only strangers. No one she might recognize, no tall figure, his eyes on the house. She hurried on.

By the time she reached Madame Ducharde's house, she had made her decision. It echoed in the firmness with which she pushed the doorbell. There was no answer and she remembered that Madame did not like to be disturbed by unexpected callers. She rang again. She was contemplating the fleur-de-lys knocker when the door opened on a crack. The maid was new.

"I must see Madame Ducharde, please."

"She's—she's not at home, Miss. I mean to callers. She's busy."

"Would you tell her that Miss Tremont . . . ?"

"Miss, I dasn't disturb her."

But the little maid, under the spell of curiosity, had opened the door wider. Noel slipped past.

"I'm sure Madame Ducharde will see me. She's a friend. It's quite important."

"I don't know, Miss. She said . . ."

"I'll wait. Don't worry. It's all right."

To the young maidservant, duty in this house seemed a perilous task but the young lady was so pleasant, so friendly.

"You'd best wait in the grand parlor, Miss. I'll tell Madame when she's free. I—I don't know what else to do."

"Then do nothing." Noel gave her a confiding smile. "I've always found that simplified things. I'll take all the responsibility."

Alone, Noel could hear voices coming from Madame Ducharde's office down the hall. A man's voice, husky, dominating. Then a low murmur. Noel recognized Madame Ducharde, sounding drained of authority and speaking only at intervals, as if she were merely listening or complying.

Aware she was eavesdropping, Noel went quickly into the long drawing room. She took a chair out of sight of the hall but within line of the front door. She would see for herself when Madame was free. She had never come to Madame Ducharde without an appointment. She was as well aware as the little maid was of the rules. But it was not for herself she came today.

Not even for Posie. Noel could imagine her upstairs at classes, or in the rear garden at play. For a powerful moment, the whole house held her child's presence. So powerful it stirred the stale air of this unused room. But she would not ask to see Posie. Her purpose was as different as it was single.

She had not been in this grand parlor before. Its furnishings had the elaborate grace of another era, gilded, finely carved. Yellow silk, embroidered with Chinese figures, draped the windows. The large painting above the marble mantel was framed in heavy gold—the three young girls in their filmy dresses, their rosebud faces laughing.

Forcing her thoughts from Posie, Noel tried to imagine the people who had occupied this home so long ago. A large family, loving and happy, cousins, relatives, friends filling this damp emptiness, their chatter, their laughter, their quarreling and making up, the flow of small acts and daily living, so important to the hour, so quickly and finally vanished.

The voices were at the front door. She saw the heavy black of a man's coat, a balding head. When he turned she saw a cleric's collar. He was gone.

"Miss Tremont!"

Madame Ducharde stood erect and very tall in the entrance, her face chiseled in anger.

"Madame, forgive me but I must—"

"Miss Tremont. You know my rules. You knew them the first day we talked. When you needed haven for your child I gave it. You knew the conditions. Now you ignore them. I see no one, no one, Miss Tremont, without a previous understanding. Without a precise appointment. I am a burdened woman, Miss Tremont. It is not easy to do all I do. I have business to attend to. I will, I must, have the privacy of my own house!"

It seemed to Noel that Madame Ducharde's anger carried her far beyond the needed chiding.

"I'm truly sorry, Madame—"

"I cannot see you, Miss Tremont!"

Noel stood stiffly, as erect as the Frenchwoman.

"Madame Ducharde. I must talk to you." Her eyes met Madame Ducharde's and held them. "Jenny Crater was arrested yesterday. It was in this morning's paper."

The mustiness of the room thickened. When she spoke, Madame Ducharde's voice came distant and dry, as if the blaze of her anger had dropped to ash.

"The affairs of Jenny Crater have nothing to do with me."

"But they do, Madame. And with me. The paper said there were even doubts that Jenny was a doctor, but that she had been associated with Mrs. Restell."

"I read the article, Miss Tremont."

"Then you know—"

"I know that Genevieve Crater is a very unwise young woman. Oh, Carrie thought a great deal of her. She trained her. But the girl had no idea about the world. She chose to leave Carrie and set up for herself. As if she could."

"She wanted to work among the poor. Poor women who—"

Madame Ducharde interrupted harshly. "Work, work without funds, without friends, without people who could protect"—Madame caught herself—"people who could advise her. No, Miss Tremont, what happened was inevitable. Mr. Anthony Comstock found her and had the pleasure of arresting her. Your father's friend, I believe."

"I came here, Madame Ducharde, to talk about Jenny Crater. Not my father. I came here to ask you what we could do?"

"We?"

"We both knew her. She'll go on trial in three weeks. I thought something must be done."

"Why?"

Noel realized not for the first time how very little she knew of this woman to whom she had entrusted her child. What dark secrets governed her thoughts, moved her mind? They were no more to be understood than the emotions, the creeds, that had once stirred the hearts of the medieval granite statues to which Madame Ducharde seemed to belong.

"Madame, Jenny Crater was my friend. No one on earth could have been kinder to me. She loved Posie as if she were her own child. She cared for her and for me in those terrible days as if we were all that mattered in the whole world. She made me feel I had done nothing wrong, only something wonderful in having a baby. In those days at Mrs. Restell's house, she would come often to my room, bring me a flower or a sweet, or a little story about her own life. She made it possible to face my own life. My future—and go on. I'll never cease to be grateful. I must go see Jenny, wherever she is," Noel said quietly.

"You are a fool, Miss Tremont. A sentimental fool. What do you think the press will do to you, to your child, your precious father, and to me, Miss Tremont, when they learn about you and Jenny and Carrie Restell?"

"That is something they will never learn, Madame. I promise you."

21

The demise of the great political swindler, William Marcy Tweed, provided welcome drama for scandal-loving New Yorkers. Though it had been two years since the mighty Tweed, three hundred pounds in weight, absolute in political power, had been brought down by an underling's jealous betrayal, the old stories were revived. Few readers of the penny journals knew what thirty million dollars was, even when it was written out in digits and ciphers. But they knew what a Fifth Avenue mansion looked like, they could imagine the luxurious country estate, the stable of racing horses, the trappings of the enormous wealth of Boss Tweed. Hadn't they feasted on such a diet with the respectable Vanderbilts, Astors, and Goulds? And what had the rich done, pray, for a poor man in need of a job, or a tenement family with the windows broken out and no coal in the stove?

Big Bill Tweed was one of their own, as near Irish as a Scotsman could be. Hard of hand, harder of will, he started as a humble fireman, and had risen rapidly, taking the tiger, emblem of Engine House 66, as the symbol for his own Tammany Social Club. His climb was a glory, his . . . devotion to his wife and eight children an inspiration, and his two flamboyantly conspicuous mistresses, the accepted accessories of power.

When his fall was inevitable, his imprisonment had its titillating details. It was said that Mr. Tweed was installed in the furnished comfort of the warden's office, the warden presumably having to officiate from a vacated cell. The prisoner's bed was soft, his meals served from Delmonico's, and he was permitted the freedom of afternoon visits to his home in company of his son and two guards. His escape had all the style of a Dumas tale. On one afternoon's visit, the great man went upstairs for a nap in his own bed. When his son went up to remind him it was time to return to jail, Mr. Tweed could not be found. Somebody recalled having seen a closed vehicle, like a fishwagon, at the rear door.

Even his eventual recapture two years later had style. A United States gunboat was sent to bring him back.

Boss Tweed was as missed as he was remembered. A feisty, competitive press kept his name, his grandiose style, and even more grandiose crimes afloat as long as they sold papers.

Against all this, the upcoming trial of a drab little female practitioner named Jenny Crater was lost. The day before the event, on a back page between Bankruptcies and Horse Sales, the notice appeared.

TRIAL OF WOMAN ABORTIONIST
SET FOR TWO O'CLOCK TOMORROW.

Anthony Comstock, renowned defender of civic virtue, expected to add another victory to his career.

To a fashionably clad woman walking past the untidily middle-class houses of Perry Street, none of this mattered. She paused uncertainly, searched a house number and walked on.

"Lookin' for someone, Miss?"

The man pushed back his cap and grinned. He smelled of beer, his clothes were wrinkled, his beard ragged and, if one noticed, his fingers were stained.

Adrienne Tremont had not anticipated this. She should have taken a cab, but the day was fine and on foot the adventure held more excitement. Besides, she had intended to find the house, ring the doorbell with no carriage wheels to announce her arrival.

The man confronting her was not overtly rude, just sloppy.

"No, thank you. I can find the number."

"Some of these old houses don't have numbers. Lot of people here don't want to be bothered."

He was well spoken, the features of his unshaven face well formed. He might, she realized, be one of the coterie of artists and bohemians said to live on Perry Street. Beer and slovenliness were what she saw. She resisted wrinkling her nose, even while she had to make the best of it.

"I'm looking for number eleven," she said primly.

"Ah. Well, I happen to know Davy's in. I've just been having a taste of the brew with his new model. Third house down on the right, ma'am. Apartment number two."

She passed quickly, so quickly she did not add a thank-you. The ghost of a shadow had fallen across the afternoon's adventure. The nameplate in the dim vestibule of number 11 verified what she had been told. DAVID TREMONT APT. 2 NO BELL. WALK UP.

In the strong, clear light of a north window, David stepped back and surveyed his drawing. Then he lifted it from the easel and laid it tenderly on his worktable. He stretched. He had worked hard but what he had done was good. In sparse pen and ink, it said what he intended. He would have it in his editor's hands in an hour. It would run in tomorrow morning's paper, to be seen before the trial started. It was the best he could do to shake a hard-shelled, thrill-seeking public from its complacency. His idol, Tom Nast, had brought down the villainous Tweed with pen-and-ink cartoons. Perhaps he, David Tremont, "Goodfellow" on his drawings, could run to earth the piously sanctimonious Anthony Comstock.

He had been too engrossed to hear the footsteps. The light, imperious knock on the opening door surprised him.

"Good afternoon, David."

"Adrienne! What in the world . . . ?"

"You never asked me here, David. So I thought I would come and see it. Your studio, my dear stepson . . . where you do whatever you do."

She was drawing off her gloves, unpinning her stylish bird-trimmed hat as she walked around the studio. A large square room, it was in incredible disarray, except for the tidy work-table and easel at the window.

David watched her as she moved, as always fascinated by the sinuous grace of her body, the artful swing of her narrow skirt. But this was not what he wanted, this peremptory invasion of his privacy. He had been satisfied with temptation, boyish longing, the playacting of passion for a woman adored, unattainable, a forbidden dream, his father's young wife. But not this, dear God, not this.

"You look tired, David." She had circled the room and returned, the delicate scent, the cool beauty close. "You've been neglecting me. You haven't come to the house in weeks."

He could banter, plead work, but she had brought with her something so demanding, if unspoken, that he must be direct now if he ever intended to be.

"I thought that was the idea. Absence."

"Did you?" The meaningless little laugh he had so often heard at her dinner parties rippled around him. "Well, you're quite wrong. After all, I am your stepmother and I do deserve—"

"Stop it, Circe."

She dropped the tiny feathered hat on the worktable and on his finished cartoon. He lifted it from the drawing.

"Oh, your work. I am sorry. I hadn't noticed. Something new, David? What is it?" She scrutinized the white paper. "A woman kneeling at a grave . . . a man whipping her . . . oh, David! And the headstone—Restell. Oh, it's horrid, horrid. That miserable business all over again. You draw so beautifully! Must you waste it on sordid things like this? Isn't it enough that your father's getting himself involved with politicians and corruption and everything ugly that happens in this city? Getting himself laughed at in the papers? But I don't care about that. Let him if he hasn't anything else to do. I care about you. And all the beautiful things you could paint!" She drew a quick breath, the threat of hysteria in her voice. He saw violet shadows beneath her eyes, where none had been. They made her lovelier.

"Glad to have your opinion of my work. But speaking of ugliness, where shall I put this monstrous little hat?"

"David!"

It worked. Indignation steadied the tremor in her voice.

"Well, look at it, girl. Why would any woman wear a whole hummingbird on a hat? Do you know that little creature once beat its wings five hundred times a minute? And in the sun those feathers shone like jewels? Now, a dead bird sewn on a piece of cloth! For fashion!"

For an instant Adrienne looked stricken. But she understood more of the moods of men than David suspected. She smiled, snatched the hat, and tossed it on the floor.

"I shan't wear it again if you don't like it. Oh, David, why do we scold each other for things that don't matter? I came to tell you something. I'm going to Europe."

"When?"

"There! You would miss me, wouldn't you? Walter's going to the shore for the summer. Noel's going with him. She had some sort of illness while she was away and Walter thinks the sea air will do her good. Oh, no doubt it will. She can encourage him in all this sordid political business he likes. Noel's always been interested in poor people and doing good. But I'm not, David. I'm really not. I don't know how. That's my confession. I don't understand all those wicked things that happen and I don't want to. I like pretty things around me. Pretty music and flowers and clothes that make me feel pretty.

And pretty rooms to live in. And people who are amusing. I like to give pretty parties that make my friends happy. Oh, David, is that so wrong? Does that hurt anyone else? Does it?''

Her eyes shone with unusual brilliance.

''David, come to Europe with me. Paris. We could have a little house with a garden. Maybe in Passy. You could sit all day painting beautiful things—flowers and trees and sunsets and moonrise. And I'd wear a white dress with a blue sash and a big hat, and bring you fruits and wine and good French bread . . . and at night when the moon shone on our little garden and there'd be no one . . . no one but us, David . . . we'd be together!''

She was irresistible to him. He felt a desperate need to touch her, hold her.

''And what would we live on, Circe? Will that French bread be baked by your own lily white hands? Dishes washed, slops emptied in that white dress, while I painted pictures no one wants?''

''Come with me, David!''

''No, Adrienne! No! My God, don't you know what you're doing? Don't you understand a man at all? You're my father's wife. . . .''

Her breath was on his cheek. In a single motion, he could sweep her up, carry her through the doorway to the darkening bedroom, and the single cot that would hold them both. His arms stiffened at his sides.

''Go home, Adrienne. Go home where you belong!''

She moved from him, her face pinched as he had never seen it. At the worktable she picked up the cartoon drawing of Jenny Crater kneeling at the grave of Mrs. Restell, looked at it, then slowly tore it from top to bottom and across and let the four pieces flutter to the floor. With a movement of windblown grace, she stooped and picked up the humming-bird hat.

''You're really a little boy, aren't you, David?''

The door closed.

The heat of anger, frustration, and desire closed his throat. ''Boys don't cry, Davy.'' Oddly, it was his father's voice.

The courtroom was narrow and high-ceilinged and held its usual quota of aimless citizenry. In winter they found it a shelter against the icy winds from the harbor, in summer a temporary relief from the hot, fetid streets.

In his robing room Judge Rudnor exchanged his frock coat

for the heavy black gown of justice. Ordinarily he preferred to wear the coat beneath the robe, as an enhancement of personal dignity, but the first week in June brought its discomforts and wool was one of them. The judge was a stern, cadaverous man. When he put on the black cap of a death sentence, he became to the courtroom the grim personification of terror.

Actually Judge Rudnor was a rather mild man and at this moment his thoughts were far from the afternoon session. In two weeks he would be marrying off the last of his three homely daughters to a successful middle-aged hay, grain, and feed merchant from Newark. After that he would go fishing. For a moment the anticipated welter of faces in the courtroom dissolved into swaying shadows of speckled trout in the Beaverkill River.

His clerk opened the door. "Now, Judge?"

"All rise!" The bailiff's enjoyment of his thunderous moment of authority often amused the judge. Today His Honor was merely grateful that the trial would be brief. The defendant had signed a confession and waived trial by jury.

He took his chair high above the room and, with a quick and practiced eye, scanned the courtroom. The prosecutor, an assistant district attorney, was in place. Poor plodding Howard, at the dead-end of his ambition. For the defense, a young sallow-faced attorney assigned by the court to the defendant, who had not wanted one. Well young Josiah could use the ten dollars even if he didn't and perhaps never would know the difference between a habeas corpus and a nolo contendere.

At the rear lounged the usual riffraff, one of whom was already being ejected on rubberized legs. Amid the customary prurient idle men and hard-eyed women was a scattering of high-bosomed ladies, well but sensibly dressed, wearing the yellow-and-white rosette of the suffragettes. The judge could have expected that. On the extreme left of the second row his eye fell on a young woman, simply dressed, head high, staring straight ahead. She had an air of quiet, untouchable elegance. Poise and polish, thought the judge. Poise and polish not often in attendance in his courtroom.

In the front row, center, he saw, as he might have anticipated, the six-foot bulk of Mr. Anthony Comstock, red whiskers masking his narrow mouth and the righteous severity of his expression. Even more than Judge Rudnor disliked a summer session, with its half-opened windows and swarming flies, he disliked the presence of Mr. Comstock. Too often the great man was under the delusion that the court was his.

The judge cleared his throat.

"Is the State ready?" he intoned. "Is the defense ready?"

Through the side door, between two bailiffs, walked Dr. Jenny Crater.

Noel leaned forward in her second-row seat. She had debated this step. She had not succeeded in seeing Jenny in jail. She had met a wall of hostility—conspiracy, as she saw it—against the accused. It had stiffened her determination but it had not erased an undercurrent of doubt. Would her presence at the trial hurt Jenny? Was she risking exposure herself? All that vanished as she watched the small, drained woman, not more than five feet tall, stop while the guards removed the absurd handcuffs. Then she walked meekly and alone to the defense table where the assigned lawyer sat twisting his pencil. He did not look up. Jenny Crater did not look at him.

Noel was shocked, not only by the vulnerability of the young doctor, but by her dulled expression, her bewildered hopelessness.

The prosecutor rose.

"Your Honor, we have here the case of the people of the State and City of New York against Genevieve Crater, accused of the fraudulent practice of medicine and the illegal practice of abortion. She has signed a written confession of guilt."

Jenny was on her feet, eyes blazing.

"Your Honor, I did not sign a confession of guilt. I am a licensed doctor. I confessed only to performing medically necessary operations."

Male boos erupted in the courtroom. A woman shouted, "Hang her!" Noel half rose. The judge's gavel beat down the uproar.

"We will have order in this Court!"

In the reluctant silence, the judge's voice was almost kindly.

"I have read the arraignment. You have pleaded guilty, Miss Crater—"

"*Dr.* Crater."

"I would like to ask you a few questions. You need not take the witness stand. Just step up here to the bench."

Most of the courtroom could catch only a glimpse of the small woman facing the bench, which was perhaps what Judge Rudnor intended. He had an unprofessional compassion for the erring human race and a special aversion to this case.

Noel found herself listening to something beyond the proceedings, something that could be meant for herself.

"Dr. Crater, you say you are a licensed physician. Where did you obtain your degree?"

"Utica Missionary Medical School. Six years ago."

"You look young for such responsibility. What form did your, uh, practice take?"

"Whatever is needed."

"Answer specifically, please. Do you practice female medicine?"

"Yes."

"Dr. Crater, you have admitted to performing abortions. Did you understand the practice is illegal?"

"I am a doctor, not a lawyer, Your Honor. When a woman is in trouble—when she has been abused—or when a mother of ten cannot feed another child—"

A murmur rose. The judge lifted his gavel.

"Dr. Crater, you are not under oath. You have signed a confession. You do not have to answer if you do not wish. I am asking this to understand before I consider your sentence. Did a woman ever die under your ministrations?"

Jenny Crater turned a white face of innocence to the judge.

"I repeat you do not have to answer."

"I will answer, Your Honor. I wish to tell the truth. A woman came to me. She had seven children and was far gone in consumption. She could not have carried another child to term. I—tried to save her." The light voice shook. "I—failed."

The crowd stared, hushed.

"Dr. Crater, did you know the late Mrs. Caroline Restell?"

Jenny's head came up. "She was my friend."

"Did you work with her at any time?"

"Oh, yes. For nearly two years."

"You knew Mrs. Restell was charged with murder for her practices?"

Jenny drew her dignity closer. "Your Honor, Mrs. Restell never committed murder. Those who say so, lie!"

Judge Rudnor sighed. He had tried but this young woman was determined to jail herself. "You may return to your seat."

"Your Honor! If you please . . . !"

Judge Rudnor took pride in never being startled but here standing before him was the young lady he had noticed with appreciation in the second row. "Madam, I do not allow interruptions in my court. If you have anything to say that might bear on this case the Court will permit you to testify, but only from the witness stand."

"No, no!" Jenny Crater's face was ashen.

"It's all right, Jenny!"

Distantly Noel heard the gavel. Distantly she saw the rows of human faces. Distantly—

"Do you swear to tell the truth, the whole truth, and nothing but the truth. . . ."

She had acted impulsively. She saw it now. The goading, the innuendos, the false assumptions had brought her to her feet. She had forgotten the necessary limits of her own life, forgotten the warning of Madame Ducharde, forgotten, God help her, even the safety of her Posie.

The judge was speaking.

"I will question the witness myself, Mr. Prosecutor." Judge Rudnor was puzzled. "Your name, Madam?"

"Noel Tremont."

"You know the defendant, Genevieve Crater?"

"Very well. She is a doctor, honorable and kind. She has helped many people. She asks nothing for herself. Whatever she has done—"

"I think, Miss Tremont, we understand. Where did you meet the defendant?"

"I knew Dr. Crater when I served as a volunteer in the charity wards of the Good Shepherd Hospital."

"Judge Rudnor, I think this questioning is entirely unnecessary." Mr. Anthony Comstock had taken center stage, his voice silky with piety. "Miss Tremont is the daughter of my honored colleague, Mr. Walter Tremont, president of the Citizens League. Miss Tremont's presence in this courtroom is evidence that the city's noble, pure-minded women want to see depravity erased and decency restored. Her innocent heart is understandably torn by the spectacle of a once-trusted friend who has added to that depravity. I bow to your Christian forgiveness, Miss Tremont."

Mr. Comstock sat down. Noel felt her face heat with resentment.

"Is this so, Miss Tremont?"

"Your Honor, I don't know anything about the city's depravity except there seems to be a lot of it, bottom to top."

A ripple of laughter brought the gavel. "Pray continue, Miss Tremont."

"Dr. Jenny Crater is my friend. I am here because there doesn't seem to be anyone else to stand by her."

Judge Rudnor had had enough of the whole matter. Let

Tony Comstock interfere at a trial and the whole pattern of orderly justice went awry. He knew the Comstock political power. But he would be damned if he would let the old predator have the last word.

"Miss Tremont, I have only one more question. When you befriended the defendant, did you know of her association with the late Mrs. Caroline Restell?"

In the instant it took to understand the question, Noel saw the chasm ahead. She was under oath. If she told the truth, there would be more questions. If she denied knowing Caroline Restell, she would commit the crime of perjury. She would lie under her given oath, publicly, deliberately. For a drowning instant, she saw all Stuyvesant Square pass before her eyes, her father's kindly, wise decency, her mother's faith in the best of all possible worlds, her brothers, all those who trusted her. And through them all, she saw a little ghost figure who stood at the heart of her life, hers to love, to shield with her very soul.

"Miss Tremont?"

She lifted her head. What was perjury compared to the falsehood she had lived for so long, the daily lies society forced on her? Her present life was a lie, her future held nothing else.

"I did not know Mrs. Restell."

Noel barely heard the judge dismiss her. As she returned to her seat, she glanced at Jenny. The girl sat with bowed head, staring blankly at her hands.

"The defendant has pleaded guilty. Date for sentencing is July twentieth, ten o'clock in the morning. The prisoner is remanded to the Sheriff's custody."

The judge left the bench. The hot, fetid room began to empty. Noel sat barely aware of it. She would visit Jenny tomorrow. This had been a trial not of fairness, but of prejudice.

"Miss Tremont! We are proud of you!" A large woman wearing the yellow-and-white rosette on a large bosom leaned over. "Very proud! If only that poor young woman hadn't confessed! Well, we shall continue to fight."

The courtroom finally cleared. Alone, Noel slowly made her way to the street. Ignoring the gawking and the curious, she stood letting a breeze cool her thoughts. How easy it had been to commit a crime—public perjury. Was this how it was, when a man had lost his honor, when a man had stolen or killed, was it easier the next time, and the next? Had she come to this same point? Did she no longer separate truth from falsehood? Worse, did she no longer care?

She made a second, even more astute discovery. She had expected a sense of anguished guilt, of self-accusation. Instead she felt, in this early summer air, a bracing freedom, a momentary lightness, a release. If she must live outside respectability, she would, as long as this mood lasted, enjoy it.

Down the street she saw a welcome patch of shade. Then her heart skipped a beat.

The grass in the little enclave was already wearing brown despite the partial shade of a giant sycamore tree. Ned, seated on the solitary iron bench, stretched his legs, tilted his hat against the sun and waited. His eyes were fixed on the entrance to the courthouse.

He had been astounded to see Miss Noel Tremont at the shabby trial. He had been even more astounded when she rose to testify. He had been filled with admiration at her gallantry, but he had resisted the impulse to rush up to her in the courtroom. He had left ahead of her, not only with a sense of elation, but of a simple happiness at this twist of chance.

His own compulsion to attend the trial had been painfully clear, although he could admit it to no one. He had asked Dr. Lendler for the afternoon's freedom. He would make up the hours lost. Dr. Lendler had quickly granted it. Sometimes Dr. Lendler's easy tolerance disturbed him, as if the little professor did not really need him. But today it made no difference. Today Ned had a single motive born of one name in the newspaper notice announcing the trial. That name was Restell.

He had tried and more often than not succeeded in putting Mrs. Restell from his mind. But he could never entirely banish the memory of the black-haired woman lying, contrary to all newspaper reports, in death in her office. No expected questions had been asked him. No expected knock by the police on the door of Mrs. Luskin's boarding house. The whole affair had evaporated. All that had remained was the tantalizing memory of the young, veiled woman he had seen leave the Restell house that night. Noel Tremont, with her slenderness, her proud, quick grace, had for a mistaken moment reminded him of her.

He had indeed been wrong. This afternoon in court he had heard her clearly, righteously, and somewhat acidly deny knowing Mrs. Restell. Putting that windbag Comstock back on his heels. Ned had thrilled to that lofty performance.

Suddenly he was on his feet. He had let his thoughts distract his vigil. She was coming toward him from the sun-baked street. He should have been surprised, but like each meeting he had had with her, rare as they had been, to see her seemed as natural as breathing.

He thought of the last time, her hand as light as a leaf on his arm, the night enclosing them. He wondered what her mood would be after the overheated emotions of the court. But he had made the right decision. Not to seek her, but to wait. She was not a woman to be cornered.

He lifted his hat. "Good afternoon."

"Why, Mr. Fitch. How you surprise one."

Had she seen him? Had she come into the enclave deliberately? There was no way to know, not in her impersonal little smile, her careful manner.

"Would it surprise you to know I've been waiting for you?"

"Not exactly. Although everything you do seems to be surprising."

He grinned.

"I'd like to say I followed you down here. But that wouldn't be quite the truth."

"How disappointing."

So that was to be the tone? Proper, well-bred, slightly mischievous, playing the coquette? He would deal with it, his way.

"Oh, come now. I was in the courtroom. Didn't you see me? I certainly saw you. I might say you were quite splendid. Portia bearding the law."

She did not answer. He flipped out a handkerchief and brushed at the bench.

"Pretty dusty, but the shade is the best around." He bowed.

"Why thank you, Mr. Fitch." She sat down.

"Ned. Easier to remember."

"Yes, isn't it?"

He sat beside her, not close, but closer than need be. He did not yet believe her presence. Nor was he sure how to keep her there. He stretched an arm along the back of the bench. He thought of closing it around her shoulder, brushing away the escaped lock of hair from her cheek, a reminder of their lingering night stroll. But this was the all-revealing light of early afternoon. And her eyes were again far away.

He withdrew his arm. "Sycamore shade, the very best. So is the wood. Hard enough for cricket bats, milk buckets, and peg legs. Brought to England from the continent for the express purpose of shading the royal corpulence of Henry Eight."

"How fascinating."

She seemed to be relaxing. He would like to understand this new mood. He would like to hear her giggle.

"Isn't it? When you know me better, which I assure you, you will, you'll find I'm a walking wastebasket of misinformation. Comes from working for a professor who owns too many books. Your friend, Dr. Lendler. Or hadn't you heard? I should warn you, we're neighbors now."

Neighbors! Every day, anyday, she might meet him in the little park across from her home. Every day, anyday she would be made aware of him. Was she disciplined enough for that? She should get up and leave now, make it plain . . . make what plain? That this moment beside him, this little green leafy place held a sweetness she could not bear to lose?

He was watching her closely, his banter continuing.

"The good professor employs me to put too many books on too few shelves. Takes muscle for that. I open one of 'em sometimes. Would you like to know about the meerkat?"

"The what?"

"A ten-inch little chap who stands on his hind feet and wigwags his paws." Ned's forefingers waggled. "Like smoke signals from your Indian laddies."

A giggle escaped her, then, quite without reason, rippled into laughter. His deeper laugh joined hers. Those who think that tears bind, that sighs draw lovers closer, that melancholy is the true route to passion have read too much, lived too little. Laughter is the secret gift of Eros, that insidious spark of lightning that leaps from mind to mind, nerve ending to nerve ending, until, as suddenly, the gale past, the air now cleared and shimmering reveals an unsuspected landscape.

In the new silence, Noel's gloved finger traced the outline of a leaf shadow on the bench between them.

"Why did you come to the trial today?"

His answer was sober.

"If you really want to know, I have friends who depend on Dr. Jenny Crater for medical care and want her back. They'll be very grateful to you."

"I'm not sure I did much for her."

"You did more than anyone else."

But Jenny Crater was part of what she had briefly and irrationally put aside, part of the painful reality she must face tomorrow. And the next day. He spoke of friends. She wondered who they were. It had not occurred to her that this man who had stepped out of nowhere, who had interrupted her life, disturbed the careful pattern of her days, her thoughts, and who now sat beside her in almost unbearable nearness, might have a world of his own. Places unknown to her, friends, another girl? But that thought rang hollow. In the complex emotions of this day, she was experiencing a singular sensation. A simple peace at being here beside him on this dusty bench, as if after a long darkness she had come home.

They fell silent again, and the silence lengthened. The summer's softness, the muffling city itself, the luminous play of leaf and shadow of the ancient tree, spun an invisible web. Again and again, he glanced at her. Once or twice he met her eyes. Still nothing was said, nothing to break the spell. In the privacy of these moments, nearness was enough.

It was Noel who finally spoke.

"I should be starting back."

Ned's hand covered hers and tightened as he drew her to her feet.

"Where shall we go?"

22

The light of the June afternoon gilded the street, more intensely than Noel had ever remembered. They walked, as young lovers have since time began, hand in hand, unseeing, as if there were no hurrying passersby, no store windows reflecting them, no rattling wheels beside them. At the cross street, Ned took her arm, in close protection, as if he had always done so.

"There's a livery stable a block from here. They have a trap for hire with an honest little cob. We could drive up along the river."

At this hour of a summer day every carriage in New York would be out on the river drive. Perhaps Adrienne with her fashionable friends, although Adrienne took care to shield herself from the summer's sun. Noel, to her surprise, discovered that it didn't matter. Nothing mattered but these golden hours that lay immediately ahead.

"Well?"

"Lovely!"

A heavy man sat tilted in a chair against the wooden walls of the livery stable, a broken straw hat tipped over his eyes, a battered spittoon within range.

"A trap you want, is it, young sir?" He eyed Noel. "Ladies waiting over there." His thumb indicated three worn wicker chairs lined up the far side of the stable. Noel went meekly to one of the chairs and sat down. She found it inexplicably pleasant, part of the inexplicable spell of the hour, to be told what to do.

"A trap, you said, sir? I have a little beauty, yellow, new painted, red wheels. But if you don't mind my saying, young sir, I wouldn't take a young lady out in a two-wheeler on these streets. Too crowded. Where did you have a mind goin'?"

Ned was suddenly aware of how little he knew of the city's roads and carriage drives.

"Up along the river."

The man nodded knowingly. "Nice day for it. Up to Jones Wood maybe. The Dutchman's Inn. A little refreshment for you and the young lady." He spat with precision. And winked.

Ned restrained a fist, partly because he knew of no other livery stable nearby.

"I'll take the trap."

The man shrugged. "As you say, sir, but if you'll hear my advice you'll take a four-wheeler. I've got a little green buggy out there, almost new, safe as a wagon. And a fine little cob, part Morgan." He continued to talk as he led Ned through the partial darkness of the stalls. "Not that one, sir. She's Galway and fresh off the track. Needs some breaking."

Ned put out a hand and heard a whinny as the bay mare touched her soft nose to it. Big boned, deep chested, her legs black silk, her eyes large and dewy. Thoroughbred all the way. God, that was a mare for him. He wondered if Noel could drive.

In the end he sensibly took the green buggy and the cob. Nearly white as the half moon showing in his left eye.

"Nothing to that." The stable owner passed a hand close to the eye and the horse tossed his head.

"Sees as good as you do, sir, Little Caesar does. Best you could find for that buggy."

Ned paid five dollars in advance, ten more on deposit to be held against delay or accident. It was a rate of expenditure he was not accustomed to but everything about this unfolding day was rare.

"Take the East River Road north to Yorkville, pass Gracie's orchard, and turn left on Mill Rock Road. You'll be in the Wood. Take the right fork to the Dutchman's place. Tell 'im I sent you."

Ned was glad to escape. The air of the place was rank.

The sparkling day, the river breeze, billows of clouds, and the river alive with white sail brought a glow to Noel's face that took Ned's mind off his route and his driving. But the little cob was trustworthy. He kept a steady trot through the stream of carriages, past the great estates whose lawns and gardens went down to the river, the solid houses of brick or fieldstone, pillared or gabled, that were New York's country playgrounds for those wealthy enough to have two city homes.

Ned slowed the horse to a walk. They had left traffic, and

passing the little farm village of Yorkville had turned into the dirt road that led into thick, arching woods, filtering a golden green summer light.

"Oh, lovely, lovely!"

Noel's face wore the raptured delight of a child. He could have thrown all sensible restraint to the June breeze. And lost everything, he told himself.

"Like to drive?"

"Oh, yes!"

Caution, he told himself. "Can you drive?"

"Of course. We had a pony cart at the shore when I was little. My brothers were never fair about it, though." She had already slipped her gloved hands onto the reins. "What's his name?"

"Little Caesar."

"Dear Little Caesar. Come on!" She slapped the reins smartly. Whether it was the lightness of her hands or the warmth of her voice, the little cob broke into a canter.

"Whoa there! Take it easy!"

"He loves it. So do I!"

Ned reached for the reins, caught her hands, and brought Little Caesar to a standstill.

"Miss Tremont. I am responsible for this buggy, this horse, and you. If it's a runaway you want, we'll go back to the livery stable and I'll find you the mare who'll give it to you. Meanwhile . . ."

But his hands, covering hers, tightened. They were alone on the dirt road. He spoke her name. She whispered his.

"Noel. . . ."

"Ned. . . ."

His lips touched hers. He had only now to take her in his arms, to kiss her deeply, possessively, as he had so often imagined, to let their bodies say what their minds knew, to feel her yield, as her eyes promised.

But fate can use small chips to stem strong currents. Little Caesar's ear went up, he moved his feet restlessly. Ned heard it, too, approaching hoofs and the light whisper of high singing wheels.

They were sitting stiffly apart when a flashy blue sulky came up beside them. They saw a young man in a straw boater, a striped driving coat, and a diamond stickpin in his neckpiece. He had a full dark mustache and his eyes were appreciatively on Noel.

"Nice day." The stranger lifted his hat.

Ned took the reins firmly in both hands.

"Yes," he answered shortly.

"Like a race?"

"No, I wouldn't."

"Oh . . . yes!" He heard Noel breathe beside him.

The stranger might have heard her, too. At least it was what Ned speculated later. "Just to the fork?"

Little Caesar stirred. Ned quieted him. "I said no. Not with a lady beside me."

"Too bad." The young man grinned openly at Noel and moved his sulky off. As he passed, he leaned from his seat and with his long whip gave Little Caesar a cutting lash across the quarters. The startled cob snorted, half reared, found his feet, and broke into a gallop.

"Hold tight!" Ned shouted to Noel. He tugged on the reins. But somewhere in Little Caesar's tough little body flowed the blood of conquest. The bit in his mouth meant nothing. Ears laid back, he was deaf to command. And the sulky was ahead. Ned found himself sawing helplessly on the reins.

He snatched a glance at Noel. One hand clung to the seat railing, the other clutched her hat.

"Never mind your hat! Hang on with both hands! I'll stop him!"

"Oh, don't," he thought he heard. A second glance told him the worst. She was leaning forward, her eyes sparkling, her cheeks flushed with excitement, her lips moving, not quite soundlessly.

"Go on, Little Caesar! Go!"

The little cob, one ear flicked back, heard her.

Was she out of her mind? The buggy was careening, the sulky was beside them now, wheel to wheel, the young man whipping his horse, laughing. The fork lay ahead. With a prayer, Ned with one arm caught her to him. The sulky veered left. Little Caesar veered right and came to a shuddering halt.

"We won!" Her hat was gone, her hair windblown and tumbling, her glove torn and her face alight. "We won, Ned! Good Little Caesar!"

Ned hung the reins over the dashboard. The spent little horse would not worry at them now. Silently Ned held out an aloof hand to Noel as she stepped down. The quiet was immense.

"It was my fault, Ned. I so love a race!"

"You might have broken your neck. To say nothing of mine. And the decent little cob's."

He was impersonally inspecting a wheel of the buggy. When he looked at her again, his face was hard.

"Do you always take offers from passing strangers?"

She flushed. That stung, deeper than he could know. Or find out, she told herself grimly. The bubble had burst, the day was over. She could not have imagined such a change in one man. But then it had to end sometime. She knew how to retire to a shell.

"I've lost my hat."

"It blew off fifty feet back, just beyond an outcropping of rock. I'll get it when I've walked this horse to the inn and found a stall for him."

"What inn?"

"Beyond that sign."

She stared back down the road.

"Where are you going?"

"To find my hat. You take care of Little Caesar. He needs you." And I don't, she added to herself. At least not until I turn around and see you again. She turned around and saw Ned leading Little Caesar toward the inn. To her horror, the cob was limping.

She was to blame. Yet was she, really? Little Caesar had been running in a headlong gallop. Nothing Ned did with the reins stopped him. Her half-breathed encouragements could not have goaded or slowed him. Ned must know that. Yet he had turned from—from all that he had been into a stranger. It would come to Noel later that an impassioned lover was a jealous man. But now as she walked, the very air around her was dead.

Her hat, small as it was, hung caught on a wild blackberry bush, the crown torn, beyond repair.

She slowly walked back. The day's light had passed its zenith. Through the trees she saw the dark outlines of a building, as somber as her own thoughts. She would rather wait here in whatever patch of brightness that was left. He would see her when he had attended to the cob. She had no wish to hasten the moment. There was still the long drive back beside him. A man like that—who could change so swiftly. . . . Not only had she let him kiss her, she had wanted it, almost asked for it.

"Do you prefer to stand in the middle of the road like a gypsy or come in and have some tea? The place isn't much, but it will do."

He had not forgiven her.

"How is Little Caesar?"

"Lost a shoe, then picked up a stone. Same hoof. I won't drive him back tonight."

"What will you do?"

"There's a coach stop a quarter mile from here where they change horses. The innkeeper sent for one of the blacksmiths. It'll take time. The city omnibus comes through on the half hour. I'll put you on it." He glanced sideways at her. She was looking straight ahead. "That is, if you can manage alone."

"I can manage, thank you."

Ahead a path curved from the road into the woods.

"Shortcut," he said.

They turned into it. A hint of twilight dusted the air. A bird called the day's ending. They walked, steps, hands, eyes apart. But nature does not easily surrender to artifice and gradually, their steps slowed.

Ned stopped and faced her.

"I'm sorry," he said. "I shouldn't have said what I did."

"I earned it."

"Perhaps."

She saw that this was as close as he would come to an apology. His pride, too, nearly matched her own.

Through the woods, a single light faintly flickered.

"That's the inn ahead."

"I'd like to tidy my hair. That's all. And put on my hat. It's a bit battered, but it will see me home."

"Noel!" It was a cry as elemental as the woods surrounding them, and all the whispering, scurrying life within it that knew the cycles of time, of sunrise, moonset, spring, summer, knew rising need in that cry, the wonder of fulfillment.

She had heard. She was in his arms, his kisses on her face, her throat, against the silk of her dress, rapturous, fiery, savage in their need to possess.

"Oh . . . Ned! Let me go!" But she was slack and soft against him.

"Never!" His arms tightened. Where could they go? Not the inn with its faces to leer knowingly. Not into the woods he did not know, with summer strollers still idling. He thought of those dingy hotels on the city side streets, "Overnight" rooms. "No luggage required." Where in hell could a man with no money, with nothing over his head but a lodging house, take this rare and lovely woman, this woman who had for a wild moment turned to fire in his arms. The answer came swift and bitter. Nowhere. The gulf between them lay slashed wide by the black truth. He had nothing. She was a woman bred to delicacy, to all that was decent. He was risking everything.

She had stepped back, breathless, staring at him with eyes large, overbright, eyes he could not read.

"I want you, Noel. I'll let no other man on earth touch you. Oh, my darling!"

Because she did not answer, he took her in his arms again, felt her tremble and bent his head to her. Their kiss, long, lingering, with the sweetness that follows passion, might have been the last to be exchanged by lovers anywhere on earth.

"I'll never let you go, Noel."

The Dutchman's Inn had seen palmier days. A half century ago the old Dutch colonial building of faded red clapboard had been a stop-over for the New York–Boston stagecoach. But the city, voracious and unstoppable, was sweeping north. Rumor had it that Jones Wood itself was soon to be lost, its great beech trees and oaks, chestnuts and elms, sacrificed to city plans for a greater Central Park.

But for the time being, the Dutchman's place could still turn a dollar. He had divided the old house in two, a saloon on one side, and what a paint-flecked sign announced as FAMILY EATS on the other. Along the wall, posters announced local entertainment—"Prize Fights to 26 Rounds, Bare-fisted. Bets on Each Round." "Mermaid Frolics, Girls in Fishtails Until Midnight." And, incredibly, "Bullfighting, Harlem Village." Anyone in the know could tell you that Farmer Kane's Holstein bull had better be returned in sound shape. So the horns were balled, and rosettes instead of banderillas were stuck to its sides. The farmhand toreadors with blunted blades knew that an enraged bull could thrill the crowd, so what they lacked in grace they made up with speed and a fast leg over the high-board fence.

The lone waitress in "Family Eats" peered through the window to watch the couple approach. Lovers, she told herself. You could always tell. Yet they were not like most seen around here. Elopin' maybe. Or maybe he's married and leading her down the primrose path. Or maybe she's married and leadin' him all innocent into temptation. Or maybe—the penny novels failed her. But not before she noted that they were young, the lady fine dressed . . . the gentleman? He could put his boots under her bed any time he liked.

She straightened her apron, pushed her sleeves up to her reddened elbows, and touched the piled friz of hennaed hair.

"That table's set if you'd like it, sir."

It was a wood triangle wedged into a dim corner. The white-globed gas fixture in the center of the ceiling was unlit.

"We don't light up until nearer dark. But if you'd like, sir—miss—ma'am . . ." She snatched from the next table a thick white saucer into which a candle had been stuck, and lighted it. A golden glow encased them. More romantic, that. The glow revealed the young lady's eyes. They were sad. Don't wonder, the waitress decided, if it was her elopin' she'd want some place fancier than the Dutchman's.

"What'll it be, folks?"

"Tea, Noel?"

"Yes, please."

"Cake plain or plum, sir?"

Ned was aware of the waitress's fixed eyes. "Plain," he said shortly.

They were sitting in silence when the waitress returned. She set down the tray noisily, her glance traveling from one to the other. Slowly she put out cups, saucers, teapot, and a plate of two fat slices of what looked to be purple cake.

"Out of plain. Oh, I've forgot the hot water!"

"It won't be necessary."

It was a dismissal, but the waitress loitered. They didn't talk much, this pair. Herself, she'd like a bit of gaiety, some dancin', heel and toe. It didn't bode good for a young couple to have nothing to say to each other so soon.

She gave an audible sigh. "Anything else, sir?"

"No, thank you."

Reluctantly she left them alone.

Ned closed his hand over Noel's. "That took a bit of doing."

Noel seemed to come back from a long way. "She meant well."

"That's the trouble, isn't it? Everybody means well. And everybody gets in the way. but that's over now for us. Noel, I'm going to say one thing I've never said to any woman before."

To his surprise, she shook her head. "Not yet. Not right away. Let's just sit here a little while."

"Haven't I the right to tell you I love you? And to believe you love me?"

The candle's flame had become a ring of light sheltering them from an outer world. Noel let seconds, heartbeats, pass before her answer. "And if I do . . ."

In another woman, Ned might have suspected coyness. But in Noel, it was again that elusive quality, as if at the very moment of discovering her, she had gone. He was left an image, a wisp of spirit, not in the mockery of flirtation, but in the enigma of a mystery he could not fathom. Yet he wanted this woman with all his being, wherever she would lead him, at whatever cost. Those moments on the wooded path had told him what he wanted.

"Tell me about yourself, Ned."

She was sipping her tea, her voice as matter-of-fact as if he had just walked into the Mission house. Was she measuring him? He looked at the play of light on her face, the lovely line of her throat, the curve of her breast that had lifted against him. He, too, could be matter-of-fact.

"The first thing you should know about me is that I am a jealous man. What's mine is mine, not to be had or touched by anyone else. I was ready to punch that fellow on the sulky for the way he looked at you."

She half smiled but then her face turned from him for a moment. When she looked at him again, it was serious.

"Ned, I haven't thought to ask! What about our little horse?"

The change piqued him. "Little Caesar? He'll be glad, no doubt, you thought of him. A fine honest character. With a horse, a man knows where he stands."

What a firebrand he was, so easily touched to the quick, changeable, lashing out. Too much like herself, Noel thought. Like unto like—disaster. But a man was luckier. He could indulge his moods. She had long learned to govern her own. Now he was looking at her with a tenderness that could have made her weep—had she been a woman who wept.

"Noel, would you like to go home now?"

"I—I haven't finished my tea. What else—about yourself?"

He grinned. "How many of my faults do you insist on knowing?"

"All of them."

He lifted an eyebrow. "*All* of them?"

The tea had restored her. His hand held hers. She cared little for his words, only his presence. The ring of light had been made whole.

"For a start, I was called Julien Edmond Abbingdon-Fitch. My mother's folly. At school I knocked a boy down for calling me Julien."

"I like Julien."

"I don't. To continue. I was born in Avebury, Wiltshire, where they raise nice pigs. My father was a pig farmer. My mother thought I was meant for better things. Like being a gentleman and having a carriage. She was full of such notions. It was my grandfather who set me straight. He had been a schoolteacher and used to say that the only way a man could get ahead was to use his muscles and his mind. I was to work hard, learn a lot, and go to America. Here I am."

He would go on forever if she would keep those luminous eyes on him. He wondered if she were truly interested.

"Don't skip! Tell me about your grandfather."

"He was a great man in his way. He sat mostly in the corner of the fireplace. They said he was daft, but I never thought so. Maybe being young is the same thing as being a little daft when you're old. I thought he was the wisest man I ever knew. He made me believe the world was made up of heroes and giants and that I'd have to fight all the way to become one. Oh, I had my fights, but when I grew up I found that everybody was pretty much the same size I was."

He liked to hear her laugh.

"My grandfather had one passion. The Hanging Stones. They're a circle of huge upright slabs of rock called Stonehenge. My grandfather would take me out to see them. And I'll tell you how daft he was. He believed the Stones could predict the Great Comet, Halley's, that comes every seventy-five years. Well, now they've discovered two circles of holes around the Stones. One has thirty-seven holes, the other thirty-eight. Seventy-five in all. Wouldn't that have pleased him . . . to know his theory was correct."

"Marvelous!"

"Noel! My God, how I love you!" But he said it to himself. Had he talked too much? She made no move to leave. For him time had lost its meaning.

For her, his images had become her own. The haunting Stones at night. The farmland, the flowering springtime, the country lane where she might have met him, a country girl in a summering world. How *right* it would have been.

"Why did you leave the farm, Ned?"

"That's another story."

"Oh."

He didn't like the small sound, as if she had been shut out, as if there were something secret, furtive. There must be nothing like that, nothing but the truth between them. The truth was not for a girl's ears, it could shock her, but she had asked.

"I'll tell you. I'll tell you anything you want to know. That's the way it must be between us. Driving me away was the only thing my father could do, by his lights. My mother was a bit foolish about me. Making me better clothes to wear, teaching me to talk better than others. There was talk in the village. My father took the notion that I—wasn't his son."

Noel looked at him so oddly he decided she had not understood.

"To put a point on it, my father got the idea I was illegitimate. A bastard. My mother, as they said in the country, had gone over the stile."

"Was it true, Ned?"

"No. My mother was a good woman. Foolish, maybe. But a decent, honorable woman. My father was hard on her."

Her silence puzzled him. Then she spoke.

"Ned . . . if it had been true. If your mother had . . . done that, how would you have felt about her?"

"Are you serious?"

"Yes."

Something had gone wrong, taken a false turn. He blamed himself. Love, as his grandfather had once told him, can twist a man's wits. No woman should be told everything. Yet she had asked. Now she sat as if looking through the walls at something past them both.

"That, my girl, is a silly question. But I'll tell you something for your own good. While you were growing up in your neat little dresses, and your neat little house, and your neat little park, the world was going on, as it always does. There are good people and bad people. There are good women. And bad women. Not that there's so much difference when you come right to it." He reached for her hand. She had dropped it in her lap. "Noel, a man needs a woman he can put on a pedestal. When he's a boy, it's his mother. When he's a man, it's the girl he wants to marry. That's the way men are.

"That's where I've put you, Noel. On a pedestal. Don't stop me, because I'm going to say it. I love you, Noel. I haven't a cent in the world. I make twelve dollars a week. I want to marry you. But I can't ask you yet. I can only ask you to"—he gave a boyish grin—"stay on that pedestal. Wait, for me. Someday I'm going to be able to do it all properly. Have things the way they should be. Your father's a rich man. But I don't want it that way. I want it my way. I want you. And I'll work to win you. All I ask is that you give me time. Time, Noel—and I can do anything."

She heard the rich timbre of his voice. And the words, marriage, a future together, a life beside him, day after day, year after distant year, until death shall—*no,* shall *not* part.

But even as he had talked, a transparent little figure had

slipped invisibly to her side. Posie, her child, flesh of her flesh, Posie, just outside the ring of light.

"Noel." Ned's face was shadowed. "You gave me your answer out there in the wood. That is enough. When I have the right, I'll ask you properly. On my knee if you like." He reached for her hands. "My darling girl. Mine forever." As if no longer comfortable with solemnity, he grinned. "Unless you fancy another slice of purple cake, which I don't advise, we'd better start home. We have something of a trip."

He looked at her closely. "I've tired you, Noel."

She shook her head. The small ghost beside her was growing more vivid. This man, with his power to attract, was becoming almost a stranger. Had she really spent this glowing day with him, had she wanted to yield? Or had she moved through a dream? She could almost feel the touch of Posie's small fingers in hers.

On the long journey home she made no effort to talk. There was nothing to talk about. Marriage, he had said. Wait for me. But she had no way to wait. No pedestal on which to stand.

At long last the omnibus reached the city. He found a cab for them. Finally the iron picketing of Stuyvesant Square came into view. The cab was stopping.

"How soon can I see you, my darling? I'll call on your father properly. Anything you want."

"I—I don't think that would be possible, Ned."

"Why not?"

"I—I don't think I can see you. We're going away for the summer. To the shore," she finished limply.

"When?"

"Maybe this week."

"I'll see you before you go. Tomorrow evening?"

"I can't, Ned. I'm sorry."

He swung around on the cab seat, to face her. "Sorry? Sorry for what? What are you talking about?"

"I'm sorry, Ned." She was looking straight ahead, her face tight as her words. "I can't see you again."

"Now wait a minute. We need to straighten things out. What's happened, Noel? What's changed you? I thought today . . . I thought you and I . . . my God, girl, I love you. You gave me to think—what are you up to?"

She could find no ready answer. Her silence stung him. The black anger that lived always just below the surface with him surged into his voice.

"What are you trying to tell me? That you've been playing

the flirt with me? That your fancy upbringing has taught you how to tease a man, lead him on . . . ?''

''No!''

''. . . or don't you know what you're doing? Haven't you ever met a flesh-and-blood man before? In that case I'll teach you. And I won't be so mind-my-manners next time. Oh there'll be a next time. I'm not the man to be brushed off like last night's party trimmings!''

He swung her around by the shoulders.

''Ned . . . no, please!''

The cab had stopped.

His arms dropped. ''All right, Miss Tremont, if that's the way you want it. But before you go, I want the truth! Was this your day out for a bit of larking?''

''No! No!'' Her anger had risen to meet his. ''This day meant everything to me that it meant to you. I'll never forget it!''

''But it's over, is that it? There's someone else—''

''No!'' It was almost a cry.

If he heard her, Ned was past believing. ''Someone more suitable to Stuyvesant Square, to the Tremonts? In that case''—he would give her no time to answer—''in that case, give him my congratulations. Tell him he's got himself one hell of a woman!''

''That's despicable!''

''What did you expect?''

He was out of the cab, holding the door open. She flew past him, running up the steps, aware in the pounding of her heart that there had been more passion in the fury of their quarrel than in the kisses they had shared.

Without looking back she heard the cab depart. She stepped into the unwelcome security of her home.

From the drawing room, Adrienne emerged in a cloud of evening tulle.

''Where in the world have you been? It's nearly eight. Noel! You look dreadful! Your hat!''

Noel caught her breath. Nothing brought the walls of her world closer than that cool voice.

''Your father is at his club. Kitty is expecting us both to dinner to meet some very important friends from Chicago. You couldn't possibly be ready.''

''No.''

Adrienne glided toward her, eyes lidded, mouth thinned. Snake-like, Noel thought. But Adrienne was Adrienne. ''I happened to be at the drawing room window when you arrived in a cab. I saw the man with you when he stepped out. He didn't have the manners apparently to help you. I think it is my duty—"

"It is not your duty, Adrienne."

"How dare you!"

"I am a grown woman. I do not need to be supervised. You and my father have a happy marriage. I don't think my activities should concern you in any way."

"Who was the man?"

The day had dissipated, its treacherous passions blown to smoke. Wearily Noel picked up the thread of falsehood that stitched her days.

"One of the students in my philosophy class at Cooper Union. He was on his way to Grand Central Station."

"I know better."

"What do you know?"

"I've seen him. He's the man—the Englishman—who came calling at the house when you were away. Shabby clothes, unpardonable manners. Bringing you flowers—violets—as if he had the right to when no one in this house had ever seen him before. A fortune hunter if I ever saw one. Oh, I didn't tell your father. I didn't want to upset him. I couldn't believe you'd ever been willing to see such a man. What is he after?"

"That's enough!"

"Oh, no it isn't! He'll be back. That kind never gives up. Not where there's money. What do you think your father would say to such a marriage? Believe me, Noel, weak as your father is about you, he would never consent to it. Never! Nor would I!"

Both heard the sounds of a carriage stopping. In another moment the doorbell would ring.

Adrienne smoothed her face. "That must be Senator Walsh. He was to escort us both to Kitty's tonight. I'll make your apologies." She composed herself, and her evening. "I think we understand each other, Noel."

"Except for one thing. Why was I not told about my caller and his violets?"

"I thought there was no need for you to know."

Noel heard a man's voice in the vestibule. She looked directly into her stepmother's eyes, which were now wide and sweet.

"You may assure my father that he has nothing to worry about in this house . . . from me."

23

The music hall was stifling. Piano, trombone, and drums rose to an ear-shattering climax. In the flare of the candle footlights the not-so-young soubrette in black tights and spangles came downstage and blew kisses. The line of girls, in pink tights and fixed smiles, kicked their fleshy legs once more, turned, bent double, and with the black bustle bows on their ample hips waved naughtily. The crowd cheered, the curtains swung together. The "Luscious, Triumphant Concert" at the Broadway Gardens was over for the night.

"Next time, Neddie boyo, we'll sit down with the swells in the front row. Get a real look at the daisy legs, eh?"

Ned felt the jab of his companion's elbow but he did not answer. From the balcony that rimmed the hall he looked out across the crowd. Clerks, storekeepers, road drummers out on a lark, salesgirls, milliners' helpers, office stenographers furtively escaping drabness. But many more were the rouged young women with high breasts and feather boas a man might pass any evening along Twenty-second Street and Seventh Avenue. They were a lively lot, shrill laughter mingling with coarser male voices and the smell of beer, the air thickened by the crush of human bodies on this August night.

Mrs. Luskin, their mutual landlady, had brought Ned and Ernie together when she moved Ned in his new affluence to the second-floor best bedroom. Ernie had arrived to occupy the attic.

"He's English like yourself, Neddie. And he's honest enough. Told me right off he'd been picked up poaching on the Duke's land and packed off by the parish vicar to America with only five pounds to his name. If you ask me, old England is emptying itself of everybody but the gentry and the royals. And the Queen, enjoying her widowhood more than most of us, I dare say. There was talk of a law, once, stopping the English from dumping their paupers and thieves here, but nothing much came of it. If you ask me, too many Americans would like to be dukes themselves. Well, I don't ask questions. I'll take a boarder who gets honest work and pays his rent."

It had been one of Mrs. Luskin's not-too-subtle reminders of Ned's own debt. Yet when he had offered a part payment, she had taken his hands in her own two, pressed them to her bosom and looked into Ned's eyes.

"I don't want you to worry yourself about that, Neddie. Twenty-six dollars isn't going to send me to the poorhouse. And now that you have such an elegant position with Dr. Hugo Lendler, you have to fit yourself for the part. Put your money in good clothes and don't think about me. Stuyvesant Square will be the making of you. Besides, a young man should have a little pleasure now and then." It was advice Ned was willing to take.

Ernie Beech had turned out to be affable, enterprising, slippery as an eel, and, in no time at all, on resourceful terms with the city's temptations. In short, Ned found an outlet for his restlessness, his inner misery during the dragging summer. If in Mrs. Luskin's calculating eye, Stuyvesant Square offered visions of splendor, to Ned it had turned to ashes, as stifling as the upstairs study in which he still worked over Dr. Lendler's dull books.

He had not had even a glimpse of Noel since that one golden day. He had not expected to, or wanted to, at first. She had said she was going away. It would give her time, he hoped, to think, to remember. It would give his angry pride time to cool. But as the empty weeks passed, he found himself looking for her. In the long twilights, on his way home through the Square, he would imagine her coming through the trees toward him, her face brightening, their quick awareness of each other, their reunion.

As the empty weeks passed, he found his longing deepening to resentment at the hold she had taken on him. He had always professed scorn, even contempt, for a man who let himself be lost to love or ensnared by passion. One girl was much like another, he told himself. Flirt a bit. If she were willing, as she often was, go further. But no entanglements. Nothing lost, nothing given. Even Millie, who had offered him all that she knew of warmth, loyalty, trust, had never possessed him. Now he was obsessed.

Once, driven by a need to see her, he had walked boldly up the steps of number 269. On the second ring, the door had opened halfway, a thin, straight-mouthed woman in a plain dress, hair drawn stiffly back, had eyed him narrowly.

"The Tremont family is away."

"Could you tell me when—"

"I am Mrs. Tremont's housekeeper. I do not give information."

He had wished for the blushing little Irish maid who had welcomed him on his one previous call. She would have told him what he wanted to know.

Then there was Dr. Lendler, his employer, with his curious habit of coming in on Ned, without warning, and scrutinizing the papers and books piled on the study desk.

"Excellent, young man. Excellent. You have a sense of order that I envy. I shall now find Tacitus where he belongs beside Socrates, two volumes from Seneca, and six from Marcus Aurelius. I advise you to dip into the old emperor someday. Aurelius had a perspective on life that would enrich any man. A time for work, a time for pleasure and no waste on self-pity or self-indulgence. Use the books whenever you want, Ned."

All complimentary, all impersonal, and to Ned, irritatingly irrelevant. He saw no promise in the work except for the unescapable fact of good pay. At times the close study, with its black couch and mustard walls, was opportunity, at others, imprisonment. Occasionally during work hours, Dr. Lendler would summon him down to the parlor. There, with the afternoon sun glancing off the brass pendulum of the mantel clock he would sit listening while Dr. Lendler talked. Too often Ned found his attention wandering, his mind drowsing as the little sun-struck pendulum swung back and forth. But the interludes had their use. He could think, uninterruptedly, of Noel. In the deeper layers of his mind, his senses remained resistant, alert only to her image.

The parlor visits regularly ended when Frau Gruen entered, with a tray of coffee, sliced sponge cake, and a bowl of whipped cream.

"*Schlagober,*" Dr. Lendler would say with a smile, delicately removing the white stickiness from his beard. "Whipped cream. The soul of the Viennese coffee hour. So you learn about the world, Ned."

The scene had become monotonous. It fed his restlessness as it thwarted his ambitions.

One day, in his loneliness, he took a rash step. He walked up to the heavy oak door of number 15, the home of Miss Phoebe Bliss. Almost immediately his ring was answered. A slight, dark-skinned man in immaculate white coat and pressed black trousers bowed. The left side of the man's face was deeply puckered. When he smiled the ridges fanned to his temple, closing one eye. The other was warmly alert and intelligent.

"May I ask who is calling on Miss Bliss?" the man's voice was softly cultivated.

Ned made a quick decision and opted for the hyphen.

"Edmond Abbingdon-Fitch."

"Won't you step in, Mr. Abbingdon-Fitch? Miss Bliss is on holiday but she would appreciate your signing her callers books."

Ned followed the man through a wide, dim hall into a twilight drawing room and saw at a glance the summer custom of Stuyvesant Square. A clutter of assorted furniture stood shrouded in pale dustcloths. The carpet lay in a heavy roll at the edge of the bared floor. The windows, freed of the weight of draperies, lost identity behind drawn blinds. The room had the mustiness of a tomb.

The only unswathed object was a small, fluted fern table near the entrance. But it bore no living plant, only a white leather-bound book, embossed with golden violets and the word "Callers." The houseman, or custodian, Ned was unsure, held out an ostrich-quilled pen.

"Miss Bliss takes great pleasure in knowing what friends call in her absence."

Ned discovered he was to sign the first line of the first page of that hopeful but virginal little book.

In the hall he took time to note the faded portraits in heavy gold frames lining the walls, nudging each other through the decades. He noted the embellished carvings of the oak lintels, the fine etched glass of the inner door. Not a cheerful house, but it bore the stolid dignity, the unassailable confidence of old money and even older self-assurance. A house of a quality and kind Ned had never before entered. The dark-skinned man bowed.

"My name is Christopher, sir. If you should require any further courtesy of the house, it will be my pleasure to offer it. Good day, Mr. Abbingdon-Fitch."

That night, eating his mashed turnips and charred pork ribs in the cramped shoddiness of Mrs. Luskin's, Ned contemplated his prospects. Not much better off than in old London, if the truth were told. Maybe the promises were richer here, but denials came just as quickly. London had its distances, rich and poor, its East and West ends, its Mayfair and

South Bank. A man had someplace to belong. Here a man could walk from the filthiest tenements to lace curtains just by crossing a street—if he could pick up a fortune on the way. But to Ned that envisioned fortune had lost its luster, unless Noel were beside him. Yet it was not his uncertain future that had turned Noel from him. He could not even convince himself that it was his background, a pig farmer's son. It was something else, something he had not begun to fathom. The mystery of Noel Tremont had returned.

So on this lonely August night at Mrs. Luskin's supper table, he had listened to Eddie Beech.

"What do you say to a bit of 'igh life, Ned boyo? I got two passes to the Broadway Gardens. Won 'em I did, wrestlin' at the Greek's. They figured a little guy for a loser. They'll know better next time!"

The Broadway Gardens was a low-class music hall on West Broadway. Ned would have liked better Niblo's Gardens, that vast theatre crowded every night with New York's most buoyant audiences to see the most "Stupendous Extravaganza" the city had ever known. *The Black Crook* had been first produced twelve years ago, but it had returned to satisfy New York's insatiable appetite for gorgeous costumes, luscious women, enormous spectacles, and a hundred and fifty pairs of the shapeliest legs in the silkiest tights in all the entertainment-loving city. The price of a ticket was as high as their kicks.

There was also a play by a new team of Irishmen, Harrigan and Hart, said to be reducing audiences to tears and laughter. Ernie was adamant. "They got more Irish in this city than a dog has fleas. Who'd *pay* to see 'em?"

And there was, most elegant of all, Tony Pastor's, where the singers came from Paris and ladies in the audience carried fans.

But it was Ernie's night, and as usual when his newfound friend had a plan, the burden of ambition slipped from Ned. He knew well that later Ernie would have another plan. It was tactily understood that for this latter part of the evening Ned would pay. He did not mind. He found it pleasant to play gentleman on the town, with a wallet no longer flat.

Now, as the last of the bouncy, thick-legged kicking and coarse humor of the Broadway Gardens was ending, Ned sat not unhappily looking across the crowd. He was watching a girl in the audience who had caught his eye earlier. She had brown hair in a straggly semblance of curls topped by a minimal hat with two green roses. She was wearing a brown dress and sitting beside a beefy young man with sandy hair and an inclination to put his arm around her. The girl sat stiffly, seeming to vacillate between animation and embarrassment. As the hall was not darkened during the entertainment Ned could watch her steadily. At the entrance of the ladies in flesh tights, her hands went to her cheeks. The soubrette's show-stopping song, with its appropriate winks, "He knew what to do and how to do it," tipped the green roses so far to her lap that she did not hear the last mocking line of "He fixed the wagon wheel and drove her home." Ned waited now to see her full face. The crowd sluggishly began to leave.

"If you're going to stand here, Ned, like a wooden Indian the birds'll have flown. I have a little oyster place in mind, with private booths. . . ."

The girl in the brown dress, pushing and being pushed through the crowd, was now about twenty feet from him. Drawn by his gaze, she turned her head, looked up. He had seen her before.

"Come on, will ya? There's a shortcut to the stage door."

"You go on, Ernie. I'm going out through the lobby."

Ernie knew better than to lose his source of cash. He followed.

On the pavement outside, where the crowd was beginning to separate, Ned caught up with the girl. The color came and went in her round dimpled face before she could manage to speak.

"Why, Mr. Abbingdon-Fitch."

"Good evening." Ned bowed. She blushed again.

"It's me, Annie-Mae. I didn't think you'd remember, sir."

"Of course I remember."

"Mr. Abbingdon-Fitch. This is Denny. . . ."

"Good evening, Denny."

The young man's broad face was redder than Ned had at first seen. Though he was short, his shoulders were thick under his green linsey-woolsey jacket, and his biceps pronounced. His eyes had the glow of beer and his nostrils quivered like a hound on scent.

"It's Denny Reilly. Mr. Dennis Reilly. Mr. Dennis Thomas O'Hoolihan Reilly, if you do it proper. Me mither and father bein' sound of mind and body and lying dacent and at peace, God rest them, in the pure and holy soil of County Mayo. And I don't take kindly to yer speakin' to me girl, forward like that."

"Denny!" In her agitation, Annie-Mae's hand flew to Ned's

sleeve. "Please don't pay him mind, Mr. Abbingdon-Fitch! He has a good heart. He carries meat for the cats and—"

"Oh, ho. So now it's the cat man I am in front of yer fancy friend. Or does this dirty blackguard of a limey think—"

"Denny, don't talk like that!"

"Who's callin' my friend here a dirty limey?"

Ernie had emerged from behind Ned, his face brightening with anticipation.

"Oh, it's the two of you, is it, you murderin' English swill of the divil's umpire, who've brought holy Ireland to her poor broken, starvin' knees. Put 'em up, both of ye, and ye'll see Mr. Dennis Thomas O'Hoolihan Reilly make crow bait of the both of ye for the disrespect to my girl and the abuse and suffering you've done to God's holy Ireland!"

"Stop, Denny! Stop! Oh, stop him, Mr. Abbingdon-Fitch!" Annie-Mae's voice rose to a wail.

Denny had lowered his head like a bull. Ernie was dancing up and down, fists clenched. The crowd around them slowed to a stop, faces shining under the gaslight with sweat and the promise of the best the night had yet to offer. Relevancy did not matter. "Let 'em kill each other!" "America for Americans!" "Down with the cross-backs!" "Git the Pope out of the country!" One shrill female voice rose to a scream, "We got rid of the King once! Go to it, Kelly!"

By this time, Annie-Mae in her terror was clinging to Ned.

"He'll hurt yer friend, Mr. Abbingdon-Fitch. Y' don't know Denny. He's the battlin' terror of the Hibernians. . . ."

"Maybe. But I'm getting you out of here. Come on!" Taking her hand, Ned pulled Annie-Mae out of the crowd, down the street crossing Broadway, between the crush of wheels and bobbing horses' heads like the veteran of the streets he had become.

"He's a madman, that friend of yours."

"Oh, no. You mustn't say that, sir. It's only his dander up when he has taken to drink. But I'm that sore afraid fer the little runty man."

"I wouldn't worry." He was looking at her intently, at the rise and fall of the little round bosom, and the shimmer of the rich brown silk that covered it, rich indeed for a servant girl.

Annie-Mae blushed.

"I'm that grateful to you, Mr. Abbingdon-Fitch. I can get home safe now."

"I'm going to make sure you do. There's an empty cab."

Annie-Mae froze on the pavement. "Oh no, sir. I couldn't. Not a cab."

"What's wrong with a cab?"

"Mrs. Jessup waits up. It's my first night off and I was given it only because things have been upset, the family still being away. If Mrs. Jessup saw me comin' home in a cab she'd know for sure I was ruint. I'd be sacked and given no character."

Ned looked down into the pretty little face. His mind went back to another mild night in the drizzle of Leicester Square and another lonely frightened girl. Millie had clung to him as this girl did, and in the end left him her wisdom. *You'll go far, Neddie, with your looks and your quick tongue, but it's our kind you'll come back to for your true happiness.*

Maybe. This little housemaid had a melting warmth about her. But tonight she was a mere footnote to all he sought. It was not the girl, it was the dress she was wearing that was significant. He had to be sure.

Annie-Mae was drawing away.

"All right, Annie-Mae. I'll walk you home, if that will please you."

"Only to the corner of the back alley."

"Only to the corner of the back alley." He grinned. "But I'm a man who gets hungry around this time of the evening. A bit of pastry, an ice? Mrs. Jessup wouldn't consider that ruination, would she?"

"Mr. Abbingdon-Fitch, I'm only second maid, just up from tweenie. I don't know all that's proper and I daren't be late. But . . ." She hesitated, her round face dimpling, her eyes suddenly alight.

Ned held out his arm. Annie-Mae took it daintily.

The dead center of his life, Ned told himself, had begun to move.

At the tiny marbleized table in the discreet rear of the ice-cream parlor, Ned leaned back. The chair was too small, the curved metal back too short, but otherwise things were going well. He found he had no need to ask more than a few priming questions.

In this brief glimpse of unexpected heaven, Annie-Mae sat drawing a teaspoon piled with pineapple ice in and out between her small teeth. Freed for the moment of her burden of fears and responding to the natural buoyancy of her nature, her prettiness bloomed.

"Sure, an' yer paying me compliments now on my dress. You're not thinking I could buy a silk dress like this for meself now are you, Mr. Abbingdon-Fitch? It was Miss Noel gave it me, comin' home one night, she was, with a piece of the hem ruffle torn clear out. I did my best, but sure I'm all thoombs yet with needle work, Mrs. Tremont says. I was that nervous I'd be sent back to parin' potatoes for Cook but Miss Noel, lovely she is too, sez nobody could mend a tear like that. She tossed it away and then said the dress was mine if I wanted it. Oh, to be sure I kept it, laid it away in tissue paper beneath me mattress"—the tip of her tongue licked at the melting yellow ice in sheer pleasure—"and I took off the bottom ruffle, for I'm shorter than Miss Noel. And I made an inset with it at the back for Miss Noel's got a slender reed of a waist. . . ."

Annie-Mae's color quickened. "Now I shouldn't be talkin' about sech things here, being ladylike. But you were kind to remark about it, and when I get home I'll put it away. I've had me night and I won't be havin' another one soon."

"Why not, Annie-Mae? Every pretty girl has a right to a little gaiety."

"It's not for me to say that bold like, Mr. Abbingdon-Fitch. You see, when Miss Noel came home from visiting her friends, up the river, she was as thin and white as a ghost. Seems her friend up there had took sick and died, Cook told me, and Miss Noel took it that hard. When Mr. Tremont saw her he said she must go down to the shore where the fresh sea air'd do wonders. He'd go with her until she felt stronger. Well, by that time, all of a sudden like, Mrs. Tremont had took off on the steamer to Europe. With all the packin' and the house so upset, everybody goin' every which ways, it was a fair wearin' down time. Then it got so quiet that one day Mrs. Jessup sez to me I might have me night off and that's how it all went and I'll never forget this evening and that I'm beholden to you!"

He looked directly at her. "How soon are they coming home?"

She misunderstood the intent of the question and blushed.

"I don't know. Mrs. Jessup says I'm to do my work reg'lar and not be bothering about what doesn't concern me. But it does. Because I'm that fond of Miss Noel. And besides, Mrs. Tremont once asked me if I thought I could learn to be a lady's maid."

"And could you?"

"It's turrible dainty work and all hours night and day, no time off if me lady wants me and my hands that awkward with all them laces and finery. Anyway"—she licked the last drop from the spoon and scooped up another melting mound, holding tight to the stemmed metal cup as if it might fly away like this mirage of happiness—"anyway I do be likin' to work second floor and parlor maid and doin' what I can for Miss Noel. Though goodness knows she never asks for much. She's a fine young lady and I do miss her and I'll be glad of the day she meets a fine young man." The red little hand went to her mouth. "Now I shouldn't be sayin' that, either, but it's talking to you, Mr. Abbingdon-Fitch, and the kind look on you." She giggled. "And the dizziness in the pineapple ice."

"Enjoy it, Annie-Mae. They'll all be home soon enough, won't they? Before the month is out?"

"Cook says maybe, then again . . . but it's glad I'll be. It's not to my likin' to be workin' in a house that's quiet as a tomb."

She scraped the ice cup clean. She folded her paper doily neatly into four parts and thrust it into the cup, then pushed it to the far edge of the table.

"I do thank you, Mr. Abbingdon-Fitch. I'll never forget this."

Ned reached for the check, bypassed it, and covered Annie-Mae's hand with his own.

"I thank you for coming with me, Annie-Mae. I won't forget the evening, either. It was company for a lonely man."

It was a mistake. Annie-Mae pulled her hand free and dropped a tight little fist into her lap. He had frightened her. Oddly, he had meant what he said.

"I'll be goin' now, sir, if you please."

Withdrawn, arms held tightly to her sides, she walked beside him out of the ice-cream parlor. He wondered if she would run from him, but he had no time to speculate. The unpredictable surge of the city suddenly swept them up.

Bells clanged, coming nearer and nearer. A horde of people came yelling, tearing, down the street past them.

The change in Annie-Mae was astonishing. Her face glowing, she ran to the edge of the running crowd. Standing on tiptoe, she cupped her hands around her mouth and to Ned's awed amazement, let out the yell of a Gaelic warrior.

"Fire! Where's the fire?"

A shout came back.

"The old brewery by the river! Burnin' like hell was in it!"

The next moment she was pushed back by the surge of onlookers. Down the avenue it raced, the red-and-gold fire engine, billowing smoke and vapor from its steamer, three galloping horses abreast, nostrils wide, manes flying, the helmeted driver laying on an unfelt whip. Clinging to the stubby water tank as to salvation itself, six helmeted firefighters shouted futilely to clear the way.

"And there's the hooksie!" screamed Annie-Mae.

The hook and ladder wagon followed with its load of wooden ladders, pike poles and more hose, the horses plunging and curvetting against tight reins.

Annie-Mae turned a radiant face.

"Oh, Mr. Abbingdon-Fitch! Did ye iver? I do think a flaming fire is the glory of all to see! And nothing burns more glorious than whiskey wood!"

"Do you want to see it?"

For an instant all the intensity of Annie-Mae's toil-smothered longing shone in her face.

"I'd be that late."

It was indeed late. So late that when at last Ned was able to find a way through the crush of people, it was necessary to take a cab.

A silent Annie-Mae sank into the far corner, in the ashes of the evening.

"There'll be another fire to see, Annie-Mae. Why, they say there are a dozen a day in this city. It clears out the old rotted wooden houses so they can build grander buildings of brick. Once, they say, half of New York burned down—"

"It's not the fire I'm thinking of, Mr. Abbingdon-Fitch."

"What are you thinking of?" The question was softer than he intended.

"It's something I have to say to you, and it's sure I don't know the words to say it."

"Annie-Mae, I thought we were friends."

"That's just it, sir. You'll be callin' on the house again. The fine gentleman that you are. And you'll be seein' Miss Noel. And I wouldn't have her know for all the world."

"Know what?"

"Where I been tonight. Where you seen me. With all those naked women dancin' and all. I didn't know of such a place and Denny didn't tell me. And I wouldn't have gone with him atall, atall, if it hadn't been my cousin Bridie at the Hibernian picnic . . . before I came to work for Mrs. Tremont . . . introdoocin' me and him askin' me if I like music." Her voice trembled. "And him fightin' in the street like a common tinker and yer friend bleedin', maybe dyin'. . . ."

"I doubt that, Annie-Mae." Ned had forgotten Ernie.

"And me comin' home in a cab, like I was a lady or ruint. . . . I see my wrong, and I'll make my confession to Father Doyle Saturday, but you won't tell on me, will you, Mr. Abbingdon-Fitch? You won't tell on me no matter wot?"

Her brief young happiness, evaporating before his eyes, touched Ned to a depth that surprised him. He would like to have comforted her. Yet the breadth of the seedy cab seat was the distance of their separate aspirations.

"I won't tell, Annie-Mae."

"Ever?"

"Ever."

She sank deeper into the corner. The turning of wheels, the measured rhythm of the horse's hoofs, filled the space between them. When she spoke at last, her voice was far away, self-absorbed.

"I'd take it kindly of you to stop at Fourteenth Street where Third Avenue crosses. I'll walk up from there, please. Alone."

The night was milk mild, the streets still busy with shoppers, late strollers, tardy homegoers. She jumped from the cab, ignoring his outstretched hand. "Good night to ye, sir."

He watched her turn up the avenue, the green roses disappearing as she fled from the yellow pool of street light into the dark.

The parlor lamp in Mrs. Luskin's boarding house was still lighted, an ominous sign. Ned opened the door cautiously to the reality of the stale smells frying and lye soap. He had only to reach the stairs, missing the board that squeaked.

"Well, a fine evening you've made of it, Ned Fitch! You and that miserable Ernie!"

Bleached curls quivering, jet earrings shaking, Mrs. Luskin filled the small hall.

"Good evening, Mrs. Luskin. So Ernie's back?"

"Back? Indeed he's back. With his head in a bandage and an eye black as coal soot and a policeman leading him up the front steps. I told the copper to be on his way. Then I told Ernie it's no use babbling about how the other fellow looked. I'll have no rowdies in my house. He's to pack up in the morning. I'm surprised at you, Neddie, going out with a little runt like that whose mother country wouldn't have him for his thieving ways. I'm surprised indeed. You, with your expectations."

"I'm surprised at myself, Mrs. Luskin. If I have expectations I owe them to you and your kindness. I should think of that when I'm tempted."

"Well now, Neddie, I guess there isn't a man alive who hasn't sowed a few wild oats in his time. But for your own good . . ."

By this time a film of remorse had settled on Ned's face, looking for all the world like tenderness to Mrs. Luskin's gimlet eyes.

"It's only you I care about, Neddie, and your fine prospects. You know that."

"I do, indeed. In these days of trial you've been like a"—he hastily skipped the word mother—"a guiding angel to me. I apologize for any worry I gave you."

"Now, that's all right, dear boy."

"And I'd like to say just one thing. Ernie Beech is far from home and he likes a little pleasure. But I should never have left him on the street with that Irishman putting up his fists."

"Irishman? Was that who started it? Why didn't he say so? My husband, the late captain, used to say it's not safe for a respectable Norwegian to go out nights with the Irish filling the streets. Well. Well. Poor Ernie. Doing policeman's duty, maybe, clearing the streets of such riffraff."

"That's what it looked like, Mrs. Luskin."

"I'll make him a nourishing herring stew in the morning. And give him a little talk on watching his step."

Ned moved toward the stairs.

"And, Neddie, I must tell you. There's a dreadful waste of kerosene going on in this house. And at these prices! So I've put candles back. But *your* lamp is filled and ready for you. Don't use your eyes too late on those books of yours."

He had only one book, a penny guide he had bought. *The Gold, Gloss and Guilt of a Great City.* But the woman was inescapable.

He locked the door and sat down. He opened his wallet and, with an impatience he had barely been able to restrain, drew out the ragged piece of brown water silk he had kept like a lodestone for his fortune.

There was no doubt in his mind. The silk matched the gleaming brown dress Annie-Mae had worn this evening, as her story fitted what he had seen outside the Restell house that March night. The girl tearing her skirt, leaving a flounce of brown silk at the bottom of the gatepost. The girl was Noel.

Yet in the witness box in that obscure courtroom, she had taken an oath, and under oath had denied knowing Caroline Restell. He should be at least grateful that the press had not bothered to cover the trial.

Who was she? What was she, this girl Noel Tremont he could not give up? She had perjured herself. So she was as easily capable of falsehood as she was of fine manners. If she had lied to the court, had she lied, too, with her kiss, her witchery? Or had she lied when she had denied her own emotions, refused to see him again?

The whole mystery should have dismayed him, angered him, swept her from his life. Yet, inexplicably, it held a kind of reassurance, even hope. Whatever had brought Noel to perjury must have been a burden so heavy that no one could offer her help, a loneliness so deep that she dared not share or reveal it.

He could not imagine what had taken her to the Restell house that night. Any more than he could guess what had happened after she had left. What had occurred between the time he had seen with his own eyes the Restell woman lying dead in her office and what the papers reported as her blood-ridden suicide in her bath?

The case no longer mattered. It had slid from public consciousness. All that mattered now was this telltale fragment of silk in his hand. Could he tell Noel what he knew? Could he offer to share, even carry her secret burden? Or would the telling take her from him forever?

When sleep came at last, it was fitful. Through layers of uneasy dreaming, the fragment of brown silk spun like a leaf in a whirlpool. Below, alone and elusive, drifted the white face of Noel Tremont. Lower than that, in the depths, floated a distant figure with a gaping mouth, staring eyes, a tumble of black hair, ivory ruffles. A figure of death.

24

The sea lay flat in silvered streaks. The sky was lost in a thick, patternless cloud cover. The air itself seemed to have been sucked into a vacuum in which the only movement was the drift of a white seagull hanging on rigid wings in an air current of its own discovery.

The girl at the water's edge, a white shawl drawn close, her brown hair tied indifferently at the nape of her neck, watched the bird's progress. A single stir of its wings could change its course. It would soon need to, as the promised storm neared. But for a few more moments, it had chosen, like herself, to float, suspended in space. And time.

From the veranda of the big weathered house above the dunes, Walter Tremont watched his enigmatic daughter. He marveled that she could stand so quietly for so long with nothing to look at but the sea. At other times, he marveled that she would walk so endlessly along the sea's edge of the now deserted beach.

For the summer people had left and with them the visiting, the porch tea parties, the croquet games, the rivulets of family news and gossip in which Maria had delighted so long ago. The seashore house to Maria had been, like her now abandoned rose garden, a place of sunshine and renewal. He was thinking too much of Maria.

He rose and paced to the end of the veranda, hands behind his back. He was always restless when the barometer was falling. It had been a family joke. "Don't bother your father now, children. The glass is dropping." But at least he recognized his disquiet now for what it was. Not the emptiness of the sprawling old house. Nor Adrienne's precipitous departure for Europe, nor the frustrations of his own summer. It was, as it had always been, the breathless uneasiness that inevitably preceded a storm. Got on a man's nerves. Always had, on his. Walter retraced his steps to the opposite corner of the veranda.

Noel, silhouetted against the dull sky, had not stirred.

There was no doubt that the weeks at the seashore had been good for her. Each time he came out from the city she seemed improved, a tinge of color in her cheeks, a more frequent smile, though her silences were still long, her thoughts fixed on something he could neither share nor guess.

"She's eating better, Mr. Tremont." Mrs. Kroll, the caretaker's wife who served as housekeeper, had made her report. "That'll cover some of the awful thinness sitting on her bones." Walter had not been aware of the awful thinness sitting on his beloved child's bones. To him, Noel had always been a slender reed of strength.

"If you ask me, Mr. Tremont"—Mrs. Kroll settled herself on her large capable feet to talk—"Miss Noel's suffered more than grief for her dear, departed friend upstate. If you ask me, Miss Noel took the fever herself. You can tell by her hands. I know from my own little Mabel when God took her to heaven, may she rest in peace, her fingers were so thin you could see through them. But Miss Noel's coming around, Mr. Tremont. I wouldn't worry if I were you or bother her with too many questions, though it must be hard to sit with her when she says nothing at all. But don't you fret, Mr. Tremont. I've known these children of yours since they were mites. I'm taking good care of Miss Noel."

Walter had been grateful if not reassured. If Noel had been seriously ill, why had she not been forthright about it? But he would not press her. The quiet closeness shared with his daughter these evenings of his lonely summer was as fragile as sea spume. It could be blown away at a word.

Noel had turned and was walking now, not back to the house as he hoped, but along the deserted beach in the direction of the lighthouse on the point nearly half a mile away. She won't make it, not there and back before the rain starts, he told himself. She should know better. He was aware that his irritation had less to do with her ill-judgment than with the distance that seemed always to surround and isolate her.

He had done his best. All his life, as he remembered. It wasn't a man's duty to understand the whims and moods of the women in his family. He would love them, protect them, provide for them. After that they were best left to themselves to run the household, bring order to his home and comfort to his life. What they did with their spare hours was not his concern, though Maria had never seemed to have any. And he had always been generous. Noel should know that. Perhaps he should have a straight talk . . .

He seemed to hear an echo of Maria's little laugh. "There you go, Walter, thinking about things and making decisions when the glass is dropping. It never works out. I'll turn up a lamp and bring my sewing and you sit there and read to me. 'Lives of great men all remind us we can make our lives sublime, and departing leave behind us, leave behind us. . . .' Mr. Longfellow. Such a dear man. Do you remember when we heard him read at Cooper Institute that night? 'Leave behind us . . .' "

Walter had obediently taken his chair but finished for her from memory, " '. . . footprints on the sands of time.' "

Her laugh had been girlish. "That's it, Walter. How many things you know!"

But Maria was not here, not where she should be, to cheer him.

He looked up the beach. To his relief, Noel was walking homeward, her step brisk, her head lifted. The daughter he liked to see.

He went indoors. The sitting room—Maria had always said you couldn't call it a real parlor—ran the width of the house. It was sensibly furnished in maple and rattan to endure the buffetings of children, and papered in blue stripes and yellow climbing roses. On fair days it was bright with sunlight, as once it had been with toys.

On this darkening afternoon, mist already pressing at the windows, Mrs. Kroll was lighting the lamp at his chair. Her market basket stood beside her.

"Cass's come with coal for the grates. Got his wagon, so he'll take me over to the market. He says it looks like a real September blow. I could have told him that. I'll want some supplies, so if you're all right, Mr. Tremont?"

"I'm fine. Fine. Go ahead before the storm gets here. You know I'm going back to the city in the morning." He liked the dependable, round-faced country woman. She was part of a comfortable past, a reminder of a long-ago close-knit family. "Mrs. Tremont is returning from Europe on Thursday."

"So you won't be coming down again, sir."

He did not resent the implication. They had an unspoken understanding.

"Probably not."

Mrs. Kroll picked up her market basket, her face heavy. There was obviously something on her mind.

"Will Miss Noel go back with you?"

"That's up to her."

Mrs. Kroll turned full square on him. "I wish you'd take her with you."

"You must have a reason for wishing that."

Mrs. Kroll drew a deep sigh of decision.

"I do, sir. And it's not because I wish her away. She's like one of my own to me, since she first came here with her ribbons gone and her hair flying, running with her brothers like a wild young thing. I've watched her all these years. She's changed. I'm not sure it's for the best."

The wind was rising. He wondered what the woman was getting at. Mrs. Kroll resettled her basket.

"She had the fever bad, all right. You could see that. But if you ask me she's taken all the cure she needs here at the seashore. She needs some liveliness. Oh, I don't expect a man to notice things like that. It takes a woman's eye. But all I seen her do is walk up and down that beach, up and down, always alone. If you ask me, she's moping."

"Moping? For heaven's sake, moping over what?" Walter felt uneasily out of his depth.

"Well, maybe I shouldn't say, but I don't like to see Miss Noel moody. It isn't like her. And I take it all the way back . . . four years maybe, you remember. No, I guess that was the year you were in Europe, Mr. Tremont. I was here with her. She must have told you—the young man . . ."

Walter sat motionless. He did not permit himself to discuss his family with the servants. He disliked even more to learn things from them.

". . . as I say, I mind my business, Mr. Tremont, as you know, and it's only for Miss Noel's sake. My land, I'd see them both that summer, walking the beach all the way to the point, him as blond as a Greek god, her like a brown sparrow, laughing, gathering shells. Holding hands like a couple of children. Nothing wrong, you understand, Mr. Tremont. Just happy. Cass told me the young man worked on one of them fancy yachts come down from Newport and that he could sail anything with a mast on it, take a boat through the slip like a pup on a leash and never mind the weather. Cass told me he'd rent a ketch for the day at the boatyard. They always knew when he was taking a girl out for he'd throw a few pillows in for comfort. I never saw him again after that summer. But I guess you know all that."

Mr. Tremont's silence made Mrs. Kroll uncomfortable. But then the barometer was falling and Mrs. Tremont, the real

Mrs. Tremont in Mrs. Kroll's opinion, used to warn her about his ways when the glass fell.

"That's all, Mr. Tremont. But if you ask me Miss Noel's been alone long enough. She has need of her friends in the city."

From outside the kitchen door came the whinny of a horse. Mrs. Kroll thrust her market basket over her arm.

"There's Cass come for me now. I hope you won't take it wrong, Mr. Tremont, what I said. I was only relieving my worry over Miss Noel." She departed heavily, her voice rising to a bellow when she reached the kitchen. "I'm coming, Cass. If you can't hold that mare quiet, then get one you can."

Walter sat, staring unseeing at a worn place in the rug. Noel and a young man. Four years ago. That was the summer after he had met Adrienne. His feelings stirred, he had departed for Europe for his father's beloved home city of Strasbourg to probe the complexities of his own life, his age, his widowhood. He had allowed his responsibilities, for the first time he could remember, to slip from him. His children were grown, his sons could take care of themselves. But his cherished Noel he had left unguarded to the indulgence of a doting housekeeper and the interest of a passing stranger. A young man whose name she had never spoken, whose visits she had never mentioned. Walter permitted his anger to rise over his deeper sense of guilt. Noel had been carefully brought up. She should have known better than to accept even the most casual attention from a man unknown to her family, a paid hand on a yacht, a common beach loafer.

The glass door to the veranda opened with a gust of wind.

"It's begun to rain, Father."

"Where have you been, Noel?" He heard his own unnecessary sharpness.

She looked at him, then gave a little laugh. "Up to the lighthouse. Where I always go. I ran most of the way back. So you see I must be quite cured."

Indeed she seemed to be. Her face glowed from the exercise. Her hair, swept back by the wind, was darkly tangled with mist, her forehead gleamed with the first drops of rain. But it was something about the lift of her chin, the clarity of her eyes that held him. It was as if in the long loneliness of sea and beach, she had reached some kind of peace with herself. If so, at least he now understood.

"Better get into dry things, Noel. Then perhaps you

wouldn't mind making me some coffee. Mrs. Kroll's gone to market. Cass came for her."

"So I heard."

"So the whole township heard. So we'll have the place to ourselves."

"Which means you have something on your mind." Noel dropped into a chair. "My clothes are quite dry. It isn't time to change for dinner. And you know Adrienne said that you're not to have coffee in the afternoon. What did you want to talk about?"

Walter had never become used to her directness. In his sons he might have admired it. But David was usually facetious and Orrin too often devious. In women he expected cajoling or coaxing. Or, as in Maria's case, a small hint with the effectiveness of a muffled hammer. But Noel could put him off balance. He wondered silently if that beach cad had also found her directness diverting.

"If you're going to scowl like that, Father, because the barometer's dropping, I shall find a book. Otherwise, I have something on my mind, too."

"Good. Then we shan't waste the day." He tried for geniality. "Turn up that lamp, will you? How your mother hated that shade. She used to say it was a pity Mr. Tiffany couldn't find something better than blue turnips to put on his glass. She would never admit they were hydrangeas. But she took care of it. She took care of everything, always." The last was almost to himself. He came back to the present. "You'll allow me a pipe, won't you?"

Noel lit the lamp and returned to stand quietly before her father.

"I don't allow or forbid anything, Father dear. To anyone. I don't think grown people should treat each other that way. I'll make you coffee if you wish. It's your responsibility whether you drink it or not."

"Oh, sit down, Noel. I count on temperament in most women. Not in you."

He had managed quite well, he told himself. It was not the time to accuse or seek redress, or even to reveal his own hurt anger. Besides, what could be accomplished? An argument now might alienate her, hold her here at the shore when he wanted her home. As so often happened, his heart stirred at the sight of this light, steely daughter, encased in pride, who might, as he had learned today, have been hurt in a way he never guessed. Damn the fellow!

"I'm returning to the city tomorrow, Noel. Adrienne's ship

may be delayed a day or two by this storm. I want you to come home with me."

She sat motionless. He could read neither her expression nor her silence.

"I dislike staying in that empty house. I have some business matters to attend to. I should like to have my daughter at home with me." He paused, filling the wait with a smile. "You're a very intelligent young woman, Noel. I like talking with you."

She turned her head, her eyes fathomless. Her silence nettled him.

"Besides, I don't think it's appropriate or proper for you to stay on here alone with only Mrs. Kroll to chaperone you."

That was a mistake. It brought from Noel only a light, almost soundless laugh, mocking or indifferent he could not tell, yet it left him uneasy.

"Do you find that amusing?"

"No, Father. I find it sweet. As if I had never been alone here. As if every June and September since Mother died, I had not come down to open and close the house."

"You had Mrs. Jessup with you." He was getting off the track. The point he was making was weak. She was right. He had depended on her for so much. But he was still in charge of his family.

"Noel, Mrs. Kroll could close this house with her hands tied behind her." He paused, for she had turned her face from him. He was not to see her answer. "I have never talked much about myself to you. I have never believed that a man's business was a subject to interest a woman. Especially a young and pretty one." He was surprised at his own need to reach her. He had never had a base for confidences in his own home. Perhaps no man of his generation did. Perhaps, too, that was the essence of an orderly and responsible life. A man set the moral stamp of his home. Those principles, multiplied over and over, were the very structure of a civilized society, the basis of human progress and human contentment.

Not all of those thoughts flowed through Walter Tremont's mind. Rather they lay at the root of his being like a rich humus nurturing his days. Self-revelation was weakness. Yet at this odd, isolated hour, wrapped in the rising winds and gusts of rain of the coming storm, Walter wanted for once to talk of himself, to be seen not as a demanding parent, but as a humane man burdened, like the humblest, with unfulfilled needs.

Don't bother your father, children. The barometer's falling! Walter smiled to himself at the gentleness of the memory.

"To tell you the truth, Noel, in the last few months I have begun to ask myself what I was really doing with my time. Orrin is running the business, not the way I did perhaps, but then I didn't run it the way my father did. Old men must be very careful about interfering with young ideas. No use shackling a young man before he's tried his wings. I accepted the presidency of the Citizens League, but what have I done with it? I accepted the Mayor's appointment to his Committee for Decency. I have been to the White House. I came home with a good deal on my mind. I wasn't sure I liked the way Anthony Comstock conducted his investigations, though he is a good Christian man and certainly fighting for the cause of morality. There is great corruption in the city. In my opinion, one of the most sordid cases in New York's history was closed too quickly."

He glanced at his daughter. She was sitting, hands folded, eyes lowered to the circle of lamplight on the floor. Maria would have had her needlework, Adrienne would have stirred restlessly, but Noel was listening.

"What case was that, Father?"

"I don't wish to go into it, Noel. But I believe that even the basest creature is entitled to justice. And if the woman's death was not self-inflicted—"

"What woman?"

"I use the case only as an illustration. It involved a woman of such corrupt practices . . ."

"Father, if we are to talk, let's be candid. Mrs. Restell?"

"I forget how modern you are."

"What are you thinking of doing?"

Walter tapped his pipe. He had begun to regret the whole dialogue.

"Nothing, now. The Mayor, the district attorney, the police commissioner are all satisfied with the verdict. Your brother, Orrin, had the presumption to tell me that I'm a damned fool, begging your pardon, my dear. Adrienne was distressed. David"—a half smile revealed the ghosts of old affections—"I'm afraid David prefers flippancy to serious thought these days. All David had to say was go ahead, stir 'em up if that's what you want to do. That was hardly my purpose. Perhaps they're right, all of them. The case is probably best forgotten. But the corruption that tolerated it cannot be. Bribery, shamelessness, indecency, open violation of the law. I am not a lawyer. I never had the advantages of college study. I'm a simple man, I began as a humble tailor''—he smiled again, warmed by her presence, her attentiveness—''though I assure you, an expert one. As a mere citizen I may be, as one newspaper said, tilting at windmills. But if I enter politics as the Citizen League urges me, I would have a base for my opinions. I believe that integrity, a high sense of morality, should be as much a part of a city's governments as of a man's family. But it takes men willing to say so. I think I owe my country that, as I owe my family.''

Noel studied the circle of light. She was so quiet that he wondered if she was still listening.

''I've thrust too much on you. You're a young woman. What interests me would naturally bore you.''

''It hasn't.''

Her mood had changed. She was what she had been earlier this summer, withdrawn, guarded. He glanced at the bent head. The lamplight burnished the straight brown hair, highlighted the delicate strength of her profile. Didn't the girl know herself? The blond stranger on the beach strode into his thoughts—brash, faceless, daring to take her hand, no doubt whispering words that would turn any girl's head. He would not mention it now. It was over, and it would not happen again. He would take better care of her. See her comfortably, safely married. He would listen to Adrienne.

''If I promise not to bore you again, will you come back to the city with me tomorrow?''

''If you wish, Father.''

He remembered. ''I haven't given you your chance yet. Have I? It's your turn. What did you want to ask me?''

The windows were darkening. The wind had begun to keen. The white gull would no longer be coasting on his secret current. Instinct heeded, the sea boiling beneath him, the gull would already have found the high, safe haven of flight.

Her father was looking gently at her. It was her last chance, Noel told herself, like the gull's to find safe haven. To trust her father's kindness, to say to him what would set her free.

Father, I have a child. I need money. I need your help.

The silence hung weighted and waiting between them.

''Father . . .''

A shutter banged. Her father glanced impatiently upward.

''I don't like it, Noel. You look white as wax, as your mother used to say. The shore's not done you much good that I can see. I insist you come back to the city with me. You're still my little girl. I'm going to take better care of you. What was it you wanted to say?''

His testiness reflected the barometer. It also stopped her at what she saw as the edge of peril.

''I'll see to the windows, Father. It—it wasn't really important.''

The storm struck at midnight. Noel, in the narrow imprisonment of her bed, released her frustration to the fury of wind and rain, letting her thoughts ride the thunder of the angered sea. The storms were the ritual of summer's end, the awesome apocalypse of change.

As a child, Noel had both loved and feared them. Orrin told her they came to take her away. David told her that they were born out of faraway hurricanes. She had seen kittens born. She had imagined each new storm emerging, round and wet and dark, from a mysterious violence somewhere beyond the horizon. Full grown by the time it reached their own house, its obvious goal, it would claw at the doors, shriek at the windows, tear at the shutters. Snug beneath her sprigged quilt, Noel would thrill to its savagery, wondering what would happen if she went downstairs and let it in. But it would never come in. It belonged, free and untamed, with all wild things. Like herself if only she had been born a storm not a girl. Sometimes she imagined it lifting her from her bed and sweeping her aloft. David had told her that above the black rolling clouds there was blue stillness and sunlight. She had never believed that. She would like to see for herself. Yet, after the paroxysm of the night, the sky would be washed clean and blue, the sea sapphire and at peace, stirring only to the white ruffling of a west wind.

The three of them, David, Orrin, and herself, would run outdoors to pick up fallen shingles, whole shutters flung on the grass. They would find their beach a tantalizing reshaped world, one dune in retreat, another vanished. Best of all they would collect a fantasia of driftwood, shaped to the eye of the finder—a horse's head, an old man with a cane, a witch's face, a pirate's wooden leg, the turret of a drowned fairy castle. The storm, spent and defeated, had never failed to leave its magic.

But that was childhood, a millenium ago.

Tonight the outside violence wracked the joints and timbers of the old house, as it wracked Noel's thoughts. She had determined to put Ned from them as well as from her life, to brush away the memory of those few shining, impossible hours as the stuff of make-believe. Her rebuff to him had been as misleading as it had been abrupt. But it had been quick, surgically quick. Had she told him the truth, he might have accepted it, and Posie, with that carefree airiness that delighted her. But looking down the narrow corridor of the years to come, would the spell hold? Would the day not arrive when he would look at her with the words unspoken but living? "A loose woman." "An indecent woman." And what then of Posie?

She had passed the stage of girlish romance, of trusting "love to have and to hold from this day forward. . . ."

The wind rattled the window, a stark reminder of where she was. Her father's house, her father's encirclement. She had one purpose now and only one. To provide for her child. To make one more effort to talk to her father, to obtain her dowry, and banish forever the threat of a marriage that now seemed even more debasing. How many long summer twilights had she sat in the porch swing, looking at the familiar shape of his massive head, his broad comforting shoulders against the deepening sky and imagined herself saying, "Father, I have a child." He would be hurt, bewildered perhaps, but in the end he would take her hands as he had the day she had broken her mother's French bisque vase, and say, "I understand." And Posie's safety would be secure. Yet in the reality of his presence, the words had locked in her throat. When he had seemed most content, she could not bear to end that contentment. When he had seemed burdened, she could not bear to add to that burden.

Once she had brought up the matter of her dowry.

"Noel, my dear girl, you ask for so little. What do you want? I'll buy it for you. But your dowry . . . you must leave these matters to me. It does not become a young lady to discuss money."

Her father had risen and left the veranda as if his very manhood had been under attack.

Tomorrow he would return to the city, to the euphoria of an imagined and unlikely political career. And to Adrienne. Next week she must meet with Madame Ducharde for the final disposition of Posie's future.

The storm was reaching its peak. On its fury came unbidden, unwanted memories she had tried to banish forever. Memories she had walked the beach these past weeks to crush. The man who had betrayed her, the false ecstasy of that long-ago summer.

He had swept her off her feet with words no man had ever spoken to her.

"I adore you, Noel. I need you. We'll be married. We belong to each other. Forever."

She had lain in his arms, deep in the dune grass, the sound of the sea in her ears, the summer gold of afternoon above his head. Slowly he had freed her from her white dress, her white lawn delicacies, from all the constrictions that womanhood had brought her, until at last she lay, her whole body washed in light and air.

She had returned his desire with an innocence, then a passion that must have surprised him. She had let her heart, her body, her whole being soar to heights unguessed and forbidden by every precept of her known world. She had drunk to intoxication his words.

Near the end of summer had come the shocking revelation. He was engaged to another girl.

"It was a mistake, Noel. Millicent doesn't love me."

Millicent?

He never told her the girl's full name, but she knew Millicent, the girl with the candy box face and the doll curls, whose father, they said, dangled his fortune before every probable suitor. She had met Millicent—at Kitty's, at Mrs. Wilberforce's.

"I don't love her, Noel. She doesn't love me. She'll find plenty of escorts to take her to parties. That's all she wants of me. I'll go up to Newport. Take the steamer Friday and break it off before she comes home. And every moment I'm there I'll look at the sea and think of you, of us, together."

"Oh, my own, my darling . . ."

The parting had its ecstasy.

Ten days later, back in the city, a stark, two-inch headline of the afternoon *Globe* had paralyzed her in the street. COLLISION AT SEA. FALL RIVER STEAMER *STAR OF THE WEST* ON FIRE. 108 VICTIMS. . . .

Numbly she had bought a paper. "Among the victims"—the name jumped, solitary for her, from the page—"Gordon Keith, New York."

In her room she had forced herself to read the article. Then again. The disaster had occurred not on Gordon's trip north to Newport, but on his return. He had at last been freed, he was to be hers.

She had barely faced her grief when the girl he had been engaged to reached the city. In deep and becoming black, pale and anguished, Millicent publicly mourned her fiancé.

Her wedding dress had hung ready, she proclaimed. She vowed that she would wear forever the black velvet ribbon of mourning for her beloved. She won every heart.

So he had not kept his promise. The engagement had not been broken. To put the best face on it, Millicent may have refused to release him. But in the end he had not been willing to be released from Millicent's trivialities, Noel told herself savagely, or from Millicent's wealth.

She heard it at first with disbelief, then gradually with honesty. It lay within her, a stone of betrayal never to be admitted, never to be held to the light. She found it possible to endure at last by the simple process of not thinking of herself, of giving her days to rigid monotony. And the child she would bear. The child that was not his, she told herself fiercely, but hers, hers alone, in a kind of immaculate conception, drained of treachery, blanched of sin, bitterness held at bay.

Now as she lay in her bed, anguish surfaced like the cutting edge of the wind. She could not erase the past. Yet no one on earth could chain the human heart. Suddenly, strong and laughing, Ned was with her, as vivid as the brief day they had spent together. Why had there not been a good angel, an ancient wisdom to stand between her own innocence and the hot words and hot hands of a stranger? But Noel had long forced honesty on herself. Would she have listened in those first hours of self-discovery with the sea light in her eyes? How did any woman know the one man for her until he appeared? Ned. Ned. She breathed into her pillow. Why didn't you come sooner? She could hear his answer, that voice that had become a buoy bell to her thoughts. "Why didn't you wait, Noel?"

She needed to breathe. She flung aside the bedcovers, lit the oil lamp, and drew the curtains back from the streaming windows.

It was at that moment that she heard the crash. It came like the crack of a revolver shot and the splintering of wood. It was in the house or very near it. Slipping into the plain wool dressing gown she used for country emergencies, she picked up the lamp and hurried down the dark well of the stairs. There was nothing amiss in hall or dining room. In the living room, pressing her face and the aureole of lamplight against the black glass doors to the veranda she saw what had happened.

"What is it, Noel?"

Her father was on the stairs in his old plaid robe, the tasseled cord tied so unevenly that he was in danger of stumbling on it. Above the lamp in his hand, his face showed deep lines, matching the grey of his tousled hair, his unkempt mustache.

Why, he's old, thought Noel. My father's an old man. This is what he will look like when he is dead. Her heart turned over in pity. But beneath it, treacherous, frightening, ran thoughts like beetles from a lifted log. When he is dead . . . my part of the estate, my burden over . . . Posie's turn.

She shivered, hating her own truancy. How many aging parents, how many greying aunts and uncles were given fond lip service while, hidden in their thoughts, the devoted heirs were calculating their real usefulness?

"I'm sorry you were disturbed, Father. It's Mama's rocker. I forgot to push it back in the corner when the storm came. The wind blew it over the railing."

He peered beside her into the night. Barely seen was the shattered white railing, like a row of missing teeth. The space in front of it was empty. The familiar old rocking chair was gone.

And with it, to Noel, a dim and faded transparency, wisp-like, fragile, of the small woman who had occupied it so continually her last summer at the seashore.

Her faiher had turned away.

"I'll get the repairs started tomorrow, Father. We'll find the rocker on the lawn. Mr. Rosalli can mend it, I'm sure."

When he turned back, he was composed. "It's done its time. Your mother always hated the thing anyway. She could settle her pillows well enough in it, but she said her feet never properly touched the floor. If there was one thing your mother liked, Noel . . ." Was he talking because it was easier than stopping? He had moved from the blackness of the glass doors. ". . . one thing she always wanted was to have her two feet square on the floor. Pretty small they were, for all that determination. She wanted mine there, too, when she could manage it."

He looked at her with sudden intensity.

"And I wish to heaven, Noel, she were here now, to see that your two feet were square on the floor. She wouldn't have stood your moping around like this, week after week, by yourself. Not because you lost a good friend up in the country, but because your head is full of something I can't get at. And maybe don't want to. Some imaginary romance or day-dream that girls indulge in, I understand, when they happen to meet someone who is flattering, and quite unsuitable or unacceptable. It isn't like you, Noel. Perhaps I haven't been all the father I should have these past two years, but long before that you were brought up to be a sensible, practical young lady. Oh, I gave in to all those studies you wanted to take up at Hunter College. And the lectures you wanted to go to at Cooper Institute, and the meetings on giving the vote to women. They'll no doubt get it someday, with or without you. And then I'll wager they won't bother to use it. Meanwhile, what are you doing with your own life? Becoming what they call the 'New Woman'? Going your own way? Doing only what pleases you? Thinking of yourself and ignoring everybody around you who loves you and wants to see you happy? New Woman—Advanced Woman! Fancy new ideas, no doubt. But you're still a woman. God hasn't made you any different. If your mother were here she'd tell you that. Get married, Noel. That's what she'd say. Find the right young man. You'll have my blessing. Marriage is a woman's true life. Marriage and the children she was meant to bear. Your mother knew that. She was a happy woman."

He was looking past her, out to the darkness of the veranda, as if Maria, freed of her ghostly chair, were coming toward them, her eyes warm, her smile loving. He was talking, Noel knew, out of the emptiness of his life without her.

Yet what he had said stung. She had never heard him so blunt, so racked. She longed to fling out the four beseeching words, "I have a child." But it was not the time. It never would be. He had evoked the spell, the sanctity of Maria. She was silenced. The family code held firm.

He seemed unable to end the painful scene. "I want you to be happy, child."

"Whom would you have me marry, Father?"

He shook his head. "I'm not a tyrant. I'd trust you to find your own young man, decent, honorable, suitable."

"Or let Adrienne or Kitty or Mrs. Wiberforce do it for me?"

"That is beneath you, Noel." But the gentleness had returned to his voice, a sort of apology, she guessed. "You'll find Mr. Right, as your mother used to say. When you do, you'll have no need to ask me about a dowry. I'll be generous. No worry about that. The day I escort you down the aisle of St. George's Church, you'll be as well provided for as any young woman need be."

Suppose I don't love him, Father?

But she did not ask that question aloud. He had made it a matter of business. So would she.

"Would the dowry come directly to me?"

"That's an odd question, Noel. Where do you get these notions?"

"I'll make it simple. The money that is to attract this—husband, would it come to me, or to him?"

He was tired. He had had enough with the perplexities of this night. He retied the cord of his bathrobe so that the tassels hung even.

"Yes. Yes. If that's the way you'd want it. Though for the life of me I don't see"—he picked up his lamp—"go to bed, Noel. The storm's blowing itself out. I wouldn't be surprised if the barometer's begun to rise. Feels like it."

At the bannister, he stopped.

"Life doesn't usually repeat itself, child. No matter what those books you read say. Not many second chances. You take what it gives, when it gives. You're an attractive young lady, Noel. But every one of us must get on with the business of living."

On the stairs, his step was firm. He no longer moved like an old man. Against the wall in the lamplight his shadow loomed large.

In her own room, she found that at last she could open the window. A rush of fresh air had cleared the night.

She blew out the lamp and settled into the darkness. There she saw her decision, plain and clear. Impersonal as an invoice, precise as a bank statement. She would get on with the business of living.

She had merely to make her bargain. Use her womanhood and keep her child.

As the wind dropped, she slept.

25

New York City, once observed Mr. Ralph Waldo Emerson, self-proclaimed trumpeter of the New England conscience, was a sucked orange. Few of the nearly million assorted souls jostling their daily way through the city's clamor would have agreed. Babylon yes, Sodom and Gomorrah, yes, indeed. But a city drained by the past, never. The garishness of its sins, the enormity of its unshared wealth blanketing the frightfulness of its poverty, the prodigal thievery of its politicians, were the very excesses that gave New York its special immediate glory. The past was gone. Its modern evils were said to surpass Singapore's, its glitter compared to Paris.

At no time of the year was its earthy abundance more evident than at the coming of the winter season. The signs were everywhere. The splendid carriages, drawn by fat, sleek horses breathing heavy vapor. The bright windows of the huge A.T. Stewart department sore, glowing with the temptation of ladies' furred and elegant winter wear. Profits were reflected ten blocks uptown in the marble mansion of A.T. Stewart himself, with its art gallery a half block long.

For those less fortunate there were also welcome signs of the season. Straw spread on the plank floor of the omnibus, the small round coal stove placed up near the driver. It would not give warmth until after Thanksgiving, but it signaled hope.

For pedestrians pushing against the river's winds, old Sadie made her appearance on the corner of Broadway and Twelfth Street, her feet wrapped in burlap, her tongue as biting as the air, stirring her rusted grate. "Hot roasted chestnuts, a half-penny a bag." But as neither Sadie nor her customer possessed a non-minted half-penny, both parties understood that a whole penny would have to do.

Another block downtown, a little Nell set down her bucket,

nose blue, young red hands totally inadequate to her burden. "Hot corn, steaming hot corn, two ears a penny." After three minutes in the frosted air, corn, water, and fingers were as cold as city charity.

Nowhere in the city was the season heralded more precisely than in Stuyvesant Square. Promptly on the fourth of November each year, a much anticipated mauve envelope was hand delivered at the front door, the address in violet ink in the careful Spencerian flourish of Miss Phoebe Bliss. There wasn't a parlor maid worth her salt who didn't know the contents and didn't recognize the impeccable black suit, the scarred brown face, and the faultless courtesy of "Mr. Christopher," Miss Bliss's . . . what was he, anyway? Butler, houseman, major domo, or palace guard? Upstairs and front it was gossiped that Mr. Christopher did not occupy a cramped servant's room under the attic, but lived in comfort on the third floor, with his own sitting room. Against Miss Bliss's silence, talk eventually faded. Gossip proved less satisfying than the receipt of one of Miss Bliss's coveted invitations.

It was Miss Bliss's only social affair of the year. It was Mr. Christopher's one annual public appearance in the Square.

Frau Gruen's hands were deep in flour when she heard the front doorbell. A glance at the clock and the calendar told her what to expect. She wiped her hands and removed her apron. It was against her principles to have anything delivered at the front door, but Dr. Lendler had been firm in this matter. "No discipline, no proprieties, everything changing," she invariably muttered, which brought her unsmiling to the front vestibule.

Mr. Christopher, thin as a broom handle, removed his black bowler, held out the mauve envelope, and bowed.

"I have the honor to present this, Madam. . . ."

Frau Gruen managed what she considered a gracious nod of her head. After all, the little brown-skinned man did make her feel like the mistress of the house.

"Thank you." But she could not go so far as to call him Master.

Frau Gruen laid the envelope in Dr. Lendler's walnut letter tray, and made a surprising discovery. There were two envelopes. One addressed to Dr. Hugo Lendler, the other, to her pleased astonishment, addressed to "The Honorable Edmond Abbingdon-Fitch." To *Herr* Fitch, her private pet and joy, *der schöne Mann!* It was a great honor.

Frau Gruen debated. Should she leave the envelope with

Dr. Lendler's mail or should she take it upstairs to Herr Fitch herself? The debate took less than thirty seconds. She plodded upstairs.

Somewhat to her curiosity the study door, usually open, was closed. Perhaps the room was chilly, perhaps the coal scuttle empty. She would speak to that careless Billy. She knocked and turned the knob. The door was locked. Never, never was that door locked, even when the *Herr Professor* was at work in the room, or took his rest. Frau Gruen's back stiffened. There was something offending about the matter. She knocked again.

"*Herr* Fitch. *Herr* Fitch."

She heard the lock turn.

The door opened halfway. Ned, his tie awry, his coat off, peered at her.

"What is it you want, Frau Gruen?"

"I have a letter for you."

"A letter? Come now, who would write a letter to me? I don't know anybody in this town."

She was used to his teasing but not to the tone.

"Here. It's addressed to you. Take it."

She turned on her heel.

"If you please, Frau Gruen, I don't wish to be disturbed again."

It was harsh, Ned knew. She did not deserve it. Alone, locked again in the safety of the study, he glanced at the mauve envelope. For a false instant, he imagined it might be from Noel. The violet penmanship flowed gracefully.

Miss Phoebe Hortense Handon Bliss
hopes for the privilege of the presence of

The Honorable
Edmond Abbingdon-Fitch
the evening of November 27th
commemoration of the Evacuation.
Eight o'clock.
Fifteen Stuyvesant Square.

The favor of a reply is requested.

Ned reread it. Then he read it again. He had no idea what "the Evacuation" might mean. Nor did he care. He had received what he had longed for all his life, a prestigious invitation to meet people of wealth and importance. Even that paled beside the stunning likelihood that Noel Tremont would be there.

That is, if he were able to accept.

He stuffed the invitation in his pocket and picked up the jacket that he had hastily tossed over the table at Frau Gruen's knock. There it lay, his stunning discovery of the morning. A long narrow newspaper-wrapped tube that had slid toward him when he had opened the closet door. He had taken it down from the shelf and unwound it. Now he could only stare again, unbelieving, at what he found within it. An ebony cane with an ivory head carved in the shape of a lotus blossom, the head joined to the cane by a tarnished band of silver. It could not be the same cane he had carried that fatal night into the house of Mrs. Restell. It must be a duplicate. Yet something deeper than memory, some warning told him differently. He twisted the top and felt it loosen. He gave a savage yank, the ivory knob came off in his hand. There, where it should be, was the narrow strip of gummed paper bearing the name and address of Mr. Elias Monk, 23 Bowery.

The first shock sent his heart thudding. Then came a hot resentment, rising to fury. How did the cane come into this house? Who was Dr. Hugo Lendler that he could have gotten his hands on it? What game was he playing with Ned, duping him into a false sense of secure well-being?

As anger congealed to resentment, it occurred to Ned that however startling the appearance of the cane, Dr. Lendler might not yet have found Elias Monk's label. Nor yet have traced the cane through Mr. Monk's secondhand store to Ned. He might not yet know of Ned's impulsive, ill-considered intrusion into the Restell mansion, linking him to that grim scene of death.

On the other hand, Dr. Hugo Lendler might know all that and more. Ned was coldly alert now, with the well-honed instincts of the hunted fox.

He went to the door to make sure of the drawn bolt. Then he carried the cane to the window and carefully removed Elias Monk's label leaving enough of the gummed label to hold the ivory top fast. He rolled the cane up in its crumbling newspaper and pushed it back on the shelf. Dr. Lendler would not be home until late this afternoon. Ned would put the hours to good use.

By four o'clock Ned had searched and returned to its place every letter, every record, every book title in the study. At last he found what he wanted. The "professor" was deeper than Ned had suspected. The discovery came in two water-stained books on an upper shelf, two of the volumes Ned himself had brought from England, the journey that had opened this door to false opportunity.

The titles were in German so he paid no attention. But they were in English character, not German script. He looked at the two titles intently. *Der Theoretischer Hypnotismus* and *Der Praktischer Hypnotismus.* A single word leaped at him—*Hypnotismus.* A hypnotist was nothing more, in Ned's mind, than a showman, a common faker. A dance hall act. The slick-talking man with the black mustache and polished black hair, the flowing tie, and the pointed shoes, with the "subject" supposedly lured onto the stage from the audience. The "hypnotist" would put the man to "sleep," then order him to walk on all fours, bark like a dog, and lift a leg against a chair. The audience would howl with delight.

Humbuggery, nothing else. Ned remembered Dr. Lendler's talk of experiments. He recalled the professor's long monologues droning on over afternoon coffee. Was he, Ned himself, in this house? Dupe to a charlatan? Or something more sinister? There was the unanswerable presence of the cane. Was Dr. Lendler probing him to confess to something he hadn't done?

Or was he, Ned, imagining too much? Putting two and two together and getting five? Nothing had yet happened to him, except that a forgotten fact of life had emerged that he now saw as a threat. Not only to himself but to the girl who was never very far from his mind. The events of that night in the Restell house came rushing back as if they had happened yesterday. Worse, Noel had been in that shadowy mansion, as he had. He knew that now. Anything that Dr. Lendler might choose to reveal about the cane, about Ned himself, would only hurt Noel. That must never happen. Ned had an impulse to open the closet and take the cane with him. But that would indeed put him under suspicion, if only for thievery. Or he might confront Dr. Lendler, deny everything, trusting the amiable little professor's seeming friendship.

But Dr. Lendler was not a friend. He had become a mysterious and devious enemy. Ned's streetwise instincts told him that as long as he remained in this cloistered little house, he was vulnerable.

And, ironically, today had come the opportunity he had so long imagined, an invitation to a social event at the most distinguished residence in Stuyvesant Square, the home of Miss Phoebe Bliss. He had no doubt that Noel would be there. He could meet her properly, in her own world, with her father, her friends, perhaps even accepted as a gentleman. He would talk of his prospects, his future. His now uncertain future.

It was getting late. He did not want to meet Dr. Lendler. Not now. He put the study to rights, straightened his necktie, removed his sleeve bands, picked up his coat and walked out.

The brisk October twilight lifted his spirits. He had never closed one door that another had not opened. It had usually been his sardonic destiny that whenever Fate held out one kindly hand she managed to strike him with the other.

A carriage passed him in the Square. For an instant he thought the lady inside it was Noel. He reminded himself that he was no longer part of the pleasant life of the Square. But he might be again. The mauve envelope still lay in his pocket.

His pace quickened. He walked westward toward the brighter street lamps. The crowds thickened. A girl looked directly at him. A cabbie slowed for him. To each he shook his head. But the excitement of the city was reaching him. It would not defeat him. This was where he belonged. Not buried in books, growing dull before his time. But out in this teeming, high-living city, young, alive, challenging his fortune anywhere he could find it.

He had never feared that challenge. Tonight he welcomed it.

Nowhere did the ebullience of the coming season ring louder than at the fifty-foot long mahogany bar of the great Hoffman House on lower Fifth Avenue. By four o'clock of the shortening afternoon, a visitor could barely push his way through the crowd. Stockbrokers, shipping merchants, lawyers, gamblers, actors, politicians, railroad builders. Men who had made fortunes, men who were risking them, with tall top hats set firmly on their heads, polished boots firmly on the gleaming brass rail. Equally gleaming cuspidors were well spaced among them. Once in place, a visitor could satisfy himself with the finest of whiskies, the richest of dark ales, a free spread of sliced beef, ham, turkey, smoked goose, well-ripened Stilton cheese, and as much herring and potato salad as a healthy man could down before dinner. Through a haze of superior Havana cigar smoke, he could muse on the rosy flesh and opulent nudity of the full-blown women in the enormous painting above the bar.

A half hour of all this and the visitor might well murmur, if he could be heard, that the city not only earned but embellished its more apt name of Gotham. The medieval village in Nottinghamshire in England, from which the name came, only pretended madness to forestall the royal visit it could not afford. This modern Gotham had no need of pretense. It could afford anything it wanted. If pride and ambition, greed and gluttony, were mortal sins, here they were flaunted like flags in a stiff wind. A man with his foot on the brass rail of the Hoffman House bar, his glass refilled, could easily believe that in the gaslit blue twilight beyond the door, anything on earth could be his.

For Ned Fitch, leaning with assumed ease on the far end of the bar this early November evening, there was no such euphoria. In the past weeks, with Dr. Lendler's generous wages in his pocket, he had cultivated the expensive habit of stopping in at the Hoffman House to catch a glimpse of the famous and infamous, the surge of rich living, to imagine himself someday among them, one of them.

That was coming to a swift end, as were the funds in his pocket. Ned had already discovered that the pleasure of having money was being able to ignore it. Not having it was paralysis.

"Look where you're setting your drink, young sir." The bartender was condescending. "Might have spilled it on the gentleman's glove there."

Ned came back to his surroundings. A heavyset man, black bowlered and black bearded, had pushed his way into a narrow space beside him and dropped an expansive black-gloved fist on the bar. Ned had seen the man at the bar before.

"My fault, young sir, my fault, I assure you." The black-gloved hand slid away. "Busy time here, what say? But then it always is." The man signaled the bartender. "Might I have the privilege of offering you a drink, young sir, for the inconvenience I have caused?"

"No, thank you. I have my own glass right here." Ned pulled his drink nearer. Somewhat to his surprise it was nearly empty. Lost in his dilemma he had been unaware of drinking.

"Come, come, sir. Shank of the evening. And for a young man like yourself . . ."

Ned did not like the man. Nor was he sure of how much he had already drunk. But he would not be driven from this bright cocoon of anonymity so easily.

"No, thank you."

"Wise, very wise I'm sure. Bartender"—the black glove signaled—"two . . . your best brandy. If my young friend isn't inclined to join me, well a man can't walk on one leg, now can he?"

Ned would have backed away, but there was no place to edge. On his left a man had squeezed closer to make space for another customer. The Hoffman House bar at five o'clock of a fine November evening was no place for the uncongenial.

"A stranger in town, young man?"

"No. I live here."

"Ah. I'd have taken you for a foreigner. English?"

"I do come from England."

"Well, now. It just so happens I had a great aunt there once. Lived in Cheltenham. A lively old girl. One night, between the fog and the grog . . ." The man laughed, showing big teeth. "Or maybe you heard that one?"

"Yes, I've heard it."

"Ah yes, I took you for a young man who knows his way around town. If I can't buy you a drink, I can give you at least a little memento of our meeting." The man drained both brandies in quick swallows, reached into a vest pocket and produced a white card. "If you like a bit of gaming and something more"—he lowered one eyelid in what appeared to be a wink—"you'll find it here, lad. The best in town. Tell 'em the Parson sent you."

The man laid a two-dollar bill on the bar, swept up the change, and with surprising lightness moved away. Ned picked up the card. GEMINI CLUB, WARREN STREET. Gemini. Where had he heard that name before?

"That will be sixty cents, sir."

Sixty cents. It was not so long ago that sixty cents paid for his food for an entire day. But Ned reached into his pocket with the assurance of a man who could easily afford such an exorbitant price. Seventeen dollars still fattened his wallet. He carried that small security with him for the simple reason that he had no place to leave it. He kept it stowed in the inside pocket of his coat. Or had he put it in the hip pocket of his one pair of dove-grey trousers. He searched, trying not to show haste or panic.

"Maybe you dropped yer wallet to the floor, sir?"

"No. I didn't take it from my pocket."

He recalled with chilling sobriety the nearness of the bearded man.

"It's been stolen," he heard himself blurt.

The bartender's eyes hardened.

"This is the Hoffman House, young sir. Better look sharp for it." But it was now obvious that Ned had no wallet. The bartender leaned toward him. "Look here, young fellow, you're not fooling Joe Malachy. I seen you coming in here, playing the swell, and now not a cent left to pay the piper when you've done. Is that it? Maybe there's a gentleman of your acquaintance here who might help you. . . ." The sarcasm was heavy.

The threat dangled. Ned saw a dozen pair of eyes fasten on him, and in the mirror a row of heads turn. He had an impulse to swing at them, as he passed. But as his foot slid from the brass rail he felt something semisoft beneath his foot. He bent over. The wallet lay half under the rail, precisely where his heel would find it if he moved.

With what he hoped was a lordly gesture, Ned retrieved the wallet, opened it. It contained two single dollar bills. The other hoarded fifteen dollars, his total savings, was gone. Between the bills was thrust a torn piece of paper. "A small price, lad, for the rewards of Gemini. Good evening to you."

With all the arrogance Ned had learned in observing social manners, he pushed one of the bills at the bartender.

"Keep the change."

He did not wait to hear the bartender's mealy thank you.

The night was thick with a chill drizzle. Ned had no need of it to clear his head. He was already cold with outrage. He would go down to Warren Street, find the Gemini, and thrash the old ruffian, if need be, to get his money back. That is, if the old ruffian were there. Common sense told him that it was unlikely. The man was a sharper, a tout, picking up what extra money he could in his own way. In New York, as in London, every other man on the street might be a pickpocket. It took only practice to acquire the skill. He remembered Artie in Millie's room, then turned his mind abruptly from that long-ago guilt.

The deepening fog suited him. It muffled all movement, put human abrasiveness at a distance and let a man come closer to himself. He liked to think he could walk all night through the fog and come clear of it in the morning a different man.

"Watch where yer goin' there now. Haven't ye eyes to see a poor old woman with her chestnuts? Half-penny a bag."

He found a nickel in his pocket. He still had loose change before he had to part with his last remaining dollar.

"Keep it. Would you know where Warren Street is?"

"God's blessings on you, sir. Warren Street, you say? Now what would you be doin' down there on a night like this? Wantin' yer pleasure is it and be damned to the weather. Well, you've a fine strappin' pair of young legs now and they should carry you easy to West Broadway. You walk no further than you'd throw a stone, turn west. If I was twenty years younger, no, maybe ten, I'd take you there myself. And you'd get the best.

A hoarse cackle followed him into the night.

By now the fog enveloped him. Vague figures passed, at a distance he could not guess. Street lamps emptied their glow into mist. Even the traffic was muffled, as if the city had vanished, leaving only a shadow skeleton of itself.

A rattle of wheels, two faint lamps, and a horse's head loomed suddenly above him. He could feel the warm hay-sweet breath on his face. A hulking figure leaned down from the box.

"If you want a cab, sir, it'll do you no good askin' my horse. I'll take you where you want to go. It's my last trip. Mollie's got one blind eye, and I haven't had a morsel since breakfast."

Ned reached to the bottom of his pocket. He had three coins left beside the single dollar. He would not part with that.

"Warren Street."

"Yes, indeed!"

Warren Street, a brief ride, proved a river of mist between two rows of faceless houses. They might have been dwellings, warehouses, or mere facades in a landscape of the imagination. The cab stopped.

"Where is it you want, sir?"

"The Gemini Club."

"I figured. Right there, across the street." He pointed a whip handle to the faint outline of a door. "That'll be two dollars."

For two dollars a man could ride a cab the length of Manhattan. The cabbie was cheating him. No guardian of the law was visible, now or in broad daylight, Ned suspected. Customers to this address paid whatever was asked.

"Thirty cents is a fair price. And ten cents for the horse." Ned handed up his change. "Take it or leave it."

He heard the oath. With it a crack of the whip so close that he jumped.

"Hell's luck to you tonight, you and your kind!"

The cab disappeared, its rear lantern winking, as if with a secret knowledge of the night Ned was yet to learn.

It was not an auspicious beginning.

The entrance indicated by the cabdriver might have been any door up four steps to any brownstone front. Through filaments of mist Ned saw two exceptional details. One, a small stone alcove, the lintel carving refined, unobtrusive, of the Zodiac sign, the Gemini twins. The other, a six-inch square panel inserted at eye level in the door. Before he could find the bell, the panel had opened, casting a streak of pale greenish light on his face.

He was not prepared. What he wanted was confrontation, not silence. No sound came from behind the door, nor did it open. He realized he had been groping in vain. There was no visible doorbell.

"I was told to say the Parson sent me," he said to the silence.

The panel slid shut. Once again he was standing on an ordinary stoop, in a night smothered in fog without even the visibility to find his way home. But for the carved twin figures above the door and the white card in his pocket he would have ended the night's wretched adventure. But not without one more effort.

He lifted an angry fist to knock when the panel slid back. A circle of green light framed his face and the door swung open.

He walked boldly through a vestibule, into a generous hall, and stopped. He had been outside the most famous and exclusive gentlemen's clubs in London. Never had he imagined anything like this. The walls were paneled in polished walnut, the squares enriched with heraldic emblems. The deep carpet yielded to his step. Ned would have labeled it Oriental. The more knowledgeable would know it was Persian, its glowing jewel colors a fifteenth-century art. But it was the left-hand wall, against which a staircase curved with the grace of a lyre, that fixed the eye. The tapestry hanging there was at least fifteen feet square. It breathed life. Few who patronized the house might know the number of fine stitches to the inch, but in the ruby glow of the several lamps life-sized figures were three dimensional. The splendidly nude young god, Dionysus, held triumphantly aloft an alabaster jar from which poured a continual stream of golden coins. Clustered at his feet, his thighs, young girls offered up goblets of wine, platters of fruit, and their own special enticements. They were neither nymphs nor goddesses. They were as human as blushing flesh could make them.

So erotic, so titillating, was the scene that for an instant Ned wavered in his sense of purpose. The tapestry was not so much an ornament as a seduction that set the ambience of the Gemini Club.

An attendant stood waiting at a double door to the right.

Six feet in height, thin and spare as a heron, with the grey beaked face of an aristocrat, he might have stepped from the pages of *Burke's Peerage,* except for the uncomfortable fact of a butler's striped vest.

He bowed to Ned and slid the doors open. A heavy man behind a claw-footed desk stood up.

"So, young sir, you didn't disappoint me. I'd have given you another hour, perhaps another night. But you're here as I knew you would ultimately be. I don't misjudge people. That's my value to society. I recognize weakness, I recognize strength, and I understand predictability. I assure you if our politicians, our lawyers, our ministers practiced the same skills, the world would be a different place—pleasanter, and possibly a safer place. Sit down, young sir. A brandy? Madeira? Or perhaps we'd better have our little talk first. I noticed you haven't a full-grown drinking head yet. Sit down, young sir."

The black beard was gone, but the sharp unblinking eyes, the large white teeth were unmistakable. Ned summoned his fragmenting anger.

"I came for my money."

"Of course you did. And you shall have it. Now sit down. I dislike anyone to stand while I talk."

"I'd like to take it and go."

"Ah! Suspicious, too? That's all to the good. There it is, young sir. You can count it if you wish." He drew a narrow envelope from his pocket and dropped it on his side of the great mahogany desk. "But it will be to your advantage to stay. And to put as polite a face on it as you are capable of. You are an interesting young man. But your knowledge of the world is sadly inadequate to your ambition. Sit down!"

A chair had been drawn up on the opposite side of the desk. Fluted and graceful, it was upholstered in pristine burgundy satin, patterned with gold-thread bees. Ned glanced around. The bee motif was everywhere, woven into the carpet, emblazoned on the pillows of a long divan, carved into the back of his host's tall chair. A single bee lay embalmed in amber, a paperweight on the desk.

"Ah. You notice my bees. Napoleon's favorite. Symbol of industry, organization, and survival. I liked that. So I took it for myself." The white teeth showed for an instant. "As I took your wallet. Not that I needed it. But I had observed you. In fact, on several occasions. A young man in mediocre tailoring. At the Hoffman House bar. Your linen. So-so. Your shoes"—the round head shook—"too shiny, young sir. And of inferior quality. You had an air that said you'd own the world if you could just get your hands on it. But you were troubled. I saw that. Too troubled to finish your own glass or accept one gracefully from a stranger. Inconsistencies, young sir. Inconsistencies interest me. They are the detritus of human secrets. I decided it would be worth an evening's hour to meet you. On my terms."

The unblinking eyes fastened on something above Ned's head. The ends of the long fingers tapped gently together. The bulky man leaned back.

"Now tell me something about yourself."

Ned sprang angrily from his chair. The day's frustration had its limits. "I don't know why I should, Mr. . . ."

The large teeth showed in a momentary smile. "The Parson. Your Reverence would do nicely."

". . . I don't know who you are or what this place is, though maybe I can guess. All I know is that you stole my money and I'm here to get it back!"

"Because it's all you have?"

"Because it's mine. I'll take it now and—"

"Never reach, young sir. It reveals a certain desperation. Puts you immediately at a disadvantage. There you are. Count it. Satisfy yourself. Fifteen dollars, exactly. A full week's salary and you haven't saved anything? In debt for that fine coat on your back? And to a tolerant landlady? Grinding away merely to stay alive. Waiting for something more suited to your ambitions. A rich marriage. An inheritance from an unforeseen source. Possible, of course, but unlikely. You haven't taken the right steps. Oh, sit down! I haven't brought you here tonight to talk twigs and pennies. I believe a young man of your style and brashness could be useful to my business. I pay well to those who are."

Whether it was the headiness of the whiskey, lack of food, or the sheer relief of money in his pockets, Ned could not have said. He sat down uncertainly.

"That's better. What's your name?"

"Ned Fitch."

"When did you come from England?"

"That's my business, I'd say."

"Precisely. Where do you live?"

"I board."

"You make about ten dollars a week? Maybe twelve? At what?"

"That's my business, too."

"How would you like to make twenty a day?"

The figure took Ned by surprise. A man could be rich in a year. . . .

"Maybe more?" The Parson's voice was as friendly as it was soft.

"Wouldn't any man? If it was honest."

The Parson chuckled. "A pious thought. I like it. Though it's been my experience that when piety slides under the wheels of ambition it soon wears thin. At least we're getting on, Mr. Fitch, as I thought we would. Now what do you say to a little supper? Then we can discuss details."

Ned saw no movement but as if on cue the elderly, hollow-eyed attendant entered, nodded, and withdrew. He returned with a tray. So quickly that Ned had an uneasy sensation that in this curiously soundless stage set, he had become a puppet figure, manipulated by unseen strings. But he was hungry. The tray held a cup and saucer of fine china, a silver coffeepot and an oval plate containing a whole roast bird, truffles, and white asparagus. A dizzying repast. He raised the knife and heard the Parson's thick chuckle.

"Remove it first, Mr. Fitch."

It was a trompe l'oeil, a covered dish so skillfully made that only close inspection could tell a man that it was false. Beneath the "bird" and its trimming lay a beef stew.

"Illusion, young sir. Your first lesson. This is a house of illusion. Men come here in the illusion of hope. And pay well for it. But I am delaying you." The Parson rose. "I am an admirer of an ancient practice among the East Indian aristocracy. I believe, like them, that eating is a coarse process. Like them, I prefer to eat alone. I allow my guests the same privilege."

Soundless as a cat, he was gone.

Ned ate rapidly. The stew was as lusty as it was hot, the coffee black and strong. The attendant materialized again, as if on invisible cue to remove the tray.

Ned sat back to consider his situation. Out of this extraordinary, maddening evening, he had heard an offer of incredible wages. More than five thousand a year. He had never thought in such terms. He had dreamed of wealth in a vague way, but this was concrete, calculated. Five thousand . . . for doing what? The question sobered him. He did not trust the Parson. He had the soundest reason not to trust him. But when had he been able to trust any man, or any woman, for that matter? He had learned early that trust was a dangerous indulgence for a man who had to make his own way up the ladder. Indeed, he had trusted Dr. Hugo Lendler too far.

He looked up to see the Parson moving soundless to his desk.

"Feeling better, Mr. Fitch? Good. No man should come to a decision on an empty stomach. Leaves too much blood in the brain for clear thinking." The man resumed as if there had been no break in the dialogue.

"What I am looking for, Mr. Fitch, is an ambitious young man of well-bred appearance, cleverness of mind and"—the Parson was standing beside his chair. He was taller than Ned had realized—"most important, I may say, the ability to mingle with people and to hold his tongue. I believe you have the qualifications. What do you think?"

"I haven't walked out."

"Excellent. We can improve your manners. But you don't give much away. That suits me. Come this way."

Ned hesitated, then made his first decision. *When a way opens, follow it, boy. Go, while the Comet's on the other side of the sun.* His grandfather, not quite as daft as he would make out.

Ned followed the Parson through a rear door, up a narrow flight of stairs, and down a dimly lit corridor into a very small room that he judged was at the back of the house. The room was bare of all furniture, except a high-legged stool, a standing desk, and a shelf of clothbound ledgers. Like the stairs, the corridor and every room he had seen was deeply carpeted and richly paneled. The effect was of unabashed, assured opulence.

The Parson went directly to the rear wall. At what would be eye level to a man sitting on the stool, he slid open a panel.

"If you'll just sit here, Mr. Fitch."

The aperture was as large as a saucer. Ned found himself looking down a heavy round table, surrounded by six red leather chairs. The rest of the room was out of sight.

"Do you play poker, Mr. Fitch?"

"I have. Don't know too much about it."

"Ah, of course. Poker is not an Englishman's game. *Le poque* came to us by way of New Orleans. It's not so much a game of skill as nerve. Now over here . . ."

On the side wall, Ned peered through a similar opening. And it all became clear.

"As you see. *Chemin de fer, rouge-et-noir,* the wheel, dice, faro . . . a gentleman can satisfy every whim. Now come with me."

The place, Ned thought, must be a rabbit warren. There

was another half of it, he could guess. The Gemini were the twins.
"Well, Mr. Fitch, how do you like it?"
"What are you looking for in me, a tout?"
"You use harsh words, young sir. The Gemini Club has no need of a decoy or a lookout. Our guests number among them the wealthiest, most influential men in New York. The late Mr. T. had his special chair, number five at the table you saw. In his time, he siphoned millions from the city treasury into his own pocket. But he was a generous man in siphoning some of it on to us. He liked to play Widow Wild. Then there was Mr. G. He made a fortune cornering the gold market, thereby impoverishing thousands of honest citizens. But no man more lavish in his playing. And well, it's hardly an indiscretion to say that a former President of this nation kept his special brand of whiskey here." The Parson smiled. "My young friend, you will learn as I did that the difference between a thief and an honest man is merely opportunity."
From somewhere a bell sounded, silvery, faint.
"The house opens in an hour. I will come to the point. I see in you a man capable of sitting among such distinguished guests and carrying it off."
"Carrying what off?"
"When a man is losing heavily, you will see that he begins to win. When a man is winning too much, you will see that his luck changes."
"How would I do that?"
"You will learn."
"You want me to cheat your own customers, is that it?"
"Dear, dear, young sir. What unfortunate language you employ. In an establishment of this stature, we do everything possible to keep our guests happy."
"And if I'm caught?"
"Ah, we come to the crux of the matter. You are afraid, Mr. Fitch, is that it? You have something to hide. You stole a bit of money once or jewelry? You stabbed a man in a fight . . . ?"
"Look here, if you're trying to fix something on me, you can't do it! I've done nothing in this bloody city except try to earn an honest living. What you're asking me to do—"
"—is to improve yourself. That's all. Faster than you have apparently yet been able to do. Let me see . . ." The Parson studied him with small unblinking eyes. "Is it possible you jumped ship to stay here? Ah, I see I've hit it. I should have

guessed at once. Naturally you have no wish to come to the attention of the authorities."

The Parson put his fingertips together and shifted his gaze to some point beyond Ned.

"Among our guests is a man who likes to play faro. Obsessed with it, you might say. He comes in two or three times a week, usually around midnight. He likes to win. After a run of good luck he is always happy to take care of any little matter we may have at hand. He happens to be a deputy captain in the police force. Does that make him any less human? Not at all. One might say more understanding, more willing to help where help is needed. For twenty dollars a week, the deputy sees that any well-run brothel in the district stays open and prosperous, the public served. Not ten blocks from here, a school for girls. It is run by a French woman. But they are not your usual run of schoolgirls. Oh no. These are the children of the rich. Children the rich would not care to have known. Bastards, my friend. She takes them in, educates them, and sends them to Paris for a comfortable future. What kind of future? She does not say. She pays five hundred dollars a month for her privacy. Why not? Such obviously worthy work should continue. So you see, everybody profits and the world spins. The purpose of a true democracy, is it not? And now, young sir, I have been quite frank with you. I must ask a few essential questions. . . . Are you presently employed?"

"No."

"Where were you last employed?"

"I was a clerk for a professor."

"A professor?"

"A college professor."

"Ah. Why was your employment discontinued?"

But Ned had begun to understand the nature of his host.

"Can't make a decent living putting books on shelves, can a bloke? Not my sort of living, not my way at all."

The Parson seemed to smile at this sudden earthiness in London street talk.

"Where is the professor to be found?"

"At the college, uptown. Forty-sixth Street. Columbia, it's called."

"Ah yes, an oasis of learning. I know it well." A thick chuckle erupted. "But not for you, eh?"

Ned breathed easier. He had not mentioned Stuyvesant Square. Nor would he. He would say nothing that could possibly lead to Dr. Lendler's house, or more important, to the existence of Noel Tremont.

"I couldn't ask better, Mr. Fitch. You would run no chance of being known here. One final question. Have you any female attachment?"

"If you mean am I married, I am not."

"I mean, as I always do, precisely what I say. A female attachment."

"No."

"Curious. I would have guessed differently."

He put his hand into his coat pocket and drew it out slowly. Ned saw a torn fragment of brown watered silk.

"What the devil . . . where . . . ?"

"Your wallet, Mr. Fitch. The lady wears superior quality."

Ned was on his feet. "I want that back!"

"You say no attachment?"

Ned had not honed his wits on the rawness of poverty without learning a thing or two. He had not walked the streets of this city, mean or respectable, without seeing deceit rewarded, greed made decent. Every day had brought him confrontation of some kind, wits matched with wits merely to survive. The Parson was a fraud. He could see it now, in every careful word, every studied gesture. Perhaps a dangerous fraud. But he had sought Ned out, not the other way around. He had opened a door, dreamlike in its vision of wealth. Ned had only to keep his head.

He managed an easy, knowing grin.

"An attachment? Well, you might call it that. For an evening. That bit of silk was a souvenir. May I have it?"

The Parson smoothed the silk with lingering fingers. Then he dropped it indifferently on the desk and rose.

"I've made you an offer, Mr. Fitch. Twenty dollars a night to begin. Your salary will progress as you do. We are closed Sunday, the Lord's day." Here the Parson lifted his eyes heavenward. "And Thursday. I attend the Opera. Observe, please, that we use no full names here for the guests. As for me—Parson will do. It was my dear mother's wish that I study for the ministry. But in coming to this city I soon realized that for a man to repent his sins, he must have sins to repent. I would provide that step essential in the process of salvation."

He had reached the double doors to the hall.

"As I said, I do not make mistakes in judging human nature or I could not have survived in this, uh, line of endeavor. I believe you can be useful to me as I to you, with subsequent profit to us both. If, on the other hand, for some reason I have failed to perceive, you decide to stand on piety and poverty, my assistant will show you through the rear door into a back alley. Thereafter you will forget, if you are sensible, that you ever had this privileged view of the Gemini Club. If you accept my offer, you will, within four minutes, touch that knob on the left corner of my desk.''

Ned was alone.

Four minutes. Why not five or two or ten? Four minutes, like a boiling egg, he thought wryly. Four minutes for a man to turn a corner in his life. To clutch the sharp edge of opportunity or to stumble into a quagmire. This curious, underground world in which he suddenly found himself offered no firm meanings. Right and wrong, good and evil, flowered together in lavalike streaks, mingling the dark and the bright until a man could not tell which was which. What benefit to him if he tried? He could rot his life away as a faceless clerk and die without having lived.

The silence pulsed in his ears. He had the odd sensation that time was racing by, yet he was held, imprisoned, motionless, like the bee, spread-winged in amber.

He stood for another moment, thinking, not thinking.

Then he stepped forward and pressed the knob at the edge of the Parson's desk.

26

The narrow stairs took Dr. Lendler's breath. Another ten minutes of morning exercises, he told himself. Or an hour's less thinking about today's young heedless students who persisted in living before learning.

Actually, as he knew, it was neither. What made Dr. Lendler puff this afternoon was a burden he could neither discard nor share. So he had come on impulse to the most congenial relaxation the city offered him, the cramped parlor above the Lion's Head Bookstore, Saul Joram, Prop.

Saul was his oldest friend. They had been students in Vienna together. When Saul with a small inheritance had founded a newspaper *Die Hoffnung*, Hugo Lendler had written for it. It was a young voice of tolerance, attracting a young readership. But it had been too loud for the authorities of the rigid empire. Saul had arrived one morning to find his type cases smashed, his books and papers in shreds. He had recognized beneath the politics of opinion, the lengthening shadow of persecution.

Six months later, with his wife and son, Saul Joram had sailed for America. A year later, Dr. Lendler had arrived in New York.

After assuring himself of a teaching post, Dr. Lendler had called at the slit of a bookstore four blocks west of the college building. Here Saul Joram had established a foothold. The Lion's Head was as cluttered as any bibliophile could wish. Saul specialized in books about his new country—about American history, American literature, American politics. And one rarity for his patrons, foreign newspapers. Although they arrived sometimes two or three months after their original issue, they were eagerly bought up.

In the tiny living quarters above the Lion's Head, Dr. Lendler had found old country warmth, old family ties.

Now as he sat waiting for Saul to finish with a customer downstairs, he wondered whether he should have come at all. Saul had transferred his natural volubility from the pages of the lost *Die Hoffnung* to the glories of talk in this marvelous land. Their visits rang with free-soaring arguments. Today, however, Dr. Lendler's troubled mind clouded the easy give and take. However, he realized with an inward smile, the talk would flow, one sided or two. Perhaps that was what he most needed.

"Well, there, Hugo. No more interruptions. I've left my son Matthew in charge downstairs. Seventeen now. Maybe a few book titles should rub off on him. Times change, my friend, times change."

Saul Joram was a slight, balding man with merry eyes, a sparse fringe of hair above his ears, a high forehead, and gold-rimmed spectacles well down on his nose.

He opened a cabinet and drew out a decanter of wine, the rich, soul-savoring plum wine made by his wife, Frieda. He darted to the rear of the flat and returned with a plate of Frieda's honeycakes. It was always a disappointment to Hugo that the bustling, well-informed little woman would never join them for his visits. Only at dinner, when a wife's place was at the table, did he occasionally meet her.

Saul lifted his glass. "To your health, my friend. *Prosit!* And to living! Well, and how are affairs at the Seventh House?"

Dr. Lendler had delighted his old friend with the legend that in the early Dutch Nieuw Amsterdam, every seventh house was obliged to provide light after dark, thereby making up for the absence of both street lamps and streets. In the square named for the old Dutch governor, Peter Stuyvesant, Saul believed his friend must indeed inhabit a seventh house.

"It depends from which end of the block you begin counting." Dr. Lendler had been amused and, in a quiet way, touched. Loyalty was an increasingly fragmented commodity in this complex city.

"Affairs as usual go a little unevenly. Frau Gruen sends a message. She wishes me to beg you to bring Frau Joram with you to dinner the next time you come."

The merry eyes were veiled for an instant, but the talk remained light. "Hugo, is that estimable woman tyrannizing you again?"

"I'm afraid it's the fault of the honeycakes your wife sends me for the holy days. My housekeeper has a competitive streak. She wants to learn how to make them."

"Tell her it takes the daughter of three generations of rabbis to make honeycakes right."

"I'll tell her nothing. Not in her kitchen. Saul, would you bring Frieda next holiday?"

Saul shook his head.

"She hasn't changed. The openness of this city still frightens her. She will go no more than three blocks in any direction from this flat. Generations of living within walls without exit, of knowing she is not wanted beyond them. That she cannot forget. But she is happy enough. I do not want her upset."

The shop bell below jangled. Saul half rose, then sat down.

"I'll leave it to Matthew. That son of mine! First year in college. Good sound mind. I had hoped to see him a scholar, a teacher. Last week he came home to say that he has changed his mind. He wants to be a banker and be rich. I tell him riches of the mind don't slip through the fingers like riches in the pocket. This week he comes home to say he thinks he will change his name. To what, pray, I ask? To Jordan. He says the boys in school call him that anyway. They don't know Joram. 'Don't know the name of one of the great Kings of Israel?' I say to him. You want to change to the name of a muddy little river?"

Saul's sharp eyes twinkled through a sigh. "But he will be a banker if that's what he wants. He will change his name, too. He will have a carriage and fine horses. Why not? His history will not be my history, his memories not my memories, his years not my years. Change, my friend, is it the lifeblood of human existence? Or the unwelcome potion a man must inevitably swallow?"

"I would say it depends on how old he is."

Saul refilled the glasses, went to the kitchen, and returned with another plate of cakes. Dr. Lendler found his spirits lifting but what lay hard and tight in his mind still frozen.

The shop bell jangled below. Saul went to the window.

"Ah, that is a customer I should have seen to myself. Come look. Do you know her?"

A thin, dark-haired young woman was walking down the street in a firm but slow stride. She carried a bundle of tied-up newspapers.

"Our famous poetess, Miss Lazarus. You've read her."

Poetry was not a specialty of Dr. Lendler's but the name Emma Lazarus was known to him as to all of literary New York. Her poems appeared in newspapers, cultural journals, art magazines, ladies weeklies, and in books of her own. He had seen her at Cooper Institute, a dedicated young woman whose intensity awed her listeners almost as much as her scholarship.

"Yes, indeed," he answered. *"Songs of a Semite.* Very nice!"

"That's the trouble. Very nice. She was invited by Mr. Emerson to Concord to meet the great ones. Mr. Emerson told her she wrote with a winged pen. But she must find a purpose."

The girl turned the corner. Saul returned to his chair. "She found it with a vengeance. She has become obsessed with the oppressions in Europe. The pogroms, the poverty, the stirrings of the masses against the harshness of their lives. She comes here regularly for newspapers that will tell her more. She informed me last time that she had been asked to write something for the Liberty Statue when they finally put it up somewhere. She goes down regularly to Madison Square to see that gigantic arm holding the torch."

Saul chuckled. "I think she is the only one in the city who can imagine the thing three hundred feet up in the sky. But she will write something and it will be remembered." His voice sobered. "But fate, my friend, has a cruel way sometimes with rare talent. Emma Lazarus is not well. She will die young. Her parents want her to give up her work. That, of course, she will not do. We can all pray that she will live long enough to see her words in granite on that enormous statue, if that is what is to happen. She is trapped by a perversity of fate, I'd say. As we all are."

He picked up the decanter. Dr. Lendler held up a restraining hand. "Enough today, my friend."

"Ach, as Frieda says, I talk too much." He glanced shrewdly at his guest. "Tell me, Hugo, about yourself. Your young Englishman. Is he coming along as you hoped?"

It was the subject Dr. Lendler wanted both to avoid yet lift from his mind. He decided he would do neither.

"He has left my employment."

"Ja, so. When?"

"A week ago. He wrote me a letter announcing he had found other work. Frau Gruen told me he had seemed quite upset the afternoon before. She accused me of being too severe with him."

"You, Hugo?" Saul chuckled. "But he is young. Books can be dull. He wants to make more money?"

"That, too, I suspect." Now that he was here, Dr. Lendler found himself unable to share or even allude to the matter in his mind. He might admit to failure but he would admit to no one the matter of the cane. He had found it misplaced on the shelf, the newspaper wrapped awkwardly around it, and, on closer inspection, had discovered the label of Elias Monk removed. It was living evidence that Ned had been where he had no right to be. Yet he knew, he alone, perhaps, that Ned had committed no crime at Mrs. Restell's house. Why he had been in that house, was the only mystery.

"Yet your theory about the young man was interesting, Hugo . . . that you could take an untutored but intelligent young man and educate him through mind control. That was your motive, yes? I had great hope for it."

"I haven't disproved it. Ned soaks up learning like a sponge. I believe he can go far. Will go far. But I'm afraid he has yielded to impulse. Or too hasty ambition."

Dr. Lendler hoped that would satisfy his friend. As for his real motive, that was another matter. He had probed it unsparingly after Ned's defection. Motive behind motive, wave behind wave. He had come to the truth, as he always must about himself. His motive had been nothing more or less than a desire—no, a need—to understand the young man on whom Noel Tremont had bestowed such radiance he had inadvertently witnessed on a spring day that now seemed so long ago.

The afternoon was nearly spent by the time Dr. Lendler dismissed his cab at Lexington Avenue. He liked to enter the tranquility of Stuyvesant Square on foot. He liked to look up at the solid old church in its somber stewardship. *May the Lord make His countenance to shine upon you and give you peace. . . .* The ancient Hebrew benediction was spoken within these same walls every Sunday.

Were we all so different?

No, Dr. Lendler told himself as he walked along the north side of the Square, men do not differ, not in hope, not in humanity, not in aspiration. Only in the burden each one is destined to carry, born of his own unique spirit. Therein lay the separateness, the loneliness, the burdens of each man, each woman, in the long walk through life.

He thought with gentle amusement of that fine, aging gentleman in Leopoldsville, who was his father. "You want to grow tall, my son. You never will. That is your burden. But let me tell you what the Lord once did about burdens. There was a certain village where everyone complained. So one day the Lord told them if they were tired of their troubles, they could bring them, each one of them, to the village square and leave them there. Everybody did and everybody felt fine. But, of course, that left a whole mound of trouble right in the center of the village. That, said the Lord, is an unsightly mess. You'll have to get rid of it. So each one of you must take one burden away with you." His father would pause, lift a solemn forefinger. "Hah, Hugo, you know what happened? In the end each man chose his own burden to carry home."

All this brought Dr. Lendler almost to the end of the block, and number 269.

"Dr. Lendler!"

He had been unaware of the cab stopping ahead of him, of Noel Tremont descending, carrying boxes. One of them, absurdly small and round, had slipped from her hand and rolled to his feet.

He retrieved it with a bow.

"Dear Dr. Lendler! Thank you!" Her smile was quick and, it seemed to Dr. Lendler, too bright, her face thin. He had not seen her since late spring. He knew that she had been ill but he had not expected such a change. Another flashing smile. "How do you always manage to be just where I need you?" She held the box up by its silken cord. "Can you guess what this is?"

"I should guess a small teacup."

"Wrong! It's a new hat. Very fashionable. It's for husband catching. Irresistible. Every girl must have a husband, shouldn't she? If I wore it for you do you think you would ask me to marry you?"

The brittle teasing did not become Noel any more than the shallow little laugh that followed. Noel made an unlikely flirt. But he could not deny a sudden thrust of pain.

"No, I would not. I'm much too old to ask any girl to marry me. But I think that the right man, when you find him, will not care what hat you wear."

"Oh, you're very wrong about that, Dr. Lendler. A hat is very important. The ladies all tell me so. Besides, what is a right man? Or a wrong man? I don't believe there is really such a difference. If there is, how can a poor simple girl tell?"

"You know very well, young lady. If you don't, your mother should have told you. I'm sure she did."

"Oh, she did. She did. Besides, I was only practicing. I'm being quite social these days and if I can't try the proper flightiness on friends how shall I ever learn?" A shadow crossed her face, her tone changed. "I have missed the duets, Dr. Lendler."

"So have I, my dear. But the pianoforte is always in tune. And I can still find true A on my old fiddle."

The small laugh was genuine. "Oh, I did love the music. I loved so many things! Perhaps someday—I don't know."

To his acute ears there was a hint of unsteadiness in the chatter. To his keen sight, there were new shadows under her eyes. Still she was Noel, the young woman who at an unconquerable distance had become a part of his inner life, seducing his scholarly detachment and turning him from a book-walled, middle-aged professor into a kind of uncomfortable conspirator.

He disliked such a role. But he knew he would change nothing if he could continue to serve her, an all but invisible—what? Guardian angel? More likely Cerebus or Caliban, that helpless spirit of the dark.

He was aware of looking at her closely.

"You profited by your holiday at the shore, I see." It was quite apparent she had not.

"Oh, yes. I love the sea. It . . . it swallows everything, doesn't it? As you see I'm quite well now. No more coddling. I'm a changed woman!"

"I hope not, my dear. But I am glad indeed to hear of your good health."

"Dear Dr. Lendler." She did what she had never done before. She brushed his cheek with a light kiss. "Thank you for humoring me!"

She dashed up the steps.

He was not yet ready to turn the corner to the brown silence of his own house. Afternoon light still filled the Square, and there was a fading warmth in the air. The sun had not begun its drop behind the church towers.

He turned into the park, walking slowly through the dry leaves until he came to an inconspicuous bench where someone had discarded a newspaper. He sat down and opened it. It would not divert his thoughts, but it might serve to conceal them.

Noel! What had happened to her? What in the name of all things sensible was she up to? "Husband catching" she'd called it. Not that way, Noel my child. Never that way!

Again the image returned of the bearded man who had governed his boyhood. "When you cannot solve a problem, my son, let your thoughts float, and leave the problem in the depths of your mind. That is where God walks, my boy. When you do not interfere."

Dr. Lendler could smile now at the old-fashioned phrases. But he knew their truth. He let God walk while his mind drifted idly to honeycakes, to the hour just past, and, oddly, to the young poetess, Miss Lazarus. He had heard her read her poem for the Liberty Statue to a room of admiring students, her tired voice trembling with emotion.

"Send me your struggling masses, the wretched refuse of your shores. . . ."

"No!" he had wanted to shout. What man or woman ever saw himself or herself as refuse? Didn't every human being, impoverished or oppressed as he might be, have his own self-dignity? Didn't it take courage, lonely courage, within his own soul to leave all that was known for all that was unknown? Wretched as they were, didn't they bring each one a gift as yet unnamed? Dr. Lendler had hated the poem as much as he had felt compassion for the ardent young woman who wrote it.

As he sat on the bench, avoiding what was deepest in his mind, words idly took shape. "Bring me your ancient wisdoms and your faith . . . your dreams of youth, your steadfastness of age. . . ."

Dr. Lendler drew an ever-present notepad and pencil from an inner pocket. He was an old fool, he told himself, but there it was, words flowing through his head. "Bring me your strengths, your talents and your pride—your visions that have yet to find a stage"—his pencil hovered—"bring loyalty and breadth to these new shores, your hearts as well as needs, give them to me. Here you shall stand as tall as any man. . . ."

Unconsciously, he straightened his own shoulders. He finished quickly. "My gift to you is priceless liberty."

He read his scribblings twice, then tore the pages and crumpled them. The young poetess, Miss Lazarus, was already doomed. It was not for him to trouble her impassioned songs.

The sun had reached the tops of the church towers. Much of the park was in shadow. It was time to go. Dr. Lendler gathered his voluminous old coat, then abruptly sank back into it. He picked up the discarded newspaper at his side and opened it.

Ned Fitch was walking slowly, yet purposefully, on a side path, his direction due north.

He had not seen Ned since his defection. Nor had he wanted

to. The questions he had for the young man were better left unasked. The Restell case was closed. Except for the evidence of the cane, Dr. Lendler had found no way to associate the brash young man with what had happened in the Restell house that last night. Yet, why had Ned been there? How had he gained entrance? And, most important, what had he seen? What did he know? *Who could he hurt?*

Dr. Lendler half rose, thought better of it. Ned had not seen him. In fact, the young man had looked neither left nor right. He was exceedingly well dressed, his face in the half-light looked older. Whatever prosperity he was finding did not seem to have lightened his step. He had, thought Dr. Lendler, the air of a man who had found a better place and was not comfortable with it.

He watched Ned through the bare trees and saw him stop, almost at the iron fencing directly opposite number 269. Dr. Lendler remembered an unexpected visit Walter Tremont had paid recently. Remembered Walter's seriousness.

"Hugo, these are not matters I make my concern. This time I must. Adrienne tells me she has learned the young man, your English clerk, has left your employment."

"That is true."

"Then I can say frankly I am very glad. Otherwise he would have been a source of considerable embarrassment. Did you know that he made an improper and inappropriate call on Noel while she was away earlier this summer?"

"No, I did not."

"I was incensed that a young man would presume to call on Noel without requesting permission of the family. If he had come to my door again, I should certainly have been forced to deal with him quite severely. I know how you share our family interest in Noel's welfare. Indeed I'm happy to tell you that a young man who made Noel's acquaintance at Cooper Institute has written me for permission to call on her. He dined with us last week. I find nothing objectionable about him. I want Noel settled and happy as any father does."

"Yes, Walter." Inwardly Dr. Lendler had resented it all. Two old men reshaping youth. And Noel . . . Noel.

A blue mist was rising from the dampness of the park. Dr. Lendler glanced toward the Tremont house. Ned was still standing motionless at the park fence. In a little while the lamplighter would be making his rounds. Already a house light or two flickered here and there. As abruptly as he had appeared, Ned turned and walked toward the west gate, the gate across the street from the church.

But the pantomime was not over. A slight figure, with a film of scarf over her hair, was entering the east gate of the park. With light, careful steps she turned into a transversing path. Dr. Lendler held his newspaper higher with a sense of guilt. Ned and Noel both here? Lovers missing each other by some malicious fate? Or a separation too heavy to be endured? And he, a reluctant witness, sitting as if shackled, humbled by the intensities that seemed to propel these two figures.

Ned had not left the park. Instead he moved slowly, aimlessly, among the trees. Noel's steps had led her to a bench, her white face catching all the lingering light as she stared, unseeing, into the dusk. Then she rose and walked again, drifting to the west gate he had passed.

Wait! The trees, the dusk, the rising wind stirring the dead leaves seemed to call. Wait! Even Dr. Lendler, with all logic and common sense on his side, felt the urgency. Wait! But they were far from him now and from each other. They had become phantoms, seeking each other in the deepening dusk. As if all lovers, all passions of the heart were playing out in these two, a shadowy *pas de deux* among the trees, passing, parting, coming closer, passing to make at last the breathless discovery of each other.

Dr. Lendler shivered. At least he had done no harm. He had lost sight of Ned. His last glimpse of Noel, ghostlike, still within the west gate. He heard his own wish. "Wait, Noel! It will come right for you!"

Darkness filled the now empty park.

As night deepened a world away, in the black alley behind the Gemini Club, Ned, his face harsh, entered the familiar realm of the Parson, dispenser of vast illusions and vaster deceits.

At her window, from where she had first seen him, Noel stood another moment, only her eyes alive as she drew the curtain against the dark.

Dr. Lendler, on his leather couch, lay staring at nothing, in that soundless vacuum of foreboding where no bird sings.

27

Kitty Merriman, adrift in pink satin ribbons, negligee, pillows, and coverlet, sat cherishing the midmorning comfort of coffee in bed. It was an important hour. This was when she read the morning papers—that is, the society columns—made notes, in an unstudied hand, of names and events and took a perspective on what might be useful.

She knew that the old, aristocratic New York names would not be there. No lady of true breeding would permit her name or her family's to appear in print. But Kitty was not interested in what was old. She followed the new, larger fortunes, in their new uptown grandeur.

At this season of the year her morning study was especially concentrated. The Merrimans did not receive one of Miss Phoebe Bliss's mauve invitations. Kitty regularly dismissed the omission with a toss of her black curls.

"I don't evny you, Adrienne. You have to go. Walter I know wouldn't miss it. But how dull. So unfashionable. Poor Miss Bliss, I understand, only invites people she knows won't refuse. We have a box for the opening of the new revue. They say it's quite naughty. Everybody in town will be there."

This morning, within days of Miss Bliss's coming soiree, Kitty scanned the mail once more. There would be no likelihood after this late date of finding the square mauve envelope.

She returned to the society pages.

Suddenly she sat bolt upright, the cup in her hand splashing coffee on pink satin. She jumped from the bed, furiously tinkling the silver bell on her side table.

The maid lumbered upstairs. She served downstairs, ordinarily. It took her a few moments to climb to the second floor for temporary transformation to Kitty's personal maid. Kitty saw no reason why a girl who had only to wait on table, clean silver, polish furniture, and keep the downstairs clean should sit idle the rest of the time.

"Herta, has Mr. Merriman left for his office?"

"Ja."

Kitty sighed in exasperation. But this was no time for servant training.

"Fill my bath. And take out my dark blue twill suit, the seal cape and muff and, oh, yes, the hat with the dove wings."

"Dove—winks?"

"Never mind. I'll find it myself. Hurry."

Kitty returned to the newspaper and read the item a second disbelieving time.

> Mr. and Mrs. Walter Charles Tremont of Stuyvesant Square take pleasure in announcing the engagement of Mr. Tremont's only daughter, Miss Noel Elizabeth Tremont, to Mr. Clarence Herman Briggs, son of Mrs. Herman Briggs and the late Mr. Herman Briggs of Beacon, New York. The wedding is planned . . .

Kitty dropped the newspaper. Her hands were shaking.

An hour later she was at the door of number 269 Stuyvesant Square, finger pressed on the bell.

Annie-Mae was prompt and smiling.

"Is Mrs. Tremont home?"

"Yes, Mrs. Merriman. She's upstairs."

"And Miss Noel?"

"She's in her room, I think."

"Tell Mrs. Tremont I'll be up immediately. I'll go and see Miss Noel first."

"Yes, Mrs. Merriman." Annie-Mae could never repress delight. "Oh, ma'am, isn't it lovely, Miss Noel and all?"

"I have no idea."

For a moment Kitty stood alone in the hall. Catching a glimpse of thirty-six of herself in the bull's-eye mirror, she steadied her breath. She must not let indignation age her face.

It occurred to Kitty the house had a curious emptiness. After such an announcement there should be flowers everywhere, the silver tray on the hall table loaded with visitors' cards, an air of bustle, of excitement. Instead there was only silence.

She found Noel sitting cross-legged on the floor of her bedroom, surrounded by newspapers, and what seemed to be mementos, dance cards, souvenirs. A wastebasket stood nearby.

"Noel! No, don't get up. I came at once, as soon as I read it. Who on earth is he? I really think I should have been told. I've taken the place of a mother to you for too long to be treated like this. Not that I was at all prepared for that responsibility, but I saw it as my duty although Henry always said I looked much too young. But I have always seen myself as your closest friend, have I not? Can't you imagine how shocked, how stunned, I was to read—how could I not have been told that a young man was calling on you with the object of matrimony? Who is he, Noel? Where on earth did you meet him?"

Kitty was doing exactly what she had not intended. She reminded herself again that outrage was never worth its wrinkles.

Noel sighed and rose. She gathered up the newspapers spread before her, crumpled them, and jammed them into the wastebasket. There was never any real need to answer Kitty. She asked so many questions, one had only to wait and she would find her own answers. But Noel would be kind if she could not be honest.

"I am sorry, Aunt Kitty, if you are distressed. Mr. Briggs did not come calling on me with the object of matrimony. He sat beside me in a class in the Principles of Philosophic Thought, at Cooper Institute, walked with me one afternoon over to Gramercy Park, and wrote me a lovely note asking me if I could be interested in a missionary school in Amoy, China. He had been offered a position but he had to be a married man. It was not easy for Mr. Briggs to talk of these things but I understood. I accepted."

Kitty was staring at her. "Amoy, *China?* Where is Amoy, China?"

"On the other side of the world, Aunt Kitty. Clarence explained to me. When we are sitting down to breakfast here, they are having lunch the next day in Amoy."

"I see. That's where you intend to go?"

"That's where Mr. Briggs is going. But he must be married to be accepted for the position. It's quite understandable."

Kitty was never quite sure of Noel, or at ease with her. At this moment, Noel's face was bland as milk, her tone held a slight edge of—what was it? Amusement? Obstinacy? Kitty gave her a long, probing look and came to essentials.

"Has he any money?"

"Oh goodness no, Aunt Kitty. He serves God, the church, and the uneducated. It doesn't take money."

Details were easier.

"When do you plan to marry this—this gentleman?"

"He's not what you mean by gentleman. But he's very polite. And sincere. The wedding will be on January tenth."

"I . . . I don't know what to say, Noel." Kitty marshaled the only forces she knew. "I hope you'll be happy, of course. I . . . goodness, if you're going to wear a white gown and walk down a church aisle you'd better get some color in your face. You look more like a ghost than a bride."

Noel's reply was gently tolerant. "I am not going to wear a white gown and walk down a church aisle. The ceremony will be performed here, in the parlor. I have told Adrienne she will have nothing to do or to worry about. I shall wear a traveling suit. Mr. Briggs and I shall leave directly after the ceremony with Miss Eloise and Miss Euphamia Briggs, Mr. Briggs's older sisters. They are coming to Amoy with us."

"With you?" Unexpectedly, Kitty's bright shrewd eyes misted. She had never been without sentiment. She put an arm around Noel's shoulders. "Noel, are you sure this is what you want?"

There was a quick step, a light rustle, and Kitty had gone.

She would have to get used to a great deal of this, Noel told herself. But not for too long.

On the floor below, in Adrienne's little yellow-and-white sitting room, Kitty sank into the divan and let her anger explode.

"How could you, Addie? How could you have let this happen? A nobody. Poor as a church mouse. You must have been out of your mind! If you didn't care about Noel, didn't you have any thought of your own position? Or mine?"

Adrienne, languid on the chaise lounge, raised cool eyes. "Yours, Kitty?"

"Of course, mine. After all I've done for you, all I've taught you, haven't you learned anything? Don't you see? Noel was your trump card, as Henry would put it. I got you married off to Walter and look where you are now. But Walter is getting along. When he dies you'll have only what he leaves you. No social connections, no rich family connections you can count on. If Noel married the right man—and she could have, it doesn't seem to me she cared whom she married—you'd have those connections. My God, Adrienne, do I have to spell everything out? What good is she to you as a schoolteacher's wife in Amoy, China? And you might have considered me! I've worked and planned all my life to be comfortable and rich. Because I knew what being poor meant. Now, when everything is going so well, you let this happen.

Didn't you tell Walter how ridiculous it is? You could have refused to have Mr. whatever-his-name-is. You could have rounded up a suitable young man, introduced the girl. Goodness knows, I've been trying! Why didn't you talk to me? I'd have helped you."

Adrienne looked into the distance.

"Addie, I never counted on you to do more than to play your part. You remember when you first walked into the manager's office and didn't get the singer's job? What were you? A mousy music teacher. Too thin, too cold. I felt sorry for you. But you looked like a lady. I thought you could be one. You liked the background I invented, English parents, English schooling. You liked being the widow of a young lieutenant in the Queen's Guard. Your late husband, what was he really, Addie, a hod carrier or a no-good gambler?"

Kitty was flinging the words like stones. Bitterness turned her voice shrill, her face pinched and drawn into deep lines.

"You should have thought of those things, Addie. You should have thought of me. You had no right to let this happen behind my back. You sit there, barely listening, comfortable, rich, well taken care of. Well, I won't let you. You will do something about this, for my sake. You owe me this. You will stop this marriage. You will go to Walter and insist on it. You will tell Noel you are mistress of this house and you intend that she will do as you say. Addie, do you hear me? You are to stop this marriage at once!"

Kitty had exhausted herself, the futile plans of her life drifting in ashes around her.

Adrienne had not moved, her cool perfection seemed frozen. She turned her head and looked directly at Kitty.

"What would you say if I told you I do not want this marriage stopped? I would have the wedding tomorrow if it were possible."

To Kitty's astonishment, Adrienne's light blue eyes misted. Then the light voice turned harsh with something Kitty had never heard in Addie before. Something near desperation.

"I want that girl out of this house. I want never to see or hear of Noel Tremont again. Do you want to know why, Kitty? You shall know. You talk about what you've done for me. But do you know anything about me? In all your plans have you ever mentioned the word 'love'? I've never known it. Not real love. I thought I was incapable of it. One of those women born to go through life without feeling. I know better. Kitty, have you any idea what my life has been the last six months? Walter forgave me for running off to Europe. But he asked one thing. You pay for forgiveness, Kitty. He asked me, as he put it, to take Noel under my wing. Do you know what that meant? The girl on my hands every day, every evening. No time for—for any life of my own. But Walter's in politics now, away a lot. Noel will be gone. Out of this house, out of my life, completely. I shall . . . find my own peace."

There was little more to say. Adrienne said it.

"I am grateful, Kitty. You must believe that. Grateful to you for all you have done for me. But grateful most of all that the time has come to—refuse it. But I will make you one promise. I will persuade Walter that Noel must have the most beautiful wedding we can manage. And you, Kitty, will fill the church with everybody you wish."

Kitty walked unseeing out of 269 Stuyvesant Square. She knew as surely as she knew defeat that a chapter was ending. It was not what Adrienne had said that was significant. It was what Adrienne had not said. All of Kitty's well-tuned woman's instincts told her that there was another cipher in the equation. Had Adrienne taken a lover?

Kitty's natural ambience was optimism. By the time she reached home her spirits had rebounded. Not everything was lost. There had been a shift of currents beneath the surface. But the surface would, must, remain smooth.

Henry surveyed his wife, almost smugly, down the length of the dinner table.

"So Walter told me."

"Did you see Walter today?"

"I thought it sensible to call on him. You see, there's the matter of Noel's dowry. When we were a bit strapped last spring, you remember, he drew on it to make me a loan. Of course, nobody then thought Noel was ever going to marry. As you know, instead of repaying it directly, I invested it. West Shore Railroad stocks. Very sound. The shares have fallen a bit, but when that railroad is built, Noel will be a very rich woman. And we'll share in the profits."

"What did Walter say?"

"I think he was relieved to know the money was invested. He said Noel wouldn't have any use for it anyway. Not in China."

Kitty regarded her husband thoughtfully.

"What if the railroad isn't built?"

"Where did you get that idea?"

"Senator Walsh. He told me Mr. Morgan is opposing it."

"Stop worrying your pretty head, Kitty, about things you

don't understand. If the railroad isn't built, Noel loses her dowry. What the hell! We'll be out of debt anyway, my pet, and she'll be in China.''

The day was not ending badly.

Kitty indifferently let Henry into her bed, endured his heavy desire. At last in tired freedom her reliable instinct for survival stirred. Her mind began to race.

A wedding to plan. A reception. A careful guest list. Noel in white. That thin, strained face . . . in unbecoming white. Noel a bride.

It would, in a way, be a relief to them all.

28

The path leading to the rear of the house had the unkempt look of coming winter. Noel chose it to avoid the sordid alley in front. The old curate, crossing to the vestry, had merely nodded piously and asked no questions. Indeed, he had seemed not only to condone but to conspire with her need of secrecy.

She opened the gate into the garden, remembering with a surge of warmth that gentle green enclave of sunlight and magic that still lived deeply in her mind. But the hard light of the afternoon drained it of color. The ivy clung to the walls in sere tatters. The willow tree bent yellowed branches to a chill earth. The bushes, like the grass, had browned—the gravel walks were littered with their small dead leaves. No bright ribbons danced, no young laughter etched the still air. Quiet lay everywhere, the shroud of summer past.

The brick house, looming beyond, had the close containment of a fortress.

All of which Noel might have expected had she thought sensibly about it. She had postponed this visit as long as she dared, giving Madame Ducharde time to read of her engagement and to know that Miss Tremont had kept her word. It was also Posie's name day, November seventeenth, the day she had been promised a visit.

The maid who answered her knock was unknown to her. Madame would receive her in the upstairs sitting room, which in an unexplained way, was something of a relief. The room she remembered as pillowed and gracious. Talk would be easier.

As she climbed the main staircase, it seemed to Noel that the house was even more quiet than the garden. But she had come at the hour of rest. The singing, the lively little games, would come later.

"Come in, Miss Tremont."

Madame Ducharde was seated in her tall carved chair, the curtains behind her drawn. A fire brightened the room. Tea in silver service lay ready on a side table. Madame wore the same grey nunlike draped gown in which Noel had first seen her, as if summer and winter were one. There was one difference. From a heavy metal chain around her neck hung a black cross larger than one would expect. Occasionally the long thin fingers caressed it.

Madame waited until tea was poured and the maid gone.

"First, Miss Tremont, I think we should clarify an awkward subject. I understand that, despite my advice, you attended the trial of Jenny Crater."

"Yes, Madame, I did."

"I also understand that you testified for Jenny on the witness stand."

Noel waited. There had been no account of the trial in the newspapers. She had searched for it. Her father, to her infinite relief, had apparently learned nothing about it. Not even one of David's lurid cartoons had appeared. The same vacuum that had followed Carrie Restell's death had swallowed poor little Jenny Crater.

"You are wondering, I presume, Miss Tremont, how I knew. I must tell you it is my concern to know whatever has to do with Carrie Restell. There are always ways. I am grateful at least that you preferred perjury to submission. Perjury is man-made. We, you and I—and others—live according to a higher law. Do you wish to say anything about it?"

"I have nothing to say. I went back to the prison the week after Jenny's trial. They would tell me nothing. Nothing . . . as if she had disappeared."

"Jenny was not in the prison, Miss Tremont. Two nights after the trial she hanged herself in her cell." Noel gasped. Madame seemed not to have heard her. "Mistakes bring their own resolutions. If one chooses a different path, a different morality, one must be sure of the moral stamina to pursue it."

"Poor darling Jenny. . . ." But Noel sensed she must let her shock, like the tragedy, like her choking sense of loss, fade into the imperviousness of the room. Distant, self-absolved, Madame sat. When she finally spoke she was blandly conversational.

"Well, Miss Tremont, you are looking better."

"I'm well, thank you."

"And you are enjoying yourself these days?"

Enjoyment was not the subject of the visit, as Madame well knew. Was it possible this tall gaunt woman, with her rigid sense of business, her calculating detachment, had not read of Noel's engagement? By her own admission, the woman read the papers daily and thoroughly.

"Ah, Miss Tremont, why should you not enjoy yourself? When one is young, there is always a quickening of the pulses at this time of year. The balls, the new gowns, the sleighing parties, the beaux, the invitations to Court, and all the laughing, the scheming, the sighing. . . ." She gave a wraith of a smile, and Noel thought, as she had thought before, it must once have been an enchanting smile.

"That has hardly been my life, Madame—"

"Nor mine!" The words came like the crack of a whip. The smile was gone. "You have been more fortunate than I, Miss Tremont."

The fire crackled in the silence. Pleasant as it was for the moment, Noel told herself she must get the matter over with and settled. Posie was somewhere in this house. She longed for the sight of her.

"Madame—"

But Madame spoke simultaneously.

"You have brought the tuition, Miss Tremont?"

"You read then of my—my engagement?"

"I presumed that was the purpose of your visit. You do not have it?"

"Madame, my father is an old-fashioned man. He has promised me my dowry on the day before my wedding."

"And that is when?"

"January tenth."

In the bleak light, Madame Ducharde looked even older than Noel might have guessed.

"I would have preferred payment before the first of the year."

"My father asked me to wait until after Christmas to be married."

Madame lifted an impatient hand.

"Miss Tremont, little Elizabeth is a bright, lovely child. She has done well with us. She is worthy of the best we can do for her. I have kept her longer than I can afford. If funds are not available—"

"They will be, Madame!"

"Then our arrangement will be this. As soon as the funds are in your hands you will notify me. I will give you the name of the bank where you will make your deposit, and the number of the account. A concealed account. It is for your protection, Miss Tremont. You will give me a bank draft. What is the sum you intend to pay?"

All passion, all emotion, had drained from the woman as if winter had laid its coming chill on her as on her garden.

"I will pay the full amount, Madame. For Posie's board and schooling, through the convent in Paris, her debut, and dowry. I wish to do it this way because I—I may not be on hand to make the second payment. We, uh, Mr. Briggs is to teach at a mission in China."

It was not possible to read the stiffened face.

"I see. Nevertheless, our agreement, Miss Tremont, is for the first payment of five thousand dollars to be delivered to me, it is to be hoped, before January first. At the very latest, I repeat, at the very latest it must be here by January ninth."

"Yes, Madame Ducharde."

Madame rose.

"You have made the correct decision, Miss Tremont. I bid you—"

"Madame, I would like to see my daughter now."

If she had been counting she would have heard the clock tick four times.

"But the children are resting. After that they have their music classes."

"But this is her name day. November seventeenth. You said—"

"You were promised name day, Miss Tremont, after Elizabeth had been properly enrolled in school. That has not yet happened."

"Madame!" Noel hated herself for begging. "I must see her. I must talk to her . . . just once!"

The Frenchwoman's face hardened to the sarcophagus mask Noel had first seen.

"For her sake? Or yours? I ask that because it is a question you have not asked yourself. Elizabeth has been here nearly six months. During all that time she has never asked for you. She has never spoken the curious name 'Mistaffy.' For her, her mother is happy in heaven with the angels. You are part of all that she is mercifully forgetting, the wretched drudgery of her first years."

You're wrong, wrong! Noel heard the words inside her. It wasn't like that for Posie. She had love . . . the countryside . . . the great river . . . the walks . . . Posie's hand in hers. . . .

"I am not a harsh woman, Miss Tremont. But I have lived

a long time. I have acquired some wisdom and long vision. You have made the right, the only decision. Do not look back. You will know moments of regret, of second thoughts, of bitterness, even toward me. You will despise yourself. But you will go on. Because your purpose is honorable. Because you will learn as I have that sacrifice is noblest when it is hidden. You will go and God will walk with you. You are, Miss Tremont, not the first woman to go to her marriage bed without love."

Madame left her tall chair. Noel was dismissed. She found herself alone, descending the wide stairs into the dim oppressive quiet.

Then she heard them, shards of sudden light in the gloom above her, the burst of small voices, laughter, the quick patter of steps. The children. Posie would be among them. Noel knew the house, she had only to run up the stairs, find her child, hold her for one quick moment. She turned. At the head of the stairs, taller than her own shadow, stood Madame Ducharde. She wore a half smile.

"Good day, Miss Tremont."

In the lane Noel turned only once to look back at the house, its curtains drawn, its windows sightless, its heart, if any, invisible.

A cold river wind slapped her cheek, a reminder of reality. She would walk home, walk until balance returned, until the comforting shawl of common sense warmed her body. She would walk until the older woman's words no longer stung. Her purpose honorable? Where was honor when she had been left without choice? Where was pride when the gold-and-garnet ring had been slipped on her left hand? From here, every step she took would be a deceit, every word she uttered a lie.

If God walked with her, she thought defiantly, He would need patience and a pair of stout boots.

The salt wind off the river swung to the east. The sun was sinking, blood red, into shreds of sullen cloud. Traffic was beginning to clog up in its usual late-day standstill. Yet as she walked, she felt, as always, buoyed by the very strength of the city. From Varick Street she followed West Broadway into Broadway. She might have taken the quieter side streets. Today she needed the full stream of life, of hurrying people, the cacophony of wheels and shouts, blurring into a wall around her. Gradually her own inner turbulence was subsiding, into a false calm born, like the hurricane eye, of emptiness.

"Noel!" At the crossing of Twelfth Street and Fifth Avenue, a round cheerful woman in an expensive suit thrust a leaflet into her hand. "We read about your engagement! How lovely! We all wish you happiness! Will you be here in the spring for our conference?" Her clear voice lifted. "Rights for Women! We want the vote!" Something passed her shoulder and splashed on the sidewalk. Noel could smell the rottenness. There was a jeering shout. The woman turned warmly. "Don't mind, Noel! Be happy, dear! Be happy!" The spring. Where would she be in the spring?

At the Academy of Music on Irving Place, she slowed. She was nearing home and not quite ready for it. She loved the fine old opera house. How often she had sat inside, losing herself in floods of music. Once she had gone with Dr. Lendler. He had sat stiff and remote and not asked her again. Her father's friend, the kindliest man she had ever known. Yet walled from her by something mysterious, she had never understood. She would miss him.

As she passed, she thought of Adrienne with a smile. Adrienne's carefully arranged "opera nights," her father slumping into a doze. Adrienne announcing prettily that next season they would have a box, like the Schermerhorns, the Minturns, the Van Renssalaers, tossing the names off lightly, knowing full well that in the whole house there were only eighteen boxes, all held like bank vaults by the oldest families. There would have to be a brand-new opera house to accommodate all the come-latelies.

The future again . . . empty of herself.

At Seventeenth Street she turned east to Stuyvesant Square.

"And the top of the afternoon to you, Miss Tremont!"

One of her favorites, Nully, the cat meat man. She could still hear her mother, "Noel, get the scraps, Nully's at the back door!" Nully was getting old, his face redder, the wen on the side of his veined nose a little larger, his laugh uninhibited by three missing front teeth, but his sharp eyes still danced with the joy of his dismal days.

Noel gave him her warmest smile of the day.

"How are you, Nully?"

"Couldn't be better, Miss, thank ye. Sure and it is a fine lass you've got in your Annie-Mae!" Nully always took the circuitous route. "Hasn't she half filled me pail now with lights, livers, and wings for me beauties. And in the way of tellin' me you're to be felicitated, my lady. All in the paper, too, I understand. I would have known, but for the fine print those divils be usin' to blind a man's eyes so he won't know what the dirty politicians are doin' next. And she's after tellin' me you'll be goin' halfway round the world to live, and I tellin' her you'll be takin' the sun and stars with you. But it's your happiness I'm wishin' to you, my lady, and the soft days for you both.''

Nully shifted on his peg leg. It was the private belief of the neighborhood that the thump of that wood appendage brought every cat in Manhattan to Nully's path, while the scraps in his pail relieved them of any need to catch mice.

Noel found a little-girl delight as two or three shrewd-eyed felines now appeared, tails straight up, legs stiff in the ancient heritage of territorial cats.

''I'll be off, Miss Tremont, me beauties are trailin' me already. But I'll be goin' first to Bridgie, the baker's cat. She's after havin' six new ones. I tell that Eyetalian, Mr. Spudomi, that no nursin' mither can live on flour paste. God's blessin' go with you, me lady.''

Noel turned into Stuyvesant Square, never more welcoming it seemed to her than on this late November afternoon. The sky, silvered above, burned in red and purpled streaks behind the dark church towers. The rows of well-kept houses, aloof in summer, were now visible through the bare tree branches, laced in ink against the pewter light. The Square drew closer to itself, neighbor to neighbor, at this time of year. Here and there, a light went on like a wink of recognition.

Its familiarity, its dearness, to Noel was like a sudden knife cut.

In the lighted warmth that was still home, Annie-Mae was waiting in the hall. Noel noticed the girl's face, unusually flushed, her eyes overbright.

''Miss Bliss left her card, Miss Noel, and one of them lavender envelopes there for Mr. Briggs.''

''Thank you, Annie-Mae.''

''And that there box came for you, Miss Noel. Grand, now isn't it?''

Grand it was and enormous, with an abundance of rich satin ribbon that trailed its bow on the table top. Annie-Mae was lingering.

Noel smiled at the little maid's rapt curiosity. Less certainly she removed the cover. There lay a profusion of parma violets and white roses, glowing and heady with the scents of summer. She heard Annie-Mae's gasp.

There was a card. Noel picked it up slowly as if it might be hot to the touch. ''To happiness wherever you find it. I am indebted for the day." Then a signature as if an afterthought, "Little Caesar."

She choked back something that threatened to become at once a laugh and a sob.

"What is it, Noel?" Her father had emerged from his study. "Another wedding present?"

"Just—some flowers."

He approached her. "Well, well. I should say so. Quite a display. Who sent them?"

"Just somebody I knew—"

"May I see the card?"

He took it gently from her fingers. "Little—what is this? Little Caesar? That's hardly a name."

"It's kind of a joke, Father. Nothing, really."

"Rather lavish for a joke, I'd say. Do you know who sent them?"

It would have to be another lie. Or would it? She had done her part. She had agreed to everything they had wanted of her, even to a marriage she despised. Perhaps the truth was needed now, if only for her own soul. A breath of fresh air into a curtained room.

"Yes, I know."

"May I ask who? You are betrothed, Noel. Any such attentions are not suitable now. I have to protect you from them." The damning card was firm ir his strong hand.

"He was someone I knew, briefly," she said tonelessly.

"Yes . . . ?"

"I shall not see him again."

"I'm glad to hear that. This sounds rather capricious of you, my dear. Does this gentleman usually sign himself, uh, 'Little Caesar'?"

"That's a—a horse, Father."

"And the man's name?" Walter was hurting himself as well as Noel. Yet he was angered, angered by this beloved daughter so unaccountably stricken, so far from him.

"His name is Ned Fitch. He worked for Dr. Lendler. I knew him for a little time. That's all. Now you know everything!"

Noel brushed past him and fled up the stairs.

Walter tore the card and dropped it on the flowers. He knew nothing. He could guess anything. He longed for Maria, yet he could hear her reprimand. *She's young, Walter. And high spirited. Don't be harsh. She'll settle down.*

He raised his voice. "Annie-Mae! Annie-Mae!" The girl

came running. "Take these flowers out, will you? Throw them away."

"Oh, sir . . . !"

"I want them out! They are not appropriate for this house."

He returned to his study, older than when he had left it.

Upstairs in her room, Noel stood, stiff and tight, her eyes dry, her hands clenched. Then it happened. Her will, that inner wall that had for so long sustained her, gave way. A sob broke from her throat. She threw herself on the bed, this woman who never wept. She let the release come, long sobs that shook her uncontrollably, and at last, the tears, as kindly as they were searing.

29

Evacuation Day was the personal prerogative of Miss Phoebe Bliss. It had not been celebrated in New York for half a century, but behind the facades of the city's older brick houses, a few claimed an ancestor, an uncle, a cousin twice removed, who had witnessed that great day, at the triumphant close of the American rebellion, when the British troops evacuated the city.

Miss Phoebe made no such claims. She did not have to. Everyone who was anybody knew that Miss Phoebe's own Grandfather Handon had stood on Battery Place that thrilling morning among the new, lustily free Americans to watch the defeated enemy officers and men march for the last time down Broadway to the harbor. There the Royal Fleet waited to take them away.

Crowds had gathered as far north as Canal Street, hooting or cheering as the British troops came on, as splendid as they were scornful in red, gold, and white. A few girls blew kisses. More than one damp-eyed matron sat behind half-drawn curtains, remembering lovely balls, dashing British officers. But in the streets many in the crowds raised clenched fists in bursts of newfound patriotism.

But generally, as Grandfather Handon had reported, the day had been one of good nature and high celebration. The British had stopped long enough on the Battery to raise a tall flagpole, slick with bear grease, atop which a spanking new British ensign stood out, snapping in the breeze of the Upper Bay.

It would take a bit of doing, even some broken Yankee bones, to pull the wretched symbol down. But as the royal sails filled toward the Narrows, martial restraint was lifted and the crowds surged in. Before the end of the day the Union Jack was successfully torn from its masthead, as grease-stained as its celebrants. Kegs of beer were rolled into the street. A whole ox was roasted. New York's city fathers, in the heat of deliverance, decreed the great day a holiday forever.

So it had been for five or six decades. More than one family claimed ancestry to the gallant lad who had brought the Union Jack down. Some even claimed to possess the flag itself. All of which Miss Phoebe knew to be nonsense. Hadn't Grandfather Handon given five shillings to the lad who had done it? Hadn't Grandfather, by folding the prize under his cloak and running like the devil over cobblestones and through back alleys, brought it home to Perry Street? There it had remained, to find safe harbor at last in Miss Phoebe's cedar linen chest in Stuyvesant Square, torn places mended, grease stains faded, tucked between Grandmother Randall's candlewick bedspread and the handwoven sheets for the trousseau Phoebe Bliss would never need.

City-wide, Evacuation Day continued in a desultory fashion. The prosperous had no time to look back. But for the poor who had little to feed on but their own abuses, and needed distraction from the spectacle of others' wealth, any celebration meant relief. For another quarter century, the events of the Evacuation were repeated, greased pole, Union Jack, ox roast, beer, and all. As time passed, the celebrants found themselves too drunk to climb the pole, or even to recall any reason for doing so.

Miss Phoebe saw her duty to keep alive the flame. So her Evacuation Day ritual became an annual event. She would produce the stained Union Jack itself and, in light, breathless tones, remind her guests that while the British had occupied the city, they had done so as gentlemen, and left us all the priceless inheritance of the Magna Charta. Miss Phoebe stood firm on the Magna Charta, though it was doubtful that more than one or two of her guests could define that shadowy parchment.

Stuyvesant Square viewed it all with tolerant affection, and eagerly awaited the violet-ink invitation. For it was well known that while Miss Phoebe had long given up Society, on this single occasion she would receive the oldest, most respected names in the city. It was said, *sotto voce*, that she adhered so rigidly to her guest list that some of the bearers of those names had been dead twenty years.

She also showed an increasing penchant for inviting a few unknowns who had taken her fancy. One never quite knew where these unexpected guests came from, but they always offered diversity, plus the spice of speculation.

In a generous mirror above the dresser of Mrs. Luskin's best bedroom, Ned Fitch critically surveyed himself. In his growing affluence from the Gemini Club, Ned had contemplated moving uptown. Yet he had the impression that his employer, the Parson, approved of his obscurity. Mrs. Luskin had been grateful. Thus the mirror, thus the embellishments of a potted plant and a book stand.

Ned knew she waited, high-bosomed, jet earrings bobbing, at the foot of the stairs.

"How fine you look, Neddie. A true-blooded gentleman to the manor born. Saw it from the first. I hope you won't forget me in your rise in the world."

"No man could, Mrs. Luskin."

But he said it absently. He had one thought in his mind. He would see Noel tonight, and among the best of circumstances. After that he drew a blank. After that—everything or nothing.

Promptly at eight he stood in the shadows surrounding the wide doors of 15 Stuyvesant Square. The night was brittle-cold and clear. (It was noted that for this event Miss Phoebe regularly and inscrutably enjoyed the blessing of good weather.) The polished carriages had already begun to roll into the Square. There they slowed to a solemn procession, their kerosene lamps twinkling to rival the diamond pinpricks in the winter sky. They came from the north, the northwest, the northeast. But very few from the south. The Square was considered now the southernmost boundary of New York Society. Downtown, the tree-shaded, brick-walled grace of the old days, had long given way to clutter, squalor, slums, commerce, and a variety of strange tongues, presaging like remote thunder an unimagined future of change.

Mrs. Mortimer Wilberforce herself, in the fourth carriage, assured everyone that she never set foot south of Twenty-third Street nowadays, except of course, for Dear Phoebe's Evening. Still, the Square itself retained a position. A few lustrous names such as Rutherford, Livingston, Fish, still gleamed on brass doorplates.

By 8:20, Mrs. Wilberforce would be ensconced on a tufted green satin settee, commanding a view of the drawing room and the cream-paneled ballroom into which its sliding doors led. Miss Phoebe's newer guests were inevitably surprised at the size of the old house. Beyond the ballroom they would find a smaller sitting room refurbished in rose brocade. Beyond this, a mere alcove of a room, hung ceiling to floor in the same rose brocade. Few knew that the winter draperies concealed glass panels that opened onto a high-walled garden, tended by unseen hands to a summer profusion of flowers for Miss Phoebe's single delight.

An ensemble of strings was already playing the waltzes and polkas of Johann Strauss and the newer pirated melodies of a talented pair of Englishmen, Gilbert and Sullivan. Miss Phoebe, tiny as a doll in rose-sprigged yellow satin of a half century ago, had taken her place in the front drawing room, her white lace-mitted hands clasped tightly on a white-lace fan.

"Phoebe!"

Mrs. Wilberforce leaned forward, spreading her jet-trimmed skirts the width of the settee, insuring solitude unless she chose to share it. "Phoebe, I'm not well enough to walk tonight. Bring every interesting person to me. But not the drones, dear. Not the drones."

Fanny Wilberforce had grown up on a farm and could still carry a full scuttle of coal up two flights of stairs if need be. But she considered her social presence a favor and had persuaded most of society of the fact. Miss Phoebe nodded indulgently.

The tide of arrivals quickened. At midpoint in the hall, black-suited and immaculate, stood Mr. Christopher—butler, major domo? No one quite knew. Occasionally he turned his head toward the drawing room and Miss Phoebe. The evening must go well.

Outside in the bracing night, Ned still watched the file of guests from carriage to door. He had already walked around the empty park. Not in uncertainty or fear, but to see the carriage waiting at number 269. There was no way of making sure that Noel would attend. But he would not let himself doubt it. Now he stood savoring the new luxury of knowing that at the moment he chose, he could enter the brilliantly lit house, expected, accepted.

He had come a long way since that day he had jumped ship and pushed through the rough waterfront crowds. He had not forgotten his anguish when, in rented clothes, he had made an entrance, unbidden, unwanted, into a splendid candlelit mansion, only to be contemptuously directed out. No one would do that to him again.

He had gulped down every opportunity this mirage of a city offered his starved ambition. He had honed his English farm accent to one he thought nearer London's, until he realized that Americans couldn't tell the difference. He had read copiously, even indulged in dancing lessons, fencing lessons. Recently he had made the discovery that money in his pocket, a good tailor, and a túrn of the wheel of chance were the quickest steps up the ladder of gentility.

He felt no remorse or need for an apology for his abrupt departure from Dr. Lendler's employ. He had been threatened. He had escaped the threat.

Remorse, like regret, was weakness. It meant looking back, doubting oneself, unsure of the turn taken in the road. He had sat too many nights at the Gemini Club in the company of men who never doubted, who knew what they wanted and the shortest distance to it. He heard talk of "deals" in the millions, Wall Street gambles that made fortunes overnight, speculations in land, in railroad shares, that yielded untold profits for the bold and the sure. Even when the railroads were not yet built! He learned of something called Tammany Hall and old Boss Tweed, discredited four years ago, dead six months now. But the System was thriving again, a balding man with diamonds in his shirt studs had assured him. Political power, pools of enormous hidden wealth, all there again for the taking. Young blood was needed, certain loyalties sworn to . . . anything could be arranged. Tammany would run the city as long as the city stood.

Heady talk. Especially when Ned's own shrewdness was being noticed. His earnings had been raised twice. He had learned to sit easily, discreetly, with the grim-faced men at the tables. It had occurred to Ned that a gaming table was not unlike a church pew. One man differed from the next only in the amount he dropped on the plate.

The line of carriages lengthened. Music drifted in fragments through the open doors. Miss Phoebe's house, lit from top to bottom, soared like a proud ship into the night. Through the first-floor windows, Ned could see silhouetted the slow graceful passage of guests.

It was time to make his appearance.

"My dear Mr. Abbingdon-Fitch! How kind of you to come! Isn't it a pleasant evening?"

Miss Phoebe stood, twinkling and diminutive between two Ming vases full of white chrysanthemums. She looked at once twenty years older and twenty years younger than when he had first met her on the bench in gentle half-skip through the Square. This startling inconsistency might have been accomplished by the girlishness of her figure, the taut cords of her throat or, most astonishing, the tiny flirtatious black circle on her powdered left cheek. How long since anyone had seen a beauty patch?

"I shall quite rely on you tonight, Mr. Abbingdon-Fitch. We shall stand together in our loyalty to our dear America and our ties to our dear England. I shall ask you to be honor bearer of the original Evacuation flag . . . ah, there's Dr. Lendler, going into the smoking room . . . with Mr. Horace Vanderlind. One of our primitive Dutch families, but you might like to know him, anyway. Noel hasn't arrived yet . . . oh dear, what am I saying? She's promised now, isn't she? Well, I'm sure we all wish her happiness. . . . Yes, Fanny?"

Miss Phoebe's eyes darted toward the green satin settee to catch the wave of command. Her small hand propelled Ned's elbow.

"Mrs. Wilberforce, may I present the Honorable Edmond Abbingdon-Fitch, second son of the second son of the Marquis—"

"Sit down, young man."

Ned found himself bowing and sitting abruptly on the edge of the settee, where on one hip he faced a tête-à-tête and a copious lady, without any possible view of the entrance hall or of the new arrivals. Still, the lady was New York's Mrs. Mortimer Wilberforce. Ned at least knew the importance of the name, thus the honor of his perch.

"The Queen is well, Mr. Abbingdon-Fitch?"

"Respectably well, mum." He guessed that was the way the long deceased Marquess might have addressed the Presence, had there even been such a man. Mrs. Wilberforce decided he was not mocking her.

"Respectable, I'm sure. That is her difficulty, dear boy. I lost dear Captain Wilberforce four years—or was it five?—after her Albert. But I did not wall myself up in seclusion, forbid dancing, and turn hundreds of eligible young women into early spinsters with one frown. Victoria had eight, or was it nine, children? An illuminating, if fatiguing experience, to be sure. When it ended for her, should it have ended for every other woman in the Empire? In this country, Mr. Abbingdon-Fitch, we women carry on. We must. How would matters have gone? You can't leave a whole wilderness to men. Who would put up the drapes? And you certainly can't leave Society to them! The dear Captain couldn't even arrange place cards properly."

Mrs. Mortimer Wilberforce drew a well-corseted breath. Ned, by twisting his neck, could see more guests arriving.

And, as the black-jetted bosom swelled with yet another deep breath, Ned saw her.

Noel Tremont had arrived.

Mrs. Wilberforce leaned forward. "Ah, Noel did come. That's her fiancé, Mr. Clarence Biggs, or Briggs, whatever it is. Whatever on earth does she see in him? But then without a mother . . . imagine announcing it in the newspaper first! And that's her father. . . ."

Ned at last could turn full around. Noel was entering the drawing room. She wore ruby silk, held her head too high, and let her hand rest on the arm of a weedy young man with a pale mustache. She looked neither left nor right.

". . . Mr. Tremont's in trade, but such a kindly man. I understand he's quite accepted in the Square. And Mrs. Tremont, the second of course, quite ravishing but so thin. One of those women who can surround herself with men without saying a word. So useful to a husband rising in the world, don't you think, Mr. Abbingdon-Fitch? There's Orrin, the eldest son. I never like a young man whose hair falls out early and who wears a pince-nez. Soul as pinched as his nose. That's his wife. Does she ever wear anything but puce? She was a Van Broot. Got them all into Society, I daresay. I don't see David yet. He's the black sheep of the family, but then every family has one. He's quite delightful. He never fails Phoebe's party."

The Tremont party was approaching Miss Phoebe.

"I did hope Noel would make a brilliant marriage. Even a good one . . ."

Ned returned to his captor.

". . . but there's a mystery about Noel. Just when she reached the age when she should have been thinking about beaux, she changed. She simply turned her back on the things that most girls like. Went to lectures, read books, as if she had gone into retirement. Most people thought it was her father's second marriage. I don't believe that for a moment. Noel has too much spunk. But now this ridiculous engagement! To a man who's going out some place to teach the heathen Chinese. If you ask me, the heathen Chinese know more than he does, always have, and should be left to their own devices, which have served them quite satisfactorily for four or was it six thousand . . . ahh!"

Mrs. Wilberforce smiled, showing large even teeth and what some called her horse-stealing expression.

"There's Dr. Lendler!" She waved a heavy, ring-encrusted hand. "He's an Oriental, you know, like your Mr. Disraeli and our Mr. Belmont. So intellectual. He speaks six . . . or is it seven . . . languages. Most people I know don't speak even one well. Phoebe is quite in love with him. Or would be, if he were thirty years younger. I can quite understand. Such eyes! I don't think we shall ever pay our debt to the Semite people.

"Ah, Dr. Lendler! We meet again! Have you met Mr. Abbingdon-Fitch?"

It was inevitable. Ned rose, feeling conspicuously tall and transparent, as if everyone in the room could see through him.

Dr. Lendler bowed gravely. "Good evening, Ned."

"Good evening, sir."

Mrs. Wilberborce beamed. "I might have known. The pleasure of Phoebe's Evening is that one meets the most extraordinary people who all turn out to know each other. How she does it I'll never know, but I go uptown feeling quite deprived. . . . Do sit down, Dr. Lendler." She patted the edge of the settee and lowered her tone to conspiracy. Social position for Mrs. Wilberforce included the privilege of making mischief.

"Mr. Abbingdon-Fitch, do go ask poor Noel for the first quadrille. That young man of hers doesn't look as if he knows what to do with himself, much less his feet." The voice rose to its usual social command. "And I insist you come to my Christmas Eve Reception. It's in honor of Sir George and Lady Bathhurst. Seven o'clock. I shall expect you!"

Ned managed a bow. Dr. Lendler sat down, his face expressionless.

"Dr. Lendler"—the large voice melted with reproach—"last year you told me that the most passionate poetry in the world was in the Bible, though I'm sure our Reverend Twilling doesn't know that. Well, I started reading from the beginning, but I simply cannot get through the begats. . . ."

Ned was dismissed.

For the moment he had lost sight of Noel. But he needed time. Dr. Lendler had not given him away. On the contrary, it was the gentle courtesy that bothered him. He had much to learn, much to think about. He must think carefully about his approach to Noel.

The smoking room proved to be Miss Phoebe's private sanctum. Papered in blue chrysanthemums and ladies in rickshaws, it was, eleven months of the year, what Miss Phoebe called her Room for Thought. Tonight, the upholstered rocker and footstool, embroidery basket, Wellington's ottoman, and that imposing feline himself were gone. They were replaced by two delicate japanned wall tables bearing heavy bronze ashtrays, and three shining new cuspidors. Miss Phoebe obviously believed that when one entertained men, one must see to their creature comforts.

The simple windows stood wide open. The room was hazy with rich Havana smoke. It was also remarkably cold.

Ned hesitated uncertainly in the doorway before the cluster of black-clothed backs. Confident men in old-fashioned evening dress, strong of face, as solid as their massive gold watch chains, were a new breed to Ned. New Yorkers who had known for generations who they were. In church pews, in gentlemen's clubs, in oak-paneled offices of law or commerce, they took pride in the stamp of integrity, of excellence, they put on their city. Or part of it. They had guided New York out of provincialism. They had seen it grow until it was now often linked in a single sentence to London or Paris. They had done it simply by being themselves, true to duty, firm in moral principle, sound in investment, orderly in last will and testament. And by raising their children to do the same.

Ned saw Mr. Walter Tremont among them. Oddly, for an instant he thought he glimpsed something familiar in another greying head on thick shoulders. Then the illusion was gone. He was being haunted tonight by his own inadequacy. He was here, where he wanted to be, an invited guest. He would not lose his grasp on that.

He turned from the room. And saw her.

She was seated in one of a row of gilt chairs along the wall of the ballroom. The chair beside her was empty but its proximity told Ned that it might at any moment have an occupant. For this moment, Noel was alone.

He crossed the empty ballroom floor directly to her.

"Good evening, Miss Tremont."

She had seen him approach. She glanced up without smiling, without visible recognition.

He gestured to the empty chair beside her.

"May I?"

"My fiancé will be back in a moment, Mr.—Fitch. He has gone to get me some punch."

Artificial as the whole damned scene. He looked boldly at her. "I hardly think so. If you'll bend that lovely, stiff neck of yours and look through the doorway you'll see your, uh, whatever he is talking to a man at considerable distance from the punchbowl. Besides"—he was started. He'd risk the whole thing now—"I don't want his chair. I want"—he grinned—"his . . . lady. For the first quadrille. Oh, it's not my idea. It's an order from a lady of whom I am in mortal terror."

The corners of Noel's mouth deepened but her face remained cold.

"Mr. Fitch, why do you persist . . . ?"

"Don't say it. If I've made a mistake, I'll apologize. Let's begin over . . . I've seen you for the first time, I'm enchanted. . . ."

The musicians struck an opening chord. Couples began to move onto the dance floor.

Ned held out his hand.

"Will you? Or shall I be hanged at sunrise?"

For an instant for Ned, the music, the ballroom, the universe waited. A riffle of sparks shot upward, whether it was from the violins or her sudden laughter, he could not tell. She put her hand into his.

"Now please look as if you're enjoying it, or the empress will send in the troops."

He would never forget the next quarter hour. In the old-fashioned pattern of the dance he would see her forever, lithe, glowing, slipping in and out among the faceless dancers, parting, meeting, parting, until he found her again in the ordained patterns of the dance.

It had to end, high and exultant, she breathless, with a tendril of dark hair loose from its evening polish. She did not look at him, nor did she turn away. The music had crystallized around them, holding them in a bright, invisible vise. But before they could break away, the violins erupted in a different strain, sensuous, head-spinning. A waltz by Mr. Strauss was still considered dangerous by the elderly. But it was danced rapturously by the young, desire in motion, longing set free.

Ned's arm slipped around Noel's waist. Wordlessly he guided her into the music. The lilt quickened. In the pier glass mirrors, on opposite sides of the room, Ned saw their figures reflected. Noel in his arms whirling through distant room into distant room, farther and farther, smaller and smaller, until she was a tiny jewel, he the possessor in an infinity of escape.

As suddenly as it had begun, the waltz ended. Applause rippled into erotic tremors of high-pitched laughter of release. For a second longer he held her.

"When can I see you?"

"No, Ned!"

"You can't marry that man!" His arm was a vise at her back.

"Ned, the dance is over! Let me go!"

"You don't love him."

"People are looking!"

The break in her voice, the unsteady breath he could feel beneath the silk at her back relaxed his grip. He tightened it for another instant, his mouth against her hair. "I love you, I want you. I'll spend the rest of my life trying to deserve you. Noel, I won't give you up!"

But she had slipped from him. Only a delicate scent hung in the air, a straw to be clutched. Then it, too was gone. He felt conspicuous and alone. There was a general movement toward the front rooms, of chattering couples, groups. He followed.

"Ah, there you are, Mr. Abbingdon-Fitch!" Miss Phoebe's small hand caught his sleeve. "I've been waiting for you, but I just couldn't bear to interrupt the lovely waltz. You and dear Noel. How charming she looked. Englishmen always dance so beautifully. It put me in mind of Mr. Willoughby, though he came from Boston. He said I did the German polka better than any girl he had ever met. And how I loved it! But of course that all ended, I mean Mr. Willoughby ended, with the Comet. My. . . ." Her sigh bridged the decades. Miss Phoebe returned to business.

"Now this is what we do. Mr. Christopher will bring the two flags, our original Evacuation flag and our own American flag, down the stairs to the landing. You will take the Union Jack and Colonel Hastings the Stars and Stripes. The Colonel was wounded at the peach orchard at Gettysburg and you can't find anything more American than that. I always wondered why they had to fight in such a lovely place as a peach orchard. Oh, well . . . then you and the Colonel will carry the flags to the bottom of the stairs, and stand one on each side. I stand on the fifth step up, so everybody can see me. I'm not very tall. Then I will recite two lines of our Constitution and two lines of the Magna Charta . . . which really began everything, didn't it? Oh my, it is so thrilling to do it properly with a real live Englishman, Mr. Abbingdon-Fitch. Then we all salute and sing 'My Country T'is of Thee' and 'God Save the Queen' in alternate verses. I hope your dear Queen will understand that in America she must take the second verse!"

Miss Phoebe's cheeks looked paper thin, a faint webbing of lines had begun to show. Her beauty patch had disappeared. But no one could doubt that she was enjoying her golden hour.

Ned felt himself oddly touched by her faded intensity. He did something that, showy as it was, he meant. He picked up her small hand and carried it to his lips.

"Your devoted Household Guard, Miss Bliss. Your colors on my shield."

"Oh . . . my. Goodness me. That's very nice, I'm sure. Yes indeed. I do thank you. . . ."

She turned so quickly that she walked directly into a heavy-set man in an immaculate clerical collar, a well-fitted black suit, a luxuriant growth of black hair, and a black beard. He had been deep in conversation.

"Oh, dear me, I am sorry. Reverend Culbertson, have you met Mr. Abbingdon-Fitch, one of our English cousins just come from London? Ned, Reverend Culbertson is one of our Thursday-nighters at the opera. We have a little club of the "alones," as we call ourselves. He is partial to Mr. Verdi, whom I consider quite rough. I prefer Mr. Mozart and the delightful Mr. Offenbach. But we do agree on Mr. Wagner, don't we, Your Reverence? So dissonant. And endless. . . ."

Ned found himself looking into the fleshy bearded face, the thin-lidded, steely eyes of the one man on earth he had no wish to see—his employer, the Parson. Like a horse or a dog, Ned thought angrily, who knows by instinct the hand that feeds him, he would know the owner and overlord of the Gemini Club anywhere. To his surprise, he felt a sudden loathing for the man in these surroundings. And for himself for knowing him.

The Reverend Culbertson's eyes met his without visible recognition. Ned managed a nod. The moment passed. The man turned back to his conversation. Ned followed his hostess. The evening had taken a momentarily sinister turn but he would dispel that. He looked over the heads of the throng for Noel. He did not see her.

"Such a lonely man"—Miss Phoebe was chattering—"he's without a church . . . minister-at-large, he says. I think the opera is his only interest. I thought perhaps an invitation might cheer him. I think he's enjoying himself. We must never judge people from the outside, must we? Now I shall give Mr. Christopher the signal and we shall start our little ceremony, Mr. Abbingdon-Fitch." She twinkled up at him. "I think I shall call you Ned. You're a dear friend!"

But Miss Phoebe's flag was not destined for its display. Not yet. Looking over her head, Ned saw the front door open and a latecomer enter the hall. A young man with a disheveled shock of blond hair, his overcoat flung wide open over rumpled street clothes. Beneath the smudged soot on his forehead and a long plaster strip on his right cheek, Ned saw the proud, drained face of Noel's brother, David. He walked unsteadily to the center of the hall.

"Evening, one and all. I'm not here to sully the party. I'm here . . . thank you no, I'll keep my coat. Ah, Mr. Christopher, how goes the night?" He threw an arm across the little brown man's shoulder. "Man of the future! Like me! The world is out of joint, my friend. But we shall put it right! By God we shall! Is my father about?"

Miss Phoebe darted into the hall.

"David dear, how nice! I was afraid you wouldn't arrive—"

"This is the east and Juliet the sun!"

Miss Phoebe stopped uncertainly. Mr. Christopher edged in front of her, gently maneuvering her back into the ballroom.

David made a low, stumbling bow.

"My apologies, dear Miss Bliss. I'm not dressed for the greatness of the occasion. Not even clean. The cardinal sin, ain't it? Not to be clean, not to be nicely scrubbed in soap and water. That's not to be godly. But it was quite a rumpus. A real donnybrook until it turned worse. . . ."

Ned heard a rustling. Noel was pushing her way through the growing circle of onlookers.

"Excuse me, excuse me please. . . ."

David was leaning now on a high-back wall chair.

"Ahh, sister mine. How now, gentle Ophelia!"

Ned could not hear her answer.

David shook off her hand. "Go home, you say? Have I a home? If I have, tell me where. Get thee to a nunnery, Noel. If you would marry, marry a fool for wise men know what monsters you make of them! *Hamlet,* act two, scene . . ."

Ned reached her side. "Let me, Noel. I'll help him out."

But David, upright, careful, moved from him.

"Not me, you won't. I can stand on my two legs as well as any trained dog. Noel, dost thou know this water fly?"

Laughter fluttered uneasily from the circle of guests. The air was thick with embarrassment.

Ned saw the portly figure of Walter Tremont moving through the crowd toward the hall, Adrienne beside him.

"Ahh, yes, I do know you. You come courtin' my sister, didn't you? Last summer. With violets and sweet talk. And no one there! Fitch, that's who you are. An honest name for an honest face. Haven't you married the girl yet? Listen and you'll learn something . . . ahh, here he comes, poor ghost. My father's spirit, complete in steel. And the Lady Adrienne, my stepmother. How is it with you, Lady? Your heart ever the seat of your Kingdom. Circe who turns men to swine, then gives them wings—"

"David!" The name like a thunderclap silenced the hall. Walter's face had purpled, his voice trembled, as if the specter of age had gripped his shoulder. "How dare you?" He lowered his voice. "David, you're drunk. Go home. Do you understand? Go home and don't come back. Here or to my house—"

"Father. . . ." Noel grasped her brother's arm.

Walter looked first at his son, then his daughter.

"Adrienne, get your wrap. I'll make our apologies to Miss Bliss. Then we'll have the carriage called."

"No, wait!" The wildness had drained from David's face, leaving it ashen and spent. Only his eyes, shadow-rimmed, blazed with a dark honesty. "I'll call your carriage, Father," he said evenly. "I'll make your apologies. Everyone's apologies. The world's apologies. Then I'll leave. But first I'll say what I came to say. You have nothing to fear from me, any of you. Whiskey . . . after the cold. Twists a man's tongue." He drew a deep, slow breath. "But I have to explain, don't I? You taught me that, Father, when I was late. You see the trouble hadn't started when I got down to Gum Alley this afternoon. You wouldn't know Gum Alley, any of you. It's a dark old slit off West Street. Wooden tenements, a sailor's flophouse, a couple of brothels. Forgive me, ladies. The truth is not always dressed for the evening. Well, it seems the landlord's agent came around today with a little advance Christmas present. To raise the rents. Going to make 'improvements.' That means dividing the flats. A family who lived in two rooms would now live in one room. Another family would move in with them to help pay the increase."

The guests stood silent. Walter took a step toward his son.

"Let me finish, Father. I want you to understand. The people in Gum Alley didn't like what they got. A fight started. Then another. Everybody wanting to hit out at something. Somebody threw a burning flare into one of the buildings. And that was it. Those old timbers burned like straw. By the time the fire wagons got there it was too late. They couldn't get near the buildings for the crowds. There was no one to clear the alley, no one to push the crowds away. No one to help the people out of the buildings. A few of us got in. I pulled out three children and a sick woman. Someone got a few whores out, one of them not more than twelve, her hair on fire. We found a blind man, three sailors alive." David looked around the silent circle. "Don't you understand? The police weren't there. No one ordered out the guards. It was only a rotted, rat-infested slum. The land is worth more than the houses and the people in them. The lords of the city know that!"

David swayed, gripped the carved newel post of the stairway.

"Oh, my God, Father! They let it happen!"

Ned reached him and caught him as he slumped. Noel was beside him. There was for a moment no sound. Together they led David through the hall, past Walter, stonelike, aged. Past Adrienne, her face pinched, white. From the drawing room, the Reverend Culbertson watched thoughtfully.

Someone brought Noel a shawl. The trio moved through the silence, through the vestibule, out into the night.

The moon rode high and small and cold above the square, lengthening the shadows of all that stirred. A Hunter's Moon. At the iron balustrade of number 269, the trio stopped.

David shook himself free with a "Thank you, friends."

"David, you must come inside! Father will get over it. I'll fix you something hot. You can lie down."

"Always the little mother, Noel." But he said it without malice. He had the face of a tired boy. In the faint street light, Ned could see the resemblance between brother and sister, the wide forehead, determined chin line, slight flare of the nostrils. Rebels both, he thought.

David stiffened. "I'm pretty drunk, girl, but not that drunk. And I'm not sorry. Poor old Father. He'll suffer in noble silence, one son gone to the dogs, the other . . . I don't want anything Orrin has!" He squinted at Ned. "Ned, eh? For God's sake, marry the man, Noel, while you've got the chance. Y'know, Ned, if you weren't so togged out I'd take you over to Billy Mould's on Fourteenth Street . . . famous for its razzle-dazzle . . . brandy, ginger-ale, absinthe . . . stir well, drink down . . . hair of the dog. . . ." David stiffened, straightened his coat, pushed an ineffective hand over his unruly hair. "Razzle-dazzle . . . make a man do anything he knows he must. Good night, dear sister . . . try to be happy. It's not easy. Come on doggie . . . nice doggie. . . ."

He started down the street, his elongated shadow lurching among the trees.

"I'll go with him!"

"Yes, please, Ned!"

It was not hard to catch up. David leaned against the iron paling. "How now, me hearty? Leave a lady alone in the night? I don't know who you are or how you got to this place. You don't look a bad sort but the cut of your jib don't suit you." David suddenly lifted his voice in an offkey tenor.

"It's the rich wot get the pleasure, it's the poor wot take the pain. . . ."

Ned burst into a laugh, threw an arm around his new comrade.

"It's the same the whole world over," he roared the old song with him.

"Ain't it all a bleedin' shame!"

David pulled away.

"Go to the devil, old friend! Get the girl! Don't leave her standing at the gate, with her eyes hot as coals on you!" He walked off. A few steps away he broke into a series of hops, a little boy's game of jumping the shadows threatening his feet.

Noel had not moved.

"I guess I owe you another apology," Ned said.

"Not at all. You might have asked me to join the fun."

She was as distant as the Hunter's Moon. Yet, he told himself, she had not gone up into the house.

"Shall I take you back to the party?"

"No, thank you. They'll be coming home soon."

"Your fiancé?"

She spoke quietly. "Clarence left early to catch a train. His sister's suffering quinsy throat. I'm sorry you saw David like this."

"Why?"

"He wasn't always this way. But he never lacked for courage or opinions."

"I hope he never changes." He was standing very close, their shadows one in the moon's cold silver.

"When do I see you again." It was not a question.

She shivered.

His voice came low and intense.

"Noel, listen to me. We can't change what's happened. We can't wipe out that day we had together. Tonight you were in my arms, where I wanted you and—I'll say it—where you wanted to be. I have nothing on earth to offer you. I can't ask you to marry me yet. I can only ask you to give me time. I don't know what you're looking for in a man. Maybe something I can never be. But I'm a man who loves you. Better than my own life. If I'm never to see you, say so! I'll walk out of this Square and I'll never trouble you again. I give you that promise."

He had not intended to say so much. He had intended only to sweep her into his arms, but the Square itself, the distant flickering carriage lights, the watchful houses, restrained him as they always had.

Her face told him nothing. The bare branches above them creaked and snapped. Dried leaves spun across the deserted sidewalk, their sound magnified in his ears. He wondered if she would answer at all or turn away forever, into that inner secret place in which she lived.

"Do you know the Hudson River?" she asked.

The irrelevance piqued him.

"I know the docks."

"I mean the real river, up beyond that. The cliffs of sheer rock. And north where the river widens between the hills . . . there's a collection of paintings of it all at the Art Academy. . . ." He heard a quick intake of breath. "I shall be there. Tuesday. At three."

She disappeared up the steps as if someone were always waiting to close a door behind her.

A carriage turned the corner and slowed. Ned had no wish to confront Walter Tremont. He had seen the look in the older man's eyes. A reality he was not yet ready to face.

He walked rapidly into the shadows, his footsteps making a ticking clock of the night. Tuesday at three. Tuesday at three.

30

"Wild oats! Just wild oats," had been Mrs. Mortimer Wilberforce's fond and commanding judgment. Miss Phoebe Bliss had touched Walter's sleeve gently with her lace-mitted fingers. "Don't be too harsh with him. He's a fine boy." As for the rest of Stuyvesant Square, what family did not share the distress of a "black sheep" on its escutcheon? Young David was certainly no worse than the others.

But it was not his younger son's misdeeds that lay at the core of Walter Tremont's anguish following the Evacuation party. It was another, deeper matter that had become anathema, even a threat, if anything could be said to threaten the Tremont family. Or did it all lie in his imagination? He could confide in no one. He well knew that the gathering years tend to turn a man's thoughts to his past, to all he had accomplished, perhaps even to overvalue the buttresses of his security. Maria would have known how to reassure him. "It's nothing, Walter. Nothing. They're young. They'll do what's right when the time comes. Don't you remember when we were young?"

The memory of Maria could always touch his lips with a smile.

As for the ugly Gum Alley Riot, the press had relegated it to the back pages of a single edition with one editorial.

> It is well to rid the city of such fetid sore spots. They spawn crime, are unfit for decent citizens and are too narrow to admit the city's fine modern firefighting apparatus. The monthly visit of the disinfectant wagon into those foul alleys has proved totally inadequate. If we are not to be regularly threatened with epidemics of plague and disease, two visits a month are minimal, at a cost not likely to find favor. . . .

But civic conscience gave way to livelier interests. The coming winter season promised not only brilliance but something for everyone. Mrs. Astor would give her annual January ball. Any shopgirl passing the Renaissance mansion on Thirty-fourth Street and Fifth Avenue could dream of the hostess's diamond stomacher, the ropes of diamonds falling from the Valkyrian waist, the enormous marbled rooms filled with $30,000 worth of hothouse roses, and the gold table service said to be finer than the Queen of England's.

The sporting pages gossiped that "the prominent Mr. H. H. would give a hunt dinner for his gentlemen friends at Louis Sherry's new restaurant. The guests would be their Thoroughbred horses led into the dining room by their owners to stand at a horseshoe-shaped table, set with carrots and hay." Omnibus riders could warm themselves with indignation and saloon patrons with bad jokes.

For the masses, the indefatigible Tony Pastor was presenting a new sensation at his Variety Hall on Fourteenth Street, a delicious cream-and-gold morsel who was transporting every male worth his salt into imagined infidelity. Miss Lillian Russell was the overnight goddess of every newsboy, her pure, girlish high C's were the bane of every visiting diva. Madame Melba herself would be heard to wonder why any woman thought she had to sing so many in one performance.

Into all this diversity came political news of significance. President Rutherford B. Hayes, Republican incumbent, halfway through his promised single term, was considering a visit to New York.

The announced date was February twelfth.

In the sedate Union Club on West Twenty-sixth Street, old Colonel Hastings waved a cigar at a fellow member.

"I certainly hope, Tremont, that the President has no intention of honoring Abraham Lincoln's birthday. Surely Mr. Hayes must know that when Lincoln began his war, the Mayor of this city, and the Governor of this state of New York threatened secession. They had solid support, too. All that bloodletting! Oh, I had my share of that, but what did New York get for it? English markets closed. Southern cotton cut off. And then what happened? Two years later Lincoln was in such trouble that he had to call for twenty thousand more men from New York. Not as volunteers, mind you, but drafted. *Drafted!* Never happened before. Well, New York gave him his answer. Riots! The most disgraceful breakdown of order in the city's history. Remember them, Tremont? I was here at the time. For five days the streets were solid with the most disreputable people, thousands and thousands pouring out of the slums, the tenements, heaven knew where . . . smashing stores, breaking into houses, tearing down street lamps and telegraph poles, running down every black man, woman and child they could, blaming the poor niggers for starting the war. Some said the rioting was the work of Confederate spies, but if you ask me, it was the Irish immigrants, who are never satisfied"—a long cigar ash trembled to the carpet—"and the whole police force helpless until the Mayor put pistols into their hands. First time in the city's history. Disgraceful, Tremont."

Walter let his mind wander. He had his own reasons for remembering the terrible draft riots, the hottest week of that long-ago summer. He had sent Maria and the children to a rented cottage at the seashore. It was then he had discovered Maria's rapture with the sea and planned their Far Rockaway home. That lonely week in mid-July, he had walked uptown on Lexington Avenue to the store front on Forty-sixth where the great wooden drum of draftee names was turning. He had seen the men in sullen groups muttering as each name was called. It was to be a poor man's draft. The well-to-do could pay three hundred to be exempted.

The second morning of the draft the crowds had thickened and by evening lavalike masses pouring from every side street had begun to move downtown toward City Hall. The riot was out of control. Walter remembered how he and his father had escaped through the back door as maddened mobs smashed through stores and houses, even into the neat Duane Street premises of the original Tremont & Sons, Gentlemen's Tailors, looting, wrecking, and burning. His father had never quite recovered.

There was Maria, at the seashore with the children. He had reassured her by fast post that the disturbances were exaggerated, but she should remain with the children where she was. So he had been left free to do what he could for the city's agony and to discover how thin was the surface of pleasant living, how close beneath lay violence. That riot-torn afternoon as he approached the south side of Stuyvesant Square, he ran headlong into another mob. They had hold of a black man and were dragging him toward an ancient pear tree, the last it was said of old Peter Stuyvesant's long gone orchards.

Unable to reach the terrified black man, cut off by throngs of yelling men and women, Walter had jumped on a stalled wagon. Over the heads of the mob he could see men with ropes, a can, a torch. Then to his astonishment he saw in the rear garden of one of the fine old houses on the Square, a small woman in summer silk and three maid-servants open the gate and push their way to the pear tree.

They carried a stepladder and four buckets of water. In the tiny woman's hand flashed something that looked like a knife. He could not hear what she shouted, but the crowd pulled back. The woman reached the tree, doused out the first flames, set the ladder against the trunk. The tiny woman climbed it, slashing at the rope with her knife. The victim, half dead, fell free.

Walter struggled through the mob. But before he could reach the women, they had managed to carry the black man through the garden entrance, the tiny woman, now limping, had shut and bolted the gate.

The next day Walter made his first call on 15 Stuyvesant Square.

"How very kind of you, Mr. Tremont. We haven't met, but how thoughtful."

Miss Phoebe Bliss was sitting in a cushioned chair, a bandaged foot propped on an ottoman.

"That poor man's going to be all right. His face and left side are burned. The doctor said he will be scarred but he will recover. His name is Christopher. That was all I could get from him. He's upstairs in my best guest room and that's where he'll stay. As far as I'm concerned, he shan't ever have to leave this house. But oh, Mr. Tremont, those people, those sad terrible people, so poor, so ragged, half-crazed. Doing such terrible things! If you ask me, they're not tearing this city apart because of the draft. They're fighting against their conditions. So unfair. Such poverty. Such suffering. One does what one can. My injury? Nothing, really. A little bone snapped. That isn't very important anyhow. The doctor said I may be a little shorter on one side than the other. Perhaps I shall have to skip. I adored skipping when I was a child."

Five days of rioting had ended when the police arrived with their new pistols and, with the armed militia, had finally driven the mobs back to their slums. Officially a thousand were counted dead, the uncounted were said to reach two thousand. The cost to the city was nearly five million dollars. It was months before many citizens could return to their torched and looted property.

"If President Hayes wishes to remind New York of all that. . . ." The old Colonel had reached the end of his cigar. He was speaking out of a deepening reverie, an old man's nearness to the past. "But make no mistake, Tremont, the

President's visit is important. Very important. Election coming up. Hayes won't be running. He's promised one term and I think he'll stick to it. He's a Republican all right but he's from Ohio. We've had only two presidents from New York. Millard Fillmore, a Whig. Martin Van Buren, a Democrat. And a disaster. What we want is a Republican President from New York. Show those damned Middle-westerners that Ohio isn't—what the devil do they call themselves out there?—the 'valley of democracy'."

The Colonel's head tipped back, he began to snore lightly. Walter waited uncertainly.

He was not yet entirely comfortable in his new membership in the prestigious club. He would like to sit and think a little longer of his quiet friendship with Miss Phoebe, her wreath of lilies when Maria died, her kindly letter at his remarriage. "I think young Mrs. Tremont might find Stuyvesant Square quite pleasant. Such friendly, nice people. I know of an available house. . . ."

Enough of the past. History's only legacy was relevancy. Without it a man's lifetime, all he had built and believed, would dissolve into mist as distant as the smoke of Homer's battle camps, the lost colors of Greek statues.

Today was here and it was different, as today would always be different. But it was his day and his duty.

The Colonel had sunk deep into the armchair of an old man's memories. Walter quietly picked up his hat and cane and walked into the thin November light.

It was already mid-afternoon. He was dining at the Mayor's house that evening. He had agreed to serve on the President's reception committee. It was a step toward the larger stage of national politics, which he had never sought. But larger loomed the other question in his mind. His family. All that he had believed in as settled and right had been turned upside down in one evening at Miss Phoebe's. He could not dismiss David's behavior in that forgiving phrase, "wild oats." The boy had publicly defied him. He had had an impulse to go around to David's flat and issue an ultimatum. He had thought better of it. It had an old-fashioned sound. Out of date. Therefore useless. Besides, he had visited David's flat once and seen a tortoise-shell hairpin near the easel. Through the half-opened door to the bedroom, a woman's chemise on a chair. David was no longer a golden-haired son. He was a man. Increasingly, a stranger.

Even as that outrage returned to his mind, he knew that its real source was not David but Noel, his beloved, his cherished daughter, in whose light figure, fine features, quick smile of mischief he could glimpse Maria. A man's love for his daughter was unique. Protective, sheltering, an idealized part of himself. He could believe that no man gave his daughter to another in marriage without a quickening of his male mind, an imagery that would remain secret, distasteful forever.

Yet he wanted Noel married. He had been prepared to accept her judgment, her inherent sensitive taste.

He had found nothing unacceptable in young Clarence Briggs. But he had found nothing in his favor, either. If, beneath her reserve, Noel believed her happiness could lie with this too earnest, bloodless young missionary teacher, Walter would accept it. But he had yet to believe it. Twice she had asked about her dowry. Twice he had reassured her. Privately he was relieved that it was bound up safely in railroad stocks, which both Orrin and his old friend Henry had assured him would yield a fortune within a decade.

As for Clarence, he had spoken clearly and commendably. "I am not concerned with Miss Noel's dowry, sir. I have no interest in money matters. Nor will she have any use for such money at the Mission in Amoy. I would think it best to keep it here for the security my employment may not bring her. In any case I would be guided entirely by Miss Noel's desires."

Whatever the arrangements, Walter thought, there seemed to be precious little desire anywhere. Not as he and Maria had understood that young fire so long ago.

So matters had remained until the night of Miss Phoebe's party. Standing in a group near the ballroom, he had watched Noel dance. She seemed to float on the music, close within the man's arm. He recognized the fellow. The young Englishman who had clerked for a while for Hugo Lendler and left without notice. Walter would not have held that against an upstart, an opportunist, or an honest man come to America to make his way by honest work. Hadn't his own father done just that? But this was no shy-mannered hopeful. This man was an adventurer. Overdressed for his place, brazenly confident. He had already called improperly on Noel. How dare he publicly embrace her under the pretext of a waltz? Or, was it more likely, to embrace her inheritance?

Yet his anger was directed as much at himself as at Ned Fitch, toward something he could not define. It lay in Noel's face, as he had seen her whirl past, head thrown back, lips parted, eyes wide and radiant, an impassioned night blooming, a glowing fantasy of womanhood come alive.

It was not the face of an innocent girl. It was the face of a woman he did not know. He could not erase it.

Had the times become unmanageable? After a life spent working for the stability of his home, the future of his children, protecting them, guiding them, a man had a right to something more than worry. He had a right to his dignity, a right to have his wishes respected. And a right to order in his household. He had consented to Noel's coming marriage with less than enthusiasm. He would have liked, indeed he had hoped for, something more substantial, a place in society that Noel would have graced. Yet he had long known that this daughter of his had depth, taste, a steeliness of mind with which he was not easy in a woman. Perhaps the young schoolteacher, bloodless as he was, had qualities of the mind. But the matter was done. And he had agreed with Adrienne that Noel should be married properly in St. George's Church with all Stuyvesant Square in attendance. Maria would have wanted that.

But now, Walter found himself of a different mood. Noel's wedding might be not only a relief but a salvation. With a father's instinct, he had sensed danger in the man, Ned Fitch. The sooner the girl was married the better. Walter would do everything possible to make her wedding day happy. He was walking too rapidly. He slowed to catch his breath. The Colonel's talk of the draft riots had depressed him. His own father had suffered the first of his strokes after that vandalism.

A shiver of mortality brushed him. He smiled faintly, remembering one of Maria's many small merriments. "A rabbit running over your grave, Walter!"

The day was shortening. Stuyvesant Square was enveloped in a four o'clock hush. Walter let himself into his house and sat down for a moment in the high-backed hall chair, then slowly he went upstairs.

In the second-floor hall he met Mrs. Jessup coming up the backstairs. Her arms were overflowing with black lace ruffles.

"Mrs. Tremont's dress for the evening, sir. She's resting, so I'll hang it in the spare room and not disturb her."

He would not disturb Adrienne either. He would take his own rest in the spare room. As he removed his boots and lay heavily down on the unfamiliar bed, he found himself gazing at the voluptuous black gown that would encase the body of his beautiful wife, as he so seldom—he let the thought die.

He had had no idea that her evening at Kitty's was to be so formal.

On the Monday after Thanksgiving, the press announced that on his February twelfth visit to New York, President Hayes would honor the eighty-seventh birthday of that city's venerated philanthropist, Peter Cooper. A fortuitous coincidence, dug up by a sharp-eyed political hopeful. The President would speak at Cooper Institute, that enormous bulk of arched brownstone on Ninth Street and Fourth Avenue, which Mr. Cooper had presented to the city. President Hayes would pay respects to that unique institution, as the first universal college in the nation for men and women of all creeds, races, and ages. The President would also be shown the equally unique system of pipes and conduits through which giant basement fans propelled cool air in summer, warm in winter, up and under each seat in the auditorium. It was another of the city's marvels.

So the modern New York would greet the President. The ghost of Abraham Lincoln would not walk. The visit would please the city leaders. It had the right American overtones.

But it was not enough. In their Tammany-run, sin-and-glitter city, wise political heads realized that if New York was to influence the choice of a presidential successor, Rutherford Hayes, tedious as he might be, must be made to feel not only welcome but at ease.

Reform was in order.

Tuesday morning's newspapers carried the announcement of the Mayor's choice to head the Reception Committee. He was:

> a man known for his dedication to civic reform, a man who came to New York a poor immigrant boy from Strasbourg, who followed his father into the simple trade of a tailor and rose through hard work and honest principles to become one of the city's most respected leaders, a man who has always stood for decency, honor, and solid family life. He is the distinguished head of the Citizens League, Mr. Walter C. Tremont of Stuyvesant Square. Later in the month Mr. Tremont will address the City Council on methods of fighting the twin vipers poisoning our magnificent city, Corruption and Vice.

In the dubious ease of his rooming house bedroom, Ned Fitch lay on his back reading very word. Since the night Noel had breathed a promise to meet him, Ned had linked himself indissolubly with the Tremont name. In the ensuing days fantasies had glowed in his mind, frozen scenes in a magic lantern show. He saw himself with Noel at his side, welcomed by Mr. Tremont's outstretched hand, mellow smile. He saw himself at the family table, witty, courteous, winning them all with his devotion to Noel. He saw himself in the inner offices of Tremont & Sons, being pressed to join the company. He saw himself at ease at the Hoffman House bar with free-spirited young David, his friend, soon to become his brother. "So you're going to marry her, Ned. She couldn't do better. Nor could you!"

How pleasant it was going to be, accepted, able to be at one's best.

But mainly he thought of Noel. Of stripping away that shield of pride, as he would strip the silken layers of her clothes, to reveal a body of slim loveliness, lifting to meet his.

How intense those imaginings, culminating in that single, never-to-be forgotten day, the most propitious of his life. On a hidden woodland path he had taken her into his arms, as sure of her love as of his own. Then as suddenly the magic, the promise, had been swept from him. She had changed as completely as if some invisible, hostile spirit had touched her. Had it been the solid walls of Stuyvesant Square, or the shadow of her father's house, or the name of Tremont, as it would someday be carved in granite in an imposing cemetery plot?

But he would not give her up, he had told himself in the hopelessness of the summer. Never. Even after he had read with disbelief of her engagement. Then one brief, spangled night, it had all changed as suddenly again. Noel, enticing, yielding, in his arms as they danced. Noel, her eyes, the suppleness of her body, again promising.

Today, this very afternoon at three, they would meet. He would be at the Academy of Art long before that. He had already made the long, extravagant trip up Fifth Avenue by cab. He would be there ahead of her waiting. He had no doubt of the outcome. Noel had come to her senses, broken her engagement. He would not even ask her how she could have even considered the fellow.

He tossed the newspaper aside. In the new leather collar-button box in the dresser drawer he had stashed six ten-dollar bills, gleaned weekly from his winnings. It would be enough to see them out of the city. He could see Noel's eyes dance at the prospect of an elopement. . . .

The knock at the door was as light as it was unexpected. And playful, a habit his landlady had acquired.

"Come in, Mrs. Luskin."

"A message for you, Neddie." His landlady's perfume had not diminished in impact. But it would not be much longer endured. "I gave the boy a nickel."

"How kind you are, Mrs. Luskin."

She moved closer as he opened the envelope. He read the message, folded it quickly, and thrust it into his pocket.

"Business." He said it shortly and patted her hand because it was now expected. It was also, he had discovered, a method of dismissal.

When she was gone, he reread the slip of paper. Four words. The very lack of signature carried authority. "Be here at noon."

In the euphoria of the last days, Ned had dispelled any significance or premonition he might have attached to meeting the Parson at Miss Phoebe Bliss's ball. The Parson's eyes had been cold, but then they always were. He had barely acknowledged Ned, but he rarely did. On the other hand, he might have been impressed meeting his new assistant in such surroundings. Ned had not seen his employer at his post in the Gemini Club for the last few days. No doubt this hasty summons from him was good news—a raise, a promotion. Not that it mattered now. In three hours he would be with Noel.

As he dressed he rehearsed his plans. He knew precisely where the museum was, the heavy glass door, the tall, narrow brownstone building. He knew how long it would take by horsecar, or cab. He would have to allow a little more time from Warren Street and the Gemini Club. Whatever the Parson's business with him, it would not take long. Time was not something the Parson wasted on his underlings.

Fastening his collar button into a stiff and immaculate white linen collar, he smiled at the mirrored image. "You can tell a gentleman by his linen and his shoes. . . ." His mother would have taken pleasure in this image. He wondered fleetingly what she would have thought of the gambling skills that had provided it.

But the past had faded to the sepia of a long-lost daguerreotype. The day was here, as immediate as the quickening of his own blood, the future opening as wide as the sky. At the museum he would watch her enter the room, see him. They would look at each other. And that look would hold all that they knew and wanted of each other.

He would tell her of his plans. She would go with him this very afternoon. They would take the ferry at Twenty-third Street to Jersey City. A train to Trenton. On the outskirts he had heard there was an accommodating justice of the peace . . . 'Do you, Edmond . . . Do you Edmond Abingdon . . .'? What name would it be? It didn't matter. I do, oh, I do take you, Noel!

Tomorrow a train to New Orleans and quick fortune . . . or west to San Francisco where with a pair of dice it was said gold rolled into a man's pocket. He wondered how Noel would enjoy being married to a gambling man. He would make sure that she loved it—the days when he could show her the world, the nights when they would lie together, forever one.

He glanced at his new watch on its heavy chain, hung properly in his watch pocket. He would give the Parson a half hour, no more. But he would not antagonize him. The Parson had unseen powers Ned had no desire to test. Time enough to notify him when he and Noel had safely left the city.

Promptly at twelve, Ned was seated in the hushed inner office of the Gemini Club.

The Parson wore a benevolent smile. His jowled face was clean shaven and pink in another of his guises. All evidence of a beard was gone. Today, a plain black frock coat and the pious white collar of a cleric added to his air of serenity. He looked like nothing so much as a benign country vicar.

"Good of you to come so promptly, Ned."

"Happy to be of service, sir." Ned was emboldened by the morning's fantasies. "I have nothing until an afternoon appointment."

"When?"

"At, uh, two."

"Ah. Well, we won't keep the, er, lady, I presume, waiting." The jest was clumsy, the smile continued. "You read the morning papers, I assume."

If amiability was to be the mood, Ned would adapt. He gave the Parson an easy grin. "Yes, sir. I understood reading the papers was expected of me."

"So it is, so it is. I like my people to keep up with the world. It's changing too fast these days." The Parson sharpened his gaze on Ned. "I believe you once told me that you were employed by a college professor?"

The question was unnecessary. The Parson knew the answer.

"Yes, sir. Office clerk to Dr. Hugo Lendler. Teaches languages. Never knew a man to know so much—"

The Parson cut him off. "He lives in Stuyvesant Square, I understand."

"Yes."

"You worked in his home?"

"Yes."

"Then undoubtedly you know a Mr. Walter Tremont, who lives in the same area."

Ned felt the first stir of uneasiness. The man had attended Miss Bliss's party, heaven knew by what ruse. He had seen Ned there. Undoubtedly he had seen him with Noel. He would keep her out of this.

"I have never met Mr. Tremont." Which was the narrow truth.

"That is not to say you haven't exchanged words with him."

Ned was wary now. The direction was faint as mist, vague of shape or purpose. Yet he sensed it.

"Exchange words? I should say a few."

"Ah." The Parson pulled from his desk drawer a sheet of yellow paper. His eyes were no longer benevolent. "Read this."

Ned saw on the sheet of paper a handwritten column of names: Le Cirque, Josie's, Allah's Garden, Seven Sisters, Blue Grotto, Angela's. He knew what they were. Halfway down the list he saw, circled in red, Gemini Club.

"The police captain sent that list around to me this morning. It is, as you will recognize, a list of the best protected houses of pleasure in the city. Tomorrow it will be on the Commissioner's desk. In a week or two, those houses will be publicly raided and closed. Politics. A show of reform to make the city look good for the President's visit. They'll open again, but at considerable cost in loss of business. That's their affair. Mine is the Gemini Club."

The Parson leaned forward. His movements were so spare that the slightest shift could seem threatening.

"The Gemini Club has never been on such a list. This is a gentlemen's club, operated for the sole pleasure of its members."

It was a good deal more than that, but Ned with the well-trained instinct of underdog began to sense danger.

"The question is"—the gravel voice softened, a warning,

as Ned knew—"how did the Gemini Club happen to be on that list? Who thought it might be of interest to the reformers, a feather you might say in Mr. Walter Tremont's silk hat?"

Ned might have blurted a quick denial, protested honestly he knew nothing, but even as the words formed in his mind, he could hear his own entrapment. In the Parson's world of half-truths, untruths, a man's word meant nothing. Only power made for safety, and the bulky, motionless figure across the desk embodied it.

"There would be reasons, of course," the Parson continued almost dreamily. "Mr. Tremont has a daughter, a very attractive young lady, is she not? Someone interested in the daughter might understandably wish to find favor with the father."

Ned's fists tightened. So did the muscles of his jaw. He could not, he must not, lose his temper. His only purpose now was to leave the premises, to escape this man's realm of evil, this miasma of secret information and secret influence that seemed to Ned without limit and devoid of decency.

But to hear Noel referred to in this poisoned talk was almost more than his self-control could manage. She would be dressing now to meet him. She would be thinking of him, only of him, as he must think only of her. Nothing, he told himself as his knuckles whitened beneath the desk, nothing else mattered.

"So, Mr. Abbingdon-Lord-Fitch"—the Parson's voice held—what? Amusement? Satisfaction?—"if that's what you like to call yourself in high society, you might also have found it convenient to report the activities of the Gemini Club to the president of the Citizens League."

The trap was sprung. The Parson had seen Ned with Noel, had watched them dance their ecstasy. He could guess the rest. He was waiting for Ned to lie.

Ned looked directly into the small, cold eyes. Uncertainty would indict him. Fear would be a confession. Denial, like the truth, was useless. It flashed through Ned's mind that the inclusion of the Gemini Club on that telling list might in itself be a trap, set by this charlatan who trusted no man. He, Ned, was being tested, probed for treachery. If the Parson could prove it to his own satisfaction, Ned would disappear from the surface of this teeming city as surely as rain into the sea. The rules of the game. In his own way Ned had played it himself. In the streetwise cynicism of London's alleys, it takes a gull to catch a gull.

Ned forced a smile, his face and voice brightening with street slyness.

"Well, Parson, it couldn't be that you're taking a big jump to the wrong conclusion? Maybe you don't know me yet. Maybe you don't know how much I've learned here. What counts. How to get rich on my own. Where the power lies. You've taught me that. Why would I chase any girl now, much less one who's already promised? I don't know Mr. Tremont. Sure, you saw me dance with his daughter. I was told to, by the fat old lady. I figured that was why a chap like me was invited. To dance with young ladies left sitting along the wall. But if you think I'd give up a good living and expectations for that, you take me for a fool."

The Parson sat back, folded his hands across his stomach, and closed his eyes. It was one of his more disconcerting habits. Then he permitted himself a thick chuckle.

"I don't take you for a fool, boy. I don't make mistakes like that. You're sharp, I saw that at the beginning. So we're two of a kind, are we?"

He picked up the list of New York's best known brothels, but he did not destroy it. He laid it carefully in the shallow center drawer of his desk. "Maybe so. My father used to give me two pieces of advice. One, never trust a sleeping dog, a horse's health, or a whore's tears. The other, never hire a man smarter than yourself. I never have."

He lifted the lid of a silver-banded mahogany humidor on his desk and pushed the box toward Ned.

Ned took the cigar. What he wanted was a glimpse of the watch in his vest pocket. But there had been a subtle change in the Parson's manner, a hint of menace, made more threatening by his easy geniality. Ned sat stiff, immobile, waiting as he had once seen a dog wait in a bearpit.

The Parson blew a ring of smoke toward the ceiling.

"You should have known my father, Ned. He was a traveling preacher. Had me trained to the cloth, too. Oh, yes, I've earned my collar. That surprise you? Get over that, boy. Never show surprise at a poker table."

The Parson blew another smoke ring. He was taking his time and savoring it.

"As a boy I traveled with him. We had a small covered wagon, black with a black canvas top. I'd drive the horse until we got near a village. Then my father in his black cloak and hat would take the reins, looking like the wrath of God had come to town." The Parson chuckled. "I'd climb back and ride under the canvas cover with the big Bible and a set of wooden type faces. Tell you about that, too. We'd go out through Pennsylvania, Indiana, down into Tennessee, always just two weeks behind Dr. Archibald Snow."

The Parson settled deeper into his chair, looking not at Ned but at something above and behind him. To Ned, the slow words became minutes.

"You never heard of Dr. Snow, boy. A pity. He was an expert. Claimed he was the most honest man in the country. He told people what they wanted to hear and sold 'em what they wanted to have. He wore a white suit and a broad white hat, and drove a white wagon with gilt wheels hitched to a pair of white horses. He'd stop at a village, take out a white bottle of something he called Spirits of Retaw, which if you can spell, which most of 'em couldn't, is water, backwards. Guaranteed to make men manlier, women hot-blooded. It would also purge bile, cure rheumatism, remove wood ticks, and improve business. It cost a dollar a bottle and tasted bad enough to fix anything."

The Parson emitted one of his thick chuckles and waved his cigar.

"You've let your smoke go out, boy. That's high-priced Havana. Light up. The girl will wait. If not, there's always another, I've found. We have a lot to talk about. Never have really gotten to know each other. Well, to go back to Dr. Snow, it took about two weeks for the yokels to realize they'd been swindled. Two weeks was just when my father would drive into town, preaching sin and salvation at the top of his voice. He told them it was lust that made them buy that stuff. Lust and greed. Two deadliest sins in the Good Book. Didn't they know that? Didn't they read the Bible? To him that hath shall be given, from him that hath not shall be taken away! There's a word missing there. The Lord wanted it that way. To him that hath what? He wanted each sinner to find that word for himself. Repent, brothers and sisters. Repent! That's the missing word. To him that hath repented shall be given. Then he'd take a white card from a stack in his pocket. 'It says so, right here on this little card. Repent! The Lord hath taken your hand.' Then he'd give each and every one of them one of those cards. Their own name printed on it. Fifty cents. Fifty cents, folks, buy Repentence! That's when I'd go to work there in the back of the wagon. I got to be pretty quick. I could print any name, Josiah Smith, Tilly Jones, on that card in no time at all and hear the money dropping into my father's leather pouch. But that's not the end of the story."

The Parson studied Ned for a long minute.

"You in a hurry, Ned?"

"I told you I had an appointment, sir."

"I've no doubt. But I'll need a little more of your time, my friend. Because what I'm explaining to you is how I operate, which I don't think you've taken in."

The small eyes now looked dangerous.

"Well, to finish the story, I soon saw, while I was printing names in the back of that old wagon, that Dr. Snow was making a dollar on the side of sin by cheating people while my father was making fifty cents on the side of salvation. I said that to him and waited for him to take off his belt and give me a 'soul strapping,' he used to call it. Instead he burst into a laugh, which he didn't do very often. And gave a lecture instead. . . . 'You're smart, son, good and smart. Mighty young to have seen the light. Sin and Salvation, two sides of the same coin. Old man Snow and me, both of us doing the Lord's work for a profit. If he wasn't out there leading people to sin, I wouldn't be coming along saving 'em. If I'd seen that twenty years ago I'd be a rich man now. But I'm too old to change. But you, son,' my old man said, 'you've figured it out. You get your preacher training and then you decide which side of the Lord's work'd suit you best.' "

The Parson smiled, as chill a smile as Ned had ever seen.

"It didn't take me long, Fitch. I took the side of Sin. Every thousand dollars I take in here at the Gemini Club gives some preacher a soul to save." He rubbed his cigar out in a cloisonné bowl and rose.

"Time now for you to see another branch of my operation."

Ned had at last managed a glance at his watch. It was nearly two. He had a long trip uptown. He had never heard the Parson talk so much. He knew the man did nothing without a purpose. The "other operation," he could guess was the twin side of the Gemini Club, known to the Parson's employees and clients as the "Opera House."

Entrance was forbidden to the employees, but Ned had seen it. He had been smuggled through the draped second-floor door one night by an exuberant, grateful, and very drunk dice winner. Ned had looked into the circle of red velvet boxes. Each could be made private by red velvet hangings, each contained a divan. He had seen the gold-and-white paneling, the small but superb crystal chandelier, an exact, diminished replica, his guide said, of the Paris Opera House. With a difference. He had caught glimpses of the erotic rites performed by the youngest, loveliest harlots in New York, some of them convent bred, accomplished as debutantes, their nudity lustrous as pearl. It was said the girls never lasted long at the "Opera." They became courtesans, mistresses, even wives of men bearing some of the most famous names and fortunes in the city.

The Parson was now on his feet. "If you are thinking of your appointment, Ned, I'm afraid the lady will have to wait. For your own good, you'd better come along."

The threat was open now. As Ned knew, the Parson was never alone. Behind any door, in any corridor of the building, there could be a guard, a watcher.

The Parson opened a side door. Ned followed him into a corridor he had never before seen, down a long flight of stairs. He found himself in a long basement, clean, well bricked, and lighted by two oil lamps. Overhead was a web of pipes. More unusual were a large table, a half dozen or so straight chairs, and a couch with a quilt over it. A not impossible place to stay if staying were necessary.

From the size of the basement he could guess that it extended under both houses.

The Parson's geniality had returned.

"I will also show you why the Gemini Club remains in this not-very-stylish section of the city." He took a lantern from the wall, lighted it, and opened a narrow, iron-banded door in the wall. "Look down there."

Ned peered into the darkness. Below he could discern a kind of tunnel, twenty feet wide. The faint light struck two dim metal rails on the ground.

"My private tunnel, boy. Without a lantern a man could get lost down there and never be heard of again. And the rats are bad." He chuckled. "Charlie Beach's folly, they called it, when it was built. That was a dozen years ago. Beach had the idea he could send a railway car underground blown by air through a pneumatic tube like a piece of mail. When it had gone a full block it would be drawn back. Sucked back by the same air power. A subway he called it. It worked all right. It ran from Warren Street to Murray Street. Beach decorated the waiting room. Paintings, a piano, a fountain, plants. People lined up for the ride."

The Parson swung the heavy door closed. "Trouble was, Beach couldn't get a charter for his subway. Boss Tweed couldn't see enough profit in it for himself. So it was abandoned. When I bought the old Gemini, I discovered it. I thought it might have its uses. So I rebuilt the old house and stayed and bought the one next to it. Now, as a trusted employee, you know all my secrets."

He chuckled.

"This way, now."

He led Ned to the far end of the long brick cellar up another flight of stairs, into a narrow hallway papered in conventional brown stripes. At the end of it, they entered what Ned guessed was the front room of the next house. Whatever he had expected beneath the opulent Opera House upstairs, it had certainly no relation to this pleasant little parlor with its commonplace Brussels carpet, brown looped curtains, plain oak furnishings. A glass-fronted bookcase, with its rows of leather-bound books, filled half of one wall. A deep chair drawn up to a coal grate, and a cage with a canary chirping at the visitors, completed the middle-class domesticity.

The Parson was no visitor.

"Good afternoon, Aggie." He smiled benevolently at a watchful little maid in black uniform and white apron in the doorway.

"Good day, Reverend."

"I'm expecting callers. Have they arrived?"

"Yes, your Reverence. A few minutes ago. They're in the side room."

"Show them in, Aggie, if you will." He might have been an avuncular bishop.

"Yes, sir." The girl curtsied to his kindliness, as if she had already set a foot in heaven.

She departed. In another moment she had ushered in the Parson's callers.

Ned saw a gaunt erect woman, taller than average, rail thin, her grey hair drawn tight, her black dress beneath a black shawl unadorned as a shroud except for the small gold cross at her throat. Her strong, thin features bore the stamp of aristocracy. Her heavy-lidded eyes were the most tragic he had ever seen in a human face.

With her, clutching the black-gloved hand, was a child.

"Ah, Madame"—the Parson rose—"you are prompt, indeed. It is a pleasure to see you. You are well, I hope. And the little one."

"Well." The syllable seemed to have been forced from her, grating and leaden.

"And why not? You walk in God's grace, Madame. This is my young associate, interested like myself in human nature." He turned to Ned. "Madame runs a school, an excellent French school, though you would not find it listed in the city's educational institutions. I have taken an interest in it. You might say I like to think of myself as the protector, the spiritual adviser, to Madame's excellent work."

But Ned, if he was listening, had only half heard. He was looking at the child, with such intensity that she stared back. She could be no more than four or five. Her hair fell straight and fine as silk from her dark blue bonnet. Her dark blue coat reached almost to her neat little white boots. But it was her face that held him, her face, an expression, an image, a face he knew. Who was it? She gave him a faint smile, shy, fleeting.

"Ah, little Elizabeth. How are we today?" The Parson held out a thick hand.

"Fais ta révérence, cherie."

"English, Madame!" snapped the Parson.

The woman's heavy-lidded eyes flashed for an instant.

"Make your curtsy, Elizabeth."

The child obeyed dutifully, woodenly. She did not move forward or extend her hand. Her gaze returned to Ned.

"Sit down, Madame, won't you? Be at ease. As you see, Ned, Madame's pupils are not only talented but charming. They are from some of New York's finest families but, alas, if their existence were admitted or even known, many of those families might lose their social status. Little Elizabeth, for example, is—"

"No!" Madame was on her feet. "You dare not! You shall not!"

The Parson raised a commanding hand. "Ah, Madame, you disturb yourself. You are perhaps overtired. You work hard. Your responsibilities are heavy. I must remind you as your adviser, your counselor, that it is I who make the rules. For your own protection. However, I think it is hardly necessary to say more. My young friend here sees for himself."

Ned took his eyes from the child. Bewilderment, frustration churned in a violent impulse to sink his fingers into the thick throat of the fraudulent cleric. He saw indeed. He saw in childhood innocence, the face that had filled his thoughts for so long. The tip-tilted nose, the fine modeling of brow, cheekbones, chin. Noel.

"The resemblance to the mother is remarkable, is it not, Mr. Fitch?"

Ned was not prepared for sparring. Realization was sweeping through him, answering as many questions, as it left dark. This was Noel's face. This was her secret. This elfin child with Noel's dark eyes, her seriousness, even the half smile that revealed hidden humor. Noel's child. By whom? His mind rejected the question, as it rejected disgrace. His own background, his poverty, had not taught him to censure. He felt to his own surprise a rush of tenderness, a protectiveness, he had never in the course of his mottled ambitions known. He wanted only to find Noel, to reassure her.

The Parson was still talking. "As Madame knows, I demand little from those around me. Loyalty. Nothing more. Or less. Treachery I do not forgive. You have been foolish, Ned, in your choice of new friends. Were you to continue, to my disadvantage, you would force me to reveal the existence of this child. A pity, would it not be? To the family of a man who now advises the Mayor, who associates with the President, who stands publicly for the noblest standards of family life . . . ?"

Ned found himself meeting the stare of the small girl pressing against Madame's black skirt. He had no idea what she was thinking. But no one can guess what magic fragments fill a child's mind. Lights and shadows, colors and shapes, size and space. Looking up at the tall man, she suddenly spoke.

"Mistaffy doesn't come to see my anymore. . . ."

"Tais-toi, ma petite," Madame commanded.

Ned bent down to the child. "Who?" he whispered.

She stepped back to the safety of the black folds and looked up at him, a smile flickering for an instant on her serious mouth.

"Mistaffy. My friend. Do you know her?"

"Perhaps." He searched the child's face.

"That's enough. Take the child up, Madame." The Parson had risen. He seemed to fill the small parlor, to hover over the three figures like a bird of prey. But the child was unaware. She pulled away from Madame's arms and stared up at the tall stranger.

"Will *you* come to see me?"

"Yes." A promise that he swore to himself to keep.

The Parson pressed a wall buzzer.

"Show the gentleman out, Aggie." His displeasure was as apparent as the underlying finality. Ned heard in it the cold challenge of an enemy now totally revealed.

He looked once more at the child, meeting her eyes with warmth, engraving her face on his mind. Then he followed the maid out. He did not glance at the Parson again.

The Parson reseated himself, gazed at nothing in his fashion, then swung his attention to the gaunt woman, clutching Posie's hand.

"Well, Madame—"

"Never ask me to do this again! To bring any child here!"

"I will ask you, Madame, whatever I wish. I must remind you that you're again behind in your account."

Madame Ducharde's aristocratic head lifted, her disdain intact but a look in her eyes of trapped fury.

"I have had expenses."

"So have I. You are not running a charity school, nor am I protecting one. I might ask how long you intend to keep that child without receiving payment?"

"That is my affair. I run my school as I think best. I pay you well for your—services."

"Without them, I remind you again, Madame, how long could you keep your pretty little bastards before the police asked to see your license and the press demanded an inquiry?"

"How much time will you give me?"

"That is better. Shall we say two weeks?"

"Three."

"Always at your service, Madame. Three." He buzzed for the maid. "Madame is leaving. Send for a cab." He bowed his heavy head toward his visitor. "You see. It is all made simple. As usual. Three weeks, then. Good day, Madame."

She nodded. "Elizabeth, *fais ta révérence.*" Her lips wore the whiteness of death.

Riding uptown in a driving rain, Ned struggled to sort out the turmoil, the conflicts, in his mind. He was late. It was already past three. But the museum would be open. She would wait. Surely she would wait. His need to see her, the strength of his love for her, the power of his will, bent entirely on her, would keep her there. Invisible tendrils holding her there until he could reach her.

The shock of his discovery had passed. Only tenderness, an obsession to be with her remained. With it the surfacing of a deep sensation he had only begun to define. Relief. Noel was no longer the remote, the unreachable woman he had known, separated from him by the wall of proprieties, of solid wealth that no one would discuss but everyone must have, the artificial rules and manners by which Society protected itself. Noel stood human and flawed. But in his eyes, clear and whole as the morning light. He was the man who loved her. Noel and her child.

The cab broke free of the shouting, wheel-locking crush that was Broadway and turned up Fifth Avenue. He would be late, but she would be waiting. She had not given her word idly.

Looking through the rain-blurred window, he was jolted by the unexpected sight of a stark, gothic mansion, the house of the late, notorious Mrs. Restell. On that side street he had caught sight of Noel, running into the night mist. He understood now. Like the lowliest frightened servant girl, she had turned to the only woman who could help her in her betrayal. As the cab passed, Ned saw that the huge house was boarded up, doors and windows. A chain hung across the spiked iron gate. Scaffolding rose along the sides in preparation for demolition. Demolition of the past, Ned thought, for Noel and himself.

The cabman reined up at a tall brownstone building that was the art museum. Ned bounded up the steps. The opaque glass door was locked. A white card noted HOURS TEN TO FOUR. EVENINGS SEVEN TO NINE. It was ten minutes past four.

The darkening sky told Ned that the afternoon, like Noel herself had vanished.

He rattled the handle. She would not be there now. But he needed desperately to know that she had been there. In that lay his life.

He pressed his face against the door and saw a shadow. He shook the handle again and called out. A withered old man in the uniform of a guard peered out.

"Closed."

"I don't want to come in. I want to ask a question. Please. Just a moment. I was to meet a lady here, young, brown hair . . . elegant."

The old man had dignity. He was also tired.

"We have had many young elegant lady visitors today. I couldn't tell you."

"But she was waiting. At the Hudson River pictures, maybe sitting on a bench. You must have seen her."

"There is no bench in that room."

"Then in the hall, or another room, a young lady waiting?"

The old man coughed. "There was one, overstayed. Against the rules. Don't like that. When it's time to close a man should do his duty. Good day."

The rain lashed the street. Ned turned up his collar. He heard the sound of bells, the merry ring of harness bells, the first of the Christmas season.

It was the loneliest sound of his life.

31

Christmas was the healing time. Hurt forgotten, error forgiven, ruptures mended and the essential bonds of life renewed. Walter Tremont was given to such thoughts at this season because for so many years Maria had lived them.

She had loved Christmas as a child does. For weeks ahead, the old brownstone house on East Sixteenth Street would be scrubbed and polished, the closets filling with mystery, the rooms with the scents of cloves, cinnamon, spices, mincemeat, candied fruit syrups, and the ultimate triumph, roasting goose.

"I do believe, Walter"—her eyes would sparkle beneath the white frill of what she called her cookie cap—"that the Scriptures haven't explained all of it. Not the anticipation. The getting ready. Thinking of all the people you don't think enough about, what to give them, what to do for them. Beginning all over as if all the troubles of life had swept away. But of course the Scriptures couldn't tell about all that because they only had the Star and the Baby." She'd brush a bit of flour from the tip of her nose. "I think about that Baby sometimes when I'm decorating the cookies. Suppose he hadn't been the Savior? Wouldn't that be a miracle, too? Wouldn't it be like making a long journey and finding you've come home? There's nothing on earth to make people feel warm and good and belonging to each other like a new baby in the house. Oh, my"—she'd laugh up at him—"I do go on about Christmas, don't I? Now you leave my kitchen before you get flour all over that fine frock coat!"

Then would come the day, much like this one, frosted, with snow in the air, when she'd walk with him through the crowds of shoppers on lower Broadway, past the gaudily trimmed holiday windows, one hand tucked under his arm, the other holding her small moleskin muff to her chin.

"I'm going to be quite extravagant this year, Walter. I'll need a dozen more angels for the tree, some new drums and a box of assorted carved birds, a half dozen sleds with those tiny elves on them, and some Norwegian trolls. The children do love them. And oh, a few new sheep and cows for the farm underneath and a new cradle for the creche. Tiggie ate the old one. But no cornucopias. They're papier-mâché and they can catch fire too easily. The children will have their candies in their stockings."

It was Maria's glorious hour. Walter denied her nothing and always doubled the order. Her face when she opened the packages at home was his reward.

Christmas, without Maria. It was for others now. He must take time tomorrow to select a pearl brooch for Adrienne.

As he walked toward Bleecker Street, he told himself he should be a man at peace. His speech on reform had gone well. It had been quoted in the papers. He had been asked to join the National Republican Campaign Committee. This would mean visits to Washington, a widening of his horizons. It was good for a man of his age to have so much to look forward to.

As for David, he had come to dinner and, like a man, apologized for his behavior. When Walter had broached the subject of six months abroad to study art, David had surprised him. He had looked from his father to Adrienne and back. He had agreed. If you do not push too hard, Walter told himself, doors will open. David was still boyish but he was learning.

Adrienne had changed, too. She had matured to the dignity of a young matron. He must not, in the nostalgia of Maria's long-ago Christmases, forget that Adrienne was his to protect. She had entrusted herself, her life, her happiness, to his care. She was his wife. Whatever one did, life could never be entirely seamless.

All this left only one cloud on his pleasant holiday horizon. Walter could not quite name it or justify it. But there it was and it had brought him today to the dark green door of Tremont & Sons. Overhead the entrance was suitably hung with a holiday garland. One of the loops had slipped from its hook. Walter reached up and with the tip of his cane replaced it. Beneath was revealed a chipping in the gilt paint of the name. No doubt Orrin intended to have it retouched, but it brought to mind Orrin's suggestion that the name be changed from Tremont & Sons to Tremont & Company.

"It will give us a broader business base, Father. We're

expanding. These are new days. We need new blood, new ideas. My little Freddie may not be interested in the old firm when his time comes.''

Neither new blood nor his frail seven-year-old grandson occupied Walter's mind at the moment. He saw his own father, newly come to America, bent over pattern board and scissors twenty hours a day in the dim area behind his first Duane Street store. Years later, his father's misty-eyed pride when the gilt lettering finally took shape on Bleecker Street, Tremont & Sons. That pride would remain alive as long as Walter breathed. He had said no and the matter had been dropped. Now, as he entered the familiar premises, he saw other changes. More clothes displayed, a dapper young salesman in a striped shirt. He hurried to the rear office.

Orrin rose abruptly from a cavernous black leather chair. It had been designed for Walter. Orrin had yet to fit it comfortably. The arrival of the older man never failed to remind him of his own slighter dimensions. It takes bulk to fill that chair, his father's presence seemed to say—bulk, physical and moral.

''Stay where you are, son,'' Walter waved him back. ''You run the business now.'' He lowered himself into a side chair. Orrin started to sit down, thought better of it, and came around the desk to another side chair.

''You're looking well, Father.''

''Always do at this time of year. Spending money is like drinking a fine cognac. Does a man good on special occasions. How are things going here?''

''Very well, sir. Very well indeed. We have an order for forty lightweight cheviots from Stewart's and twenty-five pongees for summer from Wanamaker.'' Orrin glanced at his Father, who seemed to be studying the curved handle of his cane. ''Our private clientele is holding up well, but there are a million people in this city today. Before the century's out maybe two million—''

''I know, I know.'' Walter had been over this argument before. He had either to let Orrin run the business or run it himself and he had passed that option. He had not come today to discuss the population's need for coats and trousers.

''I suppose Charlotte told you that Noel has decided on a large wedding.''

''Yes. What made her change her mind?''

''What makes any woman change her mind? She simply announced last Wednesday at breakfast that if everybody wanted a big wedding, she would agree.''

Orrin sat silent. He had no interest in Noel's nuptials. Her engagement had been a dismal disappointment to him. Orrin understood thoroughly the principles of family aggrandizement. His own marriage had brought them social position. The least Noel could have done was attach herself to one of the new fortunes. Then how they would have expanded! Instead . . .

"It's going to cost you a pretty penny, Father."

"I hope so. And I know it would please your mother. But I haven't come here to talk wedding fripperies. The house is already full of them, Adrienne and Kitty are flying in and out like a pair of demented sparrows. I have other uses for my time these days. I've been thinking again about Noel's dowry."

"What about Noel's dowry?" Orrin's voice was careful. "I thought Henry Merriman had invested it in West Shore Railroad."

Walter had regretted that revelation since the day he had made it. But he had had no choice after Henry had confessed to the investment. Walter had little knowledge of the quicksands of financial dealings.

"Oh, I'm sure Henry invested it wisely, Orrin. I happen to have read this morning that the West Shore might not be built after all. Mr. Morgan is objecting."

Orrin was not only tired of the subject, he could see no reason for money in any shape to go out of the family. Especially as Noel had made her impossible choice.

"It's only rumor, Father. Mr. Morgan has not made a final statement. If he approves, the shares will triple the next day. Besides, what difference can it make now to Noel?" Orrin, as usual, gave way under stress to peevishness. "What use could she have for it in that godforsaken place she's going to live? Except to let Clarence drain it away buying privies for people who don't use them?"

Orrin was capable of offensive vulgarity. Walter rose abruptly. He found that even with the best of intentions he was never able to sustain a discussion with Orrin.

"It is Noel's money. It has been promised to her. Since we cannot discuss it as gentlemen, I shall do what I think best."

By the time he had taken his silk hat from the antlered rack, Walter regretted the scene. He knew his elder son. It was a father's duty to show understanding. There must be no hard feeling. Not at this time of year. Not at Christmas.

He changed the subject. "Remember my old Lieder Singing Society?"

"Indeed I do, sir." Orrin's relief was audible.

"They're paying me some kind of undeserved honor."

"Very much deserved, Father. That speech of yours last week at the Citizens League was splendid. I wish I could be at the celebration tonight."

"A little old-fashioned for young men these days. But there was a time. Family Night, remember? Once a year, I'd take your mother and all three of you children?"

The tightness pinching Orrin's thin mouth lessened. He managed the smile that Noel once said made him look like a chipmunk.

"Of course I remember. Mother used to be so proud of you. I also remember that right after refreshments you'd bundle us all into a cab and hurry us home. David and I knew why. The Haymarket girls came to the party at midnight."

"So they did."

They were at the door. Orrin held to the ease, the safety, of the past.

"David and I used to make bets. When you got us all home on Family Night, did you ever go back to see the girls?"

Walter chuckled. For an instant a lifetime of differences evaporated.

"Always, son. Always."

Out in the street Walter found his mood, like the day, clouded. It was, he realized, no more than a recurrence of the vaporous depression so unlike him. Increasingly these visits to his office had come to seem intrusions, Orrin masking impatience with careful respect, family chatter, irrelevancies of the past. Perhaps that was the way today's youth edged age aside, with not-too-subtle reminders when a father's sway was over. He swung his cane at the invisible shadow across his steps. Uselessness. But it was not for him. He had a new life ahead, an important career. The Mayor himself would be dining at his house. But first he had a different objective. To see Noel happily married, to see her radiant, her eyes shining, as he escorted her down the aisle of St. George's Church.

With that image warming him, he turned downtown and walked directly to his bank. Christmas was the time to make a gesture. The brown envelope he took from his safe-deposit box contained the railroad stocks that now made up Noel's dowry. Orrin had reassured him. In another four or five years, Noel would return home, a woman of fortune. He wanted her to know that.

It had been a tiring day. Ahead lay a night that despite its honors loomed long.

* * *

The much admired hall of the Lieder Singing Society was ornate with white plaster cupids, angels, garlands, and muses, all said to account for its excellent accoustics. It also had a regrettable tendency to grow cold during an evening despite its crush of deep-breathing participants. Walter, a last glass of Rhenish in his hand, moved among friends and fellow members thanking them for their toasts, their good wishes. The night had been a triumph, one of the finest of the Lieder Society's concerts. Walter scarcely remembered what he had sung. He was aware that his middle-aged baritone in which Maria had once delighted had failed some of Handel's rousing Alleluias, and left to others some of the ceiling-ringing notes of the Third Act Prelude to *Lohengrin*, startlingly set to the sentiments of the season. Culture satisfied, the Christmas carols had suited him better. And last, Maria's favorite "Just a Song at Twilight."

As he stepped into the night, the fur collar of his overcoat muffling his hoarse throat, his hat pulled well down, he heard it again in Maria's high girlish tremolo . . . "Though the heart be weary, though the day be long, Still at twilight, Love's old sweet song. . . ."

How he needed her tonight. He had never wished to be here or anywhere without her.

He mounted the steps of his house slowly, surprised to see full lights on.

Adrienne was not yet home.

He would not admit his disappointment. He had not asked her to refuse Kitty's elaborate dinner that night for a Chicago friend whom the ladies had met abroad. Mr. Cotter, Adrienne had explained, owned a private pullman car and would invite them all to Palm Beach in the spring. Too rich for his blood, Walter thought, but again he had to remind himself that Adrienne was young and in the full tide of her life.

The lamp in his study was on. He found Noel seated on a hassock before the grate fire.

"Still up, my dear?"

"I've been waiting to make your hot cocoa."

"Thank you." He lowered himself carefully into his chair. "The celebration was a little overpowering."

"In that case I'll make you ginger tea."

He was struck again by the delicacy of her face, the inscrutability of her expression. Since the day she had surrendered to the idea of a formal wedding, she had walled herself within her own thoughts, as if nothing outside concerned or touched her. She had agreed mechanically to dress fittings. She had surveyed the boxes of linens, fabrics, trousseau patterns poured into the house daily by Adrienne and Kitty. She had smiled faintly and approved everything. It was, Adrienne complained, as if Noel were observing it all from a far distance, for someone else.

"Stay here and talk to me, Noel."

"What shall I talk about?"

About yourself, he thought, what you are thinking. Are you happy? But he had never been on terms that close. The schedule of well-ordered family life had left little time for confidences.

He had a momentary glimpse of lost years.

"I stopped in to see Orrin today."

"Charlotte was here this morning." It was part of Noel's new isolation that she followed statement with statement as if what had been said had no relevance to her.

"How is Charlotte?" The question was perfunctory. Walter wanted only to keep her talking.

"Two of the children are sniffling. Little Freddie has the croup. The second maid left because the bedroom furniture is too heavy to be moved every day for cleaning as Charlotte wants and—"

"Enough!" Walter chuckled. "What else did she want?"

"She wants to borrow Annie-Mae for Christmas Eve and she wants to make sure that I'll be Saint Nicholas as usual."

"And you will?"

"Why not?"

Walter cleared his throat, perhaps to steady his voice. Noel made Christmas live as Maria had.

"I'm very glad, Noel. You'll make us all happy. You know I might have that cocoa after all. And wait up for Adrienne."

"Adrienne is home, Father."

"She is? So soon?"

"We had dinner together."

The tightness that had lately settled in the region of his heart seemed to thin a little. The small room seemed to brighten.

"I thought . . . I must have confused the date. Wasn't this the night of Kitty's dinner party for that rich Chicago fellow? Yes, I'm sure it was . . . the same night as my Lieder Society . . . or am I getting old?"

"No, Father, you are not." She touched his hand. "You never will be. Kitty canceled the dinner. The Chicago man,

Mr. Cotter, received a telegram late today that his eldest boy has caught scarlet fever. He took the next train home."

"Oh. Well, indeed. I'm sorry to hear that. I didn't know that Mr., uh, Cotter was a family man."

"Neither, I'm afraid, did Kitty."

An ember broke in a spray of sparks. Walter watched them disappear.

"Adrienne must have been disappointed."

Noel lifted her head and looked directly at him.

"No, Father. I don't believe she was. I think, in her own way, she was relieved." Something in her father's face impelled her to go on. "We had a very lively time. Mrs. Jessup fixed us what she calls a ladies' supper. You've been spared that. Creamed chicken, diced potatoes, white turnips, blanc mange for dessert. All white. Ugh. I thought we should pour your ruby port over everything. Adrienne suggested cough medicine. We settled for plum jam with the chicken and blackberry sauce on the pudding. I can't imagine where Mrs. Jessup gets her ideas. Maybe Scottish winters."

Walter was tired. But it was a good, gratifying fatigue. His household was whole and under his roof. Noel's eyes had momentarily brightened. Adrienne was upstairs, safe. Perhaps waiting.

He took Noel's hand in his two.

"I'm going to miss you, my little girl."

"I'm going to miss you, Father."

He drew a slow breath. He had had something on his mind for weeks now. Perhaps this was the time to say it. The moment might not come again.

"Noel, I'd like to ask you one question. I hope you'll forgive me if you consider it an intrusion. . . ."

"I shan't, Father."

"It's more of a favor that I want to ask of you. You might even call it a promise."

"What is it, Father?"

Intimacy did not come easily. This was properly a woman's matter. He felt clumsy. He longed for Maria's sure touch.

"Noel, my dear, you and Clarence are going into an unknown future. In an unknown country. Noel . . . if there should be a child"—Walter felt her hand slip from his—"my little girl, when there is to be a child, will you come home to us?"

A hiss of flame filled the silence. Her answer when it came was small and distant as if she were already half a world away.

"I'll—yes, Father."

For a long moment after he left, longer than she would guess, she sat motionless before the coal fire. Her father's question had no more to do with her than the drapings of white satin and lace taking shape at the seamstress's. Her plans were complete now, as tightly interlocked as a Chinese box. Nothing would alter them. She had only to go through the steps day by day, through the motions. She had only to obtain the promised dowry, deliver it to Madame Ducharde and secure Posie's future. She would see Posie on Christmas Eve, Madame Ducharde had promised that, in the squat little church at the end of the path. She would see her distantly, but she would never admit to herself that it could be for the last time.

The rest of the plans had become a blur, the awfulness of the wedding, her father's arm down the long aisle, the undemanding facelessness of her bridegroom, the empty words, the rites of well-wishers, flowers, toasts . . . then at last the Overland train. She had even decided at which station she would disappear. Clarence would be momentarily hurt but more likely stoic. He could claim marriage and desertion. His sisters would fill the vacuum with a consoling prophylaxis of pity and duty.

And she would be free. Free to work or go hungry, free to find oblivion, free to return a veiled stranger for the rare, permitted glimpses of Posie as her child flowered.

Already in the rigidity of these last conforming days Noel was aware of a new breadth to her life. Now that she had surrendered, now that she was doing what was expected, they had begun at last to leave her alone. She could sit here, in this tight little study, as late as she liked. She had done all that had been asked of her. She would no longer hear in the morning even Adrienne's admonishing, "But a bride needs her beauty sleep."

Noel stirred the grate, added coal from the scuttle, and settled herself again on the low hassock. Ripples of blue flame ran across the coals, ripples as blue as that June sky above her in the woods, in the woods with him. She had come perilously close that day to breaking out of her shell, shattering her careful plan, destroying all the careful order she had brought to her life and Posie's.

She had waited until closing at the art museum that rain-sodden Tuesday. She had wandered from one room to another seeking him. If he had come late, she would have accepted his apology. But he had not come. The minutes of her watch ticked on. Ten, twenty, forty-five. . . . Time, at first her ally, had become her chastiser, at the end the chilling arbiter of her decision. She would not undo that decision.

She jabbed a fire tong at the coals, sending the flames higher. She would think of Christmas Eve, the clutter of small tasks at hand. Charlotte calling on her to ask her to do what she had done every Christmas Eve since her mother had died. Why were they all treating her as one apart? Was it the mythical sanctity attached to the coming wedding, the weight of innocence and virginity seen to set the bride apart, too fragile, too tremulous now for a normal day's pursuit? What a woman must conceal!

It would be her last Christmas Eve. Except for one momentous difference, it would be exactly as it had always been. The family, gathered in the old brownstone house on Sixteenth Street now occupied by Orrin, adults and children together in the parlor, the ceiling-high tree not yet lighted. At eight o'clock promptly the parlor door would open. A single orange would roll into the room. The children's eyes would widen with a mixture of terror and delight. A few seconds of unendurable suspense, then Saint Nicholas himself would appear in the doorway with his sack of rewards and punishments. He would call on each child to sing or recite a verse prepared with increasing anxiety during the weeks before. According to the merits of the performance, the child would receive an orange or a piece of coal.

In Noel's childhood, Maria's spinster sister, Lena, played the role of the good Saint Nicholas. At the insistence of Maria, however, the sack never contained coal. The shame of failure was enough to spur any little miscreant for another year. There would be no tears at Christmas in Maria's house.

By common consent, Noel had taken over the task for the children of Orrin and Charlotte and their small cousins. She made a slight Saint Nicholas, but a pillow fore and aft and some strategic toweling had filled the red suit and rounded out the image. Despite Charlotte's severe admonitions against indulgences, Noel, too, never carried pieces of coal. Worse, in Charlotte's eyes, Noel seemed to know every child's game, verse, and song ever created. She could prompt the most numbed, foot-twisting child to triumph. Her Saint Nicholas invariably finished his visit with a romp of children giggling through the old carols.

Ten minutes after Saint Nicholas's departure, Noel in party dress would rush in, full of apologies for missing it all. The children would smother her with their triumphs. Buckets of sand and water would be set in readiness against the ever real possibility of fire, and the tree would be lighted, each tiny white candle on the tip of a branch bursting into lovely bloom.

Presents exchanged, the evening meal ended in a lively march along Sixteenth Street and around the corner to the poinsettia splendor of St. George's Church.

How beautiful it had always seemed, how close, how loving. Noel would gladly do it once more, she longed to do it, before she would find the excuse to slip quietly, quickly away to the little church behind Madame Ducharde's school. To see the serious little face of her child.

A knock shattered the vision.

Annie-Mae thrust an uncertain head around the door.

"Miss Noel?"

"I thought you had gone to bed, Annie-Mae."

"Oh, that I did, Miss Noel. But I can't lay my head aisy, for not keepin' a promise."

Annie-Mae flushed. The long thick braid that dropped from under her ruffled night cap gave her the look of an abashed schoolgirl.

"What promise, Annie-Mae?" The night seemed a thicket of demands and promises.

"The gentleman . . . the English gentleman. . . ."

Noel felt her heart pound. All she had once wanted. Now the last, final hurt of this long night.

"What, Annie Mae, are you trying to say?"

Annie-Mae was plainly suffering. It was an added burden to pronounce a name that inevitably brought a deep red to her face. "Mr. Fitch . . . Miss. . . ."

Time enough, Noel told herself, to wonder how or why at this hour the girl would come to her with that name. It was not her way to be cold or show unkindness to the servants. Hadn't Ned done enough without making her a subject of backstairs gossip?

"Annie-Mae, please go back to bed. I made it clear to you and Mrs. Jessup that I am not at home to Mr. Fitch. I am betrothed. I do not receive gentlemen callers. Whatever excuse you have for this behavior—"

"He didn't call, Miss. I—I saw him—Mr. Fitch, in the back alley—"

"What?"

"No, no. It wasn't that way. It was dark. I thought he was the cat-meat man. I went out with my pail. It was him, Mr. Fitch. He asked me to give you this. He made me promise."

She thrust out an envelope.

Noel made no move to take it. "Annie-Mae. . . ." She spoke gently. The girl was trembling. "I want you to understand very clearly. You are employed in this house. We do our part to make you comfortable and content. On your part you are not to make promises or take on obligations to anyone outside this family. Anyone. Can you remember that? Now go to bed. Please."

Annie-Mae dropped the letter, bobbed, and fled.

For a long moment it lay on the floor. Slowly, Noel stooped, picked it up. *For Miss Tremont*. The writing was as near and as distant as the man himself. Whatever it contained, it could change nothing now. Everything was arranged, everything complete. Her child, her beloved Posie was safe. In the days just past she had found new strength. Only her weakness surprised her. If she opened this intrusive message, what then? How easy it would be to yield . . . how fatal.

She knelt beside the grate. Time stopped. Her thoughts spun among the flames as she had once spun, his arm close around her. She gazed into the brightness of an impossible world, forever young, forever carefree, forever shut. But she knew, as she would know for the rest of her life, that this man, wherever fate would take him, this man as earthy, as intense, as alone as herself, possessed her.

She clung to the letter another instant. She saw him standing beside her, as real as mind could conjure him, holding out his hands, his eyes fixed on her. He was laughing. That laughter! That greening of her life, that sorcerer of love, making seamless the days, radiant the night.

With a final thrust of denial, she flung the letter into the grate. The flames caught it, twisting, searing, consuming. In the hissing of the embers, her cry went unheard.

32

"Got a penny for a poor man on Christmas Eve? I've starvin' young 'uns at home."

Ned's usual response to such a plea was an automatic thrust into his pocket, a gentleman's gesture. He knew firsthand the specter of need. Tonight instead his arm shot forward. He collared the man and held him under the misted street light. He had seen him before. Twice in the late afternoon across the street from Mrs. Luskin's lodging house. And on each of his futile visits to Stuyvesant Square, the last time as a lurking figure in the darkness of the back alley when he had pressed his letter on Annie-Mae. Nothing had come of it all, and now he vented his frustration on the hapless man in his grip.

"Who paid you to tail me?" He knew the answer, of course, but for a moment it was like having the thick neck of the Parson by the collar. "Never mind. How much is he paying you?" He shook the man like a terrier. "How much?"

The man's face was so ordinary that it could be lost and found a dozen times over in any street crowd. He was skinny with a wiry strength, but even that had gone slack in his fear. Not so much fear of his captor, Ned suspected, but of his having been discovered. Forgiveness was not in the octopus nature of the Parson.

"How much?"

"Ten cents an hour." The words were barely audible.

"You're lying."

"Twenty-five cents."

"What else?"

The man was crumpling. Ned shoved him against the iron paling. "What else?"

"Twenty-five cents for anything I could bring back."

"Like what? My visits to this Square, or maybe number 269, front or back? Is that it?" Ned clenched his free fist.

"Please, Mr. Fitch. Lemme go. I'm not a fightin' man."

"You're a sneak and a liar. Go back and tell your boss that if I catch you again it'll go badly with you. And for him, too!" Ned shoved the man away, watched him stumble and vanish in the night shadows.

He was not surprised. He knew the last time he had seen the Parson, in that little parlor in the presence of the child, that he had made an enemy. An enemy who would track him as long as he lingered near the home of Walter Tremont. He had not returned to the Parson's employ. His obsession with Noel was still an obsession. He had not accepted defeat. He had made attempt after attempt to see her. He had presented himself at the front door, to be met by the black-clad housekeeper with the pinched mouth. "Miss Noel is not at home. . . ."

Once Mr. Walter Tremont had materialized in the hall behind her. For an instant the older man's eyes had met his. No words had been exchanged, but in that icy stare Ned had seen the authority. *My daughter is engaged to be married. If you come to this door again with your unwanted attentions, I shall be obliged to summon the police. . . .*

Ned had made his final assault through the rear alley, his last hope in the innocent trust of little Annie-Mae. With a touch of her shawled shoulder, a light pressure on her hand, he had persuaded her to take his letter into the house. It contained the most impassioned words he had ever put on paper. He had gulped down his pride, his desperation, even caution in a single plea. "I must see you, my darling, not only for the love we share but for your precious secret I have so painfully discovered. We belong to each other, for all time, against all obstacles. I pledge, I swear, to devote my life, to love, to honor, to protect you and your child as long as life is given me. . . ."

In the darkness of the alley he had waited for her answer until every light in the house had gone out. When at last he turned away, his frustration had hardened to anger, as iron cold as the night. It was not her father, nor the servants who barred him. It was Noel herself. Let her marry that unlicked cub of a missionary! Let her take her bastard child and herself to China! Or to the moon, and find out for herself what life without him would be. There were other fish in the sea for him.

But he could no more sustain anger against her than he could obliterate his longing.

Now, once more, on this Christmas Eve, he had been drawn

to Stuyvesant Square. Number 269, like every house in the Square, was alight from top floor to bottom for the season, a spray of holly on the door, candles in every parlor window. Yet as he walked to and fro he had no sense of the festivities within. The lighting was too uniform, the house too quiet. The Tremonts were not at home.

Then it came to him, not as lightning out of the dark but as a stupid failure of memory. Christmas Eve. At Miss Bliss's party hadn't Mrs. Mortimer Wilberforce, the dowager lady herself, invited him to attend her—what the devil did they call it in Society—her Christmas Soirée? Seven-thirty. Be prompt, dear boy. Wasn't that where the Tremonts would surely be, Noel, beautiful in silks, her head sleek and high, her smile knowing . . . there would be a corner somewhere, a sheltering of palms where they could be together, everything made sure and clear, and forever.

His watch with its fashionable fob told him it was seven-fifteen. There was no time to go back and change into the dress suit he now possessed. He found himself running to where the hansoms stood in line on Irving Place.

The snow had begun to fall thin and wet. Within her magnificent mansion Mrs. Wilberforce was irritated. She would have preferred one of New York's thick, white storms that, while adding to the miseries of waiting coachmen and carriage horses, topped every cornice and turret, picket railing and slate roof of Fifth Avenue with charm.

Her Christmas Eve reception was well under way. Her several grand salons of gilt and ebony, velvets and looped satins, were thronged with the best names she could cull from a sadly expanding Society. Holly, garlands of Christmas greens, enormous wreaths, and living firs festooned with mistletoe were everywhere. French pier glass mirrors in the marble foyer reflected the dazzling twelve-foot Christmas tree alight with a hundred candles, under the careful guard of Cobb, her English butler, and two footmen.

Cobb was a source of comfort to Fanny Wilberforce. Worth every bit she had spent to bribe him away from her dearest friend, Dolly. Cobb knew precisely, flawlessly, what to do and say on all occasions. Especially important tonight because she had managed with her well-known social dexterity to snare a title, the son of a genuine English Earl and his Lady, when everyone knew that British peers were as scarce as plovers' eggs in New York during the Christmas season.

Sir George and Lady Cynthia Bathurst had arrived promptly, and suitably splendid in ribbons and tiara.

And therein lay another cause of Mrs. Wilberforce's irritation.

Sir George, Cobb had whispered, was known to favor frequent brandy and sodas before the buffet, followed by a noticeable loss of interest. Mrs. Wilberforce had bowed her welcome to Lady Cynthia with a throaty promise of a handsome young Englishman as supper escort. Lady Cynthia had been very gracious in a light-voiced way.

"Abbingdon-Fitch?" Sir George had trumpeted. "Never heard of a Fitch, have I, m'dear, but I knew old Abbingdon well. Shared digs with him at Harrow. Used to visit the family place regularly. My grandfather foxhunted with the last Marquis. The old beggar used to run more girls to ground than foxes."

Now with supper so soon to be served, Mrs. Wilberforce found herself bordering on anxiety, a condition she deplored. She could have forgiven young Ned for arriving after the guests of honor. He was not yet in sight. Worse, her copious black velvet bosom had begun to harbor an unpleasant hint of suspicion. Just who was young Edmond Abbingdon-Fitch? She could trust her own judgment, but dear Phoebe Bliss was not improving in reliability.

Nor was that the sum of her worries. A short man perched alone on her lime-velvet loveseat waved a commanding cigar at her.

"Well, Fanny, you got me out of my comfortable house on this miserable night, leaving a good fire and a good brandy to come to one of your blooming receptions where I shall overeat and spend Christmas with a hot water bottle and a bad case of dyspepsia. No, I didn't bring m' daughters. They've got their own friends and their Aunt Clary's giving 'em a party in the grand parlor. Where's the young Englishman you want me to look over?"

Mr. J. M. Watkins tapped his cigar with a blunt finger and sent a shower of ashes on Mrs. Wilberforce's Aubusson carpeting. He was heavy of paunch and jowl, sharp of eye. He might have been a cartoonist's favorite tycoon, except for the fringe of grey hair, halolike around his bald scalp, and the fringe of grey whiskers, ear to ear. That, with a startling dimple in his left cheek gave him the look of an aging, misplaced cherub. He was worth millions.

Mrs. Wilberforce looked him in the eye. "He's not here yet, Jimsie."

"Late, eh? Don't like that."

"No, not late. Just independent. In fact, I'm not even positive that he'll be here at all."

"Well, well! Not toadying, is he? I like that. Better than the last two clerks I had. 'Yes, sir No, sir, . . . Whatever you wish, sir.' One eye on m'daughters, and the other on m'dollars. You know, Fanny, being born on the wrong side of the track gives a man a sensible suspicion of people. But I wasn't born on the right side of the biggest copper lode in Montana for nothing. I've made good use of what I've learned. We've been old friends, Fanny, you and I. You tell me this young man will make me a good secretary. Maybe. But he'll have to be where I can meet him and watch him."

J. M. Watkins planted his feet firmly and lit another cigar.

"What I've got in mind is this. I'm takin' the girls to Paris in the spring. One of 'em's engaged and wants a Paris—what does she call it—trousseau? Clothes. The other fancies a title and I hear it's no trouble to pick one up if she takes to the fellow. Then I've got a little business to do before I go down to Cannes to take over my yacht. A real beauty, Fanny, four marble bathrooms, pipe organ in the main salon and tiger skins lining the den top to bottom. I expect to have it in Newport all summer. Meanwhile I've got to see the Duke Napoleon in Paris, and the Prince of Alba in Madrid. Oh, I can talk the copper market to those boys, but I'm not comfortable sitting on those teeny-weeny gold chairs, holding a thimble-size glass, making thimble-size talk in a language I don't understand. If this young man of yours can handle 'em . . . well, you get the idea?"

"I do indeed. He'll be perfect, Jimsie. I promise you. In fact"—Mrs. Wilberforce gave him one of her best Cheshire smiles—"he's distantly related to an old English family. Second son of a second son."

"What's that?"

"Don't worry, Jimsie. Just promise me you'll get him back to Newport by summer for my tennis week houseparty. My niece will be with me. A lovely girl. Quite unmarried."

Her jet-encrusted fan tapped his arm in light conspiracy. She might have winked, but her wink, like so many other things, she was aware, was becoming cumbersome.

It was nearly eight. Her annoyance with young Ned quickened. Whatever he was, this handsome young man might miss the greatest opportunity of his life. Experience had long taught Fanny that opportunity was not a knock on the door. It was a brass ring to be caught before someone else grabs it. Ned's failure tonight could be the tragedy of his life. But Mrs. Wilberforce's emotions stirred at a deeper level. She was a woman. Beneath the armor of social prestige, beneath the layers of black velvet and satin, the proppings of whalebone, the unsheddable layers of flesh, was a woman who had once been a girl. It was that girl who now felt rebuffed.

Restlessly, she moved through her guests into the vast gold-and-walnut-paneled dining room, where she stood for a moment alone.

Cobb had seen her. "Is anything amiss, madam?"

An unseeing eye swept the dining room, as much to distract herself as to calm its stiffened custodian.

The buffet was fully laid, thirty feet in length. Mrs. Wilberforce was aware that Americans preferred to sit squarely down at tables to be served, but she had determined to demonstrate that she could serve a proper English sideboard. Seating would be at tables of eight, set in the brilliance of vermeil, holly, and bayberry candles.

"Everything looks quite perfect."

"Thank you, Madam. I took a few liberties." He gestured with as much freedom as tradition permitted. "*Terrapin au madere*, oysters in heavy cream. Grilled quail. The woodcock was not choice. Pigeon pie. Wild duck. Pheasant *asperge*, whole salmon in aspic, a lobster *mousse*, particularly fine tonight."

"Very nice," Fanny Wilberforce's attention was on the hall.

". . . for the *viandes, beouf* Wellington, a saddle of lamb *au menthe*. I took the liberty, Madam, of including boiled mutton garni for Sir George. . . ."

"Of course."

". . . a very nice suckling pig *roti*, cranberry glaze . . . two medallions of veal . . . unusually delicate." Cobb drew a sustaining breath. Not often had he the opportunity to orchestrate his talents before an American employer who he suspected had not half a notion of *haute cuisine*. "For cheeses, Madam, brie, Roquefort . . . an especially well-aged Stilton for Sir George . . . raspberries, hothouse peaches . . . a *bombe . . . petits gateaux—*"

"Yes, Cobb, I recall the menu—"

But Cobb was not to be stopped. He well knew the price of his hire and he considered his employer's intrusion in the dining room at this hour an affront. Her place was in the salon.

"The sorbets, Madam, will be served in an ice replica of

Sir George's ancestral home, details of which I was able to obtain at the British Consulate."

"Very thoughtful."

But Cobb's triumph was his own. Mrs. Wilberforce had moved with unexpected alacrity into the hall.

Ned was walking slowly toward the drawing room, his face somber, his head moving slightly from right to left as if searching among the guests. Worse, he was in street clothes, a far cry from the lively and impeccably turned-out young man she had met under the sponsorship of Phoebe Bliss.

"Dear boy, I've been worried about you!"

"My apologies, Mrs. Wilberforce. I—I was detained." Totally inadequate, but it was all he would say. He had come for one purpose only.

"No matter, Ned. I shall call you Ned. Like one of my own dear family. I've promised you. . . ." Mrs. Wilberforce hesitated. Street clothes? Still one never knew about the English. Lady Cynthia was young. She might consider it simply an American eccentricity. "I've promised you to Lady Cynthia for supper. You'll find her charming. But first there is a gentleman you must meet. Very important. Many times a millionaire, dear boy. He is interested in offering you a position."

If Ned was pleased, he did not show it. In fact, his hostess could find no change of expression in his rather pale face. Byron, she said to herself. No, not Lord Byron—an earthier man who might enthrall any girl. Any girl that is, except Noel Tremont. But one girl's loss was another's chance.

"Now do come with me and meet Mr. Watkins."

"I wonder if I might first pay my respects to Mr. Tremont."

"Mr. Tremont . . . ?"

"And his family."

Mrs. Wilberforce glanced at Ned. While her lofty status was due to Pennsylvania oil, her basis for success was a gift for shrewd analysis of human nature, bereft of the artifices of social conduct.

"My dear Ned," she began. Then quite inappropriately she chuckled. "If Mr. Tremont and his family were here, I'd have promised you to Noel for supper. Even if she is to be married in less than two weeks. Oh yes—a formal wedding. The invitations are out. Didn't you know? But the Tremonts never come to my Christmas Eve. They spend a family evening, quite bourgeois, I should say! Children, Saint Nicholas, midnight church, that sort of thing. Your respects are rather futile now. So, for heavens sake, brighten up and let me keep my word to Jimsie."

Ned liked the old dowager. If he had understood correctly, she was about to lead him through the widest door of opportunity he had ever known. *When a door opens, Boy, go through. Go through! Don't let anything or anybody take you off course!* But his grandfather's advice was spectral beside the image of Noel. Her wedding in two weeks. Invitations out. Noel a bride, veiled and white, walking down a church aisle, to another man. . . .

He came back to his surroundings on a whiff of cigar smoke.

"Ned Fitch, eh? Well, young man, I'm glad to meet you!" The fat little tycoon came barely to Ned's shoulder but managed to run an appraising eye up and down Ned's street suit. "Not too big for your britches, eh? Not afraid of what other people think. I like that. We'll have a talk a little later." Ned felt a nudge in his ribs. "The old girl keeps a good cellar. A little of the Bell's Best and we'll get to know each other. But she's hooked a couple of titles and you've got to meet 'em first."

Sir George was not in sight. Lady Cynthia, her back to them, seemed to be at the mercy of a hawklike woman in maroon silk bristling with jet and rubies.

"Oh, my," Mrs. Wilberforce breathed her annoyance. "Elsie Cannonsby! She's determined to have a title for her Monday night opera box. Wagner. So dull. Lady Cynthia is so young, so much younger than her husband, I'm sure she's quite defenseless."

Deftly she maneuvered Edmond Abbingdon-Fitch around the formidable lady and into the presence of the titled guest.

Ned saw a lavish draping of pink satin, a three-inch collar of diamonds, a tiara set high on fluffy blond hair. The narrow smile, showing small white teeth, and the light blue eyes could not be mistaken.

"Good evening, Neddie," said Millie. She held out a hand encased in a shoulder-high white kid glove.

Ned bent over it to get his bearings.

"You did that nicely, Ned. You've learned a lot. I was sure you'd be real elegant by this time."

"*You* are Lady Bath . . . ?"

"I'm Millie, Neddie, like I always was. It's just that I've got a different name now. It's really all thanks to you. I have so many things to tell you. . . ."

Unbelieving, he moved her out of the mainstream. It was

indeed Millie. Ned, who believed in neither coincidence nor Fate, had to admit to both. Suddenly he was back in the turkey-red warmth of that preposterous little attic flat off Leicester Square, with the gentle, undemanding girl who had shown him the only tenderness he had ever known.

"I hoped, Neddie, that when George and I got to New York I'd see you somewhere fashionable. I wanted to see how you'd gotten on. You look different."

"We all change, Millie."

"I mean older. I mean . . . are you happy, Neddie? I guess you must be, being here with all your friends in a place like this." Millie did not wait for an answer. Her breath was coming as quickly as her words. "I did so want you to know about George and everything that's happened. So many times. I did feel bad when you went away. I guess a girl does. But you remember the parasol, the one you gave me, all pink and lavender? When the weather turned warm, I'd carry it into Hyde Park, the way I used to with you. Sort of in memory. Remember the day you saved the lady on the horse? Well, there was a gentleman who rode along there every day. I used to watch him. I guess he noticed my parasol. He'd tip his hat to me when he went by. One day he got off his horse and came and spoke to me. And then, another day, he came by without his horse and asked me if I'd like to have an ice. And I did. The next time we had tea in a bun shop and I told him I could make much better tea at home. And cheaper. He liked my little room. He didn't talk much, but he said he didn't like being in the dark alone either. He told me that's where he was a lot when he was a little boy. It made me feel bad—badly—for him. One day I was making him tea on the red linoleum table—you remember it? Very strong, George liked, with half hot milk and three sugars. And he said, 'Millie, you make the best damned tea, and you're the quietest woman I ever knew. Would you like to be Lady Bathurst?' "

She paused.

"I didn't know, Neddie. I hadn't an idea of such a thing. I told him I thought he should think it over. Take his time. And then maybe talk to me again if he wanted. Or not. Oh . . . I forgot. Artie. Poor Artie. He went to the clink—I mean prison—once too often. The last time he went, he died. No lungs, they said. No lungs left at all. Poor Artie. Anyhow the next time I saw George I could tell he had been drinking. He said I'd be a great help to him if I became Lady Bathurst. I think there's nothing you can do better than help somebody, so I said yes. We went down to meet his family in Sussex.

Oh, Neddie. That house. It was spread all over. Like Old Bailey. Fifty-six rooms, George said. But I only saw three of them. Anyhow, Lord Bathurst, that's his father, didn't like me, but he pinched me on the way into dinner. The Countess, George's mother, said I couldn't expect her approval, but I'd have to change my name to Cynthia anyway. But George was just as determined. We were married in that house in the darkest room you ever saw, all full of old paintings. So now we're on our honeymoon. It's to take two years around the world and afterwards we're to live in Punjab. I don't know where Punjab is, but George said he'd explain it to me when we get there.

"But it isn't all bad, Neddie, because the Countess said I had to take a lady's maid. And she found Bessie . . . Bessie Boggs. I was to call her Boggs, but of course I wouldn't do that. She's Bessie and she's my very best friend and we talk a lot in common. Now that we're traveling, when George is off somewhere Bessie and I go shopping and see the sights."

Ned saw Mrs. Wilberforce hovering, her expression puzzled.

"Oh, and another thing, Neddie. . . ." Millie, Lady Bathurst, who had revealed so little of herself in that long-ago intimacy, now felt a compulsion to talk. Was it a measure of the affection that he had returned so lightly? He was uncomfortable before the candor in her eyes, more uncomfortable than in any deceit he had practiced in the cause of ambition.

". . . we were on the boat, Neddie, George and I, when he told me the truth. I wasn't feeling very good. I made them take all the flowers and candy George had ordered out of the cabin. Then he told me. He's an only son, Neddie. When his father, the Earl, dies, George is going to be one of the richest men in England and he'll have to go sit in the House of Lords, or some such place, a lot of the time. He looked so miserable that I just put my arms around him and told him it didn't matter to me at all. We'd manage somehow. And we will, too."

Chimes of "Tannenbaum" sounded through the salons. It was the signal for guests to pair off and move into supper.

"I just wanted you to know, Neddie. Because I really owe it all to you." She was looking around as if, her immolation over, she had returned him to the past.

"Millie—"

"Yes, Neddie. . . ."

It would not do to kiss the cheek of Lady Bathurst. Ned lifted her gloved hand, remembering the stubby little work-plain fingers. Gently he touched it with his lips, dreading to see her eyes mist, her mouth tremble. But as he had done before, he underestimated Millie.

Neither happened. Millie giggled.

"Oh, Neddie, weren't you always the one. There's George now."

A burly man was approaching. Ned saw a reddened face, a mustache that cascaded over prominent front teeth, and an unfocused gait. Millie took his arm, lifted her tiara-decked head, and with careful dignity moved with her husband into the flow of guests.

Mrs. Wilberforce was bearing down, full sail.

"Sir George told me he prefers to escort his wife. So very English isn't it? Or perhaps a new fashion. Ned, Mr. Watkins, I've arranged a little collation in the library, where you can talk privately."

"Mrs. Wilberforce, I'm afraid I must make my apologies."

She hesitated only an instant.

"And—Mr. Watkins? It's a splendid opportunity. . . ."

"My thanks to Mr. Watkins and my regrets."

Fanny Wilberforce could be very human. "I—quite understand. I believe you will find all the Tremont family at Orrin's house. Mr. Tremont's elder son. Sixteenth Street just off the Square, around from the old church." Her eyes were amused. "You know Lady Cynthia?"

"Lady Cynthia . . . she reminded me of someone I once knew." He looked directly at the shrewd aging lady. "I'm deeply grateful to you, Mrs. Wilberforce. You have been so very kind."

Her smile was girlish. "You are a charmer, Mr. Abbingdon-Fitch. Someday perhaps I shall hear more of you."

33

The snowfall was increasing, wet snow now clung to the pavement. Ned dismissed his cab and walked quickly along the brownstone stoops of Sixteenth Street. No one drew the drapes on Christmas Eve. He could see easily into the brightly lit parlors at the pantomime of moving figures, large and small. He knew Orrin Tremont's house. He had pursued every available detail of Noel's encompassed life. Directly across the street from that settled, comfortable house, he took his stand.

He would not have been human if he had not once, even twice, glanced back at the opportunity he had this night rejected, a future as glittering with promise as he had ever dreamed or would ever be offered again. Yet stronger than that was the memory of the emptiness of Mrs. Wilberforce's crowded, fashionable rooms without Noel and the wrench within him—Noel, to be married in two weeks!

Two weeks! Urgency possessed him. Noel was his, at whatever distance, across whatever barriers. He had only to wait. Noel must come down those brownstone steps, walk the half block to the Square and home, or around the corner to the brilliantly lighted church. He did not consider the man who might be with her. He had no plans except the numbing determination to wait. Then he heard the whispers.

"There's a rummy swell!"

"Drunk as a toad, you bet!"

"You get his hat. I'll go for the money!"

Ned whirled. In the shadows he saw two boys, neither more than twelve. He caught them, sent them sprawling, pulled them to their feet and saw, in their hunger-thin faces and ragged coats, himself.

"Go home, you little idiots, if you have a home. If not, go around to the Mission and get some food and somewhere to sleep that'll be better than jail.'' He pushed a half dollar into each one's grimy hand. With the silent hope it would not be lost to beer or bigger bullies, he released them to the dark.

He turned his collar up against the wet and settled himself to wait.

In Charlotte Tremont's overdraped parlor, the heat was rising in waves. Noel, gasping for breath, adjusted her pillow-stuffed Saint Nicholas suit. Not for the first time, she wondered how any woman could be as fearful of fresh air as her worry-ridden sister-in-law. But it would be soon over. The hall chimes had just sounded nine. She would be in ample time for the Midnight Mass, at which Madame Ducharde had promised her she could see Posie. For the last time. She would not think of that now. Instead, she distracted herself imagining Posie, her long hair gleaming, among these properly born, properly cared for, nieces and nephew, Posie—accepted.

She scanned the room. Only one child was left for the wretched trial. Freddie, the pale, delicate youngest. For him she would play it out, sweetly, gently, to the end.

''Your turn, Frederick,'' commanded his mother.

Freddie's face had turned the color of skim milk. His thin hands clung to the security of his jacket.

''You remember, Freddie. We learned it together.'' But Noel's whisper, like her smile, was lost in the wealth of white beard.

Freddie gulped. ''Snow, snow . . . beautiful snow. . . .'' There was silence, bottomless as his fear.

''Go on, Frederick!'' commanded Orrin.

''Snow . . . snow—''

''You said that,'' taunted his sister.

''Falling gently soft and—'' added the other, scornfully.

''No prompting!'' snapped Charlotte.

Noel came as close to the suffering little boy as pillowing permitted. ''Anything, Freddie! Make it up!''

Something familiar in the eyes, the tone, a warming he could not name, reached him. His hands let go their tight hold on his jacket. He stood staring at St. Nicholas. Suddenly merriment like a stray strand of sunlight lit his face.

''Snow, snow, beautiful snow''—he paused, then he dared—''Step on a lump and down you go!''

A burst of smothered giggles. Noel swung him up, holding him close, laughing with him at his triumph.

''Frederick!'' But Charlotte's outcry was lost.

Noel handed him her last orange, went to the piano stool, twirled it twice to watch the children's glee, and, resettling her pillows, sat down to play. "Deck the halls. . . ."

Walter crossed the hall to the den that had once been his. He was ashamed of his sudden emotion. He wanted to conceal it when he thanked his beloved daughter for the pleasure she always brought them at this season. He was sharply aware that this indeed would be her last Christmas with them. For how long, he could not guess. He would miss her, yet it had all turned out to be sensible and complete. He would add his own token.

He heard her at last coming down the narrow staircase from the bedroom. "Noel. . . ."

She entered, changed into street clothes, slight as Maria, but her dark head high with a pride Maria never had seemed to need.

"Yes, Father." She was, somewhat to his surprise, dressed plainly, drably, he would say, and wearing a hat. But he would put the best face possible on the entire evening.

"Thank you, my dear, for all you do on Christmas Eve. . . ." He found a need to clear his throat.

"I always enjoy it. Poor little Freddie. He loves to laugh but they don't give him much chance."

"You're coming to the midnight service with us?"

She hesitated. "No, Father, not this time, if you'll forgive me."

"I don't think Clarence will mind if you come without him. He's doing quite the proper thing to spend this last Christmas with his mother."

"Very proper." She was impatient now. She must not be late. Not on this night, her last chance to see Posie until—until heaven knew when. "But there is something I must do tonight. I—I made a promise."

"At this hour?"

"There's an orphanage I've been visiting. The children asked me to come to their Christmas Eve Mass. It's the last time I'll see them. I gave my word."

"I see."

She knew that he was hurt. He would retire into that stiff courtesy that was more painful to her than any open opposition.

"Where is this place, Noel?"

"Downtown. Near Varick Street. I'll take a cab and have it wait."

"Then someone must go with you."

"*No,* Father"—she was aware of his sudden sharp glance—"I mean, I'll be quite safe. Really. And to have both David and me away tonight, well, it would spoil things, wouldn't it? I'll just go out quietly. I'll be all right." And then, as if to break out of the warp of lies she lived, she said something she had not intended. "I can't disappoint those unfortunate children. They have no friends, no place in the world. They belong nowhere, they are outcasts. But they are children, aren't they? No different from those children here in the parlor. Some people treat them differently. But I don't!"

If Walter was startled by the intensity in her words, he would not show it. He was aware that too often these days he found himself resentful of any time she spent away, for any reason.

"Very commendable, I'm sure. . . ."

"They are illegitimate, Father."

He wished again that he could understand this daughter, who bore the very name of Christmas. He had tried to shelter her from all that was ugly, all that was immoral, indecent, sordid. Tonight once more he had a sense of indefinable loss. Maria might have sympathized with her. Or might not. Perhaps the world itself was turning from his values.

"You've been brought up not to know of such matters, but you are grown now. I can only trust your judgment. If I couldn't, I don't think my life . . ." He cleared his throat again. Sentiment was a private matter. He would remain safely with the business at hand. "You must do what you think right. Since you will not be here when we exchange our gifts, I want you to have a very special one from me. I would like your last Christmas at home to be as happy as I can make it." He was on safer ground now, finding relief in words.

He drew a tan, string-tied envelope from an inner pocket. "May this be the first of many blessings in your new life ahead."

"What is it, Father?"

"Your dowry, my dear."

He was expecting one of her quick radiant smiles, happiness dispelling the strain he saw too often these days in her face. A moment of closeness, a daughter's kiss. . . .

She opened the envelope.

"Securities, Noel. Five thousand shares of railroad stock to be kept safe for you until you return. By then, according to the best advice I have gotten, you will be a very rich woman. I have also deposited a fund in your married name in San Francisco so you—"

"Father, I thought my dowry was to be money. In the bank. . . ." Her face was drained.

"Money!" Walter's forbearance had suffered too great a strain. "Since when does a properly brought up young woman discuss money? I cannot, I will not, discuss such matters with you, Noel. That is your dowry. Keep it until you leave for Amoy. Then you will give it to me for safekeeping. Good night, Noel."

"Father, I am sorry if I've offended you."

"You have, Noel . . . deeply." But the sight of her distress, as always, could melt his anger. "Oh, my little girl—my little girl! How much I've wanted your happiness!" He kissed her cheek and turned abruptly from the room. In his ears, through his disappointment, he could hear Maria's light voice. *There, you see, Walter? You got angry. But it's all over. A kiss always settles the matter!*

Noel stood tensely, hardly aware he was gone, the envelope in her hand. Shares of stock? What on earth could she do with them? Sell them? Was there time? Would she need her father's consent? Her mind stumbled among the possibilities. There was only one. To see Madame Ducharde tonight after the service and explain. Madame Ducharde might be willing to accept them. Especially if they were so valuable.

From the parlor window, Walter, watching, saw her hurry into the night. He had not made her happy. But perhaps by tomorrow, Christmas Day, she would be herself. His attention was caught by another movement in the street. A man on the opposite side was running in the direction Noel had taken. His imagination, no doubt, but for an instant, through the thin veil of snow and darkness, the man looked familiar.

"Walter, do come! It's time for the gifts!" It seemed to Walter that Adrienne's voice was growing querulous. But it was Christmas Eve. A time for healing.

On the sidewalk outside, Ned quickened his pace. Noel was just ahead, hurrying away from the Square toward the cab stand. Her sudden departure from the house had taken him by surprise. She was alone. His spirits lifted. He had found her. He would not lose her again.

She was at the step of the single waiting hansom cab.

"Noel!" he called.

She turned and stared. She had drawn a veil over her face. She was without doubt the woman he had seen fleeing the Restell house so long ago. But he understood, now.

"*Noel!* I'm coming with you!"

"No! No, Ned. Please. Not now!"

But he had stepped into the cab beside her and taken charge.

"Cabbie, the lady gave you the address?"

The cab moved out. In the close darkness, lit fitfully by the yellow glow of street lamps, he put his arms around her and felt her return his kiss.

Those who have not known the desperation of renounced love may need a more articulate reunion. But for the two riding south in the darkness of a hansom cab on that snowy Christmas Eve in New York, this very private world was enough. Time later for words, for the implacable twists of duty and fate. They were together, not daring to speak, not daring even to look at each other. A turn of the carriage threw them closer, shoulders, arms, knees, touching, as if in pent-up fires within them they were one.

"It is forever, Noel."

She straightened, her thoughts now toward her destination. Ned sensed her change of mood. Should he tell her that he knew of her child? Yet it came hard, so quickly had she changed. Whatever her purpose tonight, he would respect it. He would wait until she was again pliant in his arms to demolish her hidden fears, her pretendings. They would laugh together in relief, in the wonder of belonging.

The cab jolted to a halt in the darkness.

The driver leaned down. "Can't get through this way, ma'am. Looks as if there might have been a fire."

"Then go back around the last block. Turn the corner and stop. I'll get out there."

She seemed already to have left him.

"Where are we going, Noel?"

"I'm going to church, St. Giles of the Angels. You'll have to leave me, Ned."

"I'm not leaving you, as you well know. Now or ever."

"Please, Ned. I must go. There's something I must do."

"What?"

"I can't talk now!" She had become the other Noel, remote, escaping. He suspected this visit had to do with her child. Good God, if he could only talk to her.

The cab had come to a halt.

"There's the church, ma'am. Down the block where the light is."

"Thank you."

"Noel, give me a minute. I must tell you something."

"No. Not now."

"Then let me come with you!"

"No!"

He helped her out of the cab. "I'll wait. I'll be here. I won't leave you!"

She broke from him and began to run.

The driver leaned from the cab.

"That'll be a dollar, sir. It bein' Christmas Eve."

"Will five dollars do for waiting, and another five for taking us back?"

"God bless ye, sir."

The grizzled old man climbed down. He tossed a ragged blanket over the old horse and hooked a near-empty bag of oats under his chin. He dropped a weighted rope to the ground, climbed into the cab, and closed his eyes. The snow had begun again. In the eternal symbol of numbing service, horse, man, and vehicle became a frozen silhouette in the night.

Ned stared down the block, keeping Noel in sight until she turned into the patch of light thrown from the church's open doors. A neighborhood, brooding, dark, faceless, encompassed church and street. He was sure now of what had brought her to this place, at this hour.

A couple passed, a man in work clothes, a shawled woman beside him.

"Excuse me, sir, uh, mister," Ned amended. He could frighten the fellow off with such a show of courtesy. "I'm a stranger around here. Can you give me some directions?"

"What do you want to know?" The man eyed him with surly suspicion.

"Is there an orphanage or a school near here?"

"Don't know nothing about no school."

His wife had noticed the tall young man. "Yes, you do, Joe, if you'd use your wits. You mean, maybe, the Frenchwoman's place. It's not on this street at all. You get to it around the block. Two full turns. The children come every Christmas Eve, pretty little things they are, too, coming down the aisle, singing. Or used to—"

"That'll do, wife!"

The man moved away. The woman hurried after him.

"Tellin' strangers everything you know. . . ." he growled.

Ned had heard all he needed. The school must lie directly behind the church.

The little church was crowded. Moving in on the tide of worshippers, Ned found a seat in a row of camp chairs behind the last pew. He remained standing and looked around. Men in rough coats, women in black shawls, girls in tawdry Sunday best, some carrying artificial flowers, children with scrubbed faces and wide eyes, babies already heavily asleep on tired shoulders, crowded the pews. A sharp look from the woman beside him reminded him that he must kneel.

If the worshippers were poor, faith was radiant. Pots of poinsettias, placed among bunches of artificial white roses, rimmed the altar steps. Below, a spread of straw contained in papier-mâché patience the foot-high ox, the ass, a too-white lamb. The Family was as rough-clothed as the congregation come to worship. But the doll-child lay in white silk and lace. To the left, in her own niche, stood the ever-promising Mother, blue-robed, gilt-crowned, lily hands outstretched in painted compassion above the flickering prayer lights. High above all hung the blanched Agony of her Son, tonight the Child again.

A young acolyte, scuffed brown street shoes and skinny ankles showing beneath his cassock, was lighting the tall white altar tapers with unsteady hands. A wheezy organ commanded silence.

Noel was here somewhere within this packed humanity, this human tide of belief and hope.

The procession began, the gangling crucifer, his grip white-knuckled on the staff of the cross, followed by the acolyte of the tapers, and another beside him, out of step. Then came a double line of solemn boy choristers, and lastly the priest, a round-shouldered, sturdy-looking man. Endurance seamed with kindness in his blunt features. But there were no little schoolgirls in the procession or among the worshippers. Perhaps they would come later.

The congregation knelt. Ned standing a moment longer searched the crowd again. The priest had turned to the altar.

In nomine Patris et Filii et Spiritus Sancti. . . .

Mass had begun.

For an hour, Ned told himself all he needed was a glimpse of her. She was here within these walls. He would locate her soon.

The chanting continued. The worshippers rose, knelt, and sat again in waves of movement. Incense drifted on the thick air. Once Ned thought he caught sight of her, far to the front and left. But he could not be sure. Broad, thick backs barricaded the front pews.

When the communicants pushed into the aisle, many pressing in from the street where they had waited in the cold, Ned realized he had small chance of finding Noel here. He rose and moved toward the open door. If she had slipped out ahead of the communicants, he would be waiting where he had promised. He stood watching the solid human tide move up the aisle in its journey to grace. He found himself envying their moment of transfiguration, their return with faces quiet, hands folded in the quick miracle of peace.

Missa est.

It was over. To a burst of triumph from the aged organ, the congregation moved sluggishly past him again into the night, loath to leave the sweetness and the glory for the cold reality of the street.

Noel was not among them.

Ned pushed his way down the three steps. He could not have missed her. She would have looked for him. He had only to wait. The last worshippers came out slowly, an old woman leaning on a small boy. The doors were closing. Ned sprang back into the building.

The acolyte, now with a broom in his hand, showed no surprise.

"You can come in, sir. The doors are not locked tonight. We're tidying up for six o'clock morning mass. Do you want to meditate?"

"Is there any other way out of the church?"

"No, sir. This is the only entrance."

"Is there a rear door, or a side door?"

"Not to the street, sir. Is it Father Michaels you want to see?"

"No." Ned heard his own harshness on this gentlest of nights. "No, thank you."

"There is one door. It's at the rear, there on the left. It's to the path to the parish house. It's private."

Ned dropped a coin in the poor box, walked up the length of the aisle, sat down. At the left he saw the door. But the acolyte began sweeping up the small debris at the chancel rail. The smothered tapers were sending up threads of smoke. The air had the staleness of crowded humanity. At last the acolyte shouldered his broom and departed. Ned rose, went quickly to the door opening to the private way, and stepped into the night.

The snowfall had dwindled. The sky had the pallor of a moon still prisoner behind the clouds, blanching the path to the priest's house. Then Ned saw a second path. It led straight back from the rear of the church. On it, black against the thin snow covering, lay a single set of narrow footprints. They marched steadily through a lane of leafless hedgerows. Behind and above loomed a whitened expanse of roof.

The school. The Frenchwoman's school where Noel kept

her child, directly behind the church. Those must be Noel's footprints, her light hurried steps from church to school building. Yet something had gone wrong. There had been no children at the Mass. There were no returning footprints in the snow.

Ned found himself running between the hedgerows. Ahead the house loomed. There were no lights. At the end of the path he came to a gate, unlatched. He stepped through it into what seemed a brick-walled garden and saw a blackened willow tree bent to the ground. Black clumps of bushes bordered the winding path, turned watery in the snow. Any footprints here would have dissolved.

The building before him must once have been a handsome home. Now it stood, stark and apparently deserted, its windows sightless, its shutters hanging awry. The entrance from the garden gaped black and doorless. But on the brick step leading to it, snow still clung. There Ned saw a single narrow footprint.

He placed a sheltering boot over it and pushed his way into the unlighted house. The fire must have been recent. Pools of water, black as tar, lay on the floor. The interior reeked of ash and smoke. In the faint light from the whitened sky he could just make out a wide hall and the silhouette of a curved staircase. It must have been a gracious house. Silence hung as heavy as air. He listened. There was no sound, no evidence of life anywhere.

"Noel!" he called. "Noel!"

Not even an echo returned. He cupped his hands. "Noel! Are you here?"

A slit of light showed on his left. He went toward it, pushed open the door, and found himself in what appeared to be a small office. A candle flickered at the edge of a desk. Behind it, in a high-backed chair, sat a woman. The tattered sleeves of her dress clung to her arms like fog, her hair, lank and grey, fell to her shoulders. He recognized her. He would never forget the granite features, the dark, hollow eyes, of the Frenchwoman he had seen with the child, Noel's child, in the sitting room of the Parson.

"Good evening," she said.

Her politeness caught him off guard. He must not stare.

"Uh, good evening. I'm looking for . . . a young lady who came here. When I saw what happened. . . ." He must not frighten this woman.

"Do I know you?" She lifted the candle, searched his face. "Do I? No matter. Yes, Miss Tremont came here. You have come after her? Is that it? How fortunate for her. To have such a handsome young caller. But as you see I am not quite prepared to receive visitors. The house has been disturbed." Her voice, low, modulated, was oddly mechanical, the heavy eyes unfocused. "Too many visitors. Now if you had come properly announced—"

"Where is she?"

Madame Ducharde's eyes returned to measuring him. When she finally spoke it was with the patience needed for the slow-witted. "Miss Tremont should not have come here tonight. It was quite wrong of her. All I promised was that she would see her child at Mass. I was very good to Miss Tremont. But she was not honest with me. She did not keep her word. The money—her dowry, she said—where was it? I could do nothing with the printed papers she brought . . . for that, for that she wanted her child! I am not such a fool. The children are mine! Mine!" Her voice thinned. "I suffered for them. God meant me to have them. No man or woman shall take them from me!"

She rose and picked up the candle. "Miss Tremont is not here. Nor will she find her child!" The candle came closer to his face. The woman gave a small cry. "Oh . . . you! I know you! Yes, yes. I have seen you before. You were there that day—in his house! *Le diable!* The king of hell! He wanted money, always more money from me. He said he would take my children. He would take my records! He would find out whose children they were . . . !" She was peering into his face. "You knew he came here tonight. That's why you came, isn't it? The devil's messenger. When he failed, you thought . . . you thought"—her features contracted into such a mask of fury that she might have sprung harpylike out of the night's evils—"but you'll find nothing! Nothing! I burned it all!" A sweep of a ragged-sleeved arm encompassed the disaster. As suddenly, the fury vanished. He saw what might have been the ghost of a young smile. "I burned everything," she said gently.

She blew out the candle and melted into the darkness as if she belonged to it. The steps sloughing through the wet snow faded. Ned stood for another moment listening. There was no sound. Nothing but the light stinging of new snow against a broken window.

But Noel had been in this house. She had come not only to see her child but to insure her safety, with payment of all she had to give. The bitter explanation of Noel's marriage swept through him, so clear, so searing he wondered how he had failed to guess. Her dowry was to be the little girl's security. Standing in this blackened devastation, Ned felt for this girl a surge of his love beyond passion, a quickening of hope, of meaning in his life. She would never face such degradation again.

He listened. Silence. There were no footsteps, no human sounds. The children must be long gone. The madwoman haunting this stricken place could not hide their whereabouts forever. If Noel had not left the house as she had come, through the hedgerow path, she must have known another route, most likely through the main hall and the front entrance.

Making his way through patches of dark and light, stumbling over the debris of the fire, Ned found himself again in the shadow of the great curving staircase. Then he saw something else. There in the stairwell, in the faint pallor of a high window lay a figure, bulky, inert. A vestige of light struck the white clerical collar. Death, recent as it had been, had already sealed the sensuous cruelty, the flabby indulgence of the face. In death, as never in life, the Parson lay revealed.

But he had delayed too long. A lantern glowed in the garden. He heard hard, quick steps. It was the young acolyte, his voice loud ahead of him.

"Sir! Sir! You shouldn't 'a come here! It isn't safe, after the fire! Eh!" The boy squeaked in terror. "God preserve us!"

Ned took him by the shoulders. "There's been an accident. Nothing will harm you. Go fetch the priest!"

"Oh Lor,' Lor' . . . I ain't never seen nothing like—"

"Go, will you! Get the priest! I'll wait."

The boy ran like a frightened cat.

Out of the questions racing through Ned's mind, only one mattered. Had Noel seen this evil thing? Was she still in the house? Then came another, wordless, faint memory, a mere fragment inexorable as this whole night had been. He was recalling another house, another death, and Noel fleeing. He must search every inch of this shell of a house. He must stand between Noel and whatever happened here tonight.

Ned looked down at the dead face. The clouds had drifted, he now saw a glint of metal protruding from the black coat. And he saw, too, in a flash of insight, the implications. The Parson had again become the nemesis of his destiny. Any future Noel had dared believe in was guttered like a match by the murdered man at his feet. He must find Noel. If she had left the house, he must give her time to reach the cab.

He must wait here, he must divert. He was thinking the unthinkable. Noel could not possible have known any of this. It was the Frenchwoman he feared.

He heard voices. A shaft of yellow light fell across the floor. Father Michaels, slightly out of breath, appeared above his lantern's glow. He bent over the figure on the floor, made the sign of the cross and tidily closed the eyelids. Then he straightened and looked hard at Ned.

"Who are you?"

"I came here tonight"—Ned had an inspiration—"to see the children."

"Do you know this man?"

"Yes, sir."

Father Michaels sighed. More tired than he would admit after the long Mass, he was not prepared for sin of this magnitude, not tonight. More than that, he recognized the tall young man. He had glimpsed him at the rear of the church.

"The police must be called. Even the Church must answer for such, uh, irregularities. It is not my duty to ask questions. But they will." The priest's eyes were sharp. "You knew a child here?"

Had Ned understood Father Michaels better, he might have forgiven him the bluntness. Beneath it lay a burden of confessed human error, a deep-buried knowledge of human weakness and deviousness too long borne for niceties. But Ned was wary now, of every nuance, every shadow, that might trespass on Noel's safety.

The priest continued as if his question had been answered. "God takes care of his innocents. One question more, if you will bear with me. Did you kill this man?"

"No."

"Did you know him?"

"I knew him. I did not kill him. But if the chance had been mine, I might have."

Father Michaels lifted a pious hand.

"I did not hear you, my son. God's will be done. You'd better go now."

"I don't think so, your Reverence."

The priest's head came up sharply. "Do you want to be here when the police come?"

"I don't mind."

"And let them take you in?"

"It's likely I'll be taken in anyway. You've found me here."

"Don't be a fool, young man. Give the police a chance at their work. As it is, they'll be in no mood for this. More mistakes are made from bad weather and bad digestion than all the processes of logic put together."

Ned's anger was rising at the trap before him. He would not leave this place until he knew where Noel was. Yet he dared not mention her. He would deny with his last breath that she had been here, even to this feisty priest with his raised hand, like Moses at the tablets. They had been struck down, too, Ned told himself grimly. He would, if he could do nothing else, provide the police with a diversion.

"I'll take it as it comes, your Reverence. I'm staying."

The horror on the floor seemed to retreat beneath the clash of wills. Father Michaels bent his head prayerfully. He had met young, misguided obstinacy often. More than once he had pleaded with the angels, but even they had insisted on his finding his own way out. Ultimately, he would. His colleagues liked to call it divine intuition. But to Father Michaels it was simple common sense. This embattled young man had been that night in his church. As had the frightened and pretty young woman he had found after Mass at the parish house.

Father Michaels told himself he had neither the time nor temperament for such matters. Yet did they not provide what small glint could be found in the dross of human behavior?

"As you must know, the young lady is on her way home. Now will you oblige me by doing likewise? You cannot help here. You can only make matters worse. Good night."

Unseemly as it was, Ned flashed the priest a twisted grin. "Thank you, your Reverence. Good night."

Father Michaels watched the long stride, the stubborn thrust of chin and shoulders retreat into the new thickening snow. For no more than a missed heartbeat in the rigidness of duty, Father Michaels found himself envying that unfettered young brashness.

Alone with death, the priest stood listening for what he knew would return from the upper darkness. He had long ceased to indulge in the excesses of surprise. God had His inscrutable design to which a mere priest could be no more than servitor. Father Michaels bent over the stiffening body at his feet, straightened, and composing himself, made the sign of the Cross.

Recrossing the garden, Ned followed the hedgerow path back to the empty church. Only the votive lights glowed and a single lamp over the Holy Mother's head. His footsteps echoed. The place was haunted for him now, with the invisible presence of Noel, a ghostly illusion that she might still be there.

In the deserted street, he saw, to his immense relief, that the cab was gone.

As he braced himself into the wind for the long walk to his lodging house he heard it. Or did he imagine it? The distant thudding of hooves, the faint but insistent clanging of the police wagon bell.

She was safe. He would be the hunted fox.

34

Early Christmas morning, the first storm of the winter struck. The snow, heavy and clinging, blanketed the streets muffling iron-shod hooves and wheels, wrapping the city in silence. By afternoon, the wind changed, whipping clouds of snow on the city, piling it in drifts, snapping telegraph wires, toppling poles. Horses slipped and fell, wooden axles broke. Omnibuses, wagons, carriages were abandoned while their teams were unhitched and led to whatever stables could be reached. By the following day, the omnibuses had stopped running and it was considered too dangerous in the high wind to ride the elevated railroad. The flow of life, with the flow of traffic, came to a halt.

It was not the greatest of New York's winter storms, merely worse than most.

In Stuyvesant Square, the citizens were content to sit by their grates, hoping the coal supply would last and sending the handyman frequently, uselessly, to clear the steps. Any boy willing to brave the weather could earn pocket money as a messenger at double pay.

For two days no newspapers were published. Not that they were missed. At this season of the year in properly run households, newspapers were sent backstairs either to divert the servants or to wrap the fish. What concerned society matrons was whether Fifth Avenue would be cleared far enough north to permit carriages to reach Mrs. Woffard's nouveau mansion on Fifty-fourth Street. More than one imprisoned dowager consoled herself that it would serve Althea Woffard right if none of the Old Families came. The new rich in their uptown Renaissance castles were making society quite unmanageable.

Two nights later the storm blew itself out.

Miss Phoebe Bliss, eclipsed in quilts and pillows, sat

propped at her bedroom window. The damp and the cold increasingly brought her reminders of mortality, rheumatic joints, which she chose to ignore except for the inconvenience on winter nights of sleeping upright. Now, as the first dawn streaked the sky, she listened to familiar sounds.

Stroking Wellington, who opted for her lap on such nights, she reached for the delicate blue-and-gold enamel French opera glasses she kept on her side table.

"There it is, Wellington! The big wagon! The lanterns, those huge horses. I can even see their white breath—I think."

Whatever Miss Phoebe could or could not see, she could hear. These were the sounds she had listened to from childhood, strong, rhythmic, assuring her again that the world had returned to normalcy, the sounds of shovels clearing the snow.

Soon there would be light enough to see her beloved park in white drifts. Sensible hedgerows turned into grotesqueries of camels and turtles, bushes into demons and angels. Fir trees now hooded white nuns. Every spike of the iron fencing wearing a goblin's cap. An enchanted world that the abiding child in Miss Phoebe Bliss was not prepared to let go.

Suddenly she sat upright as far as her bundling permitted, sending Wellington scrambling to his ottoman.

"I do believe there's a light across the Square!" She rubbed the lenses of her opera glasses with a handkerchief. "Yes, there is! I can see it quite clearly. A front room! At this hour!"

Gaslights in the rear top floors of Stuyvesant Square would have surprised no one. The servants would already be up, grates shaken and refilled, the kitchen stove ablaze before dawn. But a light in a front upstairs room? If it were illness, the lights in the hall would be on, too. Miss Phoebe made a tour of the Square again with her glasses. The light was still there, too high for the parlor, too low for a star.

She regained the cat and settled herself. "I do not snoop, Wellington, as you very well know. But I do observe. That is Mr. Tremont's house. And that, that window with the light must be Noel's on the third floor. I know because young Mrs. Tremont was annoyed about it. Now what do you suppose . . . ?" Her fingers wove themselves into the cat's fur. "Wellington, do you suppose she's decided to elope? I almost eloped once—but there was Papa. . . ."

She lifted her glasses again. "It's still there! Oh, Wellington, I would be so glad, so very glad if Noel didn't marry that dismal young man. If you should ask me, though you never do despite your feline curiosity . . . she'll go through with it, mark my word. She's promised, and Noel Tremont would never go back on her word. Even Mrs. MacWhittie next door says so. And she pounces on gossip the way you pounce on some poor miserable little mouse. But oh, I'd like to think that Noel has a secret love, which is the best kind. Secrets, Wellington, are what give plain everyday its magic. Otherwise, wouldn't it be tiresome if we were all exactly what we see on the outside?''

The delicate glasses swept the Square once more, lingering on the narrow brownstone front of Dr. Hugo Lendler's house. With another sigh, Miss Phoebe set them down. Her other hand quieted the cat's back. A mist of light began to drift into the park, shaping the trees. To the lull of scraping shovels, Miss Phoebe's eyelids drooped. As was her prerogative, Miss Phoebe had monitored the dawn. Across the Square the troubling gleam vanished.

At the now darkened window of her bedroom, Noel stood fully dressed from her sensible unadorned hat to her sensible boots. The heavy black shawl in which she wrapped herself did little to keep out the room's cold, but once outside, moving, she told herself, she'd be warm again. One wool-gloved hand clutched a small carpetbag, the other a note. She was thankful she had written it the previous night. In this bitter dawn, the ink had crusted in its container.

She had put out her lamp and now stood waiting, as she had waited in torment the last two days. She had survived the mockery of Christmas. Made captive by the blizzard, the three of them, Adrienne, her father, and herself had dined at the shortened Christmas table, the goose had been carved in the kitchen, and the Tiffany crystal in which her father served his finest wines had remained in the cabinet. Adrienne had been distantly amenable and obviously bored. Her father had made a heavyhanded effort to observe the dwindling day. Noel had found herself incapable even of pleasantries.

Throughout that endless day and night, and the next, the horror at Madame Ducharde's school had washed over her, returning again and again until it seemed that Posie's name must be stamped in living color on her face. Last evening, her father had scrutinized her closely. "I think, Noel, you should have a little talk with Dr. Sanborn, as soon as we can get out. A tonic, perhaps, a little iron for the blood . . . we want you a rosy bride, child."

As if she had ever been rosy. Now it was nearly over. The snow had stopped. Below, the shovelers had nearly reached number 269. She could get through, if only they would *hurry*.

Light was seeping into the Square. It would soon reach into the sleeping house, into the dark corners of her room, and her mind. Would she ever be able to erase from her memory the blackened walls and corridors through which she had run?

In all that devastation, she had at last found Madame Ducharde. She would never forget the bedroom, lit by a single candle, the enormous bed, heaped in a luxury of pillows and silk coverings, above it, in the starkness of heavy black wood, a four-foot crucifix. The room, like the bed, was empty. The candlelight came from what looked like a prayer closet. The Frenchwoman was kneeling, her grey hair fallen loose, her grey draped gown in dry pools around her. Her head lifted.

Then she spoke, her voice oddly light. And as sunny as a girl's.

"Is that you, Carrie? I knew you'd come, Carrie. I have told Him everything. He has forgiven me. You must, too. I did—what I had to—for the children. You know that now. I loved them. My way was better—" The flow of words broke with a choked scream. "You are not Carrie! Who are you?"

"Madame—"

"What are you doing here? I don't know you!" She picked up the candle, thrusting it toward Noel like a weapon.

"Madame! You know me! I'm Noel Tremont. I came for my child. . . ."

"What child? There are no children here!"

"My little girl! Posie. Elizabeth. Here, with the others. *Where are they?*"

As long as she lived, Noel would never forget the hollowness of those eyes, the vacancy stamped on those gaunt features, as the woman stared at her.

"Madame," Noel spoke carefully, steadily, "I came to bring you the money. For my little girl. It is here in this envelope. What you asked for."

Madame Ducharde snatched the tan envelope, then carefully felt it, the long skeletal fingers plucking at it as if at reason itself.

"Miss Tremont. . . ." She said the name slowly, studying it. "Yes. Yes, of course. I do remember. *Miss Noel Tremont.* I have so many things to think about. Everything is out of order now. You were in Carrie's house that night—that night. You knew what happened. Didn't you, Miss Tremont? You *knew* I didn't hurt Carrie. She was my friend. Willow-bark tea is kind. She died—sweetly—so sweetly. The rest . . . was nothing. Nothing but what had to be done."

Reason that flashed for an instant in her face slipped into cunning.

"But you knew, Miss Tremont. You knew. You knew. I was not safe until you were here, you and your child. You see, I have lost everything. Did you know that? To the Devil, Miss Tremont. He is in this house now. But he won't have this!" She clutched the tan envelope tight against her flat breast. "I shall keep it. I shall spend it—buying pretty ribbons, Miss Tremont . . . blue and pink and yellow . . . he shan't take it!"

The candle tipped dangerously. Noel caught it as it went out. Darkness enveloped them. Noel could not remember fleeing the house, only running, running, until she reached the parish house. The cold air, the welcoming sanity of Father Michaels restored her.

"The little ones are safe. The Church has them in charge. You can see your child tomorrow." He gave her an address. Through the mullioned windows, she saw the silhouette of the waiting cab.

So the nightmare would end. Ned would be with the cab. She would tell him everything on the way home. Tomorrow she would take him to see Posie. . . .

The sleepy cab driver, rubbing his eyes with a knitted fingerless glove, crawled out of the cab.

"The young gentleman, Miss? Last I seen he was harin' it down the street. Ain't seed hide nor hair of him since." And because he had been roused so suddenly, and the wind bitter, the night long, and Christmas a dim memory belonging to the rich, the old man spat his spleen into the dark with the ancient ruse, "And him not givin' me my fare, Miss, nor waitin' money."

"I'll pay you double. Please drive me home."

In the two desperate snowbound days that had followed she had forced Ned from her mind. Once she had weakened.

"Annie-Mae, if a messenger gets through the snow to our door, please call me. It—it might be important."

No messenger had come. Now the long wait was over, her plans fixed. First dawn had become faint morning light. The shovelers had cleared the street past her house.

She had one small duty to perform. She tiptoed from her room and into the spare room where her wedding dress hung, a ghost of herself swathed in white tissue, the train spread below on a white sheet. She even managed a smile. The long slither of lace and satin reminded her for one ludicrous instant of nothing so much as a transparent snakeskin David had found for her one early summer.

But the snake isn't in it, David!

He's out growing another. He doesn't need the old one.

She pinned a square of paper on the satin folds and went down the familiar staircase. She could hear stirrings in the kitchen. Annie-Mae would be coming soon with her scuttles of coal. Her father would be sleeping heavily in the room he now used next to Adrienne. As for Adrienne, Noel could only wish her the contentment that would never come.

She placed her note on the mantel. "I shall not come back. Try to forgive me, Father, and remember me only as a loving daughter. . . ."

In what light there was in the hall she caught a faint glimpse of herself in the bull's-eye mirror, thirty-six glimpses of a small, dark-shawled woman, fulfilling her only possible destiny. Never to be separated from her child again.

In the vestibule she permitted herself a last look back. All that she had once held dear lay behind her. Fading memories of her mother, the smothering kindness of her father, her brothers coming, going, the uneven but enduring weave of family living. She imagined them all waving good-bye. She touched her hand to her lips, as if to blow a kiss into the empty hall, a kiss they would never know.

Soundlessly, she stepped out of the house. The new light was already drifting through the Square. In the center of the street, a carriageway had been cleared, straight and narrow. Drawing a deep breath, she clambered over the drifts toward it.

35

The city slowly emerged, a sunken city, from a sea of dirty melting snow, telegraph poles and wires snapped and downed astride the streets, alleys, still choked, here and there a shattered wooden roof jagged against an innocent sky. In the perversity of New York's weather, a deceitful thaw had brought softness to the air, five inches of slush underfoot, and, to the citizens, trouser bottoms and skirts so mired in mud that only boiling water and raw lye soap could restore them.

Dr. Lendler, at his desk in his upstairs study, wondered if any house in the city could be as redolent of hot wet wool as his. He must make a study someday of the effects of this unpredictable New York climate on the behavior of its inhabitants. Already the skies were overcast and the temperature falling.

He glanced out across the Square to the reassuring bulk of the great church, its doors half open to winter's caprice, where Noel was to have entered as a bride.

The note had been delivered a half hour ago.

Dear Dr. Lendler,

It is my unfortunate duty to inform you that the engagement of Mr. Tremont's daughter, Noel, to Mr. Clarence Briggs has been terminated. Your thoughtful wedding gift will be returned as promptly as. . . .

Faithfully,
Adrienne Tremont

He had read it twice. There would have been security in that marriage, unfortunate as it was in every other respect. What would she do now? He could almost feel his hands bound behind his back, helpless even to ask for her confidence.

He tossed the note aside and picked up a volume that he invariably found soothing. But he did not read. He wondered instead of his own role in the turn of events. He had long been content to serve human error, human pain, distantly. This time it was his own. He opened the little leather-bound book of *John Donne's Thoughts.* "All these women we might think upon, and yet love but one. . . ."

But even that impassioned divine could not this morning save him from the world's intrusions.

"Herr Professor!" It was accompanied by a light rapping.

Frau Gruen was clearly out of breath. It occurred to Dr. Lendler in the interest of anatomy that if she didn't lace her stays so tight, she might achieve the two flights from the kitchen to his study without panting. Then he realized her lacings had nothing to do with it. Her face bore the makings of outrage.

"Mein Herr Professor, there is a woman downstairs who will not go away. She will not give her name. She says she has no appointment. I told her you could not be disturbed at your work. She says she must see you."

"Did you show the lady in?"

Frau Gruen's mouth tightened. "She walked in. She is in the parlor now with her wet boots."

"Thank you, Frau Gruen, I'll go down." Sometimes, he thought, the kitchen could be more strident in its social distinctions than the parlor.

His caller was above average in height. The thickness of her black knit shawl and the thinness of her black cotton gloves revealed an existence of less than ease. Her rather large features were heavily rice-powdered and he suspected a touch of beet juice on her set lips. Above a commanding pompadour of frizzed blond hair perched a black hat that seemed to consist of a single wing of a crow. The effect was heightened by a pair of elongated jet earrings that dangled with a kind of inbuilt ferocity.

It was the lady's eyes that held Dr. Lendler. They were steel blue and sharp with fear.

She was already seated on the edge of a brown velvet chair. Her boots were indeed wet.

"Good morning, Madam. You wished . . . ?"

"Dr. Lendler, my name is Mrs. Greta Luskin. I am a widow. I run a lodging house, 34 Park Row. Very respectable. Recommended. A credit to the neighborhood. Or was''—she reached for a handkerchief, clutched it tightly to hard dry eyes—''until . . .''

''Yes, Madam?''

''It's about Neddie, uh, Mr. Ned Fitch. One of my boarders, one of my best boarders, Dr. Lendler, in my best room. You know him.''

''Yes, indeed. He was in my employ.''

''He told me. I got your address off those books he brought from England. I took him in when he first got here because . . . well, he seemed such an honest, nice-spoken young man. The kind a widow like me . . .''

''Quite.'' It was not so much distaste for the highly scented intensity of Mrs. Luskin that Dr. Lendler felt, but foreboding. ''And so?''

''They came and arrested him early yesterday through the snow and all. The police, Dr. Lendler . . . with the wagon. Everybody on the block could see. Never, never have I had anything like that happen at my door. People were staring at me and talking behind my back when I left the house this morning.''

Whatever shock Dr. Lendler sustained, and it was considerable, he must contain it. The sluice gates of Mrs. Luskin's feelings were about to open. *Mental disturbance, female, stage I, could approach hysteria.* But as soon as he had classified it, Dr. Lendler knew he was wrong. This woman was not given to hysteria but to drama.

''What was the charge against Mr. Fitch?''

Mrs. Luskin sat back more comfortably.

''Murder, Dr. Lendler. Murder, when he was caught . . .''

''I am not the police, dear lady.''

''Oh, I know. That's why I've come here. I wouldn't ever talk to the police like this. You see, Dr. Lendler, I *know* Neddie. Very well, I might say. I gave him my best room. But he worried me. A lot. He went out nights. And recently he seemed to have plenty of money. He wouldn't tell me where he got it. But my, he was so handsome in his evening dress. I couldn't think of him murdering anyone. . . .''

''Nor can I, Mrs. Luskin.''

''Can't you, Dr. Lendler? Then I do feel better. But that's not what bothers me most. You see, I think Neddie was a jump-ship . . . and when that gets out, too . . . Dr. Lendler, I've never run that kind of rooming house. I'm a respectable woman—''

''Quite, Madam. But there's no reason it should, as you say, 'get out.' ''

She tightened her grasp on the dry handkerchief.

"But you see, Dr. Lendler, it is out. The police asked me what I knew about Neddie and I didn't want them to think I would give lodging to a murderer without suspecting something. What would they think of a decent woman as stupid as that? I told them I had suspected Neddie had jumped ship, but I thought . . ."

He was anxious to get rid of her. His thoughts were far ahead of her. Noel's wedding had been canceled. Ned had been arrested for murder. If there was a common thread to all this, it was nothing this woman should properly know.

"I came here, Dr. Lendler, because I don't know anybody else to tell me what to do."

That was it, the basic threat to survival that can drive a lonely human being to self-pity, to folly, and in the end to betrayal. Beneath her apparent strength lay insecurity, a fear of the unknown, the need to lean.

"I think, Mrs. Luskin," he said gently, "that the best thing you can do is nothing. I do not think the police will bother you again. You are not responsible for your lodgers' private lives. As for your neighbors, what could be more interesting than a police wagon after a blizzard? I doubt that your estimable reputation has been blemished. I suggest you put the matter out of your mind. And"—he smiled reassuringly—"when you get home change those boots. They are deplorably wet."

Mrs. Luskin's expression was so embracing that Dr. Lendler knew an instant of panic.

"Is it safe, Dr. Lendler, to rent out my best bedroom if Neddie, I mean. . . ."

"Quite safe, I should say. Good day, Mrs. Luskin."

Dr. Lendler was in overcoat, stormboots, and his old slouch hat when Frau Gruen grimly entered the hall. "I am going out, Frau Gruen."

She peered into the empty parlor, opened her mouth, shut it, then yielded to a lesser irritation. "Your scarf, *Herr Professor.*"

She knitted them regularly for him at Christmas, each one as brown, durable, and scratchy as the last.

"Thank you, Frau Gruen." He meekly wrapped it around his neck, with a silent plea to the Deity for an early spring.

Cell 37 in New York's infamous heap of brownstone, known aptly as the Tombs, measured ten feet by eight. It contained a floor pot and a shelflike bunk. Water dripped continually from the stone walls and the chill could congeal the lungs of any man not as preoccupied as prisoner number 201.

Ned lay on the bunk, a newspaper limp in his hand, barely readable in the dirty light that managed to penetrate the tiny barred window above. The privilege of the sleazy paper had been the result of the warden's unhappy conclusion that a bit of indulgence might succeed with his stubborn captive where threats had failed. Besides giving his name and address, Ned had maintained a lofty silence, made more impressive by his frequent, if denied, demands for soap and clean linen.

The guard had thrust the paper at him and leaned cosily against the grilling of the door. "If I was you, limey, I wouldn't trust me luck too long. They got ways of making people talk here that don't get known outside."

Ned had not opened the thin, damp pages of the paper. He lay instead contemplating with uneasiness his dilemma. He had been here, how long? Too long. He had expected—what? That the killer would have been caught? That Father Michaels would have come to see him by this time? That there was no longer any danger to Noel?

Where was she? In the long hours of the night he could feel her, full fleshed, rounded, warm in his arms. Holding her, her heart against his, until the piercing cold, the stench, awakened him to his prison cell. He would stay here, he swore to himself, if hell itself froze over, until he had word that Parson's killer had been found.

He picked up the ragged newspaper. First on the streets, the sensation-loving *Gazette* had abandoned private notices and given over its first page to the plight of the city. Thirty-two fires had been started as snowbound inhabitants exhausted their coal supplies and turned to paper and wood. Four citizens and three horses had been found frozen. A woman with a baby had jumped from a collapsing tenement.

On the second page was an account of a train plunging from a snow-weakened trestle into a Mohawk valley. As no details were available, the paper obligingly supplied three prewritten columns on the moans of the injured and dying, and two pen-and-ink sketches, already on hand, of shattered cars, broken windows, mangled bodies. News, as usual, was less in fact than in the eye of a circulation-minded editor.

On the fourth and last page was an account of a knife stabbing of a sailor on South Street.

No mention of the late Reverend Culbertson. No mention of a fire in a French orphanage. The very blankness was ominous, as if the city, which had never known him, had already forgotten him, going on about its business as if Ned . . . as if Julien Edmond Abbingdon-Fitch . . . had never existed. Had he?

The thought he had tried to keep submerged stung him again. In a few—how many?—days, Noel was to marry. Would she go through with it? Why not? That would be her safety. Had he condemned himself to this for another man's pleasure? He tossed the paper to the floor. He rolled over in his bunk, burying his head in his arms to shut out the images he was conjuring up—Noel and another man.

Lost in his own frustrations, he barely heard the rattle of the keys as the guard returned.

"Prisoner 201!"

Ned jumped to his feet. "At your service, sir."

"Not mine, you ain't." The guard lifted a sheet of paper to the wan light. "Prisoner number 201, Julien Edmond Abbingdon-Fitch, alias Ned Fitch, is hereby notified that bail has been duly posted—"

"Bail!"

". . . with Precinct Captain Joseph Schwartz, in lieu of Judge, not sitting due to snow."

"Wait a minute. I didn't ask for bail!"

". . . said Ned Fitch remanded to custody of—"

"Who the devil did this? I was at the scene of the crime. I knew the victim!"

"You can tell that to the Court when yer turn comes . . . said prisoner 201 remanded to the custody of a Dr. Hugo Lendler who is expecting you. 72 Stuyvesant Square. Come along, step lively!"

The guard gave Ned a shove. The cell door clanged behind him. In the street he filled his lungs with clean air and freedom. Sweet freedom. A man never knows how sweet until he's been without it. His careful plan to keep the police distracted, to be bird in hand, to shield Noel, had been blown away. Instead he would be under the watchful eye, the hypnotic eye, of that meddling little man who appeared and disappeared in his life like an unbottled genie.

He had never understood Dr. Lendler's interest in him. He'd be damned if he'd try now.

But Dr. Lendler could wait. Freed at last, Ned had only one purpose. That night, beside the grim bulk of the Reverend Culbertson's body, Father Michaels had told him that he had sent Noel safely home. But that was four days ago. The storm had passed. Everything Ned knew abut Noel told him that she would have left Stuyvesant Square by now. She was somewhere in this city with her child.

His jailers had returned to Ned his overcoat, his watch and chain, and his wallet. He swung briskly north.

Ned knew where to find her.

The short winter day had ended by the time Ned came to the address he had been given. The street was narrow, the buildings unlit, the house itself squeezed between what might be two larger warehouses. The smell of the river docks filled his nostrils, the never-to-be-forgotten mixture of brine and tar, refuse, and wet manure. He could hear, as if beside him, the occasional moan of a passing ship.

The house he approached offered a blank front except for the small cross on the door and a dim light above the transom. He knocked loudly, then, not waiting, he knocked again.

"My goodness!" The nun who opened the door showed a face not so much startled as long-suffering.

"Oh." She looked Ned up and down. "Whatever do you want, young man?"

"Miss Tremont, please. I've been told she is here."

"Miss Tremont? Yes, she is here."

"I must see her. Father Michaels gave me your address."

The Sister, who was not as old as she looked, hesitated.

"Yes, of course. But you can't see Miss Tremont now. It's not visiting hours." She had not widened the door.

"It's important, Sister."

"There is nothing so important that the rules of God's worship should be interrupted. Our residents are permitted visitors between two and three on Wednesdays and Saturdays, which Father Michaels should have told you. A dear man but so very busy."

Ned saw that against the single-minded strength of these disciplined women even Father Michaels could not prevail. Strategy would be needed.

"Sister, I am Miss Tremont's cousin. English on her mother's side. Edmond Abbingdon-Fitch. I must see her. I explained to Father Michaels. He knows."

"Sister Frances!" A stern voice called from within. "Whomever are you talking to?"

"A visitor, Mother Celia."

The voice neared. "You know the rules. No visitors at this hour."

"I've just said so, Mother Celia."

The young nun lowered her voice. "I can't tell you anything except . . . the children are well. They are being taken to a convent in Paris. The sailing has been delayed by the storm. Miss Tremont has applied to go with them. You must leave!"

"Sister. . . ." Something so desperate in Ned's voice compelled the young nun's attention for another moment, perhaps a reminder of her own binding vows, perhaps of a long-abandoned dream.

"Mr. Fitch, I cannot change the rules. Please don't ask me." She hesitated, the color touching her blanched face. "If—if you wish to send a message, I could take it to her."

"You are very kind." Ned meant it as deeply as he had meant anything in his life. "Tell Miss Tremont . . . tell her I will be here at nine tomorrow morning. Tell her to be ready . . . with the girl."

As the door closed on him, Ned wondered if God looked deeply enough into the hearts of these, the humblest of His handmaidens.

In the street, Ned found himself walking, almost blindly, enmeshed in his own turmoil, toward the river. The smell of salt and coal again enveloped him. He saw the dark shapes of the packet ships, the thrust of their bowsprits over the street. He imagined one of them, swinging out, belching smoke, turning downriver into the great bays and the limitless unknown of the ocean. A phantom ship, to a phantom port, carrying Noel.

It must not happen. It would not happen. He turned from the river and walked until he found a hansom. His order was blunt.

"Stuyvesant Square."

36

Dr. Lendler surveyed his caller mildly.

"I had expected you earlier, Ned."

"I was detained."

"So I am aware. Well, one man's expectations are another man's pitfalls. You just missed Captain Schwartz."

"He wouldn't wait?"

"He didn't come for you. Cognac?" Dr. Lendler filled two crystal glasses. "Said to warm the soul, soothe the heart, and lie sweetly on the brain. Though I wouldn't vouch for the last." He had seated Ned beside the closed piano. Through the bay window, Ned could see the Square coming to life, street lamps glowing, carriages beginning to appear.

"I'm grateful to you for putting up bail, Dr. Lendler."

Oddly, he felt at ease in the little parlor. If, as it seemed, he had lived a lifetime since he had first entered it, it no longer posed a threat. He had come only to distance himself for another twenty-four hours from the police. After that . . . he had not yet given thought to the future. He must see Noel, he must prevent her from going away. If she boarded the ship, then by everything he could swear he, too, would be on it with her.

"Bail, my friend"—Dr. Lendler's tone was matter-of-fact—"was not the difficulty. I felt no risk in standing bail for you. I am quite sure—you might say I know—that you did not dispatch the late unlamented Reverend Culbertson to his untimely death."

Ned threw a startled glance at his host.

"The difficulty is you, Ned. The police find this an awkward case. Like another case that has remained unsolved, it lies too close to the body politic. And that body contains a fever in its bloodstream. Corruption that reaches everywhere. The Reverend Culbertson's demise would best be forgotten.

But now you appear, refusing to explain your presence, to give any alibi for your whereabouts, or say anything that might give the police a sensible reason for releasing you. I provided bail for you before you brought the entire order of things down.'' Dr. Lendler finished his cognac and carefully dabbed at his trim beard.

''You see, Ned, I know who murdered the Reverend Culbertson—the Parson, as you knew him. Very simply, I was a friend, a confidant, to that courageous woman, Caroline Restell. I may have been the last friend she had. She told me things that no one else knew. The eternal strength of the confessional, my friend . . . the human hunger to share a burden.

''But she lived in fear. She knew that if she were to go on trial, the many people she had helped would become her enemies, terrified of what might be revealed about them. She even suspected she might be killed. Her days became a little easier knowing that there was one human being on whom she could completely depend. I gave her my word that I would never reveal anything I knew of her work or her patients. She needed that.''

Ned shifted his long legs uneasily. The memory of that night he had entered the Restell house and discovered the dead woman could still haunt him. But he had begun to believe he was safe from its threat. Now he wondered.

''There was someone in Mrs. Restell's house the night she died. Other than yourself.'' The professor's deep brooding eyes lighted for an instant with something like a twinkle. ''*Lieber Gott!* Ned, you have a good mind but an absolute talent for being where you shouldn't be. I would diagnose it somewhere between unshaped ambition and overblown curiosity. No matter. The woman with Mrs. Restell that night was a long-time companion. She was also a woman who longed for children, even to desperation. She was mortally afraid that when Caroline Restell was brought to trial, the children in her own keeping would be taken from her.

''Murder, Ned, is not difficult for one who has suffered intensely, who does not flinch at death and who is skilled in method. Madame Ducharde knew Mrs. Restell suffered headaches. A well-known relief is willow-bark tea, and overdose can be lethal. That is what Madame Ducharde gave Carrie that night. I can only surmise that after Caroline Restell's death, Madame was powerful enough in purpose and physical strength to stage the grim facade of suicide in Mrs. Restell's bathroom, making sure that all blood drained away, and with it all traces of willow-bark tea. What Madame Ducharde did not know was that blood does not drain entirely from a body when the heart has already stopped pumping. Carrie Restell had been dead some time before she was placed in that tub. The authorities chose to overlook that discrepancy. Only a superficial autopsy was made."

Dr. Lendler rose and refilled the cognac glasses.

"A little more warmth, yes? For the winter's chill." He glanced out on the square, as if familiar verities would banish old ghosts.

"So Madame Ducharde was safe, with her beloved children. Until the Reverend Culbertson found her. He had been unable to threaten Carrie. Her friends were too rich, too powerful. In the Frenchwoman he found a source of immense profit. Blackmail. The threat to reveal the prominent families whose sins had been made incarnate in the young innocents under Madame Ducharde's care. But the Reverend Culbertson called for his payments once too often. A woman as strong, as desperate, as Madame Ducharde did not hesitate to strike again. Murder can be an intoxicant, Ned. It destroys its victim but it habituates its perpetrators. . . . Madame Ducharde died yesterday."

It occurred to Ned that he was expected to speak. He sat waiting.

"So you have no accuser. In the last rites—I am not fully acquainted with them—Madame Ducharde made her confession. You might be said to be a free man."

Ned sensed there was more.

Dr. Lendler reached to the table beside him and took up a thick envelop tied with string.

"Did you ever see this, Ned?"

"No, sir."

Dr. Lendler opened the envelope and took out five heavily imprinted parchment papers. "One thousand shares each of West Shore Railroad stock. If they are worth anything, they are worth twenty thousand dollars. Police found them in Madame Ducharde's desk and held them as a motive for your entering the building."

Ned was on his feet.

"I don't know a thing about them! What are you getting at?"

"Oh, sit down, Ned, and hear me out. The stocks have been traced to the ownership of Mr. Walter Tremont, transferred to Miss Noel Tremont. I suggest that they were Noel's dowry, that she had given them to Madame Ducharde for tuition.''

Dr. Lendler walked to the window, his back to Ned.

''You somehow discovered the one secret I have devoted my life to keeping. I don't know how you learned it, but I can guess you were with Noel the night she took her dowry to Madame Ducharde.'' He paused. When he turned, Ned saw a visible difference, as if a mask had momentarily slipped from his face, revealing a man, human and in pain. The little professor regained himself.

''I have known from the beginning of Noel Tremont's child. It was the heaviest burden I had to bear among Mrs. Restell's confidences. I had to watch helplessly while the young woman I most honor in this world fought her hidden battle against the conventions, the cruelties of her own society. Then you came along.''

Dr. Lendler gathered up the papers and returned them to the brown envelope.

''I saw your attraction to her. I knew the harm you could do her. I had to know who you were, what kind of man. How foolish is anyone who thinks he can govern the human heart in its passions. It is not my business nor my privilege to ask more. These stocks must be returned, of course, to Walter Tremont.''

Ned spoke at last, almost reluctantly.

''Then he will know?''

Dr. Lendler nodded. ''Everything that Noel never found a way to tell him.''

It is in the silences, the spaces between words, that life is lived. How often had Dr. Lendler thought of a future when, through a twist of destiny, Noel's child would be revealed. He had seen himself standing defender of this girl he had so long, so distantly, worshipped.

Yet at this moment, as a final seal to his role, stood a young man to take the sword from him, by the one right he, Dr. Lendler, could not claim—Noel's love.

The question he expected came too soon.

''Dr. Lendler, would you let me return that envelope?''

Wordlessly, Dr. Lendler handed it to him.

''I think I should remind you, Ned, that when you are freed of the charge of murder there may still be a little difficulty for you. Shipping records show that last March twentieth the packet ship *Boedicia* from London docked in New York. An able seaman, one Ned Fitch, departed the ship under certain irregularities. The police, hard put by the political pressures of the case, may vent their frustration by having you deported. I should advise you to leave the city for a while."

"I hope to, sir."

Dr. Lendler walked with him to the vestibule. From his Viennese umbrella stand, he drew a cane, of black ebony, its top a lotus flower of carved ivory.

"I'd like you to have this, Ned. It never fitted me."

"Nor me, sir."

On a clear winter night, Stuyvesant Square was at its best. Houses fully lighted, their fine facades in close eminence, the guardian towers of old St. George's Church solid and enduring against the stars. It would be his last night, Ned told himself, in this small, once coveted, world. Tomorrow? But what man knows tomorrow?

He walked slowly around the Square, past the lofty church doors, past the firm humility of the Friends Meeting House, past that gentle chatelaine, Miss Phoebe Bliss, and finally to the wrought iron balustrade of number 269. Looking back, Ned had an odd illusion. Beyond the silhouetted rooftops, in ghostly shadow, he saw the Hanging Stones of his boyhood. Two thousand years or more ago, they, like this Square, had contained within their circle people, lights, movement, the full surge of life. All vanished now, except a skeleton of stones, as this Square would in time become.

Ned shook his mind free of the image. He was young. His own years lay ahead, fettered neither to the distant past nor the remote future. Nothing can be lost while a man's dream rises like the ancient Stones themselves above the flatness of time. As his grandfather had promised, the Great Comet was again on its way back from the Sun to remind him and all generations of Earth's wonders and touch all living things with the spark of change.

The Tremont windows blazed with light. Through the rich draperies of the drawing room Ned could see groups of men in evening clothes—men of importance, he guessed, men of power.

Mr. Tremont had guests. Ned had not thought of that possibility. He must do what he must. The maid at the door was as plain as she was unsure.

Ned felt the buoyancy of freedom.

"Is Annie-Mae not here?"

The new maid eyed him suspiciously. "No, sir. The young lady wot went away left Annie-Mae her wedding dress.

Annie-Mae said with a fine dress like that, it was best to get married."

"Very sensible."

"Yes, sir. Who shall I say, sir?"

"Mr. Fitch to see Mr. Tremont."

The new maid's glance sharpened. "And he's expecting you?"

"Not exactly, but I think he'll see me."

"Sir—I—he has guests, sir. I'm not sure I dast disturb him." She lowered her voice. "The Mayor hisself is here."

"Then I'll wait until the Mayor hisself leaves."

In the bull's-eye mirror in the hall, Ned gazed at thirty-six tiny reflections of black-coated civic authority and order. He tried to imagine Noel among them, Noel and her child. Yet this is her home, he told himself grimly. This is where she belongs.

Walter Tremont was coming toward him. Ned was startled by the difference in the man, the aging heaviness of his face, the invisible weight that seemed to bend his shoulders.

"What is it you want of me, Mr. Fitch?"

Ned thrust his hand into his inside pocket.

"Only to give you this, sir."

Walter stared at the thick, string-tied envelope as if it were a living thing.

"Where did you get it?"

"That's a long story, sir. It would keep you from your guests."

The older man's hand was shaking as he took it.

"My daughter's. Noel. Is she with you?"

Ned would like to have spared Walter Tremont, but only the truth would serve now.

"I would like to say yes, Mr. Tremont. I can only say not yet."

Instinct told Walter Tremont that he had rightly feared this man. Ned Fitch, whoever he was, wherever he came from had robbed him of all that he most cherished in life. Yet he had one ally the young could not command. Time.

He straightened, an aging lion, denying defeat.

"I can only ask, Mr. Fitch, that someday you will bring Noel home. When—if—she is willing. I have lived a long time. I know how to wait."

At nine the next morning, Ned entered the visitor's room of the little hospice near the river. The young nun had done her best. She had had him admitted as Miss Tremont's cousin from England. But for five minutes only, Mr. Fitch.

He positioned himself near a dingy window that looked out on a brick wall, out of sight of the curious Sisters, yet within view of the entrance. He had imagined, no, he had believed Noel would be there already. He had presumed too much. The minutes plodded on, heavy as footfalls, the entranceway empty as a cave.

Suppose she did not come? Suppose at the last moment she had chosen that waiting ship and the assured future for her child? Suppose that his longing, his passion had never been matched by hers? He was beginning to think the unthinkable.

"Cousin?"

She was there, the radiance around her, her tiny hat tipped slightly awry. One hand grasped a valise, the other reached to the child beside her, eyes fixed and wondering.

It was Posie who spoke.

"You came to see me!"

"A gentleman's word."

Noel stared at him. "When on earth? You know Posie!"

"We're old friends."

There would be time for explanations later. A lifetime. He took her in his arms. Doubt dissolved like the walls themselves. Ahead their road lay, yet unknown. But beckoning was the glory of the morning.